THE FANCIFUL TRAVELS OF D. LIEBER

BOOKS BY D. LIEBER

Minte and Magic

The Exiled Otherkin

The Assassin's Legacy

Intended Fates

Intended Bondmates

Intended Strangers

Intended Enemies

Council of Covens

Dancing with Shades

In Search of a Witch's Soul

Also by D. Lieber

Conjuring Zephyr

Once in a Black Moon

A Very Witchy Yuletide

The Treason of Robyn Hood

THE FANCIFUL TRAVELS OF D. LIEBER

OMNIBUS VOLUME TWO

D. LIEBER

Ink & Magick, LLC
Kenosha, Wisconsin
contact@inkandmagick.com

Hardcover ISBN: 978-1-951239-16-9
Paperback ISBN: 978-1-951239-17-6
Ebook ISBN: 978-1-951239-18-3

Cover by Maria Spada

ORIGINAL COPYRIGHTS & CREDITS

Once in a Black Moon

Copyright © 2019 by D. Lieber
Cover by GetCovers
Edited by Cover to Cover Editing

A Very Witchy Yuletide

Copyright © 2020 by D. Lieber
Cover by Bryan Donihue, Section 28 Publishing
Edited by Cover to Cover Editing

The Treason of Robyn Hood

Copyright © 2020 by D. Lieber
Cover by GetCovers
Edited by Cover to Cover Editing

CONTENTS

D. LIEBER

Once
in a
Black
Moon

ACKNOWLEDGMENTS

To Aunt Debbie, who instilled in me an unquenchable wanderlust both in reality and in reading.

I want to give a special shout out to all my betas as well as those who helped me with the many languages, folklore, and the sensitive topics surrounding the First Nations. Thank you, John, Laura, Amy, Iuliana, Gen, Rebecca, Odessa, Julieta, Abi, Sandra, Tammy, P.E., Kerry, Vijaya, Tracy, Beth, Aria, Linda, Sharon, and C.J.

DEFINITIONS AND PRONUNCIATIONS

CHINESE

Aiya (Eye-yah) = exclamation of dismay or surprise

FIRST NATION/NATIVE AMERICAN

Čanotila (chawn-oh-tee-lah) = a forest-dwelling creature similar to fairies from Lakota folklore
Wechuge (Way-chu-gay) = Of varying descriptions. A man-eating monster of Dené or Athabaskan people folklore. In use here as a person who has been possessed or overwhelmed by the power of one of the ancient spirit animals.

FRENCH

Belle (Bell) = Beautiful
Bonjour (Bohn-zhurh) = Hello
Chambre (Shahmbr) = Bedroom

En français (Ohn frhohn-say) = In French
Madame (Mahd-ahm) = Mrs
Mademoiselle (Mad-deh-mwoh-zelh) = Miss
Merci (Merhe-si) = Thank you
Mon amie (MohN Ah-me) = My friend
Monsieur (Muss-yuh) = Mister; Sir
Non (Noh) = No
Oui (We) = Yes
Romantique (Rhoh-man-teek) = Romantic
Ton amie (TohN Ah-me) = Your friend
Tout pour toi (Tooh-poorh-twah) = All for you
Très bien (Trhey byen) = Very good

NAMES

Alejandro (Ah-lay-HAN-droh)
Alexandru (Ahl-lick-SSAHN-droo)
Amélie Roussel (Ah-may-lee Rhoo-sell)
Buvons (Boo-vohn)
Camila (Kah-ME-la)
Capreanu (Kah-pREHA-noo)
Chloé (Klow-ay)
Chuthekii (CHOOT-key)
Crina (Kree-nah)
Delaforet (Della-forh-ay)
Dumitru (Doo-mee-troo)
Dzindo (TsEEN-doe)
Grigore (Gree-gor-eh)
Ion (EE-yohn)
Jacques (Szahk)
Langundo (LANE-gun-doo)
Laurier (Loh-rhe-ay)
Likinoak (LEEK-een-oak)

Louis (Loo-ee)
Marguerite Dubois (Mar-geh-rheet Do-bwah)
Mariana (Mah-ree-ana)
Mitica (Mee-tEE-kuh)
Montmartre (Mohn-marh-trhuh)
Piyiets (PIE-ee-yets)
Pówahkai (POH-wah-Kai-ee)
Testooklah (Tess-TOO-klah)
Tsesikó (Tseh-TSEE-ko)
Yejeták (YEH-jey-tak)
Xi Lin (Shee Leen)
Xi Wei (Shee Way-ee)

ROMANIAN

Balaur (Bah-lAH-oor) = A type of Romanian dragon
Bou (bOW) = Asshole; Bull
Bucuria mea (BOO-coo-re-ah Mheh) = My joy
Bucurie (boo-COO-ree-eh) = Joy
Ce? (che) = What?
Crugul Pământului (KrOO-gool Pa-mUHN-too-loo-ee) = Where the hultan are trained
Da (dah) = Yes
După ploaie, vine soare (Doo-pUH plo-AH-ee-ey vEE-neh Ssoo-ah-ray) = After rain comes sunshine
Ești frumoasa (Yesht froo-moh-AH-suh) = You're beautiful
Făt-Frumos (FUHT froo-mohs) = A Romanian hero of folklore akin to Prince Charming
Hora (HKor-uh) = A circle dance
Hultan (whOOl-tahn) = Romanian wizard, also known as Șolomonar
Iele (Yell-eh) = Type of Romanian fae
Iti dau inima mea (its dOW ene-mah mheh) = I give you my heart
Mamă (MAH-mah)= Mother
Noapte buna (Nu-AHp-te bOO-nuh) = Goodnight

Nu (noo) = No

Pentru totdeauna (pent-rOO TOT-dyeha-una) = Forever

Sânziene (SsUHN-zee-en-nay) = A festival in honor of the fairies

Tărâmul Celălalt (TUH-ruh-muhl CHEl-lal-alt) = Otherworld

Tată (TA-tah) = Father

Te iubesc (TAY you-besk) = I love you

Zână (Zzuh-nuh) = A type of Romanian fae

Zgrimties (Zgreem-tee-es) = In folklore, another name for a hultan. In this book, the governing council of hultan

Zmeu (Zzmeh-oo) = Romanian shapeshifting dragon

SANSKRIT

Dhyana mudra (Dee-ahn Muh-drah) = A hand position used in yoga and meditation

SPANISH

Canta Hermosa (Kahn-tah Ehr-MOH-sah) = You sing beautifully

Con gusto (Kohn GOOS-toh) = With pleasure

Fantastico (fahn-TAHS-tee-koh) = Fantastic

Gracias (GRAH-syahs) = Thank you

Hola (OH-lah) = Hello

Por favor (Pohr Fah-bohr) = Please

Señora (SEH-nyoh-rah) = Ma'am; Mrs.

Sí (SEE) = Yes

Usted también (oo-sted tahm-BYEHN) = You too

WYBOKA

Amâwe (Ah-MAH-way) = Mother

Azeohkwii (Ahz-ay-OH-qwe) = Sister-in-law

Ni'aze (NEE-ahz-ay) = Older brother

Ohkwii (OH-qwe) = Wife

Seyko (SAY-koh) = Son

Seyohkwii (SAY-OH-qwe) = Daughter-in-law

Wic'aze (WEEK-ahz-ay) = Younger brother

Wyboka (Why-BOW-ka) = A First Nation created for the purpose of this story

ONE

I ground my teeth, stomping toward my editor's office. I didn't bother with my usual courtesy knock as I pushed open the glass door.

"What the Hell is this, Bill?" I demanded, waving tomorrow's edition at him.

He raised his eyebrows at my question, waiting for me to explain.

"Why didn't you print my article?"

"It was unsubstantiated. Give me proof, and I'll print it." He leaned back in his chair and laced his fingers, peering over his glasses at me.

"Unsubstantiated? Are you fucking kidding me? I have electronic account transfers and sources in the mayor's office who swear he's embezzling money from the widows and orphan's fund to finance his re-election campaign."

Bill shook his balding head at me sadly and used that infuriatingly calm voice to try to soothe me. "Erin, I know your father was a Chicago police officer, and I understand you're upset the department is getting fewer funds from the city, but that's no reason to accuse the mayor."

"My father has nothing to do with this," I growled, prying my clenched jaw apart.

"I'm not printing your article. End of story." He turned to his computer, dismissing me.

I froze, having never been shut down by Bill without a proper explanation. *My story is breaking news. My evidence is solid. Why won't he print it? Unless...* "No," I whispered.

Bill looked up at me.

"Tell me it's not true. Bill, are you...in the mayor's pocket?"

His face reddened in anger, but not before I saw his eyes flicker with guilt. "How dare—"

"How could you? My mentor, the man who taught me ethics in journalism..." My shock gave way to determination, and I steeled my gut. "This story is getting out. I'll sell it to another paper. I'll go to the Internet if I have to."

Bill stood slowly, his face pale as he removed his glasses. "Erin, listen to me. Don't do that."

"Oh, it's happening."

"You're leaving me no choice. You're fired."

My stomach rolled. "Fine! I can't work for a dirty editor anyway. And guess what, Bill? The mayor is going down, and you're going down with him."

I strode from his office, not heeding his angry protests.

The office was too quiet as my heart raged. Most of my previous coworkers had left for the night, heading home to trick-or-treat with their kids.

My limbs were tense and my movements jerky as I emptied the personal belongings from my desk. I couldn't believe the last six years of my life at *The Chicago Telegraph* fit into one empty printer paper box.

Pausing, I stared at that day's edition and the last article I would ever write for the paper. "Black Moon Day Before Halloween" the headline announced on the bottom corner of page two.

I closed my eyes when they started to burn. *No crying. Not yet.* Letting out a steadying sigh, I grabbed my belongings and went toward the elevator.

As I tried to resituate my box to press the down button, another employee beat me to it.

"Thanks," I mumbled to him.

"No problem."

The large elevator felt small as the two of us shuffled in. My box of shame, the signal that I'd been canned, made my self-consciousness take up most of the breathing room. With a bowed head, I peeked at the tall man with dark hair as he pressed the button for the first floor, then looked down at his smartphone. *I don't think I know him. He must be new. Working extra to get in good with the boss? Good luck with that. They will burn your soul and dance around the ashes.*

Outside, I paused on the sidewalk, breathing in the chilly autumn night. The streets of downtown Chicago were not nearly as busy at eight at night on a Sunday as they would have been on Friday or Saturday.

With my box getting heavier by the minute, I considered hailing a taxi back to my apartment. I decided against it since I no longer had income. *Besides, I might as well take advantage of my CTA card the paper pays for while I still can.*

I readjusted the weight and hunched my shoulders against the lake wind as it whipped my short, brown hair in front of my glasses. I blew up to clear my vision. When that didn't work, I tilted my head back and shook the hair from my face.

The sky is never truly dark in the city, light pollution makes sure of that. However, if it's not cloudy, sometimes you can see the moon. Of course, that night was a new moon, so the clear sky was an empty void above the haze of city lights.

What's out there? I knew the stars and planets were there, even if I couldn't see them. I'd gone to the planetarium on a school trip once. Having lived in the city my entire life, I'd only ever truly been able to appreciate the night sky when I went to Wisconsin for sixth-grade camp.

I remembered making a wish on every star I could see. There were a lot of them, but my wish was always the same.

If I saw a star right now, what would I wish for? My job back? No. I know what I'm doing is right. The predicament I was in reminded me of the feeling from my favorite poem. I hadn't read it since college, but I still knew it by heart:

Were I away with my love fair,
Her eyes are shining emeralds rare,

Upon my breast she'd often lie,
Before we had to say goodbye.

I travel to the dragon's lair,
Cowardly and brave men, beware!
I came here for wealth, not to die,
Were I away.

As I approach with cautious care,
I find I miss my true love's hair,
I miss her laugh, I miss her sigh,
I wish I would have kept her nigh,
Were I away.

The regret and longing from the poem made my heart ache as I stared into the cave-like sky. *I can't turn back now, even if I wished to. I must move forward.*

I sighed, my resolve giving me strength, and readjusted the box again. I tried to look around it as I descended the stairs to the red line subway station, the feat making me slightly off balance.

At the bottom of the stairs, I put my box down so I could dig my CTA pass out of my jacket pocket. Through the turnstile and down the escalator, I sat on a bench on the platform, placing the box on the ground between my Converse.

A street musician played "Somewhere over the Rainbow" on his violin a few feet away. He played it in minor, giving it a sad, chilling quality I'm not sure Judy Garland would have approved of. I quite liked it. The longing that usually accompanied the tune was haunted by the feeling that over the rainbow was a place I would never see.

I reached into the pocket of my skinny jeans and pulled out the change left over from my morning's mocha frappuccino. The coins clinked together pleasantly as they fell into the velvet-lined violin case, and I smiled my appreciation at the musician.

The clacking of a train echoed in the subway tunnel. I hefted my box into my arms and stood at the tactile paved, blue edge of the platform.

As the clack, clack, clack got closer, the train's headlights appeared.

Passengers crowded the edge, preparing to board. Just as the train was about to pull into the station, I felt someone behind me.

The hand that caressed my shoulder gave me a nudge. It wasn't a hard shove, but it was full of purpose. I lost my balance, and my box and I fell onto the track.

There wasn't enough time for my short life to flash before my eyes. I only remember my heart screaming in fear, echoing the screech of the train's brakes as it crashed into me...

...I couldn't move. All I felt was pain as my foggy consciousness resurfaced. My heart pounded in my ears, but I heard a distant chanting. I couldn't understand the words the baritone sang, but I could feel the plea in his voice.

I struggled to open my eyes. Through the haze of semi-consciousness and the dim, flickering light, I could only make out a flash of red before the void pulled me under again.

TWO

*T*hwack...thwack...thwack...*What is that sound? Is Bryan doing something weird again?*

I strained my ears. Besides the repetitive sound, it was way too quiet. There were no car or train sounds. I couldn't hear Mrs. McTim's television upstairs or the college students, Chad and Mike, blaring their heavy metal next door.

All at once, I remembered being pushed in front of a train. *Am I in the hospital?*

But no beeping monitors, sterile smells, or bright lights shining through my eyelids answered my fears. Just silence and the distant thwack...thwack.

I took a tentative breath, expanding my lungs. It didn't hurt as I'd expected. I twitched my fingers and toes. They seemed to work just fine. Finally, I squinted my eyes open.

The ceiling was rustic wood and four empty coat hooks hung just above the headboard of the bed I was lying on.

Seeing light from the corner of my eye, I turned my head toward it. The small room had another bed near the window, an iron stove in one corner, and a small table with two chairs in the other. The walls were made of the same rustic wood as the ceiling. Outside, the repetitive sound stopped. A few moments later, the door opened to reveal a man carrying an armful of wood.

His scarlet coat and Stetson hat announced his profession.

"What the shit? A Mountie?" I gaped, jolting upright. My joints ached, and my skin smarted as though I was covered in bruises.

"I see you're awake. How are you feeling?" the Mountie asked.

"Who are you? Where am I? How did I get here?" My panicked voice sounded unfamiliar in my ears.

He walked over to the corner and stacked the wood near the stove. "You must have hit your head pretty hard there. I'm Constable Delaforet. You're in Farrloch. As for how you got here, I found you in the forest near the barracks, half-clothed, unconscious, and chilled to the bone. I carried you in here."

Farrloch? Alberta?

I eyed the Mountie, squinting suspiciously, as he removed his hat and placed it on the table.

His steady voice sounded as though he was trying to calm a frightened animal, and his light blue eyes were soft with pity. His brown hair was tousled from his hat, and his face was shadowed by what looked like two-day stubble. He seemed to be in his mid-twenties, around my age.

I took in his strong, broad shoulders and solid frame, and I knew I wouldn't make it past him if he tried to stop me.

I was unconscious in a forest in Canada after I got hit by a train in Chicago? I looked under the blanket at what I was wearing. *He said I was half-naked.*

I wore what seemed to me to be pajamas: white cotton capris with lace cuffs and a short-sleeved chemise. *What the...? Okay, this obviously isn't real. I must be in a coma somewhere.*

I nodded to myself before swinging my bare feet out of bed.

"You should rest, Miss," Constable Delaforet advised as I got to my feet. When the blanket fell away to reveal my pajamas, he cleared his throat and averted his eyes.

"I'm fine," I assured him. *I mean, what can happen in a coma dream anyway?* I marveled at how vivid everything was. It didn't feel at all like a dream. Then again, I'd never been in a coma before, so maybe it was normal.

I took a few steps toward the Mountie, amazed at the feeling of the cold floorboards under my feet. Delaforet instinctively reached out to steady me when I wobbled a little. His large hands were warm on my shoulders.

"Miss, I really must insist you rest until you're well. At the very least, you can't go out in your undergarments."

Undergarments? What kind of coma dream is this? "Tell me, Dudley, what year is it in this coma-created world?"

His eyebrows pulled together in concern. "Miss, this is very much the real world. We just celebrated the turn of a new century. It is 1900. Please, it's clear you're disoriented."

I allowed him to lead me back to bed. *1900, huh? My subconscious is amazing. Everything is so detailed.*

I stared at Delaforet's profile as he tucked my legs under the blankets. *Have I seen him somewhere before? I've heard that your brain never dreams faces it hasn't seen. Where would I have seen such a hot guy? I feel like I'd remember that. A movie? Well, since this is a dream, I can do whatever I want. Right?*

I grinned mischievously and grabbed the front of Delaforet's red tunic. He turned to me, eyes wide with surprise. I leaned up and kissed him full on the mouth. It had been a while since I'd kissed a man. I put all my pent-up passion into it. His lips were soft and warm. They sent a thrill through me, my body heating in an instant. He gently distanced himself from me.

I breathed hard, my eyes wide as the blood drained from my face. *There's no way. It feels too real, and I've never been rejected in a dream before... But how is it possible?*

"Miss," he said gently. "You're distressed. You should rest." If not kissing me back and pulling away hadn't made his rejection clear, his unmoved mask as he called me crazy certainly did.

How can I rest? I'm more than a century in the past in another country, and I just kissed a complete stranger. Calm down, Erin, calm down. This guy helped you, right? As he said, he brought me in here when I was in trouble. Even when I threw myself at him, he didn't respond. He's a Mountie for christsakes! He's a police officer. I'm safe with him.

I tried to swallow my panic and took a few slow, deep breaths.

After watching me calm myself, Delaforet asked, "Do you know who you are?"

I nodded, peeking over at him. "Erin Nichols," I mumbled.

"Do you know how you came to be in the woods, Miss Nichols?"

"No."

"All right. Do you know where you're from?"

"Chicago."

"An American? Chicago is a long way from here. Do you know why you might be here?"

I'd love to know that. Any ideas, Universe? I sighed. *But I can't tell him I'm from the twenty-first century.* "I don't remember," I said.

He nodded gently. "I'm sure it will all come back to you in time," he soothed. "Can you tell me anything else about yourself? You remember your name and where you're from. Do you have a family?"

"Just my mother." *Mom is going to be distraught when she can't find me.* "And I guess Bryan will notice I'm gone eventually."

"Bryan is your brother or...?" he trailed off suggestively.

Is he asking if Bryan is my boyfriend or husband? Of course, at my age in 1900, I would've been an old maid. Then again, I did just kiss him, which is definitely not proper, even by modern standards...Maybe he thinks I'm a prostitute. Oh, jeez... The confidence I'd had while I'd thought this was a dream crumbled under the reality of the situation. My face and neck flushed in the fiercest blush of my entire life. *I totally just kissed a complete stranger, likely the most attractive stranger I've ever met.*

"Bryan is my roommate," I mumbled, averting my gaze and trying to not think about the kiss. *Yeah Erin, good one. I'm sure it's not suspicious that you're living with a man.*

Delaforet nodded thoughtfully.

"It's difficult to afford housing in Chicago on a journalist's pay. Bryan is a friend from college. He's a..." *software developer.* "H-he's a writer...of sorts," I rambled.

"You're a journalist?"

I nodded.

"Perhaps you were sent by a newspaper to write a story?"

"That would explain why I'm so far from home..." I mused, grabbing hold of the explanation.

"Could you be a travel writer? Since the railroad was completed and the hotel opened, there have been quite a few newsmen who've come to town."

I nodded. *It's as good a cover story as any.* "That sounds familiar. I think you're right."

"Of course, that doesn't explain how you came to be in the forest in such a state. You could be the victim of foul play." He eyed me gently. "I think perhaps you should stay in the barracks until you're well enough to remember. Since the railroad was finished, I'm the only Mountie stationed here, so you need not fret over inconveniencing anyone."

It's not like I have anywhere else to go, and he seems safe enough. I smiled sheepishly and nodded. "Thank you very much."

After we'd agreed I would stay with Delaforet, he left to go get breakfast for us. He'd told me to stay in bed, but I ignored that directive entirely. I slipped out from under the blanket and moved toward the window. As I passed a pitcher and washbasin on a cabinet, a light flashed off a small shaving mirror.

When I saw my reflection, I cried out and rushed toward the mirror.

"What the Hell?" I demanded of the blonde-haired, blue-eyed woman in the mirror. I blinked hard a few times, hoping my green eyes would appear.

Bringing my shaking fingertips to my cheeks, I caressed my new face. My hair was long, much longer than I ever would have bothered with. It was blonde where it should have been brown. My face seemed a few years younger, and my usually warm skin seemed paler. I hadn't noticed before that I wasn't wearing any glasses, but I could see perfectly without them. I looked down at my new body. I was slightly thinner than before, having none of my city-walking leg muscles. I was also a few inches taller. I grabbed my breasts and found they were smaller.

"Jesus Christ," I cursed in a voice not my own. I'd noticed I sounded strange before, but I'd thought it was panic that had made my voice higher. "What the fuck is happening to me?"

I looked away from the mirror, my stomach flopping and my head spinning. Closing my eyes and bracing my hands against the cabinet, I took long, steadying breaths.

After the feeling had passed, I continued to the window, determinedly avoiding my reflection. I knew I was in Alberta, so I'd expected to see mountains. But nothing had prepared me for the breath-taking sight that lay before me.

The snow-topped mountains towered over a clear, frozen lake. The rounded rocks on the shore had small patches of snow between them. Evergreens flanked the sides of the lake, dwarfed by the surrounding peaks. The clear sky dyed everything blue.

"Wow" was the only exclamation my brain could come up with. I couldn't pry myself away from the view, not even when Constable Delaforet returned with a basket of food. He frowned at my complete disregard for his orders but set the basket on the table.

"I brought chicken and dumplings," he informed, unpacking a pot, bowls, and spoons.

I reluctantly left the window and went to the table.

Deliberately averting his eyes, he said, "We need to find you some clothes if you're going to be out of bed. We can go down to the church to see if they have any extra dresses they can spare, but for now..." he crossed to the foot of the bed I'd been lying in and opened a trunk. Rummaging around, he continued. "I believe Subconstable Taylor left some things behind. They will likely be too big, but ah, here they are."

He pulled out a buckskin pair of pants, a buttoned shirt, and a coat. "I'm sorry to ask a lady to wear men's clothes, but it's far better than you freezing."

I took the clothes from him, and he went toward the door. "I'll get more wood for the stove," he said delicately.

After he'd left, I pulled on the clothes over my undergarments. I would've just removed them, but the pants wouldn't have stayed up without the extra layers and the shirt tucked in. The clothes were comfortable and would certainly keep me warm. I vowed to fight the Mountie on exchanging them for a dress. Beside the bed was a pair of impractical women's boots. *Whoever's body I'm in, she didn't seem to walk around outside much.*

I dug through the trunk for alternatives and found a pair of moccasins. They were too big, but they would have to do. *Being soft and flexible, it shouldn't be too difficult to walk in them, even if they are too big.*

By the time Delaforet returned, I was dressed and dishing the meal into our bowls. The soup was warming and pleasant, and I told him as much.

"No one makes food like Mellie," he commented.

I raised my eyebrows at his compliment. "Is Mellie your sweetheart then?"

He nearly choked, and it took him a moment to settle his coughing. "No, Mellie operates the best restaurant in town." He paused before continuing. "I don't have a sweetheart."

I smiled to myself as my stomach twanged with unwarranted satisfaction. "So what exactly does a Mountie do besides keep the peace?"

"Well, being that this is a tourist town, or aims to be since the railroad was finished, Ottawa stationed me here to make visitors feel safe. I do keep the peace, but I also patrol the area for criminals, deliver mail to settlements farther out, and work with the Indian agent when need be."

"The Indian agent? Is there a First Nation around here?"

He tilted his head at my question. *Oh, I guess they aren't called that yet.* "There's a reserve near Farrloch?" I rephrased.

He nodded. "The Wyboka Reserve is very near here."

"How long have you been stationed here?"

"Nearly half a year. I was posted in the Yukon before this."

Oh, that's right. There was a gold rush there around this time, wasn't there? I nodded to show I'd heard him and the conversation lapsed. *What am I doing here? I've no place in 1900 western Canada. I need to figure out how to get home. Well, I suppose all I can do at the moment is get my bearings.*

Before we'd even finished our food, a man burst through the door. His eyes widened when he saw me. "I'm sorry to interrupt Constable, but they found another one."

Delaforet sighed and shook his head. He grabbed his hat as he headed for the door. "Stay here," he told me before leaving.

"Pfft, yeah right," I said to the empty room.

I opened the door quietly, and a large, brown horse watched me sneak toward a nearby stable. I listened to the two men talk as Delaforet saddled a black horse.

"Who was it this time?" Delaforet asked.

"A boy around fifteen. His name was Testooklah," the other man responded.

"This is the third Wyboka found dead in as many weeks."

"And this time it was a kid. I know."

"How are the elders taking it?"

"As one would expect. Some are scared, and some are on the warpath. We need to figure out what is going on before we have an uprising on our hands."

"I intend to," Delaforet declared, his tone shifting as he climbed into the saddle.

I ran to hide behind the stable so he wouldn't discover me. As I watched the two men ride away, I wished I had the means to follow them.

"Damn." The cold wind off the lake carried my curse after them.

I knew I should probably listen to Delaforet and rest, and had his steady, blue gaze been on me at that moment, I know he could have persuaded me. But what's a journalist without an unhealthy sense of curiosity?

I left the barracks and the lake behind me as I hiked down the hill toward what I'd rightfully assumed was town. The temperature seemed to be in the upper forties, and I was grateful for my long hair, which I used to cover my chilled ears in lieu of a hat. The ground was still frozen, but there was an unmistakable promise of warmth to come. Early spring birds called to one another. My body hummed with every step, the fresh mountain air invigorating me.

As buildings started to flank the main dirt road, I read their signs. There was a blacksmith—whose hammering echoed from inside his forge —a laundry, a trading post and dry goods store, Mellie's Restaurant, a recreational outfitter, a tavern and brothel, and a bank.

There weren't many people about, but there were enough that I got the distinct impression I was being stared at. *I wonder whose body I'm in. Do any of these people recognize me? Or does this body not belong to someone else? Perhaps it was just created as I showed up. I don't know! Stupid time travel.*

At the other end of town, there was a train station. I considered asking people if they knew me but thought better of it. *If I did steal someone's body, I'm sure their loved ones will come to Delaforet to report a missing person. Where do people in 1900 get information? God, I miss the Internet.*

After walking to the train station ticket booth, I whistled at the clerk through the bars to get his attention.

"The next train isn't for a couple of days," he answered before I'd asked anything.

"All right." I nodded. "Does this town have a library or bookstore?"

He shook his head. "City records are kept at the mayor's office, the local newspaper keeps an archive, but if you're looking for books, the only library is up at the hotel. It's only open to guests and those who have Mr. Broadstone's permission."

I nodded my thanks. *A high-class hotel may have books on the occult. I mean, snobby twentieth-century toffs love that stuff, right?* I looked down at my borrowed clothes. *There's no way those types would even let me in the door. I bet Delaforet has access though. Maybe he would borrow a book for me, or better yet get me access.*

Not knowing when he would return, I thought it best to head back to the barracks. Hiking up the hill was more tiring than I'd expected. *Woman has no leg muscles.*

I ate the rest of my cold soup and took a nap.

THREE

Constable Delaforet didn't return until late in the afternoon, but he brought food with him. I awoke with a start as the door creaked open when he entered. Upon seeing it was only him, I took a deep breath through my nose and stretched my stiff limbs before sitting up in bed.

"How are you feeling?" he inquired as he set down the basket and removed his hat.

"Better," I lied, making my voice light. I knew if this was going to work, he had to believe it.

He raised his eyebrows. "Did you remember something?"

"Bits and pieces," I said, sitting across from him at the table. "I do remember my editor sending me here, and it did have to do with Farrloch being a tourist town in a way."

"How so?"

"Well, I'm supposed to write about the mysterious deaths of the nearby natives."

I watched his reaction closely. He gave nothing away.

"You know how tourists love mystery," I continued.

He frowned. "People are dying, and you want to use it for entertainment?"

My stomach clenched at his disapproval. "Of course not. A journalist's job is to report the truth. I never sensationalize. I'm only pointing out that the story would probably bring curious tourists. I was explaining how my being here had to do with tourism. You suggested I might be a travel writer, remember?"

He nodded, his eyes still guarded.

"Well, people dying mysteriously is always newsworthy, but especially so in a tourist town. I was sent to find out what's going on. So, Constable, do you have anything to say on the subject?"

"No comment."

"Aw come on, Dudley," I prodded. "I'm just going to make a nuisance of myself if you don't tell me."

He slowly chewed his food, never taking his eyes off my face. I resisted the urge to squirm, hiding behind an innocent smile.

He sighed. "Three Wyboka died in as many weeks."

I nodded slightly, encouraging him to continue.

"We do not yet know the cause."

"But you're investigating?"

"At the Wyboka's request, yes. And I will discover what happened."

"Will you take me with you during your investigation?"

"Absolutely not," he said firmly, shaking his head for emphasis.

Undeterred by his expected response, I continued. "You said you found me roughed up in the forest, right?"

"Yes..."

"You suggested it could have been foul play."

He nodded slowly.

"So perhaps, while I was investigating this matter for my story, I uncovered something I wasn't meant to know."

"That's a reasonable assumption."

"Well if that's the case, then it would stand to reason that whoever hurt me before could come after me again. If that happens, then the safest place for me is with you." Despite the long lie I was weaving, my words felt accurate, their truth echoing through me like the reverberated hum from a bell strike.

He frowned, realizing I'd led him right where I wanted him.

"You would also be safe if you stayed in the barracks all the time. No one is going to harm you here."

"Perhaps. However, if I join your investigation, I might recall what happened to me and why I was a target in the first place. I can't stay here forever."

He paused, his features neutral, and I could only hope that he was considering my words.

"Besides," I added quickly before he could make a decision, "I'm a journalist. I may help with your investigation. I have my own set of detecting skills, and sometimes people are more willing to talk to the press than the police."

His distant eyes drifted back to me, locking with mine. I stilled, hoping the warmth that spread through me wasn't showing on my face.

"Any story you write will have to pass through me before you send it on to Chicago."

Normally, I wouldn't have agreed to the police editing my article. But since I knew I wasn't even writing a story, I beamed and held my hand out to shake on the deal.

His sturdy hand enveloped mine, and I shook it firmly. His eyes widened ever so slightly.

"So tell me about the case," I pressed.

Delaforet explained that the three Wyboka who had died were all found in a sacred hot spring on the reserve. He knew about the first two deaths but was not permitted to investigate the matter. With the third death, the Wyboka had asked for his help. He'd examined the most recent body and could not determine the cause of death. There didn't appear to be any signs of foul play. He'd requested to view the site but had not yet been given access. The elders were to convene the following day to discuss allowing him into their sacred space.

After I'd been caught up and we'd finished eating, I asked the question I'd been dreading since I awoke that morning. Delaforet pointed me to an outhouse about a hundred feet from the stables. It was not a pleasant experience. I swore to myself that if I ever made it back to the twenty-first century, I would never complain about gas station bathrooms or their tissue paper again.

When I'd returned, Delaforet had put on his hat and held a basket in each hand.

"Are you returning those to Mellie?" I asked.

"Yes, would you like to accompany me?"

I blinked, surprised he hadn't told me to stay put.

"If you're feeling well enough that is," he added, concerned.

"I think I will join you." I smiled. *I have to show him I'm well enough, or he won't let me go with him when he investigates tomorrow.*

"Very well. Then shall we stop at the church and see about getting you more appropriate attire?"

"No, I won't be wearing a dress unless Subconstable Taylor comes and removes these clothes from me himself."

His mouth hung open, his eyes following me as I closed the door behind us.

"It's just an expression," I waved my hand dismissively at his shocked sensibilities.

"They seem to have many strange expressions in Chicago," he commented.

"Oh Dudley, you have no idea how differently we speak where I'm from."

"Miss Nichols, why do you keep addressing me as Dudley?"

I giggled. "He's a famous Mountie. Haven't you heard of him?"

"I have not."

"Well, I'm not fond of honorifics, and you haven't told me your first name."

"We have not yet known each other a day, Miss Nichols."

"And yet, you've carried me in your arms, saw me in my undergarments, and I kissed you. I'd say all that puts us on a first-name basis." I flushed despite my flippant demeanor.

He tilted his head, using the brim of his hat to hide his face from me. I liked to think I'd made him blush too, but I couldn't picture it.

"Very well, Miss Nichols."

"Erin."

"All right, Erin. You may call me Wynn."

I bent forward so I could look at his face below his hat. "That wasn't so hard. Was it, Wynn?"

I grinned at him, and he rewarded me with a gentle smile in return. My breath hitched as my heart skipped a beat. I averted my gaze to the trees lining the road, crinkling my brow at my reaction. *I never thought I was the swooning type.*

The walk into town was much the same as it had been earlier in the day.

Mellie's was what I imagined high tea at a Cracker Barrel would be like. The rural sturdiness of wood and iron were juxtaposed by white tablecloths and delicate tea services. It was both functional and pleasant in its contrast.

A young woman with big, brown eyes in a blue dress and a frilly apron came out from a back room when she'd heard us enter.

"Back already?" she smiled at Wynn, giving him sheep eyes.

I smiled just as brightly and stepped forward. "Hi there. Erin Nichols. It's nice to meet you."

She shook my hand with a delicate grasp. "Mellie Barker," she answered, a little hesitant at my overfriendliness.

"Mellie from the sign. Your food was excellent."

This compliment turned her hesitant smile genuine. "Well, thank you. I was wondering why Constable Delaforet had asked for double portions. How do you two know each other? Relatives?"

You wish.

"Miss Nichols is a journalist from Chicago. She's here to write about our town," Wynn informed.

"Oh? Wonderful. I do hope you will mention my little restaurant."

"Of course."

"How nice of you to welcome her, Constable Delaforet. Are you staying at the hotel then, Miss Nichols?"

I looked over at the Mountie, wondering if I should lie. He just stood there, all tall and honest.

He cleared his throat. "No, she's—"

"Made other arrangements," I interrupted. "I have a friend in the area, you see." *There's no need to potentially tarnish this man's reputation when he's helped me so much.*

None the wiser, Mellie smiled. "That's well then."

"Miss Nichols will be eating with me quite a lot as I show her around, so please keep making double portions."

"Oh." Mellie's frown made her large eyes puppylike. "All right then."

"Thanks, Mellie." Wynn handed her the baskets and touched the brim of his hat at her.

Her cheeks flushed.

"Yeah, thanks so much, Mellie," I chipped in. Her smile twitched as we turned away to leave.

"Mellie is very pretty," I commented as we walked back to the barracks. "Is she married? I didn't see a ring."

"She's a widow."

I feel a little bad for poking at her now. "That sucks. And she's so young."

He eyed me.

"I mean, how unfortunate," I amended.

He dipped his head in agreement.

"Still, she's done well for herself," I continued, hoping to get any little bit of information from him.

He didn't respond.

"Oh, come on, Wynn. You're telling me you can't see that girl wants you?" I demanded, taking the direct approach.

He sighed. "Are all journalists as nosy as you?"

"Uh yeah. They can't be very good if they aren't." I smiled at having finally gotten a reaction from him. "Hmmm?" I pushed harder when he still hadn't answered.

"I am aware of Mellie's affections, and I cannot return them."

"Why not?"

"Because I just don't feel that way."

"Have you told her that?"

"She has not verbally expressed her interest, so no. I do not wish to embarrass her."

"You think you're being kind," I murmured.

He didn't say anything.

"Well, you aren't. She'll be more hurt the longer she gets her hopes up."

He remained silent for a while. "You seem to know a lot about the subject," he said finally.

"How perceptive of you, Constable Delaforet. I've had my share of heartbreak. I mean, just this morning I was rejected when I kissed this guy.

It was so embarrassing. You should have seen it, but I'm glad you didn't. It might have tarnished your image of me." I laughed at myself, humor having always been my way of coping with uncomfortable situations.

"And this broke your heart, did it?"

I smirked as he played along. "Well, it was mortifying to be sure, but I wouldn't say I'm heartbroken about it. The whole thing sort of endeared him to me in a way."

"Is that so?"

"Yeah, I was in a vulnerable situation, and he didn't take advantage of me. He's quite admirable. Wouldn't you agree?"

He didn't say anything.

"Of course, there's always a chance he found me unappealing."

He paused so long, I thought he would again opt for silence. "I can't imagine that to be the case," he said finally.

My heart skipped a beat, and my face flushed. I looked at my moccasins, thinking I was silly for being embarrassed when I'd instigated the conversation. "That's nice of you to say, Wynn," I murmured, smiling to myself. Then I took a deep breath. "But I'd still like to apologize for my behavior."

He nodded, acknowledging my apology. "I am curious though," he said, his eyes momentarily meeting mine in a sidelong glance before he directed them forward once more. "Why would you suddenly kiss a man you had just met?"

I laughed self-consciously. "An excellent question. To be honest, I'd thought I was dreaming. I mean, an attractive Mountie shows up in your dream. The only logical thing to do is kiss him, right? Isn't that what you would do?"

"I can't say I would."

I laughed sincerely. "Your loss."

I peeked sideways at Wynn as we walked. The shadow of a smile curved the edge of his lips. *I'll get him to laugh yet.*

As we reached the barracks, Wynn stepped on a letter that had been shoved under the door. He picked it up and read it.

"What is it?" I asked, noting his frown.

"Mr. Broadstone has requested my presence at the hotel. Why don't you stay here? You must be tired from the walk."

I hated to admit I was. "All right. Oh, I forgot to ask you. Do you have access to the hotel's library?"

He nodded.

"Do you think you could request access for me? I want to do some research for my article."

"I will inquire."

"Thanks."

Once Wynn had left, I didn't know what to do with myself. If I were home, I probably would have watched Netflix or spent a few hours on social media. As it was, I was too exhausted to do anything useful. Having slept that afternoon, I wasn't tired enough to take another nap. I decided to sit by the window and soak in the views nature had provided.

After a while, I found myself humming to fill the silence. Then I began to sing. I had been in choir in school and had performed in talent shows and competitions, though I'd never won first place. Singing had been such a big part of my everyday life for a long time, and I couldn't remember when I'd stopped. I sang the tunes I'd always enjoyed and realized this body's range was different from my own. I could hit high notes I'd never dreamed of as an alto.

Eventually, Wynn returned. At the creak of the door, I cut my song mid-note, biting my lip. My face heated at the thought he may have heard me belting out with reckless abandon, but he didn't give anything away as he removed his hat and put the basket with our dinner on the table.

As we ate, I asked him why Mr. Broadstone had wanted to see him.

"He heard about Testooklah, and he was concerned. He wanted to ensure I was looking into it."

"What does he think? I mean, you're a Mountie. How could you not?" I defended.

"He wanted me to know that I have support should I need anything."

I pursed my lips. "Rich people..." I muttered, not entirely ready to let go of my protective stand. "Did you ask him about the library?"

Wynn nodded. "He said you can have access whenever you need. Your name was left with the front desk."

"Great. Thank you."

He inclined his head in acknowledgment.

FOUR

I fell asleep immediately that night, though it wasn't terribly restful as I had a recurring nightmare, reliving memories I would have preferred stayed in the past.

I snuck away from the group of students singing silly songs around the campfire.

My arms and shoulders were already sore from having paddled a canoe all afternoon.

I strolled down the wooded trail to the lake and sat on the edge of the dock. It was a relief to be alone, to not have to smile and pretend everything was all right.

The grief counselor my mom and I went to kept telling me that what I felt was normal, but I knew my friends were burdened because they didn't know how to act around me. So I tried to be the same old Erin, even if she no longer existed.

I shifted my gaze from the calm lake to the night sky. The waning half-moon peeked out just above the surrounding trees. I stared up at the star-speckled sky and remembered cuddling up on the couch with my dad watching sci-fi movies.

Every Saturday night, we would watch space movies while eating popcorn and Raisinets. I'd probably seen *Star Wars* over a hundred times. We'd recite the lines along with the film, and sometimes we would have lightsaber battles with cheap extendable toys. The stars blurred as a sob rose in my throat.

I closed my eyes and took a few deep breaths.

My dad used to tell me we were all made of stardust. As I gazed up at my first view of a night sky full of stars, I hoped it was true. Because if it was true, it meant we were all connected. And if we were all connected, maybe the stars had some power to bring my dad back.

I made a wish on every star I could see. I wished things could go back to the way they were. I wished I could have stopped my dad from going to work that night. I wished we would have gotten to go to the Cubs game as he'd promised. But all of my wishes really came down to the same desire: I wished my dad was still alive.

I awoke from my dream with a lump in my throat, afraid to go back to sleep, afraid to be pulled back into that same time and place. I rolled over and whispered into the completely dark room. "Wynn, are you awake?"

His silence answered me.

I slipped out of bed and pulled on my clothes and moccasins. Feeling my way, I crept out into the night. I followed the path and stood at the edge of the frozen lake.

With a sharp intake of breath, I stared up at the sky. I'd been fooling myself into thinking I'd seen stars in Wisconsin, but nothing could have been further from the truth. The night sky I stood under by the lake seemed to belong to a different planet. It appeared to me that there were more stars than sky. They clustered together in bright smatterings as if someone had accidentally pressed the tab on a white spray paint can.

My breath came out in a long, frosted sigh as ribbons of murky light tinged with green rippled across the sliver of moon. I'd seen pictures of the aurora borealis. And though it wasn't nearly as bright as it appeared through the camera lens, it was breathtaking all the same to see it in real life. The entire spectacle was reflected in the clear, frozen water of the lake. I marveled at the mirror-like surface.

This was the sort of thing I would have shown Bryan on the Internet; I smiled at the thought. In fact, it was probably around the time of night I would have dragged him from his computer and told him it was time to sleep. *No one is there to look out for him now. He will just program all night, drinking meal replacement shakes instead of eating real food. How long will it take for him to notice I'm gone? Will he remember what day it is in time to pay the rent?*

Just as homesickness squeezed my chest, a shadow moved across the lake. My heart hammered, and I looked up. The dark form had large wings, and a shining yellow light on its forehead illuminated its reptilian face.

"D-d-dragon...Holy fuck. That's a dragon." My strangled scream came out an airy, high-pitched squeak.

The dragon landed on the shore of the lake near the edge of the forest. In the glow from its forehead, a man climbed down from its back. Then he and the dragon disappeared amongst the trees.

I was frozen in place, not daring to move. *That can't be right. No way. Dragons aren't real. I must have misinterpreted something else.*

Then I heard a song on the wind. The mellow baritone seemed familiar in a way I couldn't place. Following after the man and the maybe-dragon felt like the stupidest thing I'd ever done, but that was the direction the song beckoned me, and I wasn't about to quell the curiosity that crept over me.

At the edge of the tree line, I momentarily worried if there were bears. I laughed at myself, shaking my head in disbelief of my own thoughts. *Really, Erin? You're walking toward a dragon, and you're worried about bears?*

As I got closer, I realized the song was in a language I didn't understand. Eventually, I came upon two men sitting by a fire. The dragon was nowhere in sight. *I knew I wasn't seeing right.*

The man with crimson hair stopped singing and I froze; my mouth hung open when they both looked up at me. They were devastatingly gorgeous. Otherworldly. Ethereal. The kind of beauty no man had a right to. I blinked stupidly at them.

The man with raven-black hair and eyes that glinted gold in the firelight moved toward me and took my hand. I shivered as he kissed my fingers. And when he stared into my eyes, his eyes glowed the same color that the dragon's forehead had. His gaze surrounded me, penetrated me, engulfed me. As he smiled seductively, I started to lose myself in his presence. The world around me blurred, and everything but him drifted from my mind.

"Grigore, that is enough," the other man chided in an eastern European accent.

Grigore clicked his tongue and moved away from me.

"I am glad to see you well," the man with the crimson hair told me.

"Do I know you?" I whispered, my mind slowly gaining traction.

"We have met in a way. I saved you last night."

"Wynn saved me," I contradicted automatically.

He nodded. "Da, but I brought you to him."

"What do you mean?"

"Did he tell you he found you in the forest?"

I nodded slowly.

"When I found you, you were near death. Your body lay broken near the railroad tracks. I healed you and brought you here."

I didn't want to argue with someone I'd just met, especially not someone who I could just sit and look at for days on end, but I couldn't let the obvious lie go. "That can't be true. There's no way you could have healed severe injuries so fast."

He stared at me silently for a while, his eyes analyzing me. But I stood determinedly by my statement despite the blush growing hotter the longer his gaze was on me.

"Anyone ever tell you it's rude to stare?" I asked, more self-conscious than offended.

He took a step closer to me as if drawn in. I lowered my head a little but stood my ground.

"There is something different about you," he said uncertainly, squinting as if trying to figure me out.

"Okay..."

His blue eyes stared deep into mine, and I couldn't look away.

"You are...dissonant."

I frowned. "That doesn't sound like a compliment."

"You do not belong here."

You're right. I don't. Even with that thought, my stomach dropped as if I'd been scolded.

"Could it be...?" He murmured to himself. After another contemplative pause, he asked, "Do you believe in magic?"

A week prior, I would've answered I was an agnostic and all-around skeptic. But in light of the circumstances, I'd become a believer in the impossible. Well, time-travel at least.

"I suppose..." I answered hesitantly as if tasting a new dish I wasn't sure I was going to like.

"It was through magic that I was able to heal you."

"Uh-huh," I grunted sarcastically, my conditioned reaction coming through, though it wasn't like I had a better explanation for everything that had happened to me.

"You need more proof that magic is real?"

"That would be...helpful."

"Grigore, show her."

Grigore stood and walked a few feet away, grumbling under his breath the whole time. When he'd stopped, his eyes glowed bright yellow. The light engulfed his body, and he turned into the dragon with a shining yellow gem on its forehead.

"Holy fuck!" I cursed, leaping toward the crimson-haired man.

Grigore didn't look quite like the dragons from the fantasy movies I'd seen. He was more humanoid, with longer limbs and clawed hands, though he didn't stand completely upright like a person.

"There's no need to be alarmed." The man held his hands up in a soothing gesture. "Grigore is under a spell that binds him to me. I can stop him if he does anything to harm you or anyone else."

"What he means to say is: I am his slave," Grigore mourned, his accent the same as the man's.

"If you were not bound to me, you would be out there burning, raping, and causing chaos."

"I take issue with the word rape. I *seduce* women."

"It is rape if you use magic to seduce them."

I could tell this conversation could go on for a while. "Let me get this straight: you magically enslaved a dragon?"

"He is a zmeu. To keep him from harming people, yes."

"And you're a...what?"

"I am the product of a hultan and an iele."

"What's that?"

He frowned, searching for the right words. "I suppose you would call a hultan a wizard and an iele a fae."

"A fae? Like a fairy?"

"A soul born of the wild."

"Meaning?"

"Fae are magical beings whose magic comes from their souls' connections with wild nature."

I didn't say anything but stepped closer to the crimson-haired man, searching his eyes. He had a similar build to Wynn: tall with broad shoulders. "What's your name?"

"You can call me Mitica."

I nodded, eyes still locked on his. There was something in his gaze, something that said I could trust him. I made a decision. "I'm Erin Nichols, and I think I'm in trouble, Mitica."

"You are in danger?"

"I'm not sure. But if I tell you something crazy, will you believe me?"

"I will consider your words carefully."

I bit my lip. *I mean, it can't be crazier than fae and dragons, right?* "Mitica, I'm from the future."

His gaze didn't look away from me as he searched my eyes. "That is not possible."

"Hey! Consider more carefully," I said defensively. "I'm telling you: yesterday I was in 2016, and now I'm in 1900."

His eyebrows pulled together in thought. Finally, he said, "I think we need to ask someone with more knowledge of spirit travel. I know a woman who may be able to understand what has happened to you. Will you go with me to meet her?"

"Right now?"

"No, I need to talk with her first. Tomorrow night."

I nodded. "Okay, if you think she can help."

He placed his hand gently on my shoulder and smiled in a soothing manner. "Do not be afraid. I will help you."

I felt the anxiety I'd been carrying around since I awoke that morning slip from my body as the calming warmth of Mitica's hand seeped into me. I shivered in relief as my eyes unwittingly filled with tears. I smiled up into Mitica's kind face as the tears leaked down my cheeks. "Thank you for believing me, and thank you for saving my life."

He slowly lifted his hand and caught a tear with a bent finger, his blue eyes softening with compassion. My chest ached from either my impossible situation or the heartbreaking look in Mitica's eyes. I wasn't sure which. I took a deep breath to fortify myself.

"Until tomorrow," I whispered before stepping away and leaving the ring of firelight.

As I departed, I heard Grigore say, "I think I like her."

"No, Grigore," Mitica said firmly.

"You never let me have any fun."

"Because your idea of fun is destruction and mayhem."

I smirked at their exchange and snuck toward my empty bed in the barracks.

FIVE

The next morning, Wynn told me he'd arranged transportation for me while he was in town fetching breakfast. I couldn't hide my surprise when he led a tan horse from the stables.

"You expect me to ride that?" I asked doubtfully as the horse stared back at me.

Wynn stroked the horse between the eyes. "His name is Langundo, and he is quite gentle."

"That may be true, but I'm still not getting on his back."

"How are you going to get to the reserve then?"

"Wynn, I've never ridden a horse before. I wouldn't know the first thing about it."

He looked at Langundo and frowned. "You've never been on a horse at all?"

I've never even been this close to a horse before, or any animal this massive. I've only ever seen them in real life at a distance as they drive tourists around in carriages. "Never," I answered.

He rubbed the back of his neck. "Well, you're going to need a way to get around, and this is the easiest way. Are you open to learning? I can teach you."

I bit my lower lip. *If I don't learn, I'm going to get left behind.* "Will you take it slow?" I asked nervously.

He smiled at me kindly. "I won't do anything you're uncomfortable with."

I lowered my head but met his eyes, nodding my agreement.

"Come here." He beckoned me to him and Langundo with an outstretched hand.

I inched closer and put my hand in his. He grasped my fingers gently and brought them to Langundo's neck. Placing his hand over mine, he showed me how Langundo liked to be pet.

The horse's coat was soft, and Wynn's hand warmed mine. I held my breath as my heart pounded with nerves.

Langundo looked back at me, and I jumped away, gasping. My back smacked into Wynn's chest, and he caught my shoulders to steady me.

"You're making him nervous," he murmured near my ear.

As my heart hammered in my chest, I knew it wasn't only because the horse had startled me. "He's making me nervous," I corrected in a soft voice.

"Horses can feel emotions. If you're nervous, he will be nervous, too."

"How can I get used to him without starting out nervous?"

Wynn paused, his expression neutral. "Why don't we let Langundo rest in the stables for the day, and you can ride with me?" he asked, his tone soft as he soothed both me and the horse.

The thought of actually climbing onto a beast that size made me instinctively shake my head.

Wynn turned me around and stared deep into my eyes. My breath caught in my throat.

"It's all right, Erin. I won't let anything happen to you. You can trust me."

The firmness of his tone, his expression, and his hands on my shoulders convinced me to agree despite my inherent unease.

He nodded once, satisfied with my answer, and led Langundo into the stables. The black horse he returned with seemed even bigger. The horse snorted when he saw me and moved toward me. I internally recoiled but stood my ground. Once he'd reached me, he nuzzled his head on my neck and lipped my ears.

I giggled, and Wynn pulled him away.

"He seems friendly," I said, wiping horse spit from my ear.

Wynn didn't respond.

"What's his name?" The horse and I both looked at Wynn for an answer.

"Bou," Wynn responded.

Bou groaned at hearing his name, and I laughed. "I don't think he likes it."

"Probably not."

After tugging on his saddle to ensure it was secure, Wynn motioned for me to come to him. He talked me through climbing into the saddle. The ground seemed very far away from Bou's back, but I wasn't scared for long.

Once Wynn got into the saddle behind me and wrapped his arms around me to hold the reins, I couldn't concentrate on anything but his solid chest on my back and his breath in my ear. He explained how the reins worked, how I should hold them, and how to use my legs, but I wasn't really paying attention.

I shivered, my breath coming out in an uneven sigh. It had been so long since a man held me. The tingling I felt told me it had been far too long. It was funny how I hadn't noticed until now. Never had a man as sexy as Wynn paid me any attention. Touching me, holding me, whispering in my ear? The probability of any of that happening was incalculably small. The sensations, the images, that arose were wholly inappropriate considering the platonic and instructional nature of the situation.

I sat up straight and chided myself. *Come on, Erin. He's trying to teach you something. Get your mind out of the gutter. He's eventually going to expect you to get on a horse alone. Pay attention.* It wasn't easy to ignore how good it felt in his arms, but I eventually managed to wrestle my libido for control of my brain.

He instructed me very slowly, just like he'd promised. And Bou walked at a steady pace the entire way to the reserve.

The edge of the reserve was marked with a small sign. Beside it, astride his brown horse, was the man who had burst into the barracks the day before.

"Miss Nichols, I'm Albert Clark. I'm the Indian agent. I apologize for not introducing myself yesterday. Constable Delaforet informed me you are a journalist from Chicago."

I nodded.

He continued as he turned his horse to walk beside Bou. "I'm sorry we could not have met under better circumstances. I do hope you will be fair in your reporting of this matter."

"I report the facts as they are. Fair has nothing to do with it," I stated, slightly irritated at the suggestive pressure of his comment.

He acknowledged my assertion with a nod and a frown.

The trail into the reserve was surrounded by trees and was a rather steep ascent. At the summit, the land evened out a bit, though it was still insulated by trees and felt enclosed by mountains. Eventually, small, ramshackle houses started to appear among the rocky hills. At first, there weren't any people in sight. But the farther we went, the more they began to show themselves.

My stomach clenched as I looked at them. Their thin frames hunched under the tattered blankets in which they were wrapped. Their weathered faces looked haggard, but it was their eyes that truly got to me. Their eyes were lifeless, beaten, as if the world had taken their spirits.

I tried to hold back my tears, my heart aching for their pain and the injustice of it all.

As we continued, I witnessed a wider range of expressions from the Wyboka. Some ignored our presence entirely, going about their chores. Others glared at us with malice, which I couldn't really blame them for. And still, some welcomed us, nodding and raising a hand in greeting as we passed.

We finally stopped in front of an elderly woman with feathers braided into her long, gray hair.

Delaforet slipped out of the saddle to greet her. "Good morning, Likinoak," he said.

She responded in a language I didn't understand, then smiled cheekily at him.

He dipped his head in response and returned to my side to help me out of the saddle.

Once safely on the ground, Likinoak approached me and grasped both of my hands in hers. I met the older woman's gaze as she did so. Her dark eyes were deep, and it felt like she was staring into my soul. I had no idea what she was looking for, so I just stared back curiously. After a while, she beamed at me and cupped my cheeks as my grandmother used to do.

"Come," she instructed.

We followed her into a giant teepee. Inside, a group of grave men and women sat around a small fire. I took a seat on the ground between Wynn and Likinoak.

"Delaforet has requested entrance to the sacred hot spring. Who here would like to speak?" Likinoak asked.

"We cannot allow an outsider into our sacred space," one man spat. "They have proven many times that they have no respect for what is sacred to us."

"Why does it even matter now, Pówahkai?" a woman with scared eyes countered. "The space is already defiled with the blood of the People. It is cursed."

"Piyiets is right. No one should be allowed until the area is cleansed," the man beside Piyiets said.

"Perhaps it is the presence of the whites that has cursed us," Pówahkai muttered.

"I agree with Dzindo. The sacred space needs to be cleansed," another woman stated, ignoring Pówahkai's comment.

"I have received no message about a curse," Likinoak mused.

"Three people are dead. Is that not message enough?" Piyiets challenged.

Likinoak sighed, shaking her head. "I hear what you all say." She turned her dark, gentle eyes on Wynn. "As tradition dictates, only Wyboka will be allowed in the sacred space." Her gaze seemed to say something her words did not.

Wynn lowered his eyes in defeat. "May I at least speak to you in more depth as to the particulars?"

Likinoak met the others' eyes, then nodded.

"Each person who died was found in the hot spring?" he asked.

"In the water, yes," Likinoak confirmed.

"I know the deaths were roughly a week apart. Are there any commonalities?'

"As you know, they were of different ages. Two males and a female," Likinoak stated.

"Were they there for a particular purpose?" Wynn asked. "Or were they there just to bathe?"

"Each entered the spring to be cleansed before communing with The Great Spirit," Piyiets said worriedly.

"That's right," the other woman agreed. "Testooklah went to be cleansed before his first quest in the bush."

"And the others?"

"Tsesikó was a healer. He was there to be purified before healing one of our sick. Yejeták was seeking a vision."

Wynn nodded thoughtfully. "Has anyone else gone into the spring?"

"No one else has gotten into the water that we know of," Likinoak informed.

"Excuse me for interrupting, but is there a process for this type of ceremony?" I asked.

Everyone was quiet for a moment before Likinoak spoke. "There is a lot of preparation for these types of rituals. It begins with fasting for two days, during which the seeker meditates and chants the ancient songs. Only water is allowed during this time of fasting. The songs depend on the purpose of the ceremony. The seeker drinks the ceremonial tea, then enters the sacred spring for a purification bath. After being cleansed, he or she is ready to commune with the spirits. He may enter the bush in search of a vision or a song as Testooklah was to, or he may visit the sick like Tsesikó."

I turned to Wynn. "Is it possible they just drowned? I mean fasting for two days and getting into a hot bath could make anyone pass out."

"It's hard to say as there will not be an autopsy. It's possible, but how likely is it that all three of them drowned in such close succession?"

"Good point."

Delaforet sat silently for a moment, his eyebrows crinkled in a pensive expression. "Without more information, I don't know what I can do to help solve this mystery." He frowned, clearly not happy with his conclusion.

"I told you asking for his help was useless," Pówahkai muttered.

"It seems we must handle this matter ourselves," Likinoak pronounced.

My heart was heavy with disappointment as we left the teepee, but as Wynn had said, we needed more information.

Albert was particularly distressed as he remounted his horse. "What am I supposed to tell Ottawa?" he asked Wynn.

"Let's just wait and see what happens for now," Wynn counseled. "If enough time passes without event, it very well could have been drowning."

Wynn was pensively quiet while we rode back to the barracks. I couldn't see his face because I was riding in front of him, but I could feel his frown.

"What are you going to do?" I asked.

"There is nothing I can do."

"You need more information?"

I felt him nod.

"Why don't we just break into the hot spring and check out the crime scene?"

He shook his head. "We cannot do that."

"Because you're the law?"

"No, because it is wrong. We cannot desecrate the Wyboka's sacred space. Too much of what was theirs has been violated already. We must respect their boundaries."

A government agent respecting the rights of indigenous populations? How novel. "But wouldn't you say this is an extenuating circumstance?"

He was silent for a moment before he answered. "They were able to do just fine without our help for thousands of years. I'm certain they are more than capable of taking care of their own in this matter."

Then why did they ask for help, and why are you so upset that you couldn't help?

After we'd had another delightful lunch cooked by Mellie, Wynn left to patrol and check in on some outlying settlements. I thought about disregarding his directive to stay at the barracks, but I decided to listen just this once.

To show my thanks and to pull my own weight, I gave the barracks as best a cleaning as I could with a bucket of water and a rag. It seemed my new body wasn't used to any kind of manual labor. Even with it being winter, I had to remove my extra layers to cool down from sweating.

Of course, after all that work and not having lived up to modern standards of hygiene for a few days, I was appalled by my own smell. I took advantage of the fact that Wynn was out to strip down, hand wash my clothes, and then wash myself. I hung my wet clothes over a chair near the stove and tied a blanket around myself like a toga.

I was huddled near the stove in my blanket toga when Wynn returned.

His eyes swept the space, taking stock of things in a few seconds. He crossed the room and pulled the blanket from his bed. Then he wrapped it around my shivering body.

"I miscalculated," I explained, trying to keep my teeth from chattering.

He went outside and brought in more wood for the stove. After stuffing in a few more logs, he sat cross-legged near the stove and pulled me into his lap without a word.

His body heat soon relaxed my shivers and brought warmth back into my limbs.

Neither of us spoke as I rested my head on his chest and listened to his heartbeat. The dim light from the stove reflected off the brass buttons of his red tunic. I watched the buffalo on the button dance in light and shadow.

As my body warmed to its normal temperature, our current situation turned from comforting to enticing. The moment I thought how good it felt to be in his embrace, I stiffened and then shivered without chill.

He seemed to notice the change because he pulled back a little to meet my eyes. "Are you warmer now?" he whispered into the hushed cabin.

I nodded without looking away.

He reached out a hand slowly and felt my clothes on the chair. "Your clothes are dry. You should get dressed."

Though he'd said that, he didn't make a move to release me from his embrace. For a tense moment, we gazed at each other in silence. I sighed a shuddering breath, then licked my dry lips. It was then that his arms loosened, and he looked away. Taking the hint, I climbed out of his lap and watched as he left the room for me to get dressed.

SIX

It felt like it took forever before I heard Wynn's slow, steady breathing, indicating that he was asleep. When I was able to sneak out again, I made my way to the place where I'd met with Mitica and Grigore. They were nowhere in sight.

I huddled beside the cold, ashy stack of logs that had been a fire the night before.

After a few minutes of waiting, the dark and quiet of the forest hovered in close around me. A shiver of fear ran through me, and I regretted entering the woodland alone. The world seemed so much bigger since I'd learned magic was real. *How can an unremarkable human like me hope to survive?*

"Here you are," Mitica announced his arrival.

I let out a relieved sigh and turned toward him. "And how are you this evening, Mitica?"

I could hear the smile in his voice when he said, "I am with you. How could I not be well?"

My heart skipped, and I gave a self-conscious laugh. "Oho there, you charmer. What are you trying to do? Give a girl a heart condition?"

He chuckled in his rich baritone. The sound sent a thrill through me. I remembered how his eyes had softened in compassion as he'd comforted me the night before.

He reached out and gently took my hand. My heart danced at how natural it felt.

"Are you ready?" he asked.

"To meet your friend?"

"Da."

"Lead the way."

He led me back toward the lake, his large hand enveloping mine in its reassuring warmth. I felt a shameless moment of regret when he released it as we reached Grigore.

"How's it going, Grigore?" I asked the dragon.

"How well can I be, chained as I am for an eternity of servitude?"

Mitica sighed at him. "First of all, it is not for eternity. It is just until I die. And secondly, would you rather I had let Făt-Frumos kill you? You are supposed to be repenting for your past deeds. If you do not change your ways by the time you are released. They *will* slay you."

"They would have to find me first," Grigore muttered.

Mitica sighed again and shook his head.

I smirked at the pair. "You guys should just admit that you're actually fond of each other."

They both made sounds of disgust, and I laughed.

"How far is your friend from here?" I asked Mitica.

"Just a short flight."

"A short what now? You're not expecting me to *ride* Grigore. Are you?"

"I like the way you said that." Grigore grinned, his sharp teeth gleaming in the light of his forehead gem.

"Shut up, Grigore," I snapped.

Mitica took my hand again and stepped close to me. His blue eyes beckoned mine, pulling me back from the edge of my growing panic. "You have nothing to fear. I will protect you from any danger that may threaten you. You can trust me."

His vow loosened the knot in my stomach.

"Do you trust me?" he asked.

I let out a shaky breath and nodded.

His answering smile was devastating. My heart pounded as if it wanted him to hear.

Mitica led me to Grigore—who hunched down accommodatingly—and helped me onto Grigore's back, just behind his wings. Then he climbed on behind me.

"Are you ready?" he whispered in my ear as he adjusted my body to rest against his.

A shiver of heat ran through me, my body very aware of his chest on my back, his thighs along mine. A dirty little thought surfaced in my mind as I wondered whether my backside pressed against him would produce a reaction from his manhood. I squashed the idea. *What is wrong with me today?* Taking a deep breath, I realigned my priorities.

"As I'll ever be," I answered, grabbing at Grigore's scaly back for something to hold on to.

"Do not worry," Mitica assured. "I will not let you fall." He produced a length of pliant wood from his jacket. After muttering a few words in a language I didn't understand, he flicked the stick. It elongated and threaded itself between Grigore's lips before the other end landed in Mitica's free hand.

With his magical reins in each hand, Mitica's arms encircled me. The feeling was familiar, probably because I'd been in a similar situation with Wynn earlier that day. The major difference was that Bou couldn't fly, so I was far more nervous on Grigore.

"Here we go," Mitica warned.

I squeezed my thighs tighter to hold my balance. With a click of his tongue, Mitica signaled for Grigore to go ahead. He spread his massive wings and pumped them hard. I felt us leave the ground, and my entire body tensed.

"Relax," Mitica urged, his breath hot in my ear.

I would've found that a total turn-on had I not feared for my life. Still, I forced my muscles to unclench in an attempt to follow his advice. I took a steadying breath and finally looked past Grigore's back.

The treetops were about a hundred feet below us, and we'd already left the lake behind. The cold air whipped the hair from my face and chilled my nose and throat. The mountains still towered around us, but the stars, swirling in the Milky Way, felt close enough to touch.

I tentatively removed one hand from Grigore's back and extended it toward the sky in wonder.

I could hear Mitica's smile as he said, "Catch one for me, too."

We soared above the dark forest, and my heart raced joyfully. I laughed a breathy sound of delight.

Not long after, Grigore began to slow and descend. I could see a large fire with people around it ahead of us. We flew a ways past the fire and landed behind a simple, log house.

Mitica and I slipped from Grigore's back, and Grigore retreated into the forest.

To my surprise, the back door of the house opened, and Likinoak emerged holding a lantern. She smiled warmly at us and motioned us in. Once we'd shut the door behind us, Likinoak turned to me.

"You have come a long way to be here," she commented.

I nodded.

"Do you know anything about time travel?" Mitica asked her.

She simply looked at him and smiled. "You did well to bring her to me, Seyko."

I looked at Mitica, quirking my eyebrow at her form of address.

"I will explain later," he assured.

As she had the first time we'd met, Likinoak approached me and took my hands in hers, staring deep into my eyes. "You are you but not you," she said as if that were enough of an explanation.

"Could you be more specific?" I asked.

"First, come and sit. Then tell me your story."

She pulled three chairs close to the roaring fire, and we all sat, cupping the tea she'd handed us.

I told them what I remembered from the day I'd time traveled. She asked questions about what time of year it was, what the moon cycle was, and what I was feeling before I was pushed in front of the train.

I had been so distracted with everything that I hadn't bothered to wonder who had pushed me until that moment. *I suppose it's possible it was an accident. More likely, Bill alerted the mayor to my plans, and he'd directed someone to "take care of me."* I clenched my fists. *Crooked bastards.*

After hearing my story, Likinoak nodded and turned to Mitica. "You say you found her by the railroad tracks in Farrloch?"

He nodded. "She was in a horrible state. Her injuries certainly were consistent with being hit by a train."

"And the body you are in now doesn't look like the one you left in Chicago?" she asked me.

"That's right. I look totally different."

"I see." She pursed her lips in thought, and we waited in a silence that grew heavier with every passing moment. Finally, she presented her theory on the matter. "The desire you felt as you stared into the sky, it was like casting a spell. The black moon is a time of heightened magic, and in your time, it fell on a night when the veil was thinning. When your spirit left your body, it sought to realize that desire. The night you arrived here was also the night of a black moon. Your spirit jumped to a previous incarnation."

"But how did I cast a spell? I'm not magic."

"Everyone has a little magic because we all live on energy from the sun and earth," she informed. "But you may be right. Perhaps more is happening that we do not know."

She turned her gaze to Mitica, who appeared deep in thought.

"So you're saying that this was my body in a previous life?"

"Yes, your spirit sought a compatible vessel."

"How does that work? Does that mean I died in 1900 in a previous life and was reborn in 1989? And then what? I died in 2016 and returned to my vacated body in 1900?"

She listened carefully to my explanation, then nodded her agreement.

"But why can I remember everything from 2016 but not 1900?"

Mitica answered, "You did not return to the spirit realm. That is where memories are cleansed between lifetimes. If you knew your true name, you would have access to the memories from all of your lifetimes."

"My true name?"

"Your name during your first lifetime."

"Oh." I fell silent for a while, considering everything I'd just heard. "So...I died in 2016?" The thought made me lightheaded. "Does that mean I can never go back?"

"I am uncertain," Likinoak said. "The trauma was enough that your spirit left your body. But Mitica healed your body in this time. So if your body in the future was healed, you may be able to return."

"How would I know? And if it isn't, what happens if I try to go back? And if it is, how do I get back?"

"I do not know, but I can try to find out," Likinoak answered.

"I will also look into the matter," Mitica promised.

I sighed at my predicament. "What am I supposed to do now? I mean, I can't stay with Wynn forever. How do I even start to build a life here? I don't know anything about this time. Wait. If I'm in my body from a previous life, that means I could have family and friends here. But I don't remember anything." I moaned, frustrated.

Mitica reached out and took my hand from my lap. "Do not worry. We will figure this out."

I met his eyes as they danced in the flickering light of the fire and nodded. "Thank you."

The low, steady pounding of a drum interrupted our moment, followed shortly by voices raised in song.

"It is time," Likinoak announced, rising from her chair and going outside.

"Time for what?" I asked Mitica as we followed her out the front door.

We walked along the dirt path, which led to a large clearing with a huge fire in the center. A tall scaffolding-like platform stood at one end, and men and women danced and sang around it.

"Time for a funeral," Mitica answered solemnly.

Looking closer, I saw an oblong shape wrapped in a blanket atop the platform. I assumed it must be the body of Testooklah.

We watched the funeral progress for a long while, silently bearing witness to the mourning and celebration of Testooklah's too short life.

"Why did Likinoak call you Seyko?" I asked Mitica quietly.

"Seyko is the Wyboka word for son. I am an honorary Wyboka," he replied. "I saved Likinoak's son, Chuthekii, not long ago. We performed a kinship ceremony and became brothers."

I nodded slowly and then jumped as a thought occurred to me. "Wait, does that mean you can enter their sacred space?"

"Da."

I turned to him, pleading with my eyes. "Would you do me a favor?"

"Whatever you need."

"Wynn was investigating the unusual deaths here on the reserve, but he's hit a wall. He needs to examine the crime scene, but he's not allowed in because the hot spring is sacred. The Wyboka didn't find anything wrong, which is why, I assume, they asked Wynn for help. Will you go in and take a look around, then tell me what you find?"

He smiled gently at me, and his eyes, sparkling in the light of the bonfire, praised my cleverness. "Of course," he said.

"Thank you." I beamed at him.

After a while, Likinoak rejoined us, and we told her our plan. She nodded her approval and promised to stay with me as Mitica left to have a look.

"Mitica told me about your son. Where is he now?" I asked the older woman.

"Chuthekii is escorting the children back to the residential school. Two others had come home to seek a quest or a song in the bush at the same time as Testooklah. We felt it was not safe for them, so he took them back."

I knew about the abominable institution of native residential schools where children were separated from their families, languages, cultures, and religions in an attempt to beat the native out of them. My stomach turned in revulsion.

"How often do the children get to come home?" I asked.

"Not often enough. We had to lie to the school to take those three home. Some children try to run away to come home. Others want to stay. With the traditional ceremonies outlawed by the government and the children taken at younger and younger ages, I fear our ways will be lost."

I didn't know a lot about the Wyboka in the modern-day other than their environmental activism and their high rates of alcoholism and suicide. I honestly had no words of comfort to ease her fears besides that her First Nation still survived.

"So Mitica became a Wyboka after he helped your son? What happened?"

Her wrinkled face darkened as if remembering a particularly horrifying nightmare.

"My son is an animal person, a dreamer. He receives magic from animals. While communing with one of the ancient spirits, he became overwhelmed and turned into a wechuge. Mitica saved Chuthekii before he could hurt anyone."

It was at that point in the conversation Mitica returned. "There did not seem to be anything amiss," he informed us, shaking his head in apology.

After that, Mitica said it was time to get me back, and Likinoak promised again to look into my plight.

I was much less scared while riding Grigore the second time. My lack of fear allowed me to feel other sensations, like Mitica's broad chest warming my back, ensuring I felt no chill from the wind.

"Thank you for taking me to see Likinoak so we can figure out what happened to me," I said to take my mind off his proximity.

"I am sorry you are going through this, though I will not say I am sorry you are here," he murmured into my ear.

Warmth spread through me, and I took a deep breath.

Once we'd landed, Mitica slid to the ground first, then held his hand up to me. He pulled gently and steadied my descent with his strong arms. Feet on the ground, I stood gazing into his eyes, still wrapped in his embrace.

"When can I see you again?" I asked in a hushed tone.

He smiled softly down at me, and my heart jumped as my cheeks heated.

"Do you think you can fool the Mountie again tomorrow?"

My chest tightened at his choice of words, and I bit my lip. *I feel bad for deceiving Wynn when he has been so kind to me. He even offered me a place to stay, and he feeds me every day. But he can't help me with all this time travel stuff.*

"Wynn is not a fool," I defended, squirming out of his arms. "He's just trusting and honest. And he's my friend, so don't speak badly about him."

He gave me an appeasing smile, which irritated me somehow. "I apologize for my phrasing. I will remember you care for him in the future."

Care for him? My heart skipped at the thought, and my gaze wandered to the starry night sky. I was quiet for a while. Then I sighed and met Mitica's eyes once more.

"I'm sorry for snapping at you. I'm sure you didn't mean anything by it. You've helped me just as much, if not more, than Wynn. I also consider us friends."

Heat radiated through my chest as he flashed me a delighted smile.

"I have something for you," he said.

"What is it?"

He dug into his jacket pocket, pulled out a corked vial, and handed it to me. "Give this to your Mountie. It is water from the hot spring. If there is something wrong with it, maybe he can find out."

"Wow, thanks, Mitica... But he's not *my* Mountie."

"Is he not?" He grinned.

"Shut up." I pushed his chest playfully to distract myself from the growing heat in my face.

He chuckled and snatched my hand, bringing it to his lips. His kiss was warm and soft on my fingers. My breath hitched, and I trembled at the sensation as goosebumps raised on my arms.

"I have something else for you," he murmured against my hand.

Then he placed a crimson pouch in my palm.

My face and ears aflame at where my mind had gone, I swallowed my embarrassment and took the pouch. There was a lot of money inside.

"I forgot to give this to you yesterday. It is yours. You had it on you when I found you that night."

The pouch was dark crimson, stained with blood, a lot of blood, my blood. My stomach dropped, and my head spun. I sucked in a breath.

Mitica grabbed my shoulders to steady me, concern knitting his brow. "Erin, are you well?"

I took a few slow, calming breaths and nodded. "How...if my change purse is this stained, what happened to the rest of my clothes? My undergarments weren't stained," I wondered.

"I had to rip them open to see your injuries. They were ruined. I found you the only clean clothes I could, then I washed and changed you before leaving you for the Mountie to find."

I looked at him sharply. "You washed me?"

He nodded. "But that is all," he assured.

I pursed my lips. "That was good thinking though. Thank you." *It was alarming enough for Wynn to find me dressed that way. I can't imagine*

*how he would have reacted if I'd shown up covered in blood without a
scratch on me.*

He smiled, relieved I'd understood.

"I can meet you tomorrow night?" I asked.

His eyes sparkled, and he nodded once.

"All right. I'll see you then," I said, taking a step toward the barracks.

"Sleep well," he called like he wished for nothing else.

SEVEN

My legs were sore when I awoke the next morning. *I guess riding is more of a workout than I'd thought.* Wynn was nowhere in sight when I stiffly rolled out of bed, groaning at the pain.

When he returned with breakfast, he found me doing yoga poses to stretch my tight muscles. He quirked an eyebrow but didn't say anything.

I laughed at his confusion. "It's called yoga," I explained.

He nodded once and asked for no clarification.

"It's a form of exercise and meditation. I was doing it to stretch."

"I imagine your legs must be sore from riding yesterday."

You're imagining my legs, are you? I wouldn't say no to a massage. Instead of voicing my inappropriate thoughts, I simply hummed my assent to his deduction and thought of us cuddling by the stove for warmth. I frowned at my breakfast when I remembered how he'd pulled away.

"Is there something wrong with your food?"

"No," I muttered.

"Then you should eat it. You're going to need the strength."

"Why is that?"

"Because I'm going to show you how to care for Langundo."

My aching muscles throbbed in protest, but I knew it wasn't right to complain. *Wynn can't keep taking care of everything for me. If I'm going to ride the horse, then I should know how to care for him. Plus, I don't know how long I'm going to be stuck here. I need to learn as much as I can.*

"All right," I agreed.

If I'd thought I was sore before, it was nothing compared to how I felt after I'd cleaned Langundo's stall and brushed him. I was more comfortable around the animal after having ridden Bou the day before, and no horse could compare to riding Grigore.

I listened carefully to Wynn's instructions about how to approach and take care of him. He was quite the happy horse once he'd been brushed and given food and water. I rather thought he was growing fond of me, though not as fond as Bou seemed to be.

Once we'd finished, Wynn went into town and brought back lunch. After we'd eaten, he said he would return the basket on his way to patrol.

"I can take it back," I offered.

His eyebrows crinkled in concern. "I'm not sure it's a good idea for you to wander around alone. What if the people who hurt you find you?"

"I'll be fine," I assured him and myself.

"I don't like it," he declared.

"You're being overly protective," I accused.

"I don't agree."

"It's fine. I won't stay long. Besides, people saw me with you when we went into town the other day, and I'm sure Mellie has mentioned my presence. That means people will know you will ask questions if something happens to me."

He frowned and met my eyes. "You will not stay long?"

"I'll be back before you are," I vowed.

He reluctantly agreed though I would've gone even if he hadn't.

After sending him off, I took out the money pouch Mitica had given me and dumped it onto the table. The coins were crusted with dried blood, and it took a lot of scrubbing to make them spendable. *If I tried to spend them like this, people would think I murdered and robbed someone.*

I wasn't surprised when Mellie took the basket from me with a stiff smile.

"How is your article coming along? You heading home anytime soon?"

"Hard to say," I answered vaguely.

After leaving Mellie's, I went down the street to the trading post and dry goods store. The shop seemed to have two distinct sections. On one side, there was a long counter that separated customers from shelves of cans and tins. On the other side, there was another counter, behind which were a wide variety of items, anything from hatchets to animal pelts.

I approached the clerk as he straightened the dry goods side of the shop. He had a thick mustache and neatly trimmed hair, and he wore a gleaming white apron. He gave me a smart, all-business smile.

"Good afternoon, Miss. How may I help you?"

"Give me a moment to take it all in."

He nodded and went back to organizing.

I scanned the cans, tins, jars, and bottles on the shelves and was surprised and pleased to see they had toothbrushes for sale. I immediately asked for one.

"Would you also like some dental powder?" the clerk asked, holding up a small jar.

Knowing how no one really regulated products like that at this point in history, I declined his offer and asked for baking soda instead. I also requested a few bars of soap.

As the clerk was wrapping my purchases, I wandered the trading post side of the shop. Scanning the variety of tools, blankets, and cookware, a flash of blue caught my eye. *Oh God, is that what I think it is?* I requested the clerk retrieve the blue fabric from a stack. He handed a bundle to me, and I squealed, unable to contain my joy. *It is! Jeans!*

The strait-laced man smiled in the face of my enthusiasm. I knew they were undoubtedly for men and probably for outfitting miners or lumberjacks, but I didn't hesitate to find what looked like my size and buy them.

As I paid, I asked the clerk where I could find a barber, and he was kind enough to point me in the right direction.

The barbershop was practically a hole in the wall. The room had only two chairs beside a counter, which held the barber's tools. Hanging on the wall, there were shelves full of mugs.

The old barber smiled kindly at me as I entered. "Are you lost, Miss?"

I smiled back brightly. "Nope, I'm in just the right place."

He tilted his head.

"I'd like you to cut my hair."

His face fell into a troubled expression. "Pardon?"

"Don't worry," I assured him. "I'm sure you don't cut many women's hair, but I don't need anything fancy."

"Miss, I have never cut a lady's hair. I don't know anyone who has."

"Well, I can be your first then."

He frowned. "I'm sorry, Miss. But it is not proper."

"Look, I know it's an unusual request. But if you don't help me, I'm just going to do it myself. Then it's going to be all lopsided and messed up. Please, it won't take long."

He reluctantly gave in to my pleading and bright smile.

I sat in his chair and looked at the mirror as he put a towel around my shoulders and pulled my hair out from under it. His hands shook a little, but I smiled reassuringly at him in the mirror.

"You would like me just to trim the ends?" he asked, grabbing his scissors from the counter.

"No, I'd like it cut to my chin."

"Miss," he gasped, eyes bulging. "That is not advisable."

"That's what I want."

"Are you certain?"

"Absolutely."

He pulled a little clump of long, blond hair toward him and raised his scissors to it. "Miss, are you *truly* certain?"

"Please," I begged.

He sighed deeply and snipped, going a little pale as he did so.

After he'd gotten into the groove, he seemed to do a little better. When he'd finished, I was delighted with the job he'd done.

"You did beautifully," I congratulated.

He stared mournfully at the pile of blond locks on the floor as I paid him.

"If anyone asks, I'll definitely send them your way."

"Please don't."

Poor guy, I think I traumatized him. As I gathered my packages, I asked, "Do you know if there's a place I can purchase undergarments?"

He sighed in defeat like I'd dealt him a killing blow. "Madame Buvons has a shop the next street over." He pointed in the direction I should go.

"Thank you."

I'm sure he was glad to see me leave.

On the way to the ladies' underwear store, I found something of a hobby shop. It was smaller than the hobby stores in modern-day, but it had enough. I meandered the shelves of embroidery and needlepoint supplies and finally found what I was looking for: yarn. Knitting was the only craft I was good at, and I needed a warm hat. I normally would've chosen green yarn, but with my body change, I thought blue would look better. I couldn't find any circular needles, so I just grabbed some straight needles and a yarn needle.

The clerk raised one eyebrow at my short hair but didn't comment.

Madame Buvons's was indeed a ladies' shop. I had never seen so much lace in my life. There were ribbons and bows, corsets, skirts, capris, chemises. I cringed at the delicate atmosphere, afraid of soiling all the pretties with my crude and unworthy touch.

A refined woman with a long neck gasped as she came out of the backroom and saw me in her shop. Her wide eyes blinked a few times before she donned a neutral and professional expression.

"May I help you?" she asked in a French accent.

"I'm looking for some of those," I pointed at a chemise, planning on using it as a shirt.

"Very well. Suzette," she called coldly. A young woman with dark curls appeared. "Please assist this young...lady."

"Of course, Madame," Suzette answered.

Madame retreated back through the door she'd come from.

"Do not mind Madame," Suzette whispered, no doubt taking in my stony expression as I watched the older woman leave. "She is like that with everyone."

I looked at the young woman's earnest smile and couldn't help but return it.

"You are looking for a chemise? Could I also interest you in a corset?"

I stared at the torture devices she gestured toward. "You couldn't pay me."

She giggled as I shuddered at the thought. Something about her youthful joy and musical laugh endeared this woman to me. I held out my hand to her.

"I'm Erin. I'm a journalist from Chicago. It's nice to meet you, Suzette."

She took my hand gently. "An American? No wonder you are so modern. I like your hair. It is rather daring. Very fresh."

That's it. I'm adopting her. "Thank you very much. The barber was pretty scandalized."

She giggled again. "I can imagine."

Madame returned to issue Suzette a reproachful look. Suzette sobered and led me to the chemises.

I purchased a couple. As Suzette wrapped my shirts, I asked her where I could get a warm bath.

"There is a public bathhouse one block over," she informed me.

I lowered my voice to a whisper so Madame couldn't hear. "Suzette, would you like to grab a cup of coffee with me when you're free?"

Her eyes sparkled at the suggestion. "I am available Wednesday afternoon."

"Great." I smiled and gathered my packages. "Today is...?"

"Monday," she laughed.

I nodded. "I'll come by the shop on Wednesday then."

The term public bathhouse had surfaced images in my mind of ancient Roman baths. But if I'd thought I was going to bathe in such open splendor, I was sadly mistaken. The bathhouse had two doors on the outside, one for men and one for women. I entered and was asked by the attendant whether I would like a private room. I had no idea what the not-private room would entail, and I didn't want to find out. I requested a private room and was led up a set of stairs to a plain room with a clawfoot tub, a chair, and a little cabinet.

The young woman who'd led the way asked me to sit as she went to fetch the water for the tub. It took quite a few trips for her to fill the tub up. I felt like I should be helping her, but she outright refused when I'd offered. They gave me soap and what appeared to be shampoo made with honey. I used it as shampoo anyway.

I couldn't believe how good it felt to sink into a hot bath. My tense muscles eased, and I let out a long, satisfied sigh. I was able to scrub myself far better than I had in Wynn's little washbasin. When my skin was clean and pink, I dried off and changed into my new jeans and a chemise. Then I pulled on Subconstable Taylor's warm coat before I left the bathhouse.

I stopped by Mellie's to pick up dinner before heading back to the barracks. She sneered at my transformation as if that would give her a better chance with Wynn. *Whatever. I look this way because I like it, not to impress him.*

I hadn't known how much the money in my pouch had been worth in this time period until I looked at how much I had left. *I must've been wealthy in this lifetime, or I was a thief.*

Wynn returned to find dinner ready to eat and me knitting by the stove.

"I went to Mellie's to pick up food, but she said you'd already gotten it." He stopped and stared at my change in appearance, his mouth hanging open.

I smiled broadly at his dumbfounded expression. "I told you I'd make it back before you."

EIGHT

"It seems you did a lot more than just go to Mellie's," Delaforet commented without taking his eyes off me.

His steady gaze made my skin tingle.

"Yeah, I found a purse of money in one of my boots, so I stopped a couple more places. I even made a friend: a woman at Madame Buvons's shop."

"Did anyone suspicious approach you?"

"No, everyone seemed fine. They probably found *me* suspicious if anything. It's a nice tourist spot. I can see why you thought I was a travel journalist. Oh, and this was waiting when I returned," I lied smoothly, handing him the vial of sacred spring water.

He unwrapped the paper I'd put around it and read the note I'd sloppily written saying what it was.

"So what is it?" I asked.

"It's water from the spring," he informed.

"Oh? So we can run tests on it to see if there's something wrong with the water that would kill people." I hesitantly reached out and touched his arm, smiling up at him. "This could give you the information you need to crack the case."

He met my eyes and nodded, the shadow of a smile telling me he was pleased.

Thank you, Mitica.

Then he gently pulled away and sat at the table.

"What are you going to do with it?" I asked, sitting across from him to eat.

"I will wire headquarters and ask them where I should send it for testing."

I nodded.

As we ate, I told him about my experiences in town that day. He didn't say much, but I could tell he was listening.

When he'd left to return Mellie's basket and send his telegram, I went outside to give the horses more food and water. Then I continued knitting by the stove. I was able to go pretty fast since this body wasn't plagued by carpal tunnel from years of knitting and computer use. I was about a third of the way done with my hat when Wynn returned.

"What do you do when you have free time?" I asked him as he removed his hat.

"Different things. Mostly, I read."

"Oh yeah? Read any good books lately?"

"I finished *A Tale of Two Cities* a few days ago."

"That's a great book."

"You've read it?"

"Of course, I've read a lot of..." *classics.* "Dickens's work."

"Have you read this?" He crossed to the trunk at the foot of his bed and pulled out a copy of *Dracula.*

"Yes." *Read it, saw the movies, even saw the spoofs. I wonder if the vampire craze took off right after Dracula was published or if it took a while.*

"I have not yet started it," he said.

"Well, it has been a while since I've read it. Why don't we read it aloud together?" I suggested.

He agreed.

Wynn read for a while, but Jonathan Harker hadn't even reached Castle Dracula before it was time for bed. I wished I hadn't promised Mitica I would meet him that night because I was pretty tired, though I couldn't deny I wanted to see him. I had a difficult time staying awake while lying in the dark room waiting for Wynn to sleep.

Like the night prior, I was the first to arrive at our secluded meeting place. I settled in to wait for him, trying to ignore the oppressive silence around me. A prickling crept over my skin, and I turned around, expecting to see Mitica. But no one was there.

Squinting, I searched the dark forest for what could've alerted me to its presence.

That's when I heard it: the sound of an ethereal flute playing on the wind. The song put my mind at ease. It was so enchanting that I felt compelled to discover its source. I followed the tune deeper into the forest, pausing every so often to ensure I was going the right way. I lost track of how far I'd walked, but that didn't matter.

Eventually, I came to a, circular clearing where the song seemed to play all around me. I looked up into the naked limbs of the surrounding trees. Sitting on a low branch, just out of reach, was a tiny person about as tall as my hand.

The little woman had long, black hair and shiny black eyes. She sat comfortably on the branch in her tan dress with her ankles crossed, playing her tiny, wooden flute.

I would've said she was a fairy of the Tinker Bell variety, but she didn't have any wings.

Her black eyes sparkled at me as I slowly approached her.

"Hello," I whispered in a voice that told her I meant her no harm. "Are you all alone out here?"

Right when I stood beneath the branch she was sitting on, she pulled the side of the flute away from her mouth and smiled. Just as she brought the flute to her mouth again, Mitica came busting into the clearing and forcefully waved a hand toward her. A strong wind blew from his direction, and the woman tumbled out of the tree.

I gasped, reaching out to catch her, but Mitica pulled me away.

"Let's go before the others show up," he urged.

"What others?" I asked.

But it was too late. The others had already arrived. On every free branch stood a tiny person with hate in their shiny, black eyes.

"Run," Mitica said calmly. "Run now!" he yelled, pushing me ahead of him.

He didn't have to tell me again. I ran in the direction he'd pushed me, trying not to fall in the dark. He was right behind me. Unfortunately, so were our pursuers. They leapt from tree to tree, shooting blow-darts from their flutes. My heart pumped adrenaline through me as I crashed through the forest. My lungs and throat burned as I panted the freezing air. Tree branches scratched my face and hands, but I didn't dare stop.

Eventually, the chase took us back to the lake, and I skidded to a halt on the rocky bank, trapped.

The wingless fairies with beady eyes smiled gleefully as they closed in on us. Mitica stood protectively in front of me, ready to take whatever came next. Just as I cringed, bracing myself. Grigore swooped down from above, breathing fire at our tormentors.

The tiny people scattered, retreating back into the forest.

I let out a sigh of relief and all the strength seemed to leave my body. Mitica caught me as I started to sink to the ground. I leaned against his broad chest and took comfort as he stroked my hair.

"What were those?" I murmured, my face still buried in his chest.

"Čanotila," he answered. He pulled away gently to meet my eyes. Satisfied that I'd recovered, he sighed and said, "We should talk."

On the banks of the lake, Mitica made a small fire among the rocks. Before he began his story, he sat me on a large stone and knelt in front of me.

"Your face is bleeding," he told me, gently caressing my cheek with his fingertips.

My breath hitched at his feather touch and the proximity of his gorgeous face. "The branches," I murmured, staring into his blue eyes.

He began to sing softly in another language. His fingers on my face glowed, and I felt my skin warm. The scratches itched as they healed.

"Thank you," I whispered.

His answering smile made my heart skip.

But before he could say anything, Grigore chimed in, "What? Do I not get a thank you? I saved both of you after all."

Grigore, the mood killer. "Thank you, Grigore."

"I take kisses as payment."

"Grigore," Mitica scolded.

"Not enough? You are right. How about—"

"Quiet," Mitica growled, cutting him off before he could say something truly sordid.

I smirked at their exchange, though I was a little disappointed at Grigore's interruption.

We settled around the fire, and Mitica began his explanation. "There are many different types of fae. Čanotila are just one type."

"Are Čanotila evil fae?"

He shook his head. "It is not that simple. Some fae are dark by nature, but Čanotila can be either or both. The problem is that many fae are being forced to utilize their darker natures to survive."

"What do you mean?"

His eyes lost focus as he stared deep into the fire's light. "There is no magic without wild nature. A fae spirit in a fae body cannot survive without magic."

"So fae without wilderness die?"

"Da, they may be reborn into a human body. They would not die without the wilderness if in a human body, but their wild spirits would not have access to their magic without being in nature. The wild places are disappearing. Soon, there will be no magic left."

He was silent for a long while. I hesitated to interrupt his contemplations, but there was something I had to know.

"You said one of your parents was fae, right? Does that mean you'll die, too?"

"I will die eventually. I am not immortal. But it will not be because of my iele mother and a lack of magic. My father is a hultan. He has magic, but he is a human. My mixed background was why I was sent here, in fact."

"Where are you from?"

"Romania."

I knew his accent was eastern European. "Why were you sent here?"

"Many of the wild places are gone. Many fae have died and lost access to their magic. My homeland has a balance of wilderness and civilization. The people there still celebrate fae festivals. Not too long ago, some Romanians immigrated here. When they were performing a hora for Sânziene, they could feel the fae here were weakening. They sent word home, requesting help. The iele and the hultan sent me to try to help them."

"And are you able to help them?"

"All I can do is try. As you saw, the Čanotila have embraced their dark natures. Even the animal spirits are having trouble controlling their power."

"Like what happened to Chuthekii," I said.

He nodded.

I sighed. *I've worried about deforestation, climate change, endangered species, and dolphin-safe tuna my entire life. But to know that humanity's lack of respect for the natural world is killing magic, too? Well, shit.*

I felt Mitica's silent gaze on me as I stared into the fire, my melancholy overwhelming me.

"You want to go home," he whispered finally.

I shrugged. "Yes and no. I mean, it's incredible here. I never thought I would have such amazing experiences. But, as you said before, I don't belong here."

His eyes softened, and he frowned. "I will help you find a way home since that is what you wish."

"Thanks, Mitica."

"I want you to be careful when you are not with your Mountie while you are here. I do not know how you came to be in the state I found you in. It is possible you were killed by that train by accident. However, it is also possible that it was not an accident."

"I'm all over it."

His eyes flickered with conflict before he nodded to himself. "I want you to call on me if you are ever in trouble. Calling a fae's true name summons him or her. If you call out my name, I will be forced to materialize before you."

"Really? All I have to do is call out Mitica, and you'll show up wherever I am?"

"That is not my true name. A fae's true name is something that is closely protected. It gives others great power over you."

"Are you sure you want to tell me then?"

He moved closer to me, looking down at me as I sat on a rock near the fire. His eyes were clear of doubt when he said, "I trust you to protect that which is precious to me."

"I'll protect you," I promised.

His smile was pure joy. He reached his hand out to me, and I took it. I didn't resist as he pulled me into his arms. My heart pounded so loudly in my ears that I was afraid I wouldn't hear him. He brought his lips to my ear, and his voice was soft and clear when he whispered, "Dumitru."

I trembled at the sound and feel of him as if knowing his name made him belong to me somehow.

"You will call on me?"

"Yes," I breathed.

He pulled back, releasing me. Reaching up, he fondled the tips of my hair. "I did not get the chance to tell you before. I like your hair like this. It suits you."

I blushed, lowering my face. "Thank you."

"I think we have had enough excitement for the night. Perhaps you should go in to bed."

I dipped my head and turned toward the barracks, but he caught my hand to stop me. "I would like to see you again," he told me.

My heart raced.

"Will you meet me tomorrow?"

I smiled my assent. "Let's meet here rather than in the forest."

"That is likely for the best," he agreed.

"Goodnight," I murmured.

I felt his eyes follow me until I was out of sight. And a little flame, one I hadn't felt in a long time, lit inside me.

<h1 style="text-align:center">NINE</h1>

ynn wasn't there again when I awoke the following morning. I practiced yoga and knitted more of my hat before he returned with breakfast.

"What are you doing today?" I asked him as we ate.

"Patrolling."

"Do you mind if I come along? I want to practice riding Langundo, unless I'll slow you down."

"I'm glad you seem more comfortable with the idea of riding a horse. You may join me if you wish. I'm in no hurry."

Wynn showed me how to saddle Langundo and went through the basic controls again before helping me into the saddle. He'd been right about Langundo being gentle. He was slow and steady, and he followed Bou with little urging.

My neck and ears were cold after my haircut, and I vowed to finish my hat as soon as I could.

We had to have ridden a few miles before we came upon a homestead. It was a simple log cabin nestled among some trees near a stream. We saw no signs of life as Wynn dismounted and helped me down.

I stretched my sore legs and followed him to the front door. A young girl with a ragdoll snuggled in the crook of her elbow answered his knock.

Wynn smiled at her gently. "Hello, Clara. Is your father or brother around?"

I'd never seen him so openly pleasant before, and a gentle warmth spread through me.

"They're out back," she informed in her cute, baby voice.

Wynn tipped his hat at the child, and she grinned, revealing a gap where her front tooth had been.

I smiled to myself, remembering the stories my parents used to tell me about the tooth fairy. *I should ask Mitica if she's real.* A pang chased my happy memories as thinking of my parents made my heart sore. *I'm either dead or in the hospital soulless somewhere. Mom had a hard enough time with Dad's death. I don't think she'd survive mine.*

We left Clara and her doll in the house, and I trailed Wynn around to the back. The door of a small barn was open.

"Hello? Frank? Charlie?" Wynn called, entering.

A man in his early thirties emerged from a stall, shovel in hand. His eyes showed recognition at seeing Wynn, and he nodded a greeting to me.

"Keep going, Charlie," Frank called into the stable behind him as he moved toward us.

"Right, Pa," Charlie answered from inside.

"How's it going, Frank? Any trouble?" Wynn asked.

"Everything's fine, Constable. Beatrice will be having her calf any day now."

Wynn nodded. "Well, we didn't come to interrupt your work. I just wanted to check in and see if you all needed anything."

"We're all right here, but I hear something's going on up at the reserve. There isn't anything we got to worry about, is there?"

"I'm looking into it, Frank. No need to worry."

"Because I don't need no injuns getting riled and taking it out on us."

I glared at Frank, going from zero to pissed in the space of a heartbeat.

"There's nothing to worry about, Frank," Wynn repeated.

"If you say so, I'll take your word for it."

"I do."

Frank nodded, appeased. "Yeah, you're probably right. They don't have any fight left in them anyhow. Heck, Charlie could probably take the drunken lot." Frank grinned like he was hilarious.

"Erin." Wynn touched my shoulder, and I realized I'd readied for a fight, my glare punctuated by tense shoulders and a clenched jaw. "Will you check on the horses? Make sure they didn't wander."

I nodded stiffly and stomped out of the barn. Reaching the horses, I remembered we'd tethered them. I sighed, glad Wynn had urged me to leave. I had little tolerance for ignorance, but my raging at Frank wouldn't have helped Wynn or the neighboring Wyboka.

"What do you guys think?" I asked the horses, pausing as though listening to their responses. "I agree, Bou. Maybe we *should* subject Frank to everything the Wyboka have been through and see how he does." I stroked Bou's face. "What's that, Langundo? You think violence won't solve violence? You're probably right. I should listen to you more often. You're very sensible." I smiled at Langundo and brushed the hair from his eyes.

Wynn returned a few minutes later.

"I'm sorry," I said to Wynn.

"I understand," he replied in a tone that said he truly did.

I managed to climb into the saddle without help, and I beamed in triumph as Wynn nodded his approval. As Langundo trailed behind Bou, I watched the snowy mountains around us. *I don't think I'll ever get used to this view.* I began to hum as we steadily moved toward the next settlement. If Wynn had heard me, he didn't let on.

The next settlement had a sign in front, declaring it a mission. I felt my lip curl in distaste. I had no tolerance for missionaries. They went against everything I believed in. I viewed them as hypocrites who tried to take away the one thing they would die to keep. *Treat others as you would want to be treated, my ass.*

Not wanting to cause Wynn any trouble, I told him I'd stay with the horses when he went to check on the missionaries. I used the time he was gone to look around at the splendor of the surrounding views. As much as I was enjoying my time travel adventure, I couldn't help but think I really didn't belong there as Mitica had said. *Perhaps my views are just too modern to survive in this time.*

It didn't take Wynn long to return, and we were soon riding back to the barracks. Once we'd arrived, I took care of the horses while he went to get lunch.

As we settled into our meal, Wynn pulled some paper from his pocket and put it on the table. "I received a response from headquarters about where to send the spring water. There is a society of chemists in Edmonton who can perform tests on the water to see if it's harmful."

"Great, so you're going to send it to Edmonton?"

"I have requested permission to take it myself rather than send it through the post. I'm just waiting for confirmation."

I frowned. "If they give you permission, how long will you be gone?"

"A few days."

I bobbed my head, looking down into my food.

"I..." He paused, seemingly looking for the right words. "I would like you to come with me. I don't feel...comfortable leaving you here alone for that long."

I met his eyes, and a thrill ran through me. "You could have just said you'd miss me," I teased, knowing he only wanted to bring me to protect me.

He stared into my eyes seriously, as if to say, "yes, I would."

My heart jumped into my throat at the look, and my face flushed. I looked back down into my food. *Jeez, Wynn, I was just joking.*

Wynn had planned on continuing to patrol after lunch, but it began to rain like the clouds had something to prove. Instead, he spent the afternoon answering correspondence while I knitted.

Because I didn't have a circular needle, and I never did figure out how to crochet, I made my hat by knitting a long rectangle, then sewed up the sides. The result was a hat that looked a little like cat ears when worn. I put it on and admired it in the small shaving mirror before sitting back down to start knitting an infinity scarf.

Wynn braved the downpour to bring us dinner, and he was drenched when he returned.

"You're soaked," I needlessly pointed out, taking the basket from him and putting it on the table. "Remove your jacket so it can dry."

He stilled, staring at me.

"What? Are you naked under your red serge?"

"No."

"Then you won't shock me. Come on, you're going to get sick." I reached for his buttons, threatening to remove his jacket myself if he wouldn't.

He stilled my hands with his, and my heart raced at his cool touch. I met his eyes and held my breath.

"I can handle it," he murmured.

I lowered my face and moved away, blushing at the awkward position I'd created. *How many times does he have to pull away before you get it through your head that he's not interested?*

As I unpacked the basket, Wynn unbuttoned his jacket and laid it near the stove. He wore a long johns-style undershirt, which was also wet.

"You should change your undershirt. I can go outside for a minute if that would make you more comfortable," I offered.

"No, uh...you can just turn your back. You'll get wet if you go outside."

I turned my back to him. There was some shuffling behind me, and I'd be lying if I said I wasn't tempted to see what Wynn looked like shirtless. But I honored his wish for me not to peek, not that that stopped me from imagining him peeling the wet shirt from his sculpted chest and abs. I shivered at the thought. Closing my eyes, I took a steadying breath. *Get a grip, Erin.*

"All right," Wynn whispered, much closer than I'd expected.

I jumped as he tapped me on the shoulder.

"Did I startle you?" he asked with the hint of a smile.

"Of course not," I muttered, burying my thoughts.

Dinner was quiet except for the insistent fall of rain on the wood of the barracks. Afterward, Wynn read more of *Dracula* while I knitted.

By the time we went to bed, the rain had finally stopped. As I snuck out to meet Mitica, I failed to sidestep the mud and puddles left in the storm's wake.

The clouds obscured the moon and stars while I stood on the shore staring into the sky. The still, chilly night settled within me. The world seemed asleep, the only sound the sporadic drip of water or the splunk of snow from trees to the soaked earth.

My heart reached out with the desire to see the open sky, and I remembered a song my mom used to sing to me at bedtime. I raised my voice as I sang it to the sleeping world.

"Pale Moon,
Do not hide your mysterious beauty,
For I have waited all the day to see it.

Mysterious Moon,
Share with me your ancient magic,
For I would know all of your secrets.

Ancient Moon,
Let me love you for my fleeting lifetime,
For I have long admired you from afar.

Fleeting Moon,
Remove the veil from your pale face,
For I would have you tarry a while longer."

As I sang my mom's lullaby, the clouds shrouding the moon broke to reveal a pale crescent. I sighed, admiring the sight.

"You sing beautifully," Mitica said from behind me.

I jumped at his sudden appearance, blushing at the compliment. "Did you just use magic to move those clouds?"

He smiled gently. "You said you wanted to see it."

"You can impact the weather?"

"Da."

"You said before your mother is a fae. What kind of magic do iele have?"

"The ability to become immaterial, the power of flight, to create madness with dance or song, and the power of seduction." He paused before continuing. "Most of my magic comes from being a hultan: healing, impacting the weather, dragon taming, though other hultan tame balaur. It was my mixed background that gave me the ability to enslave a zmeu."

"Wow, is that all?" I asked sarcastically.

He smirked. "Nu." But he didn't elaborate.

"It must be nice having magic," I commented.

He didn't respond for a while. "There are far more important things," he answered quietly.

His wistful voice made my heart sink. Before I could talk myself out of the impulse, I reached out and took his hand as he had done to comfort me. When his gaze met mine, the mood shifted. The warmth from his hand and his close proximity made me overly aware of my reaction to him. I quivered with anticipation, and the little flame inside me shone brighter.

"I wish you would not look at me like that," he whispered, not taking his eyes off mine.

"Why is that?" I breathed.

"Because it makes me not want to send you home."

I licked my lips. "I know what you mean."

He reached up and ran the back of his finger gently along my cheek. I held my breath and shivered.

"I cannot be selfish and keep you here. But I would like to know you before you leave."

"What do you want to know?" I murmured.

"Everything. What you love, what you hate, what makes you laugh, what makes you cry..." he paused. "What you feel like, what you taste like."

I trembled, my breath shallow and uneven. "Okay," I agreed in a barely audible whisper.

As he slowly leaned toward me, he gave me ample time to stop him. A fleeting sweetness caressed my lips, like the fluttering wings of a butterfly, as he gently kissed me. My heart cried when he pulled away too soon. An unmistakable ache slammed into me, but I stopped myself from reaching for him.

He stroked my cheek again, and I closed my eyes to better feel the sensation.

"You should go in to bed. I will see you tomorrow," he promised.

I nodded but my feet didn't move.

"Tomorrow," he vowed again, giving me a devastating smile that thanked me for wanting to stay.

"Tomorrow," I said, forcing myself to go inside.

In the dark barracks, I grinned up at the ceiling I knew was there but couldn't see. *When was the last time I've felt like this?* Butterflies fluttered in my stomach, carrying the desire to see Mitica again.

Rolling to the side, I sobered as I faced the direction of Wynn's bed. *What about Wynn? I can't deny I'm attracted to him as well.*

I tried to make out Wynn's form under his blankets, but the room was too dark. *Wynn told me he didn't find me unappealing. But every time we get into the sort of situation where something can happen, he pulls away. I thought maybe he was just too proper, but it's more likely he isn't interested. Like with Mellie, he doesn't want to embarrass me. Still…it feels like something more. Even when enveloped in Mitica, Wynn pulls on my mind, like a little tug on my sleeve reminding me he's still there.*

My sleep was restless that night as I tried to sort out my feelings in my dreams.

TEN

I still hadn't shaken off my pensive mood by the time I awoke the next morning. I stared at my uncertain, blue eyes in the shaving mirror. I knew thinking about it that hard wouldn't help me come up with a solution, but so much had happened to me in the days prior that everything seemed to pile up and make me anxious. I'd come to rely on Mitica and Wynn in that short time. I was in an impossible situation, and their help and support were really getting me through. I wasn't surprised that I'd become attached. But I began to wonder that if I was going home, perhaps I shouldn't get too involved with either of them.

I wasn't positive how Wynn felt, but Mitica seemed pretty clear in his desires. Still, I knew I didn't belong in 1900. And though Mitica had said he didn't want to let me go, he also had promised to help me get home.

Wynn entered with breakfast, and I put my thoughts away for later.

His eyes searched my face. "What's wrong?" he asked, concerned.

I plastered on a fake smile. "Nothing. I'm just hungry. Thanks for getting breakfast."

He nodded, but his brow was crinkled. I tried to be cheerful as we ate, to forcefully ignore his prodding, serious gaze. I got the feeling I wasn't convincing anyone.

We took care of the horses, and Wynn asked me if I'd like to join him on patrol again. I declined, saying I wanted to clean up before I went to meet Suzette that afternoon. He didn't press and told me he'd be back for lunch.

Cleaning myself in the washbasin didn't take very long. I thought about knitting more of my scarf but decided a walk would clear my mind a bit.

It hadn't been cold enough for the puddles from the previous day's rain to freeze. It was a brisk morning in the forties and rising. As I stood on the edge of the forest, I hesitated, remembering the angry Čanotila. I took a deep breath and strode into the wild.

The forest was a completely different world in the daylight. The weak morning sun sparkled off the snow-clumped trees, and an alluring mist crawled along the forest floor. The fog swirled about my lower legs as my moccasined feet made no sound.

Rough, natural steps led me above the mist to the edge of a cliff overlooking a river, which led to the lake. Breathing heavily from the climb, my heart pounded more from the scene than the exercise. The roaring river bubbled white in the sunlight, surrounded by evergreens. Silvery mist danced around the green and white trees on the hills below.

I sat on the edge of the cliff, my legs dangling, and stared at the mountains of varying shades of blue. For as many people who lived in the city, I never once felt small. But facing the vastness of the untamed Rockies, I felt rather insignificant. Still, even as small as I was, I never wanted to leave this enchanted place. It was on that cliff, breathing the fresh mountain air, that I knew I could never live in the city again, even when I returned home.

Without thinking much about it, I began to hum the tune from some fantasy movie based on a book. I'd only been half-watching it with Bryan because I'd been so tired. He always wanted to start movies late at night. I couldn't remember the words, but I recollected the melody.

Recalling Mitica complimenting my voice, I smiled to myself. Then I thought of his comment about there being things more important than magic and that wistful look in his eyes. *I thought Mitica was more open than Wynn, but maybe he's just better at covering his feelings with a smile. I wonder what could make him so sad.* The mist that crept below seemed to hide something I desperately wanted to know.

As I walked back down toward the barracks, I still hadn't chosen a path on how to deal with Wynn and Mitica. But I found I couldn't be sad on such a nice day, surrounded by so much splendor.

When I opened the door to the barracks, Wynn rushed at me.

"Erin, are you all right?" he demanded, grabbing my shoulders and raking my body with his eyes.

My heart jumped into my throat, mirroring his alarm. "I'm fine. Why? What's going on?"

He sighed heavily and hung his head. Then he met my gaze, his eyes flashing with anger. "You said you weren't going out until this afternoon. When I got back, you weren't here. You should have left a note."

I was so shocked by his display of emotion that I didn't even try to defend myself. "I'm sorry," I said sincerely. "I'm sorry I worried you."

My apology seemed to drain his anger away. His eyes softened. "I thought something had happened to you."

Touched by his concern, I couldn't help but smile. "I'm fine," I promised.

He froze, hands still on my shoulders. Then he slowly caressed my cheek with the backs of his fingers.

My breath hitched at the sensation and the familiar situation.

"I'm glad you're safe," he whispered.

The sweet moment was all too fleeting, and I was soon left with regret as he pulled away from me. Shame and conflict swirled within me.

"Have you heard from headquarters about Edmonton yet?" I asked him as we sat to eat.

"No, but I'm going to check again this evening when I get dinner."

I nodded. "Is there a place to get coffee or tea in town?"

"Like a tea room?"

"Yeah."

"Well, there's a dining room at the hotel, or you can go to Mellie's."

I was afraid he'd say that.

After lunch, I promised Wynn I'd be back before dinner, and I went to meet Suzette.

Madame Buvons was her same cheerful self as she greeted me. "What can I help you with today?" she asked.

"I'm here to meet Suzette."

"Erin, you remembered what day it was," Suzette teased as she came out of the back room with her hat, cloak, and gloves on.

"I did," I responded, smiling.

We bid Madame Buvons farewell and left her lace-choked shop.

"I imagine the dining room at the hotel is quite fancy and has a dress code?" I asked her.

"Oui."

"Is Mellie's all right with you then?"

She nodded her agreement, and we strolled to Mellie's.

Mellie's wide eyes bespoke her surprise when I came in with Suzette, but she managed to be polite as she showed us to a table. Suzette wasn't fooled.

"You and Mellie do not get along, non?"

"You could say that."

There was a quiet moment where Suzette watched me with her dark eyes. She didn't ask me to clarify.

"So how long have you lived in Farrloch, Suzette?"

"A few years."

"And where are you from originally?"

"France."

"Wow, that's quite a ways." *Especially by boat.*

Suzette tilted her head at my word choice.

"I mean, that had to be a long journey."

"Oui, Madame and I came here as a way to start anew."

"Oh, you came with Madame Buvons all the way from France?"

"Oui, I owe a great deal to Madame. She is like a mother to me. You could say she saved me."

"From what? If you don't mind me asking."

She nodded but stayed silent for a moment. "Since I was a child, my only family was my older brother, Pierre. He was not much older than I, but when our parents died, he took care of me. I adored Pierre."

I frowned at her use of past tense. "I'm sorry. Is Pierre gone now?"

She nodded. "He was killed. Murdered by my lover."

Holy shit. I didn't see that coming. I waited, not wanting to push her.

"I met Renard while I was searching for a job. He was handsome and charming. He was a poet. Oh, he wrote the most beautiful poetry, as picturesque as any painting. Our love was passionate. But as time went on, Renard became obsessive, possessive. He did not even like when I began working for Madame. Of course, Pierre knew nothing of this. I was young, and I knew he would not approve. One night, both Pierre and Renard came to get me from work. Renard, thinking Pierre was my lover, hit him in the head with a brick and killed him. He urged me to run away with him, but I refused. Madame took me in, and we eventually moved here."

Oh my God! I thought I had problems. I sighed and shook my head in sympathy. "I'm sorry you had to go through all that, Suzette."

She smiled sadly. "Pierre would not want me to be sad, and I like my life here."

I returned her smile.

"So tell me, what is it like in America?" she asked, changing the subject.

"I can't speak for the whole country as I haven't seen a lot of it. But life in Chicago is busy. There's always something to do. I'm never bored."

"And you are a journalist?"

"Yes." *Well, I was anyway.*

"How exciting."

"Sometimes. Other times, I just cover fluff. I mean...other times I just write superficial stories."

She smiled mischievously and leaned toward me. "And do you have a lover in Chicago?"

I laughed. "I don't even have the time. I haven't had a boyfriend since college. I went on a few dates but nothing serious."

"This boyfriend in college, what was he like? Why are you not with him now?"

"Matt was...funny. I always had fun with him. He studied to be a journalist like me. But he decided to go off to warzones to cover what was happening there. It's not like we didn't love each other. It just...wasn't enough in the end." I shrugged to emphasize my point.

She sighed, disappointed in my lackluster love story. "It seems we both will die alone."

"Hey, don't give up. I'm sure we'll find love again."

"Oui, I hope he will be dashing."

"Well, there certainly are a few of those around town," I muttered.

"Oh? I see a man has caught your eye after all?"

"Caught my eye, yes."

"Who is he?"

"There are two actually."

"Two! You must tell me."

I sighed, still uncertain about my own thoughts on the matter. But there was no way to refuse her persistent gaze.

"Both of them are the honorable, protect-the-innocent types. One is... captivating. He's...well, he's otherworldly, like a dream. It feels real at the time, but then you wake up. He's like no one I've ever met before. He's too good to be true, like my mind just made him up. He's affectionate but sort of mysterious. He seems to be hiding sadness of some kind or loneliness perhaps? I'm not quite sure, but I want to find out."

"And the other?"

I paused for a while, thinking. *How to describe Wynn...He's like Captain America. No, better still, he's like Clark Kent. Yeah, that Kansas kind of polite. Charming in that slightly awkward sort of way, but not so awkward that he's goofy.* I smiled to myself, knowing Suzette wouldn't get the comparison.

"The other is quiet and reserved. He's polite, proper. I want to figure out what goes on in his head. He's sort of stiff. I want to help him loosen up and laugh a little."

"And you cannot choose?"

"I don't even know where to start. They both...affect me. It's like I get a whiff of their pheromones, and I become someone different entirely. It takes all my brain power not to just crumble into a grinning, giggling mess like I'm a silly teenager who has no control at all. It's actually kind of irritating now that I think about it. But..." My face flushed. "I don't think I want to stop it."

Suzette grinned and nodded as if she knew exactly the feeling I was talking about. "How do they feel about you?"

"The first guy hasn't hidden his interest. He told me yesterday that he wants to know me, and I agreed. We even kissed."

"And number two?"

I snorted. "I wish I knew. He kind of told me he was attracted to me, but every time we get into a situation that could develop that way, he pulls away. I'm not sure if he's just being honorable or if he said he found me attractive just to be nice. But he does worry about me. This morning, he practically yelled at me because he thought something had happened to me."

She shrugged. "I do not see the problem. You share a mutual attraction with the first man."

"Yes, but I feel dishonest if I don't acknowledge my attraction to the second. Also, I have to go home, and they both have to stay here. So I started to think maybe I shouldn't get close to either of them. If I get attached, it will hurt too much when I leave."

"Well, I say you do not know what the future brings. Keep getting to know them if you are unsure. Perhaps your love will end like with your Matt. But 'tis better to have loved and lost' as the poem goes."

"There's no arguing with that kind of romantic logic."

"Oui." She smiled.

What a sweet person. I hope she finds someone who is worthy of her.

ELEVEN

After we'd talked about such serious topics, what kind of cake we liked and our favorite seasons seemed trivial by comparison. But those mundane bits of information about a person are important when getting to know someone. Still, I was glad that over a hundred years difference didn't change how female friends related to each other.

In the end, we promised to meet up again, but we didn't set a time. I hummed to myself as I carried the basket with dinner back to the barracks. The puddles from the previous day's rain were mostly gone, having either traveled to a body of water or evaporated in the day's sun. It was still a little early for dinner, so I didn't expect Wynn to be back from patrol yet. I entered the barracks, planning to knit while I waited for him to return.

I froze, my mouth hanging open at Wynn scrubbing in the washbasin. He was splashing water on his face, so he didn't see me enter. Droplets dripped from his chin onto his bare chest, which was everything I'd dreamt it would be. He still wore his pants, the suspenders hanging around his legs and backside. He splashed his face again, then grasped for a towel. As he reached over, I noticed a scar on his upper arm. The black lines overlapped as if he'd been cut deliberately. Just as I was thinking I should probably leave, Wynn had wiped his face and glanced over at me.

There was a heavy pause where we just stared at each other before I went red and turned around.

"I'm sorry. I didn't think you were back yet. I'll knock next time." I could hardly hear myself over the pounding of my heart.

There was some shuffling behind me, and then Wynn cleared his throat.

I glanced over my shoulder and met his eyes. He averted his gaze, which just made it more awkward. *Jeez, it's not like I've never seen a breathtakingly sexy shirtless guy before...on TV. But I know he didn't want me to see, and his reaction is making me more embarrassed.*

I moved to the table. "I brought dinner if you're hungry."

"Thank you," he said in a deeper voice than usual.

"How was patrol?" I asked, desperate to fill the silence and distance my brain from dwelling on what I'd just seen. I could still feel my face radiating with heat. *Oh my god. Stop with the blushing already! You're a grown ass woman.* But as always, I had no control over my blush reflex. After talking with Suzette, I'd realized just how silly I must look to Mitica and Wynn, blushing like some virgin who has never talked to a man. Now, it was irritating me.

"Fine," he answered uncooperatively.

I bit my lip and looked down at my meal. "I had fun with Suzette today." I proceeded to babble about all the unimportant stuff Suzette and I had talked about, leaving the serious topics out.

It was a relief when he left to return Mellie's basket. The barracks had begun to feel too small, too filled up with his presence and the images and memories that swam in my mind. I gave the horses food and water and was knitting by the time he returned.

"I received a message from headquarters," he announced upon entering.

"And?"

"They gave me permission to go to Edmonton. I also stopped at the station. The next train for Calgary leaves tomorrow. I bought two tickets."

"That's exciting! Let me know how much the tickets were, and I'll pay for half."

He frowned. "That's not necessary."

Mounties can't make that much money for him to be paying for everything all the time.

"All right. Then I will buy the return tickets."

"Really—"

"I insist," I said firmly.

He didn't respond either way, and I felt like I'd have to argue with him when the time came.

Whether it was the walk or him concentrating on our journey, Wynn seemed more comfortable than before he'd gone to town, which made me less embarrassed as well.

He let me borrow a small messenger bag to carry clothes in for our trip. After we'd packed, we had a quiet evening while he read more *Dracula*.

I didn't have to wait long for Mitica as I sat by the lakeshore that night.

"How come Grigore hasn't come with you for the last two nights?" I asked him.

"He is being punished right now."

"Why? What did he do?"

"I let him go hunting, and he tried to 'seduce' a Wyboka woman he found on the mountain."

"Oh jeez. Is she all right?"

"Da, I found them in time."

"That's good. So you grounded him?"

He tilted his head at my unfamiliar wording. "He will not be allowed to fly freely for a while."

"Sounds like he deserves that. Have you and Grigore been together for a long time?"

He nodded. "Sometimes it does seem like an eternity."

I paused in thought. "What's it like in Romania?"

"Would you like me to show you?"

"How?"

"Magic." He smiled.

"All right," I agreed.

I took his outstretched hand, and he pulled me to my feet. As I stood near him, my hand in his, all doubts I had about getting closer to him flew from my head.

"Do not let go," he whispered.

As he began singing in his sweet baritone, the landscape around us blurred. When it came back into focus, we were in a completely different place.

We stood on a mountain. The blanket of trees below dazzled me with colors in the glow of sunset. Greens, yellows, oranges, and reds all blended together in an autumn feast for the eyes. The rolling mountains in the distance faded into a thick mist the farther they were from us.

"Wow, it's beautiful," I breathed.

He smiled over at me.

"Did you just teleport us to Romania?" I asked, dumbfounded.

"Nu, this is just a memory, an illusion."

"Oh."

"Would you like to see my home?"

"Yes."

The scene shifted again, and we stood in front of a small, simple cabin with mossy stepping stones leading to the front door. It was tucked among a group of shady trees like it had grown there.

"This is where you grew up?"

He nodded. "Until I was brought to school to learn hultan magic."

"It's adorable."

"My mother and father still live here."

"Do you have any siblings?"

He frowned. "Nu."

I sensed there was more to the story but didn't push. "It's a wonderful place to live, very different than where I'm from."

"I would like to see where you are from," he said.

"Can you do that?"

"If you have a particularly strong image in your mind."

"I'm not sure it's a good idea though. A lot has changed in one hundred and sixteen years. I wouldn't want to shock you."

He nodded. "Perhaps something small then. You said you look different in your time. Will you show me what you looked like?"

I thought about it. "That should be all right. What do I do?"

"Just hold a clear image of yourself in your mind, and let me in when you feel me."

I closed my eyes and pictured my body in 2016. Mitica began to sing, and I felt a little nudge like someone was knocking on my subconscious. I didn't fight the feeling but let him in.

When he'd stopped singing and I'd opened my eyes, I wore my usual attire of Converse, skinny jeans, and a tank top. I could see the dark plastic rims of my glasses and assumed my hair and eyes were back to normal as well.

Mitica's eyes sparkled with appreciation. "You are beautiful, Erin."

I smiled awkwardly as my cheeks heated. *Stop blushing, Idiot.* "Thank you," I murmured to Mitica. "I definitely feel more comfortable like this."

He gazed into my eyes as if trying to memorize every green fleck.

After a few minutes, the illusion faded away, and we were back in Canada.

"Thank you for sharing that with me." He smiled warm and gentle.

"No, thank you. I feel like I have to go visit Romania when I get back."

His smile slipped when I mentioned leaving. "It is getting late. You should go to sleep. I will see you tomorrow."

"I can't. I'm going on a trip to Edmonton with Wynn tomorrow. We're going to get that spring water you gave us tested." I frowned at the thought of not seeing him.

He nodded once. "When you return, tie a string to that tree, and I will know to come to you that night."

"Okay," I agreed. "I will."

As I turned to go inside, Mitica called to me. "Erin," he said softly.

I stopped and met his gaze.

"Be careful," he pleaded.

I smiled at him. "I will," I promised.

"Remember to call on me if you need help."

"Your name will be the first from my lips."

His eyes widened as if surprised.

Isn't that what he wanted? Why would he be surprised? "Anyway, I'll see you in a few days. Keep Grigore out of trouble."

He agreed, and we bid each other goodnight.

As I turned from him, my heart panged, knowing I wouldn't see him for a while. Still, my sadness didn't stop sleep from overtaking me.

TWELVE

"Erin, wake up." A whisper pulled at me in my heavy sleep. "Erin," the voice urged. A gentle touch on my shoulder nudged at my consciousness. "Erin?" Concern accompanied the breath on my face.

I squeezed my heavy eyelids tighter.

The feather stroke of a fingertip pushed the hair from my face. Finally, I mustered the strength to peek through my lids. Wynn's blue eyes stared at me from much too close a distance.

My eyes popped wide, and he flinched at the sudden motion, straightening from leaning over me.

"You have to get ready, or we're going to miss the train," he explained, taking a step back from my bedside. "Clean up, and get dressed. I'm going to ask the blacksmith to look after Bou and Langundo while we're away."

I let go of a heavy breath as he left the barracks. The jolt of surprise at waking up to Wynn hovering over me had me fully conscious, but my body was still tired as I washed and changed. I was stifling yawns even when Wynn returned.

"Ready?" he asked.

I nodded and grabbed my bag.

He held out his hand to me, and I raised my eyebrows.

"I can carry that," he explained, pointing at my bag.

"So can I."

He frowned.

"Thanks for the offer, but I got it."

His frown didn't waver when he nodded.

On the walk to the train station, we stopped into Mellie's and ate a quick breakfast. She even wrapped up some sandwiches for us to eat for lunch on the train.

"You are going with Constable Delaforet on his journey to Edmonton?" Mellie asked as she handed him the sandwiches.

"That's right," I confirmed.

"Why is that?" she queried politely.

"Research," I answered.

The vagueness of my response made her ever-present smile falter if only a bit.

We got to the platform about ten minutes before a giant steam train screeched and hissed into the station. The brakes wailed, and my vision blurred. Images of the blue tactile edge of a subway platform and a printer paper box heavy with folders and picture frames swirled before my eyes. I shivered as the cool wind that proceeds the subway train rushed past the platform. My breath was shallow as my heart raced like the train wheels along the tracks.

Then a heavy hand grabbed my shoulder. I gasped, a scream sticking in my throat.

"Are you unwell, Erin? You look rather wan," Wynn asked.

My eyes refocused on his concerned face. My forehead was clammy with sweat, and my teeth chattered. I took a deep breath. Then another.

"Erin? What's wrong? Should we delay the journey?"

"No," I said as firmly as I could manage. "No, it's too important to find out what happened to the Wyboka. Just get me on the train, and I'll be fine."

He reluctantly agreed and helped me onto the train. I felt better once we'd settled into our bench-style seats. I slumped down, leaning the back of my head against the bench.

"Will you talk to me, Wynn?" I murmured.

"About what?"

"It doesn't matter. I just need a distraction. Tell me about yourself. Where are you from? What about family? Or tell me about your time in the Yukon." *Just let me hear your voice.*

"I was assigned to the Yukon because of my knack for languages," he began. "When gold was discovered, the native tribes were routed from the area that was to be Dawson City. This strained the relationship between the force and the tribes."

"Did you help the natives who were displaced?"

"As best I could." His expression and tone told me he wasn't satisfied with what he'd accomplished in the Yukon.

"What was it like there?"

"Busy. We didn't get a lot of personal time. There was always something to do. Whether it was keeping the peace, guarding the transportation of gold from the bank in town, or doing a mail run with sled dogs."

"How long was the mail run?"

"About six hundred miles one way."

"How long did that take?"

"Usually just over two weeks."

Call of the Wild *was one of my favorite stories growing up. I wonder if it has been published yet.* "The transportation of gold sounds dangerous. What was that like?"

"We transported at least five tons of ingots to Seattle each trip. We took a steamboat down the river about two thousand miles. Then we transferred the gold to an ocean vessel and took it two thousand more miles to Seattle. We never lost an ingot."

"Impressive. So where are you from, Wynn? What about your family?"

Just as he hesitated to answer, the conductor asked to see our tickets. Wynn dug into his pocket and handed them to him.

"Your coloring is coming back," he told me after the conductor had left.

"Thanks for the help." I smiled at him weakly.

"It will take us a few hours to get to Calgary. Why don't you rest a little?"

Having not gotten enough sleep, and feeling exhausted from my little episode, I didn't need much convincing. "I think you're right," I agreed.

No sooner had I leaned my head against the window and closed my eyes, than the train began to move, and I fell asleep.

I awoke at the sound of the train's bell as we pulled into the station in Calgary. As I cracked my eyelids, I realized the material of a red tunic and the shoulder it covered supported the weight of my head.

"Sorry," I yelped, sitting up straight.

"Don't worry about it," Wynn said, the corner of his mouth quirked in a small but kind smile. "I'm glad you got some rest."

I eyed the sleeve of his jacket and was relieved to see I hadn't drooled on him.

I'd thought we would have a little bit of a layover in Calgary. I didn't know much about the city other than they have a big rodeo every year called the Calgary Stampede, so I'd looked forward to exploring a little. Unfortunately, Wynn told me we only had just enough time to get on the train to Edmonton.

We managed to find a seat just as the conductor called "all aboard" and blew his whistle. He checked our tickets, and we settled in for a twelve-hour ride.

I watched out the window for a while. The winter snow had mostly melted to reveal dry pastures of brown grass. The prairie was awe-inspiring in a completely different way than the mountains. It was bare and desolate. For as far as I could see, there was just uninterrupted horizon.

I turned away from the loneliness of the prairie and said, "I don't know a lot about you, Wynn. Why don't you tell me more about yourself?"

"Well, I don't know much about you either," he countered.

Because I have a major secret I have to keep from you. Not to mention I'm supposed to have spotty memories. "All right then. I don't mind. What do you want to know? I'll tell you if I can remember."

"You said before your only family was your mother and your friend, Bryan."

I nodded.

"May I ask what happened to your father?"

It used to sting whenever I talked about my dad. But at some point, I began to take solace in my memories. "My dad died when I was in elementary school."

He nodded silently, having known before he'd asked that it wasn't likely to be a pleasant story.

"He was a police officer, like you." I smiled. "Though he wasn't nearly as serious as you are. I didn't know what exactly had happened to him for a long time. I knew we were supposed to go to a baseball game together. But there was a break in a case he was working on, so he went to work instead. He was shot and killed on the job. Later, I found out that he had been investigating corruption in his department. The call from his partner that night was actually a setup, and he was killed by other cops."

I paused and looked over at his reaction. His head was bowed as he carefully listened to my story.

"But the people who did it paid in the end. The corruption was uncovered, and they will be spending a very long time in prison."

"Do you feel your father got justice?" he asked me quietly.

I nodded. "I used to be so angry that the men who'd taken my dad away from me were still breathing. But, after a while, I remembered who my dad was and how he would have felt. His killers can't hurt anyone else anymore. My dad was a big proponent of forgiveness and second chances. I don't think he'd want me to use my energy to hate them. So why did you decide to become a Mountie, Wynn? Was it the whole protect and serve thing?"

He was silent for a long moment. "Protect and serve is a good way to put it."

I'd hoped he would go into more detail, but I could tell by his expression that he didn't plan to. After another long silence, he asked me if I was hungry and pulled out the sandwiches Mellie had packed for us.

Wynn seemed to be in a contemplative mood during and after lunch. I felt it best to leave him alone, so I took out my knitting and concentrated on it.

After we'd stopped midway to get water for the engine and dinner for the passengers, it was still another couple of hours until we reached Edmonton. I managed to finish my infinity scarf on the train.

As we disembarked, gas streetlights dimly illuminated the streets.

"So this is Edmonton," I commented as we walked past dark storefronts on the wooden sidewalk.

"No, this is Strathcona. Edmonton is across the river."

"Oh. Well, where to now?" I asked Wynn.

"Hotel," he answered.

He took me to a small establishment by the river. We entered a room with just enough space for stairs, a door, and a front desk. The clerk was a neat man with a thin mustache and well-oiled hair.

"Good evening, how may I help you?" he asked graciously.

"We would like two rooms please," Wynn answered.

"I am terribly sorry to inform you that we have only one room available at the moment," the clerk apologized.

Just as I opened my mouth to suggest we go elsewhere, Wynn said, "That's fine."

My head snapped in his direction, my eyes wide. He didn't meet my gaze.

"Very well, Sir," the clerk answered without judgment. He handed Wynn a key from the wall behind him.

Is he planning on sleeping in the same bed as me? I mean, I've shared a bed with male friends before, but not friends I was attracted to. Boyfriends don't count. That's a mutual thing.

I took in Wynn's tall, solid form as I followed him upstairs and remembered what he looked like without a shirt on and what it'd felt like in his arms.

I'm not going to get a wink of sleep. It's fine. You'll be fine.

On the third floor, Wynn unlocked our room and stood to the side for me to enter. The room was sparse with a double bed, a dresser, and a pitcher and washbasin.

I turned back toward the threshold when I'd realized Wynn hadn't followed me in. He held the key out to me, and I took it.

"There should be a small dining room through the door on the first floor. Feel free to eat breakfast whenever you wake. I will come back for you around ten."

"You're not staying?"

He looked over at the bed and back at me. "No, I should check in at the outpost, and I will stay at the barracks."

I felt a twinge of disappointment, and then my cheeks heated.

"You will be all right by yourself?" he asked, concerned.

"Absolutely. No problem at all. I will be totally fine," I assured with an embarrassed smile.

He nodded, but his worried eyes didn't waver. "I'll see you tomorrow then."

"Yep, see you tomorrow."

I closed and locked the door when he'd left. Leaning my back and head against the solid wood, I shut my eyes and sighed.

Then I looked around the bare room and tried to stifle my loneliness.

I removed my bag and put it in the dresser drawer. Checking for bed bugs didn't take long, and I was relieved to see the hotel was clean. After taking the pitcher downstairs and asking for hot water, I cleaned the travel grime off me and crawled into bed.

I laughed aloud at myself, staring at the ceiling. *I can't believe I thought Wynn would share a bed with me. I've clearly lost my mind... I wonder if I'll ever get back to 2016. It's obvious I don't fit in this time. I doubt I would have survived without Mitica's and Wynn's help.*

I sighed again.

But I'm going to miss them when I go. I wonder why Wynn is so private about everything. He never did tell me where he was from or if he has family. Normally, I'd be a lot more pushy, but I think I'd rather him want to share stuff with me instead of my squeezing it out of him.

Maybe Suzette is right. Maybe I should just move to the friend zone with Wynn and concentrate on Mitica.

But there's just something about Wynn that I can't leave him alone. I don't feel right about moving forward with Mitica without figuring out my feelings. Of course, that rationale never seems to be there when Mitica is near me.

I remembered the feel of his embrace as he whispered in my ear and the fleeting kiss he'd given me like a promise of better things to come. I shivered under the blankets and toyed with the idea of calling his true name just to kiss him again.

I sighed, knowing that wasn't right. *What I really should be concentrating on is finding a way home. I bet Edmonton has a library even bigger than the one at the Farrloch Hotel. If a black moon the day before Halloween and reciting a poem could magic me here, maybe I just need to wait for another black moon. But it could be years before there is a second new moon in one month. And, even if it's more common, does it have to be when the veil is thin like Likinoak said? Is Halloween the only time the veil is thin? Is the black moon the only celestial event with heightened magical energy? And, even if it does all line up, how will I know if my body is alive in 2016? If it isn't and I try to go back, then I may be sending my spirit into the afterlife.*

Man, this is complicated. I need to narrow it down. All I have are questions right now. First, I need to figure out when magic will be heightened next. Mitica and Likinoak promised to look into it too. If we work together, I could be home before too long.

I ignored the tightness in my chest at the thought of leaving Mitica and Wynn behind.

"I would like to know you before you leave," Mitica whispered in my memory.

There's no harm in that, right?

I curled onto my side under the blankets.

Go to sleep, Erin. You think too much.

THIRTEEN

The next morning, I awoke determined to come to terms with my crush on Wynn. It's not like I'd never had a crush on a friend before, and I usually got over it when I realized it was one-sided. In fact, some of my best friends over the years had started as unrequited loves.

I ate breakfast in the small dining room and took a cup of coffee back to my room. I was enjoying the river view from my window when a knock sounded on my door.

I opened it to find Wynn freshly shaven and impeccably dressed in his uniform. My heart jumped, and I squashed the feeling mercilessly.

"Good morning, Wynn. Did you have a good night?" I asked cheerfully, opening the door for him to enter.

His eyebrow twitched a little, telling me he'd noticed the change in my demeanor. "My evening passed as I'd expected," he answered vaguely but didn't enter the room. "Did you sleep well?"

"Yeah, after I shut my brain up. Shall we go then?"

He nodded. I grabbed my coat and room key and locked the door behind me.

Since I was staying by the river, the walk to the ferry wasn't far. The din of Strathcona was nearly as loud as modern Chicago. But, instead of cars and trains, there were the sounds of clopping horse hooves and the crunching of carriage and wagon wheels on the dirt roads. People shouted at each other as they went about their work, and horses whinnied their complaints. After we'd crossed the river, Edmonton's midmorning bustle was almost imperceptibly less than Strathcona's. I did notice, however, that while Strathcona had the railroad station, Edmonton had electric streetlights, though they weren't on as it was daylight.

The Edmonton Society of Chemists was housed in a sturdy brick building. A stiff butler-type greeted us at the door with a raised eyebrow.

"Good morning," Wynn started. "Inspector MacEvans should have sent word that I would be calling. I am Constable Delaforet."

The butler's eyes slid to me expectantly.

"She's with me," Wynn pronounced before he could ask.

Without a word, he opened the door for us to come in. The room we entered was a large receiving hall with wooden double doors leading in three directions. We followed the mute butler through the doors on the right, which led to a library. The three men present all looked up as we entered. Their eyes widened upon seeing me behind Wynn.

"Constable Delaforet and guest," the butler announced.

A wiry man with curly black hair closed the book he held and placed it on the shelf in front of him. "Very good, Shelly. I will take it from here," he said.

Shelly turned on his heel and left the room.

"Constable Delaforet, Inspector MacEvans informed me of your query. I'm William Watts." The curly-haired man introduced himself and shook Wynn's hand. Then he turned to me. "Forgive Shelly's behavior. Women are generally not permitted on the premises. Miss...?" His words sounded nice, but his tone was disapproving.

I bristled. "Erin Nichols." I thrust my hand at him and gave him a firm shake. "And why is that, Mr. Watts? Do you find women distract you from your scientific pursuits?"

His brow furrowed at my greeting. "Well, there is that. However, chemistry can be quite dangerous. We have several laboratories here, and we would not want the gentler sex to come to any harm, especially as they are uneducated on the subject."

I didn't hide my glare. *Uneducated? I wonder whose fault that is.*

Wynn cleared his throat. "Mr. Watts, can you test a sample of water to determine if it contains anything harmful?"

"Quite."

"And Inspector MacEvans has informed you as to the importance of this task?"

Watts nodded. "I should have results for you in a week, more or less."

"That long?"

Watts gave him a stern look. "Do you have any idea how many toxins I have to test for and how long those tests take?"

"I apologize, Mr. Watts. This is a matter of some urgency."

"I understand," Watts relented, appeased. "I will send you the results as soon as I can."

"Please wire them to Farrloch," Wynn instructed, handing him the vial.

"Very well," Watts acknowledged.

I couldn't stop myself from squinting my displeasure at Watts one more time before we left.

"I guess we can leave for Calgary on the early train tomorrow. Is there anything you'd like to do in Edmonton before we leave?" Wynn asked after Shelly had shut the door behind us.

"Yeah, is there a public library in Edmonton?"

He frowned. "I don't believe so. Most of the libraries are like the one you just saw: for specific pursuits, and you usually need to be a member. There may also be some wealthy citizens with extensive libraries, but those will be even less accessible."

I pursed my lips. "Well, is there a society for astronomers or physicists?"

"I don't know," Wynn answered.

Undeterred, I walked to the front of a carriage parked outside the building and knocked on the wood to get the driver's attention.

"Excuse me, Sir. Do you happen to know if there's a society of astronomers or physicists like this one for chemists?" I asked him.

The driver nodded. "There's a group of 'em what meets at Mr. Montmartre's. I've driven them there loads of times. Seems 'e 'as a telescope."

"Would you take us there, please?"

"Course, Miss."

I grinned as I went back to Wynn. "Pro tip: cabbies always know where to go."

He gave me a small smile. "I'll keep that in mind."

We arrived at Mr. Montmartre's residence by way of bakery. Wynn insisted we eat lunch before trying to bust into someone's private library.

The Montmartre home wasn't terribly large, but it was imposing in its gothic-style architecture. A young woman in a pristine maid's uniform answered the door.

"Hello, I'm Erin Nichols. I'm a journalist from Chicago in the area working on a story. I've been told Mr. Montmartre has the best-stocked library on astronomy and physics in the area. Would it be possible for us to have a look at it? I desperately need information on the subject, and my editor will have my head if I don't deliver my article on time."

"I'm sorry, Mademoiselle, but Monsieur Montmartre is out at the moment. I have been instructed to only admit members of the Edmonton Society of Physics when the master is away."

"Who is it, Chloé?" a female voice from behind the door asked.

"A journalist and a Mountie come to see the library, Madame," Chloé answered.

A woman in a well-tailored gray dress and dark hair pinned atop her head opened the door fully. Her light eyes took us in shrewdly. "A lady journalist, you say? And you request access to my husband's library for an article?"

"That's right, Ma'am," I lied.

"Well, I see no harm. Please, come in. Chloé, make some tea for our guests."

"Oui, Madame." Chloé disappeared down the hall.

"Thank you very much, Mrs. Montmartre. You can't know how difficult it is to find good information around here," I told her as she led us through her elegant abode.

"My René prides himself on his library. I am certain he will have whatever you are looking for."

Their library was indeed well-stocked for a private collection. The well-lit room was lined by floor-to-ceiling bookshelves, each of which was full of leather-bound books.

"The books are categorized by subject, then author," Mrs. Montmartre explained. "Ring the bell should you need anything, and Chloé will answer."

"Thank you again, Mrs. Montmartre."

She smiled. "Learning should never be only for the wealthy."

"I agree."

Once Chloé had brought our tea and she and Mrs. Montmartre left, Wynn turned to me. His eyes were keen and seemed to analyze me. I squirmed under his gaze.

"What are you hoping to find here that will help our case or your story?"

My heart twinged at Wynn's trusting nature. "This is going to sound strange, but I need to research moon phases and other astrological events."

He just nodded and moved to one of the shelves to help look.

Mr. Montmartre's library contained books on a wide variety of topics. Most of them pertained to physics, astronomy, and natural philosophy. However, he didn't neglect literature, mathematics, history, or other such subjects.

It took me a while to find an almanac with a list of moon phases for the next one hundred years. Mrs. Montmartre had made it sound like the library was perfectly organized, but I found only someone familiar with all the intricacies of physics's subtopics would see it as navigable.

Eagerly flipping through the volume, I was disappointed to discover the next black moon wouldn't happen until August 1905.

Shit. I can't stay here for another five years.

I sighed and put the book back. Finding Wynn across the library, I saw he was engrossed in whatever he was reading.

"Whatcha got there, Wynn?" I asked, peering around him at the book.

"It's not really related to what you're looking for, but I found it interesting. Listen to this: 'a full solar eclipse is always during a new moon when the sun and the moon are in the same sign of the zodiac. The alignment amplifies the effects of that sign.'"

"What is that? A book on astrology?"

"Yes, it goes on to say that some cultures perform special rituals during solar and lunar eclipses as they believe it is a time of heightened magic. Isn't that curious? I wonder if the Wyboka have a ritual like that."

My skin tingled with excitement. *A time of heightened magic?*

Wynn blinked when I rushed back to the almanac. "What is it?" he asked as I scoured the pages.

"Here!" I pointed animatedly at the page. "May 28, 1900. There will be a total solar eclipse. Wynn, you're a genius."

I beamed my thanks at him. My fervor seemed to be contagious because Wynn graced me with a full smile for the first time.

My face flushed, and I looked away, my stomach flopping.

"Well, I don't know what I did, but I'm glad I could help."

I barely heard him over the sound of my own heart. After taking a deep breath, I cleared my throat and asked if I could see the astrology book he still held.

Skimming through the sun sign dates, I found that the sun would be in Gemini on May 28. The Gemini section mostly talked about personality traits of anyone born under that sign, but there was one line that caught my eye. "Gemini represents duality. It could refer to two opposing forces or aspects of one being, for instance, the spirit and the body. As such, the sun in Gemini is an excellent time to explore the astral plane or attempt past life regression."

If a solar eclipse amplifies the effects of the sign it's in, and Gemini is a time to explore your past lives, maybe I could harness that energy to send me back to 2016. I have to tell Mitica about this. Maybe he or Likinoak can figure out a way to magic me back. I hope a little less than two months is enough time.

I closed the book and handed it back to Wynn.

"Did you find what you were looking for?" he asked.

"I believe I did."

I was surprised at how much time had passed while Wynn and I had been searching Mr. Montmartre's library. Before leaving, I rang the little hand-bell Mrs. Montmartre had indicated. Chloé appeared within a minute.

"We're ready to leave now, Chloé. Would you convey our thanks to Mrs. Montmartre for her hospitality?"

"Of course, Mademoiselle," Chloé assured, showing us to the door.

Wynn tipped his hat at the maid before she shut the door behind us.

"Would you like to get supper before we go to the ferry?" he asked.

"Sure, you know any good places?"

"I do."

He started down the dirt road, and I skipped to catch up.

"You've been to the place we're going before?" I asked.

He nodded. "We stopped in on our way to the Yukon. They make the best meat pies I've ever had."

"That's quite the praise coming from you, Wynn. Don't let Mellie hear you say that." I grinned at him.

We had to walk for a while before we got back to Edmonton's main street, but I didn't mind. It was warm compared to how it had been. It had to be near sixty.

The square, wooden building had a balcony on the second floor, which provided the porch with shade. The sign nailed to the balcony proclaimed the establishment as The Winchester. I followed Wynn into the tavern.

There was a bar at one end beside a set of stairs leading to the second floor. Round tables filled with thirsty patrons sat between the door and the bar.

One of the waitresses looked toward us as we entered. She beamed at us with hands on her hips. "Wynn Delaforet, as I live and breathe. I never expected to see *you* out this way."

Wynn nodded to the voluptuous brunette. "Sparrow," he greeted. He didn't exactly smile at her, but his eyes showed a recognition that was easy to decipher.

I sucked in a breath like I'd been punched in the gut, but I plastered a tight smile on my face.

Sparrow prowled over to us. "So you came to town and just couldn't stay away, eh Wynn?"

"Well, my friend here was hungry, and The Winchester has excellent meat pies," he explained.

Sparrow looked at me and smiled. "Be careful of this one, Honey. He's a real heartbreaker."

I nodded awkwardly but didn't respond.

Her smile didn't falter. "Take a seat, and I'll grab you a couple of those pies you came all this way for."

"Thank you." Wynn nodded, and I trailed him to an empty table in the corner.

He gestured for me to sit, then went to the bar and brought us each back a beer. I nodded my thanks but didn't look at him, busying myself by watching Sparrow serve the other customers.

"Hey," Wynn said low, trying to grab my attention.

I reluctantly met his blue eyes.

"I'm sorry about Sparrow. The last time I saw her, she said she was going back to Toronto. I didn't expect her to be here."

I smiled at him like he was overreacting. "What are you talking about? I still would've wanted to try the best meat pie you've ever had. I don't mind meeting your old girlfriend. In fact, I can head back to my hotel early if you want to...you know, catch up."

He frowned at my nonchalant tone. "No, I—"

"Here you are," Sparrow announced the arrival of our food.

I smiled up at her. "Thanks."

I watched her buxom figure flit about the crowded tavern, and the image of her wrapped around Wynn, her beautiful features twisted in pleasure, came all too easily to my mind.

I concentrated on eating to hamper any continuation of conversation.

"Mmm so good," I praised, forcing myself to swallow the food that turned to sawdust in my mouth.

Wynn ate but watched me carefully. I couldn't let my guard down as his eyes prodded me. Somehow, I managed to eat everything around the lump in my throat, though I wasn't sure how long I'd be able to keep it down.

After we'd paid for our meals, Sparrow caught up to Wynn as he opened the door to leave. I waved to him, telling him I was going on ahead.

"I'm free tonight if you want to—"

I closed the door behind me, cutting off their conversation. Then I took a deep breath and let it out all at once.

This is good. I nodded to myself. *This will help me let go.* I felt the tell-tale burning in my nose and closed my eyes. *Nope. Not going to happen.*

I was a few buildings down when Wynn caught up to me. I didn't ask him why he hadn't stayed or if he was planning on meeting Sparrow later. It was none of my business, and I didn't want to know the answers.

After taking the ferry across the river, we stopped at the railroad station to purchase our tickets back to Farrloch. I couldn't convince Wynn to let me buy his ticket, but I managed to purchase my own.

As we said goodnight at my hotel room door, I could tell Wynn was hesitant to leave. I felt torn. I wanted to be alone. But I knew if he left now, there would be no turning back. The door would close on any potential feelings I could have for him.

I stood inside my room, my hand on the door, and met his gaze on the other side of the threshold. "So...I'll have breakfast here and meet you at the train station tomorrow morning. Okay?"

He nodded, and there was a heavy pause.

I smiled up at him as cheerfully as I could manage. "All right. Well, goodnight then."

When I started to shut the door, he stopped it with an outstretched hand. I held my breath, my heart hammering in my chest. Another tense silence dragged out as his eyes bored into mine.

He squinted softly and frowned, regret written all over his face. "Erin..."

I smiled sadly at him. "Goodnight, Wynn."

He didn't resist as I shut and locked the door.

Sinking to the floor, I wrapped my arms around my knees and finally allowed the tears to flow, mourning the premature death of our potential romance. When my aching chest had hollowed out and my throat was too raw and swollen to voice any more sobs, I washed my face with cold water and crawled into bed.

My heart was still sore, but I felt better after my outpouring of emotion.

"You'll be fine," I told myself in the dark. "You always are."

FOURTEEN

My heart hadn't healed by the following morning, but at least I was getting my head on straight.

This is no different than the boys I had crushes on in junior high. There's no point in chasing someone who isn't interested. Wynn will never look at me with the recognition he watched Sparrow with, that gaze that said he knew her inside and out.

A twinge in my chest chased that thought.

He's had more than a few chances to make a move.

His look of regret from the night before flashed in my mind. I knew what that look meant, that look of apologetic rejection.

All right, Erin. That's enough. You're a grown woman. Put your big girl pants on and get over it. It's not like it was that serious anyway.

I ate breakfast at my hotel and paid my bill. When I saw Wynn waiting for me on the train platform, I didn't even flinch.

"Hey, Wynn." I smiled and waved at him. "How was your night?"

I could feel him analyzing my demeanor. "I'll be glad to be back in Farrloch. I didn't sleep very well."

"Aw, I'm sorry to hear that. Well, you can sleep on the train if you want."

He nodded.

The train rides back to Farrloch passed similarly to our trip to Strathcona, except we talked even less, and I didn't have anything to knit. We both took a nap and did a lot of looking out the window.

It was late when we arrived in Farrloch, and I was grateful to stretch my legs as we walked back to the barracks. It must have rained that day because I had to dodge puddles.

I wonder if I put a string on that tree tonight if Mitica would see it. It's late, but not as late as we usually meet. Maybe I should put it there first thing in the morning. Then he'd have all day to see it.

As we approached the barracks, I saw a candle burning through the window. I stopped short and turned to Wynn.

"What's that?" I whispered. "Is someone in the barracks?"

He brought his finger to his lips. Then he showed me his palm in a "stay here" gesture.

After pulling a revolver from his gun belt, he crept toward the door. He silently turned the knob and thrust the door open.

"Hands where I can see them," he demanded to whoever was in the room.

I held my breath and strained my ears. A few moments passed without event. The longer the silence went on the more nervous I felt. Finally, I picked up a handful of rocks and snuck to the door.

I mean, rocks aren't much compared to Wynn's gun, but I have a pretty good throwing arm.

As I peeked around the door frame, I could only see Wynn's back. I raised my arm, ready to pelt whoever the intruder was, and called out hesitantly, "Wynn?"

He turned to look at me, revealing a young Mountie before him.

"It's all right," Wynn told me. "It's only Oliver."

The young Mountie smiled genially and nodded. He was wiry with sun-bleached hair and light brown eyes.

"Wynn was just telling me about you, Miss Nichols. I'm Subconstable Oliver Taylor." He crossed the room and held out his hand.

I dropped the rocks I'd been holding to shake it. His eyes sparkled with amusement at the sight.

"That's a nice coat you've got there," he commented.

"Oh, yeah. I didn't have one, so Wynn said I could borrow yours. I'm sorry I couldn't ask first."

He grinned. "It's no problem. I'm glad I could be of assistance."

Wynn's mask-like expression drew Oliver's attention. "What's with the face, Wynn? You should be grinning like a Cheshire Cat, getting to spend all your time with such a lovely woman."

I blushed slightly at the compliment, and Oliver laughed as Wynn's frown deepened.

"What are you doing here, Oliver?" Wynn asked.

"Well, after we caught Wallace's gang, I was sure they were going to send me to Africa. But they sent me back here instead. Something about mysterious deaths on the reserve?"

Wynn nodded. "I'll explain."

As he caught Oliver up on the particulars, I excused myself.

Just in case, I took a length of yarn from my knitting and tied it around the tree at which Mitica had pointed. Then I went to check on the horses.

Bou seemed excited to see me. He bobbed his head and hopped on his front legs. I chuckled and stroked his face. "Did you miss me? I hope you were a good boy while I was gone."

Langundo stuck his head out at Bou's commotion. "I'm sure you didn't give the blacksmith any trouble. Did you, Langundo?"

He didn't respond but chewed his oats as I patted him.

Another curious horse poked its head out of a stall. The horse was gray and white. "Well hello there, Sweetie. You must be Oliver's horse."

I let the horse smell me before I stroked its face.

After a few minutes, I went back to the Mounties. Wynn had finished discussing the case and was telling Oliver more about my predicament.

Oliver nodded in sympathy. "That must be difficult for you, Miss Nichols. I'm sure glad Wynn found you when he did or something even worse could've happened."

I nodded. "I'm very grateful to Wynn for saving me. I hope to get myself together soon so I'm not taking advantage of his kindness for too long. And, please, call me Erin."

"It's no trouble," Wynn assured me.

Oliver nodded. "You couldn't have found a more honorable man if you'd tried, Erin. Wynn is as good as they come. Of course, you're welcome here as long as you'd like, as long as you're comfortable sharing a living space with two bachelors."

"Not a problem, but I suppose I should give you your bed back."

Before Oliver could respond, Wynn chimed in. "You can sleep in my bed, Erin."

I felt my face warm at the suggestive nature of his comment. "No, I—"

"I'll sleep on the floor," Wynn interrupted in a tone of finality.

"It's no use arguing with him when he gets like this. You may as well give in," Oliver counseled.

I pursed my lips but agreed.

It wasn't long before we decided to call it a night. As Oliver blew out the light, I stared into the dark room, trying to figure out how I would sneak out with Wynn on the floor between my and Oliver's beds and the door at the far end of the room.

It wasn't difficult to tell when Oliver was asleep. He snored like a bear in hibernation. I had a hard time hearing Wynn's slow, even breathing over the noise.

I slid quietly out of bed and felt my way to the far wall in order to avoid Wynn. I was doing well until I stubbed my toe on a chair. Clenching my teeth, I held my breath.

Oliver snuffled, and it sounded like Wynn turned over. After a few tense moments, they seemed to still be asleep. I swiftly slipped out the door.

I let out a heavy sigh and snuck around the barracks to the lake shore, our customary meeting place. The clear ice of the lake had melted a bit along the edges. *It must've been warmer here yesterday, too. Though if Farrloch is anything like Chicago, there will be a blizzard tomorrow.*

"Did you miss me?" I heard Mitica's accented whisper from behind me. I turned around and met his joyous gaze. His blue eyes sparkled as he smiled at me.

I knew my blushing grin must look foolish, but there wasn't any holding it in. "I didn't know if you'd come tonight."

He tilted his head. "But you called for me. Did you not?"

I nodded. "I guess I wasn't sure when you'd look at the tree. I only arrived a few hours ago."

He grinned at me. "You could not wait to see me."

Then he leaned in and kissed me on each cheek. "Welcome back," he whispered.

"You seem different," I murmured, pursing my lips in an attempt to get the grin off my face.

"I have been thinking about you," he said as if that was enough of an explanation.

"Okay." I waited for him to continue.

"I did not like being away from you. I do not yet know you enough to let you go."

My heart jumped. "Doesn't that seem a little backward? I mean, won't it be harder to let me go the more you get to know me?"

He shook his head. "Nothing in this life is forever. You can never truly hold onto someone. Something will always separate you. But before we are separated, I want to know you. If I can write you on the pages of my soul, then you will always be with me."

His earnest and sweet words made me shiver.

"Why do you want to know me so badly? I would've assumed it was because I'm from the future, but you haven't asked me anything about it."

He gazed down at me seriously for a moment. "I feel as though we have met for a reason. You traveled through time and space only for me to happen upon you right when you needed me. We were meant to meet in this time and place. Why did the gods send you to me? Is everyone from your time as glorious as you are? Is everyone as brave? Do they all have an inner light that would draw me to them?"

I could feel my ears get hot, and I looked down at my feet. "I couldn't say," I murmured.

"Please," he whispered. "Before you return to where you came from, please let me learn everything there is to know about you."

"On one condition," I told him.

He waited.

"That I also get to know you."

His eyes shined as if filling with tears, but he smiled gratefully. "I would love nothing more than that."

I held out my hand to shake on the deal, but he grasped both my hands in his and kissed each of them. I shivered at the sensation of his lips on me.

Seeing the breathtaking expression he gave me as his crimson hair fell into his blue eyes while he bent down to kiss my hands, it was the first time I thought it wouldn't be so bad to stay in 1900.

Of course, that thought was followed by what I'd discovered in Edmonton.

"We don't have a lot of time before I go," I admitted to him.

His eyes held many questions.

"I went to a library while I was in Edmonton. At the end of May, there will be a solar eclipse in Gemini. Apparently, magic will be heightened then."

He nodded seriously. "Then we have almost two months to discover how to get you back to your family and friends."

"I guess so."

"Let us talk to Likinoak tomorrow night. She may have an idea."

"All right," I agreed, my shoulders hunching. *I was so excited when I discovered this information with Wynn, but now I'm...not so sure.*

"Let us worry about that later. First, tell me something about yourself. How do you spend your time in 2016?"

I sighed. "Mostly, I work, or at least I did. I told you at Likinoak's I was a journalist, and I was fired the day I time-traveled."

He nodded.

"Other than work, I just..." *How do I say I watch TV?* "I guess I like stories. Sometimes I read them, and sometimes I watch them, like a play."

"I also like to read," Mitica informed. "It fascinates me that all the beings I live with every day are now viewed as fictitious. We used to be so much more a part of the world, but I guess humans stopped believing we are real when we disappeared with the wilderness."

"Fantasy and science fiction were always my favorite genres, especially the ones written in the 1800s. It's strange to think a lot of the authors I think of as classics are almost contemporary to you."

"What is your favorite book from this time?"

"My favorite book of all time is *The Count of Monte Cristo* by Alexandre Dumas. Have you read it?"

"Of course, the French have greatly influenced education in Romania."

"Yeah? I didn't know that. Did you read it in French then?"

"Oui."

"That's cool. I was never able to wrap my head around French pronunciations."

"Would you like me to teach you a little?" he offered.

"If you think you're patient enough."

"Tout pour toi," he told me.

"What does that mean?"

"It means: all for you."

I unsuccessfully tried to fight a smile and did my best to repeat the phrase.

"Try resting the tip of your tongue against your lower teeth," he instructed.

I tried again, following his advice.

"Très bien," he praised.

"Merci." I thanked him with one of the six French words I knew. "How many languages do you know?" I asked.

"Quite a few," he answered noncommittally.

"I've heard Europeans are more likely to speak multiple languages. Is everyone in Romania like you?"

"No one is like me." Though his words were proud, there seemed to be a hint of sadness in his tone.

"I guess that makes you extra special then. I like meeting unique people. They're the most interesting, and I find you can learn the most from them." I smiled encouragingly at him and took his hand.

"Not everyone thinks so," he countered.

"Well, I do, and my opinion is more important. I mean, if the universe sent me all the way here, obviously you should listen to me."

He laughed in a rich baritone, and I couldn't help but join him.

"Da, you must be right. If you say people who are unique are the most interesting to you, then I am glad to be different."

"That's what I like to hear."

He smiled at me softly, his eyes shining with admiration. "Your light heals bruised souls."

"Well, I don't know about that, but I do like to spread a little joy everywhere I go."

"Bucurie," he murmured, nodding.

"What's that?"

"Joy."

"Oh. Well then, yes. Bucurie." I grinned.

He gazed at me silently for a while, and I could feel my cheeks heat the longer he stared. Finally, he said, "You must be tired from your trip. You should go to sleep. I will see you tomorrow."

"Yeah, you're probably right."

I moved to pull my hand from his, but he tightened his grip. Grabbing both of my hands again, he kissed them each in turn. Then he leaned down and kissed me gently on each cheek, the tip of my nose, and my forehead.

"Noapte buna, bucuria mea," he whispered before placing a feather-light kiss on my hungry lips.

"What does that mean?" I murmured, feeling his breath still on my mouth.

"Goodnight," he told me, smiling gently before pulling away.

A sweet hum pervaded my body as I reluctantly bid Mitica goodnight and returned to Wynn's bed in the barracks.

FIFTEEN

The glow Mitica had elicited remained in my heart when I awoke the next morning. I knew what the feeling meant, but I refused to label it.

Wynn was nowhere in sight when I opened my eyes, but Oliver came in with an armful of wood as I fixed my hair in the shaving mirror.

"Good morning, Erin."

"Good morning, Oliver. Do you mind if I call you Oli? I've always liked the name Oli."

He chuckled. "Not at all. Though my sister is the only one who calls me that."

"It must be nice having siblings. I've always wanted a brother."

"Well, I could use another sister if you're up for being adopted."

I laughed. "Okay. But you'll have to be patient with me because I don't know how being a sibling works."

He grinned. "I'm sorry. I can't do that. There's nothing to do but jump in."

"Why do I feel like I'm going to regret this decision?"

"Too late."

We were both laughing when Wynn returned with breakfast. He raised an eyebrow at how chummy we'd gotten.

Oli put his hand on my head and mussed my hair on his way to get an extra chair from the stables so we could all eat at the table.

"Hey!" I protested, snatching a bar of soap from beside the washbasin and throwing it at him.

He dodged and laughed all the way out the door. I sighed and rolled my eyes. Then I turned back to the mirror to fix my hair again.

Wynn retrieved the soap and placed it back where it belonged. I thought he would move away immediately, but he lingered close to me. My heart pounded at his proximity, and I scolded myself. Steeling my nerves, I looked up at him. "What's up?"

He averted his gaze, shaking his head slightly, and stepped back.

I sighed internally, half in relief and half in regret.

We all ate breakfast, and they told me they would be going on patrol.

"I'd like to visit Suzette today," I told them.

"Who's Suzette?" Oli asked.

"A woman who works at a ladies' shop in town," I said. "How haven't you met? She's been here for a few years."

"I wasn't here very long before they pulled me to help with Wallace's gang."

I nodded. "In any case, I'll bring lunch back since I'll be in town."

"Bring it? Why don't you make it?" Oli teased.

"If I ever make you food, I'll spit in it."

I packed the empty dishes back into Mellie's basket.

Mellie wasn't pleased to see me. As I handed her the basket, I sighed.

"Look, Mellie, I know you don't like me because you like Wynn, so let me tell you something for your own good. He isn't interested in you. He isn't interested in me either. That's fine. Whatever. I have enough self-respect not to chase a man who doesn't want me. There are plenty of men out there. You're young, you're pretty, and you're an excellent cook. I'm sure someone will appreciate you." *Who are you trying to convince, Erin? How many times do I have to say it's fine before it is? Well, I'm not chasing him, so that part is true.*

Her already large eyes bulged, and her mouth hung open. When she closed it into a thin line, I couldn't tell whether she would cry or rage.

"That's just my advice. Take it, or leave it," I added.

"Thank you for sharing your unsolicited opinion. I will take it into consideration."

I felt bad for being so blunt. "I hope you find happiness, Mellie."

When I entered Madame Buvons's, Suzette looked up from the counter where she was doing something with ribbon. She smiled brightly at me.

"Bonjour, Erin."

"Hey, Suzette. Are you busy?"

"Non, you are my first customer, and Madame is out for the day."

"Great. I came to tell you about some developments."

"Oui? Tell me."

I leaned my elbows on the counter across from her. "I followed your advice."

She waited for me to continue.

"I chose the one who is already interested in me."

"And the other?"

"Just friends." I went on and told her about our trip to Edmonton, about meeting Sparrow, and about my point of no return on the threshold of my hotel room.

She squinted at me. "And you have truly let go?"

I squirmed under her knowing stare. "Well, I'm working on it. It'll be fine."

She nodded "I think you made the right decision."

"Me too. And no sooner had I returned, then the first guy came on strong. And let me tell you, it was like nothing I've ever felt before, not even with Matt. It's like he's slowly unraveling me, wanting me to bare my soul. It's unnerving. It's thrilling. I'm surprised at how much I want him to know me. He wants to see me, know me, touch me, and...I want to let him."

"You are no longer worried about what will happen when you return to Chicago then?"

I frowned. "I'm supposed to go back in about seven weeks. It already hurts to think about not seeing him anymore, but it's better than not getting closer to him at all before I go. I think I'd feel more regret if I left without knowing him at all."

"You make it sound like your love story is destined to end in heartbreak. Have faith. You never know what will happen."

I nodded as though I believed her. *Those sentiments don't really apply to my situation.*

"Now, if only I could find a lover," Suzette bemoaned.

"There is a handsome young man who just arrived."

She leaned forward. "Who?"

"A Mountie: Subconstable Oliver Taylor."

"A Mountie. How romantique. And this young man, he is unmarried?"

"He said he was a bachelor."

She grinned. "I think I should welcome our new policeman to Farrloch, non?"

"I'm supposed to have lunch with them tomorrow. Would you like to join us?" *There's no need for her to know I'm staying with them.*

She smiled at the invitation. "Merci. I think I will."

I told Wynn and Oli about inviting Suzette over as we ate lunch. Wynn nodded his acknowledgment, while Oli seemed more interested.

"She said she wants to welcome our new Mountie to town."

"That's kind of her," Oli said.

"Yes, she's very sweet. I think you'll like her."

During their afternoon patrol, I cleaned the barracks and did laundry. This time I was careful not to clean the clothes I was wearing.

When they'd returned, Wynn went to fetch dinner.

"So, Little Sister, where did you and Wynn sneak off to last night?" Oli asked nonchalantly as he rolled a cigarette.

I froze. "What do you mean?"

He grinned. "Come on. You don't have to hide it from me. I know you went out to have a little tryst. I almost feel bad. It must've been easier when I wasn't here."

He must've woken up when I stubbed my toe. "I only went out last night to use the outhouse," I told him.

"Yeah, I thought so too at first. But then, Wynn snuck out after you. And you didn't come back for a while."

Fear pumped through my veins. *Wynn followed me outside? Did he see Mitica and me together?* "Well, I don't know where Wynn went, but traveling always makes my stomach upset. That's why I was gone for so long if you must know."

The tip of his cigarette glowed as he inhaled. "Whatever you say," he muttered into the exhaled cloud of smoke.

Over dinner, I tried to act normal, but I watched Wynn carefully. His calm demeanor gave nothing away. He didn't even seem to notice how I watched him, which I felt was unusual. He was normally quite perceptive, but perhaps I was just good at hiding my surveillance.

I was extra careful sneaking out of the barracks that night, and I'm positive I didn't wake the Mounties.

The temperature had dropped since the sun went down. All those promises of spring seemed to have been snatched away as I shivered by the lake.

When warm arms wrapped around me from behind, my heart leapt.

"You surprised me," I said, relieved by his warmth.

He didn't speak but nuzzled his nose between my hat and scarf. I shivered as he pressed his lips to my neck.

"You like that?" he whispered. "I can make you feel a lot better."

My heart jumped into my throat at the timbre of the voice in my ear. I squirmed from his embrace. "What the fuck, Grigore?" I yelled, wiping my neck.

His yellow eyes glowed in his human face. "I missed you."

"Where's Mitica?" I demanded.

"Oh, we do not need him. He would just get in the way." He took a step closer to me.

"Back up," I ordered, glaring at him.

"There is no need to fight. I promise I will take you to pleasure you did not know existed."

I averted my eyes when I started to feel his tug on my mind.

"You liked it when I held you, when I kissed you. I could tell."

My stomach dropped, and I balled up my fists. I didn't hold back when I punched him in the gut. He grunted and stumbled back a step.

"I said back up," I explained.

He chuckled and looked up at me with a grin. "I like that."

As I tensed for a real fight, Mitica appeared beside me. He said some words I didn't understand, and Grigore growled as he dropped to his knees.

Mitica turned to me, worry in his eyes. His hands hovered over the sides of my face as if trying to ensure I was unharmed, but he was careful not to touch me. "Are you all right? Did he harm you? What happened?"

I sighed in relief. "I'm fine. He surprised me. I thought he was you."

Mitica glared at Grigore. "She is not yours, Grigore."

"Are you sure? She seemed to like it well enough." Grigore smirked.

"You think so?" Mitica challenged. "What did he do to you?" he asked me.

I told him exactly what had happened. When I was finished, he sighed away his anger and held out his arms to me. "May I?"

I nodded.

He turned me to face Grigore and wrapped his arms around me from behind, just as Grigore had. But the feel of Mitica was so dissimilar, I was ashamed I hadn't known the difference. He didn't let me feel that way for long though. He gently loosened the scarf from my neck, exposing it to the cold night air.

He exhaled warm, humid breath on the naked, sensitive flesh of my neck. Expecting a kiss, I gasped with a shiver as he flicked it once with his tongue. I pressed my back against him, urging him to continue. His answering kiss was hot and insistent. I moaned as my eyelids fluttered closed. My entire body flushed with need as his mouth sucked gently on my neck.

As my knees gave way, he supported me by tightening his arms around my stomach. He kissed up my neck and pushed my hat up with his chilled nose.

"However it feels with anyone else, it will always be better with me," he whispered, hot in my ear.

He replaced my hat and scarf and held me as my revved need lulled into a dull ache.

Irritation buzzed in my veins at my having gotten all hot and bothered without release, but I guess that always happens at the beginning of relationships.

Grigore glared at Mitica with all the loathing a fire-breathing, shape-shifting dragon could muster. A jolt of fear ran through me, though it didn't last more than a second, still in the protection of Mitica's embrace.

Mitica grinned in triumph. "That is what she looks like when she is enjoying it, Grigore. Do not fool yourself into thinking she wants you, in case her striking you was not hint enough."

My face flushed at having had my intimate moment with Mitica watched, but I couldn't bring myself to be angry. I knew Mitica was trying to teach Grigore a lesson, and I had given him permission to touch me in Grigore's presence. I never wanted to forget what it had felt like for Mitica to touch me, and his caresses had erased all traces of Grigore from my body.

I sighed out a steadying breath. "Weren't we going to see Likinoak tonight?" I asked, changing the subject entirely.

Mitica frowned. "We were, da. But I do not think it is a good idea to ride Grigore right now. He is agitated, and it will take a lot of magic to handle him like this. I do not feel comfortable putting you at risk if something went wrong."

I nodded. "I understand. Thank you for thinking of me."

He smiled softly. "I am always thinking of you."

My heart thumped. *It's not fair that I seem to be the only one aroused.* "Hey, Mitica, I'd like to give you something."

He waved his hand. "That is not necessary."

"Please."

He paused. "Very well."

"First, can you send Grigore away?"

He tilted his head but said something to Grigore in another language. Grigore stomped off. When he was out of sight, I moved closer to Mitica.

"Can I kiss you, Mitica?" I asked, stepping into his personal space.

"Da."

He bent down, running the backs of his fingers along my cheeks as if memorizing every line of my face. I could tell from his pace that he was going to give me another fleeting kiss.

I grabbed the front of his coat and pulled him to me. His wide eyes softened and closed as I pressed my lips insistently to his. I wrapped my arms around his waist, and he urged me close with his hands on my face. I flicked his soft lower lip with my tongue, and my lips tingled as he moaned against my mouth. An electric shiver ran through me when the tip of his tongue met mine.

The need that had lulled from before returned with a vengeance. As I sagged against him, worrying my knees wouldn't hold me, he broke our kiss.

"Erin," he whispered, his breath hot on my mouth and his eyes like the blue center of a flame. He grinned down at me. "I feel as though you have marked me as your own."

I quivered at the implication and his thrill at the idea.

"We had better stop here for the night," he murmured.

I could see that I'd driven him to the edge, and I was at my limit as well. *Any further and it'll be painful for us both if we stop.* I nodded.

"Noapte buna, bucuria mea," he whispered before pecking me on the mouth.

"Goodnight. I'll see you tomorrow then?"

"Da."

I could feel his eyes on me while I walked back to the barracks.

As I lay in the dark cabin, I realized I'd forgotten to mention Wynn may have seen us together. *Wynn...* I rolled over on my side, ignoring the tightness in my chest. *I should bring that up tomorrow. Maybe we should find a new place to meet.*

<h1 style="text-align:center">SIXTEEN</h1>

I wasn't surprised by how well Oli and Suzette took to each other at lunch the next day. When they left to go for a walk, I smiled to myself and hummed cheerfully as I cleared our dishes from the table.

"You seem happy," Wynn commented. "Aren't you disappointed?"

I tilted my head at him. "Disappointed? Why would I be?"

"With the way you and Oliver have been since he arrived, I thought you might be interested in him."

"In Oli?" I laughed. "Not at all. He's easy to get along with. He reminds me of some friends I have back home. He's more like a brother." *In fact, it's quite refreshing to have someone who's so easy to be around. Oli reminds me that I haven't lost my mind despite Mitica and Wynn driving me to the edge.*

He nodded thoughtfully and was silent for a moment. "Still, you seem different since we got back from Strathcona."

I smiled softly. "That's probably true. I..." *I guess there's no harm in telling him, right? It might help me put all this behind us actually. Also, I may be able to gauge his reaction and see if he saw Mitica and me together.* "There is someone I'm interested in."

"Oh? Anyone I know?"

I shook my head. "Probably not. He's a Romanian immigrant."

He dipped his head to show he was listening but didn't give away his thoughts.

"And before you say anything, I'm sure he's safe. There's no way he's involved in whatever caused me to lose my memory. He's like you. He's honorable, and he helps people."

I watched his response carefully. If he had seen me with Mitica the other night, he gave no indication.

"And he...he makes you happy?" Wynn asked quietly as if hesitating to pry.

My heart squeezed, but I smiled and answered honestly. "Happy isn't a strong enough word. I can't say how much I'll miss him when I go home to Chicago." I paused. "But I'm going to miss you too, Wynn. You're a great friend. You're kind-hearted, and I wouldn't have survived without your help. I'll never forget you, and I'll treasure our memories together."

Wynn lowered his gaze and a slight blush of pink dusted his cheeks. "As will I," he murmured.

My face reddened at the adorable expression, and I had to look away.

When I met Mitica that evening, he smiled sweetly at me, a hint of adoration shining in his eyes.

My heart pounded. I hadn't seen that look in a man's eyes for a long time. To have someone like Mitica look at me that way, I wasn't sure my heart could take it.

He kissed each of my cheeks in greeting. "How are you tonight, bucuria mea?"

Perfect because I'm with you. I felt myself flush and scolded myself internally. "Good. And you?"

He smiled more broadly and ran the backs of his fingers over my cheek. "You are blushing. What are you thinking about?" he teased.

My face got even hotter, and I pressed my palms to my cheeks. "Jeez, you aren't supposed to point it out."

He gently pulled my hands away. "Please do not cover your face. I find the expression most becoming."

I lowered my head shyly. *It doesn't matter how old I get; a well-placed compliment always makes me blush. I wish I could see Mitica's cheeks dusted with embarrassment. I bet it's even more adorable than Wynn's. I wonder if there's anything I could say to get that reaction.* "So are we going to see Likinoak tonight?" I asked, changing the subject.

"Da, I believe Grigore has calmed down a bit."

"Good."

Grigore was his usual grumpy self, but he wasn't nearly as hostile as he'd been the night prior.

The cold wind didn't bother me as we flew over the treetops on Grigore's back. In fact, I found it rather refreshing. I was feeling overheated as Mitica's chest pressed against my back while I sat between his thighs.

When we knocked on Likinoak's door, a man with long, black hair and wide, dark eyes answered. He grinned at us.

"Welcome home, Ni'aze," he greeted Mitica.

I looked to Mitica for a translation.

"Older brother," Mitica murmured to me. "Thank you. I am glad to see you back as well," Mitica answered the man. "How were your travels?"

The Wyboka shook his head. "I bear sad news. But before we discuss it, will you introduce me to your ohkwii?"

The man's dark eyes found mine, and he smiled.

Mitica responded to him in another language, and the Wyboka's eyes danced with laughter.

"Erin, this is my brother, Chuthekii. Wic'aze, Little Brother, this is Erin Nichols."

I stuck out my hand, and Chuthekii clasped it warmly. "You have finally come," he said happily.

I tilted my head. "What do you mean 'finally'?"

Mitica chided him in a language I didn't understand.

Chuthekii smiled slyly at him, unphased. The expression clearly said, "that's what you think."

"Yes," Chuthekii answered. "My mother told me about you."

I nodded but squinted at him, knowing I'd missed something.

"Please, come inside. It is cold." Chuthekii opened the door to let us in.

He ladled hot stew into small bowls and handed them to us. We all sat around the fire.

"What sad news do you bring, Wic'aze?" Mitica asked.

"When I returned the children to the school, the headmaster informed me that another Wyboka had succumbed to consumption."

Mitica sighed heavily. "Did they let you bring the child home?"

Chuthekii shook his head. "They gave him a Christian burial on the grounds before I arrived."

"How old was the boy?"

"Six."

"His parents?"

"Amâwe is with them now, burning what few belongings he'd left behind."

"Amâwe is Mother," Mitica translated for me.

"How sad," I sympathized. "Does this happen often? Is it common for children to die at school?"

Chuthekii nodded. "Yes, it happens quite often, Azeohkwii."

I looked to Mitica for another translation, but he just pursed his lips at Chuthekii. I frowned. "Is there anything we can do?"

"We do what we can," Chuthekii responded.

I nodded solemnly.

"We came to update Amâwe on what Erin discovered. She will likely not return for a while. How much did she tell you of Erin's situation?" Mitica asked.

"She told me some. Hawk showed me more." His smile implied that Hawk had shown him much more.

"What did Hawk show you?" I couldn't stop myself from asking.

"That if my brother's hair was as long as mine, you would have braided it."

"What?"

Mitica harrumphed, telling Chuthekii not to clarify.

I squinted at Mitica. *Really?* "Whatever." I sighed. "If Likinoak already told you everything, then I'll tell you what I found. You can relay the message to her."

Chuthekii nodded.

I told him about the full solar eclipse in Gemini at the end of May.

"The most assured way to send you back is to use the same magic that brought you here," he observed meaningfully. "However, if that is not possible, which I would say is the case, we can find another way. I will ask Raven. Perhaps she has a song to send you back when the time comes."

I nodded, not quite sure what he'd meant. Still, it seemed clear he would look for a solution. "Thank you."

"There is no need to thank me, Azeohkwii. I am happy to help if this is truly what you and Ni'aze want."

I frowned at his word choice. *Is this truly what I want? I mean, it's not really about what I want. It's more about what needs to happen. I don't fit in here. I need to go home to my mom and friends. I need to go back and be unemployed in a city with no magic.*

I looked over at Mitica. I'm sure his dejected expression mirrored mine.

The ride back to the barracks was cold and quiet. The thought that I wouldn't be able to feel the warmth of Mitica's arms around me once I'd returned to 2016 swirled in my mind like the clouds Grigore's wings blew away.

Mitica's hands lingered on my hips after he'd helped me dismount the dragon. The contemplative sadness in his eyes reflected my own.

"Can I see you again tomorrow?" I asked, wanting to take advantage of every possible chance to see him.

"Da," he murmured, smiling softly.

I nodded and started to pull away, but he tightened his grip.

I met his gaze again and moved closer to him. I wrapped my arms around him, resting my cheek over his heart.

He embraced me gently as if holding something precious and breakable.

"Hold me tighter," I whispered. "I want there to be no doubt that you were real."

He crushed me to him, the air in my lungs squeezing out in a satisfactory sigh.

I tried to memorize everything about this moment. My soft form yielded to his hard body as we pressed together with one of his arms around my waist and his other hand clutching the base of my neck. His arms encased me in his warm embrace. I breathed deep his scent of campfire and pine—a woodsy smell, smoky and fresh, warm and cool.

An ache in my chest told me that we still weren't close enough. *Slowly. Savor the sweet agony. Remember this feeling later.*

"You won't forget me. Will you, Mitica?" I murmured self-consciously.

He loosened his hold on me and cupped my face in his hands. His blue eyes demanded my attention.

"Never," he declared seriously. "I would forget my own name before I forgot yours. I have known what it is to be kissed by the sun. The moonlight will never be enough again."

My heart wrenched at the sweetness of his words. "Me too," I responded, hushed. "Living in the daylight will be too harsh now that I've known the magic that is you in the gentle moonlight."

He stroked my cheeks with his thumbs and smiled as his eyes shined with unshed tears, the bittersweet expression heartbreaking.

"How appropriate, right?" I said bitterly, remembering a poem I'd once read.

"The sun and the moon, eternally separated by time and space.
One of the seasons, the other of the seas, time defined by their pace.
A boundless sky of clouds or stars, a garden where they dance.
Never be they together, but for a passing glance.
Destiny and fate are cruel to lovers, as often is the case."

Mitica still caressed my face. "Our time may be short, bucuria mea. But it will be memorable."

I nodded. "Yeah, let's make memories."

He smiled down at me and kissed me sweetly on the mouth. Then he kissed my cheeks, nose, and forehead as had become our nightly farewell.

SEVENTEEN

Since the Mounties had to patrol, I offered to return the breakfast basket to Mellie's. It was a brisk morning, but I found it refreshing.

"You're going to want your scarf," Oli commented as I opened the door to step outside.

Touched by his concern, I smiled at him. "It's not that cold though."

He smirked. "That's not why you'll want it."

"What are you getting at, Oli?" I looked to Wynn for clarification, but he pursed his lips slightly, seemingly peeved.

"Why don't you take a look in the mirror?" Oli suggested, nodding his head in that direction.

I walked over to the mirror and examined my face. There didn't seem to be anything wrong with it. Then I tilted my chin up to look at my neck, giving a small cry. Halfway down my neck was a light red hickey.

"For fuck's sake," I cursed, grateful I'd worn my scarf the day before. I watched as my reflection's cheeks flushed at the thought of Mitica's mouth on my neck.

"Told you." Oli grinned.

He held out the scarf to me, and I wrapped it around my neck. I checked my reflection, and I couldn't see it anymore. Then I turned to the Mounties.

"Better?" I asked them to be sure.

Oli nodded, chuckling, but Wynn approached me.

He frowned and reached up. His broad back blocking Oli from view, he pulled down the scarf. He ran his thumb over Mitica's mark, and I quivered as he caressed the sensitive skin.

Holding my breath, I searched his eyes. A fierceness I hadn't expected burned in his blue gaze. *Don't. Don't look at me like that.*

Another tense moment and he replaced my scarf, covering Mitica's love bite.

My head spun, dazed by Wynn's reaction, and a little knot of guilt toward Mitica formed in my gut because of my body's response to Wynn's touch. I vowed to be more careful around Wynn lest my body betray me.

That night, Mitica was unapologetic when we met by the lake.

"You caused me some trouble today," I told him.

"Did I?"

"I thought I would die of embarrassment when Oli and Wynn saw the hickey you gave me the other night."

He grinned, his eyes sparkling with mischief, and I fought a smile.

"Don't look so pleased with yourself," I harrumphed, not truly upset.

He stepped closer to me and wrapped his arms around my waist. "But I am pleased," he whispered.

"Because other men saw the mark you left on me?"

He nodded, still grinning.

I pursed my lips. "I feel like there's something inherently sexist about this situation like you're marking your territory."

He tilted his head at my statement. "Would it make you feel better if you left a mark on me?"

I looked up into his gorgeous face, and my eyes traced the column of his neck to the collar of his buttoned shirt. I felt my cheeks warm. *Mitica would let me claim him? He sees himself as belonging to me?*

His eyes twinkled in amusement. "I see the thought arouses you."

My ears grew hot, and I averted my gaze.

He bent down to whisper in my ear. "You want me to be yours, da?"

I shivered and nodded slightly.

I could feel the smile on his lips as he kissed my cheek.

Taking the encouragement, I laced my fingers with his and slowly led him to a large rock nearby. I nudged him, pressing my palms gently into the unyielding muscles of his chest. He followed my unspoken direction and sat. My fingers trembled only slightly as I brushed the crimson hair from his face. His blue eyes burned, following my every move.

I boldly climbed onto his lap and straddled his hips. His sturdy hands grasped my waist to keep me steady.

My hair fell into my eyes when he gently removed my hat. His torso expanded between my thighs as he breathed heavily below me, and his fingertips left trails of heat as he stroked my face and neck.

I dropped a tentative kiss to his lips and then another, slowly building our desires. His eyes never left mine, though they soon clouded with desire. He didn't press the issue. He was patient, and I was determined to make him wait.

Our kisses grew more heated, more insistent, and I pulled back. His curious eyes watched me as I caressed his face the way he always did to me. He smiled blissfully when I kissed his cheeks.

I trailed my lips along his jaw to his ear. "Why did you mark me, Mitica?" I whispered. "Who did you want to see it?"

He shivered beneath me. "I did not mean to at first," he admitted in a husky voice.

"No?" I murmured. "Then why were you so pleased?"

"Once it was there, I wanted them to see that you had chosen me."

"Who?"

"Grigore, the Mounties, anyone who saw you."

I pulled back and searched his eyes. "You want to be claimed by me, Mitica?" The idea that he saw the mark he'd left on me as a signal to other men that I'd chosen someone else, that I'd allowed a man to touch me, that I'd given myself to him rather than having been taken, was a different approach than I was used to. I wanted to give him the same choice before I went any further.

"Whether you claim me or not, I am already yours," he said simply.

Something about his words in this situation seemed particularly intense. The certainty with which he stated he belonged to me gave me pause. I stared back into his trusting gaze and grasped at how to respond.

I like Mitica. I don't think I've met a man I like more. He's everything I've ever wanted in a lover. But that's the problem. Isn't it? If all he was asking for was sex, I'd accept him right now. But to claim him, to truly choose him as he wants, I need to make such a decision carefully. Misleading him will be worse than stopping it here.

I was comfortable giving myself to him, having him claim me, but not yet ready to take the responsibility of claiming him. The irony of the situation wasn't lost on me, though that didn't exempt me from having to make a tough decision.

"Mitica," I started, stroking his face. "I know we don't have a lot of time together, but I think we should slow down. I don't think we know each other well enough to belong to one another yet. Look, if it was only a physical thing, then I would have no problem. If you just wanted to spend the next seven weeks having fun, I wouldn't hesitate. But I get the idea you're asking for more, and I want to respect that request by taking it seriously."

My skin prickled with nerves as I awaited his reaction.

He closed his eyes and heaved a deep sigh. When he met my gaze again, he smiled softly, but he could not hide the hint of sorrow in his eyes. "I understand. Thank you for thinking of me."

I squinted at his response. "You're not angry?"

He tilted his head. "Angry? Nu, I am sad I put you in this position. I am sorry I gave you distress, bucuria mea."

My mouth fell open in what I'm sure was a ridiculous and unattractive expression. I pouted and my eyes burned. "Jeez, Mitica. Could you even be more perfect?"

He frowned at my assessment but didn't respond.

I kissed him on the tip of his nose. "Hey, don't be so serious," I said cheerfully, trying to break the tension.

My attempt to cheer him up seemed to make the situation worse. He squinted in a mournful expression. I wrapped my arms around the back of his neck and pulled his head gently to my chest. He gingerly held me back.

"Don't be sad. All right? I'm not upset with you for being honest about your feelings. It makes me so so happy that you feel that way about me. You make me feel things I've never felt before. That's why I'd like to be completely certain when I give you an answer. You're wonderful, Mitica. No matter what happens, you'll always have a special place in my heart."

He squeezed me tighter without a word. I closed my eyes and pressed a kiss into his soft hair.

We sat like that for a while, taking comfort in each other's arms. I stroked his hair as I sat in his lap by the lake. Knowing how miserable I'd be if his feelings for me weren't the same level as mine were for him, I let him decide when he was ready to break our embrace.

After I'd climbed out of his lap, Mitica looked down at me with that look of adoration. "I do not deserve you," he said. "You are far too good for me."

I smiled up at him. "Funny. I was going to say the same thing."

EIGHTEEN

After only a few days of us all together, my time with Oli and Wynn started to feel like a routine. We took care of the horses and ate together. They would go on patrol. And in the evenings, Wynn would read *Dracula* while Oli went for a stroll with Suzette.

Oli was rambunctious, and Wynn was reserved. It made me a little sad to see Wynn retreat back into his shell after we'd made such progress together. When we were alone, he'd soften a bit, but he was always serious when Oli was around. It only emphasized their contrasting personalities.

Two nights after telling Mitica we should slow down, we sat cuddling by a fire near the lake. I was wrapped in his arms as I sat between his legs, leaning my back against his chest.

"You must've seen some amazing things in your life," I commented, staring into the fire.

"I find the details of your life far more interesting."

"Oh, come on. My life is way more boring than yours. What do you say? Will you share another memory with me? I'll share one with you."

I could feel him smile against my cheek. "Very well," he agreed. "I will show you something few humans have seen and lived to speak of."

"Whoa, talk about a lead-in."

He chuckled. After a short pause, Mitica began to sing quietly as if worried someone else might overhear. As he sang, my view of the fire blurred. When the world came back into focus, we sat in the grass on the corner of a forest crossroads.

The paths were speckled with moonlight, which filtered through the thick trees.

At the center of the crossroads, a group of naked women holding candles danced facing each other in a circle. Their long hair barely covered their breasts as they executed the steps in perfect unison. The flames of their candles flickered as they danced, leaving trails of light. The fire shined through their incorporeal forms, adding to the beauty.

"Wow," I whispered as though afraid they would hear me. "It's so enchanting. What are they?"

"They are iele," he answered, arms still around me.

"Like your mother?"

He nodded.

As we watched the voluptuous women dance naked in the night, I said, "I guess I can understand why they don't want people watching them."

"Da, they have bad tempers, too. If anyone is unlucky enough to get caught observing their dance, he will surely be cursed with madness."

"You were allowed to watch because you're half iele?"

He nodded.

"But you didn't get to dance with them?"

His quiet response came after an uncomfortably long pause. "Nu."

The sense that I'd struck a nerve made my heart sink. *But I bet Mitica is a wonderful dancer.* "Would you like to see my memory now?" I asked though I was reluctant to leave the crossroads.

"Da."

"Okay. I just picture it in my mind, right?"

He nodded.

I closed my eyes and imagined the scene I'd witnessed countless times. When I felt Mitica knock on my mind, I let him in.

Opening my eyes, I held my breath at how real the illusion felt. The breeze of Lake Michigan caressed my skin and carried its unique lake-water scent. Seagulls called overhead as they soared in the golden glow of dawn. The sand was cold beneath the seat of my jeans and my bare feet, having yet to be warmed by the day's sunlight.

I let out a contented sigh. When Mitica didn't say anything, I looked over my shoulder at him. His blue eyes shined in wonder, and he smiled unhindered.

I grinned, glad he was happy with what I was showing him. "When I was in college, I used to come down here before class to watch the sunrise and get some fresh air. There's a bakery a few blocks away that makes the best chocolate croissants."

"This is something you would see often?"

I nodded. "Almost every day. It was a great way to slow down and de-stress. Everything about this place calms me: the waves, the sand, the smell, even the seagulls. I don't know why everyone hates seagulls. They're my favorite birds. Something about their call just...reminds me of home I guess."

"It seems like a very nice place to call home."

"Well, this is pretty much as chill as it gets here. It's not nearly as enchanting as your home, but I like it."

He shook his head. "You are far more enchanting than any magic I have ever encountered."

My cheeks heated, and I looked up at the horizon. I didn't know how to respond to that. Normally, if a guy said something like that to me, I'd just have a snarky remark and play it off. But it was difficult to know what to say when I knew he was sincere. "Thank you," I muttered, my usual wit falling flat, as it always seemed to when Mitica was around.

I couldn't see Mitica's face, but I felt his cheek smile against mine.

"If we'd met in 2016, we could've come down here together," I commented. "Do you think you're alive in 2016?"

"It is possible I will be reborn and living at that time."

"You would be reborn as a human?"

"Most likely."

"So you'd only have magic if you lived in a place with wilderness?"

"Da, assuming I even know I am part fae."

"What do you mean?"

"If I grew up in a city like you and I never discovered my true name, I may not know I have magic."

"Oh, right." I paused. *It wouldn't matter anyway. I could already be dead in 2016.* "We could've met and not even known it if you're a city kid like me."

"Perhaps."

I met his eyes over my shoulder. *Would I have recognized you if I've met you before? How different would you be? You'd certainly look different. How much of your personality would be the same? I always thought personality was just biology and socialization. What about your soul makes it Mitica?*

I don't know how, call it reporter's intuition, but I felt I would know Mitica if I met him again in 2016. I didn't know if we'd met before. But after making a connection with him in 1900, I knew I'd recognize him if we met again.

The illusion crumbled around us as I lost interest in the landscape and concentrated on Mitica. The summer breeze off Lake Michigan was replaced by the winter chill of the frozen mountain lake in Farrloch.

I shivered, and Mitica held me closer. Snuggling deeper into his embrace, I looked up at the nearly full moon. A contentment I couldn't remember ever feeling settled into me. I closed my eyes, enjoying Mitica's warmth and the crackling sound of the fire.

NINETEEN

I awoke the next morning and couldn't remember how I'd gotten into Wynn's bed. I recalled cuddling with Mitica, but I didn't remember saying goodnight and returning to the barracks. *Did Mitica magic me back inside, or was I just so tired that I forgot?*

"You're finally awake," Wynn said, coming into the barracks. "We already ate breakfast and cared for the horses, but we left some food for you."

As he spoke, he crossed the room to where I still lay in bed. He sat by my feet. "Are you unwell?"

"I'm fine," I assured him, sitting up.

He analyzed my face. "I was worried. I think you were walking in your sleep last night."

"What do you mean?"

"Sometime in the middle of the night, you must have gotten up. When you were going back to bed, you tripped over me on the floor."

"Oh jeez, Wynn. I'm sorry. I didn't hurt you. Did I?"

"No, did you get hurt when you fell? I couldn't tell at the time, but I helped you to bed to be certain."

"I'm all right. Thanks for looking after me." *I guess I must've walked in on my own after all.*

He smiled gently. I was happy to see how easy it had become for him to smile in front of me, and I felt my cheeks warm.

Just then, Oli entered, and Wynn jumped to his feet. I crinkled my eyebrows at his haste, but a glance at Oli explained his reaction. He grinned with a knowing look that said, "I know what you two were up to."

I sighed and rolled my eyes, but I knew I was blushing even harder. "I'm sorry if I woke you when I tripped over Wynn last night, Oli. I must've been half asleep when I went to the outhouse."

He frowned and raised an eyebrow at me. "I didn't hear anything."

"Oh. Well, good then."

"We won't be back until after supper," Wynn said, putting on his hat. "A tree fell on a barn a few nights ago, so Oliver and I are going to be gone most of the day helping to fix it."

"Oh, if that's the case, let me come help, too. If you saddle Langundo for me, I can be ready in five minutes."

"Are you certain?" Wynn asked. "You haven't even eaten, and you slept late. Perhaps you need more rest."

"No worries. I can eat some bread in the saddle. I told you I'm fine," I reassured, stuffing my feet into Oli's moccasins.

Wynn frowned, and Oli slapped him on the shoulder. "Come on. She said she's fine."

Wynn nodded once and went outside to saddle Langundo. I rushed to get ready and grabbed some bread from Mellie's basket. I held it in my mouth as I pulled on Oli's coat and ran outside.

Once we were on our way and I'd eaten my breakfast, I asked Wynn whose barn needed repairs.

"The Capreanu's," he answered.

"Will you be able to fix a barn in a day, or will you have to come back tomorrow?"

"The Romanians seem to have a pretty close-knit community. I'm sure some of their neighbors will come to help. I don't see why we wouldn't be able to finish today with everyone working together."

My heart thumped. "The Romanians?" I demanded, louder than I'd intended. Langundo's ears twitched, and I bit my lip.

Wynn looked over his shoulder at me and met my eyes. I'm sure he was thinking about how I'd told him the man I was interested in was a

Romanian immigrant. *Will Mitica be there? I mean, he's got to have a life when he's not with me, right? Maybe he sleeps during the day though and helps the fae at night.*

"Are you one of those who has something against the Sifton immigrants?" Oli asked.

"Of course not." I didn't know what that even was, but I knew I wasn't against immigration.

"I have to admit they have some pretty strange ways, but they don't seem any harm," Oli mused.

I just nodded to him, lost in my own thoughts.

When we arrived at the Capreanu farm, a group of hearty men was already at work cleaning away the broken pieces of wood. I scanned the group for Mitica's crimson head, but all I saw was brown or black.

As we dismounted, two of the men approached us. The older man smiled and shook Wynn's hand in greeting. "Constable Delaforet, thank you for coming to help with our barn."

"Mr. Capreanu, this is Subconstable Taylor and Erin Nichols."

The older man dipped his head with a smile. "And this is my son, Ion."

Ion, a man in his early twenties, greeted the Mounties and then smiled at me in appreciation. My eyes widened when he checked me out so blatantly. I had to admit he was attractive, lean and strong from farm work, but he didn't really compare to Mitica or Wynn. He didn't even attempt to hide his interest in me, and his father chuckled.

"My wife and daughter are in the house cooking for everyone. Ion, show her the way."

"I'd rather help out here if that's all right," I countered. "I'm not good in the kitchen."

Mr. Capreanu's eyebrows rose at my suggestion.

Wynn stepped close to me and whispered softly. "Erin, I know you're more than capable to help us if you say you are, but your presence is going to make them uncomfortable. They aren't used to women like you."

I pursed my lips, swallowing the retort that they better *get* used to women like me.

Ion watched our interaction with interest, no doubt wondering what the nature of our relationship was.

I heaved a heavy sigh. "Fine. I'll go off to the kitchen with the rest of the women."

Wynn placed his hand on my shoulder. "Thank you."

I gave him a resigned look and nodded at Ion. "All right. Where should I go?"

Ion smiled charmingly. "This way."

As I followed Ion toward the small farmhouse, I looked back at Wynn and Oli, who were removing their hats and jackets to get to work.

"I have never seen you before, Miss Nichols. Did you just arrive?" Ion asked, demanding my attention.

"Yeah, I haven't been here very long, and you can call me Erin."

He grinned. "How do you know Constable Delaforet, Erin?"

Wow, jumping right in, eh? "Wynn and I are friends. He helped me out of a bit of trouble."

He nodded, clearly pleased by my answer. Lucky for me, we'd reached the house. He led me to the kitchen where an older woman and a teenage girl were doing kitcheny stuff.

They looked up as we entered. The older woman said something to Ion in a language I assumed was Romanian.

"This is Erin Nichols, Mamă. Erin, this is my Mamă and my sister, Mariana. Tată sent Erin to help you."

Mrs. Capreanu nodded and waved her son away. Before he left, he turned to me. "Please let me know if there is anything I can do for you, Erin," he said earnestly.

"Uh, thanks, Ion. I will."

He gave me another charming smile and strode from the room. I turned to the two women, feeling incredibly out of place. Mrs. Capreanu said something in Romanian to Mariana, who nodded and approached me.

"Mamă said you can help me," Mariana told me, smiling kindly.

"Okay, but I have to warn you: I'm really awful in the kitchen."

Her dark eyes sparkled in amusement. "That is all right. We are going to wash and chop vegetables."

"I guess I should be able to handle that."

As Mrs. Capreanu did something with dough and a rolling pin, Mariana and I stood at a table and washed vegetables in a metal tub.

"I think my brother likes you," Mariana confessed like it was some huge secret.

"You think so?"

She nodded. "I am glad. He has not been very happy since we moved here, and you are quite pretty."

"Thank you, Mariana. You're also very pretty."

"Are you married?" she asked me. "You are not wearing a ring."

"No, I'm not married. But I am kind of seeing someone. In fact, I was hoping to see him here today. He's also Romanian."

She pursed her lips. "Is it Alexandru?"

I raised my eyebrows at her dejection. "No, it's not Alexandru."

She immediately perked up, and I couldn't hold in my chuckle.

"Who is it then?"

"You would definitely know him if you saw him. He has dark red hair and blue eyes."

She gasped and dropped the potato she was washing into the water with a splash. Mrs. Capreanu looked up at her reaction. Mariana waved her hand, telling her mother she was fine. The older woman went back to work.

Mariana shifted her eyes as if to see if anyone else was near and dropped her voice. "You speak of the hultan?"

Whoa, she knows about magic? I nodded. "You know him?"

"I have heard the others speak of him, but I have never seen him."

Oh, I guess not then. "I was hoping to find out what he gets up to during the day."

Her eyes were wide with awe. "You have seen the hultan? You met with him?"

"Yeah, I said we were sort of involved."

Her brow furrowed. "But how?" She paused. "Hultan must be celibate, or they will lose their magic."

"What? Really?"

She nodded slowly. "That is how it is in all the stories."

Are you effing kidding me? What the Hell is Mitica thinking? Why would he get so involved with me if he knows he will lose his magic if things progress? When I realized I was squeezing a carrot, I took a deep breath.

Calm down. I'm sure there's an explanation. I'll just ask him when I see him tonight.

I shrugged at Mariana. "I mean, it's not like our relationship has gotten that far."

She nodded her understanding. "I would be careful if I were you."

"What do you mean?"

"Hultan are powerful, and they can help people. But they also have dark magic. It is best not to anger them."

Jeez, so dramatic. I mean, sure. I guess Mitica could use his magic to hurt someone, but I can't see him doing that. He's all about helping people.

I acknowledged her warning and attributed her fear to the fact that she didn't know him.

I would call my first attempt at cooking in 1900 a success. Okay, so my vegetables were cut all uneven and chunky compared to Mariana's but whatever. They were just vegetables.

When the time for supper came around, the barn had been fixed. The men had worked hard and deserved the hearty meal we served them.

When I handed Oli his bowl, he stared at it suspiciously. "You didn't *really* spit in this. Did you, Erin?"

I just grinned at him and gave a bowl to Wynn before sitting between them.

Ion lost no time chatting me up. He sat across from me as soon as he got his food. He was a decent guy, so I saw no reason to snub him. I was polite but careful not to be overly friendly.

At some point, I glanced over at Wynn. He seemed to be eating very deliberately as if his food was going to bite him back. It occurred to me that perhaps Wynn thought Ion was the Romanian man I was interested in.

When they were finished, I took their empty bowls. As I got up to go to the kitchen, I saw Mariana whisper something in her brother's ear. I can only guess what she'd said to him, but he was markedly less forward when I returned to my seat.

I don't know what was so amusing, but Wynn's lips held the shadow of a smile.

Everyone was on friendly terms when we said our goodbyes, and we were told we were always welcome.

TWENTY

I managed to maintain my chilly demeanor when Mitica greeted me with a cheerful smile that night. His grin slipped, and he met my accusing squint with grave dignity.

"Have you forgotten to tell me something important?" I demanded.

He waited silently to see if I'd continue. When I just stared back, he asked, "Such as?"

I clicked my tongue. "Come on, Mitica. I don't like being lied to. A lie by omission is still a lie."

He took a deep breath. "If I have not told you, it was to protect you or others."

"What about protecting yourself a little?" I said, my worry breaking the irritable defensiveness. "Is it really true you have to stay celibate or you'll lose your magic? Why wouldn't you disclose that? I would've been a lot more careful around you."

He let out a long breath. "That is not true," he told me.

My eyes widened. *For fuck's sake, Erin. This is what happens when you jump to conclusions. You call yourself a journalist? You know better.*

I hung my head in shame. "Excuse me while I go kill myself now." I turned to go back to the barracks and hide under the covers of Wynn's bed.

"It is not true for me, but it is true for other hultan," he clarified.

I stopped my retreat.

"Because I am half iele, I do not have to stay celibate to keep my magic."

"Oh. Well, that's...good then."

He gently placed his hands on my hips as he stood behind me.

"You were quite distressed by the thought," he pointed out quietly.

"Of course I was. I didn't want to make things hard for you."

He slowly embraced me, wrapping his arms around my stomach. "I am sorry you were upset," he murmured.

"God, Mitica. I should be the one to apologize. I even accused you of lying. *I'm* sorry." *It's not like I have any room to talk either. I mean, I've been lying to Wynn this whole time.*

He paused for a little longer than I'd expected, and I started to squirm to try to look back at him. He tightened his embrace and buried his face in my scarf.

"Everyone has secrets—things they need to keep to themselves," he muttered.

A shiver raised the hair on my neck. "Yeah..." Mariana's warning about Mitica's dark magic gnawed at my mind. I could feel the curiosity bubbling up, and I knew I wouldn't be able to resist. "You said we were supposed to be getting to know each other. Right?"

He didn't respond.

I bit my lip. *Given his comments about secrets and keeping them to protect me, it's obvious there are things he isn't telling me. Establishing trust is a two-way street. Give a little to get a little. At the very least, maybe I can figure it out in a round-about way.*

"Mitica, if I show you my most cherished memory, will you share the memory that's most important to you?"

He was quiet as he wrestled with his desire to know me and keep whatever he was hiding.

"Da," he finally agreed. "Show me what you cherish most."

"Okay," I said and took a steadying breath. "Ready when you are."

I closed my eyes and imagined the memory I held closest to my heart. I'd seen it so many times that it was like watching a film rather than reliving it. It was just like any other Saturday in spring.

Mitica sang his spell softly into my ear, and he didn't even have to knock on the door to my mind. It was already ajar for him.

I opened my eyes to the all-too-familiar scene. A girl in a Cubs jersey stood behind a chain-link fence. Her Converse were planted shoulder-width apart as she stared down the barrel of a pitching machine in a borrowed batter's helmet.

A man in a baseball practice shirt leaned into the fence behind her, his fingers curled around the metal links. His blue Cubs hat hid his features, but I knew he had neat brown hair and gentle brown eyes.

"Keep your elbow up," he encouraged the girl as she missed another pitch.

Mitica and I watched them. Distant, apart, as if we didn't belong to their rose-tinted afternoon.

"That's my dad," I said finally. "He was a Chicago police officer. He loved baseball, the Cubs in particular. He taught me everything he knew about the game. He uh...he was killed shortly after this day. It's the last time I ever picked up a bat. After a while, I started to watch baseball and go to games and stuff, but I never played again. I don't know. It sort of felt like playing catch by myself. But this...this memory of when we were together and happy, it reminds me of how precious innocence is. I can't say I haven't been happy since my dad died, but I haven't been as carefree. Maybe one day... I can't get my innocence back, but I hope to be free again."

I figured Mitica would have tons of questions about how my dad died or at least about how different the modern world looked. Instead, he watched silently as younger me finally hit the ball. The ting of the ball off my bat was drowned out by my dad's satisfied cheers.

"Freedom," Mitica murmured. "A full heart has wings."

"Yeah. Maybe."

The scene shifted back to Farrloch.

"Aren't you going to show me?" I asked Mitica. As I turned to look at him, he let me loose.

Nodding seriously, he said, "I will, but I must explain first."

He was hushed for a moment, staring up at the nearly full moon. He faced me with a sigh. "There is much in this world that is hidden, dark places where even the brave dare not go. They say one should not know his own fate, but I... Ever since the tale was told to me, I knew I must go.

"Deep in the Carpathian Mountains, there is a cave. It is dark and dangerous but houses a special treasure: The Obsidian Mirror. The legend says if you go before the mirror on the night of the dead, you will see your fate. A night where the dead return to the realm of the living and creatures far more wicked than the Čanotila prowl the forests for anyone not safely huddled by the warm hearth. Even magic is no match for what some of these beings can do.

"Still, I went. I left the candles flickering in the cemeteries and traveled through the cold mist to the cave. It took me years to discover its exact location, but I found it."

"And the mirror?" I whispered.

He nodded. "That is what I am going to show you: my most important memory."

My heartbeat was loud in my ears, my breath heavy, and my fingers trembled as I reached my hand out to him. "Show me."

He took my hand and began his song. When the world came back into focus, we stood before a smooth wall of black obsidian. A torch, which Mitica held in his other hand, illuminated his dark reflection.

His frosted breath fogged the mirror as he leaned closer to it. "Are you ready to see what The Obsidian Mirror showed me?"

I nodded, not sure I could answer around the lump in my throat.

He turned back to the mirror, and the scene shifted into the memory of what the mirror had shown him.

On the bare forest floor, where sunlight never reaches to nurture plants, Mitica sat leaning against a thick tree trunk.

His weary face looked up into the dark canopy. No moon or stars could be seen through the thick foliage of the towering treetops. Still, they must have been out because their light reflected off the mist that hung in dips and hollows, illuminating the forest with an eerie glow.

From one of the hollows came a steady humming buzz.

Mirror Mitica slowly turned his head toward the sound with an expression that said he wasn't truly interested. But his eyes widened when a small chirping bird flew from the fog.

I squinted at the creature, which darted from place to place in its excitement. "Oh, a hummingbird," I said to the Mitica who held my hand.

"Da, I did not know what it was when I was shown this vision, but I have learned since coming to Canada."

"I guess there aren't hummingbirds in Romania."

He shook his head.

The hummingbird chattered happily at mirror Mitica, flitting around him.

His once tired eyes glinted in fascination as he continued to watch the little bird. His fascination turned to amusement. Soon, he smiled joyfully at the creature.

When the hummingbird flew up toward the treetops, mirror Mitica rose to follow it. As he climbed to stay with the bird, we watched him scramble not to lose it. Up the tree he went, hopping from branch to branch, the bird never far ahead.

Finally, he broke through the barrier of leaves and gasped at the open sky. He reached his hand out toward the bird, and it landed delicately on his finger with a satisfied cheep.

In the east, the amber dawn painted the sky with morning. Mitica laughed at the scene, reveling in the rosy glow.

But as the sun broke the horizon, the hummingbird flew away.

"Wait!" he called to the creature with longing.

My chest swelled, and my heart broke at the sound of his pleas.

The bird got farther away, and Mitica looked at the ground far below, his eyes flickering with desperation.

Shutting his eyes, he took a deep breath. As he released it slowly, he gazed toward the direction the hummingbird had gone.

He spread his arms wide as if he would fly, and he leaned forward. I cried out as he began to fall.

Mitica clutched my hand, reminding me he was still beside me.

As mirror Mitica's feet left the tree, he transformed into a bird and flew away toward the hummingbird.

"A nightingale," Mitica informed me.

When we'd returned to the moonlit lake shore in Farrloch, I took a steadying breath, my hand on my chest.

"That was your most important memory?"

He nodded.

"Do you know what it means?"

"In part. The trouble with fortune-telling is you never seem to know what it means until after it happens"

Well, that did little to give me insight into Mitica's secrets. I met his eyes. *But it must be significant to him in some way or it wouldn't be so important to him. I should think on it more carefully.*

"Thank you for sharing your most important memory with me, Mitica. I don't quite know what it means, but I appreciate you opening up to me."

He brushed my cheek with his thumb. "And you, bucuria mea. Knowing what you have lost and how you still share your light with others, you are even more brave and glorious than I had thought."

My face flushed at his compliment. "Mitica, I..." *I want to know more about you. I want to know everything about you. Will you let me?* "Thank you, Mitica," I whispered, unable to give voice to my true desires.

He seemed to pick up on my hesitation. "It is late. You must rest. May I see you tomorrow, bucuria mea?"

"Of course."

Before he could kiss my cheeks and say goodnight, I wrapped my arms around him and buried my face in his chest.

He must've been surprised because it took him a second to return my embrace. I breathed in his woodsy scent and floated in the timeless moment.

Just for that moment, I allowed myself to let go. With so much uncertainty in my life and so many unanswered questions, I took a chance to indulge myself. And for the length of a single embrace, the needs I never allowed myself to acknowledge were met. I was safe. I was protected. There was nothing to fear in Mitica's arms. He was there with me. I could feel him, hear him, touch him. He was solid and real, and no one could take that away from me. As long as he was with me, I didn't have to be brave or strong. I could allow myself to feel whatever I felt without worrying about whether it would harm my determination to go on.

My thoughts quieted, and it didn't matter what secrets Mitica could possibly be keeping. All that mattered were his arms around me and his breath in my hair. Patience was never something I had been good at. But as long as Mitica's secret wouldn't separate us, I didn't really care what it was.

"Mitica," I murmured into his chest. "I don't want to be alone right now."

He pulled back, meeting my solicitation with wide eyes.

I could feel my cheeks warm slightly before I said, "Don't you have someplace we can go? You must live somewhere."

He closed his eyes, wincing. His eyebrows crinkled in regret as he gazed at me. "That is...not a good idea tonight."

My stomach plummeted at the rejection, and my ears grew hot with shame.

"The Mounties would be alarmed if they awoke and you were gone, da?"

I didn't respond even though I knew he was right.

He caressed my face and lifted my chin so I would meet his gaze. I bit my lip but complied.

"Let me find another way, bucuria mea."

I frowned and squinted into a pout. He smiled gently at me.

"I am sorry to send you back inside, especially since you want to stay with me. But I want you to know: you are not alone. I will be beside you even when I feel far away."

Pretty words, but it doesn't change the fact I'm sleeping alone.

I was a little less irritated as he kissed each of my cheeks and my forehead.

"You better figure it out soon," I whispered a moment before he placed a soft kiss on my lips.

"I will," he promised with a smile.

Just as I'd expected, the Mounties' presence did little to alleviate the vulnerable loneliness I felt in the pitch-black cabin.

TWENTY-ONE

In the light of the following morning, I felt mortified by what had transpired the night before.

I can't believe I reacted that way. I was feeling vulnerable, and I took comfort in Mitica. I didn't have to suggest we spend the night together. I wanted to think carefully before going there, what with the whole claiming him thing. Am I ready to "claim" him?

I had always been a fairly balanced person, equally guided by both logic and intuition. The trouble came when my brain and my heart told me different things. Those situations usually resulted in unease followed by anxiety and agonizing over what to do.

My brain is saying I haven't known Mitica very long, and he's clearly keeping something from me. It's saying don't fully trust him until you know him better.

What's my heart saying?

I didn't even have to ask. I already knew the answer. I knew I felt it: the pull. The quickening of my pulse when I knew I would see him, the loneliness when he wasn't around. The problem was I couldn't lie to myself and pretend he was the only one I felt it toward.

I squeezed my eyes shut and gritted my teeth. *Stupid. Stupid, stupid, stupid. And don't forget wrong. I don't deserve either of them. Mitica would give himself over to me, and I don't have the courtesy to get over a crush on a man who isn't interested? What is my problem? Maybe it's because I see Wynn every day. I mean, I've never had this problem before. Maybe I should move out of the barracks. I wonder if Suzette would let me stay with her. But is leaving a good idea? I still don't know who killed me in this lifetime. Mitica brought me to Wynn to keep me safe. Why didn't Mitica just keep me with him?*

As I stewed in my own guilty juices, the devil I spoke of entered with breakfast.

"Good morning," Wynn greeted, removing his hat.

My heart thumped at the sight of him. I rolled toward the wall and curled into a ball under the covers. Unfortunately, that just meant I was surrounded by Wynn's scent as I buried myself in his bed.

He crossed the room and stood over me. "Erin, are you not feeling well?"

"I'm fine," I mumbled.

"Are you certain? Can I do anything?" He placed his hand gently on my shoulder.

I jumped at his touch. "I said I'm fine," I snapped, glaring at him.

He pulled back and nodded with a mask-like expression.

Stop being nice to me. Ignore me, be mean, just stop making it so hard to let you go.

I'm sure Wynn was confused as to why I'd responded so nastily to his concern, but he didn't ask. He returned to the table and dished breakfast into three bowls.

That day, the Mounties had business to take care of in town. They said something about buying horse feed, but I wasn't really listening. I declined their invitation to join them in favor of moping around the barracks.

After looking out the window for a while, I went to the chest at the foot of Wynn's bed. He kept *Dracula* in there, so I surmised he would have other books I could read as well.

Lifting the heavy, wooden lid, I stared into the well-organized trunk. Most of the contents were neatly-folded clothes, but on the right side, there were stationary and writing tools.

There was only one other book besides *Dracula*. I grabbed it and cracked the soft leather binding.

Opening to a random page, I had already seen too much by the time I'd realized it was Wynn's journal. His entries were short and neat.

5 April 1900
Trip to Strathcona to test spring water sample. Erin nearly fainted on train. Everything she does draws me to her. I want to protect her.

~

6 April 1900
Chemists say test could take a week. Erin found something at library. We met Sparrow at The Winchester. I couldn't close the distance. It's better this way.

~

7 April 1900
Back to Farrloch. Erin pulling away. Oliver in barracks when we arrived.

~

8 April 1900
Erin and Oliver fast friends. No word from chemists.

~

9 April 1900
I don't know how much longer I can hold out. Still haven't heard about exemption request. I am already hers.

My hands shook, and my heart pounded. My breath caught as the sound of hooves approaching came from outside. After quickly returning the journal to its proper place, I managed to shut the lid of the trunk before Wynn entered.

Wynn took in my wide eyes, open mouth, and pale face. "Erin, what's wrong?" he asked, alarmed.

I averted my gaze, not sure I could handle looking at him at the moment. "Nothing. I uh...need some fresh air."

"Would you like me to come with you?"

"No, I'll be fine. I need to be alone."

I ran past the stables and Oli putting away the horses' tack. When I reached the treeline, I didn't slow down. I ran all the way to the cliff that overlooked the river. Once I'd reached the ledge, I bent, panting and clutching my cramped side.

With nowhere to run, my mind started spinning.

What is even happening? Wynn is interested in me? How? What—?

I crouched and hugged my legs, ignoring my screaming lungs and thumping my forehead on my knees.

"What do I do?" I moaned.

Misery gnawed at me as guilt made my eyes burn. The thought of hurting Wynn or Mitica made my tears well and spill over.

"I'm lost," I told the trees, but they didn't hear over the roaring of the river below.

My mind grasped for any words of wisdom I'd ever heard. My dad telling me to "spit on it" didn't really help in this situation.

I recalled the few times in my life where I'd felt an overwhelming level of anxiety. It came up with anything from arguments with friends to worrying about which college I would get into. Whatever the reason, I always called my mom. She was busy, being a small business owner will do that, but she was never too busy to talk when I got like this.

"Mom, I need help," I told the wind.

The advice my mom gave me usually came down to three things: be patient, be honest, and don't try to take on others' emotions.

All of these phrases I'd heard her say applied to this situation. I could practically feel her stroking my hair. "Okay, take a deep breath," she would say. "So two boys like you, and you're unsure which boy you like back.

You're upset because you know you can only choose one, and you don't want to hurt the boy you don't choose. Don't take on others' emotions, Erin. I know you don't want to hurt them, Honey, but that kind of comes with the whole love territory. If you're really unsure of whom you like better, you should just be honest with them. Tell them what you're feeling, and be patient as they work out their responses. It'll all be okay. Whatever will be will be."

I took a few steadying breaths and raised my head. *All right. I'll talk to them.*

I walked slowly back to the barracks, trying to figure out what I could say. Wynn was a particular problem because I probably should tell him I read his journal, too. I still hadn't determined whom I would talk to first when I arrived.

As I turned the corner of the stables, I saw Oli and Wynn packing Oli's saddlebags.

"What's going on?" I asked them; they seemed in a hurry.

"I got a telegram from my sister. My mother is ill, so I'm going home."

"Oh, no. I'm sorry to hear that, Oli. I hope she's all right."

He nodded. "Thanks. I don't know how long I'll be gone, but I'll send word when I know more."

"Yeah, no problem. Should I let Suzette know?"

"No, I'm going to stop by the shop before I leave town."

"All right. Well, be safe."

"Will do," he assured, climbing into the saddle.

As he rode away, Wynn turned to me. "We also got word from the chemists in Edmonton. The water is safe. There's nothing in it that would kill a person at the present amounts."

"Well, shit. I guess we're back to a lack of information."

He nodded.

After a pause, he said. "You missed lunch. Are you hungry? We left some food for you."

"I'm fine, thanks. It's almost dinner time anyway."

As he gazed at me, I could feel my cheeks heat. *Can he tell I've been crying?* I averted my eyes. "I'm going to wash my face," I muttered, escaping into the barracks.

My eyes weren't nearly as red and puffy as I'd imagined, but I splashed my face with cold water anyway.

All through dinner, I tried to decide how I wanted to broach the subject with Wynn, but I couldn't get the words right in my mind. Just as I was going to jump in, he said he had some correspondence to write, so he wouldn't be able to read *Dracula* that night.

I acknowledged his plans, sighing internally. *It will be easier to talk to Mitica first anyway.*

When I heard Mitica's sweet baritone greet me that night, I flinched.

"What is wrong, bucuria mea?" he asked, tilting his head at my sorrowful expression.

"I have something I need to tell you, Mitica."

He took my hand and smiled reassuringly. "Then tell me."

I looked down at my moccasined feet. "I don't want to hurt you, but I need to be honest with you."

"Do not be distressed. You can be honest. I promise to listen."

I closed my burning eyes, willing the tears to wait. Taking a deep breath, I looked up into Mitica's patient, compassionate gaze.

"Mitica, I love you, but I'm also in love with someone else. I'm sorry. I don't know what else to say. I want to choose between you, but my heart is torn."

Mitica froze at my confession, his face giving nothing away.

Though he showed no reaction, I knew I must have caused him pain. An aching lump formed in my throat as tears rolled down my face. "I'm sorry," I choked.

His eyes softened as he watched me break. "Who is he?" he murmured.

"What? Why?"

He took a deep breath. "Who?"

"Wynn," I whispered.

He squeezed his eyes shut as if he were in pain. He was silent for a while before he said, "I am sorry."

My heart squeezed. *What does that mean? He's going to leave.* A sob escaped me, and I brought my shaking fingertips to my lips.

"I am sorry you are going through this."

"Mitica, no. Please don't apologize. I feel horrible for doing this to you. You have nothing to be sorry for. You're perfect."

He shook his head and held up a hand to shush me. "No, Erin. You feel this way because I have not been honest with you."

I furrowed my brow, trying to figure out what he meant through my own foggy misery.

He met my eyes, and his blue depths pleaded with me to understand. "I am Wynn."

His words washed over me like a bucket of freezing lake water.

"Um...what?"

"More accurately, Wynn does not exist."

My mind pulled away from the idea. "What are you saying? Of course Wynn exists." Adrenaline made my body hum with anxiety.

He sighed. "I do not know how to explain. I am Wynn, and Wynn is not real. He is a persona I created to infiltrate the North-West Mounted Police. Look. Look at me."

My eyes snapped to his face, which blurred. When it came back into focus, Wynn stood before me.

"What the holy Hell? Wynn? Mitica?"

Wynn nodded. "This is a glamour: an illusion to hide my true identity."

"What? Why?"

"That's a long story, one you deserve to hear."

Anger bubbled in my gut. "You're damn right I deserve to hear it. Jesus fucking Christ, why did you lie to me? Do you know how much I've been struggling with these feelings of guilt? And come to find out you were the same guy. Gah, I can't even tell you how pissed I am right now!"

"I understand, but please listen to my story before you get angry. Won't you?"

I ground my teeth and crossed my arms. "Fine. Go ahead."

Wynn sat on a large rock and motioned for me to join him. "This will take a while," he said when I didn't move.

"Whatever. Just go," I snapped.

He sighed. "I told you civilization is killing magic. In Canada, the North-West Mounted Police are at the forefront of this destruction. They protect settlers who tame the wilderness, they facilitate unfair treaties between the government and the natives, their main purpose is to civilize the west. When the Romanian immigrants realized the Canadian fae were in trouble, they did what they always do: asked the hultan for help.

"The hultan leaders, a council known as the Zgrimties, sent me to infiltrate the organization and discover their motives. I was to see how much of the leadership knew about the British Empire's mission to eradicate magic and to help the fae and natives when I could.

"I created this disguise and passed myself off as Canadian to join the ranks."

"But why didn't you just tell me? You had to see I was attracted to you both."

He hung his head and shifted his appearance back to Mitica. "The Zgrimties made me swear an oath to keep my purpose secret. If I was to reveal the truth, all support for my mission would be withdrawn, and I would no longer be welcome in Crugul Pământului."

I cringed. *Shit.* "What's that?"

"It is the hultan's base of operations and where they train."

I frowned. "So because you told me, you can't go home or get support while trying to save magic? Now you're an outcast?"

He stood and took my hand, squeezing it reassuringly. "This is not your fault, Erin. When you arrived and I realized who you were, I requested an exception from the Zgrimties so I could tell you."

"And what did they say?"

"I have not received an answer yet. But they have to approve it. You are too important."

"What do you mean I'm too important. Who am I?"

"You are mine, and I am yours."

I stared at him, waiting for more of an explanation.

"My parents were forbidden from being together. But they loved each other so deeply they were willing to sacrifice everything for each other. My father even gave up his magic. When I was born, it shook the magical world. A half-iele half-hultan, what an abomination," he said bitterly. "But I never knew that, not until it was time for me to be trained in magic. My parents loved me, and they fought to get me into Crugul Pământului so I could go to school.

"It was miserable. Everyone despised me, but no one could deny my gifts. When I finished school, the Zgrimties and iele both laid claim to my abilities. Neither of them truly accepted me, but I was glad to be useful. I wanted to help people and save magic. People need me. They ask for my help, and I am happy to give it. But there has never been anyone who needed my mere existence. Someone who did not need me to do anything but just be, and there has never been anyone who I needed in the same way.

"During the last dark moon, looking into the moonless sky, I knew there had to be someone out there in that void. I wanted to meet her, to know her if only for a short while. So I made a wish. That is when I found you. I was not positive until we talked with Likinoak. You are my soul mate, Erin. The gods have brought us together through time and space."

"Your magic is what pulled me through time?" I asked in wonder.

"Well, my magic coupled with your desire and the black moon."

The irresistible pull I felt around Mitica and Wynn, the sense of innate trust and safety, I'd explained those uncharacteristic feelings by the precarious situation I was in and the fact that they had helped me. *While those things still apply, is it possible there's more to the explanation?*

I searched Mitica's eyes for the answers and was again struck by the thought that I'd recognize that soul anywhere.

"You know your true name. If we're soul mates, can you remember if we've met in previous lives?" I asked him.

"We have never met before. This is my first lifetime," he whispered.

"Oh." As I gazed at him, the flame in my heart blazed. *Mitica is my soul mate.* The words echoed in my mind like ringing the bell of truth. "I guess we belong to each other after all," I told him.

He beamed, and my heart welled in my chest.

"Bucuria mea," he whispered lovingly as he leaned toward me.

"You always call me that. What does it mean?" I asked.

"My Joy," he murmured, his breath against my lips.

I smiled. "I love you, Mitica."

"Te iubesc, bucuria mea," he whispered. "I love you."

The soft sweetness of his kiss released the zmeu in my heart. I met his next kiss with a fierceness he took as a challenge. The rough fabric of his jacket rubbed harshly against my clenched fists as I pulled him down to me. His sturdy hands on my waist urged me closer. My body flushed as his tongue met mine.

"Mitica," I gasped, breaking for air.

His blue eyes, heavy with lust, answered my call.

"I'm ready to claim you now, Mitica. Will you also claim me?"

He smiled a promise, and I shivered with heat. "Da."

I yelped as he scooped me off my feet, and my face flushed. "I can walk," I protested.

"I know," he said, striding toward the barracks.

"Then put me down," I told him.

He smiled down at me. "You do not like it?"

I buried my blushing face in his chest. "Shut up," I muttered.

He chuckled as he carried me inside. Setting me gently on my feet, Mitica slowly embraced me from behind in the dark cabin, his chest solid against my back and his breath warm even through my hat.

"I always thought you were asleep when I snuck back in at night," I whispered.

"That is why I keep it so dark," he said, sliding my hat from my head.

"Well, can't I see you now?" I asked.

He pronounced a few words of magic, and the lamps illuminated the room.

"I want to know you," he whispered, his breath in my ear.

I took in a shaky breath. "Me too."

I shuddered when his cool fingertips trailed against my neck as he fiddled with the edges of my scarf. He slipped it over my head.

Goosebumps followed his every kiss down my neck to my collar as if my flesh mourned his abandonment in favor of another spot.

I shivered as he gently removed Oli's coat, eliminating one more obstacle between his flesh and mine. As it fell to the floor, I turned to face him.

While I unbuttoned his coat, I memorized the lines of his face in the flickering lamplight. The dancing light in his lustful eyes sent a thrill through me, like the feel of lighting from a gathering storm.

His coat slipped from his shoulders and joined Oli's on the floor, and I reached for his shirt buttons. With every button that popped smoothly through its buttonhole, I placed a kiss on his newly-exposed skin. The sensitive skin of my lips yielded to the firmness of his chest and abdomen.

With the last button undone, I was on my knees before him. I splayed one hand across his abs as he looked down to meet my gaze. His crimson hair fell into his fierce eyes as I ran my thumb just under the waistband of his pants.

He stilled my advance by sinking to his knees as well.

My hands pressed into his bare chest when he crushed me to him, kissing me deeply with a deep, guttural moan.

I squeaked in surprise when he shifted my weight and lay me down beneath him. His crimson hair hung in his face as he looked down at me.

My heart pounded, and I smiled up at him, brushing his hair from his eyes. His unshaven cheek scraped my hand as he turned his head and pressed a sweet, breathy kiss to my palm.

He lowered his weight on top of me and pressed a passionate kiss against my lips. I welcomed his solid heft between my legs. One of his hands slid under my chemise, and I squirmed at the sensation of his hot flesh on my bare stomach. His other hand pressed against my lower back and pulled me closer to him, drawing a whimper from me. His calloused thumb flicked over my pert nipple, and I gasped.

He smiled down at my reaction.

"You are maddening," I accused in a breathy voice.

"Am I?" he teased.

I squirmed out from under him, and he didn't resist as I climbed atop him and pinned him to his back.

"My turn," I said, straddling his hips.

A shadow of a smile that was more Wynn than Mitica played on his lips as I pulled my shirt off and freed my breasts. He cupped them with his large hands, rubbing my nipples with the pads of his thumbs.

Arching my back, his rigid manhood ground hard between my legs. He hummed low in his throat, and I flashed him a smile.

I didn't protest when he sat up to embrace me but wrapped my legs around his waist.

I removed his shirt from his broad shoulders and gave only a fleeting thought to the black scar on his upper arm.

I pressed kisses down his strong neck to where it met his shoulder and flicked the sensitive spot with my tongue.

He groaned, and I smiled before I sucked the flesh gently, marking him as my own. His breath escaped in short bursts until I bit him playfully. He hissed and refused to sit still any longer.

He rolled me onto my back again, and it didn't take him long to remove my shoes and jeans. As he settled his weight on top of my naked body, his burning skin made up for the cold floorboards beneath us.

He kissed me thoroughly as if he had nothing but time, but my core throbbed in protest. I wanted him, and I was not prepared to wait.

I trailed my hand down his abdomen and slipped my fingers into his pants and around his solid cock.

He moaned into my lips and ground his hips against me.

I broke our kiss and brought my lips to his ear. "Mitica, please," I begged.

He met my eyes with a barely restrained expression. "I am trying...to be gentle with you, bucuria mea. We do not know who you are in this time. If you are a virgin, it could be painful for you."

I knew what he was saying was sweet and kind, but I couldn't wait anymore. "Mitica, please. Just touch me. I want you now."

His concern warred with his desire as he trailed his hand down my body. When he ran his thumb over my clit, I bit my lip against my moan.

His fingers were hot and firm as he felt between my legs, and he smiled when my wetness trickled down his hand. I held my breath.

He gazed into my eyes. "Will you give yourself to me, bucuria mea?" he asked sincerely.

"I am yours," I told him. Staring at him, I slowly reached down and unfastened his pants. I wrapped my hand around his cock, letting the rigid weight slide through my fingers.

Mitica shuddered. "And I am yours," he murmured, slowly gliding his manhood into my core.

The sweet pleasure of his every inch filled my empty void. I shivered as he shook.

"Deeper," I told him. "Make sure I miss the feel of you inside me."

With every sweaty thrust, every shuddering moan, we claimed each other. And with screams of completion, I realized what Mitica had meant when he'd said a full heart has wings.

TWENTY-TWO

For the first time since we'd met, I awoke before Mitica. At some point, he must have moved us to the bed because we were crammed into his small bunk.

I was having a difficult time breathing with my face pressed against his chest and his arms around me like he was trying to smother me. I managed to wiggle loose without waking him.

I held my breath as he sighed in his sleep, my eyes drawn to his restful face. It was the first time I'd seen him by daylight. While he was still as beautiful, I noticed certain features I hadn't seen before.

I thought I'd memorized him. I reached out and traced his Roman nose.

I was concentrating so hard that I gasped when Mitica snatched my hand and kissed it.

"Good morning, bucuria mea," he murmured, smiling sleepily at me as he opened his eyes.

I shivered pleasantly. "Hey," I whispered.

"How are you feeling? Are you sore at all?"

"No, I'm fine. Thanks for asking."

I had so many unanswered questions I still wanted to ask him, but as his warm, blue eyes gazed into mine and he gently stroked my face, I suddenly didn't care about those questions.

When he softly kissed each of my cheeks, heat spread through me. It seemed once I'd had a taste, I only wanted more.

"Mitica," I breathed, not able to keep the desire from my voice.

He smiled and kissed me tenderly on the lips.

My heart skipped. And just as I thought he would give me what I wanted, my stomach growled.

He pulled back, and I frowned.

"You are hungry, bucuria mea. I will go get food."

Stupid stomach.

He chuckled at my pout. "I will return soon," he promised.

As he climbed out of bed, the relatively small space he emptied seemed a massive void. I grabbed his hand to stop him from walking away. He knelt down and gathered me in his arms before kissing me fiercely.

My mind went fuzzy, and the moan against his mouth seemed to come from someone else.

Alas, the goodbye kiss was much too short. "I will return," he repeated.

I curled onto my side grumpily, watching him dress in his red serge and change into his Wynn face.

After he'd left, I thought I might as well do something useful while I waited. Before I went to feed the horses, I washed in the washbasin. I'd never missed a shower more than when I was trying to clean our dried fluids off me.

I paused only for a moment when I opened the door to find it raining. The horses greeted me by sticking their heads out from their stalls. I fed Langundo first, talking to him as always.

When I fed Bou, a thought occurred to me. *What does Mitica do with Grigore when he's Wynn?* I eyed Bou suspiciously as he chewed his oats. Rolling my eyes at myself, I shook my head.

"No way." I laughed at the absurd notion and turned to walk away.

I halted and squinted, pursing my lips. I looked at Bou once more. "Grigore?" I asked the horse, feeling stupid.

Bou's eyes flashed yellow.

I gasped, nearly tripping as I reflexively jumped back.

"So you figured it out, did you?" the horse asked.

My mouth hung open as his human voice left the horse's lips.

"It took you long enough."

I just stared, seemingly having forgotten how to use words.

"Hmm? Or did he tell you? You look too surprised to have discovered it on your own."

"Yeah, he told me."

Grigore chuckled. "He is going to be in so much trouble."

"Is it really that bad? He said he asked for an exception."

He snorted. "The Zgrimties are an unforgiving lot. He will be an outcast for sure."

My heart raced as alarm shot through me.

"Does that scare you?" he asked.

"But how will they know? I can keep a secret."

"I can help with that if you want."

"What can you do?" I wondered.

"He will not be in as much trouble if I tell them I told you."

I bit my lip. "You would do that?"

"Of course, for a favor in return."

"What?"

"His scent is all over you." He snuffled. "Let me cover it with mine."

I stepped back, curling my upper lip.

"They already know," Mitica said from the stable entrance. "They would have known the moment I broke my oath. It's how the spell was cast."

I ran to Mitica, still in his Wynn face. "Is he right? Will you really be an outcast?"

"Don't worry," he smiled, resting a reassuring hand on my shoulder. "I'm certain they will understand."

I sighed, though my skin still prickled with unease.

Mitica took my hand and kissed it. "Let's eat."

I nodded and followed him through the rain to the barracks.

"This rain is no joke," I commented, removing my wet coat and placing it by the stove.

"I guess we will just have to stay in today," Mitica suggested.

I smirked at him. "I like that plan."

As I reached up for his brass buttons, he stilled my hands.

"But first, you eat," he urged.

I pursed my lips. "Fine."

He removed his tunic and put it by the stove. This time, I didn't hide my appreciation when he changed his soaked undershirt. My eyes clung to his every move.

As we ate, I began asking Mitica some of the questions I still had.

"You said the Mounties are killing magic, and your mission was to discover if their leadership knows about the British Empire's goal to eradicate magic."

He nodded.

"So the British Empire has been actively trying to kill magic? For how long and why?"

"Centuries. I can't say exactly why. The Zgrimties believe most of the magic in Britain was destroyed when the groves were burned. It seems after they later converted to Christianity, they convinced themselves magic was evil. And when the British started exploring the world and subjugating others, they didn't like the magic they found."

"Jeez, so what about the Mounties? Do they even know about magic?"

"I don't believe so. By now, the 'civilize the heathen' narrative is so entrenched in the culture that no one needs to know the real reason anymore."

I thought about it. "It's hard to believe someone like Oli could be that bad."

He nodded, frowning. "Good people can do bad things when they're told their entire lives that it's right. Unfortunately, there isn't a good way to educate them on what's truly happening. I can only try to help the fae and natives when I can."

I sighed. "It's like you're fighting a losing battle."

"But every bit of magic I save is worth it."

I reached out and grabbed his hand on the table. "You aren't in this alone anymore. Let me help you."

His eyes widened.

"Does it surprise you that much?"

"No, I just... I'm used to being alone."

"Well, get used to having me around because I'm not going anywhere."

He paused, searching my eyes. "You would sacrifice your life in the future to stay with me?"

I thought about my mom and how I didn't have any idea how to live in 1900. "Do you really think I could leave after the universe brought us together in such a way?"

He closed his eyes and kissed my hand, his lips trembling on the thin skin.

My heart thumped hard.

When he met my gaze again, his eyes blazed with the desire I had never dared to hope for. The answering heat in my core made a shiver run through me.

Without a word, he stood from the table, and I willingly left my half-eaten breakfast to follow him to the bed.

TWENTY-THREE

The rain fell outside, and I listened to the steady, calming sound as I lay on Mitica's bare chest in the small bed. His Wynn face was content, the quiet joy a sight I'd so longed to see. My eyes found the edge of the black scar on his upper arm.

"What's this?" I asked, tracing the raised skin with my fingertips.

"That's the symbol of my kinship with the Wyboka. During the kinship ceremony, they cut the skin. Once it's cleaned, they rub ash in the wound. That's why it's black."

"Do Chuthekii and Likinoak know Mitica and Wynn are the same?"

"I suspect they do, though I didn't break my oath to tell them. They've never said anything outright, but some of their comments lead me to believe they know."

"What was Chuthekii saying last time that you were so keen to keep from me?"

"He knew you were my soul mate. He told me you would not want to return to the future, and he kept calling you 'sister-in-law.'"

"Jeez, I guess the animals really do show him stuff."

He nodded. "We should go back to the reserve soon and ask him if he has learned anything about what's happening at the sacred spring."

"I agree. Any information would be helpful at this point. We should go tonight."

He pursed his lips.

"What is it?"

"He's going to gloat when he hears you're staying."

I laughed. "That reminds me, we have to figure some stuff out."

"Such as?"

"Well, I should probably get a job, and I can't exactly stay in the barracks forever. It's not a long-term solution."

He frowned. "I don't like the idea of you leaving. You could still be in danger."

I hadn't thought of that.

"I will just have to go with you," he pronounced.

"Can you even do that?" I asked, lifting my head and meeting his gaze.

"Nothing will keep me from your side for as long as you want me," he said seriously.

My heart gave one hard thump. "I guess we'll always be together then."

He lifted his head and kissed me sweetly on the mouth. "Iti dau inima mea," he whispered.

"What does that mean?" I asked.

"I give you my heart."

I met my lover's gaze seriously, a pleasant flush on my cheeks. "I will cherish it. Don't worry. You'll never be lonely again."

The rest of that rainy day was spent proving our love for one another. The feel of him, his taste in my mouth, his breathy whispers in my ear, all were like floating in timelessness. I didn't know what energy, what force, what deity, had made that blissful day possible, but I didn't take the blessing for granted.

I ensured Mitica knew I was his and that I claimed him as mine with every beat of my heart and with every breath I took. I never thought of how it would feel to give myself fully to another person and to truly accept him. But once I'd let go, I found a peace I didn't know was possible, like floating in a calm lake looking up at the clear night sky. I was swimming with the stars. The trust I felt for him was freeing, and I knew he would never betray it. I was safe with him.

Likinoak and Chuthekii were not surprised to see us that night.

After we were all seated near the hearth with warm tea, Mitica turned to his family. "Erin will not be returning to the future. She wants to stay with me."

Chuthekii smiled without a word.

"Be quiet," Mitica muttered.

"I said nothing," Chuthekii laughed.

"You did not have to."

When Likinoak stood, we all rose from our seats. She beamed at us. Embracing Mitica, she said something to him in what I assumed was Wyboka. Then she turned to me and took my hands.

"I knew you were special from the moment I saw you. Your light has given his heart wings."

"And he has freed mine."

She hugged me. "May the spirits bless you both."

"Thank you, Likinoak," I said.

"There is no need for thanks, Seyohkwii. We are family now."

My heart glowed in the older woman's warmth, a warmth reminiscent of my own mother's love.

"I also have bad news," Mitica told them. "The Mountie tested the spring water, and the chemists say it is fine. Have you heard anything about what may have caused these deaths, Wic'aze?"

Chuthekii frowned. "I asked Hawk again when I returned from the residential school. What he showed me seemed consistent with your conclusion that they were poisoned. But perhaps I misinterpreted the vision. I will think on it."

Mitica nodded. "Has anyone entered the spring since Testooklah?"

"No," Likinoak answered. "But we cleansed the space today. And now that we know the water is safe, those seeking the sacred spring will be permitted to enter."

"Let us hope no one else will come to any harm," Mitica said.

They all tensed in an expression of uneasy hopefulness.

"We just have to keep looking," I said confidently into the heavy silence. "If we can find cause of death or motive, we can figure out what's happening and stop it."

"Azeohkwii is right. We will not quit until we can give the dead the peace they deserve," Chuthekii added.

We all nodded grimly with renewed purpose.

Before we left, Mitica promised to visit in a few days, and Chuthekii said he would re-evaluate his visions in that time.

The following day, we received a telegram from Oli. His mother was not mortally ill, and he said he would return on Wednesday. We knew everything would be different once Oli arrived, so we tried to enjoy those few days to their fullest.

I couldn't remember the last time I'd been so happy. Every smile, every laugh, every glance from him made my heart soar. We rode our horses through the forest, staring up at the towering peaks above as Mitica visited settlers, executing his Mountie duties. We chopped wood and ate together. And every night, in the flickering light of the oil lamps, we made love, our caresses giving life to all our wordless promises.

When the day came for Oli's return, I clenched my eyes shut and snuggled deeper into Mitica's arms. "I don't want it to be Wednesday," I whined.

Mitica chuckled in his Wynn voice. "You don't want to see Oliver?"

I sighed. "It's not that. I just don't want to go back to the way things were."

"Don't fret, bucuria mea. Even if I cannot touch you every day, you will never have to suffer through not knowing whether I love you."

"That's true. Ugh, fine. I guess I should get dressed in case he returns early."

I climbed out of bed, but Mitica grabbed my wrist and pulled me back. I landed in his lap. His eyes shined with adoration as he gently stroked my cheek with his thumb.

"Te iubesc, bucuria mea," he declared.

"I love you, too."

He brushed a fleetingly sweet kiss to my lips. Then he pressed into the kiss with more purpose.

I squealed with laughter as he rolled on top of me. "What about Oli?" I asked.

"We have time."

I wrapped my arms around the back of his neck and grinned. "We better get started if you don't want him to see."

Though we didn't have long, that didn't make Mitica any less thorough. As I screamed his name, I was grateful the barracks were so isolated from the rest of the town. I was well satiated, washed, and clothed before Oli returned.

When we heard hooves approaching, we went outside to meet him.

"Hey, Oli." I waved cheerfully. "How is your family? Is your mother feeling better?"

He smiled. "Much better. She's a hearty woman. So when she fell ill, my sister panicked. Everything is fine." He climbed out of the saddle.

"That's good to hear. They must've been glad to have you home."

He nodded. "Did I miss anything while I was gone?"

I felt my face heat and glanced at Mitica. His Wynn face gave nothing away.

"The Wyboka cleansed the spring. They'll be allowing people to use it again."

"Mmhmm," Oli acknowledged, squinting at me. "Anything else?"

I laughed. "Come on, Oli. What were you expecting? Did you think you would leave and the whole place would fall apart?"

He smiled. "Don't lie to me, Little Sister. You aren't good at it."

Pfft. If only you knew. I glanced at Mitica again, and he shrugged. "Fine. Wynn and I are...courting." The word felt strange in my mouth, but I couldn't think of another way to say it.

"Oh? What's this? You two finally admitted your feelings?"

I rolled my eyes at him. "Yeah, whatever. You were right."

He nodded once in satisfaction. "Right, so some things are going to have to change around here."

"What do you mean?" I asked.

"Well, I can't very well have Wynn sleeping so close to you. I will be taking the floor from now on, and Erin will sleep in my bed until we can think of a better solution. And you two will have a lot less time alone."

"Excuse me?" I demanded.

"Subconstable Taylor, remember to whom you are giving orders," Mitica scolded.

Oli flinched, then straightened his spine. "With all due respect, Constable. Erin has no male relatives to look after her. I feel it is my responsibility to ensure her honor remains unblemished."

Is this a fucking joke?

I looked at Mitica expecting to see outrage, but he frowned as though considering Oli's words.

"Wait just a minute, Oli. You and Suzette take walks alone together almost every day. Are you saying you should be chaperoned, too?" I demanded.

"We don't live together."

"This is unreasonable. We don't have much time alone as it is with you here, and no one even knows I'm staying here. Suzette doesn't even know."

Oli pursed his lips.

"I'll agree to the sleeping arrangements, but having a chaperone is unnecessary," Mitica said.

Oli stared hard at him. "Very well. But I'll have you know, Constable Delaforet, Erin is under my protection."

I felt both touched and exasperated by Oli's display of masculinity.

Mitica nodded seriously. "Noted, Subconstable Taylor. Now, take care of your horse. She has had a long ride."

Oli led his horse into the stables to carry out Mitica's orders.

I scowled in his wake. Mitica placed a comforting hand on my shoulder. "Don't fret, bucuria mea. This won't be for long. I'll find a place where we can live together in peace. But for now, you must learn this society's rules if you're to stay."

"Whatever. They're stupid," I grumped, though I knew he was right.

He chuckled and kissed my head. "Be patient."

"Hmph."

The rest of the day was fairly normal. It was strange to see Mitica go back to playing the part of the formal Mountie. But I followed his lead and returned to how we were before Oli had left, not wanting to blow his cover.

After dinner, Oli went to visit Suzette. Before he'd left, I made him promise not to tell her about Wynn and me.

"I'll tell her the next time I see her. She'll be angry if she hears it from anyone but me," I told him.

He agreed.

I waved goodbye to him nonchalantly as he left. But as soon as he'd shut the door, I went to it and peeked out.

Watching him fade into the distance, I asked Mitica. "How long do you think he'll be gone?"

He came up behind me and pressed a hot kiss to my neck. "Long enough."

I spun around, facing the tall Mountie in full uniform.

"Do you think so?"

"Trust me," he assured, dipping his head to kiss me.

I slid my fingers into his brown hair, urging him closer.

His strong hands grabbed my bottom and easily lifted me, and I wrapped my legs around his solid torso. I hummed as he pleasantly squished me between his hard body and the door, kissing me deeply.

Never taking his burning lips from mine, he moved us to the bed and sat with me in his lap.

I pushed my palms gently on his ungiving chest, telling him to lie on his back. After climbing off him, I quickly removed my pants before mounting him again. The smooth cotton of my chemise bunched slightly at my hips as I straddled him.

His rough hands trailed heat from my knees slowly up my outer thighs. I shivered as a pleasant tickle ran through me when he brushed his thumb along the crease where my thigh met my hip. My cheeks flushed, and I couldn't look away as his lustful gaze watched me.

With unerring accuracy, he found the sweet spot between my thighs. As he expertly rubbed my clit with the rough pad of his thumb, I let my breath out in a restrained moan and ground my ass into his hard manhood.

A low rumble sounded deep in his throat, but his hand never faltered. On shaky knees, I raised myself and reached behind me to unfasten his trousers.

He didn't stop the sweet, circular motion even as I slid his solid cock deep into me.

Our mutual groans echoed off the rustic wood of the empty cabin.

I took in the sight of the still-dressed Mountie beneath me, his face twisted in the pleasure I was giving him.

It took all of my concentration to repeatedly lift myself up only to thrust him back into me. My thighs shook, and my mind fogged.

But as I heard him call my name and felt him pump into me, euphoria finally overtook me.

TWENTY-FOUR

$\mathcal{I}$'d planned to visit Suzette the following day, but I awoke to find an unexpected surprise. It was snowing heavily.

"It doesn't look like it's going to stop anytime soon," Mitica commented from the window.

"We should go to town and get provisions in case it lasts," Oli added.

Mitica nodded, his Wynn face all business. "Erin, would you go outside and bring in as much wood as you can? We need to keep it dry. Oliver and I will go to town and get food for the next few days and oats for the horses."

I agreed, and we all went to work. By the time they'd returned with vegetables, bread, and cheese to last us a few days, I'd piled enough wood to keep the stove running.

I was surprised when Mitica volunteered to cook while Oli and I took care of the horses. After we'd fed and put blankets on them to keep them warm, we returned to the barracks and settled in.

It snowed all day, all night, and the following day. It wasn't exactly a blizzard, but I was glad I didn't have to drive in it. Still, it was unusual for me to see so much snow in the middle of April, though not remarkably so.

The Mounties spent most of the time writing correspondence. Mitica read some of the time, and we all played poker. Not surprisingly, Mitica won more than not.

Over that two-day period, Mitica and I only ever managed to get a few minutes alone together. It was frustrating, to say the least, but we survived.

When the snow finally stopped, we were all relieved to go outside. Mitica offered to go into town for breakfast, and Oli and I heartily agreed. He had been right about one thing: no one cooked like Mellie.

I told Mitica I'd join him as I wanted to visit Suzette. Oli stayed behind to care for the horses.

I was concerned about walking in the snow with moccasins, but they must've been treated with something because my feet didn't get wet.

Strolling at a leisurely pace, I laced my fingers with Mitica's.

"So do you have a plan in regards to what we're going to do next?" I asked him.

"I've thought about it. It depends on how the Zgrimties respond to my request. If they approve, I will likely have to stay with the Mounties. In which case, perhaps I'll purchase some land and build a house, or we could rent a room in town."

"And if they don't approve?"

"Then we can go wherever we wish. There will be nothing to keep us here."

"So it's a waiting game."

"For now."

I was surprised to see Ion and Mariana outside the trading post and dry goods store once we'd arrived in town. Mariana sat on the wagon seat as Ion loaded goods into the back of the wagon.

"Good morning, you two," I called to them, waving the hand that wasn't holding Mitica's.

They looked up at my greeting, and their eyes widened.

"Good morning," they returned, a little shaken.

I tilted my head at their reception. From the corner of my eyes, I noticed Mellie sweeping snow from her front steps. She openly glared at me, but I didn't miss the hurt in her eyes when she turned to go inside.

"Constable Delaforet," Ion beckoned. "May I speak to you for a moment?"

Mitica nodded. "Of course."

"I'll go order breakfast," I told them, wanting to talk with Mellie alone. "It was nice seeing you again, Mariana, Ion."

Mitica released my hand, and I went on ahead.

I was glad no one else was in Mellie's when I entered. She turned at the sound of the door, and her features tensed upon seeing me.

"Mellie?"

"Yes, Miss Nichols. How may I help you?" Even in a strained voice, she kept her manners.

"Mellie, I'd like to apologize to you and explain."

"That's not necessary."

"But I want to regardless. I'm sorry if it seems like I lied to you before. At the time, I truly believed Wynn wasn't interested in me. I'm just as surprised as you are."

She sighed, defeated, and shook her head. "I'm not surprised... The truth is, I knew Constable Delaforet wasn't interested in me. And I knew... I could tell from the first time I watched him look at you that he saw you differently than he saw me."

There was a long pause.

"Still, I am sorry."

"Don't be. I'm starting to think I only fixated on Constable Delaforet because I knew he didn't want me. I'm not sure I'm even ready to move on after...after Sean..."

Her shoulders slumped, and I felt compelled to comfort her. I placed my hand gently on her shoulder.

"Hey. Take your time. Anyone who's worth it will wait."

She nodded silently while hanging her head.

"Mellie, listen to me. You're awesome. You've managed to accomplish all this at a time when women have little to no rights in society. Just do you, and you'll be fine."

"Do me?" she asked, tilting her head at me.

"Yeah, just be yourself."

She took another deep breath and let it all out at once. "You're right. I've worked hard, and I'm not going to let anything stop me."

"Right on."

She smiled shyly at me, and I couldn't help but admire her.

"Thank you," she said.

"Anytime."

"Now." She squared her shoulders. "What can I get you?"

I ordered our breakfasts, and she said it would be ready in a bit. Telling her I would return, I went out to meet Mitica.

He watched Ion and Mariana drive away, chuckling quietly to himself.

"What was that about?" I asked him.

"Ion wanted to warn me."

"What?"

Mitica turned to me, his eyes sparkling with laughter. "It seems you are beloved by a powerful and dangerous man. Ion was concerned I may get myself into trouble if I didn't leave you be."

"Are you serious?"

He nodded.

"Oh jeez, what did you say?"

"I thanked him for his concern, of course. He was worried for my well-being." He smirked. "It seems I have competition for your heart."

"Yeah, you better watch out. My boyfriend is big and scary."

He grinned. "Is he?"

"Yeah, he would totally kick your ass."

"Would he now?"

"Yep."

Mitica snatched my hand and brought it to his lips. "I'll keep that in mind."

The sensation of his soft, warm lips on my fingers brought a blush to my cheeks.

He released my hand with a smirk. "When will breakfast be ready?"

"In a few. But, hey, I'm going to run to see Suzette real quick. I'll be back in a few minutes. Okay?"

He nodded, and I hurried to Madame Buvons's.

As I approached Madame Buvons's shop, I saw a carriage parked outside. I walked around the back of the carriage and hoped Suzette wasn't too busy to talk. When I entered, Madame Buvons and a young woman in a dark blue dress and a large hat looked over at me. Madame Buvons nodded at me civilly, but the customer openly gaped.

Yeah, yeah, I get it. Oh my god, a woman wearing pants! Whatever.

"Madame," the customer gasped in a heavy French accent. "I did not know you were arriving today." She rushed to me.

I pulled back at her approach. "I'm sorry, Miss. I think you have me confused with someone else."

Her brows crinkled. "Madame, why do you look this way? I was so worried when you left without a word. Monsieur insisted you went home, but why would you not take me with you, Madame?"

My heart pounded as the young woman talked to me so familiarly. "Who exactly do you think I am?" I asked.

"Madame Celeste Broadstone," she said in a confused tone.

Broadstone. Why does that sound familiar?

"But Madame, Monsieur will be so pleased you have returned. He has been worried. I have brought the carriage. We can return immediately."

When I made no move to leave, she grabbed my hand a pulled me outside.

"Let go of me. I don't know you," I told her, my voice rising in pitch as my heart raced. I snatched my hand from hers.

"Madame," she gasped. "I do not understand. What has happened to you? Are you unwell?"

"Leave me alone. I don't know you."

"Madame, if you are unwell, let us return home. I will send for the physician."

I turned and walked away from her, but she followed. When I ran, she fell behind but kept pursuing me. I reached Mitica outside of Mellie's, and I threw myself at him.

"Whoa, what's going on?"

"There's a woman chasing me. She keeps calling me someone else. She says she knows me."

"Thank goodness," the woman sighed when she'd caught up. "Constable, you found her. I think Madame is ill. Can you please bring her home so we can call a physician?"

"Who do you think this is, Miss...?"

"Marguerite Dubois. Madame is Celeste Broadstone, wife of Monsieur Broadstone, who owns Farrloch Hotel."

Our mouths hung open as we stared at her, wide-eyed.

I turned to Mitica desperately. "But Wynn, you've been to the hotel, right? You'd recognize if I am who she says."

He turned to me, his face lined with a worry that made my stomach drop. "I've never met Mrs. Broadstone. Mr. Broadstone hasn't been married long, and she never seemed to be around when I was there."

"But what about the townspeople?" I grasped.

"Madame has never been to town except to board a train. There is no need. The hotel has everything you could ever want."

"And who are you to Mrs. Broadstone, Miss Dubois?" Mitica asked.

"I am Madame's lady's maid."

My stomach clenched into knots.

"Please, Miss Dubois. As you can see, the lady is quite shaken. Let me calm her, and we will meet you at the hotel. Then we can straighten this entire situation out."

With the assurance of an honorable Mountie, Marguerite nodded. "Merci, Constable. I will inform Monsieur Broadstone to expect you."

"Very well," Mitica agreed.

As soon as Marguerite was out of sight, Mitica grabbed my hand and pulled me down the road toward the barracks. I couldn't see his face as he strode ahead with purpose, but I had to almost jog to keep up.

"Mitica, wait," I heaved, tugging his hand in the deserted road.

He halted. Before I could catch my breath, he wrapped me in a crushing embrace.

"Don't worry. I won't take you to a man you don't know, even if he is this incarnation's husband."

My heart ached at the desperate determination in his voice.

"We'll return to the barracks, pack quickly, and leave," he promised.

"But what about your mission? The Wyboka? The fae? You can't just leave without the Zgrimties permission. Can you?"

"It doesn't matter. Even if they tell me to stay here, you can't stay where people know your identity in this life."

My stomach dropped, and my mouth went dry. "I can't," I whispered. "I can't let you run away if there's a chance the Zgrimties will let you stay undercover. The fae need you. Magic needs you." I pulled back and looked up into his unsure eyes. "Listen, if they approve me as an exception, ask for a new assignment. I'll go with you. If they don't approve, then there's no reason for you to stay undercover, and we can find another way to help magic. But we can't just leave. That woman would know we ran away together, and they would pursue us. Besides, we don't know anything about Celeste Broadstone. We need to know more about who she was so we can avoid being recognized in the future. Also, we need to find out how she died."

Wynn's face scrunched, pain in every line. "You want me to send you to Mr. Broadstone's, your husband's, house?"

"It's not like I want to go. I just think it's the least bad option. It will only be temporary, right? I'll find out everything I can about Celeste, and you'll come up with a plan to get us both out of here safely."

"Nu, I do not like it," he proclaimed, his Romanian accent slipping through as he got more upset.

I hugged him tightly around the middle. "I don't like it either, but is there a better way?"

He was silent for a while as he grasped for alternatives. Finally, with a sigh of defeat, he murmured, "I understand."

Gazing into Wynn's broken eyes, I whispered, "I love you. We won't be apart for long."

My eyes burned as tears threatened my resolve. He kissed me tenderly as if it was the last time he would ever get to kiss me. "I will come for you as soon as I can," he vowed.

The walk to the barracks was slow, our footsteps hindered under the weight of our depression.

"What took you so long?" Oli demanded as we entered. "I'm starving." He took in our sullen demeanors and our lack of breakfast. "What happened? Did Mellie run out of food?"

"Sorry, Oli. I guess we forgot in all the commotion," I apologized. "I... have to return home immediately."

"Your editor is calling you back?"

I shrugged vaguely.

"I see." He frowned. "I guess it's time for farewells. I'm sorry you have to go, but it may be best you leave the area since we never discovered who hurt you."

Mitica cleared his throat. "I'll saddle the horse and take you to the station."

I quietly packed my few belongings into the bag I'd taken on our trip to Edmonton. It didn't take long. I removed Oli's coat and held it out to him. "Thanks for letting me borrow it while I was here."

He shook his head. "Keep it. It's a long journey back to Chicago. You might need it."

I nodded my thanks.

"Hey." He plopped his hand onto my head and smirked at me. "Don't think just because you're leaving that I'll stop being your big brother. I want letters."

I smiled sadly at him, my heart welling. "Okay," I agreed softly. "Will you do something for me, Oli?"

"Name it."

"Watch over Wynn. I have a feeling he isn't going to take this well."

He nodded. "You have my word."

"Thanks."

Bidding Oli and the barracks goodbye with a slow, lingering glance, I went to meet Mitica and Grigore.

TWENTY-FIVE

*M*itica climbed into Grigore's saddle behind me, and we began our ride to Farrloch Hotel. With his chest pressed against my back, his presence brought me both reassurance and despair. I wanted to be strong for him. I knew what needed to be done, but every step closer to our destination made me want to embrace him and never let go.

"What do you know about Celeste Broadstone?" I asked him.

He sighed but answered quietly. "A while back, Mr. Broadstone took a trip to Toronto. Everyone was surprised by how long he stayed. He returned a few months ago with a new wife. Not many people have seen her. It was winter, and she was busy learning how things ran at the hotel. I heard she was young and beautiful but not much else."

I hesitated over my next question, but I needed to know what I was getting into. "What about Mr. Broadstone? He's the one who summoned you to offer help with the Wyboka, right?"

A tinge of sadness colored his soft reply. "Yes, he's an upstanding man in his mid-forties. He made a fortune with the railroad, and then he settled here to build a hotel. I don't have cause to meet with him often, but he's cordial when I do."

I could tell it was difficult for him to praise the man in this situation, but he was honest as ever.

"Was he kind to his wife do you think?" I asked.

He paused, tightening his arms around me. "I don't believe you have to be concerned about that. He will likely take good care of you. And you can always call on me should you need anything at all."

I nodded.

"I mean anything, bucuria mea," he reiterated.

The rest of the ride, we discussed our story to explain where I'd been the past few weeks.

As we approached the imposing, castle-like hotel, Mitica distanced himself as if to appear more like a lawman escorting a lost woman home.

The structure towered above the tops of the evergreens at the summit of a large hill. I counted at least five stories, three of which had balconies on one side.

Seeing the grand prison suddenly made my situation feel all too real. I closed my eyes and took a steadying breath. *You can do this, Erin. It's the right thing to do. It would be easy to just run away with Mitica, but he's too important to keep to yourself.* I gently touched Mitica's hand, which held the reins. Squeezing my eyes shut tighter, I fought nausea and swallowed a sob. *Be strong. I need to be strong. If he sees me this upset, he won't do what's necessary.*

When Grigore stopped near the hotel entrance, I took one more deep breath and resigned to meet my fate.

Mitica helped me out of the saddle. His strong hands lingered on my waist for a moment too long. As his fingertips reluctantly pulled away, I whispered, "I love you." My voice sounded shattered in my ears.

He frowned but nodded once. "And I you, bucuria mea," he murmured.

Unable to face his gaze and keep my resolve, I patted Grigore on the neck. "Goodbye, Grigore. Be good, all right?"

He dipped his head in farewell. His brown horse-eyes seemed sad to me, but perhaps it was my own emotions reflected in his eyes.

I followed Mitica into the foyer of the hotel, a few steps behind as would be expected of a scared amnesiac.

In the lobby, a man with neat graying hair and a Clark Gable mustache directed a bellhop to carry suitcases to a guest's room. He wore a high collar with a tie, a long coat, and a vest. He was the picture of a successful hotel owner. When he turned away from the stairs, his eyes immediately found Mitica and me.

"Celeste, my darling. I have been beside myself with worry," the man exclaimed in what sounded like the accent between English and American that they used in old movies.

He approached me, reaching out to touch my face.

I flinched and took a step toward Mitica. The stranger raised his eyebrows in surprise.

"Mr. Broadstone," Mitica addressed. "Is there somewhere quiet we could speak in private?"

"Of course." Mr. Broadstone nodded and led us away from the front desk to a room off the foyer.

Sliding the doors open, he revealed a library, not as large as Mr. Montmartre's but still respectable. We entered the deserted room, and he closed the door behind us.

Mitica motioned for me to sit in an armchair, and I silently complied. Mr. Broadstone sat in a chair nearby, and Mitica stood near me.

"Mr. Broadstone, I fear I have some troubling news about your wife. I found her near the railroad tracks a few weeks ago. She must have hit her head because she doesn't remember who she is. If I had known she was Mrs. Broadstone, I certainly would have brought her home. I have been looking after her, and she has yet to recall anything prior to me finding her. Miss Dubois mentioned she was traveling to visit her home?"

Mr. Broadstone's brow crinkled in a troubled expression. "Yes, Celeste had a friend from school who was getting married. She was to travel to Toronto for the ceremony. When I didn't hear anything of her arrival, I assumed she was just busy with preparations." He turned his dark eyes on me. "Oh, my dear. What a dreadful experience. Had I only but known your plight, I would have come to you immediately. But fear not, you are safe at home now, and I will have the best physician examine you." He stood and reached out a hand to Mitica. "Thank you, Constable Delaforet. Thank you for protecting my precious wife and returning her home safely. I am relieved to have such a man in Farrloch. I will be writing to your superiors to express my admiration and gratitude at the job you've done."

Mitica nodded and shook his hand formally. "I will visit again to see how Mrs. Broadstone's recovery progresses."

"That is very kind of you, Constable. You are welcome as always. But I assure you, she will be well cared for."

Mitica nodded again and touched the brim of his hat to me. "Mrs. Broadstone, I do hope everything will be better for you soon."

"Thank you, Constable. I have faith that it will."

Mr. Broadstone held out a hand to me, but I didn't take it. "Come, my dear. Why don't you rest in our room while I send for Dr. Hollander?"

I froze, my eyes wide. "Our room?" I asked.

"Perhaps Mrs. Broadstone would feel more comfortable in a separate room until she regains her memories," Mitica suggested.

Mr. Broadstone frowned. "Of course. I apologize, my dear. It was careless of me. I will have Frederick assign you a separate room. Marguerite can move your things there later."

I gave him a small smile and nodded. "Thank you...Mr. Broadstone."

His eyes saddened at my formal address. "William," he corrected.

"Yeah, sorry. William. I mean, yes, I apologize."

I trailed William past Mitica.

"Thank you again, Constable," William dismissed as he headed for the front desk.

I paused near Mitica, meeting his eyes without knowing when I would see him again. I wanted to tell him how much I loved him, how I would miss him every moment we were apart, and how he was taking my heart with him. But as I opened my mouth, his eyes flashed with a warning.

"Be well, Mrs. Broadstone," he said, bowing to me slightly.

"And you, Constable."

A gentle hand on my elbow pried my attention from Mitica as William returned. "Come, my dear. Let us get you settled," William directed, leading me away from the man I loved and toward the unknown.

I tried not to squirm as William led me to a room on the second floor. His hand was foreign on my arm, but I thought pulling away wouldn't be worth the potential consequences.

The plush rugs on the second floor were lit by the gentle glow of electric hall lights.

William stopped before a corner room and unlocked the door. I stepped in before him as he motioned me forward.

"I am sorry about the assumption that you would be returning to our chambers. I do not know what I was thinking. I suppose I was relieved to have you home safe," William apologized again as I took in the luxurious suite.

The hotel room was nearly as big as my two-bedroom apartment in Chicago. It had a large living room with a fancy couch and two chairs, the kind antique lovers keep in their houses that no one is allowed to sit in. A small dining table and two chairs were set before a heavily-curtained window.

Through a set of paned French doors, there was a bedroom with a large, neatly-made bed. An ornate fireplace sat opposite another set of doors, which opened onto a balcony. But it was the bathroom that made me gape in wonder. It had a sink with a mirror, a flush toilet, and a bathtub with running water.

I turned to William, having forgotten what he'd just said.

He smiled gently at me. "I see the room pleases you. I am delighted, my dear. Would you like to freshen up before the doctor arrives?"

I couldn't deny that I eyed the bathtub with desire. "Would that be all right?" I asked.

"Of course, I will instruct Marguerite to bring you more suitable garments."

"Oh, don't worry about it. I have a clean shirt in my bag."

William glowered. "I do not wish to offend you, dear one, but your current attire is not appropriate for your station. I would not wish our guests to see you thus."

I bit my lip. *Eck, what a pain. Whatever. I guess I'll play along for now.* "Oh, I'm sorry," I muttered. "I hadn't thought of that."

He nodded in satisfaction. "I will leave you to it then." He bowed his head at me and exited the suite.

As the tub filled with hot water, Marguerite knocked and entered.

"Madame," she greeted. "Monsieur informed me of your memory loss. How horrible! I am certain I must have frightened you when we met at Madame Buvons's. I apologize. But I am glad I found you. Had I not gone to purchase some unmentionables, we may never have brought you home."

Yeah, thanks ever so much, Marguerite. What would I have done if I had to stay with the man I love forever? I nodded silently at her.

"Would Madame like me to wash her hair? It looks like it has been a while."

"I think I can handle bathing myself. Thank you."

"Very well. Then I will go to Madame and Monsieur's chambre and retrieve some essentials, oui?"

"That's fine. Thanks." *Whatever will get you to leave me in peace.*

As I sank into the steamy bliss of a bath, I tried not to blame Marguerite. *It's not really her fault. I mean, it's her job. I wonder if we were any sort of friends in this lifetime.*

The only thing more heavenly at that moment than a bath would have been to be in Mitica's arms. I closed my eyes and swallowed around the lump in my throat. *It's fine. You're fine. You're an adult, and this is the responsible thing to do right now. You'll be together again. We have time. We have the rest of our lives. One day, this will all be a distant memory.* I took a deep breath and let it out all at once.

Knowing the doctor was on his way, I didn't take as long of a bath as I would have liked. Still, I scrubbed hard and felt refreshed when I was finished.

Marguerite was waiting for me as I exited the bathroom in a towel, and we began the epic journey of dressing in appropriate attire. I put on the undergarments she handed me, a chemise and shorts, drawers as she called them. With a suppressed sigh, I pulled on the thigh-high stockings she offered and the garters. But when she held up a corset, I started dubiously at her. "Um no," I said with finality.

She tilted her head in confusion. "But Madame, how can you—"

I held up my hand to stop her. "There is nothing you can say to get me into that thing. I've agreed to wear a dress, but I'm not going to torture myself."

She frowned but didn't force the issue. "I had no idea Madame was so progressive."

"Call it whatever you like."

Next, she tied a little pillow around my waist.

"What's this?" I asked.

"Your bum pad, Madame," she informed me.

"Of course it is."

I chose the simplest skirt and blouse from the options Marguerite had presented, and I picked the pair of boots with the shortest available heel. The thought that this wasn't so bad after all lived only a moment in my mind before Marguerite destroyed it with three layers of petticoats under my skirt, another undershirt, a blouse, and a belt.

As she approached me with a comb, I thought about doing it myself, but I just gave in.

"What happened to Madame's hair? Do you remember?"

"I had a barber in town cut it. It was far too long to maintain."

She gasped at my answer. "Well...perhaps with pins in the right places and a hat, no one will notice." She stared at me seriously, considering how to make me presentable.

I sighed, allowing her to have her way. "Marguerite, I'm sorry I don't remember you. How long have we known each other?"

"Monsieur hired me shortly after you were married before you left Toronto."

"And when was I married?"

Her face fell as if the thought of me forgetting my husband broke her heart. "Madame has been married less than half a year. Madame and Monsieur are still newlyweds."

Her sadness at someone else's broken love reminded me of Suzette. "Marguerite, could you do me a favor?"

"Of course, Madame."

"Please call me by my given name."

"Madame, I couldn't," she said, aghast.

"I have a feeling I don't have many friends here, just William and his employees. It would make me feel more comfortable if you called me by my first name."

She paused for a while, frowning as she thought. "Very well. If that is your request, then I will address you as Celeste."

My heart sank at the name. I'd almost forgotten she would know me by a name that was no longer mine. *Oh well, better get used to it after all. I need to be able to recognize it.* On the other hand, it was good she didn't call me Erin. Addressing me as Celeste was a reminder that this wasn't who I truly was, not in my soul's current lifetime anyway. It would remind me that this was temporary and that I would return to the one who knew me one day soon.

TWENTY-SIX

*D*r. Hollander was an older gentleman with a wrinkled face and a steady hand. He sat beside me on the couch as William and Marguerite stood nearby.

After checking my pulse, he asked, "You say the furthest you can remember is Constable Delaforet finding you?"

"No, I remember waking up in the barracks. The constable told me he found me and brought me to safety."

"Why didn't he contact me?" the doctor asked.

Oh, shit. "Well, my only injury was a bump on my head. I couldn't remember anything, but he said someone would report to him if I were missed. Also, we thought I would remember if just given time."

Dr. Hollander pursed his wrinkled lips but nodded. "Well, he is quite right, of course. There is not much to be done in cases of amnesia. Still, it will be much easier for you to remember surrounded by a place and people you know. Are you feeling weak at all? Fatigued?"

"Oh, no. I'm fine physically. My bump is gone and everything."

He checked the spot I'd randomly chosen on my head. "Very well, Mrs. Broadstone. I suggest resuming your routine. Read letters from your family and friends and speak to your husband about the past. In short, be exposed to anything that may trigger your memory."

I nodded like I took everything he said seriously. "I understand, Doctor."

He smiled gently and patted my hand. "Worry not, Mrs. Broadstone. I'm certain your memories will return in time. For now, rely on those around you, and let me know if you experience any headaches or dizziness."

"I will. Thank you."

"I will return next week to see how you are faring. Mr. Broadstone, would you mind showing me out?"

"Of course, Doctor," William agreed and left with the doctor to discuss my treatment amongst men no doubt.

I stared after them wondering exactly what was being said.

"It is a relief to hear your memories will return, non, Celeste?" Marguerite encouraged. "I am certain they will come back soon, now that you are home and with Monsieur."

I nodded as if comforted. *At least I have an alibi for not knowing anything. Dr. Hollander didn't seem too suspicious of Mitica. I wonder how long it will take to figure out what happened to Celeste or if I ever will. I hope Mitica hears from the Zgrimties soon. In the meantime, I should gather as much information as I can on Celeste Broadstone. It will be easier to avoid being recognized as her once I leave the more I know about her.*

"Marguerite, the doctor said I should get back to my daily routine. What exactly do I usually do all day?"

As Marguerite opened her mouth to answer, William returned and interrupted her. "That can wait until tomorrow. Today, I think you should rest. Are you hungry?"

"I am. I didn't have a chance to eat breakfast." *Because Marguerite uprooted my life.*

William frowned as if displeased at Mitica's treatment of me. "Marguerite, go to the kitchens and order a repast for Madame."

"Right away, Monsieur." Marguerite nodded and left to complete her mission.

"I don't need to rest, William. As I told the doctor, I'm feeling strong."

He sat beside me, took my hand, and kissed it lightly.

I gritted my teeth and resisted the urge to snatch it back as my stomach clenched.

"I know, my dear. However, before you concern yourself with your daily duties here at the hotel, I would like to speak to you in private at more length."

Eck. "In private" sounds too intimate.

"I'm certain you have more personal questions than how the hotel functions. Perhaps you would like to know about your family or how we met?"

That is much more valuable information than what Celeste did at the hotel. "Yeah, I would like to hear about that," I agreed. "I mean, yes, you're right."

"As I thought. Well, I have some things to attend to this afternoon, but shall we talk about it over dinner?"

I nodded. "That's fine. In the interim, would you happen to know if I kept a journal? Reading it could help a lot."

William stilled for a moment, then quirked his mouth. "I don't believe you did."

"That's a shame."

"Indeed," he answered without hesitation. Then he excused himself, promising to return that evening for supper.

Left alone, I heaved a sigh of relief. *It's going to be tough with everyone watching me so closely.* I scanned the comfortable suite again. *This place is beyond nice.* My heart sank. *But I'd rather be in the cramped barracks with Mitica and Oli, even if I can't bathe every day.* My chest tightened, and my body flushed, anxiety making me uncomfortably warm. I went onto the balcony for some fresh air.

The empty second-floor balcony had a white, wooden railing like a picket fence marking the boundary of my captivity. The balcony was big enough to hold the table and chairs in the sitting room of the suite, but it was far too cold to eat outside. I brushed the accumulated snow from the railing and leaned my elbows on it.

"Well, at least the tourists are getting their money's worth," I muttered to the gorgeous scenery.

The small valley before me was covered in snow, which sparkled in the afternoon sun. In the distance, wooded mountains climbed to picturesque peaks. Though the snow obscured it, I knew the winding trail that led through the valley and into the mountains. I had traveled it once before when I'd first visited the Wyboka Reserve. The reserve was likely a few miles away, but I would never forget that first horse ride. The scenery, the company, the thrill—I couldn't believe how much had changed in just a few weeks.

"Celeste?" Marguerite called from inside.

She frowned as I came in from the balcony. "You should not go outside in such weather without a coat. You could catch a chill."

"I wasn't out there very long," I assured her. *Besides, why would I need a coat with so many layers?*

I sat at the table, the meal she brought in front of me. It was simple, a ham and cheese sandwich more or less, but it satisfied my hunger.

"So what do you say we go exploring after I eat?" I asked Marguerite as I reached for my cup of warm tea.

She raised her eyebrows. "Monsieur said you should rest today."

I took a sip of tea and squinched my nose at the taste. "What kind of tea is this?"

"Earl Gray, your favorite."

"Oh. Well, could I have English breakfast tea with milk and sugar in the future, please?"

A line formed between her eyebrows. "Breakfast tea? Very well."

I returned the cup to its saucer. "I know he said I should rest, but I really am fine. I can't stay still in this room all afternoon. Come on. If we're careful, he'll never know the difference." I smiled encouragingly at her.

Her expression became stern. "I do not think you should go against Monsieur's wishes. If he is telling you to rest, then it is for the best."

Tch, I see where your loyalties lie, Marguerite. Fine, then. I sighed, seemingly defeated. "You're probably right, Marguerite. I'm sure William knows what's best. Instead of exploring, how about I get acquainted with my everyday things. You only moved a few essentials from our room, right? Why don't you go get the rest of my things? I bet everyday items are great for triggering memories."

She nodded in satisfaction. "Oui, that is a good idea. You rest here, and I will return."

I smiled at her. "Okay."

As soon as she'd left the door, I rushed to it and peeked outside. She went down the hall and entered another room. Smirking to myself, I slipped out of the room and quickly descended the stairs before she could see me.

When I was far enough down the stairs to see the lobby, I peeked down to determine if there was anyone there. The man William had called Frederick was the lone resident, but his back was turned to me.

The wooden stairs had a rug down the middle, but most of the lobby's floor was uncovered wood. I removed my shoes. Holding them in one hand and lifting my skirts with the other, I crept down the stairs, across the lobby, and out the front door.

Outside, I quickly put my shoes on. It was chilly out, but I wasn't cold.

I scanned the scenery before me and weighed my options. *Right is the direction Mitica and I came from. I saw a stone wall with an iron gate beside the hotel when we approached. Left it is then.*

Not far down the cobbled road, I came upon a few wooden buildings adjacent to a corral. There didn't appear to be anyone around, so I entered the wide, open door to the stable.

The unmistakable scent of horses and straw was unexpectedly comforting for a city dweller like myself. Long rows of stalls flanked the center aisle. There must've been at least ten on each side.

I peeked into stalls as I strolled through the stable. The first few were empty. When I did meet a resident, she was a dark brown pony with a white spot between her gentle eyes.

I smiled as she stuck her head out to greet me. "Hey there, sweetheart," I cooed. "What's your name?"

I found the name Saundra etched neatly into a wooden nameplate when I scanned the frame of her stall door.

"Saundra?" I asked.

Her ears flicked in recognition.

"That's a pretty name for a pretty girl." I held my hand to her nose so she could sniff me before petting her neck.

"She's sweet, isn't she?" a deep voice beside me asked.

I jumped, and Saundra snuffled.

"Jesus, you scared me," I laughed, turning to the owner of the voice.

A tall, black man with high cheekbones and a square jaw smiled down at me from under his cowboy hat. "I'm sorry. I didn't mean to startle you, Miss."

"It's all right. I should've been paying attention."

He nodded his acknowledgment. "Are you a guest?" he asked. "We don't have any trail rides scheduled today because of the snow. But you can put in a request at the front desk if you want to get a group together for after it melts. It shouldn't be more than a few days."

He must have never met Celeste. "A guest? No, I guess you could say I work here." *Maybe? I'm not really sure what I do yet.* "And what about you? Do you work here, Mr....?"

"Oh, I beg your pardon, Miss. You aren't wearing a uniform, so I just assumed. You can just call me Butch. I run the stables for the hotel."

I waved my hand. "Don't worry about it, and you can call me Erin." *Damn. I meant Celeste. Oh, well.*

He smiled kindly at me. "You like horses, Erin?"

I shrugged. "Sure. I like them a lot better when I'm not riding them though."

"An animal lover then?"

I nodded. "That's probably more accurate. So Butch, how long have you worked here? I haven't seen you before." *At least I assume I haven't since you don't recognize me.*

"Not long. Just a few months. I don't go up to the house much, and Campbell and I generally eat in the hand quarters with the lads."

"Who's Campbell?"

"Campbell drives the carriage for the hotel."

I vaguely remember there being a carriage in front of Madame Buvons's when Marguerite accosted me. Was Campbell driving it?

"I hope you guys are being taken care of out here."

"We have no complaints. A solid roof and warm food? It's better than most of us are used to."

"I'm glad to hear it."

"So you work up at the hotel?"

I nodded, not even sure how to elaborate, but Butch was nice enough not to push.

"Well, feel free to come visit the horses anytime you like."

"That's nice of you, Butch. I think I will come down when I get the chance."

He nodded. "If you'll excuse me. I've got some work to do yet."

"Go for it," I said, apologizing for distracting him.

"You have a nice day, Erin."

"Thanks, Butch. See you later."

As Butch headed out of the stables, a slender, pale man met him at the door. Whatever he'd planned to say was forgotten when he saw me.

"Losh!" the man exclaimed with a Scottish accent. "I didn't know the lady was coming to visit. You should have had the lads clean more thoroughly."

"The lady?" Butch looked over his shoulder at me, and I pretended not to overhear their conversation.

"Aye, the lady: Mrs. Broadstone."

Butch grunted. "Well, I had no idea who she is, Campbell. In any case, she seems comfortable with the way things are. She didn't complain to me, so I think it's fine."

Campbell snorted. "You best be careful, Butch, being alone with the lady. I don't know if Mr. Broadstone is a jealous man, but I would be if she were my wife."

"If anyone needs to be careful, it's you, making comments like that," Butch chided.

Campbell didn't respond.

"All right, we have work to do. Stop staring, and get to it," Butch ordered, dragging Campbell away from the stable entrance.

I sighed heavily. "Butch seems nice," I told Saundra. "I could use a friend in a place like this. Anyway, at least I can come visit you whenever I want. Next time, I'll bring you something delicious. Maybe an apple or a carrot, eh? Or how about a sugar cube? Would you like that?"

Saundra bobbed her head as if she recognized the words, and I laughed. "All right, it's a promise then."

I petted her velvety coat absently and wondered how long I'd been gone. *Marguerite is probably freaking out right now. Should I feel bad for tricking her? Maybe, but I don't. She's a little too eager to please William for being Celeste's maid. Not that I care, but that means I can't trust her. I better head back though. I don't want her to find me here. I'd rather this be a place where I can go to get away.*

"Well, have a good night, Saundra. Sleep well. I'll see you again soon." I gave her one last stroke and left the stables.

As I approached the hotel's front entrance, Marguerite exited the iron gate in the stone wall beside the building. She heaved a sigh, pressing a hand to her chest.

"Celeste, I was worried when I returned and you were gone. Monsieur told you to rest today. I thought you had gone to the garden as usual, but you were not there. Where did you go?"

I shrugged. "Nowhere special. I just took a walk. I needed fresh air." *Wait. Why am I explaining myself to her anyway?*

"And you did not even wear a coat." She tsked.

I didn't respond.

"Well, come inside before Monsieur realizes you have disobeyed him." She waved me toward the door.

I curled my lip. *Disobeyed? Really? She's got to be fucking kidding me.* I clenched my jaw instead of saying something churlish.

Frederick nodded a good afternoon to us as we passed by on the way back to my room.

"Which room is William's?" I asked Marguerite when we reached the second floor.

"Monsieur and you share this room," she corrected, pointing at the door nearest the stairs.

It appeared that Marguerite had left in a rush after having found me missing from my room. A large trunk lay near the entrance in the middle of the walkway, and an armful of garments was folded over the back of the couch.

She rushed forward to move the trunk and organize the strewn clothes. "I will take care of this presently," she assured.

Normally, I would've offered her assistance, but I wasn't feeling generous.

As I sat at the small table, I rested my head in my hand and stared out the window. *It's boring here. Lonely.* I ignored the pang in my chest as I thought about Mitica. Having always expressed myself through the written word, I wished I had a journal to ease my anxiety. *It's probably not a good idea though. Anything written could be easily found.*

My eyes slid to Marguerite, who was organizing in the bedroom. *She wouldn't think twice about handing stuff I wrote over to William. She didn't turn me in for leaving when he'd told me to stay, but that was probably to save herself.*

The world outside the paned window was snowy and perfect. My eyes lost focus the harder I stared at the freedom that beckoned me.

TWENTY-SEVEN

The rest of the afternoon was dull and uneventful in my confinement. I was almost grateful when William arrived in the evening for dinner, though I would've preferred he was a dashing brunet in a red serge or a crimson-haired Romanian with a magic all his own.

"Good evening, my dear," he greeted. "I hope you are feeling rested."

"I wasn't tired to begin with," I couldn't help but retort.

He nodded, squinting ever so slightly. "Forgive me. It is a husband's prerogative to worry about his wife."

Casually referring to me as his wife made my stomach curdle, but I tried for a neutral expression. "You said you would tell me about my past?" I asked after a pause.

"Indeed. Let us discuss it as we dine."

It wasn't five minutes before room service arrived with dinner. The smell of steak and potatoes made my mouth water as the waiter set it on the small table.

"Shall we?" William asked, pulling a chair out for me.

I know it's the manners of the time, but ugh it's a little creepy.

I sat, and he pushed my chair in. As I lay my napkin in my lap, he took the seat across.

He smiled sweetly as he said, "This almost reminds me of when we were courting."

Eck. "Yeah? How did that happen exactly? How did we meet?"

His smile softened. "We met at an art exhibition. You love art and music. You've often used your family's wealth and position to patronize artists and musicians."

"I did, huh?" *Celeste was wealthy then?* "So I was sponsoring an artist's show?"

He nodded. "Indeed, a talented young painter from Toronto."

"Is that where I'm from?"

"Yes."

"But why were you in Toronto if your hotel is all the way out here?"

"I was in town for business, looking to entice the people of Toronto to travel west."

"You were advertising the hotel?"

He nodded. "The art show had many people who enjoy travel and can afford to do so."

"I see. So that's how we met. Then what happened?"

"You were quite taken with the idea of the west, the Rockies, the Indians, the adventure. You invited me to tea so you could hear all about it."

"And we began courting after that? How did my family feel about me marrying someone who lives so far away?" *Not to mention who is twice my age.*

"I cannot say they were pleased to have you moving away, but you would hear no objections. Your father and brother were particularly sad to see you go. On the other hand, your family's logging company has a claim in British Columbia, and your father often travels there for business. It is not as if they would never see you."

That's good to know. "I have a brother? Do I have any other siblings?"

He frowned. "Jacques would be distraught if he knew you'd forgotten him. No, you have just one younger brother and your parents."

Celeste and her brother must've been close. "How much younger is Jacques?"

"Two or three years," he answered.

I nodded, internalizing the information. Before I could pull away, William reached across the table and covered my hand with his. "You're not wearing your wedding ring. Did you lose it somewhere, I wonder? The vows we made to each other still hold true, my dear."

Mitica would've noticed if I'd been wearing a ring when he found me. Did I lose it when I was killed? Was it stolen? No, if Celeste had been mugged, they would have taken her money, too. I gently pulled my hand away, using it to grab the glass of wine before me. "Which vows are those?" I asked, watching him closely.

His eyes bored into mine, and I tried not to flinch as the hair on my neck and arms stood up.

"I vowed to bring you out here and give you partial dominion over the hotel. I went to Toronto to invite guests, and you were determined to help me make the hotel attractive to polite society. You wanted a grand project in the west, and I have given you just that."

"And what did you get out of it?"

"Well, your assistance, of course. Not to mention the love and duty of a beautiful, young wife."

I cringed at the thought of this man touching me intimately. It's not that he was unattractive or that the age gap particularly bothered me. It was more about who he wasn't than who he was. *Did Celeste love him? He seems to think she did. I guess he is mature and gentlemanly. But her soul mate wasn't three miles away. I sort of feel sorry for William. I suppose she should be grateful she and Wynn never met. Then again, she is me, and we did meet. In this body, am I not Celeste?* That philosophical spiral of thought was interrupted when I noticed William staring at me intensely.

"Do you truly remember nothing? Not our courtship, our home, our wedding, not even your family?" His tone made it sound like it was all some elaborate ruse.

Why would he think Celeste would do that? "I'm sorry. I don't remember anything. I don't remember meeting you. I don't remember loving or marrying you. I didn't recognize my own name when Marguerite found me."

His stony expression gave nothing of his emotions away.

Is he upset? Angry? Shocked? Heartbroken?

"Worry not, my dear. We have time. You fell in love with me not long ago. I am positive you will again."

Not likely. I didn't respond.

"In the meantime, I will just have to be patient. As Dr. Hollander recommended, you will return to your daily routine in the hopes you will recover your memories. Tomorrow, I will show you around the hotel and explain your duties."

"Okay."

"As for tonight, I suggest you go to sleep early. I will send Marguerite in to assist you."

"I can handle changing into pajamas by myself. I'll see you tomorrow."

"Very well. Goodnight, my dear."

He reached out to me as if by habit. When I shrunk back, he froze and lowered his arm.

"Of course. Forgive me," he muttered. He bowed to me, then left the room.

After locking the door behind him, I took a steadying breath. *What am I even supposed to do in this situation?*

I numbly got ready for bed, though it was still early. Marguerite had neatly organized the clothes in a dresser, and it took only seconds to locate a nightgown. Having washed my face, I stood uncertainly in the center of the bedroom.

Mitica wouldn't risk riding Grigore this close to the hotel, and he wouldn't know which room I'm in anyway. Should I call for him? But it's still early. What if he disappeared when Oli was right beside him? I miss him, but it's not really an emergency. I feel like this isn't a reason to call his true name.

My chest ached as I came to terms with the idea I wouldn't be seeing Mitica that night. I squeezed my eyes shut against the burning in my nose, and I took a slow, deep breath.

The safety and comfort I'd allowed myself to feel with Mitica were far-gone. When I'd let him in, I'd felt nothing could take him or that security away. The hollow ache inside me at that moment told me I'd been very wrong. Even though I'd been the one to leave, I was abandoned, alone on a raft in a stormy sea. Forlorn. Vulnerable.

Still, I couldn't bring myself to regret letting him in. The brief moments when he'd given my heart wings, when he'd showed me I was brave and beautiful, it was worth the pain.

I will be with him again soon. Nothing to worry about. And I can call on him if I really need him. My mind assured me, but my heart didn't believe.

The pain in my chest told me I needed him. I refused to concede. *You're being silly. Come on. Adult time.* The agony and despair didn't subside, but my resolve didn't waver.

After opening the balcony door, I stepped into the cold night. The waning half-moon lit up the blanket of snow, creating more light than usual.

I thought about the night Mitica had overheard me singing my mother's moon lullaby, the night he'd told me he wanted to know me. So much had happened since then. Everything had changed.

In a tone too broken by longing, I began to sing the song again, hoping the light of the moon would carry my love to him when it lit upon his face. My voice nearly broke as I sang, the words soft, thick with emotion. I knew Mitica would be feeling the same as I, and I had to believe my message would reach him.

It took me a while to fall asleep that first night alone. The bed was far too big and too comfortable.

When I was finally able to sleep, I awoke in the middle of the night, overheated and sick to my stomach. Had I not experienced this feeling many times before, I would've thought I was going to vomit. But I knew. My stress always manifested physically. Of course, my stomach hadn't acted this nervous since the night before I'd started my job at *The Chicago Telegraph.*

I threw off my blankets and rushed to the balcony door before pressing my forehead to the cold glass. It cooled my clammy face, but it only gave me mild relief.

I cracked the door and lay on the floor with my face near the opening. Frozen night air wafted over my skin. I sighed in relief as the nausea subsided. After a few minutes, I started to shiver, which was exactly what I wanted. I wouldn't feel sick if I was cold. I curled into a ball on my side and drifted into a fitful sleep.

Sometime in the night, I must've gotten too cold because the balcony door was closed when I awoke. I cracked my eyelids and stared out at the predawn light through the window.

I stretched out onto my back, groaning at the soreness left from shivering for most of the night on the floor. The shoulder I'd been lying on was particularly stiff.

Closing my eyes, I took long, deep breaths and systematically willed my body to relax. My head throbbed against the hard floor, but at least I wasn't nauseated.

I hate when stress gets the better of me. I feel so weak. Maybe I should try meditating. It may help me deal. In any case, the first day is always the worst.

I didn't know when William or Marguerite would come for me, but I knew I was in no condition to receive them. I hoped more sleep would help my headache, and I crawled into bed and dozed for a few more hours.

TWENTY-EIGHT

Golden rays of sunlight filtered into the room, tickling my face. I cracked my eyelids cautiously, then took a deep breath. I felt much more rested. My limbs were still sore, but my headache was gone.

As I lay in bed, the room I'd thought was so nice the day before felt uncomfortably large and empty in the sparkling morning light. The silence smothered my ears, and my own sighs sounded too loud.

"I miss you," I whispered. "Hurry up, will you? I don't want to need to be strong."

A soft knock at my door announced a visitor. I sighed again and threw off my blankets. *I would've liked to loosen up with some yoga before anyone came around.* The floor was pleasantly cool beneath my bare feet. Before I was halfway to opening the door, Marguerite unlocked it and entered.

"Whoa there, lady," I said, taken aback. "Don't just enter someone's room without her answering. How did you even get a key?"

Marguerite stopped and bowed her head in apology. "I am sorry. Monsieur gave me the other key so I may help you more easily."

"Did you used to enter my room unbidden before?"

"Non, you usually called for me. Monsieur was concerned you would need more assistance in your delicate state."

I held out my hand, and she passed me the key. "Let's just keep it the way it was. I can call if I need your help."

She dipped her head again. "Very well."

I sighed. "When am I supposed to meet William?"

"Monsieur requested you meet him in the dining room shortly."

"All right, I'll get ready then."

It took almost an hour for me to bathe and dress, and another fifteen for Marguerite to pin my short hair under a simple hat. *Will I ever get used to having a personal maid? I don't like it, but I should probably play along.*

On the ground floor, Marguerite led me to a cozy dining room with small tables covered in pristine white tablecloths and east-facing windows alight with morning sunshine. The cheerfulness of the scene tasted bitter. I spotted William at a table near a swinging kitchen door and went to meet him. He noticed my approach over his newspaper and stood from his chair.

"Good morning, my dear. I hope you slept well."

I took a seat without answering, and he sat again.

"So what does my normal day look like, William?"

His eyebrows rose slightly. "Right to business I see."

When a young waiter in a smart butler-type uniform brought me a cup of tea and asked what I'd like for breakfast, I told him buttered toast. He nodded without judgment and left to fill my order. After he'd gone, I drank some water, leaving the tea untouched.

"You are not hungry this morning?" William asked.

More like my stomach can't handle anything else right now. "No, I'm not very hungry."

He frowned, analyzing me.

"So what do I do here?" I repeated.

He paused for a moment before answering. "In the morning, you check on the kitchen staff to ensure everything is ready before they start breakfast. Then you eat."

"Okay. Then what?"

"Then you meet with Harrison, our activities coordinator."

"What do I do with him?"

"You plan and schedule activities for the guests."

"Like what?"

"Skiing, horseback riding, cards, hunting, the sort of pastimes our guests would enjoy."

At this point, the waiter returned with my toast. I thanked him before he left.

"What do I do after I meet Harrison?"

William nodded toward my food. "Why don't you eat? I promise I will explain everything as we go along."

I nibbled at my toast, not wanting to upset my stomach.

The scene before me was so surreal. I was eating breakfast in a glowing dining room with my husband, not a day after leaving the arms of my soul mate. *If Mitica was sitting across from me now, it would be romantic.* As it was, a stranger I was supposed to know and love sat in his place. The juxtaposition turned my stomach, but I stuffed the last bite of toast into my mouth and forced it down with water. I stared out into the shining valley, knowing he was out there somewhere.

When we'd both finished breakfast, William took me to the kitchen. Two immaculate chefs went about cooking. They looked up at our presence and acknowledged us shortly with a nod.

"This is Louis and Gabriel, my dear. Gentleman, the lady is in delicate health at the moment. I expect you to be understanding."

They dipped their heads in reply without stopping their work.

William gave them no further explanation, and I made a mental note to clarify to them that I didn't remember anything.

"Every evening after supper, you come to the kitchen and set the menu for the following day," William told me.

"Okay."

On the way out of the kitchen, I officially met our waiter, Oscar.

Next, William took me to the front desk where Frederick, a pale man with light hair and piercing eyes, stood guard.

"Welcome back, Madam," he said formally.

"Uh, thank you," I muttered.

"Sometimes, you tend the front desk so Frederick may complete other tasks," William informed. "Frederick can show you how to check guests in and out later."

"All right." *Jeez, it feels like my first day at a new job. I should have brought a notebook. I wonder if Celeste knew what she was signing up for when she got married.*

Behind the front desk, there was an office with two additional desks. One was empty, and a young man with broad shoulders and wavy, golden hair poured over a pile of papers at the other.

"This is Harrison," William told me.

Harrison looked up from his work and smiled at me. "Celeste, you're back," he proclaimed happily in an Australian accent.

William frowned and cleared his throat, but Harrison appeared unapologetic.

"My wife has had an accident. She does not recall anything from her time here."

Harrison gaped at William's declaration. "Is that true? That's dreadful. You don't remember anything at all?"

I shook my head, wondering why William had chosen to tell Harrison about my memory loss but made it sound like it was only my time at the hotel I didn't remember.

Harrison's expression told me the news hurt him. *We must've been friends for him to call me by my first name and for him to be that upset that I've forgotten him.*

"I'm sorry this happened to you," Harrison said sincerely. "But don't worry. We'll help you adjust. You let me know if you need anything."

Touched by his earnest concern, I was glad to know Celeste had a friend like him.

"And you will inform me immediately if my wife is in need of assistance, Harrison," William ordered.

I blinked at William, startled by his territorial tone.

Harrison paused for a moment too long. "Of course, Mr. Broadstone."

"Through there," William pointed to a door at the other side of the office, "is my office. If you need anything, you can often find me there."

I nodded.

"Come, my dear. Let us continue the tour," William instructed, grabbing my elbow and leading me out the way we'd come.

I met Harrison's eyes and smiled gently, trying to thank him without words.

Near the library, I followed William down a hall. Through a set of double doors was a large, empty room with tall, arched windows on either side. At the far end, paned French doors led to what looked like a patio and garden.

"This is our ballroom."

Rain pelted the glass windows, and I could see it melting the snow in the garden. *The weather changes fast here.*

William pursed his lips. "I will show you the garden another day."

"Okay. Is there anything else I need to know?"

"Not particularly. You generally attend most meals with the guests and host tea every afternoon. You also have time to yourself to do with as you wish."

Host tea? I hope that's not as intimidating as it sounds. "So you've shown me the entire hotel then?"

He nodded. "Everything except the laundry and employee quarters."

And the stables, but I guess that's not necessarily part of the hotel. "I'd like to see those as well."

He raised his eyebrows as if that was an unusual request. "Very well. This way."

I followed him down a hallway near the front desk. It was clean but simple, clearly a place guests were not supposed to see.

"All employees may be housed here should they wish, though some choose to stay elsewhere," William said, gesturing down the hall of doors. "Most of the maids are local and live nearby, and the stables' staff stays nearer to the horses."

I'd like to see one of the rooms, but I don't want to invade someone's privacy. "And the laundry?"

He nodded, and I trailed him through a door and down a flight of stairs.

In the dimly-lit basement, a group of at least five Asian men labored over washtubs, hand-washing bed sheets and towels.

They chatted at each other in a language I could only just recognize as Chinese. When the man nearest us noticed our presence, he said something to the others. They all went silent and paused in their work. The men bowed far too low and for too long.

Ducking my head at their uncomfortable show of fealty, I was relieved when they started working again. I looked around the basement. There was hardly any light, the heat from the washtubs was like a sauna, and there was little ventilation. I frowned. *It would suck working in this environment. I can't believe William allows such working conditions. Maybe I can figure out a way to help them.*

The young man who had announced our presence approached and bowed again.

"My dear, this is Xi Wei. He manages the laundry and these men."

I bowed to Xi Wei to the same extent he had to me. "It's nice to meet you, Xi Wei. Thank you for your hard work."

I looked up into Xi Wei's dark eyes, wide with shock. When I got a closer look at him, I saw that he was quite pretty. I smiled, thinking he looked like a guy who would be an international pop idol back home.

"Mrs. Broadstone," he started in a thick accent. "It is an honor to finally meet you. I have known your husband for many years. My father worked for him on the railroad. He was generous enough to give us work."

"I hope you'll let me know if you or your men need anything," I told him.

He dipped his head. "We are all very well here."

I frowned at the working conditions again.

"That concludes our tour, my dear," William announced, looking at his pocket watch. "It is nearly time for the next meal. Why don't you go to the kitchen to see if Louis and Gabriel have everything they need? I have paperwork to attend to."

I nodded. "All right." I turned to Xi Wei. "It was nice to meet you," I said again in farewell.

He bowed. "May you have peace wherever you go."

I smiled and bowed back. "You too."

TWENTY-NINE

*B*ack in the foyer, I split from William and went toward the kitchen. The dining room was empty except for Oscar, the waiter, who was folding napkins in preparation for the next meal. He didn't look up when I passed through to the kitchen.

Louis and Gabriel were busy cutting meat and chopping vegetables. They spared me a glance as I entered through the swinging door.

I smiled into their uninterested faces. "Hey, guys, I just want to make sure you have everything you need."

They didn't respond.

I watched them expectantly. Louis, the older of the two, had long, gray hair, which was pulled back at the nape of his neck. His stiff expression seemed to say he was less than pleased as he expertly cut beef into even slices. Gabriel's younger face was more indifferent. He was taller than Louis, and his chin-length, golden brown hair was tucked behind his ears.

"So...do you have everything you need then?"

"Oui," Louis answered shortly.

"Okay. Well, that's good." I tried not to let their coldness affect my tone. *Did Celeste not get along with them?* "So listen, guys. I don't want to distract you while you're working, but William didn't exactly tell you the whole story earlier. The truth is: I was in an accident. I don't really remember anything about my life here. I don't want to be a burden, and I'm going to work really hard to support you guys in whatever you need. Please be patient with me, and feel free to correct me if I'm doing anything wrong. Okay?"

They stopped what they were doing and looked up at me. Gabriel's brow crinkled as if he'd only partially understood what I'd been saying, and Louis clicked his tongue in irritation. Louis muttered in French.

"We do not understand," Gabriel said slowly with a thick, French accent. "Please repeat en français."

I frowned, thinking how my Mom had forced me to take Spanish in high school, saying it would be more useful. *Mitica never did teach me very many words.* "But I don't speak French."

Just then, the door swung open as Oscar entered the kitchen.

"Oscar, do you speak French?"

He blinked. "Oui, Madame."

I sighed in relief. "Would you mind translating for me?"

He tilted his head. "Of course, but Madame speaks French very well."

"It's a long story. Please tell Louis and Gabriel what I'm saying."

After Oscar had translated, they all seemed to understand my situation.

Louis spat something unpleasantly, and Gabriel answered in a soothing tone. Then Gabriel turned and asked Oscar something.

"They would like to know how involved you will be in the kitchen if you can't remember anything," Oscar told me.

I frowned, thinking. "I'm going to be honest with you guys. I don't know anything about cooking. The only things I care about is that the food is good and prepared in a clean and safe way. If you have ideas for the menus, I'll gladly rely on your expertise. You guys just let me know what you need."

Oscar translated. Gabriel's eyebrows rose in response, and Louis's stern expression gave way to a satisfied hint of a smile.

I get the feeling William and Celeste micromanage them. "So does that work for everyone?" I asked, giving them two thumbs up.

They blinked at me. Oscar translated, and they nodded their approval. Gabriel even hesitantly raised his thumbs in a sympathetic gesture.

"Great. I'll let you get to it then," I said before leaving.

I heaved a deep sigh once I was in the dining room. Oscar soon returned with silverware. I insisted on helping him set the tables, not really knowing what else to do with myself.

After we'd finished, I sat by the window and watched the rain streak lazily down the glass. The snow that had blanketed the landscape that morning had melted into inconsistent patches.

It's so strange here, like a completely different world than when I was with the Mounties and Mitica. It's so...mundane. How long will it be before I can leave with Mitica? Will all the snow be melted? Will spring be in full bloom? I hope he's staying out of the rain. I thought of his soaked undershirt clinging to his broad chest and felt my face heat. Then sadness squeezed my heart.

Oscar approached the table at which I sat with a warm plate. "Would you like to try the dish before the guests arrive?" he asked me, setting the plate before me.

"Sure," I answered, picking up my fork and spearing a cream-covered, sliced potato. I blew on it softly before I took a bite. It's soft texture and delicate sauce melted on my tongue. "Mmm," I complimented. "It's very good."

Looking over at the kitchen, I saw Gabriel's golden-brown head peeking out around the door. I smiled and gave him a thumbs up from across the room. He returned my smile with a nod of satisfaction.

As I continued to slowly eat the meal, I wondered how Celeste had stayed so skinny with such deliciously rich food to eat. By the time I was finishing, guests began to filter into the dining room. I watched Oscar seat them and take their orders before I approached to introduce myself. I went to the table nearest me first, where a pair of older gentlemen sat. "Good afternoon, how are you both today?"

Their dulled eyes lit up. They both had thick muttonchops that led to prestigious mustaches.

"We are quite well, lady. Quite well indeed," the shorter, ruddier man declared.

I smiled. "I'm glad to hear it. I'm Er... Celeste Broadstone. I hope you'll let me know if there's anything you need while you stay with us."

"We are quite comfortable, dear lady," the grayer of the two said. "Your father, Mr. Broadstone, is an excellent host."

I ducked my head and cleared my throat. "Actually...Mr. Broadstone is...my husband." Sickness bubbled in my stomach, and I silently apologized to Mitica.

The older man blinked in surprise, but his counterpart was quick to cover for him. "We had heard Mrs. Broadstone was young and beautiful, but you are much lovelier than described. Forgive Higgins for his misstep."

I waved my hand dismissively. "It's not a problem. Don't worry about it Mr....?"

"Oh, pardon me, lady. I am Reginald Sheffield, and this is Colonel George Higgins."

I smiled and nodded at them. "Well, it's nice to meet you, Mr. Sheffield, Colonel Higgins. Please let me know if you need anything during your stay."

"Of course," Reginald promised.

Not far away, a young couple gazed lovingly at each other. I didn't want to intrude, but it was my job to mingle. "Good afternoon, are you both doing well today?"

The young lady with big, blue eyes blushed an attractive shade of pink. Her companion, a well-dressed young man, answered. "Very well. Thank you."

"I don't mean to interrupt your meal. I just wanted to introduce myself. I'm Celeste Broadstone. Please let me know if there's anything you need while you're here."

"It's a pleasure to meet you, Miss Broadstone. I'm Alfred Durant, and this is my wife Jane."

Jane blushed deeper and smiled at me.

"Are you on your honeymoon?" I asked.

"Why, yes, we are," Alfred responded.

"Congratulations. Thank you for staying with us on such an important occasion. I hope you make many happy memories while you're here."

"Thank you, Miss Broadstone," Jane said softly.

"And you'll let me know if there's anything I can do?"

"Of course." Alfred nodded.

A trio of giggles drew my attention, and I stopped at the next table as a matronly woman sat with three young women. They stifled their laughter as she censured them with a look.

I smiled at them. "Good afternoon, ladies. How are you?"

"We are well, thank you," the matron answered formally.

"I'm glad to hear it. Well, I just stopped to introduce myself. I'm Celeste Broadstone. Please let me know if there's anything you need during your stay."

"I will, thank you. I'm Elizabeth Pickens. This is my daughter, Mary, and her friends, Sarah Grant and Juniper Willis." The elder woman indicated each girl in turn.

They smiled and nodded at me.

"It's nice to meet you all. I hope you enjoy your stay."

"Miss Broadstone," Mary began. "Is there anything planned for tonight after supper?"

"I'm not sure. Let me check with our activities coordinator, and I'll get back to you."

"Thank you."

"No problem."

As there was only one more occupied table, I decided to introduce myself to the two young men before going to see Harrison. Having been slyly watching the three young ladies, the men were not surprised by my approach. Their dark eyes locked on me with polite appreciation.

"Won't you join us, Miss?" the more attractive of the two offered. He was long and lean with a confidence that said he knew of his charms.

"Oh, I've already eaten," I told him.

"Well, that's all right. Sit down and have a cup of tea and a chat," the broader man insisted, adding to his friend's invitation.

I hesitated. *Well, I guess William did tell me to be a good hostess.*

"All right. I could use a cup of tea." I sat in the free chair between them.

They smiled congenially. "What's your name, Miss?" the first man asked.

"I'm Celeste Broadstone. And you?"

They didn't seem to recognize the last name. "I'm Stewart Thomas, and this is my friend, Cole Linton."

"It's nice to meet you both. Are you here on vacation?"

"Yes," Cole answered.

"That's nice. Thank you for choosing to stay with us."

"Of course." Stewart was silent a moment, then added as if by afterthought. "Had I known such a lovely woman worked here, I would have come sooner."

I paused, uncomfortable with his compliment. "That's...kind of you," I forced out.

"What is it you do here, Miss Broadstone?" Cole asked.

I thought about all the duties William had described to me. "I guess you could call it guest relations. I ensure you have everything you need and assist in other ways."

Stewart smirked like I'd said something unintentionally humorous. "Indeed? There is something I need."

"Yeah? Well, let me know if it's something I can help with."

"Oh, I'm positive you're just the woman for the job."

I frowned at his suggestive tone. "What is it?" I asked suspiciously.

His answering smile was meant to be inviting. "I'm in room 403. Come there after supper, and I'll let you know all about it."

Eck. I stood, flaring my nostrils. *He seems like the type I need to be clear with.* "I'm not available tonight. In fact, I'm never available after hours. Incidentally, I'm spoken for." I thought about how Mitica would respond to someone making such an overt pass at me.

Before I could walk away, Stewart grabbed my wrist to stop me. "There's no need for such a response. I apologize for upsetting you. I just wanted to express my interest. There's no harm in that, is there?"

Oscar approached the table with the pair's meals. He took stock of the situation without effort. "Is there anything you require, Mrs. Broadstone?"

Cole's eyes widened, and Stewart released my wrist.

I sighed internally. "No, thank you, Oscar. I was just leaving."

"What about your tea?" Stewart asked, not quite giving up.

"I forgot that I'm busy at the moment."

As Oscar and I left, I heard Cole and Stewart whispering.

"You need to be more careful," Cole said.

"I didn't know she was married. She isn't even wearing a ring."

"Would it have mattered if she were?"

"It never has before."

They laughed.

THIRTY

*H*arrison wasn't in his office when I went to see about the schedule. I asked Frederick if he knew where he was.

"He left for the stables not long ago," Frederick informed.

I sighed. *I wanted to talk with him after his reaction this morning.* "Do you happen to know if there are any activities planned after dinner tonight?"

He reached behind the front desk and consulted a sheet of paper. "There appears to be a card game scheduled in the library," he said.

"Yeah? Okay, thanks." I turned to walk away, then turned back. "Hey, do you have time to show me how to work the front desk in a bit?"

He nodded stiffly.

"Great. I'll be right back after I tell a guest the schedule."

Mary, Sarah, and Juniper were delighted to hear there was something to entertain them after dinner. I promised to see them at tea and returned to the stoic Frederick.

"Sorry about that," I apologized for making him wait.

He didn't respond but reached behind the counter and pulled out his guest book.

"Hey, Frederick, did William tell you why you have to show me this stuff again?"

He stilled for a moment. "Mr. Broadstone informed me of your memory loss."

"Good." After a heavy pause, I asked, "How long have you worked here, Frederick?"

"I have been here since the hotel opened."

"That long, huh? So you would've met me when I first arrived."

He gave me a slight nod.

"Will you tell me something?"

He waited for my question.

"Was I happy here? With William and everything?"

Frederick was silent for so long I thought he wasn't going to answer. But after a while, his sharp eyes softened ever so slightly. "I try not to pry into others' personal affairs...but yes. I believe you were quite happy, especially at first."

"And later on?" I pushed softly.

He paused again. "I have some duties to attend to presently. I shall show you how to man the desk now."

I frowned at his evasive maneuver. "Right. So what does it entail?"

Frederick turned out to be an excellent trainer. He was concise and easily answered all of my questions. He showed me how to check guests in and out, where the room keys and mail was kept, and gave me all manner of points of interest information should the guests ask for it.

I felt confident I could handle the job for a short time, and I told Frederick I would watch his post.

Not long after I'd taken up residence at the front desk, Marguerite entered the lobby from the library. I waved her over.

"How can I help?" Marguerite asked once she'd reached me.

"How much of my stuff have you moved to my room?"

"I moved your clothes and some of your jewelry. But you will be returning to Monsieur's bed as soon as you regain your memories, so I did not move everything."

I froze, internalizing my cringe. "I think it's best if you move everything. I was hoping to read some letters from home. I hear I was close to my family. Surely, we wrote to each other."

"Oui, that is an excellent idea. I will move the rest of your things today."

"Great, thanks. Oh! Do you happen to know where I could get a candle?"

She tilted her head. "But the hotel has electric lights."

"I know, but I still need one."

She nodded. "Very well, I will find one for you."

"Thanks."

I had hoped Harrison would return before Frederick, but Frederick soon relieved me.

Maybe I should go down to the stables and look for him. No, I'd be interrupting his work. I'm supposed to meet with him every day after breakfast. So if I can't catch him today, I'll see him tomorrow.

As I stood in the lobby thinking, William appeared in a flurry. "My dear, what are you still doing here? Are you not to host tea at this hour?"

"Uh, what time is tea?"

"Why, three in the afternoon, of course."

Of course, I mean, obviously. "And that's starting now?"

"Indeed. Hurry along. You mustn't keep the guests waiting."

I sighed internally and headed for the dining room.

When I arrived, I noticed some of the guests were missing. Colonel Higgins and his friend Reginald, as well as Stewart and Cole, were not in attendance.

As the newlyweds were basking in each other's presence, I opted to sit with Mrs. Pickens and her three charges.

"Good afternoon, ladies. May I join you for tea?"

"Of course," Mrs. Pickens granted me permission while the young women all smiled.

I'd never hosted tea before, but I placed my napkin in my lap and hoped standard table manners were good enough. I had assumed I would be pouring and serving the tea and little sandwiches, but Oscar didn't leave much for me to do.

"So where are you guys from?"

The women blinked at my modern word choice.

"I mean, where are you ladies from?"

"Québec City," Mrs. Pickens answered after a pause.

"Oh yeah? What brings you all the way out here? Just a vacation?"

"My daughter is to be married."

"You are, Mary? Congratulations."

"Thank you. Yes, John and I are to be married in a few months. And since he wishes to return to England, this was my last chance to see the great west." She sounded a little regretful but not so much that I was concerned about whether she wanted to marry John the Englishman.

"So you and your friends came out here for one last adventure, eh?"

The trio smiled a little sadly and nodded. "Just so," Mary agreed.

"Well, it's an excellent place to come for adventure. What sort of things have you done so far?"

That was all the encouragement they needed. The girls told me all about their long train ride, how Juniper's trunk was lost along the way, how the heel of Sarah's boot broke, how they'd gone shopping in Farrloch, strolled the gardens of the hotel, and played cards in the evening. They were still trying to convince Mrs. Pickens to allow them to join Harrison on a trail ride, but she seemed unwilling to budge on the matter.

"We noticed your hotel has a ballroom," Sarah said.

"Yes, we do."

"Do you ever have balls or dances?"

"I'm not sure. Why? Do you guys want to have one?"

The girls nodded with enthusiasm.

"There don't seem to be many guests here at the moment, but I'll talk with Harrison and see. Maybe we could have a small dance."

They practically hummed with excitement.

"Did you hear that, girls? How wonderful. Perhaps you two will find some handsome strangers," Mary gushed.

"Those two gentlemen staying here are awfully handsome," Juniper whispered as Sarah nodded with a giggle.

Mrs. Pickens cleared her throat.

I looked around the room and saw that the four men had still not arrived.

"Oh, you won't find them at tea, Miss Broadstone," Sarah informed. "They go hunting after lunch with the two older gentlemen."

I pursed my lips. *Of course they do.*

"Indeed, they brought down a bear a few days ago," Mary said.

What do people staying at a hotel do with the carcasses?

"Oh, how do you know, Mary? We only just arrived the day before yesterday," Sarah said.

Mary flushed. "Well, I overheard them talking while we were all in the library last night."

"You did? I didn't hear that," Juniper added excitedly.

"Perhaps we should ask them tonight after supper," Sarah suggested.

My frown mirrored Mrs. Pickens's. *I'll have to keep an eye on these girls. Stewart and Cole will waste no time taking advantage of them.*

After Oscar cleared away our dishes, I was given my first bit of free time. I went to see if Harrison had returned to his desk.

As I entered the office, Harrison met my eyes as William stood over him, censuring him for being gone all morning.

Harrison winked at me, then tilted his head toward the door to tell me to make my escape. I bit my lip and nodded. William never even realized I was there as I snuck out the way I'd come.

With no work to do, I went to my room. I found Marguerite still putting things away.

"How's it coming, Marguerite?"

"Everything is moved. I am just putting things in order."

"Awesome. Did you find the letters?"

She tilted her head at my choice of words but picked up a decorative wooden box from the coffee table and held it out to me. I was finding it difficult to change my speech patterns, and all the strange looks just reminded me how understanding Mitica had been. *It helps that he knew I was from the future.*

"Oui," Marguerite said as I took the box from her. "But I am sorry. I could not find your journal anywhere. I will get you a new one when I go into town."

I sucked on my teeth. "Do I keep a journal?"

"Oui, of course. You love to write and sketch. You wrote in your journal every day."

I hummed, pursing my lips. "Well, keep an eye out for it, will you? It could be a big help in regaining my memories."

"Oui, I will."

Marguerite went back to organizing, and I took the letterbox into the bedroom. After shutting the French doors, I crawled onto the bed and sat cross-legged, resting the box in my lap.

The dark wooden lid was etched with an intricate leaf pattern, and the initials "CL." The lid was thick and heavy but did not stick or creak when I lifted it. Neatly-folded letters were packed into the box like cards in an old library catalog. I slid out a random letter near the front and began to read.

To my daughter,

I hope all is well with you out there in the west. Everything is just fine here, so you need not worry.

Are you taking care of yourself and your husband? Make sure you both get enough to eat. And wear your shawl. It is cold in the mountains, and you are forever leaving your shawl.

I am certain William is treating you well, and I wait every day for news of a grandchild.

Don't go wandering the forests, and be kind to the staff.

I love you.
Mother

I smiled to myself at the fretful nature of mothers everywhere and pulled another letter from the box.

My darling girl,

Your favorite ballet is playing at the theater on Saturday. I looked up from the paper at breakfast to tell you about it, forget-ting you weren't there. I believe I've finally turned into an old man.

I can hear your laugh as you tell me my gray hair is distin-guished, but I cannot see it that way anymore.

Was it mere months since we danced so gayly at your

wedding? It feels like years. However, I am "looking to the bright future" as you always encourage me to do.

I know you are living your dream among the snowy peaks of the Rockies, but I do hope you spare a thought for your Papa.

Stay bright, my darling girl.
Papa

I gently refolded the letter and placed it beside me on the bed. Then I reached for another one and unfolded it.

My sweet Cellie,

I could not have predicted how quiet our house would become when you married and went to live with your husband.

Father sits in his study, reading, all day with no one to interrupt him. And Mother, well let's just say she has started to turn that calculating eye toward me. I cannot tell if she is planning to find me a bride as soon as she can or if she is to confine me indoors so as to keep her other child near. In any case, I fear for my future, dear sister.

I know you were so happy to finally have your grand adventure, but did you have to move so very far away? That was rather unkind of you.

I've complained to my heart's content. Now, I shall tell you some good news. Father and I are coming to Vancouver on business in early April.

I know William is ever-busy, but perhaps you could visit us while we are there? It would mean so much to Father and me.

I will expect your reply as early as is possible.

Your loving brother,
Jacques

I closed my eyes against the unexpected burning. *Celeste's family really loved her. And when I'm gone, they'll never see her again. No, I can't think of it that way. It's not because I'm leaving. It's because Celeste died, possibly by murder. I need to figure out what happened to her.*

Jacques said they were going to be in British Columbia in April. Was she on her way to see them when she met her fate? But William said she was on her way to Toronto for a friend's wedding. Why would he lie? Either way, she never arrived. Wouldn't they have inquired as to why she never showed up?

I sighed at all the questions for which I did not yet have answers. My gaze drifted back toward the box of unread letters, and I reached for another.

In the quiet bedroom, only the soft crinkle of paper could be heard as I spent the day reading all of Celeste's letters. I read about how her family missed her, how her friends wished her well, and how the artists she'd patronized still wanted support. There was no mention of a friend getting married, but it was possible that such a letter would have contained specifics of time and place and might have been in Celeste's things when she died.

She seemed universally loved. If she'd gotten letters from her enemies, she had not kept them, at least not with the letters from her loved ones.

While her correspondents bemoaned her absence, no one seemed surprised by her marriage and subsequent move, and no one questioned her love for William. On the contrary, other than a few "heartbroken" artists, her friends commended her choice and wished such an affection for themselves.

While I couldn't comprehend her attraction, it was clear Celeste had adored her husband, or at least it appeared that way to everyone around her.

I frowned at the papers scattered around me on the bed. *If she had truly loved him, I should assume the feeling was mutual. Poor William. He's going to be devastated when his loving wife disappears. What will we have to do to make him let her go? Will I have to crush his attachment? I don't know if I could destroy someone like that. Maybe I could come up with a reason to leave, and Mitica could help me fake my death. I need to talk to Mitica.*

My stomach dropped at the thought. *When will I even see him again?*

I let myself fall to one side and curled into a ball. *Man, 1900 sucks. If we were in my time, I could call him or video chat.* I squeezed my eyes shut. "What a messed-up situation," I murmured. "Nothing I've ever learned has prepared me for this."

Not for the first time in my life, I wished I could allow myself to be childish. *It would be so much easier if we just said "screw it" and ran away.*

I knew Mitica would. Without any question, he would abandon everything just to be with me. And that only made it worse because I wasn't only fighting myself. I wasn't only struggling with my own desire in order to be an adult, to be responsible. Because he would do it, I knew I was the only thing keeping us apart.

THIRTY-ONE

William knocked on my door to escort me to dinner that evening. Taking in his change of attire, I understood why Marguerite had insisted I dress for dinner.

He smiled gently at me when I entered the hall. "You look wonderful, my dear."

I nodded once in acknowledgment and hesitated to take the arm he held out to me. I resigned myself and placed my fingertips on his elbow. An uncomfortable feeling made me want to squirm, like the sensation of dancing closely with a person I'd just met.

All the guests were in attendance in the dining room, and I dutifully smiled my greeting to everyone in turn, even Stewart and Cole.

Apparently, it was customary for William and Celeste to eat dinner together. The guests kept to their own parties and did not interrupt us, though I wish they had because it felt pretty awkward. William asked about my day, but I didn't have much to say. I'd completed my duties as was expected.

In all honesty, I was likely the one making it awkward. After reading all those letters, it felt weird being around William in Celeste's body. They had this entire relationship, and he was expecting her to wake up one day and remember her love for him.

I was relieved when dinner was over. I popped into the kitchen, and Oscar, Louis, Gabriel, and I went over the following day's menu. I really wasn't of much use, but they seemed pleased when I just agreed with their recommendations.

I was beyond ready for the evening to be over; I was done interacting with people. Unfortunately, I had to attend the night's entertainment in the library. Along with the guests, William, Harrison, and Marguerite were also there.

Harrison informed the crowd we would be playing whist, a game I'd heard of but had never played. We were instructed to separate into groups of four. As there were fourteen of us, two had to sit out. I opted to sit out since I didn't know how to play, and Harrison sat out to manage the groups.

The three groups varied in intensity as they played through a few rounds. Colonel Higgins, Reginald, William, and Mrs. Pickens seemed to take the game very seriously. The Durants, Marguerite, and Sarah looked as though they played for fun. But the most enthusiasm came from Mary, Juniper, Stewart, and Cole's table, where they were far more interested in flirting than playing cards.

I watched for a while, then decided to make myself useful. I poured after-dinner drinks for the men and went to the kitchen and retrieved coffee and tea for the women.

When everyone had played their fill of whist, they split up around the library. William, Mrs. Pickens, Colonel Higgins, and Reginald relocated to armchairs and a couch near the fire. The men smoked cigars, and Mrs. Pickens tried to hide the liquor she slipped into her tea.

Marguerite and Sarah chatted about something in French, and the newly-weds read a book together.

Once Harrison had cleaned up the cards, he excused himself for the evening. I watched him go, wishing I could escape so easily.

Mary, Juniper, Cole, and Stewart were gathered around a piano in the corner. After some pleading, Mary and Stewart sat beside one another on the bench and began to play an upbeat duet.

They laughed and smiled as if they were the only two in the room.

"That's marvelous!" Juniper praised when they'd finished. "Can I make a request?"

"Of course." Stewart smiled charmingly. "What would you like us to play next?"

"My favorite is 'Silent Woods' by Dvořák. Do you know it? Mary knows the one."

"Indeed, I do," he said, turning to Mary. "Miss Pickens, would you be so kind as to be my partner once more?"

Mary's eyes sparkled at his attention. "It would be my pleasure, Mr. Thomas."

As their melody filled the room, the other guests went silent to better appreciate the performance. Each piano hammer struck a chord in my heart, and I wished I was cuddled up by the fire in Mitica's warm embrace. I had to admit they were both very good. When the last note died out, Stewart smiled over at the blushing Mary as everyone else clapped for their performance.

The look the two young people shared unsettled me, and I moved toward them to make some space. But as I approached the piano, Juniper halted me by asking if I wanted to play next.

With everyone's eyes on me, I froze. "Um, no, I don't play the piano."

"What are you saying, my dear? You are a wonderfully talented pianist," William informed.

At his praise, the others began to insist I play something for them.

But I really don't know how to play the piano. Desperate for an out, I grasped at the only musical talent I had. "I'm not really feeling up to the piano right now, but how about I sing you a song, instead?"

Marguerite and William's eyes widened, but everyone else nodded with eager smiles.

I took a deep breath to steady my nerves, then began to sing the first song that came to my mind. The longing notes and words of "Moon River" echoed through the quiet library. I probably should've chosen a song that was written before 1900, but the chances of them living to see *Breakfast at Tiffany's* were slim. At the very least, I hoped they wouldn't remember the song if they did see it.

Unfortunately, the fact that no one had heard it before meant everyone was paying rapt attention to me. My heart pounded too hard twice at the silence that greeted the conclusion of my impromptu performance, but I was able to breathe again once their enthusiastic applause filled the still void.

Marguerite rushed to me. "Celeste, I did not know you had such a beautiful voice. You always said you sang like a crow."

Oops. "I was just embarrassed to sing in front of people," I hedged. *Probably.*

As the guests returned to their previous activities, I looked around to see if I could busy myself with something else. Panic squeezed my throat for a second when I met Stewart's fleeting gaze of lust.

I squared my shoulders and glared at him. He just smiled and turned his attention toward Mary, who hadn't noticed he hadn't been paying attention to her chatting.

This spells disaster. Something needs to be done about him.

Before I could think of how to extract Mary from a potentially dangerous situation, William interrupted my thoughts.

"You sang as beautifully as a nightingale, my dear," he praised, raising my hand to his lips.

I resisted the urge to snatch my hand away but couldn't suppress my shudder.

"Thank you," I muttered, taking my hand back as soon as I could without giving rise to suspicion. *I understand William loves Celeste, but I feel like I've been clear about taking it easy on the touching. He's kind of an ass for forcing the issue in a place I can't refuse without making a scene.*

"I'm certain you are exhausted after the day you have had. Why don't we head upstairs for the night?"

Had I not known better, I would've thought he was suggesting we sleep together.

"Yeah, you're right. I'm pretty tired," I agreed, still grateful for the out.

He smiled and nodded like he knew me so well.

We said goodnight to the assembly, and I was glad to see Mary safely back in her mother's protective bubble of propriety when we left the library.

William and I were both silent as he escorted me to my room, the awkwardness returning the moment we were alone.

"Well, goodnight then," I said, turning to enter my door.

William snatched my hand to stop me from leaving. My head snapped back to his direction, and I pulled my hand from his grasp.

"I apologize," William said.

Yeah, you say that a lot, but you just keep doing it. "What is it, William?"

His eyes searched my face with an expression that bordered on intense. "You went about your daily routine all day. Did anything trigger your memory at all?" His eagerness struck me as more dubious than solicitous.

"No...nothing has come to me yet."

As he silently gazed at me, I could not decipher his reaction. "Very well," he finally pronounced. Then he gave me an encouraging smile and asked, "Perhaps we should dine alone again tomorrow night? After all, most of your memories here are tied to me."

Is this him trying to make me fall in love with him or what? I don't really want to be alone with him. "I'd prefer being with the group actually. It was fun with everyone there."

His smile stiffened. "Very well, if that is what you wish. Go in and rest, my dear. I will see you tomorrow at breakfast."

"Right...see you tomorrow."

He didn't attempt to stop me again when I closed and locked the door behind me.

As I readied for bed, the weight of the day settled in my stomach. I knew in times such as these, it was best to stay busy. It was in the moments of stillness that Mitica's absence was felt most keenly.

While I hated the queasy sickness in my gut and the anxiety that fatigued my limbs, I wouldn't have traded them. Sure, it was easier to keep my mind off Mitica when it was occupied, but it was in these moments of longing I felt closest to him.

As I crawled into bed, I noticed a long taper in a silver candlestick on my bedside table. *Marguerite fulfilled my request after all.*

I moved the pillow from the head of the bed and sat cross-legged in its place. After lighting the candle, I settled my hands in the dhyana mudra position. Focusing my gaze on the steady flame, I took a deep, cleansing breath and let it all out. With a shiver, my body readjusted, and I began concentrating on regulating my breathing.

I don't know how long I meditated for. But when I blew out the candle, I was confident I wouldn't wake up anxious in the middle of the night.

THIRTY-TWO

I awoke early the next morning. Though I'd slept through the night, I felt far from rested. Predawn light announced the sun's approach on the eastern horizon.

As I stared out of the balcony door, a strong compulsion to be outside drove me to bathe, dress, and go for an early morning walk. The act of fully dressing without Marguerite's help made me understand why women of the time had ladies' maids. Still, it wasn't too difficult as I fastened the buttons on the back of the shirt before I pulled it on.

The hotel still slumbered; even the front desk was vacant of its stoic resident.

I took that first step outside, and the chilly mountain air stung my nostrils. But I sighed in relief as if I'd been holding my breath. Though my feet wanted to wander down the road into town, I knew I would never reach my desired destination before I was missed.

Sighing, this time in resignation, I strolled toward the stables. The walk was shorter than I remembered, and I cursed to myself for forgetting the treat I'd promised Saundra.

Unlike the last time I'd visited, the stable was bustling. Young men went about cleaning the stalls and feeding the horses. *I guess the stables' staff gets up early.* A couple of them looked over at me curiously, but no one challenged my presence.

I gazed down the row of stalls, but I didn't see Butch anywhere. I took a few steps forward and stood on my toes, trying to see if Saundra was in her stall. Pursing my lips, I decided not to get in the stable hands' ways by visiting her at the moment.

I turned to leave but stopped when I heard the deep timbre I recognized as Butch's voice coming from the tack room to my right. I couldn't hear what he was saying, but I popped in to say hello.

My head tilted in surprise when I saw the person Butch was speaking to was Harrison. As Butch rubbed oil into some leather straps, Harrison leaned his back and one foot against the wall.

I smiled to myself. *I knew Harrison and Celeste were just friends.* There was no doubt in my mind that William's jealousy was completely unfounded as I watched the Australian appreciate the sight of Butch at work.

"Good morning, guys," I called to them.

The two men stopped what they'd been doing and looked over at me.

"Good morning, Erin," Butch called with a smile at the same time Harrison said, "Celeste, what are you doing down here?"

"Wait, who's Erin?" Harrison asked.

Well, shit.

Butch's eyebrows rose, but he stayed quiet, allowing me time to explain.

"Uh...so you know I can't remember anything from before a few weeks ago... Well, they had to call me something, so I went by Erin."

"Ah," Harrison uttered in understanding.

Well, of course he believes me. I mean, it's a way more plausible explanation than: "Oh, that's my name in a future life. Yeah, sorry. I'm sort of a time-traveler."

"So you two have met then?" Harrison asked.

"Yeah, when I first came back to the hotel. I wandered down here and met Butch."

Harrison's eyes flicked to Butch, who nodded once at my recount.

"Well, in any case, I was just out for a little fresh air and stopped to say hello, so I'll let you guys get back to what you were doing."

"Are you headed back up to the hotel now?" Harrison asked.

"Yeah, probably."

"I'll walk with you then."

"Are you sure? I don't want to interrupt."

"It's fine," he assured me, looking at Butch again.

And with a locked gaze and another silent nod from the stable master, I could tell Butch and Harrison's feelings for each other were mutual.

That's nice. I'm so glad Harrison isn't mooning over someone who isn't interested. I tried to suppress my smile at their fleeting but silent exchange of affection.

We both promised to see Butch again later and left the stables together.

"I'm glad you decided to walk with me, Harrison. I wanted to talk to you."

"You did?"

"Yeah, it's clear to me we must've been friends before the accident." I watched his reaction.

He nodded slowly, frowning. "I thought we were..."

"Why do you say it like that? Did we have a fight or something?"

"I wouldn't say that."

"Then what would you say?" I pushed when he wasn't forthcoming.

"I would say we were close, and then we weren't. I could tell some-thing had upset you. But every time I asked, you told me it was nothing. And then you left. You didn't mention to me you were leaving. You were just gone. Mr. Broadstone told everyone you went to Toronto for a friend's wedding."

"That's...strange," I admitted.

He nodded his agreement.

"Well, I don't know what happened before, but I'm sorry I left without telling you."

"It's all right now. I'm glad you're home safe. Don't worry about that. Just try to get better."

"Right," I absently agreed. *Whatever happened to Celeste, it doesn't seem like Harrison knows about it. Why didn't she tell him if they were friends? Could she not trust him? Was it to protect him? Or was she just the shoulder-everything-yourself type? Now that I think about it, Marguerite also mentioned she left without a word when we first met.*

I filed my thoughts away for later. "So why was William scolding you yesterday?"

He smiled cockily as if whatever he'd done wrong had been worth it. "He wants me at my desk when I'm not leading activities even if I have no work to do."

"And you weren't at your desk when he wanted you there?"

"Well, the trail ride was canceled due to the rain."

"So what did you do instead?"

He hesitated, then smirked. "Helped Butch in the stables."

"Oh yeah? What were you helping him with?" I teased, the tone in his voice already telling me what those guys had been doing. *He must have shared his preferences with Celeste if he's so open about it with me. That can't have been easy for him knowing how society sees gays in this time period. He trusted her. At least I wasn't a homophobe in my past life.*

As he grinned like a Cheshire Cat, I couldn't help but mirror his expression.

"Oh, just some heavy lifting."

I laughed. "I'll bet."

When we entered the hotel's front door, Frederick greeted us with all the seriousness of a Buckingham guard.

I told Harrison I'd see him after breakfast and went to the kitchen.

I entered as Louis let out an angry string of exclamations, one of which I recognized as the French word for shit. Gabriel stood against the wall with his arms crossed and a pensive crinkle between his eyebrows.

"What's going on?" I asked Oscar as he chewed his lip.

"The delivery from Farrloch said the dry goods store ran out of yeast," Oscar explained.

"We don't have enough?"

"We do not."

"All right. It's okay. What did we need the yeast for?"

"Croissants," Oscar answered.

Louis spat at the word.

Ew, Dude. This is a kitchen. My mind grasped for any cooking knowledge my grandmother had tried to teach me. I'd never had the knack for it, and she'd eventually relegated me to taster and dishwasher. But one bit rose to the surface. "What about baking powder? Do we have that?" I asked.

Oscar translated, and Gabriel dashed to the pantry to see.

"Oui." He returned with the tin.

"Great. Then let's make biscuits instead of croissants."

They stared at me like they didn't quite understand.

"You know? A biscuit: flour, baking powder, salt, butter, and milk. They're stiff on the outside and soft on the inside."

Oscar translated, Gabriel smiled, and Louis clapped once and nodded. As the cooks scrambled around the kitchen, Oscar and I moved to get out of the way.

"Madame," Louis called as I pushed open the swinging door.

I paused and looked over my shoulder.

"Merci," he said, giving me two thumbs up.

I smiled and stifled a chuckle. "You're welcome."

William turned out to be too busy to sit down for breakfast. Marguerite came in, all a flurry.

"Celeste, there you are! You never called for me this morning, and you did not answer when I knocked."

Oops. "Sorry, Marguerite."

She pursed her lips. "Please call for me tomorrow."

I made no promises. "Did you ever find my journal yesterday?" I asked, changing the subject.

"Non, I am sorry. I will go into town today and get you a new one."

"Why don't we go together?" I suggested, jumping at the chance, even if it was too risky for me to actually use a journal.

She shook her head. "Monsieur has instructed me to ensure you stay close to home for the time being. You must rest properly if you want to get better."

I gritted my teeth. *An actual prisoner then.*

"But Monsieur told me you did not get to see the garden yesterday because of the rain. Would you like to walk after you meet Monsieur Harrison?" she asked brightly.

"Yeah, that's fine," I answered, not cheered.

After breakfast, I shook Marguerite off to meet Harrison.

"So what do we have planned for the guests today?" I asked him, leaning against his desk.

"The trail ride that was scheduled for yesterday is what we have in the afternoon."

"And tonight?"

"More cards."

"Okay, and tomorrow?"

"Nothing planned as of yet."

"Hmm. How about a hike? People come out here to see the mountains, right?"

He nodded. "I could guide them up the nearest peak. It's not particularly high, but it has a nice view."

"That sounds great. What about tomorrow night?"

"The ladies could get together to do needlepoint, and the men could have drinks and cigars."

"How about something really different? Have you ever hosted a bonfire?"

"No, our guests are genteel."

"Well, let's try mixing it up. We can have a fire outside. We can even sing songs. Do you know anyone who plays the guitar?"

"One of the stable lads."

"Well, invite him to come along and play if he's up for it. And if the guests don't like the change of pace, we can just go back to needlepoint and cards."

Harrison nodded. "I'll mention it to him."

"Awesome. I mean, great. Oh! Before I forget, a few of the guests mentioned wanting to have a dance. Do we do that? I know we have a ballroom."

He thought for a moment. "Sometimes we do but not often. The ballroom is usually for grand parties when we host special guests and the like."

"But it doesn't have to be a big deal, right? I mean, all we need is music and space."

"I'll look into it."

I smiled. "Thanks."

We threw around more activity ideas, but we didn't commit to anything, wanting to see how our plans went over with the guests first.

When I'd left the back office, Frederick informed me that Marguerite awaited me in the library. Upon seeing me enter, she marked her page and shelved the book she'd been reading.

"I am excited to show you the garden, Celeste. You spent so much time there. It was your favorite place at the hotel," Marguerite said as we walked through the ballroom and out the doors to the garden.

The garden was probably breathtaking when it was in full bloom. But at that time of year, it only had the gloomy death appeal found in Poe stories, not that I was opposed to that aesthetic. The even, brick paths cut the bare hedges in half, and trellises with shriveled ivy separated the paths from bony, naked trees.

All routes seemed to lead to a fountain at the center of the garden, which was empty and stagnant. At the center of the fountain was a statue of Apollo and Daphne, their marble faces twisted in despair. I frowned at the beautiful piece of art. Theirs was a story that had always saddened me. To love someone so much and have them spurn you so completely, it just made my heart ache for them.

"Monsieur had this fountain made especially for you," Marguerite told me.

I stared at Daphne, her legs and arms the roots and branches of the laurel tree. The agony expressed on Apollo's face as he reached for her was almost too real. *What an unusual gift for your new wife.*

"Why?" I couldn't stop myself from asking.

"Laurier, the laurel," she explained. "Your maiden name."

"Ah." *Well, it is a wonderfully done sculpture anyway.*

As we continued to stroll the bleak garden, the only indication that life would soon return to the sleeping plants was the birds chattering overhead. Too busy building their nests in the barren trees, they spared no attention to those below them. As I watched their labors, I hadn't noticed Marguerite had stopped to tie her boot.

I walked on without her, only halting when an older Asian man stooped on the path before me. He dug in the dirt, preparing the garden for spring.

"Oh! Excuse me. I didn't see you there," I gasped, almost tripping over him.

Looking up at me, his eyes widened, the shock clear in his face. He shot to his feet. "You...you are not supposed to be here," he hissed in a thick accent. "I thought you had left."

I pulled my head back, surprised by his reception. "Well, now I'm back?" I said, unsure.

"Aiya! You must not be here."

"What—"

"There you are," Marguerite interrupted. "I am sorry. My boot came unlaced."

The Chinese man clamped his mouth shut at her appearance.

"Oh, I see you have met Monsieur Xi, the gardener."

I dipped my head to Mr. Xi. "Yes, Mr. Xi was just telling me how surprised he was to see me."

"Oh, Monsieur. I was also surprised when I saw her in town the other day. And then I heard about the accident! I have never heard anything so sad."

"Accident?" Mr. Xi asked.

"Oui, Celeste was in an accident, and she cannot remember anything of her time with us. It is horrible, non?"

Mr. Xi's eyes softened, and his eyebrows pulled together. "I see."

"Marguerite tells me I spent a lot of time in your garden, Mr. Xi."

He nodded. "We saw each other quite often," he answered, still flustered.

"Mr. Xi, are you related to Xi Wei, who works in the laundry?" I asked.

"I am Xi Lin, father of Xi Wei."

"Oh! Xi Wei told me you worked for William on the railroad."

He bowed his head in acknowledgment.

I could tell Marguerite's presence was making Xi Lin uncomfortable. *He has something he needs to say to me alone. He said I shouldn't be here. What did he mean? What does he know? I need to come back when we can't be interrupted.*

"Well, I'm sure I'll be back very soon, Mr. Xi. I'll probably see you then. For now, let's stop interrupting his work, Marguerite."

Xi Lin bowed again and watched me walk away with his brow still furrowed.

Marguerite and I left the garden by the iron gate in the brick wall near the front entrance of the hotel. As she'd expected, Campbell waited for

Marguerite with a carriage to drive her into town. I waved to them as they pulled away and turned to go inside.

A black horse was tethered to a pole near the front door. My heart skipped a beat.

Not entirely certain what I would find, I flew into the hotel as fast as my feet could take me.

THIRTY-THREE

My heart pounded as I scanned the foyer. A flash of red between the slightly ajar library doors caught my eye, and I rushed in that direction.

Throwing the door wide, my chest ached, and I trembled at the sight of Mitica before me. I held my breath as his blue eyes found mine, his Wynn visage blurring with unbidden tears.

I'd almost started to believe I'd imagined him. I took a step toward him but stopped short when he warned me with a glance.

He's so close. My body hummed with the compulsion to touch him, and it took all my willpower to stop myself.

His usual unreadable mask gave nothing away. But I knew it was just as difficult for him as it was for me. I could feel his tension simmering below the surface.

"Constable," I started, my voice quivering. I cleared my throat. "What are you doing here?"

He held up the copy of *Dracula* we'd been reading together.

"You finished it?"

He shook his head no. "Yes, and I wanted to get a different book."

His sweet baritone was like soft kisses against naked skin. I stepped closer to him, taking the book from his grasp.

"And I wanted to check in to see how you were adjusting," he said at a normal volume. "And I miss you," he added in a barely audible whisper.

"I'm doing fine. I've been busy learning my duties here at the hotel," I answered. "I miss you, too," I added, hushed.

"You haven't called for me," he murmured.

I made a small, sad noise. "I didn't know if I should."

He closed his eyes and breathed a sigh of relief as though he'd been worried about it.

"Can I? I wanted to."

"Of course, you can. I said you could."

"But when? How will I know when Oli isn't around?"

"10 o'clock. He's usually asleep by then."

"Tonight?" I whispered, anticipation welling inside me.

"No, not tonight."

My stomach dropped in disappointment.

"I'm going to Chuthekii to see about his vision tonight."

"Oh," I breathed.

"Tomorrow," he promised

I swallowed around a lump in my throat. "Tomorrow," I agreed.

Hesitantly, I reached for his hand. But just before we touched, William burst into the library. My heart screamed.

"My dear, I hear we have a visitor."

"Thank you for the suggestion, Mrs. Broadstone. I think I will read this one next." Wynn grabbed the book nearest where my outstretched hand had frozen.

"Wonderful. I think it will be just what you're looking for."

The book he'd picked up turned out to be a collection of Greek tragedies. *Oh jeez.*

"I'm glad to hear you are settling in here, Mrs. Broadstone. I'm certain I will see you again."

"Thank you for checking on me, Constable. I do hope you enjoy the book."

"I'm sure I will. Have a good day."

"Goodbye." I waved to Mitica cheerfully as everything within me protested. *Follow him you fool. Being apart is not worth it.*

Still, I stood unmoving as William approached me. "Constable Delaforet came to see how you are faring?" he asked.

"His primary purpose was to return a book he borrowed. But, yes, he asked me how I was."

"He's a very dutiful young man."

"I suppose he is."

Too shaken by Mitica's surprise visit to withstand William's gaze, I excused myself to check on the kitchen staff. I paused in the deserted dining room and took a steadying breath.

This whole situation is so messed up.

I felt my resolve start to fray at the edges. It wasn't as if I needed to be with Mitica every moment of every day. It was more the uncertainty. At times like this, if there ever had been times like this in the history of humanity, my instinct was to keep my loved ones close. My heart said clinging to one another was the only way to survive the storm raging around us, but my heart wasn't in control. My head was. And my head thought this reaction was downright foolish.

You're both fine. Separation sucks, but it's nothing so dramatic. You've got good leads so far into cracking the mystery of Celeste. Concentrate on that, and see Mitica when you can.

Not feeling any better, I went to check on Louis, Gabriel, and Oscar. As the cooks had everything under control, I helped Oscar set up for lunch.

This time around, I dined with Colonel Higgins and Reginald. They seemed honored by my request to sit with them.

After Oscar had placed our plates before us, I asked, "So how long have you two known each other?"

"It has been nearly five and twenty years. Wouldn't you say, Higgins?"

"Good God, that long?" Colonel Higgins responded. "Yes, I suppose it has."

"How did you meet?"

"I was stationed in Africa at the time," Colonel Higgins started as if settling in for a long story. "I joined the British army at just seventeen, you know. For Queen and country, and all that. Of course, I couldn't foresee that I would be sent straight to Grey in Waikato. What a business that was—"

"Higgins, she asked how we met not for your life story," Reginald interrupted.

Colonel Higgins blinked at us as if he'd lost his train of thought.

Reginald continued. "I was a spice trader, you see. Cloves and what have you. I was in Zanzibar. This was before the war, mind you. The crown was still trying to curb the slave trade there. Terrible business that."

"Terrible business, indeed," Colonel Higgins agreed.

"In any case, I came upon a slave auction and saw a trader beating a young negro boy. Well, I couldn't stomach the sight, so I stepped in."

"Wait a moment, Reginald. I was the one who stepped in," Colonel Higgins argued.

"No, no, old boy. I stopped the boy from being beaten to death. And when the traders detained me, you knocked one fellow on the head."

Colonel Higgins stilled, thinking, then chuckled. "Quite right. Quite right. You were in a predicament when I came upon those men dragging you off to do God knows what."

"Indeed, I was. Quite the predicament."

"So Colonel Higgins hit one of them on the head. Then what?" I asked, urging them back on topic.

"Well, we ran like mad, that's what." Reginald laughed.

"Outnumbered us they did. We were lucky to make it out alive," Colonel Higgins added

"Indeed. Well, we have been together ever since."

"And what about the slaves? Institutionalized slavery isn't still happening in Zanzibar is it?"

"Indeed not, her majesty would never allow such a barbaric institution to continue in her empire," Colonel Higgins answered.

"Here here! Long live the Queen," Reginald cheered.

"Long live the Queen!" the rest of the room answered.

I didn't quite know how to respond to their outburst, especially since I knew Queen Victoria wasn't going to be alive much longer. While I was certainly glad slavery had been outlawed, I also knew all the horrors British imperialism had inflicted on the world. *I mean, India hasn't even gotten their independence yet though I suppose Gandhi is still alive at the moment.*

The magnitude of the thought hit me

Holy crap! Gandhi is alive right now.

A man whose teachings I had so admired, the words and actions he embodied helped me cope with my father's murder. To think I was drawing breath at the same time as he was surreal. I knew the man wasn't perfect, far from it in fact. But that imperfection, that struggle to be better, to free his people, to bring peace—it was inspirational.

As I ate lunch with the two old Brits, reminiscing about their adventures, I remembered a quote from Bapu: "Live as if you were to die tomorrow. Learn as if you were to live forever."

Carpe diem, a concept with which I'd always struggled. The balance between planning for the future and living in the present is not easily achieved.

After lunch, I wanted to talk to Xi Lin. It seemed like he knew something about why Celeste had left. Unfortunately, I had to work the front desk.

Not long after I stood at Frederick's post, three men descended the stairs, leaving for their daily hunt. Colonel Higgins and Reginald tipped their hats to me as they passed on the way out the front door. I smiled at them, though a little sick to my stomach at what they were going out to do.

Stewart stopped by the front desk, seemingly waiting for Cole to arrive.

"How are you this afternoon, Celeste?" Stewart asked, leaning on my counter.

"I'm fine. Thank you, Mr. Thomas," I replied coldly.

He smiled seductively as if I'd given him some encouragement.

"I must say I was rather surprised to discover you're married to Mr. Broadstone."

I didn't respond.

"Tell me, Celeste," he started, lowering his voice to little more than a whisper. "You aren't satisfied by that old fossil, are you? He's likely as old as your father. Surely, a man with more stamina would meet your youthful needs much more adequately."

Eck. I don't want to think about either of them in bed. I met Stewart's eyes seriously. "I assure you, Mr. Thomas. My needs are adequately met."

He smirked. "Perhaps, you'd like them surpassed then?"

I guess history has no shortage of men who don't understand refusal. As

I opened my mouth to snub him again, Cole descended the stairs to join him.

Stewart smiled lazily at me again and whispered, "We aren't leaving for quite a while. Consider my offer until then."

Great. Just how long am I going to be stuck with him?

Needless to say, I was relieved when Stewart and Cole left me in peace.

After hosting tea, it was early evening before I was able to get any free time.

I scoured the garden for any sign of Xi Lin, but it was deserted. Just as I turned around to go back inside, Xi Wei pushed a wheelbarrow of fertilizer down the path toward me.

"Xi Wei," I called to him, and his head snapped up at my voice.

His eyes widened, and he gently set down the wheelbarrow. Then he bowed to me, and I bowed back.

Approaching him, I told him I was looking for his father and asked if he knew where he was.

He lowered his dark eyes apologetically. "My father is resting now. Something has upset him."

"Oh, no. I'm sorry to hear that. Is that why you're helping him?"

He nodded. "I sometimes help my father when my work is complete."

I smiled. "That's nice of you. Do you think he'll feel better tomorrow? I'd like to speak to him when he's free."

"I am certain he will insist upon working if the weather permits. It is an important time for the plants."

"Right. Well, hey, I wanted to talk to you about something too when you have time."

"With me?"

"Yes, you're in charge of running the laundry, right?"

He nodded. "How can I help you?"

"Well, I noticed that the working conditions in the laundry are pretty awful. It's so hot down there. I want to try and help make it better for you guys, but I need you to explain your process before I can do anything."

He gave me that pop idol smile. "I will take this first, and then I will show you."

"No problem. That's fine."

He pushed the wheelbarrow out of the path to where it wouldn't be in anyone's way, and then we walked back to the hotel. On the way, he told me how they wash linens in the tubs I'd seen in the basement.

"Okay, and then what? How do you dry them?"

"We take them to the attic."

"What? Why would you do that?"

A doorway in one corner of the basement led to a back staircase. The plain white walls and creaky, wooden stairs looked like they belonged to an entirely different hotel. By the time we'd reached the attic, I was winded. Xi Wei seemed used to the climb.

The long attic had clotheslines strung from end-to-end with sheets and towels hung on them. Three fans in the roof spun overhead, propelled by the heat from the drying linens.

"Why don't you just hang them outside?" I asked.

"Mr. Broadstone does not want the guests to see them."

God forbid.

"And they would freeze in winter."

Yeah, I probably should've thought of that. "Hmm," I acknowledged. "I see the predicament. Let me see what I can do, okay?"

He bowed in appreciation.

I brought up the matter with William over dinner.

"Isn't there something we could do for the men in the laundry? I mean, it's awful down there, and then they have to walk up all those stairs."

William looked unconcerned. "What would you suggest, my dear?"

"There has to be a way to ventilate the basement better. What if we added an outside cellar door? Then they could leave it open while they are down there. At least they'd have some fresh air."

He crinkled his brow in consideration but didn't say anything.

"And I think we should have an area outside where they can hang the linens. Maybe the cellar door could lead to a patio. If you're worried about the guests seeing, just add a cover and maybe lattices on the sides. Then air could get in. I know we don't want the linens to freeze in the winter. Why not install an elevator so they don't have to climb all those stairs with arms full of wet sheets?"

"That all sounds rather expensive, my dear," he explained as if to a child.

I bit my lip. "Well, at the very least, digging a cellar door shouldn't be that difficult, right? And the patio is even easier."

He watched me from across the table. Finally, he said, "You are quite adamant about this."

"Well, as employers, it's our responsibility to take care of those who work for us."

"Those men would never even think to ask for this. They are happy just to be employed. There aren't many opportunities for the Chinese."

"Whether they're Chinese or not makes no difference," I declared. "They're people."

His eyebrows rose a little, his expression somewhere between curiosity and amusement. "Very well, my dear. I will make inquiries and consider it if it pleases you."

You should do it because it's right not because it pleases me, but I'll take it. I smiled in triumph. "Awesome. Thanks, William."

As curious as he'd looked by my pushing, he seemed even more so by my happy gratitude.

Perhaps Celeste would've handled things differently.

The after-dinner entertainment was much the same as it had been the night before, except I made sure to play this time. As expected, Mary and Juniper wanted to group with Stewart and Cole.

As I watched the young women heading toward the two men, I impulsively stepped in before them.

"Mr. Thomas, Mr. Linton, could I join you this time?"

The men were delighted, Stewart especially. I ignored the knot in my stomach for Mary's sake.

That night, we were playing conquinn, which I was glad to discover was similar to rummy.

"I hope you guys will help me," I said, sitting between Stewart and Cole with a shiver of unease. "I've never played this game before."

Keeping their attention on me was exhausting. Mary was not pleased. But it's not as if having Stewart's eyes on me was fun for me either. Unfortunately, the younger woman could not appreciate I was trying to keep her off the predator's radar. She did all she could to get Stewart's attention back to her.

I was just glad I didn't have to do anything overt. A smile and a little praise, and the man's slimy gaze always returned to me.

It seemed Stewart preferred experience to innocence, or perhaps it was because I'd rejected him before. *Maybe he likes a challenge. Ugh. Why am I even doing this? She's a grown woman. She can make decisions for herself.*

But as I glanced over at Mary's pouting face, I knew she was too naive. *She doesn't know. Maybe she thinks the attention he's giving her is special. She can't tell that he would seduce her, destroy her prospects with John the Englishman, and leave her flat to pursue someone else.*

He doesn't care if a woman has someone already. In fact, he seems to enjoy it more when that's the case. Maybe I should talk to her. If I can make her understand, then I don't need to call attention to myself.

THIRTY-FOUR

While I was relieved to retire to my room for the night, I was having a difficult time sitting still. I stood at the balcony door and stared out into the cold night, watching the skies for a hultan riding a zmeu.

My vigilance was not rewarded, and I eventually lit my candle to try to calm my mind. The bright, steady flame burned away my restlessness over Mitica's meeting with Chuthekii.

As my vision unfocused, my eyelids became heavy. "Tomorrow," I whispered to the flame before blowing it out and going to bed.

The following day was as busy as the days prior. I pretended to guide Louis and Gabriel with breakfast and lunch, met with Harrison to plan the evening's bonfire, worked the front desk, and hosted tea.

The guests seemed intrigued by the idea of sitting around a fire outside.

I finally got my chance to talk to Mary after trying to find an opening all morning as the dining room emptied after tea. The women were going hiking with Harrison and wanted to change into more appropriate clothes. Mary told her mother and friends she would catch up after finishing her cup of tea.

I stayed behind and waited for everyone else to be out of hearing range. "Mary," I started.

She looked up politely.

"Mary, I wonder if I could talk to you as one woman to another."

"Of course, Mrs. Broadstone. But whatever could this be about?"

"Mary...why do you suppose your mother is so protective of you?"

Her eyebrows scrunched together. "To protect me from things she feels might harm me, I'd say."

"Right. So I'm sure she's talked with you about being careful around men. Hasn't she?"

Her tone turned guarded. "She has. Though I suppose most mothers are overly concerned with their daughters' virtue and virginity."

Eh, not necessarily. "This isn't really about virtue or virginity. I couldn't care less about that."

Her eyebrows rose at my assertion.

"Look, I can't really put this delicately. There are men out there like your fiancé John, who want committed relationships. I mean, he wants to share a lifetime with you, or he wouldn't have asked you to marry him. He loves you, right?"

"Yes..." she answered cautiously.

"Yeah so, then there are men like Stewart Thomas. They aren't really interested in committed relationships, which is fine if you know what you're getting into. All I'm saying is: I know the type of person Stewart is. He'll say and do anything to get a woman in his bed. He doesn't care if she's about to marry someone else or if she's already married for that matter. He'll take from her what he wants and leave her when he's done."

As I told her how it was, her face grew more and more red, and her pretty blue eyes squinted at me.

"Mrs. Broadstone, I don't know why you feel it's necessary to slander Mr. Thomas, but I don't want to hear any more. Mr. Thomas has been nothing but kind and gentlemanly toward me since the moment we met."

"It's not slander if it's true, Mary. Look, he—"

"No, I don't want to listen to any more." She cut me off and stood from the table. "My relationship with John, or any other man, is none of your concern, Mrs. Broadstone. I will not mention this to Mr. Thomas as I'm certain it would humiliate him to know you think so low of him, but I trust you will avoid such topics of discussion in the future. Good day."

My mouth hung open as she strode furiously from the room. *Well, that could've gone better.* I sighed at my failed attempt to guide the younger woman. *If that's the way she wants it, then fine. I have so many other things to worry about. I can only hope she heeds my warning before she fucks up her life.*

I thought I'd have time to talk with Xi Lin after tea, but Harrison needed help since he was leading the afternoon hike. First, I had to choose a place for the fire. I decided behind the hotel would be fine. Some stable hands helped me collect wood and build a small fire ring with stones. A few of the cleaning staff brought wooden chairs from inside for everyone to sit on.

As I helped arrange the chairs around the fire ring, Harrison returned and drew my attention to a young man, no older than seventeen, with black, wavy hair; big, dark eyes; and rich, brown skin.

"Celeste, this is Diego. He's the fellow I spoke of who plays the guitar."

I smiled at Diego, who dipped his head self-consciously. "Señora," he greeted.

"Hola, Diego. You must be pretty good if Harrison says you can play." *I have no idea if that's true, but I'd like to believe Harrison wouldn't set him up to embarrass himself.*

Diego smiled at the compliment but seemed too shy to meet my eyes.

"We're going to have a bonfire tonight. Would you play for us, Diego, por favor?"

"Sí, Señora, con gusto."

"Fantastico! Gracias." *I guess those Spanish classes Mom forced on me came in handy after all. I'm glad I continued into college and kept practicing.*

Harrison dismissed the youth to go about his business.

At dinner, I instructed the guests to dress warmly and comfortably for the evening's activities. As Marguerite helped me change for the event, I stared longingly at my jeans, knowing it would be considered inappropriate. I sighed and allowed Marguerite to choose for me. *At least she didn't get rid of them and only had them cleaned.*

As I stepped into the cool, April night, I instinctively looked up at the waning crescent moon, hanging among an expanse of stars. I strolled through the darkness toward the bright glow of the fire. The heat warmed me as I took a seat between Marguerite and Diego.

Surrounded by mountains and watched over by the distant stars, the only sound was the soft crackling of the fire. I closed my eyes, half believing Mitica would be sitting near me when I opened them. But the mist of memory dissipated when Diego started to play a soft melody on his guitar.

A few bars in, his tender voice sang a song of sorrow as if he couldn't help but call out once he'd started playing. I smiled as I recognized the poem from a college assignment, where we had to translate a poem while trying to keep its rhythm and rhyme. I didn't know if anyone else spoke Spanish. When he finished, I asked him to play it again so I could translate. Nodding, he started over. With every line, he played the melody twice. He'd sing it first in Spanish, and then I'd sing it in English.

"The moon hung orange and low, hardly in the sky.
The candles burned in the square and where the dead do lie.
The wind, so warm in the day, held October's chill,
But Camila still came singing—
Singing—singing—
Camila still came singing, to the headstone on the hill.

"Her hair was the feathers of a raven, black as the darkest jet.
Her eyes were deep and brown, the brightest he'd ever met.
Her skirt was blood-red satin. It scarcely touched the ground.
And as she walked it fluttered—
Fluttered—fluttered—
As she walked it fluttered, but never made a sound.

"Up the hill, she climbed to visit her family there.
Her grandparents, long gone, for her, they showed such care.
His parents rest beside them upon the cliff so steep.
He watched her approach, staring—
Staring—staring—

He watched her approach, staring, Camila of beauty deep.

"She met his gaze with a smile. She'd seen him once before.
At the market in town, how he'd made her heart soar.
He had not seen her looking at him that summer day.
But he watched her now, dazzled—
Dazzled—dazzled.
He watched her now, dazzled. He could not turn away.

"'Alejandro is my name,' he said with a little bow.
'I know,' she told him truly. He did not ask her how.
She held her hand out to him. He took it in his own.
And kissing her palm gently—
Gently—gently—
Kissing her palm gently, his passion for her shone.

"That night they made a promise to meet again and soon,
At the bustling market by the fountain at noon.
Parting ways for the moment, they waited for the time,
And spent their long nights dreaming—
Dreaming—dreaming—
They spent their long nights dreaming for the clock bell to chime.

"They met throughout the autumn. They met in winter's cold.
They met with spring flowers in their hair and when the corn
    turned gold.
Then one fine day in August, under a willow tree,
Alejandro asked her to marry—
Marry—marry—
Alejandro asked her to marry. Camila did agree.

"The young man went to her father and told him how they felt.
He begged him for his daughter, upon his knees he knelt.
But Camila's father refused. She'd been promised to his friend.
He spurned Alejandro, beating—
Beating—beating—

He spurned Alejandro, beating. Camila's heart did rend.

"She would not marry another. She would not forsake her love.
She sent word to Alejandro, swearing by the stars above.
She'd meet him on the clifftop, where their families did rest,
And they'd run away together—
Together—together—
They'd run away together, run away to the west.

"Under the new moon sky, the stars the only light,
Alejandro waited for his love on the appointed night.
He held his breath to listen, but who should come instead?
Her father he came, yelling—
Yelling—yelling—
Her father he came, yelling. Camila, she was dead.

"He scarce could hear the tale over his pounding heart.
How Camila killed herself when her father kept them apart.
He tore at his chest in agony, hoping to stop the pain.
Then leapt from the clifftop, falling—
Falling—falling—
He leapt from the clifftop, falling, and as his love was slain.

"Every autumn night, when the moon hangs low in the sky,
When the candles burn in the square and where the dead do lie,
When the wind, so warm in the day, holds October's chill,
Camila still comes singing—
Singing—singing—
Camila still comes singing to her love's headstone on the hill."

The juxtaposition of language and pitch lightened my heart in a way only music could, but it also ached for the lovers' tragic fate.

Diego and I smiled at each other as those gathered clapped for us.

"Canta hermosa, Señora."

"Usted también, Diego."

The rest of the event would have been rather pleasant if I hadn't been anxious to go to my room.

Diego played more songs, Colonel Higgins and Reginald told stories, and the time until I could leave felt eons away. But eventually, the fire burned low. And though a few decided to stay and build it up again, it was safe for me to excuse myself.

I kept my footsteps slow and steady as I climbed the stairs, but my heart raced ahead.

After closing and locking the door behind me, I strode to the bedroom with purpose. My hands shook, and my uneven breathing was loud in my ears. I wasn't quite sure how this was supposed to work.

I planted my feet and thought of Mitica: his crimson hair, his blue eyes, his baritone song, his woodsy scent, the warmth of his skin on mine, his taste... "Dumitru," I whispered, my hushed, trembling voice expressing all of my heart's longing.

The empty room blurred as my eyes lost focus. I blinked to clear my vision, and Mitica stood before me. Smiling softly, his eyes shone with love and adoration.

I rushed to him and buried my face in his chest, breathing deep his scent as he pressed me to him.

"I am here, bucuria mea," he reassured. I looked up into his eyes. "We have much to discuss," he said.

"Later," I promised, pulling his lips down to mine.

His warmth spread through me as though he was breathing life into me. He needed little urging, sliding his hands up my back and kissing me deeply.

"Stay with me tonight," I gasped, breaking our kiss to plead with him.

His gaze, heavy with lust, answered before he purred, "Da," in a low, husky voice.

"I'm yours, Mitica. Love me so thoroughly that it hurts when I'm not with you," I begged, trailing my trembling fingertips along his cheek.

"Da," he murmured again, turning his head to kiss my palm.

He lifted me off my feet, folding me over one shoulder.

I yelped, surprised by his forcefulness. I didn't really mind the blood rushing to my head as I smiled at his backside. I prepared to be flung onto the bed. Instead, Mitica set me down with care.

He kissed me deeply; his hot tongue teased mine, causing heat to pool in my core. As he pulled back, a sweet fog disoriented all thought. I trembled as I panted.

His shadowy blue eyes met mine as he hovered over me. "This is not a night you will forget."

I shivered, knowing he would deliver. "Good."

I spent the next few hours covering my mouth to stifle my moans so no one would hear. His lovemaking was slow and thorough, savoring each caress, each stroke, each quiver, each kiss.

He seemed more desperate than before as if every heavy breath would be our last. He was intense and imposing; he demanded all of my attention. There were no problems, no worries, just Mitica and me and his hot breath in my ear, proving to me he was solid and real.

Completely undone, I nestled in Mitica's arms, my eyes growing heavy with satisfaction.

"Bucuria mea," he whispered, caressing my face as we lay on our sides.

"Hmm?" I asked.

"You cannot fall asleep yet."

"But it feels so warm and comfortable," I mumbled.

"I know, but I need to talk to you," he urged, kissing my eyelids.

"Okay. Tell me," I said, my eyes still closed.

"It's about Chuthekii's vision."

I sniffed hard, my eyes flying open. I sat up and smacked my cheeks, ensuring I was fully awake. Then I looked over at him. "Okay. What did he say? Did he figure it out?"

He nodded. "He thinks it was the ceremonial tea that was poisoned. Remember when Likinoak mentioned that a special tea was part of the ceremony?"

I thought back to my first meeting with the Wyboka elder. "Vaguely. So what do we do next?"

"I have sent Oliver to Edmonton with a sample of the tea for the chemists."

I nodded. "It may take them a few weeks to test it."

"Da."

"And until then?"

"We try to discover who had the opportunity and motive to poison the tea. We don't have the evidence to prove the tea was poisoned yet. But Chuthekii is confident, and he has rarely been wrong before."

"What can I do to help?"

He frowned severely. "Just think about everything you have observed so far, and try to stay out of trouble. I cannot protect you as easily as when you were staying with me."

"Are you telling me to be quiet and keep my head down right now?" I asked, lifting one eyebrow.

He smirked at my tone. "Would you listen if I were?"

I pursed my lips. "Being quiet isn't something I'm terribly good at."

He pulled me on top of him. "Then we shall have to keep that busy mouth of yours occupied."

I smiled against his lips as he kissed me.

"Still sleepy?" he inquired as I readjusted my weight to a more comfortable position atop him.

"What do you think?" I asked, trailing my hand down his body and slipping it between us to wrap my fingers around his stiff manhood. He shuddered beneath me, and I grinned.

"What do you say, Mitica? Do you still have it in you?" I let him slip through my fingers with a flick of my wrist.

He hissed with pleasure. "Do you doubt me, bucuria mea?"

The hot flesh of his ready cock slid in my hand as I continued to stroke him. He panted, his solid chest rising and lowering beneath me.

"Then show me what you're made of," I challenged.

Rolling me to my back, Mitica released himself from my grasp. "I do not think you are ready for what I am truly capable of," he taunted.

"Try me."

He smirked, amusement dancing in his eyes. "If you insist."

He pulled me to my feet until we were both standing naked in the center of the bedroom. "Close your eyes," he instructed.

I did as I was bid, and he began to sing so softly I could barely hear. I felt him knock in my mind, and I let him in.

"All right. Open them," he whispered, his breath a warm summer breeze on my face.

I gasped at the sight before me. We stood in a moonlit corridor.

Pointed archways on one side led to an open courtyard. A fountain tinkled, its water sparkling in the moonlight.

I glanced down, running my fingertips lightly over the long, white chemise I was wearing. Mitica wore tight, black pants and a tunic-like jacket with a Mandarin collar and embroidered sleeves over his bare back. Neither of us had shoes on.

"Will you dance with me, bucuria mea?" he asked, his blue eyes dark in the dim light.

"I'm not that great without practice," I admitted.

"Just follow me," he suggested, clasping my hand and wrapping one arm around me.

I gave myself over to his care, and he started a slow but simple waltz. We twirled down the corridor, moonbeams illuminating our path. Our gentle motion ruffled our hair and the edges of my nightgown. Mitica held me firmly in his grasp, and his hand on my back burned me through the thin fabric.

When we'd reached the end, we stood before a full-length mirror. Mitica had remembered every detail of my modern-day appearance and had magically rendered me thus in the illusion. He grasped my hips and pressed his chest to my back as our eyes met in the silvery surface of the mirror.

With eyes still locked, he turned his head and pressed a fleeting kiss to my cheek. Then he trailed kisses down my neck, each more insistent than the last. Watching his progress and my own expression in the mirror made heat rise to my face.

"Eşti frumoasa, bucuria mea," he told my blushing reflection. "You are beautiful," he translated, though I hadn't asked.

His gentle fingers slowly pushed the chemise's neck from one of my shoulders. My own gasp sounded loud in my ears as his mouth replaced the fabric, bit-by-bit. He repeated the gesture on the other shoulder. The smooth fabric sliding from my skin felt so realistic; I wondered how he was accomplishing it. He tugged the chemise, and it fell to the ground. I shivered more from his fervent gaze than the air on my skin.

As I stood naked before the mirror, he trailed one hand up my side to my breast. His palm was hot as he cupped it, and the pads of his fingers were rough on the sensitive skin of my nipple. I trembled, an electric tingle racing through me. Enthralled by the eroticism created by touch and sight, watching him touch me in the mirror, seeing my lips part with that glazed look in my eyes, I couldn't have looked away if I wanted to.

I leaned against him, his arms supporting me as his chest burned my back and his manhood dug into me.

Mitica grinned, a mischievous twinkle in his eyes, as he pressed a soft kiss to where my neck met my shoulder. I quivered as he hit the sensitive spot and the hair on my neck and arms stood up. His teeth bit into the soft flesh, and my moan echoed off the stone walls of the corridor. I squirmed against him.

"Mitica," I whimpered, my voice a breathy sigh as I begged for him.

He moved us forward, pressing my naked skin against the cool glass of the mirror. I watched his reflection, his features slack with lust, and a cry, low and guttural, like the grunt of a feral animal, ripped through my throat when his hard cock slid deep into my ready core from behind.

My fingerprints smeared the silvery glass of the moonlit mirror as I held myself steady so he could enter me again and again.

We didn't take long. The moon, the mirror, our screams of satisfaction echoing off the stone walls of the corridor—and him and me, our faces clouded with desire, we never looked away from each other. I was captivated by our reflections, sleek with sweat, while Mitica thrust into me. Just as my limbs shook and shuddered with climax, I felt him pump inside me.

When Mitica's illusion had dissolved, I found myself leaning against the glass of the balcony door.

"How did you do that? I even felt the chemise against my skin," I asked as I turned around to face him.

He smiled, his eyes laughing. "Magic," he answered.

I clicked my tongue in pretend exasperation and rolled my eyes. "You don't say."

After we'd climbed back into bed, we snuggled closer and finally went to sleep.

THIRTY-FIVE

I awoke with a start the following morning to a loud knock on my suite door. Gasping, I sat up and looked over at Mitica, my heart racing in panic.

He watched me with an amused smirk.

"That's probably Marguerite. We slept too late," I whispered urgently.

"I think we earned our rest," he countered in an easy tone.

The knock sounded again, even louder, and I was relieved when I remembered I'd taken the spare key from her.

"Be right there," I called to the other room. "What are we going to do?" I asked Mitica.

He sat up in bed and kissed me sweetly on the mouth.

"Stop that. I'm serious. How are you going to get out of here?"

"You will call for me tonight, da?" he asked.

"I'm more worried about right now."

He forced his gaze on mine and stroked my cheek with his fingertips. "When will I see you next?" he murmured, more to himself than me.

"Yes, yes, I'll call for you. Now, what do we do?"

He smiled. "You summoned me, bucuria mea. Only you can send me away."

My heart jumped as the knocking pounded again. "I said hold on!" I snapped. "What do I have to do?" I asked him.

"You must say my true name and tell me to be gone."

I sighed, not really wanting him to leave. "You should probably put your clothes on first."

Mitica and I both dressed, then I hugged him tightly. I looked up into his eyes and murmured, "I love you."

"Te iubesc, bucuria mea."

I did not look away from him but took a deep breath. "Dumitru, be gone."

As my vision blurred, his solid weight in my arms evaporated. When the room came back into focus, he was no longer there.

I sighed again and fought the burning in my nose as I walked to the door.

Marguerite waited impatiently in the hall. "Celeste, are you unwell? What took you so long to answer?"

"I'm fine. I just didn't get a lot of sleep is all."

She examined my face and nodded. "It appears not."

Great. I must look awful... Eh, worth it.

I rushed to get ready for the day, and I couldn't escape Marguerite's fussing since she was there before I was dressed. I did manage to take a bath in private though, which was good because there were dried fluids all over me. *At least Mitica's bite didn't leave a mark.*

I was disappointed to see it was raining again when I entered the dining room. I hoped it would be short-lived enough that I could meet Xi Lin later. The kitchen staff had everything in order, and William found time to eat breakfast with me, though I wished he hadn't. He suggested we dine alone together again that night, but I managed to fend him off.

After breakfast, we walked to the office behind the front desk. I was to meet Harrison as per usual, and William had work to do in his office.

I stopped short when I saw a man I didn't recognize sitting at the desk next to Harrison's. He was an average-sized man in a worn suit, the top-two buttons of his shirt undone as if he wore the outfit out of some contemptible requirement. He had dark, hat-mussed hair and black eyes. When I met his cold stare, I froze, my stomach dropping as I shuddered.

"Hickory, you're back," William said to the man.

The stranger nodded, the tip of his cigarette glowing, but his gaze never left mine.

"Come into my office. We have matters to discuss," William ordered, leading the way.

I held my breath until they were gone.

The angry timbre of William's voice sounded through the door, though I couldn't hear what he was saying.

"Harrison, who is that?" I asked, hushed, as I leaned over Harrison's desk.

He glanced over his shoulder at the door to William's office. "That's Winston Hickory, Mr. Broadstone's man," he whispered.

"His man? What is that? Like his personal assistant?"

He nodded. "Like Marguerite is to you."

I snorted. *Maybe if she actually worked for me and not William.* "So what? He just does odd jobs for William then?"

"More or less."

"Tell me, did this guy and I get along before?"

Harrison shrugged. "You never paid him much mind until recently."

I scrunched my eyebrows. "Around the same time you said I started to act distant?"

He thought for a moment. "I suppose it was around that same time, yes."

I pursed my lips in thought.

A loud thud from William's office, like the sound of a chair falling over, made me jump. A few moments later, Hickory exited. I averted my gaze when his hate-filled glare met mine, but not before I saw his tongue, darkened with blood, suck his teeth.

I didn't unclench until he'd left the room.

During our meeting, Harrison told me the guests enjoyed the bonfire, and we decided to continue to have one every week.

We chose to have the craft circle and drinks and cigars for that evening's entertainment since we didn't know how long it would rain.

It ended up raining for the rest of the day. I was frustrated about not getting a chance to talk with Xi Lin. I even thought about asking Xi Wei to show me where they lived but decided against it. The rain wouldn't last forever.

I'd never felt so uncomfortable working the front desk. I could hear Mary, Sarah, and Juniper giggling in the library from the other side of the foyer, but their youthful joy didn't warm me. A shiver shook my shoulders, and I peeked behind me. Hickory's black eyes glared at my back from his and Harrison's office. Facing forward, I tried to control the anxious humming of my limbs as I counted the moments until Frederick's return.

After Hickory's meeting with William, I saw him quite a bit throughout the day. I wouldn't say he watched me so much as he hovered. He just seemed to pass me a lot on his way to do whatever William had instructed him to do. He never talked to me, but I could always feel when his cold gaze was on me.

I sagged in relief once I went to my room for my afternoon break. I'd decided I should write to Suzette. I hadn't talked to her in way too long, and I had never even gotten a chance to tell her about Mitica and me. *Oli has probably told her I've left town though.*

I sighed and sat down at the small table near the window to write the letter. I took a sheet of paper and a fountain pen from the stationary box in front of me.

Dear Suzette,

I can't tell you how sorry I am I didn't say goodbye to you before I left. I was even more surprised than you when I was called away so suddenly. I hope you can forgive me.

I miss you and the life I had in Farrloch.

Did Oli tell you? I did end up choosing from the men I told you about. My choice was none other than Constable Wynn Delaforet. Surprise! Don't be angry with Oli if he didn't say anything. I asked him not to because I wanted to tell you myself.

Of course, our romance was rather short-lived since I had to leave. But, as you said, who knows what the future will bring?

You and Oli will watch over him for me while I'm away. Won't you?

I promise to write to you again, and I hope we will see each other as well.

I'm sending this letter through Wynn. Should you want to reply, he will know where to send it.

I wish you all the happiness in the world.

Your true friend,
Erin

I searched the stationary box for a stick of wax and a seal. I found what I wanted and pulled the little, wooden drawer out. Reaching for the seal, my fingers closed around something unexpected. I squinted at a pair of rings, examining them closely. One had a sizable sapphire encircled with diamonds and the other was a plain silver band.

I froze. *Wedding rings? Are these Celeste's wedding rings? But why would they be in here? I mean, they should be in her jewelry box. Or better yet, they should have been on her when she died.*

When I called on Mitica that night, I told him about all the strange things that had happened since I'd come to the hotel. He listened attentively.

"I really think Xi Lin might be the key. He seems to know something."

Mitica nodded, deep in thought. Finally, he met my eyes. "I want you to be cautious about all this. There may be more going on than we previously thought. Your safety is more important than solving this mystery."

I pursed my lips but didn't answer.

"Do you hear me, bucuria mea? It should not be long now until I hear from the Zgrimties. Find out what you can, but do not put yourself at risk."

"I hear you," I told him.

It rained for the next two days. I went about my indoor duties and was unhappy to find Hickory around every corner. His presence in the hotel was like walking through an unseen spider web. It was unexpected, distressing, and made me want to wash my entire body just to make sure it was gone.

After Saturday morning breakfast, Dr. Hollander came to visit me as promised.

"How are you feeling, Mrs. Broadstone?" he asked after checking my pulse.

"I feel fine, Doctor."

"Still haven't remembered anything?" His voice was tinged with concern, but his brow was unfurrowed.

I shook my head. "Nothing. I've been going about my regular duties every day. I even read letters from my family and friends in Toronto. But I still don't remember anything."

He nodded slowly. "Well, I wouldn't worry just yet. We mustn't live too much in the past anyway. It's important for you to concentrate on living your life. Your memories could return at any time, in pieces or in a rush."

"Thank you, Doctor."

That afternoon, I finally got the chance to look for Xi Lin. He was taking advantage of the sunshine by spreading fertilizer in what I assumed would be flowerbeds.

Though I'd made sure Marguerite and Hickory hadn't followed me, I called to Xi Lin softly. "Xi Lin, I've been wanting to talk with you. Do you have time?"

He looked around nervously, then nodded. "My son told me you were looking for me the other day."

I nodded. "It's about what you said to me that day. You stopped before you were finished. Didn't you?"

He gazed into my eyes as if looking for something, but he didn't seem to find it. "You truly do not remember?"

"I really don't."

He paused for a while, and I held my breath in anticipation.

"You left this place because you felt you were in great danger," he whispered.

"What sort of danger?"

He shook his head. "That, I do not know. One night, I came to the garden, looking for a glove I had misplaced. You were here, alone and crying. I asked you if I could help. You told me Mr. Broadstone was not the man you had thought he was and that you were afraid."

"Did I tell you why I said that about William?"

He shook his head again. "You told me it was too dangerous for me to know. I said I wanted to help, and we made a plan. I purchased a railroad ticket for you to travel west. On the night you left, I went to the stables and brought you a horse."

"And then what?" I breathed.

"I do not know. You left. You said you would not return, but here you are."

Holy shit, Celeste. What was going on with you?

"Mrs. Broadstone, you must not be here. You are in danger," Xi Lin urged.

I reached out to the old man and placed a hand on his shoulder. "It's okay, Xi Lin. I won't be here for long, I promise. Thank you for telling me this. I know to be more careful now."

He sighed in relief.

"And thank you for helping me before as well. You sound like a great friend."

He bowed at my compliment.

When I told Mitica what Xi Lin had said, he wanted me to leave immediately. Though I was scared, I couldn't show him that.

"I can't leave yet. What about the Zgrimties?"

"You know I will leave without their permission."

"But you can't. What about the Wyboka? We still haven't found out about the poisoned tea."

He frowned.

"These people, you're supposed to help them. Likinoak and Chuthekii? They're your family."

"You are my family. I will do anything to keep you safe."

"Well, I won't be kept safe at the cost of someone else. If someone poisoned that tea, then he or she could do it again."

His frustration twisted his beautiful features.

"Listen," I soothed, placing my hands on either side of his face. "I will be okay. They all think I have amnesia, and I don't really know anything. For all we know, Celeste was upset because she found out William was sleeping with Marguerite."

"Is he?"

I shrugged. "I doubt it, but that's not the point. That would've been a betrayal that would've made her want to leave."

"How would that have put her in danger though?"

"I don't know. Maybe she was upset and exaggerated to Xi Lin, or maybe she had a prenup."

His worry didn't diminish.

"The point is: we don't know what really happened. And until we do, we should follow the plan. You said you would be hearing from the Zgrimties any day, right? What are a few more days? No one has hurt me so far. And besides being a little touchy, William has been fine."

His expression crumbled into helplessness. "You will stop looking into what happened to Celeste? If she was in danger, this could be the reason she died."

"Absolutely," I lied. *I'm sure poking around a little more won't make that big of a difference. And if William is behind Celeste's death, he needs to be brought to justice.*

He pulled me into his lap and buried his face in my neck. I hugged his head, stroking his hair in a comforting gesture.

"I do not know what I would do if something happened to you," he murmured into my neck.

"You won't have to find out," I assured. *I hope.*

I started my investigation the following day. I'd already looked through Celeste's things and found little of consequence, so I decided to search their room. It turned out to be fairly easy to get the key.

"Marguerite?" I called to her as I watched the front desk for Frederick.

"Oui, Celeste?" She stopped before it.

"William mentioned something to me about not wearing my wedding rings when I first arrived. You wouldn't happen to know where they are?"

"I did not see them when I moved your things."

"I thought so. Could you get my key to William's and my room so I can look for them when I have time?"

"Of course. I will help you search as well."

"No, it's fine. I'm sure William doesn't want you looking through his personal things."

She nodded at my seeming sensitivity. "Very well, I will fetch the key and put it on your table."

"Great. Thanks so much."

I got my chance during my afternoon break. William had called

Hickory into a meeting in his office, so I knew they were both occupied for the time being. How long they would be busy, I didn't know. But I also didn't know when I'd get another opportunity.

I went to my room and grabbed the key Marguerite had left. Then I hurried down the hall to William's room.

His suite was set up the same as mine but felt as though it was missing something. Half of the dresser was empty, half of the medicine cabinet as well. *If William cares for Celeste as much as I assume, I'm sure it's difficult for him to see the space she once inhabited so vacant.*

I looked through everything: every drawer, every corner, every chest, even under the bed. Nothing of interest was there. In fact, it was as if he had only the basics: clothes and toiletries. There weren't papers of any kind.

Standing in the middle of the living room, I scanned to see if there was any place I hadn't checked. *He must keep everything of importance in his office. That's going to be far more difficult to get into.*

Just as I was turning to leave, the doorknob clicked, and William entered the room. I froze, my shock mirroring his.

"What are you doing in here, my dear?" he asked after a tense pause.

"Oh, you mentioned before that I wasn't wearing my wedding rings, remember? I've already looked through my things and couldn't find them, so I thought maybe Marguerite had left them here."

"Not to my knowledge," he said guardedly.

"Oh, okay. Well, look for them when you get the chance. Won't you? I'd hate to think I've lost them. I'm sure they're expensive."

"Certainly. I will look for them."

"Thanks." I made my escape as fast as I could.

In my room, I locked the door and took slow, deep breaths, trying to calm my racing heart.

THIRTY-SIX

I didn't mention that I was investigating to Mitica when I called for him that night. It was easy to hide because Oli had returned from Edmonton, so he couldn't stay the entire night. That meant we were too busy loving each other to talk much.

The following afternoon, I decided to go to the stables, thinking perhaps Butch might know something about Xi Lin taking a horse to help Celeste escape.

I remembered to grab a few sugar cubes for Saundra before I left the hotel. I knew William was busy in his office, but I didn't know where Hickory was. I hoped he was occupied by some enthralling task.

The stable hands must have finished most of their work because there was no one in the stable. Saundra greeted me as I stood outside her stall.

"Hey, pretty girl. I brought you something." I offered her the sugar cubes. Her velvety nose tickled my palm as she ate them greedily. I giggled at the sensation.

After a few minutes of petting her neck, I heard a shuffling sound from farther down the row of stalls. *Maybe it's Butch.* I walked toward the noise at an easy pace, greeting the horses with a pat as I passed by. At the end of the row, there was a room where they kept the hay and oats.

On the threshold, I saw Stewart and Mary kissing in earnest. A small sound of surprise escaped me. He had pinned her back to the wall of hay bales, and she urged him closer.

Oh Mary, you fool.

They stopped suddenly when they heard me. Mary's eyes went wide, and her face flushed.

A flash of irritation crossed Stewart's expression before he smiled easily. "Good afternoon, Celeste," he said cheerfully.

"Mr. Thomas, Mary," I responded, not attempting to hide my tone of disapproval.

"It's lovely weather we're having. Wouldn't you say?" Stewart asked.

I ignored him. "Mary, I believe your mother is looking for you." Of course, I had no way of knowing what excuse Mary had given her mother to get out of her sight, but I'm sure it had been a lie.

Mary cleared her throat and walked quickly for the exit. She had straw in her hair, but I wasn't going to tell her.

Once she'd gone, I glared at Stewart. "She's to be married soon. We both know you aren't going to offer her a life. So why don't you just leave her be?'

He gave me a charming smile. "Why Celeste, I had no idea you cared for me so much that you would feel jealousy."

I clicked my tongue and turned to leave, knowing there was nothing I could say to convince him.

"My offer stands when you're ready," he called after me as I left.

I strode down the row of stalls and out of the stable. Just as I turned the corner, I ran into Butch.

"Whoa there," he said, steadying my shoulders so I wouldn't fall.

"I'm sorry. I wasn't paying attention. Thanks."

"What has you so out of sorts?" he asked, tilting his head with a puckered brow.

"It's nothing. I'm just irritated by something one of the guests did."

He nodded as if he understood completely.

"Hey, do you have a minute? I overheard something I wanted to ask you about."

He bobbed his head in assent.

"So a while ago, probably late March, did one of your horses go missing?"

He nodded. "More like was stolen."

"Why do you make that distinction?"

"Because the mare's tack was missing, too. Horses get out, but they don't saddle themselves."

"Does that happen often?"

He shook his head.

"Do you know who could've stolen the horse?"

He shook his head again.

"Did you ever find it?"

"In a manner of speaking. We found her but not alive. She looked all the world like she'd been hit by a train."

"You found her by the railroad tracks?"

He nodded. "In pieces."

"Holy shit," I murmured.

Butch didn't seem to mind my lack of delicacy. "It wasn't a pretty sight to be sure. Mr. Broadstone was particularly upset about it. He even sent his man to find the culprit. I hear he never found the thief. Came back only a few days ago, empty-handed."

Mitica said he found me by the tracks, too. Was Celeste riding the horse when it got hit by a train? Does William know Celeste tried to run away? Did he send Hickory to find her, then call him back when I came here? If they found the horse all mutilated, they may have thought Celeste was injured. But why not report her missing to the Mounties? And why lie to everyone and say she'd gone to visit a friend? Did he not want people to know she'd left him? Or maybe he just didn't want people to know about his marital problems and sent Hickory to find her and bring her home so they could work it out. Maybe he doesn't think the horse is related at all, though that may be a stretch with her and the horse going missing on the same night. But this isn't enough to prove anything. It's all still speculation. I need more information. I need to get into William's office.

I thanked Butch for answering my questions and promised to visit again.

I wasn't sure how I was going to sneak into William's office, but I knew I needed help. After much consideration, I decided to ask Harrison. It was clear Celeste hadn't told him anything before, but I thought that had more to do with keeping him safe rather than not trusting him as she'd said to Xi Lin.

That evening, when we were finishing our card games, I kept a few of my cards in my lap. Harrison cleaned up as usual, then said goodnight. Right after he'd left, I pulled the cards out.

"Oh, it looks like a few cards are missing from the deck. I'll go give these to Harrison before he puts them away." It was a silly excuse, but no one seemed particularly suspicious.

After closing the library door behind me and rushing to the other side of the lobby, I caught Harrison as he was putting the cards in his desk.

"You forgot these," I said, holding the pair of sevens out to him.

He quirked an eyebrow. "Did I? Huh, I wonder how that happened. I'll go through the decks tomorrow."

"Harrison," I started, hushed. "Can I talk to you in private?"

He looked around. "We're already alone."

"No," I urged. "Anyone could walk in. Please, it's important."

With scrunched eyebrows and a frown, he rubbed his chin. "It's not proper, but you could come to my room."

"That's fine."

Harrison led me quietly to the workers' hallway and unlocked one of the doors on the left. His room was clean but simple. It was more like a college dorm than the suite I stayed in upstairs.

"Have a seat." He gestured to the only chair as he closed the door behind us.

I waited until he'd sat on the bed and was looking at me before I began. "I need your help. I still don't remember anything from before, but I've discovered a few things since I've been here. Something happened between William and me before I left. I don't know what it was, but it was awful enough that I wanted out. He lied to everyone when he said I was going to a friend's wedding. I actually stole a horse from the stables and was leaving."

Harrison kept his composure, but he pressed his thumb to his lips as he listened intently.

"I can only assume I didn't tell you before because I was trying to protect you, Harrison."

"This is terrible, but it explains a lot. What do you need my help with? Are you going to try to leave again?"

"Not yet. Right now, I'm trying to figure out whatever it was that made me leave before. I've already looked through William's room, but there weren't any clues. I need help distracting William and Hickory so I can search William's office."

He didn't respond. He just silently thought, his thumb still on his lips.

"Will you help me?" I asked, hoping I'd put my trust in the right person.

His eyebrows crinkled. "What? Of course I'll help you. I'm coming up with a plan."

I sighed in relief, and we started plotting our break-in.

I wanted to tell Mitica about the plan Harrison and I made as well as what Butch had told me about the horse. But I didn't want him to worry before I had any idea what to worry about. Even though he didn't know it, his arms around me, his kisses, his smile, his sweet whispers, he was giving me the strength and comfort to face my fears.

The following afternoon as I watched the front desk for Frederick, I heard Harrison knock on William's door in the office behind me.

"Excuse me, Mr. Broadstone. I'm sorry to interrupt, but there's a matter that needs your attention."

"What is it, Harrison?" I heard William's muffled reply.

"The mercantile in Farrloch, Sir. I went to pay the bill this morning as you asked, but the manager refused to settle with me. He will only talk to you, Mr. Broadstone. I have a feeling he wants to increase his rates, too."

"Very well, I will deal with him later."

"I beg your pardon, Sir. But this problem needs immediate attention. Because he wouldn't deal with me, I was unable to get items, which are needed today."

"Fine. Hickory, we are going into town. Fetch my coat."

A few moments later, William and Hickory left the hotel.

"All right," Harrison whispered from directly behind me. "I'll watch the desk and the door. Get moving."

"Thanks," I told him, quickly making my way to William's office and slipping in.

It's a good thing Harrison was told to settle that bill yesterday. I don't envy that manager's meeting with William, but I'm sure it won't be too terrible.

William's office didn't have much furniture, but the number of papers on and likely in his desk as well as on the shelves behind it was overwhelming.

I hope he's organized.

After pulling one of the many thin, unlabeled books from the shelf, I opened it to find an accounting ledger. Sighing as I scanned the black-inked records of every purchase William had ever made, I knew I'd never have time to go through them all.

The supple brown leather of William's chair cracked as I sat in it. I gently picked up the paper nearest me on the desk and quickly read William's correspondence to Mr. McMasters in Ottawa. It was full of nonspecific assurances that some new project was going well. I carefully replaced the high-quality paper where I'd found it.

It would help if I knew what I was looking for.

The drawer above my knees slid out easily, and I looked down at a collection of stationery supplies. The strewn blank papers were smooth under my fingertips as I pushed them aside. The irregular lines of something drawn rather than written caught my eye. I carefully extracted the large composition from under the stationary, trying not to rip the slightly yellowed map.

Not for the first time since I'd been in 1900, I wished for my cell phone. *Pictures would be a lot quicker.* The map wasn't very detailed, and I wondered what William could possibly use it for. It mostly depicted the wilderness surrounding Farrloch and the hotel. The mountains and trees were imprecisely inked, and Farrloch was just a word in elegant letters. The hotel was artistically drawn but not overburdened with detail. On the other hand, the lake and river were brilliantly done in a gorgeous blue. And through the reserve wasn't labeled, the location of the hot springs was also done in blue.

I wonder what color artists call that? It's more art than map.

I tucked it back into the bottom of the shallow drawer and reached for a deeper drawer beside me.

I bit my lip when the drawer showed resistance. *Is it locked?* But with a little more effort, I realized it was just too full. With some wiggling and one hard pull, I managed to get it open.

Not so organized after all. My eyebrows crinkled at the conglomeration of seemingly random junk. The wooden legs of the chair groaned as I slid it farther back to kneel beside the drawer. I hissed, clenching my teeth, and moved more carefully so as not to make so much noise. As I dug through the chaos, I pulled William's collection out and put it on the floor beside me.

A rusted railroad tie, a broken quill pen, a framed picture of Queen Victoria, really? The absurdity of the apparently bottomless drawer never ceased to surprise me.

Just as I was giving up to look somewhere else, I pulled out a heavy wooden box. My heart thumped hard, and I held my breath.

Slowly, I unlatched the clasp and lifted the smooth lid. My gasp stuck in my throat, and I nearly dropped the box when a large, smooth handgun stared back at me, nestled lovingly in its velvet-lined case.

Jesus. I sighed, willing my heartbeat to slow. *It's fine. This is the west, right? I mean, everyone probably has a gun. But, jeez, that surprised me.* I swallowed the nervous giggles that rose in my throat, gently closed the lid, and placed the gun box on the floor.

I saw only one item remaining in the drawer. *Finally.*

The small, black book was wrapped in a thin strip of leather. I unwound the tie, and a bundle of papers slipped from between the pages and fell to the floor. I retrieved the twine-tied bundle and read the address on the front of the top envelope.

These are...letters to Celeste? Then...

Hurriedly and with shaking hands, I flipped to the front page of the book.

Her journal. William had it all along. My heart raced, the sound of it beating loud in my ears, and I wanted to read it right then. *No time.* I reluctantly let go of the smooth leather book, setting it in the chair beside me, and began putting William's random junk back.

As I forced the overfilled drawer closed, I hoped I'd put everything in the right order. And I tried to be as quiet as I could when I pushed his chair back into place.

I wonder how much time I have left. Probably not much. That drawer took a while. I should cut my losses while I still can.

Just as I silently closed the door to William's office, I heard Harrison from the other room.

"Mr. Broadstone, how did it go? Did you settle everything?" His voice boomed in the foyer.

"Yes, and the manager seemed surprised by my presence. He claimed he'd never said he would only deal with me."

"Really? Well, that was certainly the impression he gave me, Sir. I apologize if I've inconvenienced you."

"It did give me a chance to renegotiate some of our contracts, but I suggest you be certain before calling me away over something so simple as paying a bill again."

"Of course, Mr. Broadstone."

There was a pause. "Where is my wife? Why are you at the front desk?"

Exiting their office, I said. "Thank you so much for watching the front desk for me, Harrison. I'm feeling better now. Oh, William, you're back. I wasn't feeling well earlier, and Harrison was nice enough to let me rest at his desk for a bit while he covered front desk duty."

William frowned. "You were not feeling well? Would you like to rest in your room?"

Do you even care? "No, I'm all right now. I'll rest after tea. Thank you for your concern." I smiled and nodded at Harrison, hoping he would understand that everything was okay. Then I left for the dining room.

THIRTY-SEVEN

The creamy, sweet aftertaste of tea was still in my mouth when I retrieved Celeste's journal and letters and smuggled them to my room.

I sat cross-legged on the bed, my breathing loud in my own ears as I unwrapped the dead woman's journal.

I scanned the pages, my eyes struggling to absorb the details of her inner thoughts. She was sad to leave home but excited for her new adventure. She liked but paid Marguerite little mind. She'd overheard Louis and Gabriel gossiping about how William was much too old for her before they'd known she spoke French. She became fast friends with Harrison, finding the Australian funny and kind. And she loved William. Oh, how she loved him.

She poured her heart into the ink on the page, her hopes, her dreams, her love, her adoration for this man twice her age. She thought him so wise, so cultured, so mysterious and exciting.

I blushed and shied away from reading her intimate inner thoughts about her husband, but I trudged on.

As I neared the blank pages toward the end, her entries became sparser. She went days without writing a word. And when she did write, she didn't go into nearly as much detail.

18 March 1900

I cannot perceive the light of the world as I did only days ago. Everything is dark and dismal. Has life always been thus, and I was too naïve, too blessedly ignorant, to know the truth?

The agony, the betrayal, my chest aches as though my heart has been run through.

How could a man who has never shown me anything but kindness be so callous toward others, so evil?

Was it all a lie? Can a man capable of such atrocities also be capable of love?

I am a fool, a silly, love-blinded fool.

Am I party to this sin? But, even if I know, I cannot stop it. I am lost.

~

19 March 1900

A plan has been hatched. Not a good plan, but a plan none-theless.

I see now how unforgivably trusting I have been. And though I cannot undo the past, my conscience will not allow me to stay here any longer.

Regret makes for a restless bedfellow.

I'm certain I will be condemned in the minds of those who truly care for me, but I must keep this endeavor hidden.

I'm sorry, friends. This is for the best.

~

21 March 1900

Has Hickory always lurked so near me, a shadow unnoticed until the bright sun of truth revealed his presence?

Does the devil know my plot, or has my forced awakening led me to paranoia?

~

29 March 1900

Tomorrow. Everything is set. I hope to soon be in the safety of my dear Papa's bosom.

Has fate finally shown me a ray of sympathy that my father and brother should be so near when I need them most?

My heart races like that of the smallest bird. May hope give me the rapid wings of one as well.

I held my breath and eagerly turned the page. The next was blank. I sighed, closing my eyes.

What was it that William did to so change her opinion of him? She didn't tell me anything I didn't already know or couldn't have guessed. Though, I suppose confirmation is valuable. Now I know she was going to meet her father and brother in BC.

The rough twine on the small bundle of letters pricked the pads of my fingertips as I pulled the neat bow loose. There were five of them in total, all from Jacques.

24 March 1900
My sweet Cellie,

I cannot tell you how pleased I am you've decided to meet us in Vancouver. Father has not stopped smiling since I told him.

We leave in a few days, so send any further correspondence to the enclosed address.

Your brother,
Jacques

~

7 April 1900
My sweet Cellie,

We have safely arrived in Vancouver.
I had thought you were to arrive before us. Did something delay your departure? Are you still coming?
Please write at your earliest convenience.

Your brother,
Jacques

~

14 April 1900
My sweet Cellie,

Father and I are beginning to feel concerned at your silence. Please respond as soon as you receive this letter.

Your brother,
Jacques

~

21 April 1900
Celeste,

Father is beside himself with worry, and I can hardly calm him with my own rising panic.
We had planned to stay in Vancouver for another month,

but your silence has spurred action.

If we do not receive a letter by the week's end, we are coming to Farrloch.

Please, dear sister, let us know you are well.

Your concerned brother,
Jacques

~

28 April 1900
Dearest Celeste,

I apologize for alarming you before. I had no idea you had fallen ill.

We were all packed to leave when we received William's telegram.

It is a shame we will not get the chance to see you on this visit west, but I hope you are saving all of your energy to get well soon.

You are in good hands, Sister. I am confident you will be better in no time under William's loving care.

Your brother,
Jacques

My hand holding the letter fell into my lap. *Wow, William really does have everyone fooled. To open her letters and write a telegram so they wouldn't come to check on her? Truly diabolical. It seems Celeste must've only written that she was coming to visit and didn't tell her family anything about the crisis she faced. And based on Jacques's latest letter, there's no way William told them about my "amnesia." Whatever was going on, it's clear Celeste thought she was in danger. I really should tell Mitica what I've discovered.*

I paced the length of my hotel suite, worrying my lower lip. Finally, I paused and spoke Mitica's true name to summon him to me. I was so nervous about telling him how I'd been investigating behind his back that I didn't notice his sorrowful mood, so close to my own.

"Listen, Mitica," I started, gathering the courage to look up at him. He crushed me in an unexpected embrace. I paused a moment, taking strength from the love I knew he felt for me. "I know you're going to be angry," I whispered. "But I have to tell you anyway."

"I also have something important to tell you," he said.

"Okay, but let me go first. I want to get this off my chest."

His silence was his consent.

"For the last few days, I've been investigating what happened to Celeste. Before you blow up, I want you to know that I was really careful. And now, I agree with you. I'm ready to let it go. Whatever happened to her is too dangerous for me to mess with. I think we should just wait to hear from the Zgrimties and make an escape plan."

I cringed, fully expecting his well-deserved outburst.

But his voice was even and void when he said, "I heard from the Zgrimties today."

Dread froze my stomach. His reaction was not one that foretold good news.

"Did they...did they cut you off?" I murmured.

"Nu."

I shivered, somehow knowing his next words would be worse than I imagined.

"I am permitted to continue my work for them under the condition that I never see you again."

My head spun with the dizziness his words produced. "What?" I murmured.

"They said I must never see you again if I want to continue helping the fae with their support."

"What would be their purpose in separating us?"

"Punishment. I broke my vow. Now, I must choose." His voice sounded far away over my ragged, shuddering breath.

"If you stay with me, it will be at the price of all of those people? I can't. I can't do that. Mitica, they need your help. I—"

He cupped my face, forcing me to look at him as my eyes rolled around in panic.

"Nu, Erin. Nu."

I flinched as he called my name.

"This is their doing. Not yours. They could have let it go, but they would rather see people suffer than have someone disobey them and go unpunished."

"But the fae...magic..."

"We can still help the fae and magic without them. I will no longer serve such masters. You, you are far more important. And I know you and I will help a great many fae together."

"Are you...are you sure?" I asked weakly.

"Da, there is nothing anyone can do that would stop me from being with you."

I couldn't quell the hot tears as they streamed down my face. Mitica gently kissed each one away until all I felt was the glowing warmth of his love.

"I am very upset with you, bucuria mea," he assured gently.

I nodded.

"You lied to me."

"I know," I said miserably.

"But I know you do not give up. It is one of the things I love about you. What is upsetting is that you felt you could not tell me you wanted to investigate."

"I knew you didn't want me to because you thought it was dangerous, and I didn't want you to worry."

"It was dangerous, and it is only my fear of losing you that makes me worry."

"You're right. I won't do it again. I swear."

He kissed me lightly on the mouth to show his forgiveness and seal my promise. "Now, what did you discover?"

I recounted what Butch had told me about the horse and what I'd read in Celeste's journal and letters. "I don't know what William did that so shook her faith in him, but it must've been severe."

He nodded. "It seems likely he noticed her change in behavior and sent this man Hickory to watch her."

"You think so? I mean, he must've realized she tried to run away when he found the horse. But do you think he knew she figured whatever it was out before she tried to leave?"

"Unlikely. He would have attempted to stop her before she left if he had."

"That's true," I agreed. "But he definitely knows now that he's read her journal and letters. You don't think he killed her. Do you?"

He frowned darkly, then met my eyes. "I do not know. But if he did not know she knew, then he would have had no reason to."

"Right, and if he did, he probably would've made such an attempt on me."

"Not necessarily. He thinks you have amnesia. It could be he is waiting to see if you remember something."

"So we still don't really know anything. William could be a murderer, or he could just be a guy whose wife left him and then died."

"Well, we know one thing. We have to get you out of here immediately."

I sighed. "Mitica, you're not going to want to hear this, but I'm staying."

"Nu."

"Yes. We need to pretend everything is normal until we find out what's going on with the Wyboka. In the meantime, we can make a plan to escape. If we plan carefully, we can disappear in a way that no one will ever come after us. Celeste Broadstone and Wynn Delaforet will be gone, and we can just be Erin and Mitica."

He ground his teeth. "I do not like it."

"I don't like it either, but is there a better option?"

As he glared out the window, I reached up to touch his cheek.

"Mitica, look at me."

He sighed and turned his troubled blue eyes on me.

"Everything is going to be fine. I'll lay low. I swear. I'll act totally normal, the good little amnesiac. I won't investigate anymore. We should hear from Edmonton soon. Then we will have evidence, and we can help the Wyboka."

"I have a bad feeling."

"Of course you do. All of this is potentially incredibly dangerous. You just concentrate on solving this case, okay?"

"And what will you be doing?"

"Me? I'll be planning a party."

He tilted his head in confusion. "Ce?"

"I just had an idea. One of the guests mentioned something to me about having a dance. What if I made it this big thing, invited tons of people? If there was a crowd, it would be easy for us to just slip out. Right?"

He considered the idea, then nodded slowly. "But they would still come looking for us when everyone left."

"That's true."

"I could make a false report of your death. If I claimed you threw yourself off a cliff into the river, they'd never think they could find your body."

"Right. But wouldn't that mean you'd have to stay behind?"

"Only for a little while. It is not uncommon for lawmen to retire early after facing the tragedy of not being able to save someone."

"Okay. And if you haven't solved the Wyboka case by then, that will give you extra time."

He nodded. "When should we plan for this to happen?"

"Why not the 28th, the day of the eclipse? It's the perfect excuse to have a celebration, it gives us just under a month to make sure there will be tons of people, and it gives you time to help the Wyboka."

He frowned at the timeline but agreed. "How do you plan on getting away? You are not going to steal another horse, are you?"

"No, I'll go with Grigore."

He squinted his displeasure. "I do not think that is a good idea."

"Yes, it is. Just think about it. He can get me far away much faster than a train could, and then I'd have a dragon protecting me while you're away."

"Da, and you would have a dragon trying to seduce you, too. You are not immune to his magic."

"I know not to make eye contact with him. Besides, there has to be a charm or spell or something to repel his influence. Isn't there?"

He sighed. "There is a charm, but it does not repel so much as dampen."

"That's fine then."

He didn't look happy about it, but he didn't argue either.

"How long do you think it will be before the Zgrimties realize you're choosing me?" I asked softly.

"They requested my response before the next full moon."

"So they can take weeks and weeks to answer you, but you have to answer them in a week and a half? Eck, if that's not just typical of a governing body. But then there will be two weeks between when you send word and the party. Do you think they'll sabotage us at all?"

"I do not know. However, they are not likely expecting me to choose you, and they will convene a council meeting and debate what to do with me. They are not going to like losing me as an asset."

"But they won't rat you out to the Mounties, right?"

"Nu, they will not involve the humans. They will devise a much more insidious punishment."

"Well, that's...foreboding."

He nodded. "We must disappear before they settle on a punishment."

"Right."

THIRTY-EIGHT

"William," I called over breakfast the next day.

"Yes, my dear," he asked from behind his newspaper.

"Did you know there's a full solar eclipse later this month?"

"Indeed? I did not."

"I was thinking, wouldn't it be the perfect reason to have a big party?"

He met my eyes over the top of his paper, and I steeled my nerves so as not to look away.

"One of the guests mentioned wanting to have a dance, and you said part of my job is to make the hotel attractive to easterners, right? We could invite tons of people to come to watch the eclipse and then have a celestial masquerade. I don't think it would be hard to fill up the entire hotel."

He seemed to consider my proposal as he folded the paper. "I think it is an excellent idea, my dear. When is the eclipse?"

"Yeah? May 28."

"That doesn't give us much time for a grand affair, but if we work very hard, I believe it's possible."

"Thank you, William." I beamed at him, trying to maintain the façade.

"Though if we are having a ball, I will have to ensure the digging of that cellar door and patio you requested for the men in the laundry are finished." He smiled so gently I almost believed he was a good guy.

I can see why Celeste trusted him. "You're going to go through with it after all?"

"Of course. My beautiful and compassionate wife pointed out that I must care for my employees."

What is it you want from me? Are you just trying to win me over as you said you would? Or are you trying to make me reveal what I know by keeping me off guard? "That's so nice of you, William. I really appreciate it, and I know the guys downstairs will, too."

I'd never been great at acting. I was always just in the chorus in drama club. Perhaps it was my fear that gave me the added motivation to carry out my performance. Whatever the case, I felt confident my excited expressions were flawless.

William promised he would start writing letters immediately to all the people he knew out east, inviting them to our celebration.

Thankfully, Harrison picked up that my enthusiasm for this new venture was a signal something was afoot. He jumped right into event planning with me, trusting I would inform him when we were alone.

We outlined everything we would need for the ball: food, decorations, musicians, and, of course, guests. I recalled Celeste was known pretty well in the Toronto art community. I decided to use her connections to secure an orchestra and artists to make decorations.

As for food, I had full confidence Louis and Gabriel would know what to do. The chefs ran with the task, eyes shining with the thrill of a challenge.

Harrison wrote to the press and members of the event planning community, asking them to advertise. He would also handle the logistics of travel for guests coming to the event. All-in-all, we were going to have a lot to keep us busy over the next month.

When we announced our plans to the guests that evening in the library, the young women squealed with delight. I was disappointed to hear Colonel Higgins and Reginald would be checking out before the event, as were the newlyweds. Unfortunately, Stewart and Cole planned to stay.

As Harrison said goodnight and prepared to leave the room, he asked if I could give him a hand with a detail he was struggling with. I obliged, and we went to the garden for privacy.

"So what's going on?" he asked as soon as we were outside.

"I found my journal and some letters from my brother in William's desk yesterday."

"Did they give you any idea as to why you left before?"

I shook my head. "Not really. I only know I found out something terrible, and William didn't want me to know since he kept the journal and letters from me."

"We need to do more investigating?"

"No, I'm done trying to figure it out. It feels too dangerous to dig any more."

"Then you're going to just forget about the entire matter?"

"No, I plan to leave. This time for good."

"When? How?"

I shook my head again. "I can't tell you. But I want you to know: I value our friendship, and I wish there could be another way."

He frowned at my choice of words coupled with my solemn tone. "You will be all right?"

I smiled sadly. "I will be free."

We strolled quietly in the garden for a short while before Harrison excused himself. Apparently, he had a rendezvous with Butch. I wished him goodnight but stayed.

Wandering through the garden on that cool, spring night refreshed my ragged nerves. It had been difficult to pretend all day. The gentle moonlight from the waxing crescent, peeking just over the garden wall, and the twinkling of countless starts reminded me how small I was in the universe.

"Long before you and me, the sun and moon shined down on those who breathed the fresh air of a spring night," I told Mitica as though he was right beside me.

"You and me, I like the sound of that," a voice cooed from the other side of the lattice wall I stood before.

I gasped, nearly jumping out of my skin. Stewart stepped out from behind it.

"How long have you been there?" I asked around the lump in my throat.

"Oh, I came out as Harrison went in."

I sighed internally. *He didn't overhear us then.* "What do you want?" I demanded.

"I'm a guest at this hotel, you know. Can't I enjoy the garden at night like everyone else?"

He stepped up beside me, and I edged away.

"Sure, you can. Away from me."

He gave me a charming smile, my harsh words not offending him in the least. "Is that what you truly want, Celeste?"

"Yes, Mr. Thomas. That is what I truly want."

"I don't think it is. I think you burn with passion. I can see it within you. It calls to me, drawing me to it."

My face heated. "Okay. I burn with passion, but not for you."

"You can't expect me to believe it's for your husband. I see how you look at him. He's a stranger to you. But me? You show me your inner fire."

"Are you purposely thick or were you just born that way?"

I turned to walk away, but he grabbed my wrist and pulled hard, slamming my back against the lattice wall.

My head throbbed and my wrist screamed where he still squeezed it.

"You know, Celeste," he continued in an easy tone. "You are the first woman to ever resist me. Why is that?"

"Because you're an asshole," I hissed through my teeth, which were clenched in pain.

"No, that can't be it. Women adore aggressive men. Don't you? You all just want someone to dominate you."

"You're delusional. Now, let me go," I demanded, attempting to twist my wrist from his grasp only for him to box me in by grabbing the lattice behind me with his free hand.

"How could I let you go now that your sweet scent is in my mind? I haven't shown you how charming I can be yet."

I struggled in earnest; he was too strong for me to escape. Fear instinctively pumped in my veins, but my mind couldn't seem to grasp what was happening. I froze and couldn't stop myself from shaking.

As he grabbed a fistful of hair at the base of my neck, I could feel the treacherous tears run down my cheeks, betraying my weakness. He forced my head to look up at him.

I'd always thought the eyes of a perpetrator would be cold and unfeeling, but not Stewart. His eyes burned, reveling in the power he had over me.

My mind raced, and I couldn't grab hold of a coherent thought to get me out of this nightmare. His face was too close, his breath too near, his hand too tight, too cold, too real.

Bile rose in my throat when he smiled triumphantly and crushed my lips with his. As his slimy tongue licked at me, the horrible reality of the situation cracked the ice that had frozen my protests.

He yelped as I stomped hard on his foot, giving me just enough time to cry out, "Dumitru!"

I sucked air through my teeth as Stewart yanked my hair and forced me to turn around. The crisscrossed pattern of the lattice pressed painful creases into my skin as he pushed me into it.

"That wasn't nice, Celeste. But I'm prepared to forgive you," he growled into my ear.

"Let go of me." My voice sounded weak, even to me.

I could hear his frown. "This is all wrong," he murmured almost to himself. "I want to feel that passion I see burning inside you." He nodded against my cheek. "It's all right," he reassured. "I must have to coax it out of you."

Why isn't he here yet? I must've done something wrong. He isn't coming. My mind began to pull away as if stung by the horror. "Dumitru," I whispered, not even sure I'd called him aloud.

The cool night air raised the hair on my legs as Stewart lifted the back of my skirts. Then the fabric returned to its proper place in a rush of wind as Stewart's weight on my back disappeared.

I sank to the ground, Stewart's strength, and not my knees, having been the only thing holding me up. *Run! Run!* My mind screamed, still not completely focused. My head craned to see over my shoulder as I forced myself to my feet.

And there he was: Mitica, his face flushed in fury as crimson as his hair.

Stewart's eyes popped wide as Mitica held him by the throat. He wheezed, clawing at Mitica's hand.

"Know this before you die," Mitica hissed. "You have forced yourself on the wrong woman."

"I'm sorry," Stewart choked out.

Mitica smirked. "It is too late for that."

"Mitica, don't," I murmured.

His murderous rage didn't allow him to hear.

I approached him and gently touched his shoulder. "Stop it. I don't want you to become a murderer."

His fiery eyes met mine and softened in recognition. "Killing scum like this hardly counts as murder." But his hand on Stewart's throat loosened a little.

Stewart sucked in air, coughing.

"Just let him go," I urged.

"Oh, I will. As soon as I am finished with him." Glaring at Stewart, he pulled him closer. "You have caused many harm. Haven't you? Well, now you will feel their pain." Mitica chanted something in Romanian; it sounded much like a dirge.

Then he flung Stewart away from him; he landed in a heap on the brick path of the garden.

"I suggest you leave. Now," Mitica demanded.

Stewart fled toward the hotel and didn't look back.

Before I could even blink, Mitica's arms enveloped me. I trembled, relief and residual fear mixing as my body tried to make sense of it all. A sob stuck in my throat.

"Mitica..." I whimpered.

"I know, bucuria mea. I am here," he hushed.

It took a while for my shivers to succumb to Mitica's warmth. I can't say how long I sagged against him in the moonlit garden, heaving unsteady breaths, his embrace the only source of heat in that cold, unforgiving night. Eventually, the all-encompassing strength of his presence soothed my nerves, and my heartbeat and breathing returned to normal. "Thank you," I whispered into his chest, my shame at my own weakness not allowing me to look up at him.

"Nu, bucuria mea. Thank you for stopping me. I would have killed him." Mitica sounded as ashamed as I felt. "You kept a clear head in the worst sort of situation."

"Don't make me sound so great. I should've never been in that type of situation to begin with. I should've known better."

He gently lifted my chin so I would meet his eyes. "This is not your fault. His sins are his own."

I knew his words were true, but I couldn't stop that nagging feeling that I could've prevented it somehow. "What did you do to him?" I asked.

"Instant karma. When he inflicts pain and suffering, so too will he have pain and suffering inflicted upon him."

"That's...kind of genius."

He grinned. "Much better than death."

"Mitica..." My face heated, and I felt silly as if I were a frightened child who was asking for her parents to leave the hall light on. "Would you stay with me tonight? I know Oli is still at the barracks, but I don't want to be alone." I couldn't meet his eyes as I asked something so vulnerable and embarrassing.

"Da, bucuria mea. I will think of something to tell Oliver tomorrow. I will not leave you tonight."

The knot in my chest loosened a little.

Mitica waited in the garden as I snuck to my room. I couldn't help but feel jittery walking the halls alone, worrying I'd run into Stewart, jumping at every shadow and the creak of every step and floorboard. But the stress turned out to be unnecessary once I was securely behind my locked door.

When I called Mitica's true name again, he completely obliged my need for the safety of his embrace. I was able to sleep soundly that night, snuggled deep in the protection of his arms.

Stewart and Cole's midnight checkout was all the talk the next morning at breakfast.

Apparently, they'd been in some sort of rush, but no one knew why their departure had been so hasty. No one except me that is. Frederick, being the discreet and professional clerk he was, would never think to question his guests about their personal decisions.

Reginald expressed his surprise to Colonel Higgins, insisting the lads had planned to stay through the ball. Colonel Higgins couldn't recall.

Mary quietly pushed her breakfast around her plate, her eyes red from recent tears, as her two friends speculated as to the gentlemen's motives.

I felt light as if I hadn't a care in the world. The jackass was gone, away from Mary and me. And neither of us would ever see him again.

I hope Mitica's spell taught him how to treat others with respect.

Karma, after all, can also bring good things into your life, as long as you give good things that is.

Dr. Hollander came for his third visit after breakfast.

After he'd asked his mandatory doctor questions, we engaged in a little small talk.

"I do love this time of year," he commented. "The mountain air is so fresh, and I love the feel of spring about to bloom."

I nodded. "Are you from here?"

He shook his head. "Montreal. My wife, my brother, and I came out here to start anew. My brother is a barber, you know, in Farrloch. He enjoys his work, takes pride in it, too. Though he has been rather stressed of late. Apparently, a woman came into his shop a while back and asked him to cut her hair rather short." Dr. Hollander chuckled. "Boy, that certainly shook him."

I bit my lip, grateful Marguerite had again pinned my hair under a hat. *Aww, I knew I traumatized him.*

Later that afternoon, I went back over Celeste's letters from her friends. I recalled one of the musicians she'd patronized had referred to the manager of the Toronto Symphony Orchestra.

Finding the name, I wrote Walter Baker a letter, naming our mutual acquaintance and asking if he would consider bringing some of his musicians to perform at our celestial masquerade.

I also wrote to a sculptor and a painter with whom Celeste corresponded, inviting them to the hotel and asking if they would make decorations.

It may be a little strange to meet Celeste's friends without remembering them, but I'm sure I can use the chaos of party planning as an excuse if I act in a way she wouldn't.

After I'd given the letters to Frederick to post, I thought all I had to do was wait for responses. Harrison and William were taking care of guest invites, and Louis and Gabriel had the food situation in hand. I'd thought I was done for the moment until I saw Marguerite's barely controlled excitement.

"Now, let us plan your costume!" she squealed.

Crap. I forgot about that.

THIRTY-NINE

Over the next few days, Marguerite pestered me about my costume for the masquerade. I had so many things I was worried about that I told her to just take care of it. My only condition was that the dress be easy to move in. When she told me she was going to hire Madame Buvons to make the gown, I was glad William had discouraged me going into town.

How would I explain that to Suzette? I thought as Marguerite took my measurements for the dressmaker.

I was relieved when Mitica brought me a response from Suzette. I'd been certain she was angry with me. But her words assured me she understood.

Dear Erin,

I was happy to receive your letter from your Constable Delaforet. I must say I was worried from not seeing you for so long.

Oliver did indeed keep your secret, but he was glad when I told him I knew. I laugh when I think of his expression. I thought he would burst. He claims to have known how you two felt about each other before you did. Is this true, or is he just boasting?

You need not worry about your Mountie. Oliver and I will look after him. He seems to be coping. Oliver says he was quite depressed the first few days after you left. But now, he seems almost determined. Perhaps he is planning to visit you?

I hope you get to come to Farrloch again soon. I miss you, mon amie. Would you make the journey for a wedding, for instance? I hesitate to even write this, but Oliver seems serious about me of late. I think I would like to be a Mountie's bride.

He is so kind and considerate. Speaking of which, you should write to him. He was upset when I received a letter and he did not.

That is all for now, mon amie. I am off to help Madame make a dress for Madame Broadstone. The hotel is to have a masquerade at the end of the month. It is wonderful, non? I wonder if they will send invitations to people in town. Probably non, but it would have been fun.

Ton amie,
Suzette

I made a mental note to consider inviting the townspeople to the party. *I wonder if anyone would recognize me in my mask. I hope not.*

As Suzette had suggested, I wrote a quick note to Oli. It was vague, asking him how he was and telling him to stay out of trouble.

While I waited for responses to my letters from Toronto, William and Harrison began to get telegrams from guests excited for our party. There was only a handful so far, but people had started to book rooms.

I couldn't wait to tell Mitica how our plan was working when I called for him. My body hummed with the thrill of moving toward our goal, finding purpose and balance in the activity. But when he materialized with a solemn expression, I immediately tensed.

"What is it?" I asked, reaching for him.

"We just heard from Edmonton," he told me. "The ceremonial tea was poisoned: hemlock."

There was a heavy silence. When I started to speak, it was in a slow, uncertain cadence. "But that's good. Isn't it? Now, we can find who did it."

"Is it?" he asked. "Da, we can find the culprit, but this means there is a murderer loose. It was not just an accident."

I nodded seriously. "What do we do next?"

"I will open an official investigation tomorrow. We now have evidence of foul play."

"Won't that give the murderer warning?"

"Perhaps, but what else can I do?"

"Let's talk to Likinoak and Chuthekii. Maybe they can tell us something."

"But I cannot let them know I am Wynn. I told them I left the tea on the barracks' threshold with a note last time. How would I know the results of the tests?"

"Through me, of course. I know both Wynn and Mitica. Remember? And before you argue, I'm coming with you. As long as I'm back before dawn, no one should notice."

"But will I have the strength to bring you back?" he muttered just loud enough for me to hear.

"Yes, you will. Because you want to be with me forever, not just as long as it takes for them to find us."

"Pentru totdeauna," he whispered.

"What's that?" I asked.

"Forever," he answered, sliding his arms around my waist.

I smiled as he kissed me on the side of my head. "Te iubesc," I told him.

"I love you, too," he murmured.

After releasing Mitica from the summoning call, I dressed in my jeans and chemise under Oli's jacket, reveling in the feel of the comfortable fabric hugging my legs.

Then I snuck cautiously downstairs and out into the garden. Pursing my lips at the rather narrow paths flanked by trees and bushes, I slipped out of the iron gate. It creaked as I shut it, and I flinched at the sound, so loud in the hush of night. Once it was closed, I crept along the garden wall and started walking down the street, knowing they would intercept me along the way.

I squinted into the darkness, searching for my ride. Waves of wind blew the hair from my face as Grigore and Mitica landed before me.

"Erin," the zmeu purred, grinning in the light of his forehead gem. "I have missed you."

"I hope you've been behaving yourself, Grigore," I told him.

"As if I have had a choice," he muttered.

His response reminded me of Stewart a little, and I frowned. "I wish you would change your ways, Grigore."

He blinked, surprise showing on his reptilian face.

"Mitica obviously thinks you can be saved, or he wouldn't have stopped Făt-Frumos from killing you, right? Wouldn't you rather a woman choose you because she wants you and not because you used magic on her?"

"Do you think I, too, do not crave true love?" he asked softly after a long pause. "I was not born a zmeu, you know. I was once a zână."

"Another type of Romanian fae," Mitica explained.

"Yes, a *fae*," Grigore spat in disgust. "I bestowed gifts and protected children. I had powerful magic, even for a zână. I lived among my people in Tărâmul Celălalt."

"What happened?" I whispered.

"Crina." He went silent for a long time. The name hung in the air like a spring fragrance with no breeze to blow it away. "She was a zână, and I loved her. But all of her promises were false. She destroyed me, and in my despair, I vowed to bring that same destruction upon the world."

"What did you do?"

He smiled in diabolical glee. "I stole the sun and the moon."

"Wait... What?" I looked at Mitica for confirmation.

"In a manner of speaking," Mitica clarified.

"I conjured the darkest of clouds. For an entire season, the sky was the blackest night. Nothing grew, and no rain fell. And everyone suffered as much as I."

"Jesus," I murmured.

"The other fae and the hultan could not dispel my bane, so they cursed me instead. They united for the sole purpose of defeating me. This was my punishment. They made me into a monster. But they failed in many ways. They tried to turn me into a balaur. But their magic could not entirely contain mine, so I became a zmeu instead."

"You wrought much fear and horror after that," Mitica added.

"They deserved it," Grigore growled.

"You must've truly loved her," I murmured to Grigore. "Crina. You must have loved her so much to be in that much pain when she betrayed you."

He was quiet for a while before he answered. "I did... I do."

I solemnly nodded my understanding. "It's not that you want the love of a woman. It's that you want the love of *that* woman."

He averted his eyes and didn't answer.

"Grigore, listen. I don't know how it feels to go through that kind of rejection. But do you really want to be this way? I can't believe someone so full of love wants to cause such pain."

"If she will not love me, then have her hate me."

"But it's not just her you're hurting. I'm sure you had other people you cared about. Friends or family?"

"They all left, the same as she."

"But Mitica didn't."

"Neither fae nor hultan is trustworthy."

"What about humans? I'm going to be honest here, Grigore. You're kind of an ass. And you and Mitica can say you dislike each other all you want, but I don't buy it. He's stuck with you this long, and I trust his judgment. If he says you can be redeemed, then I'm with him. I hope in time you can open your heart and find love again. But for now, you're stuck with us as friends."

He stared at me, and I didn't look away, though I knew I should so his magic wouldn't affect me. After a few moments, I still didn't feel his golden pull.

"You are both fools," he muttered, sliding his eyes away from mine.

The flight to the reserve was much too short. I was free, with nothing but the wind in my face and Mitica's arms around me. And then I was on the ground, knocking on Likinoak's door in search of a murderer.

"So it was the tea?" Likinoak asked as we stood in her kitchen.

Mitica and I nodded.

"Who has access to the tea, Amâwe?" Chuthekii questioned.

"Only the elders and Tsesikó," Likinoak answered.

"Well, it clearly was not Tsesikó," Mitica reasoned. "Since he was one of the victims."

Likinoak nodded seriously. "All of the elders must be searched, including me."

The old woman looked at Mitica, then at me. "Tell Constable Delaforet this information, Seyohkwii. I will expect him tomorrow."

I nodded, pretending like he wasn't beside me.

"You must not tell the other elders about this, Amâwe. They may get rid of evidence if they know we suspect them," Mitica advised.

"I will do as you suggest," Likinoak said wearily as if the entire situation broke her heart.

With tensions high, we prepared to leave. But right after Chuthekii and Mitica went outside, Likinoak stopped me with a hand on my elbow.

"Seyohkwii," she urged.

"What is it, Amâwe?"

"I have a feeling in my breast."

I frowned at her ominous tone. "What's wrong? Is it the investigation?"

She shook her head. "I do not think so." Searching my eyes, she said, "I will not see you again."

I smiled gently at her and wrapped my arms around her. "I know everything seems overwhelming right now, but I'm sure we will see each other again. We're family, remember?"

She clung to me as if she truly believed her fears, and I returned her embrace for a while.

With a heavy heart, I was back by the garden wall well before dawn.

"Good luck tomorrow," I told Mitica, staring into his sorrowful eyes.

"I hope this will all be over soon. The Wyboka will be safe, and we will have a new life."

I nodded. "Three weeks from now, Grigore and I will be far away, just waiting for you to join us."

"Speak for yourself," Grigore muttered.

"Oh, hush, you," I told the snarky dragon. "I believe in you, Mitica. I know you can figure this out." I stood on my toes and pecked him on the lips.

He wrapped his arms around my waist and lifted me into a sincere kiss.

Grigore grunted from over Mitica's shoulder.

"Goodnight," I whispered sweetly. "And goodnight to you too, Grigore," I added. "Get lots of rest. You have a big day as a Mountie's noble steed tomorrow."

Grigore blew air through his lips, making a vaguely horse-like sound.

I giggled.

"Goodnight, bucuria mea," Mitica told me.

FORTY

The next day, I couldn't help but worry about how the investigation was going. Even William noticed my concern.

"What is the matter, my dear? Are you unwell? Shall I send for Dr. Hollander?" he asked as I stared out the window at breakfast.

"I'm fine, William. I'm just thinking."

"What could be worrying you so thoroughly, I wonder?"

My gaze slid from the window to his face. He still held his knife and fork, but his eyebrows were raised in curiosity.

"This ball," I lied. "It's a lot more work than I'd imagined. I still haven't heard from anyone in Toronto."

"Oh. Well, I wouldn't worry about that. You are so well-loved in Toronto. I have no doubt they will accept your invitations. I should think you will hear from them next week. But if you are concerned about how much time we will have, feel free to send telegrams once you receive responses."

"Thanks."

"Might it be nice to have dinner just the two of us this evening, my dear? We can also excuse ourselves from the festivities if you are tired."

I grimaced internally at the thought of being alone with William. *But*

I've refused him a lot thus far. Will he start to get suspicious? I plastered a smile on my face. "A quiet evening is just what I need," I agreed.

"Excellent. I will inform the kitchen staff."

Marguerite was all smiles as she set my small table for dinner that night.

"What are you so pleased about?" I asked her as she hummed happily.

"You and Monsieur are dining alone tonight. Romantique, non?"

"No," I corrected her. "We are having dinner alone because William thought it would help with my stress level." *Though it's far more stressful to be alone with him.*

She smirked at me as though I wasn't being honest with myself. "Celeste, you have forgotten much of your past, so I know you do not recall your moments of intimacy with Monsieur. You are so rigid now. You must be frightened. You should let Monsieur in a little. He is your husband after all, and he has always been quite gentle with you."

Ew. My expression must've given away some of my feelings because Marguerite giggled like I was some untouched virgin who didn't know what I was missing.

After Oscar had brought our meal and Marguerite had left us alone, my giant hotel suite seemed to shrink into a coat closet. I concentrated on keeping my breathing even and my expression polite.

William started talking about how receptive the guests he'd invited to our party had been so far. Though I didn't really care to talk about the party, I soon wished he had stayed on the topic.

"Marguerite tells me she purchased you a journal in town a while back. Have you been writing about your day and thoughts and the like? Perhaps bits of memories? Doing so might help you recover."

"No, I haven't used it. I honestly haven't remembered a thing from before Constable Delaforet took me in. Maybe the habit of journaling just isn't for me, you know? I mean, you said I didn't do it before either, so I'm sure it's fine."

His eyes sharpened for a moment. But when I blinked, the look was gone.

"Quite right," he agreed. "I have to say, your change in other habits has been rather interesting."

"Really?" I tried for unconcerned. "That's fascinating. Perhaps memory is a big part of our personalities."

"Indeed."

"What's changed about me?" I asked, curiously.

"Quite a bit, in fact. I would almost believe you were an entirely different woman if I hadn't known better. Even the way you walk and talk is different."

I flinched.

"And other things, too. For instance, you always loved music, but you would never sing. You hated your own voice, and you could only be caught humming when you didn't realize it yourself. To think you would sing before a room full of strangers is incredible."

He watched my reaction intently.

"That is strange," I admitted.

"And Hickory tells me you've become quite fond of horses. He's seen you visit the stables on multiple occasions."

Shit. "Yes, I like horses as long as I'm not riding them. There's one horse in the stables, Saundra, who is very sweet. I bring her sugar cubes from time to time. I didn't like them before?"

"You never paid them much mind one way or the other."

This attack was feeling very one-sided. Before I could think better of it, I said, "I notice Hickory around a lot since he's been back. It feels like he's around more than Marguerite. It's almost as if he's watching me."

"That's very astute of you, my dear. Indeed, I have told Hickory to watch you."

My heart pounded in my ears, but I had a steady voice when I asked, "Why is that?"

"You are my wife, and I am worried for you at present. This all must seem strange to you, not remembering anything from before. I've asked Hickory to keep an eye on you because I cannot as much as I would like. You should feel free to ask him for help with whatever you need as well."

I eyed William's congenial smile. *Man, you are good. What are you playing at?* Picturing Hickory's icy glare, I thought about William's suggestion. *Yeah fucking, right.*

I could hardly wait to call for Mitica that evening. I had to know how the first day of investigations went. I stared at the clock, watching the seconds tick closer to ten. As soon as the second hand hovered over the twelve, I called for him.

He cursed in frustration. "Send me back," he urged. "He's on the run. Oliver and I are giving chase, and I don't want to lose him. Don't summon me until I give you a sign. Hurry!"

"B-be gone, Dumitru." I stumbled in my rush.

He vanished.

My heart raced as I stood, small and alone, in my dark room. I bit my lip. *Shit. I hope I didn't just screw this up.*

It rained for the next two days. The dark gray clouds hung low and oppressive, mirroring the squeezed feeling in my chest. Every night, I watched out the window for some sign that it was safe to call for Mitica, that Mitica was safe. And every night, I went to bed anxious.

When news did come, it was in the most unusual form of Dr. Hollander.

After he'd checked my vitals and asked me questions about whether I'd recovered any memories, we started to chat as we had been doing.

"How is your family, Dr. Hollander?"

"Oh, my wife's back has been sore with all this rain."

I nodded. "And your brother?"

"He's doing quite well. Much recovered from that earlier incident."

"That's good to hear."

He bobbed his head. "Did you hear the big news from town?"

"Not unless it was in the paper."

"It wouldn't have been. It just happened as I was on my way here."

"Ah, so what happened?"

"The Mounties captured a murderer."

I froze. "They did? Who was it?"

"I haven't the slightest. Some Wyboka fellow I believe. He gave those two hardy lads a difficult time, I hear. They chased him all over the mountains before they caught him."

I had to wait for the morning edition to find out the full details.

I rushed downstairs, nearly tripping over the hem of my many skirts and asked Frederick for a copy before I'd even had breakfast. The paper crackled under my hurried hands as I unfolded it to the front page.

MOUNTIES APPREHEND WYBOKA MURDERER

FARRLOCH—Constable Wynn Delaforet and Subconstable Oliver Taylor apprehended and detained a Wyboka man suspected of murdering three of his tribe.

The suspect, Talking Raven, also known as Pówahkai, declined to comment. Talking Raven managed to avoid capture for nearly three days until the Mounties brought him in 12 May.

"The higher authorities have been notified, and he will stand trial," Constable Delaforet said.

When asked to speculate as to the suspect's motive, the Mounties did not yet have an answer.

I pictured Pówahkai's dark eyes and curled lip as he'd accused the presence of white people as the cause of the curse that took three Wyboka lives. He'd certainly been the most hostile of the elders I'd met in the teepee that day. *But why would he kill his own people? He seemed like he wanted to preserve them rather than kill them.*

Later that day, I finally received word from Toronto. It seemed Celeste was as well-loved as William had said. The manager of the orchestra was more than happy to send a quartet to our ball. He was thorough in his requests for compensation and travel expenses. After talking with William about it, I dispatched a telegram via Harrison, agreeing to the manager's terms.

That evening, I stood at my balcony window, still waiting for Mitica's sign. Yet again, I waited in vain.

As William read his paper over breakfast the next morning, I ate only my toast. The stress from recent days had tied my stomach in knots.

"Are you still concerned about the ball, my dear?" William asked, his paper sagging in the middle as he looked over it. "I thought you'd heard from the orchestra manager."

I glanced up at him. "Yeah, but I haven't heard from the artists yet. Wait. What is that?" I pointed to the front page. "Can I see that for a minute?"

"Of course." He folded the paper and handed it to me, his eyes squinched in curiosity.

WYBOKA MURDERER FOUND DEAD

FARRLOCH—Talking Raven, also known as Pówahkai, was found dead in the locked horse stall in which the Mounties were detaining him.

Talking Raven was being held under suspicion of murdering three of his own tribe. The suspect was found early this morning, his death apparently suicide by ingesting hemlock, the remnants of the poisonous plant still in his mouth.

Constable Wynn Delaforet and Subconstable Oliver Taylor, only yesterday lauded as heroes, are baffled by the turn of events.

Constable Delaforet assured the public he and his counterpart are looking into the matter but declined to comment on whether Talking Raven had revealed anything about his own guilt.

I pushed the paper away from me and got up from the table. *Holy Hell. What the fuck is going on out there? I need to see Mitica.*

"Where are you going, my dear?" William asked.

"To check the mail," I lied. "I'm sure you're right about the artists. Perhaps I received a response this morning."

Instead of stopping at the front desk to check the mail, I walked right out the door.

"Oh, have you come to see us off? That's very kind of you, Mrs. Broadstone," Reginald said, slowing my steps and pulling me from my thoughts.

The two men stood on the front stoop of the hotel as Campbell loaded their luggage onto his carriage. How he'd managed to mount an entire stuffed moose up there I had no idea.

"Yeah, I couldn't let you two leave without saying goodbye," I answered, having completely forgotten they were leaving that day.

"Very kind of you, lady. Very kind indeed," Colonel Higgins agreed with his friend.

"You two have a safe trip back. I hope you'll come visit us again."

"We certainly will. The hunt was fruitful, the food delicious, and the company excellent," Reginald praised.

"I'm glad to hear it." I smiled at them as they climbed into the carriage.

I waved goodbye with a sigh, thinking better of my hasty decision to head into town. *Wait for his sign, he said.* I clicked my tongue. *I hate waiting.*

It turned out I did have another letter from Toronto. The painter Gilbert Martin was distraught he could not accept my invitation. He did, however, give me the name of an excellent replacement, who was, at the moment, expecting word from me.

"Would you like me to send a response, Madam?" Frederick asked as I finished reading the letter.

Not really. I'd rather go into town and send it myself.

But as Hickory's cold eyes locked with mine over Frederick's shoulder, I sighed.

"Yes, thank you, Frederick." I sent another telegram to Toronto, this time to Amélie Roussel.

FORTY-ONE

As I stood watch at my window for the fourth night in a row, my heart was nowhere close to as calm as the nearly full moon drifting above the mountains.

I gazed up at it, hoping its gentle glow might give me some of its peace. Curiously, a part of the moonlight broke off and floated toward me. As I squinted at the moondust, it faded in and out like a firefly.

It's way too cold for fireflies.

Mesmerized, I opened my glass door and stepped onto the balcony. It floated closer and closer, then hovered before my eyes. I hesitantly lifted my hand and caressed it.

At my touch, it faded like a sparkler that had run out of fuel.

I frowned. *I killed it. Wait. Could that have been Mitica's sign? It must be.* I closed my eyes and called for my lover and soul mate.

To my relief, he didn't yell at me when he appeared. However, he was downcast, his face full of failure and shame. Wrapping my arms around him, I waited for him to be ready to speak.

"I do not know what happened, Erin. I thought I checked him for weapons before we locked him in the stall."

"So it's true then? Pówahkai killed himself by eating hemlock?"

"It seems to be the case."

"Did he say anything after you caught him? Did he really kill those Wyboka?"

He nodded. "The moment he discovered we were searching the elders' homes, he ran. It took us days to catch him. And when we did, all he would say is that his people were blind. He said white men had taken their spirits, their fight. He thought by poisoning the tea and blaming the curse on the white presence, his people would go to war and drive the invaders out."

My heart was heavy with sadness. "I can see his pain, and I even understand his logic. But nothing at this point could've driven the whites out. He was only harming his own people. The tragedy is that his actions may result in even stricter rules imposed on the Wyboka and the rest of the First Nations."

Mitica sighed and shook his head in grief.

"Hey," I murmured, reaching up and stroking his cheek. "I know this isn't the way you wanted this to end, but at least it's over. The Wyboka are safe. You caught the guy."

He gazed down at me and said, "I have to give my answer to the Zgrimties tomorrow."

"Right... The full moon."

We looked over at the silent moon hanging above the mountains, its glow much more haunting than before.

I slipped my hand into his and led him into my bedroom. "Come here. Tonight, it's just you and me. Tomorrow is tomorrow."

Though we were weary, afraid, and downhearted, we found solace in each other's embrace.

I did not see Mitica the following night while he performed some magic to give the Zgrimties his answer. I couldn't help but feel a little selfish that he was choosing me over working for them to help the fae and magic, but I kept repeating his assurances. *We can help the fae together.*

I heard from the sculptor I'd contacted the following day. Apparently, he'd left the moment he'd received my letter. He assured me he would arrive shortly after his letter.

After William had outright told me he'd asked Hickory to watch me, I thought I'd at least feel more at ease knowing I wasn't being paranoid. But the knowledge had the opposite effect. As I went about my regular duties and helped Harrison plan for the ball, every unexpected sound made me jump. When Hickory was in the room, his presence loomed over me. And when he wasn't, I still seemed to feel his icy gaze. He still never talked to me, which seemed to make everything worse. He was just this silent menacing shadow, watching. I spent as much time in my room as I could, which was increasingly more difficult as the party drew nearer.

Only a few days after receiving his letter, the sculptor arrived with a flourish shortly after breakfast.

"Celeste, my glorious patroness, how different you look!" he called from across the lobby.

Out of a process of elimination, I guessed he was the sculptor. "Andrew Shaw, is that you? I can't believe it. I'm so glad you've come."

He approached me and kissed each of my cheeks. I smiled to hide my surprise.

"Well when you wrote, I told Michael here. I said, Michael, my Celeste needs me. We must go to Farrloch immediately."

I looked over his shoulder at the handsome young man he'd indicated. Michael smiled and dipped his head to me.

"I don't believe we've met," I guessed.

"Oh, of course. I was so excited to see you that I've forgotten my manners entirely. Michael, this is my magnificent patroness you've heard so much about. Celeste, this is my assistant, Michael Hamilton."

The youth took my hand and kissed it. "Miss," Michael greeted.

"Oh, she's married now, you flirt."

"I refuse to call such a beauty Madam," Michael defended.

"You best watch out around him, Celeste. I believe he's stolen half the hearts in Toronto," Andrew teased.

Michael smiled prettily at this compliment.

"Well, why don't you two get settled, and we can talk about the ball and what we need after lunch?"

"Always the excellent hostess, Celeste. Marvelous suggestion. Come, Michael. Let's wash up and have a rest."

Lucky for me, Andrew was the talkative type. There was no way he would notice I wasn't Celeste, chattering on as he did. He had plenty of ideas for decorations. He spared no details, and I only understood half of what he said. I told him a painter would be arriving as well, and he should consider that while he planned.

He nodded and said all he needed was space to work, supplies, and access to an oven.

I let them work in the ballroom and introduced them to Harrison for supplies.

Louis was less than pleased when we asked if we could use one of his ovens. But with many assurances that the artists would not destroy his kitchen, he grudgingly agreed.

As Andrew and Michael talked with Harrison, I went to the laundry to fetch old sheets to cover the floor of the ballroom. It was gratifying to see how the digging of the cellar door progressed. The laundrymen were permitted to wash everything outside during construction to avoid getting the linens dirty. *It won't be long now.*

Within a few days, the ballroom also seemed a construction zone.

When Amélie Roussel arrived a few days after Andrew and Michael, I didn't have to pretend to know the quiet woman since she'd never met Celeste. In light of everything going on, it was a small relief to not have to remain so vigilant in conversation.

"Gilbert has told me many things about you, Madame," the young painter said. "I will endeavor to live up to your expectations."

"I'm sure you'll be wonderful, Amélie. And please call me Celeste."

When we entered the ballroom, Andrew and Michael looked up from their work. Michael gave Amélie a brilliant smile and stepped toward her.

"Michael," Andrew warned. "Now is not the time."

Michael winked at Amélie, and she averted her gaze, hiding a small smile.

After examining the space and talking with Andrew, Amélie seemed to have a better idea of what she wanted to do. I introduced her to Harrison, telling her he could get her whatever she needed.

With less than a week away until the party, the hotel was in frenzy. Guests flooded through the doors every day, and I didn't even attempt to keep them straight after a certain point.

As promised, Harrison took care of all the logistics. I don't know how much William was paying him, but it wasn't enough. He dealt with every lost trunk, late coach, and fatigued traveler with ease.

I couldn't wait for the day I would start my new life with Mitica, and my stress and anxiety was getting the better of me. As soon as Mitica left and I fell asleep, I would awake, overheated and sick to my stomach. I didn't ask Mitica to stay or tell him about my troubles. He had enough to worry about.

The Zgrimties had yet to dole out their punishment, and he'd received word his superiors in the Mounties were coming to investigate whether he and Oli had been negligent when it came to Pówahkai's suicide.

At least everyone was too busy to notice my lack of sleep or appetite. Everyone except Hickory, that is. I had no idea how he found the time to carry out his duties and still be lurking in the shadows, but he did. I was beginning to question whether he was magic or had a twin or something.

Two days before the masquerade, the musicians arrived. I heaved a sigh of relief as they lugged their instruments upstairs.

The artists were scrambling to get everything ready, but they assured me it would be fine. I was only just beginning to see their visions come to life. *They're going to have to work day and night to finish in time. At least the cellar door in the laundry room is done.*

The day before the solar eclipse, we were packed to capacity. Every seat was taken at meals, and I had no time to myself.

After lunch, Marguerite found me, her eyes lit up with delight. "Celeste, I just returned from Farrloch, and I have your dress. You must try it on to see if it fits. If non, alterations need to be made immediately."

"All right, I'm coming."

I followed Marguerite's bouncing form upstairs. *She's pretty excited about a dress she isn't even going to wear. She may answer to William, but perhaps Marguerite really is fond of Celeste.*

She beamed with pride as she opened the box and revealed the gown I was to wear the following night.

It was a deep purple with simple lines and a scoop neckline. A moss-green strip of satin ran from one shoulder across the torso to the waist, like a sash. The hem was the same moss green. The sleeves were wide and sheer, fluttering like the wings of a bird.

Madame Buvons and Suzette really do excellent work, I thought as I admired my reflection in the full-length mirror.

"It fits perfectly," Marguerite marveled. "Would you like to see the mask?"

I nodded, Marguerite's excitement infecting me as I stared at the gorgeous gown. She handed the mask to me, and I held it up to my face. It had a long, green beak with green feathers around the eyes and purple feathers around the edges.

"Belle," Marguerite complimented.

"Merci, Marguerite."

Her reflection smiled over my shoulder.

After a little while, I sighed. "Well, I better take this off and get back down there."

"Oui." Marguerite stepped forward to help me out of the gown.

When I called for Mitica that evening, he looked as nervous as I felt.

"I heard from the Zgrimties."

I held my breath, waiting for him to continue.

"They sent this message:

A full heart has wings, or so they say.
But wings are supported by the threads of fate.
When the Moon embraces the Sun, darkness envelops the day,
Heart's blood wells, and obsidian shadows await."

"Well, that's creepy. What do you think it means?"

He shook his head. "We may not know until after it happens, but the moon embracing the sun could be a reference to the eclipse."

I nodded. "We need to be extra careful tomorrow then." I sighed deeply. "We had enough to worry about already." I wrapped my arms around him, desperately taking comfort and giving it in return. "It'll work out. Everything is all set," I said, trying to reassure us both.

"Not everything," he argued.

I looked up at him. "Are we forgetting something?"

He nodded and pulled a small pouch from his pocket. The buckskin was warm and smooth in my palm when he handed it to me.

"What is it?" I asked, loosening the drawstring.

I tipped what looked like a necklace into my hand. Red and white threads twisted together to form the chain, and a trio of dried, white buds hung from the bottom like a pendant.

"The charm to help you handle Grigore, should he turn his magic on you."

"What flower is this?" I gently caressed the petals, careful not to break them.

"A snowdrop. Some of the Romanians brought a few with them from home. They dried them when they bloomed earlier this year."

Remembering how Ion and Mariana had reacted to the hultan, I raised my eyebrows at him. "You didn't terrify anyone to get these did you?"

He pursed his lips. "Not on purpose."

I stifled a laugh. *It really shouldn't be funny. Those poor people.*

"It is a relief to see you smile," Mitica murmured, stroking my cheek.

"I guess I've been a little stressed of late. "

"După ploaie, vine soare,"

"What does that mean?"

"After rain, comes sunshine."

I smiled up at him. "When did you get so optimistic?"

"When you said I was yours and you are mine."

"I vaguely remember that night," I teased.

"Vaguely, you say?"

I smirked and nodded at him.

"This, I cannot have, bucuria mea. You must always remember."

I shrugged. "I guess we'll just have to do it again."

His answering smile was slow and full of heat. "Will you give yourself to me, bucuria mea?" he asked, repeating the words from what seemed like ages ago.

"I am yours." My answer was the same.

That night, as Mitica and I claimed each other anew, our worries felt far away. There were no Zgrimties, no party, no charade to maintain, no William or Hickory. There was only Mitica. There was the heat his kisses left in their wake. There was the sound of his voice whispering my name in my ear. There was the feel of him deep inside me. There was Mitica, only Mitica.

FORTY-TWO

Breakfast was served early the next morning so everyone could eat before the eclipse. I forced eggs and toast around the lump in my throat, knowing I'd need the energy for the long day ahead.

When Harrison announced the eclipse was beginning, everyone filed outside. Excitement hummed through the crowd like the static electricity before a summer thunderstorm as we stared at the eastern sky.

We'd told the guests not to look directly at the eclipse so as not to damage their eyes, but the urge to do so anyway was difficult to resist.

Gasps and exclamations escaped the gathering as the world dimmed. An unexpected, primal fear gripped my heart. The hush that followed was eerie and profound. Not only were the guests silent, but the birds stopped singing. Even the wind stilled.

I let out the breath I was holding as the moon released the sun from its cosmic embrace, and the sun shone brightly once more. Stifling self-conscious laughter, I shook my head at my own silliness.

I barely had a moment's peace all day. Guests were needy, and everyone wanted to talk to the lady of the house.

After tea, I had just enough time to check in on the artists. As the heel of my boots echoed in the dark ballroom, I squinted to see if I was alone.

"Hello?" I called. "Amélie? Andrew? Michael?"

All at once, an overhead light illuminated their work. Gazing up at its source, my mouth hung open at the crescent moon and stars that hung from the ceiling.

"Papier-mâché," Andrew boasted from behind me.

"Wow, you guys. They're beautiful."

The sculptor and his assistant smiled and bowed in appreciation of my praise.

The peaked windows were covered with thick, velvet curtains of dark purple and silver trim.

On either side of the room, the walls were painted to look like archways. The rich texture of stone, the sparkle of lanterns off the Venetian waterways, gondoliers steering their gondolas in the night, and revelers in the distance, celebrating Carnevale, I couldn't tear my gaze away.

"Oh my goodness, Amélie. These are incredible," I murmured, overwhelmed.

"Merci, Celeste," Amélie thanked with pride.

"You guys have done amazing work. I love it so much, and I know the guests will, too. I'm sure you're tired, but I hope you'll come to the ball tonight."

They bowed as if I'd done them some great honor and not the other way around.

"Wonderful. Why don't you go rest for a little while before it starts?"

With only a few moments to spare before I had to get ready, I went to my room and stuffed my jeans, a few chemises, Oli's coat, and the pouch with the snowdrop charm into the bag Mitica had given me for our trip to Edmonton.

Knowing I wouldn't come back to my room once the ball started, I took my bag and smuggled it downstairs. I greeted the guests who called out to me as if I wasn't doing anything suspicious whatsoever.

Since it was such a nice day, the garden was full of strolling couples, who waved and tipped their hats at me. I stood by the iron gate for a long time, chatting and smiling at people before the coast was clear. Finally, there was a break in the line. My eyes scanned the paths for onlookers, and then I stuffed my bag behind the bush near the gate.

My heart hammered as I swiftly returned to my room to bathe. The water was hot but did not release the tension in my body. The scent of rose did not soothe me as I breathed deep and released it slowly. But after a few more breaths, my pulse was forced to even.

You got this, Erin. Just keep your eye on the ball and swing. Think of Mitica. It's all for him. Mitica...Mitica.

"Celeste?" Marguerite called from the other side of the bathroom door. "Are you finished? You need to dress so I can do your hair."

"I'm coming," I answered, climbing out of the tub. I shivered in the sudden rush of cold air as water dripped off me onto the floor. The towel was rough against my skin, but the friction warmed me. I dressed in my underclothes and paused by the door.

I took one more steadying breath and repeated his name again. *Mitica.*

As nice as the gown had looked the day before, it paled in comparison to when Marguerite was finished with me. Her reflection beamed at her masterpiece as she secured the mask's ribbon over my curled and pinned hair.

When she'd finished and left, I rose from my chair and glided toward the door, the ball, William, Mitica, and my fate.

"How beautiful you are this evening, my dear," William's voice greeted from behind a white mask that was very *The Phantom of the Opera.*

I closed and locked the suite door behind me, reminding myself to leave the key somewhere Frederick could find it.

"Thank you," I said out of obligation.

He held out his arm to me, and I took it gently, ignoring my clenched stomach. *Mitica.*

"It was kind of you to invite the townspeople to our gathering," he commented as he led me downstairs.

"It's prudent to have a working relationship with them. Don't you think?" *And I could tell Suzette really wanted to come.*

He nodded. "I am fortunate to have such a clever wife."

I didn't respond and kept my expression smooth and neutral.

Just before we entered the ballroom, William stopped, forcing me to halt as well. "You will, of course, save the first dance for me?"

I got the feeling I didn't have much of a choice. "Of course, William. Who else would I dance with if not my husband?" I nearly gagged on the word as I tried to sell my performance.

"Indeed."

"Aren't we going in?" I asked after he'd forced the unnecessary pause.

"Can't I gaze upon the glorious beauty of my wife for a moment longer?"

Is this a trick question?

His eyes behind his mask crawled over me like a spider with sticky, spindly legs. I couldn't hide my shudder.

"Can we go inside? It's a bit chilly out here," I lied, covering my reaction to him.

"Of course, my dear," he obliged coolly.

Finally, he led me inside the ballroom.

The velvet curtains, which had blocked out the sunlight earlier that afternoon, were drawn back, bathing the room in starlight.

Couples twirled and laughed in their elaborate costumes as the string quartet played a waltz.

I scanned the crowd, my heart jumping when I found Mitica. He stood, tall and dashing in his red serge, with his handsome Wynn face unmasked.

He must've felt my gaze upon him because he met my eyes and nodded with a reserved smile. My heart fluttered like the wings of a bird learning to fly, and my face heated beneath my mask.

Beside him, Oli talked with a dark-haired beauty in a gilded dress and mask, whom I could only assume was Suzette.

"Constable Delaforet is here. Aren't you going to greet him, my dear?" William asked.

"I'm sure I'll get the chance later," I hedged, not wanting to approach when he was with Oli and Suzette from fear they'd recognize me.

"Indeed."

From there, William and I greeted our guests, complimenting and receiving compliments in turn. The purpose of a masquerade, of course, is so everyone can be someone else, if only for a short while. As we weren't more than passing acquaintances with most of the people there, it wasn't difficult to wonder who some of them were.

I suspected seeing Michael and Amélie on the dance floor, and I could've sworn I heard Mellie ask Ion for something to drink.

While I was listening to one lady talk about her wayward daughter, William approached me with an outstretched hand.

"May I have this dance, my dear?" he asked formally.

I smoothed my features and nodded, excusing myself from the woman's problems.

When William slipped his arm around my waist, I went rigid. My palms began to sweat, and I couldn't seem to find my feet. My eyes looked everywhere but his. Still, I could feel his gaze, insistent, as he held me in his arms.

"I'm sorry, William," I said after the third time I'd messed up our steps. "I don't think I really remember how to dance."

"I understand, my dear." He didn't sound like he understood though.

"Perhaps Mrs. Broadstone just needs a little more practice," Mitica suggested, appearing beside us. "May I? I'm a patient tutor."

"Of course, Constable. Who could say no to Canada's finest?" William passed me over to Mitica, his mask covering his reaction.

I thought about the last time I'd danced with Mitica, and my body flushed. He pulled me into his arms, and I relaxed, knowing I belonged there. Dancing with Mitica was easy, like waves advancing and retreating on a beach. The movements were natural, and the world around us blurred as if submerged below the surface.

"I couldn't stand to watch any longer," Mitica murmured.

"Because I'm so bad at dancing?"

"No, bucuria mea. Because I had to suffer another man to hold you in his arms," he whispered, letting his Canadian accent slip for his term of endearment. "You're too beautiful for this world," he added.

My face heated as his blue eyes caressed me. It had been a while since I'd seen his Wynn face, and I was surprised by how much I'd missed it.

"Wynn..." I breathed.

"I know. You don't have to say it. I see it in your eyes, so full of longing, your cheeks, that perfect blush of pink. I know." His words kissed my ears, and I warmed at the sensation.

So lost was I in the sea of his gaze, drifting on the wind of his words, that I'd hardly noticed when we'd stopped dancing.

He bowed his head to me, thanking me for the dance. "Later," he promised. "You know where to go."

I dipped my head. "I'll be waiting," I told him.

"There is nothing anyone can do that would stop me from being with you."

As Mitica tore himself away, the sounds of the party crashed into my ears. Dazed, I took a deep breath and looked around.

William was at the far end of the room, talking to some men. He didn't seem to notice me. *Now is a good time to make my way outside.*

I turned toward the garden and forced myself not to rush. I even watched my feet as I went, to ensure they didn't betray me.

"Oop, sorry," I gasped when I bumped into someone. I glanced up, and my heart stopped. *I'd recognize that icy glare anywhere, even behind a mask.* "S-sorry about that, Hickory. I wasn't paying attention to where I was going."

"And where would that be?" he drawled accusatorily.

My heart sped as if making up for the beat it missed. "Oh, I'm just a little overheated from dancing, so I'm going to get some fresh air in the garden."

He didn't stop me, but I could feel his eyes follow me as I went.

The cold, night air scraped my throat as I heaved deep breaths in the garden. I placed a hand over my racing heart. *It's fine. There's no need for alarm. It's perfectly normal for me to go to the garden. Right? Right. It's Celeste's favorite place, and there are plenty of people out here already getting fresh air. For all I know, Hickory was coming in from the garden when I bumped into him. That's right.*

I took a few more steadying breaths, the night breeze cooling my face and arms. I smiled at the people coming in and out of the garden, and my heart eventually slowed.

I took the center path to the fountain as if that were my destination, trying to keep my pace stroll-like.

Apollo and Daphne still played out their tragic fates, forever stuck in the moment of eternal loss. *Some love was just not meant to be, but ours is. Mitica, I'm coming.*

I removed my mask and tied the ribbon around the key to my suite. I left it on the wide edge of the fountain. I took a deep breath, squaring my shoulders, and cast aside my fear. Then I strode toward the iron gate, snatched my bag from behind the bush, and slipped into the night.

FORTY-THREE

The road crunched beneath my lonely footsteps. With no moon to light the night sky, I could barely see my own frosty breath. Still, I knew if I just stayed on the road, I would eventually reach town. Beyond that, the Mounties' barracks.

Of course, Mitica would tell everyone I climbed the steep, nearby cliff and jumped to my death. But by then, I would be far away, flying with the clouds on Grigore.

The lights from the hotel glowed in the distance, and with every step, I was leaving Celeste Broadstone behind. I may not have been able to see the way forward, but I could feel it. I felt the sturdy earth of the road beneath my feet, and I felt the certainty that comes with following your heart.

The cold, mountain air stung my throat, but I could breathe again. I was free again.

I didn't worry if anyone in town saw me pass through. They could help corroborate Mitica's story later.

My feet were sore by the time I saw the welcoming visage of the Mounties' barracks. The hike had been long, and I was looking forward to riding for a while.

In the flickering light of a small fire, Grigore waited by the lake. His eyes glinted gold in his human face, and his raven-black hair lifted gently in the breeze. He gave me the same charming smile he had as when we'd first met. Then he frowned.

"I thought we were friends now?" he asked.

The snowdrop charm Mitica gave me must've worked. I looked down at the dried flowers around my neck on their red and white string. "We are friends, Grigore. But I'm not an idiot."

He pursed his lips. "Where are we going anyway?"

"Wherever the wind takes us."

He smiled contentedly. "I like the sound of that."

"Don't get too comfortable," Mitica commented, stepping into the fire-light, still in his Wynn visage.

I jumped, my heart yelping, then sighed in relief. "Jeez, Grigore. You could've told me he was coming."

He smirked. "You could have told me about the snowdrop."

"You know, we really need to work on our communica—"

"Shhh," Grigore hushed, cutting me off and rising to his feet.

"What is it?" I whispered.

"Someone is coming," he hissed.

"Who? Oli?"

He shook his head. "Nu, I do not know the scent."

I strained my ears but couldn't hear anything over the pounding of my heart. The seconds dragged on, and Mitica took a step toward me. He froze before he reached me. I followed his wide gaze. My blood ran cold, and my stomach dropped at the sight of a gun pointed in my direction.

"You must think me an old fool," William stated, stepping into full view. "Did you truly believe I thought you couldn't remember?"

"William—"

"Quiet, my dear, I am speaking."

I clamped my mouth shut, unwilling to argue with the man with a gun.

"I didn't believe you for a moment. I don't care how different you acted. I knew you knew. I must say, it surprised me when Marguerite found you in Farrloch. I was rather frantic when your body wasn't discovered with the horse's. Hickory had assured me he'd done the job right, but then where were you?"

My eyes flicked to Mitica, still frozen and clenching his jaw.

"But I saw through your charade immediately. The only reason this upstanding Mountie would allow you to return to such a dangerous situation is if he needed evidence to build a case against me. My suspicions were confirmed as you snuck around, digging through my room and my desk."

My mouth went dry.

"Oh, yes, my dear. I noticed you took the journal and letters, and so I waited. I waited to see what you knew and when you would make a move. And here we are. You've come to report me to the Mountie, to betray me."

Dude, I can't believe how off-base you are. But what am I going to say? No, William, I really can't remember you and your henchman trying to murder me. Actually, I'm just leaving because I'm having sex with this guy.

"You think you'll get away with this? Do you think I haven't reported this to my superiors?" Mitica took the smarter route and played along, trying to get us out of this situation.

William smirked. "I know you haven't. Hickory silenced that Indian dolt before he could implicate me. You have your word and no evidence, but for what is in my wife's pretty head."

"Hickory killed Pówahkai," I murmured at the realization.

William frowned. "I thought you were more clever than that, my dear. Yes, Hickory dispatched the rat with his own poison. He'd had his own reasons for betraying his people, of course. But I didn't really care what they were so long as the Wyboka abandoned the hot springs. A little money, a fool to do the work, and the superstitious imbeciles would be happy to be rid of the land. Unfortunately, I need to go a different route now."

"Are you fucking serious? You did all this for hot spring real estate?" I couldn't help but shout.

William snorted. "Enough with the ignorant act, Celeste. You overheard the Indian and I arguing about it that night and ran before you thought I saw you. Stupid girl. You even wrote about it in your journal."

"What exactly do you get from telling us all this?" I demanded. "Even if you shoot me, Wynn and Grigore will still make sure you're brought to justice."

"Celeste, you know me better than that. I am nothing if not practical."

At his words, Hickory stepped from the shadows.

William turned the gun on Mitica. "Hickory, you handle the other one. My darling wife will be no trouble on her own."

My stomach dropped, and my chest tightened.

"No!" I cried, my body moving toward Mitica without a thought.

Wynn's eyes widened in horror as I flew toward him. He reached his hand out toward me, and I was forcefully blown in the opposite direction.

The crack from William's gun echoed off the calm lake and the ancient mountains.

I sat up and met Wynn's blue eyes as he gasped and clutched his stomach. His fingers shined with blood, black as obsidian in the firelight.

My mind slowed and came to a halt, not able to comprehend what was happening.

As Mitica sank to his knees, his glamour flickered. I ran to him, my hands fluttering around him, not sure what exactly to do.

Bright flames flashed in my peripheral vision as Grigore breathed fire in his dragon form. The back of my mind was only vaguely aware that William and Hickory presented no further danger.

I heard their shouts drift into the distance, and Grigore moved to chase them.

"Grigore, no. I need you. Mitica needs you. Do you know healing magic?" I didn't take my eyes off Mitica's as his bloody fingers reached up to caress my cheek.

"I cannot use such magic as a zmeu," Grigore murmured, his voice tinged with sorrow.

"Bucuria mea," Mitica whispered.

"Don't talk," I hushed, looking down at his wound to see how bad it was.

The front of his red serge glistened in the flickering light.

My eyes filled with tears, and I swallowed a cry. "We're going to get you help. Okay? Dr. Hollander doesn't live far away. Grigore, go get him."

My hands pressed into Mitica's, attempting to keep any more life from escaping him.

"There's no time," Mitica murmured. "Listen...you aren't safe here... you...have to leave."

"No fucking way I'm leaving you!"

He gave me a sad smile. "Bucuria mea...Come closer."

I leaned in, my face not an inch from his.

"Kiss me," he demanded.

Tears rolled down my cheeks as I pressed my shivering lips to his.

"Te iubesc," he breathed.

I sobbed. "I...I love you, too."

His blue eyes, which had begun to fade, sharpened for a moment. In a strong voice, he ordered the universe to obey. His song was sweet and full of longing. As the foreign words washed over me, my eyes lost focus.

FORTY-FOUR

The rhythmic clacking of a train echoed off the hollow tunnel as a gust of foul, metallic wind rushed across my skin. Through the cacophony of screeching brakes and the murmuring crowd, loud in their multitude, someone was singing, low and soft.

"Erin," the unfamiliar voice whispered, cracking under the weight of his emotion. "Erin, wake up," he pleaded.

I took a deep breath, and my chest screamed in protest. "Ah," I groaned with a hiss, squeezing my eyelids tighter.

The voice, so close to me, gasped. "Erin? Don't try to move," he urged. "They've called for help. You're going to be okay."

I cracked my eyelids with effort, the sounds around me so loud and overwhelming as to be painful like an insistent poking on a bruise.

A pair of deep blue eyes met mine from beneath a dark fringe of swept bangs. The man's face was very close to mine as he knelt on the platform of the red line, cradling me in his arms. I searched his features. He looked familiar somehow, like someone who had stood behind me in line at a coffee shop. My gaze landed on the White Sox beanie he wore, and I scrunched my nose.

"Your hat is ugly," I croaked.

His eyes filled with tears. He closed them and shook his head, a low, nervous laugh coming unevenly from his throat. His chuckle shook his body and mine in return.

I hissed as the motion brought a wave of pain over me.

"I'm sorry. I know it hurts. I wish I could have done more. The ambulance is on its way. Just hang tight, okay?" he assured, his brow crinkled.

"What happened?" I murmured.

The man glanced around at the crowd of onlookers and dropped his voice even lower. "Someone pushed you in front of the train. Luckily, you weren't hit head-on, or I might have not been able to save you."

The image of Mitica dying in my arms flashed in my mind. *So was it all just a dream? Wynn? Mitica? Even Grigore the shape-shifting dragon?* My chest ached with a sense of loss that had nothing to do with my injuries.

"So I didn't die like we thought," I muttered.

"Only for a moment," the man answered with a relieved smile.

I met his eyes sharply. "Who are you?" I asked.

"Don't you recognize me, bucuria mea?"

My eyes widened, and I froze. "You...how did you...? I saw you die," I stammered.

He smiled softly, stroking my cheek just the way Mitica used to. "I was reborn. It took me a long time to explain the magic I have in this life. But once I discovered my true name, I remembered everything: the Mounties, the hultan, the Zgrimties, and most importantly, you. I remembered where you were from and your name. And since you're a journalist, you weren't hard to find, especially not with the Internet. I'm sorry I couldn't heal all of your injuries like last time. I don't have a lot of magic in the city."

"When did you find me?"

"About six months ago," he admitted.

"Why didn't you tell me?"

He snorted and tilted his head. "How would that conversation have gone? Hi, I'm Greyson. You don't know me, but I'm your soul mate. We met in a past life when you traveled through time."

I pursed my lips. "Okay, you have a point. But you still could've talked to me."

He smirked. "I did. Tons of times. I even work in the same office as you."

"Shut up. You do not."

He nodded with a laugh. "I'm a photographer."

I squinted at him. The memory of a coworker with dark hair, staring at his smartphone in the elevator flashed in my mind. "Holy shit."

He grinned.

"You dirty stalker," I teased.

His smile dropped. "I tried to stop it. I swear I did. I knew you'd be fired from the paper and pushed in front of the train on the black moon. I just wasn't fast enough."

I reached up hesitantly and caressed his cheek with my fingertips. "If I hadn't been hit by the train, I never would've gone back."

"I know, but we still could've had a different life together in this lifetime."

I smiled at him. "You know what? I'm actually kind of pissed at you. I mean, what the fuck was that in 1900? I try to save you from being shot and you use magic to push me out of the way? You totally ruined my big heroic moment."

He ducked his head sheepishly.

"You're just going to have to make it up to me," I pronounced.

He smirked. "I can do that."

I snorted. "You think it will be that easy?"

"I have my ways." He hovered lower and kissed me. His lips were warm and familiar on mine. I giggled as he kissed my cheeks, my nose, and my forehead. Then I winced as my laughter upset my injuries. Still, it was worth the warmth that spread through me.

"That life you mentioned, can I take that as a promise?" I murmured.

"Da, bucuria mea, and all the lifetimes to come."

EPILOGUE

"**H**urry up," I called over my shoulder to Greyson as we hiked up the hill.

"What's the rush? You should be taking it slower anyway. You haven't been out of physical therapy for that long," he complained.

"It has been more than six months, and we have to get there before the sun rises. Carl wants that sunrise shot."

"You know what? Carl can kiss my ass. I don't care if he's our editor. What kind of sadist interrupts a man's honeymoon to ask for a stupid shot of a sunrise over a lake and mountains?"

I paused to let him catch up and kissed him on the cheek. "The sooner you get the shot, the sooner we can go back to the hotel and commence with the honeymooning."

He smiled slyly. "Or we could just make some memories out here."

Grabbing my hips, he pulled me toward him. I squeaked in surprised delight. My core heated as he pressed his lips and body to mine.

"Okay," I breathed. "After you get the shot."

As we raced up the rest of the way to the top of the cliff overlooking the lake we'd seen over a century before, my mind was full of Greyson. I didn't think about the mayor's office lackey who'd pushed me in front of the train. I didn't think about my previous editor feeling guilty and writing an exposé about his involvement in city hall corruption. I didn't think about how the mayor had quietly retired without any sort of real retribution. I didn't think about the clerk at the Farrloch Hotel telling us about how the founder had gone mad. I didn't think about how all of Farrloch was dragon-crazy. Or about the Loch Ness-level legend of the dragon with the yellow gem on its forehead who they swear could still be seen flying over the lake at night. I didn't think about the museum in the Mounties' barracks. And I didn't think about the two small gravestones nearby, where secret lovers rested quietly beside one another.

I only thought of Greyson, the talented photographer with a sharp sense of humor and a strong moral compass, the White Sox fan who never admitted defeat even when the Cubs broke their curse and finally won the World Series, the man who would use his magic to find me no matter how many years and miles separated us.

Once we'd reached the summit, Greyson pulled me into another demanding kiss, ignoring the golden sunrise sparkling off the clear, blue water of the lake.

"Hurry," I urged as he kissed down my neck.

"It's not fun if you rush," he teased.

"Take the shot," I barked.

"Fine." After uncapping his lens, he snapped a round of pictures.

Impatiently, I stepped in front of his camera, blocking his view. "Good enough," I declared.

"You think this will be enough for Carl?" he asked.

"I'm not worried about Carl."

"Oh?" He smirked as I moved in close to him.

"I'm worried about claiming and being claimed by my husband."

"You don't need to worry about that, bucuria mea. I will claim you over and over, as many times as you need."

"Forever?"

His smile was all the answer I needed. Still, he whispered, his deep blue eyes warm and true, "Forever."

A Very Witchy Yuletide

Yuletide

D. Lieber

To my Pagan sisters and brothers. Blessed Be.

Special Thanks

As always, I would like to thank everyone who helped me research and beta this book. A special thanks to Joyce, Amy, Wren, Kass, Laura, Aunt Debbie, and John.

Dear Reader,

Let me take you aside for a moment before you begin. While I am attached to all of my work, this story holds a particularly special place for me.

As someone who is Pagan and visually impaired, I have been pressured to share those aspects of my life in my writing for many years. People want to know what it's like. I understand. I found, to my surprise, that sharing those very personal experiences is much more difficult than I thought it would be. It puts me in a very vulnerable place.

The confrontations my characters experience in regards to their religion and Evergreen's visual impairment are all situations I have experienced in my own life. However, I did take some artistic license in regards to exact situation to better fit the story. This is by no means my autobiography. In fact, Evergreen responds to many of these confrontations in a completely different way than I did myself.

I would also like to say that my experiences do not necessarily reflect the experiences of the people who are part of the same minorities as myself. I do not speak for all Pagans everywhere. My experiences with my own blindness do not necessarily reflect the experiences of the entire blind community. Both of those things are very personal and are experienced in a myriad of ways. These are but some of the situations I've dealt with in my personal life.

Thank you for taking the time to read this little note. I do hope sharing this story, and thus some of my personal experiences, will let you see the world from a slightly different angle.

Your support is much appreciated, as always.

D. Lieber

CHAPTER 1

$\mathcal{E}$vergreen took a deep breath and tapped the submit button, sending her sparse résumé off to another company that wasn't likely to hire her. Placing her tablet on the coffee table before her, she ignored the building anxiety in her chest.

She grabbed her tea from the table, the fabric of her sweatshirt protecting her fingers from getting burned by the hot ceramic. Tucking her legs under her on the couch, she looked out at the bright, snowy morning. The snow dusted the naked tree limbs of the woods outside her apartment window, and little icicles glistened in morning sunshine.

Muir sat tall on the windowsill, his striped tail twitching as he squinted at some busy, morning birds.

Evergreen's apartment was unusually quiet this morning, her roommate having gone home for the holidays. Most of the building was quiet in fact, due to the amount of college residents. It was the pleasant silence of solitude where she could just sit, drink tea, and watch her cat.

The stillness was broken with a loud chiming melody. She jumped when her cellphone rang, hissing as hot tea seeped into the cloth of her sweatshirt and pajama pants.

She put the cup back on the table and answered the phone without seeing who was calling.

"Hello?" she said, clicking her tongue at having made a mess.

"What's wrong?" her mom asked.

"Nothing. I just spilled some tea."

"Are you all right?"

"Yeah, I'm fine. What's up?"

"Well, I know you said you weren't going to come home for break because you wanted to look for jobs, but I'm calling to ask you to reconsider."

Evergreen frowned. "I know I've always come home for Yule before, but I only have one semester left until I graduate. Between helping with preparations and taking care of the guests, it's just too busy there."

"I know, but I really think coming home would be good for you. I can tell you're stressed. You still have an entire semester to look for jobs, and being around family would help you relax."

Evergreen hesitated.

"And I called to tell you we're doing something special this year," her mom added.

"Yeah? What's that?"

"Well, as it's been a while since we've all gotten together, your dad and I talked with the old coven, and everyone has decided to come for a visit."

Evergreen's heart jumped. "Everyone...? Do you even have space for everyone?"

"Well, not everyone. I doubt Charlie will come. We don't have any retreats scheduled, so we can make room, even if you kids have to put sleeping bags on the floor."

"You're *really* convincing me," Evergreen answered, rolling her eyes.

"Oh, stop. It's been so long since we've all been together. It won't be the same if you aren't there. Won't it be nice to see everybody?"

Her answering silence was heavy. *Yes, it would be nice to see everyone,* Evergreen thought. It had been a long time since the old coven had all been in the same place. What with life being as it is, the families had moved away one by one.

A Yuletide with everyone there sparked joyful memories. So many sabbats happily celebrating the seasons. Of course she wanted that nostalgic feeling again. But things were different now. She was different.

Evergreen bit her lip and twisted the end of one sleeve between her hands. *Can I even handle it?* she wondered.

"Is...is he...?" she started to ask.

"Yes," her mother answered. "Sawyer will be here, too."

Evergreen's chest tightened, and warmth spread through her. "I don't know, Mom..." she murmured.

Her mom's voice softened into that soothing tone only mothers can manage. "You'll be all right," she promised. "It has been what? Almost five years since you last saw him? You're a different woman now. Think of all you've seen, experienced, accomplished. Surely you aren't still carrying a torch for him, are you? After all this time, how many boys have you dated since then?"

"A few."

"And you did just fine with them. Don't let an old crush get in the way of us having a happy Yule."

"You're right." Evergreen nodded curtly and straightened her spine. "It was just a silly schoolgirl crush. It's not like he ever even noticed. And I've had good relationships since then, even if they didn't turn out. I'm not the same insecure girl who used to watch him. And you know what? He's probably not the same either. He's probably nothing like the boy I knew."

"That's right," her mom encouraged. "It will just be old friends getting together for the holiday," she promised.

Evergreen smiled. "That sounds nice."

"So you'll come?"

"Yeah, just let me pack my bags and get Muir in his carrier. I'll be there by dinnertime."

Her mom let out a soft squeak. "I'm so happy you reconsidered. Be careful. Okay? I'll see you later."

"I will. Love you, Mom."

"I love you, too."

After hanging up the phone, Evergreen sat for a moment. Anxiety swirled in her gut, but she squashed it down. *I can do this. No problem,* she thought.

After dumping what was left of her now cold tea into the sink, she went and scooped up Muir. She stood at the window, the morning sun bright but distant as it hit her face. Holding Muir like a baby, she kissed him on his little forehead. "Come on, Muir. Let's get ready, eh? I'm going to pack your favorite toy and treats. I'll make sure to put your warm, fuzzy blanket in your carrier. You better behave yourself. No fighting with Larkspur and no attacking the Yule tree. I'm going to put your special Yule collar on you. We've got to make you all handsome to see everyone. We're going home, Muir."

CHAPTER 2

Sawyer could feel his cellphone silently vibrating in the pocket of his jeans, but he just let it ring as he concentrated on bottle-feeding the baby bat, which was wrapped in a towel in the crook of his arm.

"There's a good girl," he murmured to the little creature as she hungrily sucked on the bottle. "Good job," he praised.

After putting the pup back with her siblings, he washed his hands and pulled his phone from his pocket. He'd missed a call from his mom.

As he headed to the breakroom, he held and pressed the two on his screen. While the speed-dial connected, he poured himself some coffee from the communal pot.

"Why didn't you answer?" his mom asked once she'd picked up.

"I'm at work, Mom. What's up?"

"I thought you had the day off."

"Well...they were short-handed."

His mom clicked her tongue. "Aren't they always?"

"Come on, Mom. Don't be like that. The animals need to be taken care of."

"Are you still going to be able to come home for Yule?"

"Yeah, no problem. It was only today they needed extra help."

"Well, that's all right then."

"Did you need something? Or did you just call to chat?"

"There's been a change of plans."

Sawyer frowned into his coffee. He didn't like when his mom got that conspiratorial tone in her voice. But he waited for her to continue.

"Ria called. She and Wes invited everyone to come and stay with them for the holiday. I told them we would both be there."

Sawyer froze, his heart pounding hard in his chest. But he didn't speak; he'd always relied on silence to hide his emotions in situations such as this.

"Eeva will be there," his mom continued, hitting the exact point he both longed to know and dreaded to hear. "Ria tells me she's close to graduating with her Bachelor's. Did you know she goes to the college near you?"

Sawyer cleared his throat. "No, I didn't know," he lied.

His mind flashed with images from his youth: Eeva all in white at Imbolc, Eeva dancing around the Maypole at Beltaine, Eeva sitting with her back to a tree and her nose buried in a book. He'd never been brave enough to tell her how he'd felt. Animals and plants were much more his speed. The trees didn't care if you stumbled over your words.

Had she been sad when he'd gone so far away to school? He'd always wondered. But she'd never called or texted. She'd never messaged him on social media. She'd never even emailed. It's not as if she hadn't known how to find him if she'd wanted to. He remembered the last time he'd seen her. She sat on the steps of his porch, her elbows on her knees and her head in her hands as she stared at the oak tree in his front yard. She'd only looked at him for a moment as he called his goodbyes before her parents and his mom had embraced him, wishing him well on his way to the freshman dorms three states over.

"Sawyer, are you listening to me?" his mom shouted into his ear, drawing him from his memories.

"I'm sorry. What did you say?"

She sighed dramatically. "I said Ria told me she's single right now."

His chest squeezed. "So?" he managed.

"You can't fool your mom, mister. I know how you've always felt about her."

"That was a long time ago."

She blew a raspberry into the phone. "Uh-huh and those perfectly nice girls you dated in college? Shelby and Michelle and what was her name?"

"Krystal," he supplied.

"Right, and Krystal. What was wrong with them? I didn't push you at the time because I knew the problem."

His face flushed, dreading what she was about to say.

"They weren't Eeva. That's what," she finished. "And now you have the chance, and all you can say to me is 'so?' as if it all has nothing to do with you?"

"What do you want me to do, Mom?" Sawyer snapped. His stomach clenched in immediate regret.

"You're not the same scared little boy anymore, Sawyer. You've done a lot since you went away. You graduated college and got a job doing what you love. I've seen you grow into a good and confident man. But as wonderful as you are, son, you can't expect everything to just come to you like a stray cat you've coaxed into trusting you. Sometimes, you do have to put in a little bit of effort and go after what you want. Show her who you are. Tell her how you feel."

"It *has* been a long time. And you're right, I've changed a lot. But don't you think she's changed, too? She's probably nothing like the Eeva I knew."

"Well, there's only one way to find out. Are you going to let that uncertainty get in the way? Come to the gathering. You don't have to do anything right off. Spend some time together; see how you both have changed. Maybe you'll find you like her even more now."

"You know what? You're right. There's no pressure after all this time. Maybe I'll find I like her more, and I'll finally have the courage to tell her. But it's also possible I won't like her at all anymore, and I can finally move on. This is a good idea."

He could hear the smile in his mom's voice when she responded. "Excellent. So after work you'll come home? Then you can spend the night here, and we can go there tomorrow morning."

Sawyer nodded. "Sounds good."

"Wonderful. Love you bunches."

"Love you, too, Mom. Bye."

After his phone beeped in his ear, Sawyer stood in the relative silence of the wildlife refuge's breakroom, the only sounds the humming of the refrigerator and the distant chirps, squeaks, and squawks of the animals in their care. Closing his eyes, he let out a long sigh to steady his nerves. *I can do this. No problem,* he thought.

CHAPTER 3

Evergreen smiled to herself as the train slowed down, pulling into the Main Street station of Birchland. Holiday decorations sparkled and twinkled in every storefront window. The huge tree in the town square was already alight as the early sunset of winter hugged the western horizon.

After slinging her backpack over her shoulders—double checking to ensure her cane was folded inside—she pulled her luggage down from the overhead compartment. Then she hurriedly grabbed Muir's carrier, knowing the train wouldn't be stopping at the station for very long. Still, she was careful as she walked past the seated passengers, not wanting to hit them with anything.

On the platform, Muir meowed his complaints as the cold wind blew through the holes of his carrier.

"I know, baby boy," she soothed. "I will call for a ride right now."

Evergreen dug her cellphone out of her back pocket and pulled up the ridesharing app. She went about ordering a ride and headed to the front of the station.

Muir cried pitifully again.

"Don't worry," she told him. "It says our driver will be here in four minutes. Then you will be in the nice warm car."

A few minutes later, a light blue car pulled up to the curb. The door opened, and a man stepped out. He wasn't much taller than Evergreen, but what he lacked in height he made up for in good looks and fashion sense. His charcoal peacoat was pristine over his straight-legged jeans and clean, leather boots.

"Are you Niko?" Evergreen asked, trying to place the name the app had given her.

"Yes." His dark eyes glinted in his olive face, and his curly, black hair moved only slightly as he nodded at her. "You must be Evergreen," he said, his voice rich and smooth.

She nodded in turn.

"Let me help you with your bags," he offered, holding out his hand for her roller suitcase.

"Oh, yeah. Also, I have a cat. I hope that's okay."

"No problem. I love cats."

Evergreen followed Niko to his trunk and took off her backpack as he lifted her suitcase into it. She surreptitiously checked the license plate, comparing it to the one the app had provided. Then she climbed into the passenger seat.

As he got behind the wheel, Niko looked over at Muir's carrier in Evergreen's lap, lowering his head so he could see through the gate.

"He's a cutie," Niko said.

Evergreen smiled. "Thank you."

Niko pulled away from the curb. "So you're going up to the retreat center? What sort of retreat are they having this time?"

"You know it?"

"Of course. I take guests up there all the time."

Evergreen nodded. "They aren't having a retreat. My parents own it. I'm just coming home for the holidays."

"Ah."

A few blocks away, they were out of the main part of town and on the winding road engulfed by snow-laden trees. Evergreen pushed her sunglasses up onto her head, the car too dark with the added shade. She glanced over at Niko, now a silhouette against the outside light.

"Have you lived in Birchland long?" Evergreen asked.

"How do you know I'm not from here?" He sounded like he was smirking.

I'd remember a guy like you, Evergreen thought. "Well...I don't know everyone, but there's only one high school in town. And you don't look that much older than me. Unless...did you go to Birchland Catholic?"

He nodded. "I did, though I took an elective summer class at Birchland High once. You're looking at someone who survived twelve years of Catholic school. I've lived here my whole life, except for the summers I spent visiting family in Greece."

"That must have been fun."

"It was," Niko agreed. "What year did you graduate? 2017? 2018?"

"2016. You?"

"2015."

"I had a...friend who graduated that year, but he went to Birchland High."

"Yeah? What's his name?"

"Sawyer Collins."

"Collins, Collins," he muttered, searching to place the name. "It sounds familiar...Oh! Was he a tall guy, kind of quiet, with wavy blond hair and brown eyes? Yeah, I think he was in that summer photography class. He didn't really talk much, but man his nature photography was amazing."

They're amber not brown, Evergreen thought. "Yeah, he was really into photography. That probably was him."

Niko glanced over at her with a grin. "Look at that," he said. "Birchland is a small town after all."

Her skin tingled as his suave tone caressed it.

"What's Collins doing now?"

"I don't know. I haven't talked to him in a long time. But he's supposed to be coming in for the holiday, so maybe you'll run into him."

"Yeah, maybe. Well, here we are," Niko said, pulling into the round drive of The Spiral Path Retreat Center and parking.

They both got out of the car and went back to the trunk. Niko placed Evergreen's suitcase on the ground beside her, then hooked her backpack onto the extended handle.

"Well, if you ever need a ride, you know how to find me," he said with that easy tone.

She nodded. "Thank you. Happy holidays."

"You too, Evergreen. See you around."

Evergreen could feel his lingering gaze as he flashed her a smooth smile. Her cheeks warmed. Niko gave her a polite nod, got back into his car, and drove away.

She shook herself. *Gods, he was pretty,* she thought. Even though she knew he was only nice to her to get a good rating, she didn't even care. It felt good when a hot man smiled and called her name, but she had no delusions that he was attracted to her. She could tell the difference. Besides, she'd gone twenty-two years without ever seeing Niko. It wasn't likely she'd ever see him again.

As she turned toward the sturdy lodge, the calm warmth of home and hearth settled into her. Grabbing Muir's carrier and her roller suitcase, Evergreen headed up the wooden steps and in through the front door without knocking.

"I'm home!" she called as she closed the door behind her.

The cadence of small feet running on the wood floor approached her. Evergreen tensed for impact, placing Muir's carrier on the ground, as Sol rounded the corner.

"Eeva!" the little boy squealed.

Evergreen knelt to better catch the child as he launched himself into her arms.

"Hey there, Sparkler," she said, embracing him. "How did you get here before me? You must have learned how to fly."

He giggled, pulling away from her. "You're silly. Witches can't fly."

Evergreen tilted her head with a grin. "Are you sure about that?"

He nodded.

She reached out and tickled his belly. "Really sure?" she challenged through his giggling squeals.

"Yes," he screamed his answer.

"Well then. I've got news for you, sir." She picked him up, holding him by his middle tucked against her side like a football. She spun around, making zooming sounds as he laughed, his arms held out like Superman.

Slightly out of breath, Evergreen returned Sol to his feet. "See?" she said. "You flew."

"Do it again!" he demanded.

Just as she smiled, wondering if she had the endurance to pick the boy up for another go, his mother came around the corner.

"What's all this noise?" Cassandra asked, her voice smiling.

"Eeva was teaching me to fly," Sol explained.

"She was?" his mother asked. "Well, why don't you fly to the bathroom and wash your hands for dinner?"

The boy looked back up at Evergreen. "You're coming too?"

Evergreen smiled. "I'll be right there," she promised.

And Sol was gone just as fast as he'd come.

Evergreen embraced Cassandra. "Hey, cuz," she murmured.

"Hey. Glad you made it safe. Aunt Ria was starting to worry."

"Starting? When isn't she already?"

Cassandra chuckled.

"I can't believe how big he's gotten," Evergreen commented.

"I know. He's growing so fast. Almost five already. But, you know, it wouldn't be so much of a shock if you came around more often."

"Yeah, yeah. I hear you. It will be easier when I'm done with school."

Cassandra nodded and picked up Muir's carrier. "Is your mama still spoiling you, Muir?" she asked the cat, peering in at him.

"He's not spoiled. He's just loved. You have your baby, and I have mine."

"Aunt Ria already put the spare litter box in your room. Do you need help carrying this stuff upstairs?"

"No, thanks. I can handle it," Evergreen responded.

Evergreen headed up the stairs to the third floor where her attic bedroom had been. She pulled up short when she opened the door. Even though she knew none of her things were there anymore since she'd taken them to her apartment, it was still jarring to see her familiar space turned into the cozy but impersonal visage of a guest bedroom.

Evergreen let Muir out of his crate and showed him where the litter box was. After he'd hopped out, she cradled him in her arms and headed downstairs.

"Wow," she murmured as she entered the common room.

The mantle of the fireplace was covered in greenery. The small flickering lights among the green said there were also candles. A fire crackled in the hearth.

The Yule tree in the corner was bright with string lights, and the heavy fragrance of cinnamon drifted in the air, emanating from the scented pinecones that hung among the branches.

"We did good, right?" her mom said, coming from the direction of the kitchen.

"It's beautiful," Evergreen complimented, crossing the room and kissing her mom on the cheek.

"I'm so glad you decided to come, baby girl," her mother said.

"Where's Dad?"

"In the kitchen. Dinner should be done in a few minutes."

"Here, hold your grandcat while I go say hi." Evergreen handed Muir into her mother's arms.

He purred as his grandma scratched his ears.

"Something smells good," Evergreen announced upon entering the large kitchen.

"There she is," her dad said, looking over his shoulder as he stood at the stove. "How was the ride?"

Evergreen stood on her tiptoes and kissed her dad on the cheek. "Not bad. Muir wasn't happy for the first hour, but he eventually fell asleep."

Her dad nodded. "You hungry?"

"Starving."

"Well, you're just in time. Why don't you help Mom set the table?"

"You got it."

The quiet family dinner was anything but. Every few minutes, a pair of fuzzy bodies tore through the dining room while Muir and Larkspur chased each other. Cassandra punctuated the scramble by scolding Sol every time he moved to join in the race. When ten minutes had passed with no sight of them, Evergreen got up, concerned about their silence.

"Muir?" she called, her tone laced with warning. "You better be behaving yourself."

Evergreen stalked through the house, her eyes scanning for her mischievous cat.

She found Larkspur seated at the base of the Yule tree just staring into the branches. She squinted at it, creeping closer as she searched, the lights too bright for her to make out anything dark.

"Muir!" she shouted.

The cat's yellow eyes, pupils wide, stared out at her from the branches of the tree.

"Get out of there, right now," she demanded.

He didn't move.

She reached toward him, and he jumped out of the tree, running to the safety of some dark corner where she couldn't reach him. Larkspur still sat at the foot of the tree, watching the exchange as though he couldn't be bothered.

"You're a bad influence," she said to her cat-sibling. Evergreen sighed and returned to the table. "These cats," she said, shaking her head as she sat back down.

CHAPTER 4

"Are you sure it's not too early?" Sawyer asked his mom as they drove up the winding road to the retreat center.

"I told Ria last night we'd be coming in early," she answered from the passenger seat of his car, wrapped in her hat, coat, scarf, and mittens while snuggled into a blanket. The heater was blaring so high that Sawyer had taken off his winter things and just wore his T-shirt and jeans.

"Besides, she knows how traffic makes me nervous. She told us to let ourselves in," she added.

He pulled into the round drive and parked behind a blue Honda he didn't recognize. The bumper sticker proudly proclaimed that the owner was a "Tree Loving Dirt Worshiper." Sawyer smiled, knowing he was in the right place.

It had been years since he'd been to the Pendre's house, but it looked just the same as he remembered. He glanced over at his mother as she struggled to free herself from her many layers.

He chuckled at her. "Do you need some help, Mom?"

She sighed. "No, I just can't seem to—ugh, it's like quicksand!"

He laughed harder. "Let me help you."

She glared at him. "Are you laughing at me, son?"

He tried to smother his smile. "Maybe. You know, if we had gotten in a crash, I bet you wouldn't even be injured with all your layers of cushion."

She scowled, though she had to be used to him teasing her for always being cold by now.

"Do you want my help?"

"No," she said proudly without bite. "I can do it myself."

"All right. Whatever you say," he said mockingly.

She pursed her lips. "Just go."

He moved around to the trunk and grabbed their luggage. As he closed the trunk, he peered through the back window at her. She had just extricated herself from the blanket and was struggling with her scarf. He shook his head, snickering to himself, and went on ahead.

Sawyer opened the front door as quietly as he could. It wasn't super early, but people did tend to sleep in while they were on vacation. He didn't want to disturb anyone.

He took the bags through the entrance hall and stopped in the living room. *I don't know what rooms we're staying in,* he thought. *We can just hang out here until someone gets up.*

He glanced around the room, cold and still in the early morning light. Evergreen boughs and ivy twisted among beeswax pillar candles on the mantle above the hearth. The Yule tree in the corner was alight with crystal-style string lights, which danced on the holly berries and bells hung on the tree. Cinnamon scented pinecones were nestled in the branches.

Feeling something against his legs, Sawyer looked down at the grey tabby as it rubbed up against him, trilling. He smiled at the cat and crouched, holding out his hand so the animal could smell him.

It trilled again and purred. Sawyer picked it up, scratching its ear to the cat's sounds of delight.

"Muir!" A shout came from the direction of the kitchen. "I swear to all the gods, you better not be in that Yule tree."

Sawyer looked up just as Eeva stopped short upon entering the living room. She was still in her pajamas: flannel plaid pants with an oversized hoodie and fuzzy socks. Her long, brown hair was dyed a dark green, and it was still messy from sleep.

His heart throbbed in his chest, and he held his breath as he met her deep ocean blue eyes. His memories hadn't done her justice.

"Hey," he said lamely. "It's uh...been a while." He cleared his throat, his own voice sounding hoarse and uneven in his ears.

She blinked as if she'd forgotten who he was, then frowned. "Yeah, I suppose that happens in life... How is...everything? I mean, I hope you and your mom are doing all right." Her tone was distant and polite. Formal.

His stomach clenched as his raised hopes deflated. "Yeah, everything's fine. We're both good. And you?"

"Same."

As the strained silence grew between them, Sawyer grasped for something to say. Anything. "So...my mom says you're graduating soon. What are you studying?" He knew very well she was studying history. It didn't matter that he'd said more times than he could count that he didn't care. The moment his mother mentioned her, he'd always internalized the information. And he'd taken more than a few glances at her social media profiles over the years, though he'd gotten better about that.

"Eeva!" his mother called, entering the room before they could struggle on in their conversation.

Eeva smiled, her eyes alight with the same warmth and kindness he'd seen so many times in his youth. "Tara," she said as his mother embraced her tightly. "It's so good to see you."

His mom held her at arms' length. "Let me get a good look at you." She clicked her tongue in a sound of appreciation. "Oh, still as beautiful as ever."

A light blush dusted Eeva's cheeks. *She still gets embarrassed by compliments,* Sawyer thought.

"Thank you," Eeva murmured.

"I love the hair color by the way," his mom continued. "Isn't she gorgeous, Sawyer? She's grown up a lot in the last four and a half years."

He ducked his head toward the purring cat in his arms, automatically falling into his old routine of silence and self-consciousness.

But unlike while he was growing up, his mother didn't just continue on with the conversation like the question was rhetorical, allowing him to stay comfortable in his shyness. Her silence was heavy as she stared at him expectantly.

He remembered their earlier conversation about how much he'd changed, how he needed to show Eeva who he was now, show her that confidence he'd gained over the years. He looked up at Eeva again, but she wasn't looking at him.

He let himself smile that smile he'd always kept to himself, that smile that had been too telling for him ever to let Eeva see.

"As ever," he said with a nod.

Eeva's eyes snapped to his. Her face flushed, and she looked away. "That's not very nice. After all this time, you catch me off guard in my PJs and then you tease me?" She pursed her lips, clearly displeased.

But before he could tell her he wasn't joking, she approached him, took the cat from his arms, and started from the room. "You guys make yourselves at home. Mom and Dad should be up before long, and they can tell you where to put your stuff. There's coffee and tea in the kitchen. I have to feed Muir and get ready."

CHAPTER 5

Evergreen could still feel her face flushed with heat as she shut her bedroom door behind her and placed Muir on the floor in front of his already full bowl. She rushed to the mirror above the dresser, leaning far over so she could properly see. She groaned at her disheveled appearance, finger-combing her messy hair and trying to smooth it into some semblance of order.

"Why did he have to get here so early?" she murmured.

Her stomach grumbled, reminding her that she'd left her breakfast mostly uneaten in the kitchen. She scowled at her reflection. "He didn't have to tease me. The old Sawyer never would have done that. Then again...the old Sawyer didn't talk much at all let alone smile mockingly and make rude comments."

Disappointment tingled across her skin before she could brush it aside. "That's good. I'm glad he's so different. Now, I won't have to worry about getting over him again. I've met tons of guys like that in the last few years. I know how to deal with them. No problem. Right, Muir?"

Muir's only answer was to crunch his kibble, his face shoved into his food bowl.

"Right," Evergreen answered for him.

She left her cat to his breakfast and grabbed her shower bag from her suitcase. Then she went down the hall to the bathroom to get properly ready for visitors.

After putting on thick leggings, a black skirt and tank top, and her favorite upcycled sweater jacket, Evergreen smiled at her presentable appearance in her bedroom mirror just as a knock sounded the door.

"Come in," she called.

"Oh, don't you look cute," her mother said from the doorway.

"Thanks, Mom. What's up?"

"Would you come downstairs and help Tara and Sawyer get settled into their rooms?"

Evergreen quirked an eyebrow. "It's not like they haven't been here tons of time before. Why do they need help?"

Her mother pursed her lips. "Because they're our guests, Evergreen, and it's the polite thing to do."

"Fine," Evergreen sighed.

Her mom's voice smiled like she hadn't just been scolding her. "And your father is making omelets."

"All right. I'm coming." Evergreen left her door slightly open so Muir could get in and out when he wanted to and headed downstairs.

On the second-floor landing, she met her cousin, who smirked at her.

"Don't we look adorable this morning?" Cassandra said with a teasing tone that had way too much subtext.

Evergreen flipped her hair to one shoulder. "Hashtag woke up this way."

Cassandra laughed. "Uh-huh. I bet."

Back in the living room, Tara and Sawyer waited for their room assignments.

"Tara, I'm going to put you on the second floor. You'll be sharing with Hazel when she arrives," Ria told her.

"I guess Charlie isn't up for Yule," Tara said.

"Yeah, I think one Pagan is as much as he can handle. He's going to spend Christmas with his family," Ria agreed.

Tara nodded.

Evergreen reached for Tara's bag, but Cassandra got there first. Evergreen squinted at her cousin, who smiled innocently back before leading Tara to the second floor.

"And Sawyer, I'm sorry. But there just isn't enough room for everyone. Do you mind being in a sleeping bag in the meditation room?" Ria asked.

"Not at all, Ria," Sawyer answered, grabbing his suitcase.

Ria nudged Evergreen with her elbow, and Evergreen sighed and stepped closer to Sawyer.

"I can take your bag," Evergreen muttered.

"Oh, it's fine. I can carry it."

"Really, my mom is going to complain at me if I don't do it, so just give it here."

Her mom pretended like she didn't hear. "Go on, Sawyer. Evergreen will show you to your room. And she'll get the sleeping bag from the closet for you."

There was a heavy pause before Sawyer silently held out his bag. As she took it from him, their fingers brushed together. Evergreen froze as a jolt ran through her. She glanced up at Sawyer. His amber eyes met hers below the soft waves of his golden hair.

"Well, go on," her mother urged. "Only a week and a half until Yule, and we still have a lot to do before then."

Evergreen felt her cheeks heat. She looked away, glaring at whatever her gaze landed on. "Come on," she said irritably as she started toward the meditation room.

At the far end of the house was a sunroom with glass walls trimmed in cedar and a peaked glass roof. Its wooden floor was empty save for an altar at the far end and shelves with rolled up yoga mats, blocks, and pillows near the door.

The scents of pine and cinnamon wafted through the air, coming from smoking incense on the altar. The altar had a wooden dish of salt, a crystal bowl of water, a white pillar candle—which flickered dimly in the morning light—and a small bucket of sand where the incense stuck out. The center of the altar had a foot-tall statue of the triple moon goddess, her long hair flowing down from her crown with the triple moon symbol on top. Her carved garments of green soapstone gracefully held the base of a flickering tealight. There was a conspicuous spot beside her, empty of the god statue that would soon return to its rightful place upon the god's rebirth on Yule.

Evergreen placed Sawyer's bag on the floor. "I'll go get your sleeping bag," she muttered.

She turned to leave as quickly as she could, but Sawyer called out to her. "Eeva," he said, his tone clipped as he tried to stop her before she was out of earshot.

She looked over her shoulder, raising an eyebrow at him.

"Thank you." His voice was warm and welcoming, and Evergreen just knew he was mocking her.

She squinted at him and left without a word. Digging through the hall closet in search of a sleeping bag, Evergreen jumped when her mother spoke from behind her.

"Is he getting settled?" she asked.

"How should I know?" Evergreen grumbled. "I put his stuff down in the meditation room, and now I'm trying to find the sleeping bags."

"Would it hurt you to be a little kinder in your tone, Evergreen? After all, the rule of three would still apply even if it wasn't the season to be *extra* kind to others," she lectured.

Evergreen sighed; her mother always used three-fold retribution as a way to curb bad behavior. "Yeah, yeah. Ah! Here they are. Finally." She pulled out an orange sleeping bag and stuffed the rest back as the lot surged toward her. Then she quickly shut the closet door before they could change their minds about staying put.

"Take this as well." Her mother held out a space heater to her. "It's cold out there, especially at night."

"Fine," she agreed, heading back to the meditation room with her quest items.

CHAPTER 6

*A*n unfamiliar feeling came over Sawyer as Eeva glared at him before turning to go find his sleeping bag. He'd never seen that defiant look in her eyes, at least not directed at him. She'd always been so warm, so bright and joyful before.

But she'd looked directly at him. She'd met his gaze straight on. And even though she was clearly irritated, for that moment, her attention was fully his.

Of course that wasn't the look he wanted from her. But it was a strong, personal reaction, and it belonged to him.

Eeva returned shortly with a sleeping bag and a space heater. She placed them near the door.

"Thank you, Eeva. And you even brought a heater. That's considerate of you." He smiled.

She squinted at his sincerity. "My mom gave it to me to bring."

"Still, you brought it." Sawyer didn't let his smile slip.

"Do you need anything else, or can I go eat my breakfast now?"

"Of course. I'm right behind you."

Sawyer followed Eeva through the house and into the kitchen, where her dad was standing at the stove making omelets.

Wes smiled over his shoulder at them. "Toppings are on the island," he told them. "Grab a bowl and fill it with what you want."

Sawyer stood beside Eeva, edging along the island, bowl in hand. The surface was covered with bowls of mushrooms, tomatoes, cheese, cubed ham, bacon, potatoes, bell peppers, and everything you'd ever want in an omelet. An odd addition caught Sawyer's eye. At the very center of the island was a mug of cocoa, its whipped cream deflated from sitting too long, and a piece of buttered toast topped with cinnamon and sugar, a neat bite taken out of one corner.

Sawyer smiled to himself. *Maybe she hasn't changed so much after all.*

After passing her additions to her dad, Eeva went on through to the dining room.

"It's been a while since we've all been together," Wes said to him, pulling Sawyer's attention away from Eeva's retreat.

"It has," Sawyer agreed.

"A lot has changed," Wes continued.

Sawyer nodded slowly, placing his bowl on the counter beside the cook.

They were silent for a moment, the only sound the sizzling hiss from the frying pan.

"Do you still keep your cocoa in the same place?" Sawyer asked.

Wes nodded, pointing his spatula to the cupboard above the coffee pot.

Sawyer went to the cupboard and took the glass jar of cocoa down along with a mug. After spooning a few heaping tablespoons into the cup, he poured hot water atop the powder from the electric kettle and stirred. Then he went to the refrigerator, scanning the shelves.

"In the door," Wes instructed.

Sawyer grabbed the can of whipped cream from the door and squeezed a mound of it atop the cocoa. After returning the cocoa jar to the cupboard, he pulled down another with mini chocolate chips. He sprinkled the chips onto the whipped cream and grabbed the mug.

As Sawyer left the kitchen, he heard Wes mutter to himself. "Then again, maybe not so much after all."

In the dining room, his mom, Ria, Eeva, and Cassandra sat at the large table, waiting for breakfast. His mom warmed her hands on a cup of green tea while Ria and Cassandra had coffee.

They were chatting about all the things that needed to be done before Yule as he entered. He approached the table and sat in the empty seat beside Eeva, placing the mug of cocoa carefully before her.

She looked up at him, her eyebrows raised. "What's this?" she asked.

He smiled. "Cocoa."

Eeva lowered her gaze to the table, biting her lower lip ever so slightly. "Thank you," she mumbled.

His smile widened. "You're welcome."

"I'm most worried about the Yule log," Ria said, continuing her conversation without noticing their exchange.

"You didn't get it at Midsummer?" Tara asked.

Ria shook her head. "Everything else I either have or can get at the craft store if needed. Though I suppose we can go to the hardware store if we really can't find one."

Tara nodded. "Well, maybe one of the others will bring a log. You never know. When do they arrive?"

"Thursday, during the full moon," Ria answered.

"Don't worry, Aunt Ria," Cassandra said. "We still have plenty of time. And everyone will be here to help."

Sawyer felt a tug on his sleeve and looked over. A small boy, no older than five, stood beside him.

"You're in my seat," the child informed him.

Sawyer raised his eyebrows. "Am I?"

The boy nodded.

"I'm sorry about that. Just so I don't make that mistake again. How will I know it's yours in the future?" Sawyer whispered politely.

The child nodded, accepting his apology. "Because I always sit next to Eeva."

"Oh, but what if I want to sit next to Eeva?"

Eeva snorted into her cocoa, then coughed. Everyone looked at her to make sure she was all right. She held up her hand to say she was, whipped cream smeared on her nose and upper lip.

Sawyer bit back a laugh and turned his attention back to the boy, who frowned, his small brow furrowed in deep thought.

"Well," he said finally. "I guess we could take turns sitting next to Eeva."

"That's a well thought out plan," Sawyer complimented. "What's your name, my friend?"

"Sol."

Sawyer held out his hand to the boy, and Sol shook it as best he could. "It's very nice to finally meet you, Sol. I'm Sawyer. You know, your mom was pregnant with you the last time I saw her."

"You knew Mom before I was born?"

"We've been friends for a very long time."

Sol looked to his mother, who confirmed with a nod. Then the boy smiled at him. "Since you're friends with Mom, I'll let you sit next to Eeva for breakfast. But next time, it's my turn."

Sawyer nodded seriously. "Okay. You got it."

The sweet, creamy warmth of her hot chocolate swirled on Evergreen's tongue as she washed down her last bite of omelet. She glanced sideways at Sawyer over the rim of her mug. He didn't notice her looking, but then again, he never had. *It was awfully nice of him to make me cocoa, and he even remembered just how I like it,* she thought. *But why would he do that? I didn't ask him to.*

She smiled into the cup as she downed the last of it. *Don't make it into something it's not,* she told herself. *That's how you got all wrapped up in him before and look what a mess that was. It's just cocoa. He was just being nice, probably making up for teasing me earlier.*

"I have to go to the grocery store today," her dad told everyone at the table. "I've got a lot of cooking ahead of me."

"Could you also go to the craft store if I give you a list?" her mom asked. "I need stuff for the baskets and cotton thread for the candles. I'd go, but we have to get the rest of the rooms ready for everyone. Plus, I have to do laundry and whatnot."

"I can go with you, Dad," Evergreen said. "We can split the effort. I'll go to the craft store, and you can handle the market."

"Thanks, honey. That would be a big help."

"I'd like to go to the craft store, too," Sawyer added. "If you could use an extra pair of hands."

Just as Evergreen opened her mouth to say she was just fine without help, her father agreed.

"I'll stay and help Aunt Ria," Cassandra said.

"Me too," Tara seconded.

"But Mom," Sol complained. "I want to go into town, too." He held out the last word, his voice rising into a whine.

Cassandra glanced at Evergreen, who nodded.

"You can come with me, Sparkler," Evergreen told the boy. "I'm going to need lots of help carrying all the heavy packages."

"I can do that! I can carry the packages," Sol assured.

"Then it looks like you're just the man for the job."

Twenty minutes later, Cassandra helped Sol put on his boots, coat, hat, and mittens. "You're going to be good for Eeva and Sawyer, right?" she asked him.

"Don't worry," Evergreen assured her cousin. "Sparkler is always good for me."

Cassandra smiled sweetly at her son, then kissed him on the cheek. "Okay. I'll see you later then."

He wrapped his arms around his mom's neck. "Bye, Mom. I love you."

"I love you too, sweetheart."

Then Sol took Evergreen's hand.

"Make sure Muir stays out of trouble, will you?" Evergreen asked her cousin.

Cassandra nodded, and Evergreen and Sol headed into the cold winter morning.

"All good?" Evergreen asked as they approached her dad's car.

"Yep, all done," Sawyer answered, standing up from securing Sol's car seat. "You ready, my friend?" he asked, turning his attention to the boy.

Sol nodded and climbed into his car seat. Sawyer went about buckling him in as Evergreen went around to sit beside him.

"Ready?" her dad asked, buckling his seatbelt and looking around to make sure everyone else had done the same.

The rest answered in the affirmative.

They made their way toward town. "Did your mom give you the list?" her dad asked as he drove slowly down the snow-lined road.

"Yeah, she said you guys are donating to the women's and children's shelter this year."

"She found out they're running low on supplies."

Evergreen nodded, but she didn't know if he saw her.

"So, Sawyer," her dad started, "I hear you're working at an animal rehabilitation center."

"Yes, I care for the animals and give tours, lead nature hikes, and teach kids about the wildlife when they visit on field trips."

"That sounds right up your alley. You always were good with animals," Wes answered.

"Yeah, it's really rewarding, especially when we get to release them back into the wild. It makes all that patience nursing them back to health worth it."

"You seem like you're enjoying it," Wes said.

"I am," Sawyer agreed, the smile apparent in his voice.

A warmth spread through Evergreen's chest. *He's happy,* she thought. *I can hear it. He found something he loves to do. I'm glad.* And she knew it was true, even as she ignored the tinge of sadness in her stomach.

"Eeva is looking for jobs at the moment. Any luck yet, honey?"

Evergreen sighed. "Not yet."

"Maybe you could send Sawyer your résumé. He's done the whole job search thing before. Maybe he could give you some tips," her dad suggested.

"N—"

"I'd be happy to," Sawyer said, cutting off her objection. "Go ahead and send it to me. Do you...still have my email address?"

Do I still have your email? she thought. *Yeah, I still have it. Just like I still have your phone number, and we're still technically friends on social media.*

Her heart squeezed at the memory of all those checked boxes in the photo gallery of her phone disappearing into a cloud drive folder called Vault so she'd never have to accidentally see any of the pictures of animals or interesting looking trees he'd sent her. Unfollowing him on social media had been even worse. *He has no idea just how hard it was for me to let him go, just how much it tore me apart to recognize all his fleeting glances and sweet gestures for what they really were: warm, kind, and colored with the heart-rending torment of a friendship that fell too short,* she thought.

"Yeah," she murmured. "I still have it."

CHAPTER 8

"I'll pick you up in two hours," Wes said as Sawyer helped Sol from his car seat.

"Okay, Dad," Eeva acknowledged. She pulled her white cane from her bag as he drove away. She unwrapped the elastic and let the sections snap into place.

"I didn't know you could get them in different colors," Sawyer said, nodding to the purple handle and tip of her cane.

"Yeah, companies are finally catching on to just because you're blind, doesn't mean you don't want to look good."

"Eeva, why do you only carry your cane sometimes?" Sol asked. "Don't you need it all the time?"

"You're probably right, Sparkler. If I was smart like you, I'd carry it all the time. But when I'm in a place that I know really well, like at home, I don't really need it. And sometimes, like when I have a lot to carry, I just don't use it. But when I'm in a place where I can easily trip or bump into things or when there are a lot of people who have to know that I don't see them very well, then I try to carry it."

Sol frowned. "I don't want you to get hurt. You should carry it all the time."

Eeva smiled down at the boy. "You're probably right," she said again. "All right. Let's do this. You ready, Sparkler?"

"Ready!" Sol agreed, squeezing Sawyer's hand as they began walking toward the entrance.

The steady clanging from a corner Santa's bell sounded muffled by the insulating snow.

Sol frowned as he watched the man and his red bucket.

"What is it, my friend?" Sawyer asked him. "Why are you giving Santa that look?"

Sol turned his big, brown eyes to Sawyer. "My teacher was reading a book about Santa, and some kids in my class laughed at me when I didn't know the story."

Eeva met Sawyer's gaze, her brow puckered with uncertainty.

"Did your mom tell you about him?" Eeva asked the boy.

Sol frowned. "She told me he was a giving spirit. But I didn't know about any of the other stuff. I didn't know he had flying deer or that he came down the chimney."

Now inside the automatic doors of the craft store, Sawyer knelt down in front of the child. "Storytelling is a big part of how we celebrate Yule. Why don't we ask your mom to tell us the story of Santa tonight?"

"Okay," Sol agreed as if all his concerns had been addressed.

Sawyer helped Sol take off his mittens and hat and unzipped his coat. Then he stood and looked at Eeva.

Her eyes were warm as she smiled softly at them. Sawyer's heart jumped in his chest. He'd thought she would never look at him that way again with the reception he'd received.

"I've missed that," he murmured.

Eeva frowned. "Missed what?" she asked.

"Your smile."

Her cheeks flushed, and she averted her eyes.

He smiled. *And I've missed that*, he thought.

"Let's get this done before the old ladies beat us to the good yarn."

"Lead the way." Sawyer swept his hand before them.

She turned to Sol. "Do you want to sit in the cart or walk?"

"I want to walk."

"All right. Then you better stay near Sawyer or me."

Warmth spread through Sawyer as his name left her lips. Yes, she may be different from the Eeva he knew before, but it was clear she still had an effect on him. His skin tingled with the renewed desire to have her eyes only on him, to have her voice whisper only his name.

"I will," Sol promised.

"Will you push the cart?" Eeva asked, turning her attention to Sawyer.

He smiled. "Whatever you need," he promised, his voice thick with implication.

Her cheeks colored again, and her eyebrows crinkled. His grin widened.

She cleared her throat. "Um, okay. Thanks." Then she turned and led them to the back of the store.

Three full aisles of yarn stood imposingly before them.

Eeva stared down at her list. "Okay, mom wants some worsted weight wool or alpaca and some skeins of cotton as well."

"What is she making?" Sawyer asked.

"Hats and mittens with the wool, and washcloths with the cotton," she answered. "All right, Sparkler. Let's find what we need. What colors do you like?"

The trio spent the next half hour picking out yarn.

"What else?" Sawyer asked.

Eeva consulted her list. "Looks like baskets to put all the gifts for the shelter in."

Picking the baskets didn't take nearly as long as it had with the yarn. But then, they had to go all the way back to the yarn aisle because they'd forgotten the cotton thread for the candles. Next, they picked out fabric to wrap the soap in. They chose a light blue with snowflakes.

They still had time once they'd gotten everything on the list.

"Do you want to look around a little, Sparkler? Maybe we could find a craft for you."

The boy agreed. "I want to make something for Mom to give to her at Yule."

"Okay. Is there anything special you want to make her?" Eeva asked him.

Sol's brow crinkled in thought. "Something that has to do with the sun."

Eeva smiled. "That's a very appropriate Yule gift. Hmm, how about a sun catcher?"

Sol pursed his lips. "You're teasing me, Eeva. You can't catch the sun."

"Always so skeptical, my little Sparkler. A sun catcher is something you put in the window. When the sunlight hits it, it lights up, shining rainbows of color all over the room."

Sol's eyes sparkled. "That. I want to make that."

Eeva smirked. "Okay, let's make that."

For Sol's special project, they got clear acrylic discs, each with a hole drilled into it. They also found clear quilting thread, glue, and colored glass dragon tears.

Eeva looked at her cell phone as they put the last of the stuff in the cart. "I think that about does it. Unless you need anything?" she asked, turning her questioning gaze on Sawyer.

"Nope. I'm good."

"Let's head toward the checkout then. Dad should be here soon."

They got into a rather long line of elderly ladies, quite a few of whom indeed had yarn. Eeva gave Sawyer a significant look that said, "I told you so."

When it was their turn, the smiling cashier rang them up, and Eeva paid for the purchases as Sawyer helped Sol put his winter things back on.

"Your receipt is in the bag," the cashier told Eeva.

"Great. Thanks. Happy holidays," Eeva responded, reaching for the cloth bags they'd brought with them.

The cashier frowned. "We say merry Christmas here," she corrected forcefully.

Eeva froze, her face going a bit pale.

Sawyer stood from helping Sol and smiled brightly at the cashier. "Thank you so much for your well wishes. And let me also wish you a very happy Yule. May the gods and goddesses of darkness and light guide you on your journey to enlightenment."

The cashier's mouth hung open, and her eyes bulged.

Sawyer reached out and took their purchases from the counter with one hand; he gently placed his other on Eeva's back.

She glanced over at him, and he smiled.

"Ready?" he asked cheerfully.

Eeva nodded.

Sol took Eeva's hand, and the trio left the store as Sawyer flashed one more smile at the glaring cashier.

CHAPTER 9

Though Evergreen could not feel the warmth of Sawyer's hand on her back through her winter coat, the gentle pressure was reassuring nonetheless.

Sawyer's eyes swept the parking lot. "It doesn't look like he's here yet," he said.

"It shouldn't be too long," Evergreen answered. "Let's just have a seat over there." She gestured toward a bench some twenty feet from the store's entrance.

"Hey, I was supposed to carry the bags!" Sol protested as they started toward the seat.

"Oh, that's right. I'm sorry, my friend." Sawyer handed Sol the lightest bag. "Hold on tight. We don't want to lose anything."

Reaching the bench, Sol stared at it as he tried to work out how he would sit on the higher seat without dropping the bag.

"Why don't I take that, and I can give it back once you're comfortably seated?" Sawyer suggested to the boy.

He nodded, holding the bag out to Sawyer. Then he climbed into the middle of the bench and demanded it back. Sawyer obliged.

Evergreen and Sawyer took seats on either side of the child.

Staring out at the parking lot, surrounded by massive mounds of plowed snow, Evergreen snickered to herself. She could see Sawyer turn to her from the corner of her eye, and she looked at him.

"That cashier certainly didn't see that coming," she said with a chuckle.

Sawyer's voice was warm. "I'm sorry if I stole your thunder. You looked as though you could use an assist. I hope she didn't upset you too much."

Evergreen shook her head. "Nah, I was just surprised. You hang around with other Pagans too long, and you sort of forget just how few of us there are compared to everyone else. Plus, you know, you never expect someone to be so militant about something nice like happy holidays."

"You don't have campus crusaders at your university?"

Evergreen nodded. "Of course we do. But they don't know when our student group meets. And we know when to expect them. We know they'll show up to protest Pagan Pride Day and anything we actively advertise, so we're ready to put on our thicker skins and ignore them." She shrugged. "But I don't know. I guess I just wasn't ready this time."

Sawyer nodded, his silence heavy with thought and maybe a twinge of sadness. Evergreen frowned. She didn't like that feeling coming from him, and she mentally kicked herself for bringing up such topics.

"I wish people could leave us to be ourselves," he murmured. "I wish we didn't have to hide so much, that we didn't have to fight so much." He met her eyes. "I wish I could make it so you never had to be afraid to be your whole self, Eeva, that Sol could grow up and never learn what it means to keep a part of himself hidden."

Evergreen's chest ached at his words, and she had the urge to go back and give that cashier a piece of her mind. *How dare she make Sawyer feel this way!* But she knew it wouldn't help even if she did. She sighed and shook her head. "This is the path we've chosen," she said. "Just because it's hard doesn't mean we should give up. Maybe one day people will be more tolerant. Maybe by the time Sol is our age he can openly be himself without fear of retribution. In any case, that's what we fight for. Isn't it? And we will keep fighting, even if that day never comes."

Sawyer nodded. "But it would be nice if we didn't have to fight."

Evergreen smiled at his soft-heartedness. "For how many centuries have we been fighting? At least we're still around. Right? I mean, they haven't stamped us out completely no matter how hard they tried. The old ways still survive, and I don't think they're going anywhere. There will always be those who hear the call of this path and follow it."

"You've always had the heart of a warrior," Sawyer murmured, his tone distant but smiling. "I remember that time you got detention for standing up in assembly and proclaiming that forcing us all to bow our heads and pray violated our rights."

Evergreen grinned at the memory. "And you've always been the peacekeeper. If I recall, you went to the principal's office and requested that if they insisted on praying that they should have a moment of silence as opposed to a Christian prayer so all students of different faiths may pray or abstain as they wish."

Sawyer smiled warmly, and Evergreen felt that hint of sadness dissipate. "You inspired me. You always did."

A shiver ran through Evergreen as her cheeks heated. She averted her eyes, looking back out toward the parking lot. "Yeah, well. That was a long time ago. A lot has changed since then."

"So you aren't still fired up to take on the establishment every chance you get?" he asked, his voice thick with mock astonishment.

"I've learned to pick my battles," she answered. *I've learned to be more like you,* she thought.

"When is Uncle Wes coming?" Sol asked. "I'm hungry."

Evergreen squinted down the street in search of her father's car. There was no sign of it yet.

"You are? Well, then it's a good thing I just so happen to have this chocolate chip granola bar in my pocket," Sawyer said, taking the snack from his jacket and shaking it at the boy.

"Ooo! Can I have it?"

"Mmmm, I don't know. It looks awfully delicious. Do you know the magic word?"

"Pleeeeaase!" Sol begged.

"Okay," Sawyer agreed. "Let me open it for you."

Evergreen watched the exchange, warmth spreading through her chest. "You really are good with him," she murmured to herself, smiling softly.

She was relieved Sawyer hadn't heard her over Sol's squeals of delight. Because as he looked up and met her gaze again, her heart skipped a beat, and an old familiar feeling pooled in her stomach. *No,* she thought, crushing the feeling down. *Not this time.*

CHAPTER 10

as that smile for me or Sol? Sawyer wondered as they all rode back to the retreat center. Wes was telling them about how he'd gotten stuff to make suet for the birds tomorrow, but Sawyer wasn't really listening. He looked at Eeva out of the corner of his eye. She stared out the window, her thoughts her own.

He pictured the soft curve of her lips as she smiled after he'd given Sol the granola bar. His heartbeat echoed the pounding of fifteen minutes before. *It was for me. Wasn't it?* he thought. *She smiled when we talked about the past. She smiled, and I was right back to what it felt like back then. No. That's not true.* He knew himself too well to believe it was the same. When she'd smiled at him this time, he'd felt his heartbeat in his neck and fingertips. This wasn't the crush of a shy schoolboy. *This time it's worse.* It wasn't the simple attraction he'd felt for others. This was different. *This is Eeva. There's no going back after this.*

Sawyer took a deep breath and let it out slowly. *I may be feeling like this, but that doesn't mean Eeva is,* he thought. *She doesn't even know me anymore. I can't let this time be like the last time. I have to tell her this time for sure. And if she doesn't feel the same...* His chest squeezed painfully. *Well, at least then I'll know.*

Once they arrived back at the center, Wes and Sawyer carried in the bags, and Eeva helped Sol from his car seat and ushered him into the house. They put the bags on the dining room table where Ria, Tara, and Cassandra were taking a break.

"How was your mission?" Ria asked her husband.

Wes nodded. "I think we got everything," he answered before giving her a kiss. "And yours?"

She shrugged. "We got a load of laundry done and a few of the rooms cleaned. We can finish the rest tomorrow. Everything should be ready by the time everyone else arrives."

As Sol cuddled happily on his mother's lap, Tara tilted her head at Sawyer.

"What is it, Sawyer? You're wearing your stressed face," his mother said.

He shook his head. "Nothing, Mom. I'm fine. I'm just going to go outside and ground myself a bit."

Sawyer left the dining room and went out the sliding glass door of the common room. The patio had been cleared of snow, but the lawn chairs that usually sat around the stone fire ring had been put away for the winter. Sawyer shuffled to the edge of the patio and stared into the woods behind the house, the dirt path showing in patches below the tree branches, thick with snow.

He breathed deep the freezing air, the chill tickling his nostrils and making him feel like he had to sneeze.

The sliding door opened and shut behind him, and his mom shuffled up beside him. He glanced over at her.

"Mom, what are you doing out here? You're going to get cold with just a blanket," he chided.

She smiled at his concern. "Oh, I won't be out here for long."

She stood by him in companionable silence, staring at the same path through the woods. "Eeva told us what happened with the cashier at the craft store. Is that what has you upset?" she asked finally.

He shook his head. "No, I'm not upset. I'm... Mom, do ever wish you'd never married Dad? I mean, with how everything turned out."

"No. Even though our marriage ended in divorce, even if I'm not in love with your father anymore, I will always be grateful to him. He gave me the greatest gift in life. Without him, I never would have had you. And being a mother... It's what I was meant to do."

Sawyer smiled softly to himself. "You are pretty awesome at it."

"I know, right?" she said in a teasing tone. "So let me do my thing." She cleared her throat formally. "What's bothering you, son?"

Sawyer chuckled before letting his smile slip. He sighed. "It's worse this time, Mom. I can already tell. It's like while I was away from her I forgot what it was like to be in her presence, like I forgot how to breathe. And then I see her and she smiles, and it all comes rushing in like crushing water from a burst dam. I feel...desperate. Like I have to take one more deep breath before sinking below the surface."

"And the water is...?"

"It's the feeling I know is coming if I mess this up again."

"What makes you so sure you're going to mess it up?"

Sawyer shrugged. "I'm not. I'm just afraid I will. I did before. And she...she wasn't exactly pleased to see me."

His mother rubbed slow circles on his back. "You have such a good and kind heart, Sawyer. Why don't you think she will see that?"

"Even if she does, that doesn't mean she'll choose me. She didn't before."

"Well, you didn't tell her how you felt before either. And neither of you are the same as you were before. You can't control whether she chooses you or not. You can only control how you act not how she reacts. You already know what you need to do. If you hadn't already decided to be honest with her, you wouldn't be this anxious. I know you're scared. But courage is doing what's hard despite that fear, right?"

"You're right."

"Aren't I always?" his mom said with a grin. She stepped in front of him, placing her chilled hands on either side of his face. "You are beautiful, my boy. And I know you will find someone worthy of you. I feel it."

"Is this the mom or the witch talking?"

"Both."

The threatening torrent retreated a little at his mother's assurances.

"Okay, but let's get inside. It's freezing out here," she urged.

He chuckled. "I'll make you some tea," he promised as they headed back toward the lodge.

CHAPTER 11

Evergreen sat at the dining room table, her tablet propped up before her in its detachable keyboard. Everyone else had gone about their after-lunch business.

Evergreen bit her lip as her heart squeezed in anxiety. The little envelope icon on her screen showed that she had one unread email. She inhaled deeply and held it, tapping on the icon with her fingertip.

Her eyes scanned the form letter. *We regret to inform you...* she knew the rest. She let the breath go, her stomach dropping as though the air had been holding it up. She buried her face in her crossed arms on the table before her, pushing the tablet away with her elbows.

"Are you going to send me your résumé?" Sawyer asked, his voice coming from the doorway in front of her.

She rolled her head to the side, not bothering to even lift it. "Why does it matter? It's not like it's going to help. No one wants to hire me anyway," she said miserably.

His voice grew louder as he came closer. "It's tough out there, but I've never known you to give up so easily. Me giving it the once over certainly won't hurt. Will it?"

She was too despondent to argue with him. "Do what you want. It's on the home screen." She slid the tablet farther from her on the table. She didn't look up but heard him pull it toward him as he sat beside her.

He didn't speak again for a while, and she just used the silence to wallow, her slow breaths loud in her ears as she breathed into the space created by her folded arms.

"Can I ask you something?" he said finally.

"What?" She still didn't look up.

"You're GPA is amazing. You're probably going to graduate with honors. You've done multiple internships, and you even did work-study in your university library archives. But what do you want to do when you graduate? What sort of jobs are you applying for?"

Evergreen slowly raised her head and rested her chin in her hands. "What I want and what I'm qualified for are two different things," she said. "I've been applying for pretty much any job that will take a B.A. in history."

Sawyer frowned. "What do you *want* to do?"

Evergreen sighed. "It doesn't matter. I would have to go to school for a lot longer. I'm already way too far in debt with student loans as it is. I can't go for a higher degree."

His voice was tinged with concern. "You didn't get any scholarships?"

"I got a few small ones. But I went out of state my first year, and there weren't many scholarships for transfer students."

"Yeah," he agreed. "But say you can do whatever you want. What would it be?"

There was a heavy pause before she answered. "If I didn't have to worry about paying for school, I'd go on to get my PhD and become a museum curator."

"Okay, but not everyone at a museum needs a PhD, right? Couldn't you get an entry level position and get a higher degree part time?"

"What do you think I've been trying to do?" she snapped.

"Well, you didn't list that among the things you've been trying," Sawyer said softly, and Evergreen felt bad for having taken her frustration out on him.

"I'm sorry." She sighed. "I'm just really worried. I only have one semester left, and six months later, they're going to come after me for these student loans."

"I understand," he said. "Let me do some research, okay? I will get back to you."

"Thanks," she murmured.

"Have you pulled some cards for advice?" he asked.

Evergreen dropped her head in a slow nod. "Yeah, but I think I'm too emotionally charged to read myself properly on this one. So I'm not getting a clear feel from them."

"Have you had anyone else read you?"

She shook her head. "No, most of the people in the Pagan Student Association at my school have been super busy and stressed about their own stuff. I don't want to bother them."

"I could cast some runes for you if you want."

Evergreen met Sawyer's eyes. It took a lot of concentration for her to maintain eye contact what with her eyes' natural tendency to wander. But she stared at him. *Why? Why does he want to help?* she wondered. *He hasn't been involved with anything in my life for almost five years. He left for college and dropped off the face of the Earth. No texts, calls, messages, nothing. Now he wants to cast runes on my behalf?*

Whatever she thought she'd find in his gaze, she didn't. There was just Sawyer, his expression open and friendly, quite unlike the reserved introvert she remembered, unlike the boy full of shy kindness.

"You're different," she stated.

He didn't look away from her gaze. "I am," he agreed. "But not where it counts."

Evergreen tilted her head at this assertion. *What does that mean?* she wondered.

"Eeva," Sawyer started, his tone gentle but strong. "I know we were never very...close. I mean, we were around each other a lot, but we didn't much confide in each other. Still, I always thought of us as friends. Didn't you?"

"Friends..." Evergreen murmured. The word left a bitter taste in her mouth, and her heart sank in a feeling she recognized all too well despite the lapsed time. "Yeah," she agreed softly.

"I'm sorry if you thought I was teasing you this morning. I really didn't mean to make you feel that way. It's been so long since we've seen each other. I'd like it if we could get along, catch up and everything. Maybe we could get to know each other again?"

Evergreen could hear the fragile hope in his tone, and she couldn't bring herself to crush it. "Sure, Sawyer. I'd like that," she said.

And as Sawyer smiled, his furrowed brow smoothing out in relief at her answer, Evergreen repeated to herself not to let him in. She could be polite, cordial even, but she could not afford to let him back into her heart. *We won't be here that long,* she thought. *I can manage until we go our separate ways again.*

CHAPTER 12

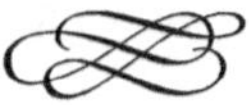

Sawyer rose from the table. "Let's go," he said.

Eeva's eyebrows scrunched together. "What?"

"I'm going to pull some runes for you. You never know, there could be good news, advice even."

Eeva bit her lip indecisively.

"Come on," he urged gently. "What's it going to hurt?"

With a heavy sigh, Eeva rose from the table. Sawyer beamed a smile.

"My runes are in my bag. The meditation room should be quiet enough for a runecast."

He led the way, and she followed. The moment they crossed the threshold to the meditation room, the temperature dropped perceptively.

"Oof, it's cold in here," Eeva said. "I'm going to set up the heater."

As she executed her task, Sawyer went to his suitcase and pulled out a red suede, drawstring bag. Then he settled cross-legged in the middle of the room. After pulling a white, cotton cloth from the bag, he spread it out on the floor before him. Eeva sat opposite him.

"It's been a while since I've studied runes," she admitted.

"Don't worry. I'll explain all the meanings as we go. Ready?" Sawyer looked up, meeting Eeva's eyes.

She nodded.

"First let's take a few cleansing breaths to center ourselves."

Sawyer closed his eyes and breathed slowly in through his nose and out through his mouth. As he breathed deep again, his muscles relaxed, and his heart slowed. On the third breath, goosebumps raised on his arms, and he shivered once. He was ready. In his mind's eye, Sawyer visualized a bright green glow emanating from his chest and engulfing him and Eeva in an orb of light. With another deep breath, he opened his eyes and met Eeva's steady gaze.

Holding the bag above the white cloth, Sawyer shook it vigorously a few times. "Pick three," he instructed.

Eeva reached into the bag he offered and laid out her choices on the cloth between them. Sawyer put the bag aside and leaned forward.

"Past, present, future," he said, pointing to each of the runes in turn. "In the past position, you have Ansuz, Odin's rune. Ansuz is a rune that represents communication. But here it's reversed. It could mean that you have received unwanted messages, like your rejection letters. Or it could symbolize miscommunication or misunderstood messages."

Sawyer looked up and met Eeva's eyes. She nodded her understanding.

"In the present, you have Kenaz, the torch. This is a rune of illumination and clarity. It is sudden enlightenment and understanding. In regards to your previous rune, I'd say that whatever misunderstanding happened in the past, it will be cleared up. It can also sometimes mean an offer, like a job. In any case, this is your present. So, if it hasn't happened already, it's going to happen very soon."

"And the future?" Eeva asked, pointing to the last rune she had laid out.

"Wunjo." Sawyer looked up from the runes, meeting Eeva's gaze once more. "Joy," he said simply.

Light crept into Eeva's eyes. "Really?" she asked, her voice only just above a whisper.

Sawyer nodded.

Eeva placed a palm on her chest and sighed, closing her eyes as she did so. "Thank the gods."

"You're going to be just fine, Eeva," Sawyer reassured.

She met his gaze and smiled softly. "Thank you, Sawyer."

His heart thumped hard in his chest. That smile, that tender look in her eyes, that was for him. He knew that was for him.

"You're welcome," he whispered, unable to get enough air to say it properly.

"Did you make these?" Eeva asked, staring down at the runes.

Sawyer nodded. "Yes, I made them from a fallen branch of ash. I sawed it into discs and used a wood burner to carve the runes into them."

"They're beautiful," she said, reaching out and caressing Wunjo.

Sawyer's chest swelled. "Thank you," he murmured.

"You always were good with your hands," Eeva said. "You even built all the sets for the drama club, didn't you? I remember the one you built for the mermaid's lagoon when we did *Peter Pan*. It was really good."

She noticed that? Sawyer thought. *I mean, she obviously knew I was set crew, but I didn't think she paid that close attention.*

"Thanks," he said. "I had to make sure I did a good job on that one. You were one of the mermaids. I didn't want to ruin your scene."

"Oh man, those mermaid outfits were awful! I could barely walk in that tail."

The image of Eeva in a seashell bikini top and shimmering blue mermaid tail rose in Sawyer's mind.

"Well, it looked good," he said honestly.

Eeva's sharp eyes flicked to his face. "Maybe," she said.

Sawyer remembered how she had fawned over Sean Ferguson. And Sean had loved every second of it. Sawyer had even overheard him during dress rehearsal talking about what he'd like to do to her with the actor who had played Captain Hook. *Would Eeva have been into a guy like that?* he wondered. *She never had a boyfriend in high school, so she must not have been. Sean didn't seem the type to be shy about his interest.* Sawyer had known that her giggles and squeals at Sean on stage were only part of the script, but that hadn't stopped his chest from hurting at the sight.

"You were a pretty convincing actress," he said.

"You think so? I don't know. I was never very good at nuanced parts. That's why I always tried out for the outrageous characters."

"Did you...stay in contact with any of the people from drama club?" he asked, trying to sound offhand. He didn't remember seeing any posts on her social media about hanging out with them, but that didn't mean it didn't happen. He tried to remember the names of the guys she had listed on her page as being in a relationship with. Tyler, Dean, and Marty, though Marty hadn't lasted more than a few weeks.

Eeva frowned. "Not really. I didn't really stay in contact with anyone from high school. I was ready to move on with my life. Start fresh."

Sawyer's heart squeezed, and his gaze dropped with his stomach. *That includes you, Sawyer,* he thought, finishing the rest of her unsaid statement.

"A-and you?" she asked.

Sawyer looked up at her.

"Do you still talk to people from high school?" Her voice was steady and unconcerned, but her eyebrows were bunched together as if his answer mattered very much to her.

"Not really. I get the odd message on social media every now and then, but everyone is doing their own thing. Plus, I went pretty far away for college."

Eeva nodded slowly.

"But I'm glad to be here now," he added. "Eeva, I never intended—"

"Here you two are," Cassandra interrupted, opening the door to the meditation room. Her eyes found the runes on the floor between them. "Oh, am I interrupting a reading?" She sucked in air through her teeth. "Sorry," she whispered, dipping her head.

"Don't worry. We were already finished," Eeva said.

"Oh, okay. Good. Well, dinner is ready," Cassandra informed.

Eeva rose from the floor. "Okay. I'm coming." Then she left.

Cassandra tilted her head at Sawyer in a question.

"Yeah, me too. Let me just clean these up first."

Sawyer picked up the three runes from the white cloth and dropped them into their bag. As he folded the cloth, Cassandra pointed to the floor beside him.

"You dropped one," she told him. Then she made her exit as well.

"Huh, it must have jumped out while I was shaking the bag," Sawyer muttered to the empty room.

Flipping the rune over in his hand, his breath caught in his throat as an X burned into the wood clarified the runecast.

"Gebo," he whispered. "Gift. The rune of union and partnership... The herald of love."

CHAPTER 13

Evergreen slipped another stitch from the left needle to the right. It had been a while since she'd knit. And though it came back to her without much effort, she'd decided to start small with a washcloth rather than daring the double pointed needles for a hat or mittens.

Ria and Tara sat on either side of her on the couch, her mother just pulling the top of a knitted hat tight as Tara made a topper pom. Seated on the floor at the coffee table, Sawyer patiently took the finished works and weaved the ends in with a yarn needle. Beside him, Sol colored in his Little Pagans coloring book, his fist clutching a green crayon.

On the floor, Wes had laid out the blue fabric they had gotten at the craft store. He was attempting to cut it into small, even squares, but Muir and Larkspur were giving him trouble by laying on it in turns.

"Tea break," Cassandra announced, entering the living room with a tea service tray. Sawyer moved the projects from the coffee table so she had somewhere to place the tray.

"Smells good," Evergreen said, placing her knitting beside her and moving her sore wrists in slow circles.

Cassandra poured each of the adults a cup before offering the cream and sugar. Lastly, she sat beside Sol on the floor, placing a cup of milk before him.

"Mom," Sol started, calling for Cassandra's attention with a very serious tone.

"Sol," Cassandra acknowledged, turning to him with an equally serious voice.

"Sawyer told me I should ask you about Santa," Sol said.

Cassandra turned to Sawyer, but she was too far away for Evergreen to see her expression.

"We saw Santa outside the craft store today, and Sol said the kids at school were teasing him because he didn't know some of the stories about him," Evergreen explained.

"Sol, honey, why didn't you tell me about the kids at school?" his mother asked, concerned.

"You have a lot to worry about," Sol murmured. "I didn't want to bother you."

Cassandra reached out and stroked her son's hair. "Sol, you could never be a bother to me. I always want you to tell me your problems. It makes me sad when you don't confide in me, sweetheart."

"I don't want to make you sad, Mama. I will tell you from now on. I promise," Sol vowed.

"Good. So you want to know more about Santa?"

The boy nodded.

"Do you remember a few years ago when you saw Santa at the mall, and you asked about him?"

"Yes, you told me he was a giving spirit."

Cassandra smiled. "That's right. Santa is very special. He is a spirit of kindness and generosity, and he is particularly invoked this time of year. So people give each other gifts in his name or perform acts of kindness. Just like what we're doing now. We're making gift baskets for the women and children at the shelter. That's the kind thing to do when they need help." She explained the same way they had been taught as children.

"But what about the flying deer?"

"Every spirit has a backstory. You know that. Some chariots are pulled by cats, some peacocks, some horses. Santa's is pulled by reindeer."

"My friends said that only good kids get toys from Santa," Sol said.

"Well that's not true at all. You know that toys cost money. What if a family doesn't have enough money to get their children presents? That doesn't mean that poor children are bad. Does it?" Cassandra asked.

"No," Sol agreed, following her logic. "But..." He hesitated, his voice uncertain as he worked through his thoughts. "But we should be kind to everyone, right? I want to invoke Santa, too. I'm going to color pictures and put them in the baskets. Do you think they would like that?"

Cassandra kissed her son's head. "I think that gifts that come from the heart are the best kind, and you have a very big heart, my boy."

Sol turned back toward his coloring book. "I have to hurry," he told his mom. "I don't have a lot of time before Yule."

Evergreen sniffed hard, wiping her eyes on her long sleeve. *Cassandra is doing such a good job raising Sparkler,* she thought. Then she leaned over on her mom, resting her head on Ria's shoulder. Ria wrapped an arm around Evergreen and kissed her temple. Evergreen wasn't really the touchy-feely sort. She liked to maintain her personal space. But when she wanted physical contact, she needed it like a wound that needs pressure.

It wasn't long after that Cassandra told Sol it was time for bed. He complained, of course, saying he had a lot of work to do for the people at the shelter.

"You have enough time to work on your presents tomorrow," Cassandra assured.

"Can I say goodnight first?"

Cassandra nodded.

Sol crossed the room to Wes and gave him a hug. Then he hugged Sawyer, then Tara, then Evergreen, and finally Ria. He went back to Wes and hugged him again. When he returned to Sawyer for another hug, Sawyer chuckled at the boy, the sound rich and sweet.

"That's enough," Cassandra said, her voice barely holding in a laugh. "You'll see everyone tomorrow."

"Just one more," Sol negotiated.

"Okay."

Sol gave another hug to Tara, Ria, and Evergreen.

"Goodnight, Sparkler," Evergreen murmured as the boy's head rested on her chest. "Sweet dreams."

"Goodnight, Eeva. I hope you have good dreams, too."

As Cassandra led her son upstairs, quiet laughter traveled through those he'd left behind.

It wasn't long until Evergreen's eyes were heavy, and her hands slowed in her knitting.

"Why don't you go up to bed, sweetheart?" Ria suggested as Evergreen leaned more heavily against her.

"I'm not tired," Evergreen lied.

"We all know you're not a night person," her father pointed out. "You never have been."

"You barely made it through our esbat rituals," Tara agreed.

"I'm an adult now. I've changed," Evergreen argued.

"There's nothing wrong with being a morning person, Eeva," Sawyer said. "They say it's much healthier actually."

Evergreen frowned, knowing she couldn't really make a good case. "I think I'm going to go to bed," she said as if it was her idea all along.

"Goodnight," Sawyer said, his voice sounding suspiciously like he was smirking.

CHAPTER 14

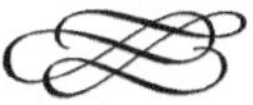

When Sawyer entered the common room the next morning, he found Eeva sitting cross-legged on the floor, leaning her elbows on the table with the television set, her face a foot and a half from the screen. Muir lay curled up in her lap, sleeping. She glanced over at him only long enough to see who had entered.

"Good morning," he mumbled, his voice still graveled from sleep.

"Morning," she responded automatically, not taking her eyes from the screen. "No one else is up yet. Feel free to make yourself some coffee."

"Can I get you anything while I'm in the kitchen?" he offered.

"No, I'm good. Thanks."

Sawyer went to the kitchen and started the coffee pot, breathing deep as he scooped the grounds into the filter basket.

With a fresh cup in his hand, he returned to the living room and placed his mug on the table.

Eeva glanced over her shoulder as he sat on the couch. "Do you need me to move?" she asked. "Can you see around me?"

"You're fine. I can see," he answered.

Sawyer watched as Margaret Sullavan insulted Jimmy Stewart without mercy, a copy of Tolstoy and a red carnation on the café table between them.

Sawyer smiled to himself. He'd seen the film many times before, every Yule since he was fourteen, since his mother joined the coven. It was Eeva's favorite holiday movie.

"You're not still calling this a holiday movie. Are you?" he teased.

"If *Die Hard* counts as a holiday movie, then so does this," she countered primly.

He agreed with her, but he took a little pleasure in getting under her skin. "Whatever you say."

She shushed him as if she didn't know what was going to happen. "Just because you don't want to watch doesn't mean I don't."

He hadn't said he didn't want to watch it. *I wonder what she'd say if she knew I've watched it every year since I saw her last,* he thought. *She probably wouldn't believe me.*

As the movie continued on, Sawyer paid little attention to it. He was too busy watching Eeva's reactions. Her eyes sparkled with laughter at William Tracy's antics, and she giggled freely. So long had it been since he'd seen such carefree joy in her. His chest warmed at the sight. *Could I ever be a source of easy happiness for her?* he wondered.

Eeva grinned, her cheeks pink with restrained delight as Jimmy Stewart finally put the red carnation in his buttonhole. She laughed as he pulled up his pant legs and sighed contentedly as he bent down to kiss the heroine. "Kissing seems so different in old movies. Don't you think?" she commented as the screen declared that it was the end. "I don't know. Somehow, it's more passionate in a way. Less sexual but more passionate. I wonder why it feels that way."

Sawyer tilted his head in thought. "I read once that there were rules and conventions back then about how long actors could kiss at a time. I think it was only three seconds. That would mean they would have to pack in all the passion that would later be able to build slowly into just three seconds. Maybe that's why."

Eeva nodded. "That makes sense. Interesting. I wonder what other kinds of rules they had." She pulled out her phone to answer the question for herself.

Sawyer followed her lead, using the time to track down some ideas he had about her job problem.

"Wow, listen to this. There were rules against cursing and certain dance moves. They couldn't show interracial couples. They couldn't even talk about sexual diseases."

"You're surprised?" he asked, looking over his phone at her.

"I mean, yes and no. This code was in effect until 1967, and how can they put restrictions on art? Where is the freedom of speech?"

"Come on, you've been Pagan your whole life. You think there is really freedom of religion and speech in this country?"

Eeva frowned, the light in her eyes dimming a little. "Yeah...you're right," she murmured. "Even if they say there is, it doesn't make it true effectively. I guess I never stop being surprised by it. The narrative is so different from the reality. They fill your head full of promises and high ideals, and so I'm just a little taken aback when I'm faced with how it really is. They tell us that we are the freest country. The land of opportunity. But that really only applies when you're the right gender, the right color, worship the right god, love the right person."

Sawyer didn't like the uncharacteristic hopelessness in her voice. "But it's like you said yesterday. We have to keep fighting. That's just how it is if we want to survive. And maybe, maybe one day we can be as free as they keep telling us we are."

She smiled sadly, curling around the purring cat in her lap. "Maybe," she murmured.

"On a side note, I think I found something that might help you with your career goals."

She tilted her head. "What do you mean?"

"Have you heard of a museum certificate?"

"No."

"It's a certificate that seems to help people break into the museum field. It's only like sixteen credits to get, and you may have some of them already. You might have to go to school for an extra semester, two tops if the classes don't line up right. And it requires an internship. I'm sure the college has museums it partners with so students can complete their requirements. I even found some people on forums saying that their internships landed them full time positions. Some said the museums are paying for them to go on with their studies, too."

"What? Really? I wonder if my university offers it."

Sawyer grinned. "I already looked. It does. Here, I'll text you the link."

CHAPTER 15

$\mathcal{E}$vergreen hadn't realized just how far into hopelessness she had fallen, just how bad her anxiety had gotten until Sawyer had pointed out a direction. She would have to do more research of course. But the knot in her stomach had loosened, and her breathing came easy.

She looked over at Sawyer as he stood beside her at the kitchen island. He was helping Sol measure out the shortening for the suet they were making. Sawyer scooped it into the measuring cup Sol tried to hold steady.

"That's it," Sawyer said with a smile, dumping the contents into a saucepan.

"Now what?" Sol asked.

"Now for the nut butter. We need three-fourths of a cup. Can you tell me what measuring cup we should use?"

Sol hummed, staring at the assembled cups. "That one." He pointed to the smallest.

"That's right! Good job," Sawyer praised. "All right, you got the nut butter?"

Sol took the jar from the counter and tried the lid, his little elbows stuck out to the sides as he grunted. "It won't open," he complained. "I need help."

"No problem, my friend. I got your back." Sawyer took the jar from him and opened it without effort.

Then he handed it back to Sol, helping him measure out the right amount into the pan.

Evergreen smiled at the pair, her chest warming at their exchange.

"How's your part coming, Eeva?" Sawyer asked. He turned toward her, his amber eyes finding hers.

Her heart jumped, and she could feel the blush rising in her cheeks, telling the tale of her spying. She looked down at the gathered ingredients she still had to assemble into her mixing bowl. "Almost finished," she lied, even though he could clearly see she hadn't put anything in the bowl.

"Okay then," he answered. She could hear the smile in his voice, but she didn't look over to confirm.

"What do we do next?" Sol asked.

"Next, we wash your hands." Sawyer picked up the boy and carried him over to the sink.

Evergreen quickly measured out the birdseed, oats, and cornmeal as the faucet ran behind her.

"I like your pentacle necklace," Sol told Sawyer as the man returned the boy to his step stool.

"Thank you."

"Where did you get it?"

"Nowhere special. Just online."

"Oh. Well it's really nice."

"I tell you what, since you like it, why don't you have it?" Sawyer pulled the black-corded silver pentacle over his head and put it around the child's neck.

Sol looked down at the pendant, which hung to his sternum, then looked up at Sawyer, beaming. "Thank you, Sawyer."

"You're welcome. Hey, can you tell me what the five points of the pentacle represent?"

"Oh sure, that's easy," the boy replied proudly. "Earth, air, fire, water, and spirit."

"You sure are smart. You obviously pay attention to all the things your mama teaches you."

Sawyer held out his fist, and Sol bumped it with his considerably smaller one.

"Okay, let's melt this and add the dry ingredients," Sawyer said, taking the saucepan and the mixing bowl to the stove.

A while later as Evergreen spooned the hot mixture into a silicone ice cube tray, her mother entered the kitchen.

"Hey, would you two mind going into town when you're done? I thought I had enough bottles for the shampoo, but I miscounted. Eeva, you know what kind I use. Sawyer, would you mind driving her?"

"Not at all," Sawyer responded.

"Can I go too, Aunt Ria?" Sol asked.

"Not this time, Sparkler. It's nap time for you."

The boy groaned but didn't argue.

I guess it can't be helped, Evergreen thought. "Sure, Mom," she agreed.

"Great. Thanks," Ria said.

As Evergreen slid into the passenger seat of Sawyer's car, she became overly aware of how close he was. His presence was heavy and insistent, and she couldn't escape his scent all around her.

"Do you mind if I put on some music?" she murmured.

"Go ahead."

Evergreen pressed the button, and the dulcet tones of Loreena McKennitt emanated from the speakers. She grinned. "Your mom pick this?"

"Hey, I like her too," he defended. Then he chuckled. "But yeah, she's my mom's favorite. If you want to change it, there are CDs in the center console."

"Let's see what you have," Evergreen said, pulling out the discs more for something to do than to actually change the music. She flipped through. *Blackmore's Night, Celtic Women, Led Zeppelin,* Evergreen read the artists in her mind. *Oh, this was always his favorite,* she thought, pulling the CD from its sleeve. She removed Loreena McKennitt and popped in the new disc, navigating to number four.

As the upbeat melody filled the car, Evergreen glanced at Sawyer. When he smiled over at her, her heart danced with the music of "Tanz mit mir."

"You remembered?"

She lowered her face, suddenly self-conscious that she had brought attention to her past weakness for him. "Well...you know, it was hard to forget. You played it so often. I mean, you even took German in high school to be able to understand their lyrics."

"I did," he agreed. "And I still remember them." He reached forward and turned up the volume, singing loudly, his voice pleasant and energetic.

Evergreen bobbed her head and tapped her foot to the beat, letting the music carry away the awkwardness she'd felt since getting into the car.

Though they didn't have to get very many bottles from the craft store, it took them quite a while as the place was packed with people just picking something up during their lunch breaks. Without any verbal agreement, they avoided the cashier they had the previous day.

As they finally returned to the fresh air and headed for the car, Sawyer said, "Gods, that took forever."

"I know. I'm starving."

"Me too. Hey, do you want to get something to eat? I haven't had Mediterranean Smoothie since I went off to college."

Evergreen hesitated. "I mean, my dad should be making lunch."

"You don't understand," he said seriously. "Now, I have the expectation of Violet Rave in my mouth. It won't go away until it's satisfied. Please, Eeva. I'll buy you lunch," he ended with a plea.

"Pff," Evergreen chuckled. "I mean, I'm not stupid. Who would say no to free lunch?"

"Yes!" Sawyer exclaimed, holding the ending S with a hiss.

"You're going to regret making this offer," she warned. "I'm not shy when it comes to eating."

"It'll be worth it for the Violet Rave."

Mediterranean Smoothie was just starting to calm down after the lunch rush, the few empty tables being wiped down by bussers. After they took a seat, the waitress appeared and handed them their menus.

"Can I get you started with anything to drink?" she asked in a chipper tone.

"I'll have the Violet Rave," Sawyer told her.

Evergreen squinted at the menu.

"You know you'll make yourself go blind holding the menu that close," the waitress joked.

Evergreen took a slow, deep breath. "Too late," she muttered.

The waitress paused for a moment, unsure what she meant.

"I have to hold it this close. I'm legally blind, and I can't read it if I don't," Evergreen said patiently as if the waitress deserved an explanation.

"Oh my god. I'm so sorry," the waitress gasped. "I didn't know. I mean, you don't *look* blind."

Evergreen let that one go. No good would come from explaining to the woman just how rude of a comment that was. Sure, she might understand that blindness could be caused by so many things. But she clearly didn't get that blindness didn't have a *look*. And really, she didn't want to make the woman any more uncomfortable by pointing out that she'd just insulted the entire blind community, especially when she clearly had thought she was giving Evergreen a compliment.

"I'll have a mango smoothie, please," Evergreen said, ignoring the comment altogether.

As the waitress walked away to fill their orders, Evergreen rubbed her eyes, having had to strain them to read the too small print.

"You all right?" Sawyer asked.

"Yeah, fine. Thanks."

"Is there—"

"Oh my goodness, Sawyer Collins. Is that you?"

Sawyer turned as a chic African American woman entered the restaurant.

"Lay-Lay?" his voice raised in confused delight. He rose from his seat and went to hug the woman. "Wow, it has been so long. How are you?"

"Oh, I'm just out here being my fabulous self as always."

"Of course. I wouldn't have expected anything less."

"But look at you all tall and handsome. I see you grew into those lanky arms after all. And you even have a girl with you. Oh, is that Evergreen Pendre?"

"Oh, sorry, yeah."

The pair walked the few steps to the table.

"Eeva, you remember Allaya, right?"

Evergreen dipped her head, forcing a smile as her stomach dropped. *Do I remember your best friend and high school crush? How could I forget?* she thought.

"Of course. I'm glad to see you again, Allaya. How are you doing?"

"Wonderful. Graduated last year and opened an interior design business."

"That's great," Eeva said. "I mean, you designed all the sets for drama club, and you were so good at it."

Allaya smiled. "Thank you."

"Lay-Lay, are you meeting someone here? Do you want to join us for lunch?" Sawyer asked. "You don't mind. Right, Eeva?"

"Of course not. Please, join us." Evergreen was quite impressed with her pleasant and convincing tone.

"Thank you," Allaya said again, taking the chair beside Sawyer.

"I'll be right back. I have to go to the bathroom," Evergreen told them. "If the waitress comes back, please tell her I want a chicken gyro pita."

"No problem," Sawyer confirmed.

Get your shit together, Evergreen thought. *Allaya has always been nice to you. And you don't even like Sawyer anymore, so there's no need for you to still be jealous.*

As Evergreen walked away, she heard Allaya say, "Boy, you are lucky I ran into you. If I had found out later you came to town and didn't tell me, you wouldn't have survived to New Year's."

CHAPTER 16

Lay-Lay turned her sparkling, dark eyes on Sawyer. "That girl still doesn't like me."

"Aw, come on, Lay-Lay. You're still going on about that after all this time?"

"Oh, don't get me wrong. I'm not taking it personally. It's your fault anyway."

"My fault? How?"

"How many times do I have to tell you? She only didn't like me because she liked you."

"You're crazy."

Lay-Lay smirked. "*I'm* crazy?"

She didn't have to elaborate. Sawyer understood her implication and sighed. "You were wrong, Lay-Lay. I have a lot of proof, as you know. And even if she had liked me back then, why would she still not like you?"

Lay-Lay raised her eyebrows significantly.

Sawyer felt his heart swell with hope, and he quickly tethered it before it flew away.

Lay-Lay smiled. "Look at that blush! You still like her. Don't you?" she teased.

Sawyer hushed her. "Yeah, I do. Okay?" he whispered. "Could you not broadcast it?"

She shook her head. "See? That has always been your problem. You were too quiet about your feelings. Maybe if you had been more honest, this whole thing could have been cleared up ages ago."

"Yeah, yeah."

Lay-Lay leaned forward, dropping her voice. "Do you want me to tell her for you? This whole thing could be over in ten seconds. Girl, Sawyer loves you. He's always loved you. I don't know where you got this idea he was into me. We have always just been friends. He's just shy. Take his coward ass home and give him some."

Sawyer's eyes scanned the room. "Lay-Lay," he admonished.

Lay-Lay sighed. "I know. Don't worry. I won't say anything. But I think you should. You two would be so cute together, raising your little Pagan babies."

"Oh my gods..."

"Who's that?" Lay-Lay asked, pointing behind Sawyer.

He looked over his shoulder at a man talking to Eeva. He looked vaguely familiar with his dark hair and olive skin, but Sawyer couldn't quite place him. His stomach clenched as Eeva smiled widely at the man, a pink blush dusting her cheeks. Eeva pointed toward their table.

"Well, we're about to find out. He's coming this way," Lay-Lay said.

"Hey, Collins. It's been a while. Good to see you," the man said, holding out his hand to Sawyer.

"Yeah, it has. Nice to see you again," Sawyer said, trying and failing to place the man as he shook his hand. Sawyer glanced at Eeva. "I didn't know you two knew each other." *I definitely would have remembered a guy like him around Eeva,* he thought.

"Oh, Niko drove me home from the train station the other day. Apparently, his uncle owns this restaurant."

*Niko...Niko...*Sawyer searched his mind to place the name. *Oh, that guy from my summer photography class. The one all the girls were silly over.*

"Cool. I always loved this place," Sawyer said.

"Are you here for lunch, Niko?" Eeva asked. "You could join us if you want."

Sawyer's eyes snapped to Eeva's face, then to Niko's.

"No, I'm just here to drop something off to my aunt."

"Oh," Eeva mumbled.

"But I could get a smoothie and sit with you guys for a bit," Niko added with a smooth smile.

Eeva perked up. "Great. This is Allaya. She was Sawyer's best friend in high school."

Lay-Lay and Niko greeted each other politely as Niko took the chair beside Eeva.

They were just starting to exchange basic information about what everyone did for a living when the waitress returned with their food.

"Oh, looks like they forgot my tzatziki sauce," Eeva said, putting her gyro down.

"You want me to call the waitress back?" Sawyer asked.

"No, it's fine. I can just go to the counter and ask for some."

She made her way toward the counter. Sawyer and Niko watched her go. Halfway there, she bumped into an empty table. She paused, hissing as she rubbed her hip, then continued on.

Niko chuckled to himself. "She's a bit clumsy. Isn't she?"

"She's not clumsy. She's blind," Sawyer corrected coolly.

Niko blinked at him. "What?"

"Eeva is legally blind, and she has a habit of walking around without her cane."

Niko scrunched up his face, his attractive features twisted in disgust.

Sawyer's stomach dropped at the sight, and anger boiled in his chest. Lay-Lay stiffened beside him.

"Do you have a problem with that?" Sawyer challenged the man, his voice low and even.

Niko didn't seem to notice the rage bubbling just below the surface of Sawyer's tone. "No, I don't have a problem with someone being blind. I would just prefer to know that before I waste my interest on a girl."

"Everyone has something to deal with," Sawyer said, trying to keep his voice steady. "It's clear you struggle with an overinflated ego. You think you're so perfect that you can call her flawed? She was born that way. She had no choice in the matter. You weren't born a narcissistic prick, so what's your excuse? Eeva is beautiful inside and out. I'm glad you showed your true colors early on. You don't deserve her."

Niko slowly rose from his seat, hovering over Sawyer and tensing for a fight.

Sawyer stood up to meet him, barely aware that Lay-Lay had risen too as he looked down at the infuriated man. "Leave now. Before she gets back."

"This is my family's restaurant," Niko growled.

"And do you think your family would be pleased to know that this is how you treat disabled customers?"

Niko glared up at Sawyer, fury flashing in his dark eyes. Then he turned on his heel and stormed away.

Sawyer took a deep breath and sat back down as Lay-Lay glared after Niko.

Drinking some Violet Rave, he glanced over at Lay-Lay, who had retaken her seat. She was staring at him seriously.

"What?" he asked, putting his cup down.

She grinned slowly. "My baby boy grew up. Look at you, all hot and manly. Why don't you show Eeva this side of you?"

Sawyer turned back to his meal without comment.

When Eeva returned to the table, she stopped short. "Where's Niko?"

"He had somewhere else to be," Sawyer answered.

"Oh. Damn. I wanted to hire him to take me home."

"Why would you need him to do that?"

"Well, I mean, you and Allaya haven't seen each other in a long time. I figured you would want more time to catch up."

Sawyer frowned. "Don't call him for a ride anymore. If you need someone to drive you somewhere, I'll take you."

Eeva's eyes widened, and she blinked a few times. "Um... Okay. Did something happen?"

"No," Sawyer said. *Maybe she knows there are men like him out there. But it would still be shocking and painful to be confronted head-on with something like this aimed directly at you. I don't think I could handle the hurt in her eyes.*

"Just let it go, girl. Let it go," Lay-Lay suggested.

CHAPTER 17

Evergreen looked over at Sawyer from the corner of her eye as he drove them home.

"I'm sorry you didn't get to spend more time with Allaya," she murmured.

"It's fine. She was only on her lunch break anyway," he said, his voice unconcerned.

"Do you...talk to her a lot?"

Sawyer turned his face toward her, just for a moment taking his eyes from the road. She jumped internally as his gaze unerringly found hers, if only for that second.

"I told you I didn't talk much with the people from school. We sometimes chat online every now and then. You know, just catch up or whatever."

Evergreen nodded slowly, her brain telling her to let it go. She didn't listen. "I'm just surprised. You two were so close."

"Yeah, we were. But then we went to separate colleges. It's not like we aren't still friends. But things change when you don't see each other every day."

Yeah. Things change. Do you still feel the same way about her? Evergreen wondered. But she didn't give voice to her question.

"Still," he continued, "I think I can always count Allaya as one of my friends, no matter how long we don't talk or see each other. I guess at this point she's more like family. I mean, we've always called each other's moms 'mom.' And she only has sisters. Her family always wanted a boy. So I guess they just sort of adopted me in a way."

Evergreen stared hard at him, hoping she didn't look surly as she squinted to try and make out his features against the bright light outside the car. His face was restful, neither wrinkled with concern or joy. He appeared to just have stated the facts as he saw them.

Evergreen took a slow, quiet breath and turned her gaze to the snow-covered trees that lined the road. *He thinks of her as a sister? Could I have been wrong about them? But he was always smiling when he was around her, always laughing. He never smiled like that around me,* she thought. *Well, that just means that whatever joy she gave him as a friend and sibling, I didn't give him. Him not liking her in that way has no bearing on how he felt about me.*

"What are you thinking so hard about?" he asked.

"Nothing," she mumbled, wondering how he knew. "I'm just recalling some memories."

There was a thick silence before he said, "You know...Lay-Lay thinks you don't like her, that you never liked her."

Evergreen's heart squeezed. "Oh? Why is that?" she asked, trying to make her tone sound only curious.

Sawyer hesitated. "She said she thinks you don't like her because you think I like her...in a romantic way."

The sounds of the heater and the engine seemed more muffled as if Evergreen's ears were plugged. She held her breath as she became too aware of the blood pumping from her heart to her brain, the artery pulsing in her neck.

"But you just said you thought of her as family," she pointed out, her voice sounding weak and unconvincing to her own ears.

"Right," he agreed, equally quiet.

"And I have no reason to dislike Allaya. She has always been nice to me."

"I told her it wasn't true." He paused. "She's just paranoid," he added softly.

"But..." Evergreen hesitated. "I wouldn't have been surprised if you, or anyone for that matter, did like her that way. She's smart, pretty, and talented."

"She is all those things," he agreed. "But you can't control what your heart wants."

Evergreen dropped her gaze to her hands in her lap. "Yeah," she mumbled.

They rode the rest of the way back in silence, both lost in their own thoughts. The atmosphere in the car was thick and uncomfortable, and Evergreen was relieved when she stepped outside into the fresh, cold air.

"Aren't you coming in?" Sawyer asked when Evergreen made no move to head inside.

"I'm just going to go for a short walk," she said. "Will you take these in to my mom for me, please?"

Sawyer took the bag with the shampoo bottles from her with a nod and went inside.

Once he had closed the door, Evergreen took a deep breath. Then she walked around the house to the back patio, the movement of walking calming her rattled mind. Without hesitating, she took the path into the woods, her boots crunching the pebbles on the frozen dirt.

"No. No, no, no," she murmured to herself. "Don't you dare, Evergreen."

She stopped, squinting up at the grey sky between the snow-laden branches of the trees all around her. She sighed; her chest warmed as Sawyer's words repeated in her mind. *You can't control what your heart wants.* She started walking again, faster, as if to outrun the phrase.

"He was just making a statement of fact," she told herself. "But...it had sounded so...heavy, so...suggestive. No, that's just what I *wanted* to hear. Wait...no it isn't. Why would I want to hear that?"

She followed the path up a steep hill to the small clearing where most of the coven's outdoor rituals took place, where they would have a bonfire, pitch tents, where her dedication had been. She plowed right through the clearing and descended the other side of the plateau.

"It doesn't matter," she insisted, her throat ragged as she took labored breaths of cold air. "It doesn't matter what he meant. Even if he came out tomorrow and told me he used to have a crush on me, that wouldn't change anything now. Right. It wouldn't change anything because a crush in the past means nothing in present day. And...I'm over him."

Her declaration sounded loud and final. Even insulated by the surrounding woods, it seemed to echo as if she'd shouted it into an empty canyon. She stopped again, startled by the sudden feeling of intense loneliness. Looking around, she saw the edge of her family's property line. The small isolation cabin used for meditation and reflection marked the end of the retreat center.

She sighed again, and her stomach churned. She didn't follow her mind's train of thought. "I better get back," she mumbled. Then she turned around and walked slowly home.

CHAPTER 18

*L*ike the evening before, Sawyer sat at the coffee table beside Sol, sewing in the ends of the knitting projects his mom, Ria, and Eeva finished. Wes sat on the floor, decorating the baskets that would go to the shelter when they were all finished.

Sawyer peeked up at Eeva as she cast off the last row of the washcloth she was knitting. His heart panged as he recalled their earlier conversation.

What was I hoping for? he thought. *Why would I bring up her not liking Lay-Lay? The way her face flushed, she knew what I was suggesting. I knew she didn't like me. But when she asked about Lay-Lay, I just got the feeling that maybe...*

Evergreen looked up as she cut the tail off her project. She glanced at him and stilled as she realized he'd been watching her.

"This one is finished," she said, leaning forward to hand it to him.

He reached out, his fingers brushing hers as he took it from her. Her cheeks pinked ever so slightly, and warmth spread through him, heat pooling in his gut.

His manhood stiffened. Her hand had been soft and warm and real, not the hand of a long-ago crush. But the hand of present Eeva. The woman she had become, not the girl she had been.

She had changed. He had seen it, even in the two days they had spent together. She was much more contemplative, less likely to forge forward without thought. But her heart, it was the same. The way she interacted with her parents, her cousin, his mom, especially how she was with Sol. How she worried about failing to find a job, her laugh. Yes, she was different, but not so much that his heart wouldn't recognize her.

Let's not think about the past anymore, Sawyer told himself. *I've long known how I felt about her in the past. I want to know the new Eeva. And it's the future I should be concerned about. The past is already done. No, it doesn't matter how she felt about me back then. It's how she feels now that matters.*

"Uncle Wes," Sol said, pulling Sawyer from his contemplations.

"Yes, Sparkler," Wes answered, pausing in his decorating.

"Will you tell us a story? My mom always says you were the best at storytelling."

Wes smiled. "Your mom was always the best listener."

"Hey, I listened," Eeva countered.

"You did when you could sit still long enough," Cassandra said.

"Point taken," Eeva conceded.

"Hmm. Let's see. What sort of story should I tell?" He sat on the floor, facing those assembled.

"There once was a wise and powerful sun god, and he was married to an equally wise and powerful earth goddess," Wes started.

"Did the god and goddess have names?" Sol asked.

Wes nodded. "They have had many names, too many to list. The goddess and god were very happy together, and their joy brought new life to the earth. In the spring, the god impregnated the goddess with his seed. As the seed grew, so did all the plants on earth, warmed by the love they shared. The seeds grew so big that they began to sprout and bear fruit. And the people and animals were happy because they had a lot to eat."

"But what about now?" Sol asked. "All the plants are sleeping."

"That's right," Wes said. "Because death is the inevitable part of life. The god died on Samhain, and the goddess was very sad. The plants slowly died with him, and the sun didn't warm the earth the way it used to."

Sol frowned, tears filling his eyes.

"But, even though he died, he left something behind: the seed he left with the goddess. Because when something dies, that death only fuels new life for those it leaves behind."

"What happened to the seed?" Sol asked.

"On Yule, the winter solstice, the seed was reborn as a new sun god. The days got longer, and the sun got warmer. And eventually, the goddess was renewed as well. That's why, every year, the people celebrate the changing of the seasons. And at Yule, we celebrate the birth of the new sun god and the return of the light."

"I hope he isn't late," Sol said. "Mom said sometimes babies come late. She said I was three whole days late."

Sawyer stifled a laugh. "Don't worry, my friend," he told the boy. "He won't be late."

Sol pursed his lips and squinted his eyes. "Are you sure?"

Sawyer nodded seriously. "Positive. The god always returns just when he says he will."

"Okay," Sol agreed, apparently reassured.

Shortly after Wes had finished his story, Cassandra took Sol up to bed. It wasn't long before everyone else called it a night as well, leaving Eeva and Sawyer alone in the common room.

"You're up late," Sawyer pointed out. "Aren't you tired? You were up before everyone else this morning too."

Eeva yawned. "Yeah, I just know I won't be able to get to sleep."

"Something on your mind?"

Eeva frowned and sighed, wrapping up her knitting and putting it aside. "It's more like trying to keep something off my mind. If that makes any sense."

"Do you want to talk about it? Maybe it will help."

She glanced at him. He put on a reassuring expression, though he wasn't sure how much of his face she could see from that distance.

"You ever have something you just don't want to face? I mean, you know when you get a tarot reading where every card just tells you exactly what you already know, but you don't want to accept it? If you hadn't pulled the cards, could you have just gone on pretending, ignoring the truth?"

Sawyer thought about it for a moment. "I always find facing the truth is the best option. If I ignore it, it's not like it will go away. The longer I wait to face it, the harder it's going to be to deal with because it's just growing there in the dark."

Eeva sighed again. "I had a feeling you'd say something like that... But what if you aren't ready to face it?"

"Hard to say. I mean, I'd never suggest you overextend yourself or force yourself to deal with something you aren't ready for. But on the other hand, sometimes we don't have much of a choice. Sometimes things just happen, and we have to deal with them whether we're ready or not."

Eeva nodded slowly.

"So which do you think it is? Do you think you have the luxury of ignoring it for the time being?" Sawyer asked.

"I'm not sure," she said. "But it will hold until tomorrow at least. I think I'm going to go up and try to sleep."

Sawyer nodded. "Sleep well," he said.

"Thanks. You too."

But just as she stood up to leave, Sawyer called out to her. "Hey, Eeva, since the suet is finished, do you want to go out and feed the animals with me tomorrow? I'm hoping to get some good pictures."

Eeva paused, and Sawyer held his breath.

"Sure," she said finally.

Warmth spread through Sawyer as he grinned. He was grateful that she left without turning back to see the stupid look on his face.

CHAPTER 19

After breakfast the next morning, Evergreen and Sawyer started putting on their coats and hats to go outside.

"Where are you two off to?" Ria asked, as everyone watched them from the living room.

"We're going to put out the suet for the birds," Evergreen answered her mother. "And Sawyer wants to see if he can get some wildlife photos."

"In that case, would you like some chestnuts for the squirrels, too?" Wes asked.

"That would be great," Sawyer answered.

"Since you're going out, would you mind gathering some things for the door wreath?" Ria asked.

"No problem," Evergreen said.

"Great. I'll go get the basket," Ria responded.

"I want to come too," Sol said, standing from his place at the coffee table.

"I thought you wanted to work on your art for the baskets, Sol," his mother pointed out before Evergreen could agree.

Sol was silent for a moment. Evergreen could practically hear him weighing his thoughts, though she couldn't see his expression from across the room.

"You're right, Mama. I'm sorry, Eeva. But I can't go with you this time. I have too much work to do," Sol apologized sincerely.

Evergreen smiled, managing to hold back her laugh at his serious tone. "That's all right, Sparkler. I understand. I'll see you later. Okay?"

"Okay," he agreed.

As her mother handed her the basket and chestnuts, Evergreen asked, "Have you seen Muir?"

"He's over there by the fire sleeping with Larkspur," she told her.

"Oh, good. If he wakes up and starts crying, it's because he wants attention. I have some toys up in my room for him."

"I think I know how to take care of my grandcat, Evergreen," Ria said flatly.

"I know. I just don't want him to wake up and be looking for me."

"He'll be fine," she assured.

"Make sure he doesn't eat any of Larkspur's food. He's on a special diet, and I don't want him to get sick."

"If you don't leave this house right now, I'm going to kick you out," her mother warned.

"Fine. We're going."

"Here, take this, too," Wes said, coming out from the kitchen and holding an insulated lunch box out to Sawyer. "There are sandwiches and a Thermos of cocoa."

"Dad, we aren't going to be gone that long. We aren't even leaving the property."

"Yeah, well, time can get away from you," he said with a shrug.

Sawyer thanked Wes and smiled.

"I don't need to tell you to watch where you're going," Ria warned Evergreen. "I see you don't have your cane with you. Pay attention to where you're walking. Take it slow. Sawyer, you'll watch out for her, won't you?"

"Mom, seriously, I was just out there by myself yesterday. I think I know the woods I grew up in by now."

"Things grow and change, Miss Smarty Pants," Ria snarked.

"All right, we're out of here," Evergreen declared.

The rest called their goodbyes.

As he closed the door behind them, Sawyer turned to Evergreen with a smile. And they shared a small chuckle.

"You ready?" he asked, his camera bag on one shoulder and the lunch bag on the other.

Evergreen nodded, lifting the basket she'd put the suet and chestnuts into.

"What's easier for you?" Sawyer asked. "Is it easier for you to go first or me?"

"You can go first," Evergreen said, reluctantly heeding her mother's warning. "Just warn me if there are any unexpected holes or tree roots."

He agreed and started on toward the path she had taken the day before.

Once they were in the woods and the house was out of sight, it grew very quiet. The birds still chirped sporadically in the distance, and there was still the odd skittering sound of creatures just beyond sight. But Sawyer's presence was heavy, like a weighted blanket on her chest. The analogous crunching of their footfalls wasn't enough to relieve the pressure.

Evergreen looked up from scrutinizing the path and watched Sawyer as he marched on before her. She couldn't see his golden hair under his beanie, and his neck was covered by a striped scarf, one his mother no doubt crocheted for him. His shoulders were wide under his winter coat, much wider than she remembered. *He really filled out over the last few years,* Evergreen thought.

Her eyes traveled down to the back of his jeans, and the thought surfaced in her mind before she could stop it. *His ass is nice, too.* Her face flushed, and her ears radiated heat under her hat. She focused her gaze on the path in front of her, concentrating on every step. *Oh my gods, no. That's not okay.*

"Are you all right?" Sawyer asked, his head turned over his shoulder at her. "Do you need to take a break?"

"No, why?" she murmured.

"Because your breathing sounds more labored than before, and your face is all red. Do I need to slow down? Am I walking too fast?"

"I'm fine," she assured. "I just have too many layers on." She unwrapped the scarf from her neck and shoved it into her coat pocket.

"Okay," he said, his tone free of suspicion.

"So are there any particular birds you're hoping to get pictures of?" Evergreen asked, filling the silence so her mind wouldn't go on its own.

"Not really," he answered noncommittally. After a short pause, he added, "I'm sorry, Eeva."

He stopped walking, and she halted so as not to run into him. He turned to face her.

"I feel like I invited you out here under false pretenses." He raised his eyes from the ground to meet hers. "I mean...I still want to get some pictures, but I was just using the tradition of feeding the animals as a way to spend more time with you."

Evergreen's heart thumped hard in her ears, and her breath came out in long puffs of frosted air. *Spend more time with me,* she thought. *Why would you want to do that?* She wanted to ask him. She wanted the answer. *What would he say? He wanted to catch up, like he mentioned before? He has a favor to ask of me? He missed me?* The potential answers varied vastly.

Evergreen gave him her best polite smile. "That's okay," she said, accepting his apology. "It's nice to get outside and enjoy the season. I've been cooped up far too much with schoolwork and job hunting lately. And I always enjoyed feeding the animals."

Sawyer watched her. She couldn't make out his expression, but she doubted it gave much away.

Her mind raged at her. *You fucking coward.*

CHAPTER 20

Sawyer stared at Eeva's professional smile. There was no warmth in it. *Did she just...?* His mind analyzed her reaction. *But she isn't angry. She isn't upset. Distant, formal, yes, but that could be caution. Eeva never had a problem with confrontation or standing up and raising her voice to fight for what is right when she thought it could help others. But when it came to something that was only for herself, she was always more reluctant, bashful almost. Did I embarrass her by saying that? But I want her to know how I feel. Fine. If she needs me to ease in, to take it slow, I can do that. But I'm not going to mince words this time. Until she indicates she isn't interested, I'm going to be open and honest about how I'm feeling toward her.*

"Thanks," Sawyer said finally. "I wanted to be honest."

Eeva nodded. "Should we keep going then? We've still got a bit before we reach the clearing."

"Yeah," Sawyer agreed and turned back around to lead the way.

As they walked, Sawyer was acutely aware of Eeva behind him. He focused on the sound of her footsteps, on the quiet hush of her even breathing. The weight of her presence was as if she was leaning against his back, embracing him from behind. And every so often, a tingle would run up his spine as if he felt the brush of a kiss on the back of his neck, and he knew her eyes were on him.

Eventually, they came to the clearing and approached the first suet cage hanging from a branch. Sawyer reached up and took the cage off the chain. Then he opened it, and Eeva popped suet cubes into it. There were two other cages, and they repeated the action at each.

"Where do you think we should put the chestnuts? On the altar?" Eeva asked.

"Yeah, I think that works fine."

They moved to the big stone that the coven had often used as an altar during outdoor rituals. Sawyer used his gloved hands to brush the snow from the surface. Eeva took the bag of raw chestnuts from the basket and piled its contents onto the cleared stone.

"Do you want to gather the wreath stuff now? If we leave the clearing, there might be some animals to take pictures of by the time we come back this way," Eeva asked.

"That's a good idea," Sawyer agreed.

He led the way down the hill, warning Eeva that the trail sloped down and to watch out for tree roots. The tone of her acknowledgement led him to believe that she was aware of the obstacles he pointed out. But she had asked him to warn her, so he did.

"What about that fir over there?" Sawyer said, pointing a little off the path.

Evergreen raised an eyebrow at him. "Really?" she asked. "You think you're just going to point, and I'm magically going to be able to see that far?"

Sawyer chuckled. "Sorry. That was silly."

"Don't worry about it. Sometimes I even forget I'm blind." She laughed. "But yeah, fir sounds good. Lead the way."

Sawyer went on ahead, warning Eeva about every fallen stick and holding branches out of the way so she wouldn't hit her face.

Once they'd reached the tree, they stopped, appreciating it for a moment.

"I'll look for pinecones," Eeva said, dropping down to search the ground.

"All right. I'll take a cutting then." Sawyer pulled out his pocketknife and reached toward the tree. "Oh great and sturdy evergreen," he murmured. "You who represent hope and renewable life. You promise the return of spring. Please lend us some of your life to get us through the darkness of winter." He paused for a moment, just existing in the tree's presence. It was calm, and a low frequency tingle hummed in Sawyer's veins. "Thank you for your sacrifice," Sawyer told the tree. "It will not go unappreciated."

Then he cut a few ends to accent the Yule wreath they were making.

Eeva held out the basket for him, and he could see she had a couple pinecones in it already.

"So what else do you think? Cedar would be nice. It would be easy to work with, too," she said.

Sawyer nodded. "I'll look for one. Let's go back to the path."

They carefully made their way back and continued walking down the trail.

"There's one," Sawyer declared. "And right near the path, too."

"Awesome. Let's get some."

The pair approached the tree, and Sawyer repeated the process of communing with the plant. But as he reached up and cut one of the thin branches, some of the snow from the nearby branches shook off and fell onto Eeva's head.

"Oh! That's cold," Eeva complained, wiggling to get the snow off her.

Sawyer laughed at the sight. "Well, why did you stand under where I was cutting then? You deserve it," he teased.

"I deserve it, eh?" Eeva asked, grinning. She placed the basket on the ground and gathered a handful of snow. "Then I guess you deserve this!" She threw the snow into his face.

"Oh, it's on now," he said, shaking his head, trying to get the snow out from the inside of his scarf.

Eeva laughed and threw another snowball.

The battle raged on. They each got some good shots in. Eeva had surprisingly good aim for someone who couldn't see well. But Sawyer made sure to make some noise to indicate his position. It wouldn't be fair otherwise.

They ran up and down the path, laughter and squeals dampened by the surrounding trees. Finally, they lay on their backs beside each other on the ground, breathless and covered in snow.

"Truce?" Sawyer asked, turning his head toward her.

She turned her head and met his eyes. She sat up, gathered a giant pile of snow between her hands, and dumped it right onto his face.

"Yeah," she giggled. "Truce." She collapsed back down beside him.

He sat up and tried to shake the snow from him but gave up and lay back down. "That was uncalled for," he complained.

Eeva rolled over on her side to face him more completely, propping her elbow on the ground and resting her head in her hand. "Well, you started the whole thing, so I had to finish it."

"I didn't start it. The tree started..." his words trailed off as Eeva reached out and brushed snow from his hat.

His breath caught. She didn't smile at him. Her face was smooth, and her lips slightly parted. Her deep blue eyes were trained on him, serious and intense as she looked down at him.

He'd seen that look before but never from her. He had only dreamed, only fantasized, about ever seeing that heated look from Eeva.

His heart thumped hard in his chest, pumping heat through his veins. His cock throbbed to life, raised by the desire in her eyes.

"Eeva," he whispered, tensing to sit up, ready to meet her, ready to give her what her expression said she wanted.

She blinked, and her eyebrows crinkled. The sound of her name seemed to shake her out of the moment. She pulled her hand back, frowning.

Sawyer's own desire waned at the sight of her change in demeanor. *She's not ready,* he told himself. *But I saw it. I know it's there. I can wait.*

CHAPTER 21

After they had gone back to the basket and finished collecting cedar boughs, Evergreen suggested they warm up and have lunch in the isolation cabin, which wasn't too far away from where they were.

Sawyer agreed, and Evergreen led the way since he didn't remember where it was.

Upon reaching the cabin, Eeva took the spare key from its hiding place and unlocked the door.

The cabin was small and chilled. It consisted of a single room plus a bathroom. In the main room, there was a fireplace, a coffee table, and a chest with blankets in it. At the far end, there was a kitchenette with a single burner on the counter and a sink. The cupboard above the sink had some snacks and a few dishes. It was a place meant for quiet reflection and meditation, a place where someone could be alone and learn to be comfortable with that.

Sawyer stood in the doorway, taking the space in. Evergreen looked over her shoulder at him.

"Something wrong?" she asked.

"No," he answered, stepping in and closing the door behind him. "I just haven't been here in a long time. I think I was only ever here once at that."

Evergreen glanced around the space. "Doesn't seem to have changed much," she said with a shrug. "Anyway, we won't be here long, so I won't make a fire. But the cocoa should warm us up soon enough."

She unzipped her coat and removed her wet hat and gloves. Sawyer did the same. As Sawyer unpacked the lunch box onto the short table, Evergreen went to the cupboard for an extra mug for the cocoa.

"Look at that," Sawyer laughed. "Your dad even put a can of whipped cream and a baggie of chocolate chips in here."

"He knows me well." Evergreen smiled and sat at the opposite side of the table from Sawyer.

As they settled into their meal, Evergreen glanced up at Sawyer only for a second before looking back at the whipped cream in her cup.

Why did I do that? she wondered. *That was just stupid. I should have had better control. But...*

She pictured Sawyer's face again, looking up at her from the ground, snow clumped to his hat and scarf.

I've never seen his face so close before. The closest I've ever gotten to seeing him in detail was photos. And it's different in person. He was...real. Warm and real, and I couldn't help but wonder what it would be like to kiss him.

Evergreen paused in her chewing, shaking her head.

It's a good thing he said my name and jolted me out of it. I might have done something I shouldn't have.

His voice echoed in her mind. "Eeva..." There was no mistaking the heat in that word. It had been thick and heavy and was all too like the whispers she'd heard countless times in her dreams.

Yes, in the feverish dreams of a lovesick teenager. Not the dreams of a grown woman who is too smart to go down that road again. Nope, there's no place for Sawyer Collins in my life anymore. I mean...he clearly wanted to kiss me. A moment longer and it would have happened. But then what? He has a whole life I'm not a part of. He has a job, which is gods know where. For all I know he has a girlfriend, too. No, we're so far past that point. I can't allow someone who had so much control over my heart in again. It's better to keep my distance. I need to have control of the situation.

Evergreen glanced at him again, glad he wasn't looking at her. *Okay, it's clear I'm still attracted to him. But so what? That's not a problem. I was attracted to him before, and I managed just fine.*

A small voice in her head countered her point. *But you were only fighting your own desire last time, not his.*

Evergreen took a deep drink from her mug, the hot liquid burning her throat on the way down.

It's not a problem, she assured herself. *It was only a fleeting thing on his part and a momentary lapse on mine. I mean, I'm not unattractive. Why wouldn't a man want to kiss me? That doesn't really mean anything. No, no, next time I won't let it get that far. Next time... Wait...no, there won't be a next time. After Yule, it won't be likely that I'll see him again, not unless the coven gets together for another sabbat. And that isn't likely anytime soon. No, we probably won't see each other for a long time after this.*

Evergreen's heart squeezed, and she couldn't ignore it. *See? This is a problem. Already, after just a few days, I'm upset about not seeing him again. I definitely need to keep my distance. I won't go through that heartbreak again.*

Evergreen and Sawyer ate their lunch in silence, the isolation cabin hollow with only the sounds of quiet chewing and the occasional slurp of cocoa drinking. After they were finished, Evergreen washed the extra mug and put it away.

"We should head back soon," Evergreen murmured.

Sawyer nodded. "It should have been enough time that the birds and squirrels have found our offerings."

"Right. Well then, let's see if you can get the pictures you want." Evergreen shut and locked the door of the isolation cabin and put the key back in its place.

The pair walked in silence through the woods. Their pace was slow, and they told themselves that it was not to scare any animals away. But it took them a lot longer to reach the clearing than it should have.

They crouched down, peeking over the hill to see if they had any visitors.

"Anything?" Evergreen whispered, unable to see that far. She squinted, trying to make out movement.

"There's a squirrel," Sawyer murmured back as he took the lens cap from his camera lens.

After a few snaps of the shutter, he looked down at the screen, then turned the camera to her. She squinted at the screen, holding it close to her face. There was a grey squirrel with a big fluffy tail. He held a chestnut between his little paws.

"Aww, look at him. He's so cute," she said, grinning at the picture. "Are there any birds?"

Sawyer looked over the hill again and shook his head.

"Do you want to wait and see what we can get?" she asked.

"Do you mind? You're not too cold, are you?"

"I'm fine for a while," she assured.

After over an hour, their only reward was a few shots of a finch and a couple of blurry sparrows.

Sawyer glanced over at her as the sparrows flew away. "Let's call it a day, huh?"

"Are you sure?" she asked.

He nodded. "Yeah, it's getting cold out here. And besides, if your nose gets any redder, it might fall off."

Evergreen held her glove to her nose, and Sawyer chuckled. The sound was rich and warm. *Eeva...* he whispered in her mind, desire coloring his voice with heat.

"Yeah, let's head in," she agreed.

CHAPTER 22

*A*fter dinner had been cleared from the table and Cassandra and Tara were doing the dishes, Sawyer and Eeva brought the supplies they'd gathered to the dining room. Wes set out some crafting paper.

"You found some really good stuff this time," Ria complimented, carefully removing the boughs and pinecones from the basket and setting them on the paper.

Wes nodded. "I'll go get the wreath ring and the twine."

With well-practiced hands, Ria and Wes assembled the bits of greenery into a beautiful Yule wreath in less than an hour. As they worked, Sawyer and Eeva used the other side of the table to help Sol make his suncatcher.

When the wreath was complete, Sawyer took it to the front porch and hung it on the prepared hook. He walked down the front steps and turned around to better appreciate it from a distance. He nodded with a satisfied smile.

Everyone else was just settling down to the evening knitting when he returned. He took up residence beside Sol in his customary place.

"Eeva," Ria said. "I'm going to need you to move your things from the attic down to the meditation room first thing in the morning. Everyone will be arriving tomorrow, and I have to make sure the room is clean."

"What? Why?"

"Evergreen Pendre, you know we only have so much space. I warned you that you might have to sleep on the floor. And Devan and Piper need the single rooms. You know Devan has a CPAP machine, and Piper's snoring could wake the dead."

"But..." Eeva's protests trailed off.

Sawyer studiously kept his eyes on his work and tried to maintain a smooth expression. But he strained his ears to hear over the beating of his heart.

"What are you worried about?" Wes asked. "You, Cassandra, and Sawyer used to share a tent all the time."

"Maybe she's worried one of us will walk in on them," Cassandra suggested.

Sawyer glanced at Eeva out of the corner of his eye. Her cheeks were pink as she squinted at her cousin.

"Oh, don't worry about that, honey," Ria said. "Just lock the door."

"Mom!" Eeva moaned, her face completely flushed.

"What?" Ria asked. "There's nothing wrong with it. You're both adults. As long as it's consensual, there's no problem."

"Stop...talking..." Eeva mumbled, covering her face with her hands.

"Eeva, we didn't teach you to be ashamed of these types of discussions," Wes said. "Your mother is right. Sex is a natural act. There's no reason to behave like this."

"Okay, it's a natural act. That doesn't mean I want to talk about it with my parents in front of everybody. And anyways, it's not right for you to suggest something like that would happen between Sawyer and I without taking our feelings into consideration."

Silence answered her.

"I'm sorry," Cassandra said finally. "I was just teasing, but I didn't mean for you to get this upset. We always used to joke about you and Sawyer getting together. I thought it would be okay."

Eeva sighed. "Things are...different now," she said.

How are they different? Sawyer wondered. *Why was it okay then but not now? Is it because now she's attracted to me? Now there is some semblance of a chance that it could happen?*

"In any case," Ria continued. "You still need to move your things to the meditation room."

"Fine," Eeva muttered.

The rest of the evening was fairly quiet, giving Sawyer's active thoughts no distraction.

As he lay on the floor in his sleeping bag, he stared at the clear night sky through the glass roof of the meditation room. The low whir of the space heater barely even registered.

"Things are different now," he murmured to himself, repeating Eeva's words from earlier that evening.

He had to agree with her. Before, things hadn't felt so real. He'd never been in a relationship before. He'd been a virgin. All of his ideas of what could happen with Eeva had been juvenile and, in some cases, downright inaccurate.

But now, they had both learned and experienced things. There wasn't the same shyness that came with stepping cautiously into the unknown.

The jokes about them being together from their teenage years felt far away, truly fantastical. And though he had wanted them to become reality, he knew now that he hadn't the courage to make it so back then.

Sawyer's dream that night was a complex mixture of memory and fantasy, the kind where his conscious mind somehow marked the deviations from the past but wasn't aware enough to change the course of the dream.

The spring night was warm, and the window to Sawyer's dorm room was open. A hard knock sounded on his door, and he called that it was unlocked.

His friend Felicity walked in at his beckon.

"I can't believe it," she said. "You really aren't going to go?"

He glanced up from his phone as he lounged on his bed. "I said I wasn't."

"Yeah, but I didn't believe you."

"I didn't go last year either."

"What is your deal with Beltaine anyway? You go to all the other rituals with no problem." Felicity climbed up on the bed, shooing his feet so she could sit down.

Sawyer didn't answer but glanced back at his phone. He stared at a picture of Eeva, a wreath of spring flowers in her hair. It had been posted a half hour ago.

Felicity crawled up beside him on the bed, peeking at his phone. She groaned. "Oh, come on, dude. Not this again."

"Leave me alone, Flick," he said, turning the phone away from her.

"It has been what? Like a year and a half since you even talked to her? When are you going to give up?"

He didn't respond. He didn't even know the answer himself.

"You know, there are a lot of women trying to get your attention if you would just get your head out of your ass long enough to see them."

Sawyer snorted. "Yeah, right."

"Dude, I'm serious. Shelby is practically begging for it."

Sawyer glanced over at his friend. There was no trace of joking on her face.

"I'm not really in a place where I can be with anyone. It wouldn't be right with my head all full of...Eeva."

"Ugh, you're so honorable. It's disgusting," Felicity moaned sarcastically.

"Well, excuse me for being a decent human being."

"You are not excused."

Sawyer laughed. Felicity always had a way of making him laugh.

"Maybe you just need to, I don't know, get her out of your system. You know?"

"Yeah? How am I going to do that?"

"You're way too fixated. Loosen up, branch out, get to know some other people. You might like Shelby if you gave her a chance."

"Yeah, and I might get intimate with her and call out someone else's name. How fucked up would that be?"

Felicity paused for a long time before she asked, "Is that what you need to do?"

"What?"

"Do you need to be with someone else and pretend it's her?"

"That's just wrong."

"It's not if the other person consents to it... I'd do it. I mean, don't get me wrong, dude, I don't want you to think I'm, like, into you or anything. But I'm your friend, and I don't like seeing you like this. We could do it on Beltaine and just go on with our lives tomorrow. I wouldn't want your first time to be all emotionally complicated or whatever anyway."

Sawyer's heart pounded, and his mouth went dry. He stared at Felicity, wondering if she was serious.

Then the memory shifted from reality. He wasn't in his dorm room; he was in the clearing at the retreat center. The Beltaine fire was built high; it would burn through the night.

Eeva was in Felicity's place. But it wasn't Eeva from his memories. It was the Eeva from the present. She did all the things Felicity had done. And it wasn't the purely physical release it had been; it was everything he'd wanted. He didn't have to pretend, and love shone in her eyes.

CHAPTER 23

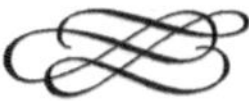

The next morning, as Evergreen packed her things to move them downstairs, she wondered if Sawyer knew why she didn't want to share a room with him.

I have a hard enough time maintaining balance with him around when I have my own space to retreat to, she thought. *It's fine. I can do this. I'm in complete control over my actions.*

She pushed aside the thought that it was her emotions she had no control over.

She carried her things downstairs, hesitating at the door to the meditation room. She could hear her dad already puttering around in the kitchen. And Cassandra was curled up on the couch watching cartoons with Sol.

She knocked gently to be sure Sawyer wasn't in there. Her knock received no reply, so she opened the door.

On the floor, Sawyer still lay asleep in his sleeping bag. As Sol's laughter filtered in from the other room, Evergreen gently shut the door behind her.

She crept to one side and carefully placed her suitcase and Muir's litter box on the floor.

Just as she turned to leave, Sawyer groaned in his sleep. She halted and went back, looking down at him.

Is he sick? she wondered. *Is he having a nightmare?*

Evergreen knelt down beside him. Sawyer's face was moist with sweat, his hair stuck to his forehead. He squeezed his eyes shut. His breathing was heavy and uneven. She reached out her hand and placed the back gingerly on his cheek. He didn't seem to be running a fever. *A nightmare then?*

"Eeva..." he whispered, his voice breathless and moaning.

She pulled her hand back with a start, certain she had awoken him. But his eyes remained closed.

He called her name again, and a shiver ran up her spine. It sounded too much like how he'd said it the day before, too much like how he'd said it in her dreams the previous night.

Feelings from her dreams, feelings she'd thought she had successfully washed away with cool water, surfaced in her mind. Eeva didn't dream like other people. She didn't see images like they did in the movies in any case. She always thought that it was because she didn't see very well. But in her dreams, she didn't see at all. She didn't even really hear. She just felt and knew. She knew people by their presence rather than their faces or the sound of their voices.

It wasn't really strange for her when she started to dream about her first time. She often did when she was sexually flustered. What was strange was the love she'd felt for Tyler in the dream. Oh, she liked him okay enough, and she had certainly been attracted to him. But she hadn't loved him, which is why they broke up in the end.

The dream started out as usual, Tyler and her making out in the woods behind the humanities building. But just as Tyler had steadied her weight against the trunk of a particularly thick oak, the dream shifted. The lust she'd felt was overshadowed by the feeling that this is what she'd always wanted. And as Tyler had smiled down at her, and she met the outpouring of his love with hers, she realized it wasn't Tyler at all. It was Sawyer. And he whispered her name in a low moan, just as he was doing now.

As the feeling resurfaced, Evergreen reminded herself that it was just a dream. She had had many sexual dreams about her guy friends over the years. And once she was fully awake and in the light of day, the feelings in those dreams always faded out of existence.

Maybe it has been too long, she thought, trying to count how long it had been since she'd broken up with Dean. She hadn't even gotten that far with Marty. *Yeah, too long. This Yuletide reunion couldn't have happened at a worse time.*

She looked down at Sawyer again. His breathing had evened out, and he no longer seemed to be dreaming. As quietly as she could, she rose and left the room.

"Is Sawyer awake?" Ria asked as Evergreen entered the living room.

"No."

"Will you go wake him, please? It's time for breakfast."

"I'll do it!" Sol said, running off in that direction.

A few seconds later, Sol's voice sounded from the other room. "Sawyer, it's time to get up!"

There was a shout and a thud.

Shortly after, Sol emerged. "He's awake," he declared brightly, clearly proud of the job he'd done.

Sawyer entered after the boy. Even Evergreen could see his hair was mussed as his socked feet shuffled on the floor.

"Well, good morning, son," Tara said. "You look wrung out. Didn't you sleep well?"

Sawyer paused for a while. "It was fine," he murmured, his voice still thick with sleep.

His mother sounded unconvinced. "Uh-huh. Well, get some food in you so you can shower before people start arriving. You look like you just escaped from being held hostage."

At breakfast, Sawyer sat across from Evergreen as Sol insisted that it was his turn to sit beside her. Sawyer didn't tease the boy. Didn't say much of anything, in fact. And as they all tucked into their French toast, Evergreen glanced over at him.

He was eating, slow and deliberate.

She squinted, trying to make out his expression. *What's he thinking about?* she wondered.

Sawyer glanced up, meeting her eyes for just a moment. Evergreen froze, her body flushing as his heated gaze bespoke his thoughts. He looked back down, the exchange taking only a second.

What the hell was that? she wondered, dropping her eyes to her own food. But she wasn't stupid, she knew what it was. And even worse, she recognized her very real reaction to it. She shivered once as if his releasing her gaze had left her out in the cold.

Glancing back at him again, she bit her lip. *Sharing a room with him is going to be much harder than I thought.*

CHAPTER 24

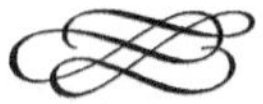

Sawyer chided himself internally. *Why did you do that? Get a grip. You're having breakfast for gods' sakes.*

Sawyer glanced up at Eeva again, carefully controlling his expression. But she wasn't looking at him. She stared down at her French toast as if it took all her concentration to eat it.

A vivid image from his dream flashed into his mind, Eeva's face stiff with pleasure, her eyes boring into his as he thrust deep inside her.

His cock throbbed. He dropped his fork, and a loud clang sounded through the dining room when it hit his plate.

As everyone's attention turned toward him, he pushed back from the table. "I'm, uh, not that hungry. I think I'll just go take a shower and eat later. Thanks for breakfast though."

He didn't wait for their responses before making his escape. Using the movement to push all thoughts aside, he gathered his clothes and headed to the bathroom.

Sawyer stepped under the rainfall showerhead and let the warmth of the water ease his tense muscles. His sigh echoed off the stone walls of the grotto-style shower. He'd kept the lighting in the bathroom low, only turning on the small, dim bulb in the shower itself.

As he began to relax, more images from his dream arose in his mind.

He clenched his teeth together, stifling a groan. His balls ached as his cock strained to get larger than his skin allowed.

He sighed again, slowly, puffing his cheeks out as the hot water streamed down his face. Then he reached for the conditioner and squeezed a decent amount of the thick cream into his right palm.

Closing his eyes, he braced his left hand against the stone wall in front of him and hung his head. The water hit the back of his head, gathering in his hair before dripping into his eyes and down his neck.

He let the myriad of images flow and closed his hand around the shaft of his throbbing cock. He shuddered, the combination of the pressure from his hand and the warmth from the water sending a jolt of pleasure through him.

Eeva's hair smelled of lotus as he buried his face in its soft waves. Her breath was hot and uneven in his ear. He could feel the weight of her in his lap, and his hands glided easily over the smooth skin of her back.

"*Sawyer*," she whispered his name. "*Come for me*," she begged.

As he tensed and shuddered and his released desire pumped out of him, he swallowed his moan of satisfaction.

He sighed, then took a few deep breaths, pressing his fingertips into the rough wall of the shower.

He'd long lost count of how many times Eeva had featured in his sexual fantasies. But this time felt different. The look she'd given him the day before, her flushed face at breakfast, never had his fevered daydreams been so close within reach.

With his sexual tension released, his mind dwelled on foggy recollections of why his heart had never let her go. The kind witch who could laugh with the carefree lightness of an untroubled soul, whose eyes flashed as she stood up to face her peers and elders when she felt an injustice had been done, who cried at others' pain be they human, animal, or plant. She had long enchanted him.

He knew any distance she set between herself and the world was only to protect her tender heart. She cared too deeply, felt too much. It was a very real problem for an empath. He had long watched her slowly build her walls, brick by mental brick. If he knocked on the door, would she let him in? He knew she was capable of protecting herself, but still... Couldn't he protect her, too? Was that so wrong?

After his shower, Sawyer dressed and finished getting ready for the day. As he entered the sitting room, he asked Ria if she needed any help preparing the lodge for everyone else to arrive.

She looked over from the mantle while she fussed over the ivy not being evenly distributed. "No, no. You're fine, hon. You're a guest too after all. And I really don't have much left to do. We already changed the sheets in the attic. And Cassandra is up there vacuuming now."

"Well, would you like anything to drink? I'm heading to the kitchen," he offered.

"Actually, I'll have a cup of tea if you're putting the kettle on. Thank you, Sawyer. You've always been so thoughtful."

As Sawyer made his way to the kitchen, the doorbell chimed. The sound of feet thumped rhythmically on the stairs before Eeva and Sol appeared.

"I got it," Eeva called as she raced the boy to the door.

"Evergreen, Sol, don't run on the stairs," Ria chided. "What if one of you fell?"

Curious to see who had arrived, Sawyer trailed after them.

"Uh, Mom...?" Eeva called, hesitating as she stood beside Sol in the doorway.

Sawyer came up behind them and looked over Eeva's shoulder. A smiling young man, probably in his late 20s early 30s, stood on the porch. He wore a well-kept suit with a tie and a winter overcoat. In his hand, he held a black leather book and a stack of glossy papers.

"What?" Ria shouted from the other room.

"Um, there's a Jehovah's Witness out here," Eeva called back.

Seconds later, Ria arrived at the threshold.

"I couldn't help but notice the wreath on your door," the man said. "Do you have a moment? I'd like to talk to you about Christmas."

Ria tilted her head. "Are you new to this area?" she asked the man.

"Yes." He smiled. "My wife and I just moved to Birchland with our baby boy."

"Oh, well, welcome to the neighborhood. I'm Ria Pendre. My husband and I own this retreat center. Would you like to come in for a cup of tea? We were just about to put the kettle on. You're a ways from town way out here, and it's pretty chilly out."

"I'd love to, ma'am," the man said. "Thank you very much. I'm Caleb."

"Well, come on in, Caleb," Ria invited.

Eeva and Sawyer stepped to one side to let him in while Ria took Sol's hand and led the way.

Sawyer met Eeva's eyes after she'd shut the door behind their visitor. "What...?" he whispered.

Eeva shrugged, then shook her head. "I have no idea," she murmured back.

CHAPTER 25

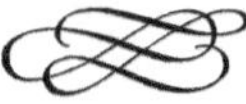

Evergreen sat beside her mother at the dining room table. Sawyer was at the end, on Evergreen's other side. Caleb sat across from Ria.

"Is black tea all right?" Ria asked.

"Yes, thank you for asking. Some of my faith do not drink caffeine, but I find I'm all right if it's occasionally and in moderation."

Ria smiled. "The middle way is often the best choice, I find. And I always ask. Running a retreat center, we encounter quite a few people with dietary restrictions."

"It's a beautiful lodge," Caleb complimented. "How long have you been running the center?"

"Oh, let me think. Eeva is twenty-two now, and we moved in when she was around a year old. Twenty-one years. Wow, I hadn't realized it had been that long. How long have you been in town?"

"About a month. I moved here for work," he said.

"Are you liking Birchland so far?"

"Yes, the people at the Kingdom Hall are very welcoming."

Ria nodded. "I'm glad to hear it."

"This is my first time out spreading the Word in Birchland. You're the first people willing to listen."

"Well, I enjoy learning other people's perspectives," Ria said.

"I noticed your home is decorated with a lot of greenery. Do you know what Christmas trees, gift-giving, and merry making have to do with the birth of our lord Jesus Christ?"

Evergreen exchanged a glance with Sawyer.

"I couldn't say," Ria answered.

"Nothing. All those things have absolutely nothing to do with his birth. Those are *Pagan* traditions. They stem from an ancient Roman holiday known as Saturnalia," Caleb proclaimed. "Jesus wasn't even born in December. That date was chosen to Christianize the festivals surrounding the winter solstice."

"I do know that, yes," Ria replied.

"The Bible tells us that only Christ's death should be commemorated."

"Jehovah's Witnesses celebrate Easter?" Evergreen asked, curious at the contradiction.

Caleb shook his head. "No, that too has Pagan origins. Rabbits and eggs? Those are symbols of false gods, of Pagan celebrations of fertility and spring. No, we commemorate the Memorial of Christ's Death."

Evergreen raised her eyebrows and blinked. "Well, that actually makes a lot of sense."

Caleb looked at each of them in turn. "This is not new information to you," he said, his eyebrows scrunching.

"That's not true," Evergreen countered. "I didn't know you have a holiday for Jesus's death."

"But everything else... You know of Christmas's Pagan origins, but you still celebrate it."

The idea seemed to baffle him as if just knowing the information would bring them to his way of seeing.

"Well, not exactly," Ria answered. "You see, we agree with you. We just—"

Ria's explanation was interrupted as Wes burst into the dining room. "Honey, look! It finally came in the mail. And just in time for Yule, too."

Wes wore a red cloak, its edges embroidered with golden Celtic knotwork. As he spun his back to them, he showed off the huge gold pentacle emblazoned on the back.

"Cool, right?" he said, turning back to them with a grin. "Oh, we have company. Sorry to interrupt. I was just excited. Hi, I'm Wes." He held out his hand to Caleb.

Caleb's eyes were wide, and his mouth hung open. He closed it and opened it again like a fish gasping for water. He took Wes's hand by reflex. "Caleb," he murmured like the wind had been knocked out of him.

"Welcome, Caleb." Wes turned his attention to Ria. "What were you guys talking about?"

"Oh, uh, I was just leaving actually. I have other people to visit, you see."

Evergreen tried to stifle a laugh but ended up snorting.

"It was nice to meet you all. Thank you for the tea." Caleb made a hasty retreat.

As soon as he was out of sight, Evergreen burst into laughter. "Oh my gods! Did you see his face? Dad, your timing was epic."

"Evergreen," Ria scolded. "Don't be unkind."

"Oh, come on, Mom. It was funny. They would like nothing better than to convert us. I mean, they love their martyrs, people who died refusing to give up their faith. But what do they do? They're out there trying to take faith from others, trying to take our gods, without a second thought. So what if I laughed a little at his reaction to finding out that the Big Bad Pagans are still alive and well."

"That's not how we educate people, Evergreen. That's not how we find common ground and understanding," her mother lectured.

"Yeah, well. You have your way. But this is my way of coping with the fact that we are *never* going to understand each other."

"That's just not true. You just told Caleb that you understood why Jehovah's Witnesses don't celebrate Christmas and Easter," Ria pointed out.

Evergreen frowned. "Yeah, but with the same information he went a completely different direction. I mean, he says these holidays are Pagan, so you shouldn't celebrate them. And we're like, yay Pagan holidays are still being celebrated."

Ria gave Evergreen a stern look, one she felt more than saw. "You wouldn't like it if people laughed at you for your beliefs, Evergreen Pendre."

Evergreen sighed. "No, I wouldn't."

"What is the Rede?"

Evergreen rolled her eyes. "Yeah, yeah. I got it."

"No, I want you to say it."

Evergreen groaned. "An' it harm none, do what ye will," she muttered.

"Good." Ria nodded with satisfaction. "Now, come here."

Evergreen plopped her head onto her mother's shoulder as Ria embraced her. Her irritation slid away the longer her mother patted her head.

"There is too much hate in the world already," Ria murmured. "We need to be better."

"I know. I'm sorry."

After releasing Evergreen, Ria stood from the table and took her and Caleb's cups to the kitchen.

Sawyer leaned toward Evergreen, resting his elbow on the table and cupping one hand around his mouth. "It was funny though," he whispered to her.

Evergreen snickered under her breath. "Right?"

CHAPTER 26

It was shortly before lunch, while Wes was chopping up fruit and setting deli meats and cheeses out on the island that utter chaos descended on the retreat center. The others began to arrive.

Piper rang the bell first, and Sawyer happened to be closest to the door at the time. As he opened it, he looked down at the petite woman buried deep in her winter things, only her light grey eyes peeking out from her hood and scarf.

"Piper? Is that you in there?" Sawyer asked.

The hood bobbed in assent.

Sawyer stepped aside so she could enter. As soon as the door was closed, Piper pulled the scarf from her face, sputtering as she tried to get the fuzzies off her lips.

"It's cold out there!" she complained. Then she turned back to Sawyer and looked up at him. He was over a foot taller than her and nearly twice as wide. She leaned back as though he were a giant.

"What the heck are they feeding you? When did you get so huge?" she asked.

"You know, that's exactly what I said to Tara when I saw him, too," Ria said, coming to see who had arrived.

"Ria!" Piper grinned as she held out her arms to the woman. "It's been too long."

Ria agreed and embraced her.

"Don't you have any bags?" Ria asked.

Piper pulled off her hood, revealing her pixie-cut, white hair. "I do, but I left them in the car. The heater is broken, so I thought I'd come in and warm up first."

"I can go grab them for you," Sawyer offered.

"Oh, no. It's fine. There's too much." She waved her delicate hand.

"It's no problem," he insisted.

"I'll have Eeva and Cassandra help, too," Ria said.

The cousins came when they were called, and the three of them carried Piper's things into a room on the second floor.

Eeva shook her head as they placed Piper's luggage at the foot of the bed. "I will never understand how someone as small as Piper can snore so loudly."

Cassandra laughed. "Remember the first time we all went camping, and I told you it was a bear?"

"Remember? I didn't sleep the whole weekend!"

"Sometimes, you're too easy, cuz."

"I don't remember that," Sawyer said as they walked down the stairs.

"You and your mom hadn't moved here yet," Eeva explained.

Sawyer had only just bitten into his sandwich when the doorbell rang again.

Cassandra, who was putting a glass of milk in front of Sol, told everyone she would get it.

A few minutes later, she reappeared, a woman with frizzy, curly, black hair streaked with grey following her.

"Look who it is," Cassandra announced.

"Grandma!" Sol squealed and raced to hug the woman, who reacted with equal enthusiasm.

Morrigan embraced Ria next. "Little sister," she murmured. "Sorry I'm late."

"Oh, don't worry about it. We know you work crazy hours at the hospital."

"Hello, dear heart," Morrigan greeted as she kissed the top of Eeva's head. "How's school?"

"Well, I thought I was about to start my last semester, but... I'll tell you about it later."

Morrigan chuckled. "All right."

"I put you on the second floor with Cassandra and Sol," Ria told her sister.

Morrigan nodded. "Cassandra, would you take my things upstairs while I catch up with my favorite grandson?"

"I'm your *only* grandson," Sol pointed out.

Morrigan blinked. "Are you? Are you sure we haven't misplaced a brother anywhere?" She looked around as if she was really searching for another child.

Sol giggled. "You're silly, Grandma."

Morrigan ruffled the boy's hair as Cassandra left to take up her things.

Devan arrived next, his booming voice carrying to the sitting room as he greeted Eeva at the door.

"Am I the last?" he asked.

"Not this time," Eeva said, leading him into the room where the others were catching up.

Devan was not a tall man, and he was stouter than Sawyer remembered. But he still had the same chin-length pale hair and the same well-trimmed goatee. He smiled his greeting at everyone. "You all thought I would be late? Didn't you?" he challenged.

"There's a first time for everything," Wes teased.

"Devan, you're in the attic. I hope that's okay," Ria told him.

"No problem at all." He patted his belly. "I could use the exercise," he declared with a chuckle.

Cassandra and Eeva carried his bag and CPAP machine upstairs for him.

It was still early afternoon when Dorian and Cory arrived.

"Can I get some help?" Cassandra called from the front door.

Sawyer and Eeva rose to assist her, realizing why she'd asked when they arrived.

Cory, a six-foot-three, ripped beast of a man, stood just inside, his foot in a splint and crutches under his arms.

Meanwhile, his husband, Dorian, held a car seat in one hand and a teddy bear in the other. He had diaper bags crisscrossed over his chest.

"What happened?" Eeva asked, staring at Cory's foot.

"Oh, don't even ask," Dorian said. "He'll give you the whole play-by-play. Short version: he got hurt playing hockey."

"Is it broken?" Sawyer asked.

"It's only sprained. Don't let him whine too much about it," Dorian advised.

"And who is this?" Cassandra asked, tilting her head at the car seat.

"Let's get inside, and we'll introduce you," Cory said.

Once Cory was seated comfortably in an armchair, his foot propped up on the ottoman, Dorian took the blanket off the car seat.

"Everyone," Dorian said, unbuckling the baby inside, "We'd like you to meet Ella."

The baby girl couldn't have been more than six months old. She looked around at them, her eyes big and blue under a mess of strawberry blonde hair.

"Hi, Ella," Eeva cooed, smiling at the baby. "Aw, look at her cute little frilly dress."

"I picked it out," Cory said proudly.

"The adoption went through last month," Dorian informed. "It has been an adjustment, but we're finally getting the hang of it."

"Don't you worry," Ria said. "We've got the crib all set up for you."

"Mom, you knew? Why didn't you say?" Eeva complained.

"Well, they wanted it to be a surprise, and they couldn't very well not tell me to prepare for a baby in the house."

"Can I hold her?" Eeva asked.

"Sure," Dorian said. "After you wash your hands."

"Okay." Eeva went and washed her hands, then sat on the couch, where Dorian handed her the baby. "Hello, Ella. Pretty girl. I'm so glad you've come to visit us. I bet you like being adopted by your daddies. You don't worry one bit. They're going to take good care of you."

Sawyer sat beside her on the couch, looking over at Eeva and Ella gazing at each other. His chest warmed, and he smiled gently.

Muir jumped up on the couch between Eeva and Sawyer, wanting to see what the commotion was about. He looked at Ella, and Ella looked at him. Then he started to meow, loud and insistent.

Eeva chuckled. "Here," she said to Dorian, holding Ella out to him. "Muir doesn't seem to like the competition."

After Ella had been passed back, Eeva picked up Muir and held him like a baby, stroking his chest and belly. "I know. I know. I'm a traitor," she murmured to the cat.

Muir purred and closed his eyes.

Just as Wes was finishing dinner and the whole house smelled of slow cooked pot roast, the last of the old coven arrived.

Eeva led Hazel into the dining room. She hadn't changed at all since they'd seen her last. She was still reedy with long, dark hair and flowing garments of varying shades of blue.

"Sorry I'm late," Hazel apologized. "Charlie was being a handful. How that man is going to survive without me for the next ten days I have no idea." She glanced around at everyone, her gaze landing on Devan. "What? Even Devan got here before me."

Everyone chuckled and sat down to eat.

CHAPTER 27

*L*ater that evening, everyone sat in the common room knitting, quilting, and just catching up. Devan, who lay on the floor near the fire, asked, "When was the last time we were all together like this?"

"Eeva's dedication," Piper answered, her memory as sharp as ever.

"That was just before Sawyer went off to college," Tara said.

"Yeah, the summer before," Cory agreed. "Because there was that huge storm the night before."

Everyone fell into a thoughtful silence, one blurry with memories.

Evergreen remembered that night, the most important night thus far on her Pagan path. Cory was right. It had stormed the night before. She recalled that the path beneath her bare feet had still been wet.

Though they had always referred to themselves as a coven, that wasn't strictly accurate. Unlike an actual coven, there was no lineage, no passing of secret truths. They were just a group of eclectic Pagans who celebrated the sabbats and esbats together. They were a group of like-minded friends who performed magic together more than anything. And so there was no initiation to be had.

Still, they did have a tradition for dedication, a practice usually reserved for solitary practitioners. The group saw their relationships with deity as unique and individual. So, when Evergreen felt she was old enough to declare that she would continue on this spiritual path, she asked to have a dedication ceremony.

The coven was there only to show support. They were there on the patio in full regalia, ready to send her on her journey. Her father gave her the lantern that would light her way, and her mother took her cloak so she could meet the gods in the same state as she'd been born.

She walked down the soggy dirt path through the woods, mud squelching between her toes. When she reached the clearing, she performed her ritual, swearing to all who would listen that she dedicated herself to the old ways, that she would honor and celebrate the Earth and its seasons, that she would endeavor to live in perfect love and perfect trust.

When she returned to the coven, still waiting on the patio, her cloak was returned, and they all had a big party.

"I've got an idea," Piper said, pulling Evergreen from her memories. "That is, if you guys want to, of course. Why don't we have a naming ceremony for little Ella?"

Cory and Dorian exchanged looks, then Dorian nodded. "That's a wonderful idea, Piper. But will we have time? I mean, we're already preparing for Yule."

"Oh, don't worry about that," Ria assured, looking down at the baby in her arms. "We've got most of what we need already. And what's most important is that we're all together. Isn't that right, baby Ella?"

"We should all go into town tomorrow," Cassandra suggested. "Then we can shop for Yule gifts and naming gifts for baby Ella. We can have the naming ceremony the day after."

Everyone agreed to the prospect with enthusiasm.

As Ria handed Ella to Cory, Evergreen could hear the dreamy smile in her voice when she said, "I can't wait to be a grandma."

"You're hurting Muir's feelings," Evergreen chided, putting her free hand over the cat's ears.

It wasn't long before Evergreen called it a night. The day had been full, and she wanted to be asleep well before Sawyer crawled into the sleeping bag beside her.

But such was not her luck. She was still staring up at the glass ceiling when he came into the meditation room.

He crept in, trying not to wake her. She could hear him suppressing his breathing.

"I'm awake," she told him.

"Oh, okay," he murmured, letting out a sigh. He turned on the dim yellow lamp in the corner.

As a heavy silence choked the room, Evergreen wished she hadn't said anything.

"Do you...need me to leave so you can change into your pajamas?" she asked softly.

"No, it's fine. I'll just change in the bathroom when it's free."

She watched as he dug through his bag. "You could just change in the corner. I mean, you're wearing underwear, aren't you? I won't peep."

His eyes slid over to hers. "I'm not shy," he told her.

"Neither am I," she stated. "But it would be rude to look without permission."

His gaze was level and serious, and she could feel him analyzing her response to what he was about to ask. "Is that something...you want? Permission, that is."

Evergreen imagined Sawyer slowly unbuttoning his jeans. *Yes*, she thought. "No, that's not what I meant. I was speaking generally," she said.

"Because..." Sawyer continued softly. "You can if you want... I wouldn't mind."

Evergreen's heart leapt into her throat. She turned on her side, facing the glass wall. "I didn't say that," she murmured. "I was only trying to make things more convenient for you. Take it or leave it. I don't care." But her voice sounded a little too uneven to be convincing.

"All right," he conceded. "I will then."

"Fine. Go ahead."

The night was dark outside the glass, and the lamp cast reflections. Evergreen watched, her eyes drawn to the movement. And though her vision didn't permit her to see anything in detail, she saw enough for her mind to wander back to her dream from the night before. A dull ache arose in her core, and she clenched her jaw.

Sawyer turned off the lamp, his now-fully-clothed reflection disappearing into the night. Evergreen sighed, hoping its retreat would make her desire wane. But as Sawyer climbed into his sleeping bag on the floor beside her, she could feel his presence behind her, his solid, warm presence. He didn't touch her, didn't even reach for her. But her skin started to tingle as if anticipating his caress.

She adjusted to lay on her back, taking a deep breath and letting it out all at once. *This is going to be a rough night,* she thought. Acknowledging her desire for Sawyer had done nothing to alleviate the feeling. In fact, if anything, it had made it worse.

Bury it, Evergreen, she told herself. *There's no relief in sight, so just bury it.*

"Are you warm enough?" Sawyer asked, his voice soft and way closer than she'd expected. "I can switch places with you if you'd like to be closer to the heater."

"I'm fine," she muttered.

She stared up at the ceiling, trying to concentrate on the clouds overhead, trying to push her body's sensations out of her.

"About what your mom said before," he started. "Does she bug you a lot about having grandchildren? My mom does."

Evergreen latched onto the conversation, anything to distract herself. "No, not really. I mean, I know she wants to be a grandma, but it's not like she pressures me or anything."

"Do you...want to have kids?"

Evergreen sighed, her desire slipping out of her under the weight of the topic. "Sure. But, you know, it's not that simple for me."

"Why not?"

"Well, my eye disease is genetic. That means my children would have a greater chance of having it, too. At the very least, they all would be carriers. And can I be an effective parent without being able to see? I mean, I couldn't even take my kids to school. I couldn't even drive them to the hospital if they were sick or hurt."

Evergreen heard Sawyer turn toward her, but she didn't look over at him.

"Would you have not wanted to be born?" he asked softly.

"What do you mean?"

"I mean, if your parents had known you would be blind, if you could make that decision, would you still want to be born?"

"Of course I would. Even a life with blindness is better than no life. But just because I feel that way doesn't mean my kids will. And I know better than anyone the struggles they will face."

"And you will be able to teach them how to face them better than anyone. And let me add that it's total nonsense that you couldn't be an effective parent. That's bullshit. You've found ways to adapt to every situation. You're telling me you couldn't adapt to motherhood? You're the strongest, most competent person I know. If you decided to be a mother, I know you'll be amazing at it, just like you're amazing at everything else. I mean, you're so good. You make it look easy, effortless."

"It's not though. It's hard work."

"I know. And you don't shy away from that work either. I think society needs more parents like you. You know...not to influence your decision or anything."

Warmth spread through Evergreen's chest, and with it, light and contentment and...*hope?* She didn't dare look over at Sawyer, afraid of what her expression might say. "Thank you," she murmured.

"Anytime." Sawyer paused for a moment. "We've known each other a long time, but I don't think I've ever heard you say. Do you mind if I ask you what your eyesight is like?"

The question she'd been asked so many times put her back in comfortable territory. "I don't mind, though I've had bad vision my whole life so I don't know how much sense my explanation will make. I don't have anything to compare it to."

"That's fine."

"I think of my vision like impressionist art. Maybe sighted people see the world like a realist painting, but my vision is a lot of guesswork. For example, if I see a round circle on a wall above a door. It's white with a dark edge. I assume it's a clock. I can't read the numbers or see the hands, but it's a safe bet it's a clock. It could not be a clock. It could be a barometric pressure gauge for all I know. I can see someone sitting across the table from me, but I can't necessarily see his or her facial expressions because facial expressions are often too minute. So I rely on how people sound when they speak, or don't speak for that matter. And I sort of feel the vibes coming off them if that makes sense. I can do a lot of things by touch, like knitting for instance. Sometimes I run into things as I'm not great at judging distance, or maybe that's just my excuse for being clumsy. I'm also color deficient, meaning I can't always tell colors that are close in shade. I might call something green when it's yellow. It's easier if I can compare them side by side. Contrast is easier, especially if the background is vastly different from an object. I'm also light sensitive, and lighting can vastly impact what I can see in any given situation. Does that help you understand better?"

"Yeah. Thanks for sharing that with me."

"No problem."

CHAPTER 28

When Sawyer awoke the next morning, Eeva was no longer in her sleeping bag beside him. The thick scent of cinnamon hung in the air, and the candles on the altar were lit, telling him she had already been busy that morning.

Once he'd changed, he went out to see who all was up and about. Eeva was in the common room with Hazel and Cory. Eeva and Hazel cradled mugs in their hands, their feet tucked under them on the couch. They watched Cory talk to Ella as he fed her.

"So what do you say, Eeva?" Dorian asked, entering the room, a steaming cup in each hand. "You know how it's done, and Cory isn't exactly up for it this year."

"Sure," Eeva agreed with a nod. "I have no problem. And I know you'll teach me anything I forgot. We have time to practice, right?"

"Oh, honey, I can't do it either. Cory is going to have a hard enough time just getting around himself. I have to help him and watch baby Ella."

"Why not Sawyer?" Hazel suggested. "He did it that one year, didn't he?"

They all turned their attention to Sawyer, who covered his mouth as he yawned. He hadn't gotten a lot of sleep the night before, too aware of Eeva beside him. "I what now?"

"You know the dance. You could play the oak king. Couldn't you?" Hazel asked.

"Oh, yeah. I mean, it has been a while, but sure."

"Great," Dorian said with a smile. "Then Eeva can be our holly king, and Sawyer can be our oak king. Don't forget to practice, you two."

Sawyer glanced at Eeva. She did not look as happy at the prospect as she had a few moments before. *Maybe I misread her,* he thought. *Maybe that whole kiss thing was just a fluke. I mean, surely the thought of partnering with me wouldn't be that upsetting if she felt something for me... anything... Should I back off? I feel like I was pretty up-front last night. Maybe I should just tell her outright instead of leading up to it. Maybe I should just tell her how I feel... But if she isn't ready to hear it, it may not end the way I want. Timing is everything.*

Once everyone else was awake and had breakfasted, Wes announced that he would be staying home while they went shopping.

"I've got to make the cakes and ale for the naming ceremony," he explained.

"What will you be making?" Piper asked.

"I'm thinking about crescent moon cutout cookies and faux mead. You know, since I won't have time to ferment actual mead."

"Okay, the kitchen witch will stay home to do his brewing," Morrigan acknowledged.

"I'm staying, too," Cory said. "I don't want to tempt falling on the ice. Ella and I can stay here with Wes. It's too cold to take her out for too long anyway." He smiled at Dorian, leaning over and kissing his cheek. "You go have fun. We'll be fine here with Wes."

Everyone else split into three cars and headed for town. Most of Birchland's shops were situated near each other in the shopping district, so they just parked along the side of the road and bundled in their winter things to walk.

The first shop they went to was Toil and Trouble, the Pagan supply store and new age shop. In the front window was a set of shelves, which held crystal balls, statues of gods and goddesses, wands, and a carved dragon that clung to the front as if scaling it. The dragon wore a tiny Santa hat. A sign in the window informed that tarot card readings were available by appointment.

The air inside Toil and Trouble was thick with the heady smell of dragon's blood incense.

The shopkeeper looked up as they all shuffled in. "Ria," the young woman greeted. "Good to see you. And I see you've brought guests."

Ria smiled. "Yes, this is most of my old coven. They all moved away before you opened the shop. Guys, this is Clover. This shop is her labor of love."

"It's lovely," Hazel complimented.

"Thank you," Clover said. "Go ahead and take a look around. Let me know if you have any questions."

Everyone acknowledged and squeezed into the space.

Sawyer was surprised to find that they had quite a few baby things. He decided to get Ella a onesie with a buckler on the front that said "Shield Maiden."

Sawyer found Eeva's green head easily across the room. She was bent over a glass case with jewelry in it. He perused the shelves, thinking of all the Yules they'd missed together. *Should I get her something again this year?* he wondered. But he knew he still had Yule gifts from the past four Yules in his bag in the meditation room. *Maybe I should just give her the gifts I've been saving. It may be a little weird to give her five gifts after all.*

He stopped in front of a shelf, a glint of light reflecting off faceted glass catching his eye. Before him was a shelf full of glass figurines. A stick with mistletoe, bright green with white berries on top stood in a mosaic cup.

He reached out and pulled the smooth stick from the cup. He'd thought it was glass, but it felt more like plastic.

"It's resin," Clover told him, appearing beside him as he examined it. "It's real mistletoe. I harvested it myself and preserved it in resin to make the hair pin. Pretty, isn't it?"

Sawyer nodded.

"How long are we going to be here?" Sol whined to his mother further down the aisle. He pulled on her hand in emphasis.

"Be patient, Sol," Cassandra told him.

Sawyer approached them. "I'm pretty much done here, Cassandra. I can keep Sol occupied if you need more time," he offered.

"Oh gods, would you?" she asked.

Sawyer knelt down to the boy. "What do you say, my friend? Do you want to go on a quest?"

"A quest? What's that?"

"It's a journey where a brave warrior goes in search of something."

"What are we going to search for?"

Sawyer grinned. "For ice cream, of course. What other kind of quest is there?"

Sol's eyes lit up at the prospect. "What about Eeva? Can Eeva come too?"

"Sure she can," Sawyer agreed. "I'm just going to go buy these things. Why don't you ask Eeva if she wants to come on our quest?"

"Okay!"

Sawyer went to the cash register and purchased the onesie and the hair pin. By the time they were carefully wrapped, Sol and Eeva had reached him.

"You ready?" he asked them.

"You two can head outside. I just have a few purchases to make real quick," Eeva said.

Sawyer nodded, glancing at her hands to see what she was buying. She didn't have anything.

"We're on a quest for ice cream, a quest for ice cream!" Sol cheered as they headed for the door.

CHAPTER 29

*E*vergreen thanked Clover as she handed her the paper bag with her purchases. She smiled to herself, warmth blooming in her chest. *It's perfect,* she thought. *Just the right size and color.*

She zipped up her winter coat and left Toil and Trouble. Sawyer and Sol were waiting for her outside on the sidewalk.

"Okay, I'm ready," she said.

"Witches! Heathens! You'll all burn in Hell!"

Evergreen's stomach jumped into her throat as a man, who seemed to just have been passing them on the sidewalk, began to yell at them.

She turned her back to ignore him; she had long discovered that arguing with his type wasn't worth it.

"Don't turn your back on me, you whore of Satan," he sneered.

Evergreen's heart pounded as fear crept across her skin. She looked down at Sol; his eyes were wide and afraid. Anger churned in her stomach. She took his hand and rounded on their assaulter.

"You don't need to do this," she told him, hoping he couldn't hear the quiver in her voice. "Can't you see you're frightening this child?"

"He should be afraid. The fires of Hell will burn his flesh and melt his soul with eternal torment. He even wears the mark of the Devil," the man spat, pointing at the pentacle on Sol's chest.

"Eeva," Sol murmured, tugging on her hand.

She knelt down to see him better. Tears streaked down his cheeks.

"Why is he yelling at us?" he asked.

Evergreen wrapped her arms around Sol, not having the words to explain to him at the moment.

The man was blocked from her view as Sawyer stepped in between them. "I think you need to leave," he said, his voice low, his threat clear.

"'Blessed are those who are persecuted for righteousness' sake, for theirs is the kingdom of Heaven. Blessed are you when others revile you and persecute you and utter all kinds of evil against you falsely on my account. Rejoice and be glad, for your reward is great in Heaven, for so they persecuted the prophets, who were before y—'"

"Daniel!" a woman scolded, firmly interrupting the man.

Evergreen peeked around Sawyer to see a short, round woman stomping toward them.

"Please, tell me you aren't harassing these nice people. We talked about this. You can't keep doing this," she censured.

"I have the freedom of speech. This is America!" the man shouted at her.

"Yeah, and that same amendment gives them the freedom of religion."

"A man or a woman who is a medium or deals with the spirits of the dead must certainly be put to death. They must be stoned to death. Their blood is on them," he countered.

"Really? Death threats now? You know, Daniel, one of these days you're going to be charged with a hate crime."

"We live in a Christian nation. Our leaders will see the righteousness of my words."

"That's enough," the woman said finally. "We can talk about this at home. Go wait in the car."

"Woman—"

"Don't you 'woman' me. Go."

The man squinted his hatred one more time before he stormed back the way he'd come. Then the woman turned toward Sawyer, Evergreen, and Sol.

"I am so sorry," she apologized, her voice thick with regret. "There isn't any excuse I can give for my husband's behavior. He's on this new evangelical kick. I have no idea what has gotten into him. I hope he didn't scare you too much. Are you okay?"

Evergreen stood, lifting Sol in her arms. Sawyer looked over at her as she moved to stand beside him. She could feel his gaze on her face, analyzing her emotional state.

"I think we're all right. It may take us just a bit to calm down," he told her.

"Well...I hope you know that all Christians aren't like that. Some of us are very accepting. Just... You have allies amongst us. Though I'm sure that doesn't mean much to you at the moment."

"That's not true," Evergreen told her. "It's a relief to have a Christian stand up to one of their own, to hold them accountable for that behavior. We're shaken up, but I'm grateful you stepped in."

The woman smiled, and even Evergreen could see the light shining from her face. "Thank you, and I'm sorry again. I hope you three have a very happy solstice. You look like such a nice family."

"Thank you, and merry Christmas to you," Sawyer said.

"Merry Christmas," Evergreen seconded as the woman nodded and followed her husband.

Evergreen heaved a deep sigh, trying to steady her still-racing heart.

"Are you all right?" Sawyer asked.

She swallowed and gave him a small nod. "I'm okay."

"How about you, my friend? Are you okay?" Sawyer asked, rubbing Sol's shoulder.

"Was that man going to hurt us?" Sol asked.

Sawyer frowned. "It's hard to say," he told the boy honestly. "But you better believe that Eeva and I would never let anyone hurt you. Okay?"

Sol nodded.

"Do you still want to go on that quest for ice cream? Or do you want us to take you inside to your mom and grandma?" Sawyer asked him.

"I want strawberry," Sol declared. "No, I want chocolate."

"Why don't we get both strawberry *and* chocolate?" Sawyer asked.

Sol squirmed in Evergreen's arms, and she put him down.

"Yeah!" he agreed.

His enthusiasm, his child's way of pushing the bad experience aside, of living in the moment made Evergreen's anxiety slip away.

"We're on a quest for ice cream, a quest for ice cream," Sol sang, holding out a hand to Evergreen and Sawyer in turn.

And as they all walked hand-in-hand, Evergreen remembered the woman saying how they looked like a family. She glanced sidelong at Sawyer. She couldn't see him well from this distance, but she just knew he was smiling. Warmth spread through Evergreen's chest, and with it returned the light and contentment from the night before. And, yes, she recognized it now. It was hope. The world paused for just a second as if her heart had taken a picture of the moment.

CHAPTER 30

Sawyer let his sigh out slowly so as not to wake Eeva as she lay beside him. He'd presented a strong front that afternoon, but if he was being honest with himself, the encounter outside Toil and Trouble had frightened him. Not because he thought the man would hurt them. No, he knew he could protect Eeva and Sol. He was afraid at the sheer magnitude of his anger. He would not have hesitated in striking that man down had he made a move toward Eeva or Sol. The image of Eeva's pale face as she clutched the crying child to her, her quivering voice as she'd challenged the man, his blood still boiled to think of it. He'd never been so angry in his life, and it left the taste of shame behind.

And for the rest of the day, Eeva had been quiet. He hadn't felt much from her. She seemed still, contemplative. And when she'd looked at him —and he'd caught her doing so quite a few times—her gaze had been open as if she were asking him a question he couldn't understand.

Sawyer lay on his side, watching Eeva's tranquil face as she slept. Muir lay between them on her sleeping bag, unconsciously purring in contentment, Eeva's hand was buried in his fur. Sawyer reached out hesitantly, holding his breath as his heart picked up speed. He stroked Muir, his fingers millimeters from Eeva's. He pulled back before he woke her and closed his eyes. Listening to her slow, even breathing, he matched his rhythm with hers and drifted off to sleep.

The next day was a flurry of activity at the retreat center. Some were getting things ready for the naming ceremony that evening, while others were playing games or doing crafts. Morrigan was looking everywhere for something she'd misplaced—swearing that the faeries had hid it because she hadn't left them a gift, which was her custom. Ria had taken over the meditation room so she could perform reiki on Cory. Piper was drawing up Tara's star chart for the coming year, and Hazel and Devan were facing off in an intense game of weiqi.

Sawyer found Eeva in the kitchen, helping her dad frost the moon cookies he'd made the day before.

"Hey, Eeva. You mentioned yesterday that you wanted to practice the holly king versus the oak king before Yule. We can do that when you're done if you want," Sawyer said.

"Oh, I can handle things here," Wes assured. "Eeva, go on ahead and practice with Sawyer."

"But Mom is using the meditation room," Eeva said. "Where are we going to practice?"

"Just go out to the patio," Wes suggested. "I'm sure you'll warm up once you start moving around."

"All right." Eeva nodded and stuck the tip of her finger in her mouth, removing the smear of yellow frosting. "Where are the practice staves?"

"In the garage," Wes answered.

She nodded. "Meet you outside in a sec," she told Sawyer.

He acknowledged and went to put his coat on over his hoodie.

Eeva joined Sawyer outside shortly, a staff in each hand. She offered him one, and he took it.

"Do you remember the steps?" he asked.

"Vaguely. As I recall they're fairly simple. It's the feeling, the rhythm that's more important."

Sawyer nodded. "Right. And since this is the winter solstice and you're playing the holly king, you're the one who loses this time."

"Yeah, okay. Let's give it a try. You got a beat?"

"Sure, I'll use the one I used to practice before. But of course, it'll be different the day of since the drum circle will be going."

Sawyer pressed play on his cellphone, and the sound of drums started from the speaker as "Punagra" played. He put it on repeat and placed the phone on the step. He faced Eeva, loosening his shoulders to the primal beat.

As Eeva shifted her weight from foot to foot, swaying in time, they started the simple steps of the dance, circling each other.

"Yeah, that's it," Sawyer encouraged. "You remember. Ready for the staff?"

Eeva smiled. "Go for it."

Sawyer struck out with his staff, and Eeva met it with hers. He did it again with the same result. And so they went on in rhythm, the mock battle playing out in a dance. They circled each other. They clashed in the middle. They retreated.

Sawyer's heart raced as the exercise made him warm in his coat. He took it off, his steps still in time. Eeva did the same, her breaths punctuated by white puffs from her lips.

"Ready to try the end?" Sawyer asked her.

"Come at me," she challenged, her voice teasing.

Sawyer attacked, bringing his face in close to hers, their staves crossed between them. This was where he was supposed to push them apart. She was to fall to the ground, defeated. But as they locked eyes, and he felt her breath on his face, they both froze.

The music played on in the background but seemed very far away. And there it was again, the look that beckoned him. Eeva's eyes were deep and serious, and they were trained on him. This time, he didn't speak. He didn't want the sound of his voice to pull her from the moment. Still, as he leaned down toward her, he did so slowly, giving her time to retreat.

Just as he felt her warm breath on his mouth, he looked at her through heavy eyelids. Her eyes were lightly shut. He smiled, then pressed his lips to hers. The kiss was soft and sweet. And though lust pumped in his veins, he reined it in, focusing on the pleasant ache in his chest. He broke the kiss but didn't pull away.

As Eeva's clouded blue eyes met his, her face flushed. He smiled gently at her. *It has finally happened,* he thought. *I did it. Surely she knows how I feel now. And she didn't resist either. She kissed me back.* Sawyer's head was fuzzy with giddiness.

"Um... Can we practice another time?" Eeva asked softly. "I think I need a minute."

Sawyer sobered, trying to quiet his inner cheers of triumph. *This is coming out of nowhere for her,* he thought. *Of course she needs time to process.* "Sure, no problem," he told her.

CHAPTER 31

$\mathcal{E}$vergreen nodded slowly. Then she leaned her staff against the side of the house and grabbed her coat. Too warm still to put it on, she folded it over her arm and started down the path through the woods.

What...? What...? What the hell was that? she thought. Her heart pounded in her fingertips, and her crunching footsteps sounded very loud in her ears.

She halted on the path, her breaths long and deep. "We kissed," she murmured. She closed her eyes. She could still feel Sawyer's lips on hers like the far away echo of a low and sweet melody.

Evergreen grinned, her entire body tingling as if she were having a pleasant panic attack. "We kissed," she breathed, soft and happy.

But her joy was short lived. Reality descended upon her, and her stomach dropped as the smile slid from her face. "We kissed," she said again, dread coloring her tone.

What does this mean? she wondered. *Why would he kiss me? I mean, other than he felt like it. Did he just feel like it? Is it that simple?*

She thought back to his reaction after he'd pulled away. *No, that can't be right. I felt...relief from him. Like he'd been holding it in for a long time. Could I have misread him all along?*

Evergreen shook her head. *No, that can't be true either. If he'd been harboring feelings for me for that long, he would have stayed in touch. Right? I wouldn't have been...so easy to forget.*

She tried to swallow the lump that rose in her throat. *It doesn't matter,* she thought. *That's not the question here. Why would he kiss me? And why would he feel relieved afterward? Maybe he was just relieved I didn't pull away like last time. Yeah, that makes sense. But what does that mean for what comes next?*

She couldn't lie to herself about how it had felt. It had been everything she'd wished for before. How many times had she prayed, begged in her mind for Sawyer to lean just a little farther down, to give her some indication that he wanted her as much as she wanted him?

But he never had. He had always been so calm and balanced. Nothing phased him. It was one of the things she'd loved about him. He never wasted words. But he always had an answer, a solution to whatever situation that had fired her up. She'd liked to think he cared in a quiet sort of way, like the base of a pillar. It doesn't draw as much attention, but it's equally if not more important. That's how she'd always seen him, an ever-present, if silent, support.

Which of course is why I was so fucked up when he'd left, she thought. *He'd been a steadying presence, something to navigate by, and then he left and didn't look back.*

But, thinking about it now, he was always the still, silent reflection type. I was the one who jumped into action, with everything but love that is. When I look at it that way, it doesn't make sense that he would have made a move back then. So what's different now? Has he changed so much?

Evergreen thought about everything she'd witnessed over the last few days. *Yes, he has changed quite a bit. He never would have threatened that man before or confronted the woman at the craft store. He wouldn't have been so forceful about me not riding with Niko. And he obviously never kissed me, even when I wanted it so desperately. Even so, it's the little things that tell me he's still the Sawyer I knew: he remembered how I like my hot cocoa, he's still polite and considerate, he's sweet with Sol, and he helped me find a better way to approach my career.*

A gentle warmth settled into her heart, and she smiled at the familiar feeling. *He's different. Of course, he is. I am too. I don't know anything about his life right now, but I can learn. I want to learn.*

And though anxiety clenched her gut, Evergreen didn't allow it to take over. *Maybe this time it will work out. There's no ignoring this feeling anyway. I might as well make the best of it.*

Evergreen took a deep breath and headed back toward the house. She entered just as her dad called that lunch was ready.

The island was packed with taco stuff, and a queue had formed.

"Don't worry, Tara, Piper," Wes told the women as Evergreen took her place at the back of the line. "I made black beans for you since I know you're vegetarians."

"Are you sure I can't take this man off your hands?" Piper asked Ria.

"Go ahead and try. You'll give him back in a week. He's needy," Ria said affectionately, rubbing her husband's back.

"It's true," Wes agreed. "I'm like a puppy."

"You mean, you aren't house trained?" Devan asked.

Everyone laughed.

After Evergreen had gotten her tacos, she made her way to the dining room. The only free chair was between Morrigan and Piper, across from Sawyer. She sank into the seat, furtively glancing at him.

Their eyes met. He smiled. And as her cheeks heated, she smiled back.

A shiver ran down Evergreen's spine as Morrigan stroked her hair. Evergreen jumped as if caught doing something she wasn't supposed to.

"So what's going on, Eeva? You mentioned something had changed with school?" Morrigan said.

"Oh, yeah. Well, I was having a hard time finding a job. You know I've always wanted to work in a museum."

Morrigan nodded.

"Well, Sawyer looked some stuff up for me, and he told me that you can get a certificate that really helps you get those jobs. Part of the program is that you have to have an internship. And it sounds like if you do really well, not only can you get a job at the museum after, but they might even pay for higher degrees."

"Wow, that's amazing. So are you going to do it then?"

"I called the university and made an appointment with my academic adviser after the holidays."

"That's excellent. I hope it works out," Morrigan said.

"Yeah, me too," Evergreen agreed.

CHAPTER 32

The sun set early that evening, and the meditation room felt enchanted as the coven filed into the space under the watchful light of the waning gibbous. Devan had already cleansed the room, and everyone was smudged prior to entering. The sharp scent of white sage and the mellow saccharinity of sweetgrass still lingered in Sawyer's nose. He felt light, the burned herbs having blessed him and banished any negative energies. A reverent hush descended as Cory and Dorian carried their daughter into the room and toward the altar.

They turned and faced the coven, who had formed a circle. Everyone had changed into their best garments from cloaks to flowing dresses to jeans and sweaters. They wore them with purpose, which was what mattered.

"We gather on this night to ask and receive blessings for this child, to give her name power, and to introduce her to you and the gods," Cory declared, gesturing at Ella in Dorian's arms.

"Please face East," Cory said, turning in the correct direction.

"Spirits of the East, element of Air, please join our circle. Hail and welcome," Dorian said.

As Dorian spoke, Sawyer imagined the wind blowing the hair from his face and the sound of rustling leaves.

"Hail and welcome," everyone responded.

Cory lit the incense on the east side of the altar. Then everyone turned South.

"Spirits of the South, element of Fire, please join our circle. Hail and welcome."

Sawyer's face was warmed by a visualized flame.

"Hail and welcome."

Cory lit the candle on the south end of the altar.

Everyone turned West, their hands raised as if to embrace each element.

"Spirits of the West, element of Water, please join our circle. Hail and welcome."

Sawyer imagined the feel of rain dripping down his face and neck.

"Hail and welcome."

Cory lifted the bowl of water from the west side of the altar, held it at head level, and nodded his head in a bow.

They all faced North.

"Spirits of the North, element of Earth, please join our circle. Hail and welcome."

Sawyer pictured the warm soil of spring and the scent of freshly cut grass.

"Hail and welcome."

Cory lifted the bowl of salt from the north side of the altar, held it at head level, and nodded his head in a bow.

Sawyer turned back toward the center of the circle as did the others. He placed his hands, one over the other, at the center of his chest and closed his eyes.

"Divine Spirit within, please join our circle. Hail and welcome."

He imagined a soft purple glow at the center of his chest.

"Hail and welcome."

"Goddess, Divine Mother, Sacred Sister, we invite you to join our circle. Hail and welcome."

"Hail and welcome."

Cory lit a candle to represent the goddess.

"God, Divine Father, Sacred Brother, we invite you to join our circle. Hail and welcome."

"Hail and welcome."

Cory lit the candle that represented the god. Then he took the bottle Wes had filled with faux mead and poured it into a bowl between the goddess and god candles. "To the Lord and Lady," he declared. "Blessed be."

"Blessed be," they echoed.

"Before we finish casting our circle," Dorian said. "Let us raise energy with a chant."

The group listened as Dorian sang the chant and then joined in as he repeated it.

"Circle, circle, circle of light, protect us as we work this rite."

Sawyer lifted his voice in song, harmonizing with those around him. And as they repeated the chant over and over, his heart lightened, and the room seemed to hum with the energy they raised.

As the last note died away, Dorian turned to Ria and took her hand. "Ria, hand to hand I cast the circle."

Ria turned to Wes, who stood on her left. "Wesley, hand to hand I cast the circle."

And so it went on around the room until Cory turned to Dorian and said, "Dorian, hand to hand I cast the circle."

"The circle is cast," Dorian declared.

"Tonight, we stand at this altar, and ask that the gods, goddesses, spirits, and elements give us guidance on the path ahead," Cory said. "May we teach Ella all she needs to know to prepare for her to stand on her own, and may she ever have love and support when she needs it most."

Cory took the incense from the altar and turned to Dorian and Ella. He moved it in a circular motion so the incense wafted around her. "Spirits of Air, we ask that you bless Ella with curiosity and communication. May she be ever curious to learn new things and expand her knowledge. May her voice be strong and clear so she may never suffer in silence."

Cory replaced the incense on the altar and took the fire element candle. He carefully circled it around Ella. "Spirits of Fire, we ask that you bless Ella with protection, passion, and courage. May she have the passion to have dreams, the courage to follow them, and the protection that her feet may never fail her."

Cory replaced the candle on the altar and brought the bowl of water to his daughter. He dipped his fingers into the bowl and sprinkled the water onto her forehead. "Spirits of Water, we ask that you bless Ella with peace and compassion. May her heart have few troubles, and may her actions heal the troubles of others."

Cory replaced the water on the altar and took the bowl of salt. Taking a pinch, he sprinkled it over her head, carefully avoiding her eyes. "Spirit of Earth, we ask that you bless Ella with prosperity and conscientiousness. May she be a good steward of the planet and all the life it supports, and may her hard work be rewarded."

Cory returned the salt to the altar and faced the center of the circle. "We call on the ancestors to guide Ella as she learns and grows."

"We call on the Mother Goddess and the Father God to nurture and protect Ella as she walks her own path," Dorian said.

"If anyone would like to bestow blessings on Ella, please do so at this time."

Dorian presented Ella to Ria. "I would like to bestow the blessing of health and vitality on you, Ella," Ria said before kissing the baby's forehead.

Dorian presented Ella to Wes. "May your belly always be full and your heart big enough to share what you have with others," Wes said. Then he kissed Ella's forehead.

Dorian presented Ella to Morrigan. "For you, Ella, I wish the fae will forever be friends." Morrigan kissed Ella's forehead in turn.

Dorian presented Ella to Cassandra. "May you have the foresight to make wise decisions." Cassandra gave Ella a kiss.

Dorian knelt down so Sol could reach the baby. "I want baby Ella to always be happy. I want her to laugh a lot." Sol pressed a kiss to Ella's cheek.

Then Dorian brought Ella to Eeva. "I hope that you will easily find love and kindness, Ella." Eeva sealed her blessing with a kiss.

Dorian approached Sawyer, and Sawyer gazed down at the beautiful baby girl in his arms. Her wide, blue eyes looked directly at him as if she knew exactly what was happening. He smiled at the child. "Ella, I wish that you will always see the wonder of the natural world around you." He leaned down and brushed his lips against the baby's soft, fine hair.

Dorian moved on, presenting Ella to Tara. "May you have balance, baby Ella, to never feel overwhelmed by what you encounter along the way." Tara kissed the child's head.

Dorian next presented her to Hazel. "May you be a force to reckon with." And Hazel kissed the baby.

Dorian then stood before Piper. "I hope that you can always find solace in the stars, Ella." Piper placed a kiss on Ella's head.

Finally, Dorian presented Ella to Devan. "May you learn from your mistakes." Devan leaned down and kissed the child.

Taking his place beside his husband again, Dorian passed Ella to him. Then he went to the altar and took a moon cookie from the plate and the chalice of faux mead.

He held up the cookie. "May I never hunger," he said before eating it. "Blessed be." Then he held the chalice aloft. "May I never thirst." He drank from it. "Blessed be."

Dorian took up the plate and chalice and turned to Ria. She followed his pattern, asking that she may never hunger or thirst. And so the ritual of cakes and ale continued around the circle, gently grounding the energies that had been raised.

After Dorian had offered the sustenance to Cory, he placed the plate and chalice onto the altar, took Ella back from Cory, and faced the circle.

"Thank you for your blessings. We will now release the circle," Cory told them. He turned to the altar. "God, Divine Father, Sacred Brother, we thank you for joining us. Go if you must. Stay if you will." Cory snuffed out the god's candle.

"Goddess, Divine Mother, Sacred Sister, thank you for joining us. Go if you must. Stay if you will." Then he snuffed out the goddess's candle.

They all turned North, and Cory continued. "Spirits of the North, element of Earth, thank you for joining us. Go if you must. Stay if you will."

They turned West. "Spirits of the West, element of Water, thank you for joining us. Go if you must. Stay if you will."

Again, they turned South. "Spirits of the South, element of Fire, thank you for joining us. Go if you must. Stay if you will." And Cory snuffed out the Fire candle.

Finally, they turned East. "Spirits of the East, element of Air, thank you for joining us. Go if you must. Stay if you will."

As everyone turned back into the circle, Cory said, "The circle is open but never broken. Blessed be."

"Blessed be!" everyone answered.

CHAPTER 33

Evergreen sat cross-legged beside Sawyer on the floor of the common room as Dorian and Cory opened the gifts everyone had gotten for baby Ella. Evergreen had given her a dream catcher for her bedroom.

Everyone's attention was on the couple as they smiled and expressed their thanks. Baby Ella wasn't much interested in her presents, but she watched curiously from her car seat.

Muir and Larkspur played with a discarded ribbon bow nearby, sometimes batting at it, sometimes picking it up and playing keep away.

Evergreen's legs started to tingle painfully from sitting in the same position for too long. She stretched them out, crossing them at the ankles, and leaned back. But as she placed her hand on the floor behind her, her fingers landed on Sawyer's.

Her heart jumped, and she glanced over at him. His wide eyes softened, and he smiled gently at her.

"Oops, sorry," she murmured, shifting her weight and moving her hand from his.

"It's okay," he answered with a nod.

She directed her gaze back to Dorian and Cory, who were holding up a handmade crib mobile with sacred symbols dangling from it. A moment later, Evergreen's breath hitched as Sawyer's hand covered hers. The slight pressure, the warmth, a jolt ran through her, and her nerves stood on end.

She looked over at Sawyer again. His eyes were soft and solicitous. "Is this okay?" he whispered.

Evergreen nodded once, not sure her voice would be stable enough to answer. Her consent was rewarded when Sawyer gave her a brilliant smile. Her breath left her in a rush as if she'd been kicked in the chest. That look, that light in his eyes. Only in her most outlandish dreams had Sawyer ever looked at her like that. It was the gaze that said all his little kindnesses had meant something. It said he'd never forgotten her.

Warmth bloomed in her chest. A pleasant ache squeezed her heart, an ache of anticipation, an ache that made promises.

Evergreen averted her gaze, not wanting to draw attention only slightly more than wanting to keep her eyes locked with his. She couldn't have said how long they sat like that, but it was long enough for her hand to miss the feel of his when he pulled away.

All in all, the naming ceremony had been a resounding success. They all welcomed Ella to the path and wished that her journey would be more full of love, laughter, and learning than theirs had been thus far.

As Evergreen lay beside Sawyer in the dark meditation room that evening, she stared up at the starry night sky, stroking Muir beside her. The room was silent but for the whir of the space heater, and that silence was thick and oppressive.

"Do you remember when we all went on that trip to the beach?" Evergreen asked, the words squeezed out of her as if from the pressure of the silence.

"Yeah, that was the summer before my senior year. Wasn't it? We went for the solstice. Piper was so disappointed that we couldn't see as many stars as she'd thought we would be able to," he answered. "She moped the whole time."

"But Hazel was happy," Evergreen countered.

"Oh, I don't think I've seen Hazel happier. But then again, she's a sea witch, so that's to be expected."

Evergreen giggled under her breath. "That's true. I think that was our first trip with Cory, too. Wasn't it?" She glanced over at Sawyer, who nodded, still staring up at the ceiling.

"Yeah, Dorian and Cory had just gotten together. Remember they kept sneaking off to be alone thinking no one would notice?"

"Oh my gods, and Devan kept getting lost," she added, laughing louder.

Sawyer chuckled, and the sound made Evergreen shiver like a string that had been plucked. "Do you think that the reason he's always late is because he has a horrible sense of direction?" he asked, glancing over at her.

Their eyes locked, and Evergreen's smile relaxed. "I bet you're right," she murmured, her response coming out quiet and confused as if she'd forgotten his question.

The silence squeezed her lungs, and her breaths were slow but shallow.

Sawyer's eyes were steady and earnest, and she knew what he wanted. She was certain her expression wasn't much different. He propped himself up on his elbow, staring down at her with intent.

Evergreen's heart raced, and the sweet ache of desire spread through her core. As he leaned down closer, she closed her eyes, anticipation making her body hum.

When he kissed her, it wasn't as sweet and fleeting as the first time. His lips were insistent, fiery and fierce as they branded hers. She lifted her head to match his urgency.

And then a loud trilling sounded in her ear as Muir complained that she'd stopped petting him.

Sawyer pulled away. He turned to the cat and laughed. The sound of his chuckle broke the moment far more than Muir's interruption.

Then Sawyer reached out and scratched Muir's ears. "Well, all right then," he told him.

The cat flopped down on his side and rolled onto his back.

"Is this a trap?" Sawyer asked him.

"No, Muir actually likes belly rubs. He must like you if he's offering you his belly," Evergreen said.

Sawyer stroked Muir's chest and stomach, and the cat wiggled, unable to sit still in his excitement. "You're a funny one," Sawyer told him.

Evergreen smiled at the pair. "You're in trouble now. He's not going to leave you alone after this."

"That's fine," Sawyer answered, glancing back up at her. His smile was soft and warm, the passionate heat mellowed in his eyes. "We should probably try to go to sleep," he said. "I'm sure your mom has something planned for us all tomorrow. We wouldn't want to miss it."

Evergreen nodded, her disappointment tempered with the thought that she finally knew what old movie kisses felt like.

CHAPTER 34

Sawyer didn't think he'd ever felt as good as he did the next morning. The sun shined brightly off the snow, and the outside world sparkled as if covered in eco-friendly glitter. His chest was warm, his heart light, and his head fuzzy as if he lay on a bed of pink cotton candy.

Eeva and Muir no longer lay beside him, but that didn't dampen his mood. Anticipation zipped through him, and he knew he wore a goofy, self-satisfied smile as he changed his clothes.

The pressure of his joy built up inside him, and he felt as if he'd have to shout at the top of his lungs just to let off some of the steam.

He took a deep breath, pushed his shoulders back, and strode into the common room. Eeva sat on the couch, Muir pawing at her as he placed himself between her and the book she was trying to read.

"Yes, yes, I see you, Muir," she murmured, bookmarking her page and redirecting her attention to her furbaby.

"Good morning," Sawyer greeted, confident she couldn't see his silly grin from this distance.

But as she looked over in his direction and visibly held in a giggle, he was certain she'd still heard it. "Morning," she returned.

He got control of his expression as he crossed the room and sat on the couch beside her, his gaze landing on the cup of coffee on the table next to her cocoa. "Is someone else sitting here?" he asked, pointing at the cup.

"No," she said. "That's for you."

"Thank you." His smile returned without consent. "Any idea what the plans are for today?"

Eeva shook her head.

Even her shaking her head is cute, Sawyer thought.

"Hmm. Well, we still haven't made the soap and shampoo for the gift baskets. We haven't made the candles for Yule yet either. And we don't have a Yule log. Dad will probably wait a few days before he really starts cooking. So my guess is one of those three things."

It turned out Eeva's guess was correct. Once everyone had breakfasted, Ria said they would be making soap and shampoo that day. Because they didn't have the knowledge to deal with the volatile chemicals involved in from scratch soap making, Eeva and Sawyer were put in charge of the essential oils that would be used as fragrance.

They sat at the dining room table while they let some of the others do the hard work in the kitchen.

"What do you think of ylang ylang?" Sawyer asked, reading the bottle he'd just smelled.

Eeva shrugged. "It's all right. I like jasmine better. Oh, how about this one." She held out the vial to him, and he leaned forward to sniff it.

"That one is nice," he said.

"It's nag champa. Yeah, I like it, too."

"Should we try mixing some together?" he asked.

"Yeah, I got my mom's chart with base, middle, and top notes." She drew the paper toward her, squinting at it as she read. Then she offered it to him so he could make his own blends.

They focused on their tasks for a bit, Eeva muttering to herself in concentration. Her eyebrows were pulled together as she carefully counted out the drops of oil from the eyedropper.

As she took a test sniff, she smiled, sighing in contentment at her creation. When she looked up at him, he realized he hadn't been focusing on his own work at all.

"Do you want to smell? I think it turned out pretty good," she said, holding it out to him.

"Sure." He leaned forward just as she moved to bring the vial closer to his nose. The glass bumped his nose, and he snuffled as the scent overpowered him.

Eeva burst into laughter. "Oh gods, sorry," she managed through her giggles. "Are you okay?"

The sound of her mirth tightened his chest in the most pleasant way. "I'm fine," he said, unable to hold back a smile in the face of her glee.

"I'll go get you some coffee beans. Maybe that will clear the scent out of your nose."

She got up from the table and went to the kitchen, returning a few moments later with a glass jar of coffee beans. "Here," she said, offering him the jar.

He opened it and breathed deep. The earthy scent overtook the smell of her blend.

Before he put the cap back on, Eeva leaned over him and stuck her nose in the jar. She breathed deep, then sighed. "I always loved the smell of coffee," she said. "I wish it tasted as good as it smells."

"It does. Your palate is just too unrefined to appreciate it," Sawyer teased.

Eeva made a choking sound, then laughed as she straightened up. "Whatever. Your palate is just so dead that you need something that strong to taste at all. That's why you like spicy food, too."

"You're just a wimp when it comes to real flavor. That's why you can't handle spicy food."

She laughed again. "It's true. I am a wimp when it comes to spicy food. But, seriously, what is everyone's deal with liking spicy food? I mean, there are other flavors: sweet, salty, savory. Why does *everyone* want spicy?"

Sawyer just smiled at her impassioned speech, reveling in the comfortable atmosphere they had found.

"Oh my gods, this one time, my friend from college—he's the president of the Indian Student Association. He invited me to their Diwali celebration. Anyway, they had tons of Indian food there, right? And I could smell that it was spicy before I even put it in my mouth. But I really wanted to try it, so I asked him which stuff wasn't spicy. He said none of them were. So I trusted him, you know? Lies, so many lies. Do you know how much naan I had to eat to cool my mouth down? Man, it's like a slow burn, too.

You take the first bite, and you're like, 'this is good.' Then four or five bites in, it just hits you. And it stays long after you've finished. Have you ever tried Indian food?"

Sawyer couldn't keep the grin from his face as Eeva told her story. It reminded him of before, when she was talkative and open. He was glad she hadn't lost that part of herself. "I have," he answered. "It's really good. Curry is great on winter days like this. It will warm you right up."

Eeva pursed her lips in disappointment. "I wish I could eat curry. It always looks so good."

"I could make you some," Sawyer offered. "If I blend my own curry powder, I can take out all the spicy elements."

"You can cook?" she asked, tilting her head.

Sawyer snorted. "I am a grown man, you know."

"I see that," she said, her tone carrying the tint of appreciation.

*E*vergreen's anxiety had started to wane as she went about making tea the next morning. Sawyer had been sweet and playful all the day prior. The atmosphere around them had been easy, much easier than in the past. There was no better feeling than the person you like liking you back.

And though the world seemed to shine around her, the anxiety didn't go away completely. There was something fragile in this stage. His actions said he was attracted to her more than he liked her, and he hadn't said anything one way or the other. She still didn't really know about his life at the moment. And the fact that they would be leaving in less than a week hung over her, a looming presence that she couldn't quite ignore no matter how good she felt.

Still, she tried her best to ignore it, having faith that they would at least talk about what would happen later before they left.

At breakfast, her mother worried that there was still too much to do before Yule. "We still don't have a Yule log," she said. "I completely forgot to harvest one at Midsummer. And now we don't have time for a fresh one to dry out before the solstice."

"Don't worry, Mom," Evergreen comforted. "I'm sure there's a downed tree in the woods. We can just go out there and saw off a log. It's better that way anyway. And then it'll only have to dry for a few days just to get the surface moisture out."

"I'd go soon if I were you," Cory said. "There's a storm coming."

"The news said we would get a dusting tomorrow," Wes agreed.

"No," Cory shook his head. "It'll be worse than that."

Ria made an anxious sound.

"It's all right, Ria," Sawyer soothed. "Eeva and I can go out today and find one. We were tramping around the woods a few days ago, and I saw a few downed trees that might do."

"Would you?" Ria asked.

Sawyer looked to Evergreen for support. "Yeah, sure thing, Mom. I'll go get the handsaw from the garage, and we can start looking right away."

Evergreen heard her father say he would pack them a lunch again as she went to the garage. When she returned, Sawyer was putting on his winter things. She put down the saw and did the same.

"Make sure you bundle up," Ria said. "The temperature is dropping."

They did as they were told. Sawyer picked up the saw, and Evergreen carried the lunch her father had made for them. Then they waved goodbye and told everyone they'd be back before dark.

Evergreen followed Sawyer through the woods, trailing him to the downed trees he'd remembered. The first two hadn't been dead long enough for the wood to season properly.

"There's one more," he said, leading the way.

Luckily, that tree had sat long enough that it would burn nicely after a few days of drying out.

"Could you hold that end?" Sawyer asked.

Evergreen got down on her knees, the snow seeping into her jeans, to hold the log steady so he could saw it.

It took a while for him to saw through it, much longer than she would have expected. By the time he was finished, it was well past lunch time.

"The temperature really has dropped," he commented. "Why don't we head to the isolation cabin and have lunch? We aren't far now. We could make a fire and warm up before heading back."

"Sounds good," Evergreen agreed, trying to stop her teeth from chattering.

"Be careful," Sawyer advised as he went ahead of her on the path, the log in his arms. "There's a slope coming up, and it's probably icy with the temperature change. Ohhhh—"

Sawyer slid down the hill, crashing at the bottom.

"Sawyer, are you okay?" Evergreen shouted, her voice raising in pitch in her alarm. She sat on her butt and slid down the icy hill.

"I'm fine," he muttered. "Only my pride is hurt."

Evergreen offered her hand and hauled him up.

He hissed in pain.

"What is it? Are you hurt?"

"It's okay. I think I just twisted my ankle. It just smarts a little. I'm fine."

Evergreen gnawed her lips, her stomach churning. "Let's get you inside. Just leave the log there. I'll come back for it. Lean on me."

He wrapped his arm around her shoulders and leaned some of his weight on her as they walked. After she'd gotten him settled on a blanket on the floor of the isolation cabin, she returned for the log, the saw, and the lunch bag. She placed the log and the saw in a corner of the cabin, put the lunch bag on the table, then went out to the wood hutch to get dry firewood.

"Will you call my mom and tell her we're going to wait a bit before coming back while I make a fire?"

"I'll be fine," Sawyer argued. "I can walk as soon as I have lunch and warm up. Look, it's not even swollen. I just twanged it."

Evergreen frowned. "Well, let's see how you feel after you eat."

As the fire crackled in the hearth, Evergreen unpacked their lunch and set it on the coffee table as before. She watched Sawyer while he ate.

"You worrying like that isn't going to make it better faster," he pointed out.

Evergreen sighed. "I know. I'm sorry. I just hate it when people get hurt."

Sawyer smiled. "I know. You sort of feel it, too. Don't you? You get all queasy in your gut, like you're going to be sick."

"How did you know? Does that happen to you, too?"

Sawyer shook his head. "No, but you aren't the only empath I know. My friend Flick is like that. She can't even take her dog to the vet without feeling sick."

Evergreen remembered the name from his social media, back when she'd still checked his profile every day. "She's a friend from school?" she asked, not sure she really wanted to know but unable to stop herself.

"Yeah." He didn't elaborate.

Evergreen's stomach hardened in a flash of jealousy. She shook her head to rid herself of the feeling.

After they'd finished their lunch, Evergreen told him to take off his shoes so she could see his ankle. The fire had sufficiently warmed the room enough that she took off her coat and boots as well. She sat on her feet, patting her thighs to tell him to put his foot there. He did.

Evergreen felt around his ankle carefully, her fingertips prodding for any puffiness. She didn't find any.

"Okay, now rotate your ankle for me," she directed. "Does it hurt at all?"

Sawyer shook his head. "Nope. I'm okay, Doc. No pain at all. Am I good to go?"

Evergreen chuckled, her worry filtering out with each laugh. "I think you'll live."

A chiming melody emanated from Evergreen's pocket. She dug into it and answered her mother's call. "Hey, what's up, Mom?"

"Evergreen Pendre, where in goddess's green earth are you?" she shouted.

"We're at the isolation cabin. We just had lunch. Sawyer fell, so I wanted to make sure he wasn't hurt before we headed back. But he's fine, so we're just about to leave."

"Oh thank goodness," Ria said with a sigh. "Listen, you guys just stay there. Okay? Don't try to come back until the storm blows over. There should be snacks enough in the cupboards, and there are blankets in the trunk."

"What storm?" Evergreen said, going to the window. She couldn't even see the trees through the blowing snow. "Oh," she answered flatly. "Yeah, okay. We'll stay put. But can you feed Muir? He gets a half can of wet food at seven."

"I'll take care of him," her mother confirmed before hanging up.

Evergreen returned to Sawyer on the floor. "I guess we're stuck here for a while," she said, putting her phone on the table beside his.

"Guess so," he murmured, shifting his gaze to the fire.

As the logs cracked in the hearth and the wind began to howl, Evergreen's awareness fixed on Sawyer. He seemed relaxed, his legs stretched out in front of him. The glow from the fire played in his golden hair.

Without really thinking about it, Evergreen reached out and stroked a shiny lock. Sawyer's amber eyes met hers.

"Eeva," he murmured, his expression serious, "I don't know if this is the best time to tell you this, but—"

Evergreen silenced his words by covering his mouth with hers. Whatever he'd been trying to say must not have been very important because he met her demanding kiss with one of his own.

A shiver ran through her as he slipped his hand into her hair, pulling her closer with urgency. She gasped against his mouth when his hot tongue flicked her lower lip.

He pulled back, his brow furrowed despite the desire in his eyes. "Was that okay?" he asked, his voice breathy and deep.

Evergreen sat up and climbed on top of him, smiling as his hard manhood dug against her through their jeans. She wrapped her arms around his neck, playing with the hair at the base of his head. "Perfect," she responded.

Sawyer didn't need any more encouragement. He kissed her again, roughly grabbing her ass as she straddled him.

She moaned against his mouth, the sensation tickling her lips.

Sawyer slipped his hands under the back of her shirt, his rough fingertips sending a thrill up her spine as he stroked her bare flesh. "You're so beautiful, Eeva," he murmured, pressing insistent kisses to her throat.

Lust raged inside her, urgent, demanding. She arched her back, grinding hard against him. "Do you have a condom?" she whispered, her voice thick and raw even to her own ears.

He flinched beneath her. She pulled back, staring at him. "No," he said with a grimace.

"It's okay. There's still hope." She climbed off him and made her way over to the blanket chest. Digging through the blankets, her hand touched the smooth plastic wrapper. She turned back around, holding up a strip of condoms in triumph.

"Why would that be here?" Sawyer asked.

"Does it matter?"

"No, I'm just curious."

"My parents keep the cabin stocked with condoms in case someone is too sexually pent up to properly meditate." Evergreen shrugged. "Easier clean up. You aren't allergic to latex are you?"

"No, you?"

Evergreen grinned. "Nope. Isn't that lucky?"

"I certainly feel like it's my lucky day. Do you mind coming over here please?"

"Oh, I do hope so," Evergreen said with a chuckle, swaying her hips as she returned to Sawyer.

He laughed at her double entendre. "Don't worry about that," he promised.

"Oooo, look who's so confident now." Evergreen smoothly climbed back on top of him and wrapped her legs around him.

"Oh, I've a right to be. Here, let me show you." He removed his shirt, his golden hair getting deliciously tousled.

"You do that then," Evergreen encouraged, placing her palm on his firm chest before kissing him.

Evergreen shivered as he removed her shirt, the cabin not nearly as warm as she'd thought. "Do you need help with my bra?" she asked.

He snorted, then smirked before unclasping it with one hand.

I guess not, she thought, grinning.

His skin burned hers as he pressed her to him, smothering her thoughts with sensations. She gasped for air, her desire even more urgent than it had been before she'd gotten the condoms.

He shifted under her, picking her up and laying her on her back atop the clothes they'd discarded.

He stroked his fingers down her body, his touch feather-light and maddening. Her clit throbbed as he unbuttoned her jeans. His eyes were fixed on hers as he slowly unzipped them. "Tell me when you're ready," he requested.

"I'm already there," she informed, not at all surprised that it hadn't taken more foreplay. *It is Sawyer after all,* she reasoned. *And I've been waiting a long time for this.*

He obligingly removed her pants and underwear, the fabric rubbing roughly against her smooth skin. He smirked, the expression confident and irritating somehow as he unbuttoned his own jeans.

"You tease," Evergreen accused.

He chuckled but didn't argue. The rest of his discarded clothes made a satisfying fwump as he dropped them on the floor.

Evergreen's breaths came out heavy and slow as she watched Sawyer roll the condom onto his ready cock. She grinned at the glistening drop of precum at the tip. She sat up and wrapped her fingers around the solid shaft.

Sawyer shuddered under her hand, his breath coming out in a rush.

"Feel good?" she asked.

He nodded, his eyes losing focus as she stroked. "I'm not selfish," he muttered, his weak voice pleasing her just as much as his shivers.

Evergreen bit her lip against her moan, her body shaking as he ran the pad of his thumb over her clit. Her hand on his cock loosened.

Sawyer kissed her, slowly lowering her back to the floor. Her thighs twitched in anticipation as his cock neared her core. And as he slid smoothly into her, the howling wind outside did not cover the sounds of their mutual pleasure.

Sawyer pumped slow and hard, his hips digging into Evergreen's thighs. She vaguely wondered if she'd have bruises the next day. But she didn't care. It was finally happening. With Sawyer. His abs stiffened with each thrust, and Evergreen clung to his neck and shoulders, her fingernails sinking into his skin. And as he drove her to her peak, she knew that he'd had the right to brag after all.

He collapsed beside her, having fully lived up to expectations and then some. His eyelids drooped.

Evergreen stroked his sweaty hair. "Tired?" she murmured.

He nodded.

She glanced over at the window. "It's dark out. Go to sleep," she encouraged, leaning over to kiss his cheek.

He nodded again but held his arms out to her.

She smiled and snuggled in close to him, his heartbeat a comforting lullaby.

Sometime in the night, Evergreen awoke. She wiggled free from Sawyer's embrace and started toward the bathroom.

The fire had dimmed, so she stopped and put a few more logs in. Standing up again, she looked back to make sure she hadn't woken him. Her phone's notification light blinked from the table, and she picked it up to make sure her mother wasn't freaking out.

By the time she'd realized it was Sawyer's phone, it was too late. She'd already seen part of the message from a woman named Maria, whose profile picture was a black cat.

> Hey, honey, call or text me when you get this...

The rest of the message was cut off, and she didn't know the password to see what else was said even if she'd wanted to.

Evergreen's stomach dropped, and she was pretty certain she was going to be sick. She put the phone back on the table and rushed to the bathroom. After turning on the cold water, she splashed her face. She took deep breaths, trying to keep her lunch down.

Who the fuck is Maria? she thought. *Does Sawyer have a girlfriend? Is that what he was trying to tell me when I cut him off by kissing him? Would he cheat on his girlfriend with me? I never thought he was that kind of guy. Maybe he isn't. Maybe he's poly. Maybe that's what he was trying to tell me. I mean, that's great for him or whatever. But poly doesn't work for me. I don't share.*

Once the initial nausea had quieted, Evergreen's chest tightened as if some witch hunter was trying to force her to confess. *I knew it,* she thought. *I should have listened to my instincts from the beginning.*

Hot tears rolled down her cheeks, and her nose burned as she tried to silence the sob that rose in her throat.

CHAPTER 36

Before Sawyer even opened his eyes the next morning, he smiled to himself. He was groggy, sore, in that very satisfying way. Eeva no longer lay on his chest, but the scratchy roughness of the blanket she'd draped over his naked body bespoke her care. He'd gotten through to her. She might have cut off his confession by kissing him, but he'd made sure that his actions spoke louder than words ever could. He breathed deep from his nose and cracked his eyelids against the morning light.

Eeva lay, fully dressed, on a separate blanket. She stared up at the ceiling, her eyes dark and puffy.

Sawyer rolled to his side, facing her. "Good morning," he greeted warmly. "Did you sleep okay?"

She didn't turn to him. She just stared ahead, her eyes unfocused and resolute. "That was a mistake," she declared, her tone deadpan.

It took Sawyer's mind a few seconds to process her words. As his heart squeezed, his stomach churned. "You regret it?" he asked, not even certain he'd said it loud enough for her to hear.

"Yes," she confirmed. "I regret it."

The room spun as Sawyer seemed to drown in a sudden sense of hopelessness. *Did something happen?* He wondered, his mind grasping for some explanation. *She certainly seemed to enjoy it last night. Did I misunderstand? But she initiated it to begin with.*

He tried to swallow around the lump in his throat. *But that doesn't really matter. Does it? She has the right to feel differently in the light of day. But...did I do something wrong?*

Sawyer analyzed her stony expression. She wasn't giving anything away. "Okay," he muttered. *What else can I even say?* he thought. *If that's how she feels, then that's how she feels.*

He averted his eyes, praying that he could hold it together. Sitting up, he held the blanket to his naked form. He grabbed his clothes, his numb fingers hardly registering the feel of the fabric in his hand. Then he went to the bathroom to dress. His movements were slow and automatic, relying on muscle memory to execute the procedure.

He glanced at himself in the mirror as he moved to put his shirt on. There were tiny indentations on his shoulders and back where Eeva had dug her nails into him. He pulled on his shirt, covering the evidence. But as the cloth passed over his face, he was smacked with Eeva's scent. *That's right,* he thought. *She lay on my clothes as we made love...had sex,* he corrected.

He turned on the faucet and closed his eyes against the telltale burning. He breathed in deep through his tingling nose, but he didn't manage to keep all the tears down. He bent over the sink and splashed water on his face, washing away the few that had escaped.

By the time he exited the bathroom, he had successfully masked his emotions. He walked over to the window and looked out. "The snow has stopped. We should head back," he said, woodenly.

When Eeva didn't respond, he glanced over at her. *Bad idea,* he thought, redirecting his eyes as his stomach flopped.

"I'll carry the log if you can get the saw and lunch bag," Sawyer said, not daring to look at her again. His voice sounded hollow even to him, and he knew he'd never talked to Eeva that way before.

She didn't respond, but she didn't argue either. Sawyer pulled on his winter things and picked up the log. Her footsteps were soft as she drifted after him.

With how bad the storm had looked the night before, Sawyer had expected the snow would be a lot deeper. Still, it was about mid-shin for him, and it took a bit of effort to stomp through it. He was extra careful when he climbed the hill he'd fallen down the day before. And he did warn Eeva to watch out, as if he were a guide she'd paid to get her home safely.

As they arrived back at the retreat center, they were greeted with exclamations of joy and relief. The enthusiasm from his friends and family was too loud, too happy, too juxtaposed to the weight that silently crushed him.

"I'm just tired," he found himself saying as someone asked him what was wrong. He wasn't even sure who it had been. Probably his mom. There didn't seem to be a lot of attention on him, so he didn't bother to figure it out.

He registered a gentle pat on the back. "Maybe a nice hot shower will sort you out." Yes, it was his mom speaking. He nodded, passed the Yule log into Wes's arms, and headed in the direction of the bathroom. He turned on the shower, the mundane task doing little to distract his thoughts.

He needed a shower to be sure. He could feel the dried sweat, no longer sticky, still clinging to him like Eeva had just hours before. The ghostly remnants of her kisses on his mouth, his face, his neck and chest, still echoed in his mind. He needed a shower, but he didn't want one. He didn't want to wash her off of him, as if doing so would wipe their too short time together away like it never happened.

No, he thought. *It had happened.* The ache in his chest was too real, and it wasn't going away just by washing the only evidence of their love... sex down the drain. He'd wished it was only that easy, that fifteen minutes of soap and hot water could rewind time, back to when he still had hope in his heart.

He stepped under the waterfall showerhead, the sound of the water splashing on the stone walls and floor too pleasantly dissonant, and went about erasing all physical traces of their night together, the night she regretted so much. How much of what streaked down Sawyer's face was tears? How much was water? He didn't give it much thought.

CHAPTER 37

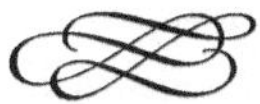

shower had not washed away all traces of Sawyer from Evergreen's thoughts. She'd said she regretted their night together, and she did. She regretted how she now had to deal with the emotional fallout. She had gone against her better judgment. Her heart had opened up to him again, called out to him again, seemingly forgetting the hurt it had gone through before. She'd been weak. Sawyer was her weakness. And now she would pay for it.

She would pay for it every time her eyes drifted toward him, every time her skin remembered the brush of his touch, and every time he didn't give her a second thought. Her legs were still sore from where his hip bones had pounded into her. And, despite her emotions, her body was still languid from the satisfaction he'd provided.

"Okay," she muttered to herself, repeating Sawyer's words to her declaration that morning.

She stood at the kitchen island, cutting cotton string into two-foot lengths. Cassandra stood at the stove melting beeswax in the double boiler.

Okay? Evergreen thought. *Is that all he could say? Didn't he want to know why I suddenly changed my mind? I thought there was going to be more of a fight. I thought I was going to get to tell him exactly why I was upset. But he just accepted it. Just like that. It must not have been that important to him to begin with. I mean, he shrugged it off so easily. Shrugged it off while I lay there despondent and hurting.*

Evergreen had tried to feel out his reaction at the time. But when her own emotions were that high, she couldn't effectively read others.

I'm so stupid, she thought miserably. *I wish I never would have come home for Yule. If I would have stayed at school, Sawyer could have stayed a relatively happy memory. Sure, I would have been hurt that he'd left and never looked back. But at least I remembered him as sweet, and kind, and solid. Now...it just stings to think about him at all.*

"Okay," she said again, clicking her tongue in disgust.

"What are you muttering about over there?" Cassandra asked from the stove.

Evergreen flinched. "Nothing," she murmured. She started tying washers to the ends of the strings she'd cut.

"Mmmm, yeah, I'm not buying it. You've been weird since you got back this morning. Did something happen between you and Sawyer?"

Evergreen turned her back to her cousin, knowing she wouldn't be able to control her expression. "No," she said, trying for unconcerned. "Why would you think that?"

"Um, I don't know," Cassandra said sarcastically. "Maybe because you two have been flirting with each other since you arrived, and now you can't even look at each other."

Evergreen didn't respond.

"Did you two have a fight?" Cassandra pushed.

Evergreen sighed. Hanging one of the strings over a wire coat hanger, she carried it to the stove.

Cassandra took it from her and started ladling melted wax over the string.

"I guess you could say he isn't who I thought he was," Evergreen murmured.

Cassandra responded without looking away from her work. "Did you think he wouldn't have changed at all over the last four and a half years?"

"No, I mean, I knew he would. Of course he would. But...it just seemed like he'd changed for the better up until yesterday."

"You want to be more specific about what exactly happened?"

"No."

"Okay...Well, from where I stand—knowing what little I know—Sawyer is a pretty good guy. I mean, I think we can both agree I have an eye for irresponsible assholes. Not to mention I'm a magnet for them."

Evergreen didn't say anything.

"We've all known each other for a long time. And let's not mince words here. You've been totally in love with him for most of that time."

Evergreen made a sound to protest, but a glance from her cousin just made her nod her head silently.

"That's a long time fantasizing and hoping and wishing." Cassandra shrugged. "Maybe you've put him on a bit of a pedestal. Don't you think that's possible?"

Evergreen frowned. "Even if that's true—and I'm not saying it is—there are certain things that...just don't mesh between us."

"Such as...?"

"Well...I mean, yeah, we have known each other for a long time. But a lot of that time, he utterly pretended like he didn't know me at all. Like, he left for college and didn't talk to me at all until just a few days ago."

Cassandra snorted. "He ignored you, did he? So you sent him message after message, and he just pretended like he didn't know you? Be honest, cuz. Communication is a two-way street. Sure, maybe he didn't reach out to you, but I don't recall you reaching out to him either."

Evergreen shifted her weight uncomfortably from foot to foot. "I mean...that's true...but—"

"Look, I'm not trying to assign blame to either one of you. I'm just pointing out that you two have a pretty long history of not being honest with each other. You never told him how you felt back then. You didn't reach out when you missed him. And he's obviously got some things to answer for, too. So don't you think it's possible that whatever you're upset about is just a misunderstanding?"

Evergreen's stomach rolled as she remembered reading the text on Sawyer's phone. She shook her head. "I hear what you're saying. And, yeah, I haven't been very good at communicating with him. But this time... I don't see how I could be misunderstanding."

Cassandra shrugged. "Well, it's not like I even know the particulars, so maybe you're right. But it's still four days until Yule. I suggest you figure something out."

"It's a big house. There are a lot of people. We can pretty well avoid each other for four days."

"If you say so."

CHAPTER 38

Sawyer had done a pretty good job of avoiding Eeva since they'd returned, though effectively doing so meant he was overly aware of her movements. Sometimes, he felt as if he could feel her eyes on him. But he told himself that was his imagination. That's what he wanted to believe. He wanted her to change her mind back, to return to the Eeva who would haunt him, the one who'd climbed into his lap with that come-hither smile.

He was exhausted, physically and emotionally. But he didn't want to go to sleep. He didn't want to crawl into his sleeping bag on the floor beside her. And he was worried what he would dream about. So he stayed up, sitting in the common room until everyone had gone to bed but him and his mom. Muir and Larkspur both lay in his lap as he stroked them in unison.

"Are you going to tell me what happened, son?" Tara asked finally.

"I don't want to talk about it," he murmured.

"Are you sure? Because you kind of have that expression like you need to."

Sawyer frowned, a tug of war playing out in his mind. "I think I fucked up."

"How's that?" his mom asked.

"Eeva..." He choked a little on her name. "We uh... Stuff happened last night while we were in the isolation cabin."

"Is that your way of telling me you and Eeva had sex?"

Sawyer nodded slightly.

"Okay. So how did you fuck up? You used protection, didn't you?"

"Yeah, we did...I...I wish I knew what I did wrong. I thought everything was great. Totally fine. Then I woke up this morning, and she's all serious... She said it was a mistake."

Tara nodded slowly, her eyes losing focus as she considered his problem. "Did she give you a reason?" she asked.

"No. And...it didn't feel right to ask. It's her body. If she regrets sharing it with me...then how can I argue?"

Tara reached out and rubbed her son's arm.

"Mom, what did I do? Why would she change her mind?"

Tara shook her head. "I don't know, honey. It could be any number of things. Maybe she got caught up in the moment and didn't really think about what it meant until after. Maybe, after all was done, she realized she felt more platonically toward you. Or maybe she's scared."

Though she had given her examples gently, each one was like a knife in Sawyer's chest. "Scared? Of me?" he asked.

Tara stroked her son's hair in the soothing gesture she'd always used when he was a boy. "Not necessarily," she answered. "She could be scared of what she felt, of what it could mean for her, for you, for your relationship."

"Like...like she's worried about getting hurt, so she pushed me away?"

"Well, that's one way of looking at it."

Sawyer frowned, gazing at the glowing embers in the hearth, all that was left of the fire that blazed only hours before. "But these explanations are really different. If she's scared, then I should reassure her. But if it's another reason, I should just leave her alone."

His mother nodded. "It is a predicament."

Could she just be scared? he wondered. He pictured the mask-like expression Eeva had worn as she'd said those three words: I regret it. *No,* he thought. *She wasn't scared. She never shied away from a confrontation. If she had something she wanted to say, she would have just said it.*

"I don't think she's scared, Mom," he admitted.

Tara sighed sadly. "I know it hurts right now. But it will get better. Believe me."

Sawyer dipped his head in a slow nod. He'd seen people go through much worse than what he was feeling, his mom included. But she was right. It didn't feel possible at the moment.

"You going to bed soon?" she asked.

"Yeah, in a bit. I'm just going to sit out here with the cats for a little while longer."

"Okay." She leaned over and pressed a kiss to her son's head. "Goodnight."

"Night, Mom."

As he turned his attention back to the glowing embers, his phone vibrated in his pocket. The cats jumped up, looking at him with disdain at being disturbed. The deal was off. They went about their own cat business.

He opened a text from Felicity. It read:

> Hey, bud. I've been thinking about you all day, and I'm getting a really weird vibe. Everything okay?

Sawyer frowned. *Even states away I set off her empath alarm,* he thought. He texted her back.

> Things are…pretty complicated over here. My mom and I are spending Yule with the old coven.

As he pressed the home button, Sawyer saw that he'd missed a text from Maria.

> Hey, honey, call or text me when you get this. I know you said you were heading north for the holiday. I just saw on the news that a big storm is hitting up there. Just wanting to know you're all right.

It's too late to call her now, Sawyer thought. *I hope she hasn't been too worried.* He sent Maria a reply.

> No worries. All good here. Hope all is well on your end, too. See you next week.

His phone buzzed with another message from Felicity.

> Oh. Eeva must be there then. Do you want to talk about it?

Sawyer's chest twinged. *I don't have the energy to talk about this anymore right now,* he thought. *Even with Flick.*

He replied with a simple, "later," and put his phone on the coffee table. With a sense of inevitability, he leaned to the side and let gravity flop him onto the couch. As he stared at the lights twinkling on the Yule tree, his eyes grew heavy, and he drifted off to sleep.

CHAPTER 39

*E*arly the next morning, Evergreen was surprised to find that Sawyer was not in his sleeping bag. *He can't even stand to be near me now,* she thought. The action only confirmed his lack of concern in her mind.

After she made the daily offering of incense and lit the goddess candle at the altar, she went out into the sitting room. Sawyer lay on the couch, Muir curled up on his chest. *Traitor,* Evergreen thought, squinting at the cat. Though as soon as Muir saw her, he knew there was food in his bowl. He leapt off Sawyer and ran for the meditation room, the motion waking Sawyer from his sleep.

He looked around the room, confused, and froze as his gaze landed on Evergreen.

Her heart rate spiked, and there was an uncomfortably thick moment before she had the wherewithal to walk on through to the kitchen to make herself some tea. After sprinkling some cinnamon and sugar on her toast, the mundane task evening out her heartbeat, she moved to the dining room table to give him space to make coffee should he want it.

The atmosphere eased a bit the more people woke and joined her at the table.

"The next few days are going to be busy," Wes said as they all ate breakfast. "I'm making cookies today to put in the baskets so we can take them to the women's shelter tomorrow. And while we're in town tomorrow, I need to get some odds and ends so I can start cooking the day after."

"What kind of cookies are you making for the baskets?" Hazel asked.

"My grandmother's chocolate chip with vanilla buttercream frosting."

Everyone made yummy sounds.

"I'm going to need help decorating them if anyone is interested."

"Oh, me! Me!" Sol volunteered.

Wes smiled and nodded. "Eeva, how about you?"

"What?" Eeva said, her name pulling her out of her fuzzy-mindedness.

"Would you like to help Sol and me decorate cookies for the women's shelter?"

"Sure, Dad."

Cassandra also said she would help.

As Morrigan and Piper were talking about making the cards to put Sol's coloring masterpieces in, Sawyer burst out laughing. Everyone turned to him. He looked up from his phone.

"Speaking of holiday cards," he said. "Maria just sent me an ecard. Check this out."

Shame and irritation flooded into Evergreen. Even hearing her name on Sawyer lips, the lips that had so recently been pressed to her naked flesh, made her stomach drop.

Sawyer passed the phone to Tara, who giggled as she looked at it. Tara gave it to Devan, and so on until it reached Evergreen. She didn't want to look, but as Hazel handed it to her, she couldn't quell the compulsion.

On the screen was a picture of a woman and her cat. They wore matching elf hats with bells on the ends. They even had matching cuffs on their wrists. As Evergreen stared at the elderly woman grinning out at her, all the blood drained from her face. The room spun, and her toast felt like it was going to make a reappearance any second.

Eeva passed the phone to her dad, who laughed like everyone else.

"Who is this?" her mom asked when the phone had reached her.

"Maria." Sawyer answered. "She's the admin where I work. She's sort of like the mom of the whole place. Always looking out for everyone. She loves to dress her cat up, and we all get a big kick out of it."

Evergreen didn't say anything, couldn't have if she'd wanted to. She rose from her chair and left the dining room as quickly as she could without downright running. She could feel her heartbeat in her neck, her head, her fingertips as she made her way to the meditation room.

"Oh gods," she whispered, her voice strangled. "What have I done?"

Tears clouded her already imperfect vision, and there was no stopping them from spilling down her face. *Why didn't I just talk to him?* she thought. *Why did I assume?*

She sucked in air, trying to breathe around her silent sobs. *It was perfect. He was perfect. And I had to go and fuck it up. He doesn't even know why I snubbed him. No wonder he can't even look at me.*

She froze, her tears halting as a thought occurred to her. *But if he really cared that much, why did he let go so easily? Because you told him it was a mistake, idiot,* she argued with herself. *But maybe...maybe it didn't mean as much to him as it did to me.*

She shook her head. *I can't know that for sure,* she thought. *Maybe he's just internalizing it like I was. Maybe he doesn't care as much as I do, and maybe he does. But I can't assume he doesn't. And I can't let my fear that he doesn't stop me from telling him. Because...because if he does...this is truly my last chance. It may already be too late.*

Evergreen sighed, squeezing her eyes shut. "Cassandra was right," she murmured. "It was a misunderstanding. If I let this stand without doing anything, I'm an even bigger coward than I was before. And anyway, no matter how it turns out, I can't let him believe that I really thought it was a mistake. Even if he doesn't care for me. That still would have hurt him."

Wiping her running nose on her sleeve, her head pounding from the tears she had shed, Evergreen crossed to the altar at the far end of the room. She dug through the cabinets underneath and pulled out three short sticks of incense.

She lit the first one from the already flickering goddess candle. "Artemis, please give me strength." She shook out the flame so that it could burn at a smolder and stuck it into the bucket of sand. Then she lit the second. "Athena, please give me courage." She shook out the flame and put it beside the others. She lit the third. "Aphrodite, please smile on us both."

After she'd put the last incense stick in its place, she closed her eyes and bowed her head. Then Evergreen took a deep breath, squared her shoulders, and let it out.

CHAPTER 40

As Ria, Hazel, and Cassandra used one side of the dining room table to start putting all the gifts into the baskets for the women's and children's shelter, Sawyer and Tara used the other end to cut circles of green cloth for the Yule charms everyone would be making.

Another tingle ran up Sawyer's spine, and he knew Eeva's eyes were on him again as she stood at the kitchen island decorating cookies with Wes, Cassandra, and Sol. Sawyer's heart squeezed in his already tight chest, but he didn't look over his shoulder at her.

Why? he wondered. *It feels like she has been looking at me constantly since breakfast. What does she want from me? Doesn't she know how painful this all is?*

Sawyer sighed, hanging his head as he leaned heavily on his hands on the table.

His mother patted his shoulder gently. "You all right?" she asked, her voice low.

He nodded. "Fine," he reassured, lifting his head and going back to his task.

It went on like that for the rest of the day. Sawyer tried to stay occupied, helping anyone with anything he could. It didn't matter if it was taking out the trash or changing Ella's diaper. He just wanted to stay busy. And through it all, he could feel Eeva's gaze following him.

I've got to be imagining things, he thought as everyone sat in the common room that evening. *I'm being paranoid.*

As was expected, Eeva headed to bed early. While she was saying her goodnights, Sawyer felt it again: the tingle, the little irritating prod. He looked up at her purposely for the first time since they'd left the isolation cabin, just to be sure he wasn't crazy. Her blue eyes were staring directly at him, intense despite her inability to see across the room in detail. His stomach wrenched, and he averted his gaze.

What the hell was that? he wondered. *What does she want from me? Is she messing with me? I never thought Eeva was someone who would play games.*

The strain that her attention caused eased as she went to bed, and Sawyer could breathe slightly better, though not freely.

Sawyer had planned to sleep on the couch again as he had the night before. He hadn't slept great, but he had slept. Still, his dreams had been full of vague feelings of impending doom, his anxiety filtering into his unconscious mind.

After everyone else had called it a night, Sawyer lay on the couch. He looked at his phone as another text came through on the group message Maria had started with his coworkers. Tim had sent a picture of him helping his daughter put the star atop their Christmas tree.

On one hand, Sawyer was grateful to Maria. She had given him the only bit of joy he'd felt that day by sharing the photo with her cat. And as everyone else had shared pictures of what they were up to in preparation of the holiday, it reminded Sawyer that there was a whole world outside of this retreat center, a whole world outside what he was feeling at the moment. Next week, he would be back at home in his one-bedroom apartment. He'd be back to work, taking care of all the injured and sick animals, covering the Christmas shift for his Christian coworkers.

On the other hand, the joy his friends and colleagues were experiencing was far different from what he was feeling. In some ways it made him feel a lot lonelier than he had before. Their smiles were foreign to him as if he couldn't figure out how to make his face look that way. And if he tried, it would be some grotesque mockery of the gesture that people would wince just looking at. Yes, next week he would be home. Eeva would be even further away than she was now, and he would be worse off than he was before he'd come, worse even than those days, months, years where he watched her live her life free of him via pictures on social media.

He was the only one now who hadn't added a picture to the group message. Sawyer placed his phone face down on the coffee table.

He shifted his gaze to the only light in the room, his eyes staring unfocused at the sparkling lights of the Yule tree. It was almost a relief to be alone. He could wallow without worrying anyone. Then again, there wasn't any pushing down his emotions when there was no one to pretend for.

"Sawyer?"

Sawyer flinched as he heard Eeva's voice whisper his name. He closed his eyes, wincing at the pain in his heart. *I'm hallucinating now. Great,* he thought.

But as he sighed deeply and reopened his eyes, Eeva really was standing there in the doorway. *Well, that's good. At least I'm not hearing things,* he thought.

He just stared at her, too tired to fight, his vision dull and unfocused. "What is it?" he muttered, his cheek misshapen against the couch as he hadn't bothered to lift his head. *Is that my voice?* he wondered, unable to believe that lost and lifeless tone came from his lips.

Eeva bit her lower lip, shifting her weight from one foot to the other. "N-never mind," she murmured. Then she turned around and headed back down the hall toward the meditation room.

Sawyer sighed again, staring at the tree lights once more. "Whatever," he muttered into the couch.

CHAPTER 41

Evergreen shook her head at herself as she stared at the ceiling of the meditation room the following morning.

"I can't believe you chickened out," she scolded herself, her disgust apparent in her tone.

But she could still hear the echo of Sawyer's voice as he said, "What is it?" Hollow, defeated. She had done that to him. She'd crushed him like that.

She'd thought perhaps he wasn't so affected by what she had said to him that cold morning in the isolation cabin. But that was clearly not the case. She could feel his despair, deep and thorny through the hum of her own nerves as she'd called out to him.

And just when she could put a stop to his sorrow, she fucking chickened out. *What if he can't forgive me?* she had wondered. And her words had stuck in her throat. She barely choked out "never mind" before she had to retreat, chased by her own fear and shame.

"Your fear got the better of you yesterday," she told herself. "But not today. Today, you are going to apologize and explain."

She crawled out of her sleeping bag and got dressed. She knew she was always the first to get up. She was the only morning person in the house. "Now is my chance," she said, trying to pump herself up. She opened the door to the meditation room and made her way to the living room.

Sawyer sat on the couch, rocking baby Ella in his arms.

"Thanks so much for holding her while I got her bottle ready," Dorian said, entering the room.

"No problem." Sawyer handed the baby back to her daddy, who sat in a nearby chair to feed her.

"You're up early," Evergreen murmured when Dorian's gaze fell on her.

"Yeah, Miss Ella here let us know she was hungry before her usual feeding time," Dorian explained.

Ella sucked happily at her breakfast.

Don't worry about it, Evergreen thought, soothing the disappointment that swirled in her gut. *You have time. You have the whole day. You got this.*

The baskets for the shelter were finished. They were stuffed full of hats, mittens, soap, shampoo, washcloths, cookies, and hand-colored pictures from Sol. It was finally time to deliver them. Evergreen got into her mom's car along with Tara, Hazel, and Piper. Wes had taken Devan and Sawyer with him to the grocery.

As Ria parked on the side of the road in front of the shelter, Evergreen took her cane from her bag and made her way to the front door. She pushed the buzzer as everyone else went to the trunk for the baskets.

"Yes?" the box crackled at her.

"We have some donations," Evergreen explained to the woman on the other side.

The door unlocked with a loud bzzzt, and Evergreen held it open for everyone, their hands full. She followed them inside, stopping behind them at the reception desk. The receptionist pointed them down the hall to where they could deliver the donations.

Evergreen could already feel a shadow falling over her heart, the pain and fear palpable in the air. "I think I'll just wait here," she told her mom. She reached her hand into her coat pocket and cursed when she realized she hadn't brought her hematite with her.

"We won't be long," Ria promised.

Evergreen turned to sit on a couch near the entrance but veered toward the water cooler nearby. She took a paper cone of water, then went to her initial destination. As she sat down, clasping her white cane between her knees, a woman in a yellow parka came down a set of stairs and got herself a cone of water as well.

She smiled at Evergreen and sat beside her on the couch.

"Good day, sister," the woman greeted Evergreen.

"Good morning," Evergreen said politely.

"Your expression says you've seen better days," the woman said.

Evergreen's eyebrows pulled together. She'd never been good at schooling her expressions, but she wasn't used to getting called out for it either. On the other hand, she was quite used to people approaching her and telling her their life stories. She steeled herself for the tale she knew was coming.

"You know what always makes me feel better when I'm feeling out of sorts?" the woman asked.

"What?" Evergreen knew she didn't really have to ask, but she didn't want to be rude.

"The Word. Have you heard the Word, sister?"

Here we go, Evergreen thought, internalizing her sigh. "Yes," she told the woman. "I've heard the word."

The woman smiled openly, and Evergreen found it hard to be irritated in the face of such friendliness. "Then you *know*. I'm sorry you're having a rough time right now. Would you like to pray for strength with me?"

"No, thank you. No offense, but I'm not Christian."

The woman tilted her head at her, her brow crinkled. "But you said you knew the Word..."

Evergreen had met with this sort of confusion before, someone who thought that if you understood what Jesus was saying, you surely would follow him. If you didn't follow him, then you must not understand. "You asked if I'd heard the word. Yes, I have heard the word, and I understand it. But that doesn't mean I agree with it. That doesn't mean it speaks to me."

Her confusion still palpable, the woman offered herself an explanation. "Perhaps, it just hasn't been expressed to you properly."

Evergreen shook her head gently. "Let me put it to you this way: you know that feeling you get when you go to church or read the bible? That feeling of belonging, of light, of hope, of peace?"

She nodded.

"I get that feeling, too. But I don't get it from going to church or reading the bible. I get it from walking in the woods, from beating a drum. The old gods give me that feeling. I don't even know you, but as one human being to another, I know how special that feeling is. I would never try to take that feeling away from you. And as a woman who clearly cares for others, I would expect you to have enough empathy to not try to take that feeling away from me."

The woman's face was serious as she carefully considered Evergreen's words. "I understand," she said finally. "I'm glad you have found that sort of light in your life. So many are lost and looking for hope. May you have peace whatever path you walk on, sister."

Evergreen sighed in relief, glad she had reached someone, glad she had met an open heart who understood. "Thank you. I'm glad you have something to get you through as well."

Just as Evergreen and the woman shared a warm smile, the others returned. Evergreen stood from the couch and nodded at the woman.

"Happy holidays," the woman said.

"Happy holidays," Evergreen responded.

CHAPTER 42

Sawyer went back out to Wes's car to get the last of the groceries. Just as he slipped his hands into the handles of the cloth bags, he heard footsteps behind him, crunching the snow as they approached.

"I've got the rest," Sawyer said. "But if you could shut the trunk, that would be..."

His words trailed off as he turned around and saw Eeva standing before him.

"Sawyer..." she started, her voice soft but clear.

He flinched at the sound he'd begged for only days prior.

"I need to—"

"I have to get these things inside," Sawyer cut her off mid-sentence.

"It's not as if anything will melt," she argued. "Don't you have a second?"

Sawyer shook his head. *I can't do this,* he thought, his chest squeezing his lungs so tight it was hard to breathe. "Whatever it is, I'm sure someone else can help you with it."

As he walked past her, his mind shouted that he wanted to know what was so important that she would approach him. *What could possibly make her ask me for something? Is it the same thing she wanted last night?* His mind wanted to know, but his heart didn't. His heart couldn't handle her saying his name, couldn't handle her voice in his ears, couldn't handle her eyes on him. It was good, old fashioned, self-preservation that made him leave her outside without looking back.

Sawyer didn't know what he'd been expecting when he'd brushed Eeva off. If he'd thought she would give up and leave him alone, he had been sorely mistaken.

For the rest of the day, she watched him, looking for any chance to get him alone. But he was not the same old Sawyer who would just give in. He couldn't be. And though he wanted nothing more than to take a long walk alone in the woods to ground his emotions, he didn't dare. He couldn't afford the possibility that she would follow him. He could barely handle being in the same room with her with the rest of the coven there. He knew if he heard her call to him again, he'd be even more pathetic than he was now.

As it was, he knew he was hardly holding it together. He knew he would be a wreck once he got home. But at least he could be a wreck all by himself. *I don't want to ruin anyone else's Yule by being all depressed and miserable,* he thought as he narrowly missed being alone with her in the kitchen. *Can't she see that?*

As Sawyer lay on the couch again that night, he counted how many hours he would have to get through before he could leave. A shuffling from the hallway made Sawyer close his eyes.

"Sawyer?" Eeva murmured.

He didn't open them, gritting his teeth against the wave of despair that her whisper brought.

The shuffling grew louder. "Are you asleep?" she asked.

He could feel the weight of her presence hanging over him as she got close enough to see whether his eyes were closed. He kept still.

She sighed and shuffled back from whence she'd come.

So what if I'm a coward for not wanting to face her, he thought. *She ripped my heart out and lit it on fire. She doesn't even seem to notice how all this is affecting me. So yeah, I pretended to be asleep to get out of talking to her. What is there left to say anyway? She regrets the best thing that has ever happened to me. The thing I longed for the better part of a decade. It's going to take me more than a few days to get over it.*

Sawyer's phone dinged with another message from the group chat. His coworkers were still sharing their holiday fun. He sighed and put his phone on silent.

The following day was set to be a long one. Wes would begin the bulk of his Yule cooking. Everyone would make their Yule charms. And, that evening, they would stay up through the longest night of the year until dawn, as was tradition.

A hum of excitement hung over the group, though they would all probably take a nap sometime in the afternoon so they could stay up all night.

Eeva was still trying to get Sawyer's attention, and Sawyer was still ignoring her, though it got more and more difficult as time went on. After lunch, Dorian brought out the stuff for everyone to make their Yule charms.

"Everyone have their green cloth and red string?" he asked.

They nodded, and Wes placed a big mortar and pestle on the dining room table in front of him.

"All right. This charm is for us to attune to the sun energy that is on the rise. We have bay, cinnamon, and nutmeg." He dropped equal parts of the herbs and spices into the mortar and began crushing them with the pestle. "Now, when we light our candles during the Yule ritual tomorrow, we're going to make wishes. But feel free to put some energy into this if there is something you want to manifest."

After Dorian had pulverized the ingredients to his satisfaction, he reached into the mortar and took some of the mixture. Then he placed it at the center of his green cloth and tied it into a sachet with the red string. He passed the mortar to his left so everyone could take some.

When it reached Sawyer, he took some of the powder and sprinkled it on his cloth. He thought of all the energies associated with the sun. *The fiery energy of the sun offers guidance and enlightenment on matters of the heart,* he thought. *This is what I ask for.*

He tied the green cloth with the red string and put the sachet in his pocket.

CHAPTER 43

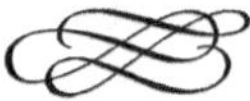

After they had made the Yule charms, they split off into smaller groups. Wes had asked Devan and Cory if they wouldn't mind going into the garage to drill the candle holes into the Yule log. The Yule log would act as a centerpiece during the celebration the following day until the candles burned down to their nubs. Then they would burn the log in the fireplace, saving only a small piece to light next year's Yule fire. Sawyer got up without a word to join them.

"Sawyer," Evergreen called out to him. Her time was running out, and she had less and less luxury to try to speak to him alone.

Tara, Cassandra, and Hazel, who were sitting on the couch, looked over at him. Evergreen kept her smile internal when he turned back to her, the peacemaker inside him unable to snub her with an audience.

"I'm still not comfortable with the holly king and oak king dance, and it's tomorrow. Do you mind going over it with me one more time?"

Evergreen couldn't see his face, but she could feel his frustration at having been cornered.

"You were fine the other day," he hedged.

"Well, we never finished the other day, and I want to make sure I get the last part down."

He sighed. "Yeah, all right."

"The meditation room is free, and it's pretty cold outside. Let's go in there," Evergreen suggested.

She led the way, and he pushed their sleeping bags to the side to make room before he faced her.

"Where are the staves?" he asked, looking around when she wasn't holding them.

Evergreen paused for a moment. "I lied about the dance," she murmured. "I just wanted to talk to you, and I didn't know another way of getting you alone."

Sawyer turned on his heel to leave without a word.

Panic lurched in Evergreen's stomach and climbed up her throat. "It wasn't a mistake," she said in a rush to get it out before he could leave.

Sawyer froze but didn't turn back to face her.

She tried to get out as much as she could while she still had time. "I accidentally saw a text on your phone and thought it was from your girlfriend. I don't regret what happened between us. The truth...the truth is I've been wanting it to happen for a long time, practically as long as I've known you."

There was a heavy silence, and Evergreen continued, her voice softer but still audible. "I love you, Sawyer." She laughed bitterly at herself. "I've always loved you. I'm so—"

Her apology was cut off as Sawyer spun around and crushed his mouth to hers. A relieved ache welled up in her chest, and tears rolled down her cheeks as she pulled him closer. A half sigh, half sob escaped her lips, and Sawyer broke their kiss, resting his forehead against hers.

"Don't cry, Eeva," he murmured, wiping her tears away. "I love you, too. I've loved you since I was a stupid teenage boy too shy to tell you how I felt."

Evergreen inhaled a shaky breath, his words making her tears flow harder. "Is that true?" she asked, her voice thick and nasally as her nose stuffed.

"It is," he assured, his amber eyes serious and true as he stared into hers.

She smiled through her tears. "I thought I'd fucked it all up," she told him. "I thought you'd never talk to me again."

He hushed her soothingly, stroking her hair.

Her breathing gradually evened out, and her eyes dried. "Will you kiss me again?" she murmured.

His smile warmed her chest.

"As many times as you want."

Sawyer kissed her sweetly, kissed her gently. And he continued to kiss her until her heated blood wanted more.

"Lock the door," she urged as she gasped for air.

He was gone but a moment, and then he was back with his arms around her as he trailed his lips down her neck.

He lifted her off her feet, and she wrapped her legs around him. His hot body pressed her against the cold glass of the meditation room wall as he drowned her in kisses.

"Do you have a condom?" he asked against her neck, his breath fogging up the window as he ground his ready cock against her equally ready core.

"Do you think we're the kind of Pagans who don't have contraceptives in the altar room?" she countered with a smirk.

"Where?" His voice was deep and husky, urgent.

The sound raised the hairs on her neck and arms, making her shiver. "In the cabinet," she breathed.

He didn't leave her but carried her over to the altar and laid her down before it, twisting at the torso to reach into the altar cabinet without having to untangle himself from her legs.

But as Sawyer fumbled with the wrapper, Evergreen released his torso and removed her pants and underwear. Before she'd even fully let go of the fabric, Sawyer slid deep inside her.

She gasped, and he smothered her moan with his mouth. Her mind went fuzzy as he settled atop her, his weight solid and real on her chest. Once he was inside her, he slowed to a steady rock, his face hovering over hers so she could see every smile, every bite of the lip, every loving glance from his amber eyes.

Evergreen had a hard time keeping quiet as Sawyer led her to her peak. But once they were finished, she was too satiated to care if anyone had heard her as Sawyer fluttered kisses on her face and neck.

"I have so much to tell you," she murmured, as she lay in his arms atop one of the sleeping bags.

"We have more than enough time," he assured. "Even when we leave, we can see each other after work and on the weekends. You don't have to rush to say everything at once."

Evergreen pulled back, frowning. "But how are we going to see each other that often? You live so far away."

"No, I don't," he informed. "I live in Marshton same as you."

Evergreen sat up and looked down at him. "What? When? How?" she demanded.

"I moved there last year when I got the job at the rehabilitation center."

Evergreen's eyes still held many questions.

Sawyer chuckled, pulling her down to him and kissing her on the mouth. "We have time," he repeated.

CHAPTER 44

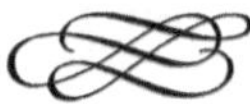

"We should probably head out there. Don't you think?" Eeva said, not making a move to back up her statement. "It's already dark out. Even if they took naps to be able to stay up all night, they would be awake by now."

Sawyer tightened his arms around her. "We don't have to," he said with a tone of finality.

Eeva giggled, the sound making his heart feel light. "We're supposed to be spending Yule together with everybody."

"Yule is tomorrow. We can spend it with everyone tomorrow. Nope. I've shared you with them too long already."

Eeva smiled, snuggling in closer to him. "As long as you don't think anyone will come knocking."

"Your mom is the one who told us to lock the door," he said.

"That's true." She laughed.

They were both quiet for a moment before Eeva said, "It's a little early, but can I give you your Yule present now?"

Sawyer pulled away, glancing down at her. "Did you get me a gift?"

She smiled and nodded. Then she wiggled out of his arms and went to her suitcase. He sat up as she dug through. She returned shortly after with a paper shopping bag from Toil and Trouble.

"Open it," she urged, holding it out to him.

He felt himself grin as his heart squeezed in anticipation. He pulled out the tissue paper and reached into the bag. His fingers closed around a cool metal object. He took it out.

A shiny copper pentacle hung on a smooth black cord.

"It's to replace the one you gave to Sol. I think this one suits you better, too. The copper will go so nice with your hair color."

He clasped the necklace around his neck. "Thank you, Eeva," he said earnestly. "I love it."

Her answering smile was an even better gift. "I know I was being kind of a brat before we all went shopping. So don't worry about getting me anything."

Sawyer tilted his head. "What makes you think I don't already have something for you?" he asked. He went over to his bag and got Eeva's gifts before returning and setting them out before her.

She raised her eyebrows. "What? So many? You didn't have to."

"Oh, these aren't all from this year. I got you a gift every year..." he trailed off, suddenly embarrassed.

Her smile widened. "You did?"

He nodded, trying to ignore the slight heat he felt in his cheeks.

"Which was the one from the first year?" she asked.

He stared down at the packages and pointed at the small packet wrapped in what was once a brown paper bag.

She unwrapped it, and pulled out the quartz pendulum he'd gotten her his first Yule away.

"It has stones for each of the chakras," he told her. "And it has a clasp at the end, so you can wear it as a bracelet, too."

"It's adorable," she complimented.

"This one is next," he said before she was even done admiring her first gift. He offered her the one that was most square.

She unwrapped it, revealing a coffee cup that read, "Hex the Patriarchy." Her lips mouthed the words, and she burst out laughing.

His chest warmed at the sound. "I knew you'd like that," he said. "Now this one." He handed her the squishiest one.

She put the mug down beside her and unwrapped the red drawstring bag. "What's in here?" she asked, opening the bag. "Oh!" she gasped. "Did you make these?"

He nodded as she shook some of the wooden runes into her palm.

"They're beautiful!" she exclaimed. "My very own runes. You're going to have to help me practice."

"I will," he promised.

"Is this one next?" she pointed at the rectangle one beside the Toil and Trouble bag.

"Yes."

She gasped when she unwrapped the hand-carved tarot box he'd made. "Sawyer, how long did this take you? It's gorgeous."

Sawyer shrugged, embarrassed but pleased at her reaction. "Last one," he urged, pushing the bag toward her.

"I feel spoiled already," she said with a smile, reaching her hand into the bag and pulling out the mistletoe hairpin.

"Clover said it was real mistletoe," he explained as she smiled and stroked the smooth resin.

"Is it?" she asked, dangling the hairpin over her head and raising her eyebrows at him expectantly.

He leaned over and kissed her once, twice, five times, one for every Yule since he'd last seen her.

Eeva snuggled up beside him, resting her head on his shoulder. They sat like that for a while, quiet and comfortable in each other's company. Then she slipped her hand under his shirt. He shivered as she stroked his stomach slow and deliberate.

"You know," she murmured. "I'm not very good at staying up all night. I think you're going to have to keep me occupied so I don't fall asleep."

Sawyer's manhood stiffened. "How many hours until dawn?" he asked.

"Hmm, longest night of the year? Give or take fourteen hours."

"I'm going to be honest with you. I might have to take some breaks, but I'm willing to try my very best."

"I believe in you," she murmured right before she pressed a hungry kiss to his lips.

By the time the eastern horizon started to lighten on December the twenty-first, Sawyer felt confident he'd made up for not being honest with Eeva for all those years.

They pulled on their rumpled clothes and shuffled to the living room like two creatures emerging from a winter's long hibernation.

"Where is everyone?" Eeva asked, blinking at the empty room.

Sawyer poked his head into the kitchen. And though he was greeted with the mouthwatering scent of glazed ham and spiced, he didn't see anyone.

"Sawyer?" Eeva called him from the front hall.

He met her there where he found a cowbell and a tambourine beside the door.

"They must already be outside," she said.

"It's almost time," he agreed.

They pulled on their coats, hats, and boots, then grabbed the instruments before heading out the front door.

Eeva slipped her arm into Sawyer's, using him as a guide in the still-dark morning.

"Watch the steps," he told her as he led her off the porch and around to the side of the house.

They found the coven huddled in their coats and hoods, their eyes trained on the eastern horizon.

Just as Sawyer and Eeva settled in behind them, the sun shone its first light.

"There it is!" Sol shouted, pointing at the first rays of dawn.

Everyone responded in a burst of noise. They hollered and whooped. They banged their drums and shook their bells. They greeted the sun, the newly reborn god, with cries of welcome.

And as he shook his cowbell and Eeva jingled her tambourine, he smiled over at her. Her face was open and bright in the morning sunshine. He couldn't help but lean down and press a kiss to her smiling lips.

The cheers of the coven turned to whistles and laughs.

"I have a feeling we will be meeting sooner rather than later," Devan said, chuckling.

"I see a handfasting in our future," Piper added.

"Finally!" Cassandra shouted.

"I know," Tara agreed. "It's about damn time."

Eeva broke their kiss, burying her face in his chest.

"Don't say finally," Sawyer argued with a grin. "Finally makes it sound like the end. It's a new day, a new season. We're only just beginning."

THE *Treason* OF **Robyn Hood**

D. LIEBER

SPECIAL THANKS

As always, I would like to thank everyone who helped me research and beta this book. A special thanks to John, Brandon, Bryan, Megan, Mary, Aunt Debbie, Abi, Sara, and Vijaya.

CHAPTER 1

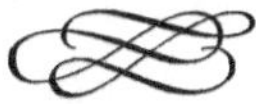

Robyn left Lackland Steel as fast as she could when the shift whistle screeched. She didn't even bother to change out of her overalls; she just grabbed her bag from the locker room and punched her time-card on the way out.

As the sound of the city streets slammed into her, she forced it to dim into the background. Car horns blared at each other, their drivers trying to navigate the evening rush to get home, or wherever they were going. The sky glowed yellow as the sun unsuccessfully struggled to cut through the smog. She adjusted the scarf over her face as she passed under the train's overpass, wrinkling her nose at the smell of rusty iron.

She followed the elevated train tracks with her eyes as they crossed over each other, all eventually ending at Central Station. She climbed the platform just as her train hummed into the station. It hovered lower than some of the newer lines, and she had to step down to board.

An older woman beside Robyn clicked her tongue, eyeing her with disapproval. Robyn looked down at her hands, which still had soot and oil from the steel mill crusted in the creases of her knuckles and stuck around her fingernails. She stared out the window as the city passed by, too impatient to care about her appearance and how others saw her.

Robyn didn't glance back at the reproving woman as she stepped off the train. She fought the flow of the crowd as they hurried in the opposite direction. After much elbowing and a few sore toes, theirs not hers, Robyn managed to escape the crush and distance herself from the train station.

Her boots made little sound on the sidewalk as she took the longest strides her five-and-a-half-foot stature would allow. Rounding the corner, she looked up at the ten-story brick monstrosity. Her stomach lurched as she stared at the apartment building turned prison.

Robyn's tongue stuck to the roof of her dry mouth as she tried to wet it. Sniffing hard, she squared her shoulders and strode toward the front door.

As expected, an armed guard halted her entrance. "What business do you have here, Miss?" he demanded.

"Don't pretend you don't know me after all this time, Charles. Today's the day. I've gone through the proper channels. I have an appointment with the warden."

Charles frowned. "The warden isn't here right now," he said.

Robyn blinked at him, and it took her a minute to process. She squinted at the guard. "What do you mean 'he's not here'? We have an appointment. After two months of being jerked around, what's going on here?" she demanded.

Charles didn't even flinch at her impotent anger. "I don't know what to tell you."

As her fury reached the boiling point, a man in a tailored suit exited the door behind Charles. His eyes focused on Robyn, taking in her grimy appearance.

"Are you Robyn Loxley?" he asked her, one eyebrow raised.

"Yes, and I'm supposed to be seeing the warden today."

"That is not possible, but I do have a message from him for you." The man handed her an envelope.

She hastily opened it.

```
Dear Miss Loxley,


I regret to inform you that I am unable to grant
your admittance to Midshire War Relocation
Center.
```

Warden James Weldon

"Is this a fucking joke?" Robyn demanded from the man in the suit.

He leveled his gaze at her and narrowed his eyes at her foul language. "I am not privy to the contents of the warden's correspondence, but I assure you that whatever he has written must be the case."

The man turned and went back inside, and Robyn glared after him. Pursing her lips, Robyn contemplated making a rush for it, but the long barrel of Charles's firearm made her reconsider.

"Don't think this is over," she warned Charles coolly.

He didn't respond.

Robyn turned on her heel and stomped through the small courtyard. Just as she was about to round the corner, she wrinkled her nose at Charles, pulled down her scarf, and spat in his direction. It was much too far to hit him, but he got the idea.

Too mad to go home, Robyn wandered around the city. The sun hugged the western horizon. She stomped through the soot-covered streets, her fury mounting with every step.

Two months I've played their game, she thought. *Two months! I shouldn't even have tried. I knew they would never let me in to see Will. I knew they would never hear me out. Well, I'm done doing it the right way. I'm not playing bureaucratic games anymore.*

Unable to take another step, Robyn looked up and saw she was at the waterfront. She leaned against a wide industrial pipe for a moment, watching as it dumped sludge into the bay. Then she climbed up the ladder on the side of the pipe and sat on top, her eyes widening as she stared at what lay on the other side.

Beyond a canal, an abandoned neighborhood lay before her. It was rusty and crumbling, and she couldn't see a window left unbroken. Under a narrow, grated bridge, the canal wall bore graffiti of a vivid Lincoln green. It pronounced the Hooverville as "Sherwood."

Of course, like most of the residents of Midshire, Robyn had heard of the shanty town Sherwood, the last of its kind. Most of the other Hoovervilles had been destroyed by the Shanty Eradication Program. She didn't know why they hadn't bothered to take this one down; likely the funds were rerouted to the war effort. Whatever the reason, it was a forgotten part of the city, overlooked and devoid of life.

Robyn scanned the other side of the canal and didn't see anyone or anything moving about, as expected. Determined to take a look, she climbed down a ladder on the other side of the pipe and approached the narrow bridge.

But the moment she stepped onto the bridge, a deep voice demanded, "state your business, stranger."

"My business is my own," Robyn snapped, glad her surprise didn't show in her voice.

A giant man, seven feet in height and nearly twice her breadth, stepped out from behind a crumbling wall. "Not just anyone is allowed in Sherwood. State your business or turn back," the man said, hopping onto the other side of the bridge, a long staff in his hand.

Robyn glared at him. "Step aside, or I'll knock you into the canal," she threatened.

The large man raised his eyebrows and grinned. "Are you angling for a fight?"

"Only if you won't move out of my way."

He nodded good-humoredly. "All right then. Much!" he called over his shoulder.

A young boy of eight or nine appeared from behind the wall carrying a staff nearly twice his height. Much handed the staff to the man, who stepped forward and offered it to Robyn.

She took the solid wood in her grip, testing its weight and wishing she and Will had trained more with the staff than the bow.

"Are you sure you want to do this?" the man asked.

"Giving me a weapon was your biggest mistake," Robyn spat.

He grinned again. "I won't go easy on you."

"Neither will I," she growled, lunging forward and aiming a blow at his head.

He parried it to the right and struck out at her stomach. Jumping back, she narrowly avoided the hit. His grin infuriated her, and she ground her teeth. Aiming this time for his feet, again her staff was brushed aside.

She wasn't fast enough to avoid his next attack. His staff cracked her right on top of the head. Dazed, Robyn lost balance and toppled into the canal.

The cold water jolted her back to her senses. When her head broke the surface, she saw her opponent had lowered a rope down to her and was looking ready to dive in after her. She grabbed the rope, and he hauled her up.

Sitting Robyn on the bridge, the man smiled at her, satisfaction sparkling in his eyes. "You're a feisty one," he complimented.

She couldn't hold in her laugh. "Thanks for not going easy on me."

He patted her on the shoulder and helped her to her feet. "What's your name, stranger?" he asked, good-naturedly.

"Robyn."

Holding out his giant hand, he enveloped hers in a firm shake. "I'm Jon Little."

Robyn raised one eyebrow at him and smirked, finding the name terribly ironic.

"So what brings you to Sherwood, Robyn?"

"Would you believe I was just taking a walk and was curious?"

Jon quirked his mouth, trying to determine the veracity of her explanation. Then he shook his head and laughed, a deep, happy chuckle one couldn't help but join.

"You sure are something."

Laughing at herself, she suddenly shivered when a cool wind off the bay raised goosebumps on her wet skin.

Jon's smile faded from his face at her shudder. "Come on, let's get you dried off and warmed up."

Robyn trailed Jon across the bridge and into Sherwood. As they caught up with Much, John ruffled the boy's dark hair.

"Robyn, meet Much Molinero."

She smiled at the child. "It's nice to meet you, Much. I'm Robyn."

The boy looked up at her, his slight frown quite serious. "You shouldn't be here," he said.

"Why you...don't pay him any mind, Robyn. He's a little scamp."

"You don't want me here, Much?" she asked the boy.

"Oh, it's not that, señorita. It's just that you're too bonita for a place like Sherwood."

"Oho, you little sweet talker!" Jon chuckled.

"In that case, I should probably find myself a strong, handsome escort while I'm here. What do you say, Señor Molinero? Will you be my proud protector?"

Much stood up straight, bright eyes shining through the bangs of his dark hair. "Don't worry, señorita. I'll make sure you get home safe."

"Gracias, Much. I'm certain I won't have any trouble with you by my side."

As the boy vigilantly scanned their path for any danger, Robyn looked over at Jon.

He smiled down at her, light shining in his eyes. "This way," he said with a gesture.

She followed Jon through the seemingly abandoned streets of Sherwood. Stepping over debris in the dim light of dusk, the soot and dust from the path clung to Robyn's wet boots.

Above them, a clang sounded. Robyn looked up at the scaffolding of a building never completed. Roughly constructed skywalks crisscrossed overhead. No one was there.

They passed deserted lean-tos made of whatever wood or metal scraps the occupants could find.

Jon Little, or Little Jon as Robyn thought of him, walked boldly on, paying no mind to the occasional skittering sounds of those just out of sight.

He stopped outside a crumbling corner store. The front window had been boarded up to keep the weather out, but the crooked, faded sign above the door still declared the place "Barnaby's Books and Stationery."

He opened the chipped blue door with a loud creak. Much skittered in ahead of them, and Little Jon nodded at Robyn to go next.

The faded wooden floorboards groaned under their steps as they entered the dark bookstore. Robyn could hear Much shuffling around farther in, past the many wooden shelves stuffed with books.

Robyn ran her fingertips along the tattered spines; these were not the new books one would usually find in a bookstore. They were old and worn. Still, they were well dusted, and she could tell someone cared for them.

She looked back at Little Jon as he shuffled behind her in the dark. The glow of firelight flickered off the walls and ceiling ahead. As Robyn moved toward it, it became clear to her that this was a small living space. Much knelt before the fire he'd just lit in a heavy, stone fireplace.

The flames illuminated a small table and two chairs to one side and a cot next to a nest of blankets on the other.

"Welcome to our home," Little Jon said humbly. "It's not much, I'll grant you. But it keeps the chill out, and we're never short of entertainment," he added, nodding to the shelves.

"It's very cozy," Robyn told him.

He smiled softly. "In any case," he started, crossing to the nest of blankets on the floor, "you can use this to warm up while I go fetch some clothes that will fit you." He handed her the blanket. "Sit by the fire. I won't be long." He took one of the chairs from the table and set it close to the fire, then left the way they'd come.

As soon as she'd wrapped the blanket around herself and settled by the hearth, Much sat cross-legged at her feet.

They stared into the fire as it popped and cracked.

"How long have you lived here, Much?" Robyn asked him.

"I don't know," he admitted. "But I know I haven't always lived here. I used to live with my parents. I remember their bakery. But when they died, Jon found me and brought me here." His voice shook a little.

"I also lost my parents at a young age. I was only four years old when they died," Robyn told him.

"Did you have someone like Jon to help?"

She nodded. "Yes, my father's friend took my sister and me in."

"That's good."

"Are you and Jon the only two who live in Sherwood?"

He frowned. "No, there are others."

"How many?"

"We're not supposed to talk about it with people who don't live here," he murmured.

"That's all right. You don't have to tell me. I was just curious."

"Where did you learn to fight, Señorita Robyn? Most people who Jon challenges just leave." His eyes sparkled with curiosity in the firelight.

"I learned from my best friend and his family while we were in school. I'm not very good at hand-to-hand, though I did practice quite a bit. I'm much better with a bow and arrow." Robyn chuckled.

"A bow and arrow? Would you show me?"

Before Robyn could answer, the door creaked, and Little Jon appeared with an armful of clothes. Robyn stood to meet him.

"I didn't know what you'd like. But they should fit, and they're dry."

"Thank you." She smiled up at him as he handed her the clothing.

"We'll be just outside. Vámonos, Much." Little Jon ushered the boy out so Robyn could change.

He'd found her a pair of men's trousers, which fit her around the waist but were loose in the legs. They were charcoal and had buttoned pouch pockets on the sides. The women's three-quarter sleeve shirt was snug in the chest and a little too short, with her abdomen just below her belly button exposed. He'd also given her a patchwork poncho of earthy colors: dark green, brown, grey, and black. It was warm and covered her exposed midriff.

After changing, Robyn folded her wet work clothes and went to meet Little Jon and Much, who leaned against the eroded bricks outside their bookstore home.

"Thank you again for these," she said.

"Ah well, it was my fault you fell into the canal after all."

Robyn laughed. "Well, I should have heeded your warning. I don't think I need to tell you I get a little blinded by my anger sometimes. I don't always make the best decisions."

He grinned. "What got you so riled, if I might ask?"

She frowned, not sure she was ready to open up that much yet. She looked up at the darkened sky, knowing she'd never be able to see the moon or stars through the smoke of the city. "Perhaps next time I'll tell you all about it. As for right now, I need to be getting home."

"Of course, I'm sure whoever's waiting for you is probably worried. A husband, a child...?"

Robyn snorted. "Nah, none of that for me. I doubt they even notice I'm gone. But even so, my sister will be worried if she goes looking for me."

Little Jon nodded. "You best get going then. But if ever you want to blow off some steam, you know where to find me. And if someone else is guarding the bridge, you just tell them you've come to see Jon Little."

"I'll do that," she told him.

Then Jon and Much led her through the dark borough that was Sherwood. When she'd crossed the bridge over the canal, she looked back at them and waved, promising herself she would visit them again soon.

CHAPTER 2

Jon watched as Robyn crossed the bridge connecting Sherwood to the rest of Midshire, her wavy, golden blonde hair windswept around her.

"She'll come back, won't she?" Much asked.

When she'd gotten across, she looked back with a smile and a wave. Jon's chest warmed at the twinkle in her blue eyes.

He smiled gently. "Yeah, I think she will."

Jon and Much stood on the Sherwood side, rooted in place until Robyn's retreating form was out of view.

He turned to Much who strained to see through the darkness and fog to find his new friend. "All right, Muchito," Jon said, rubbing the boy's hair. "It's past your bedtime."

Much groaned. "Aw, come on, Jon, I'm not even sleepy," he complained.

"Oh, no? Well, then maybe you should catch up on your schoolwork. I recall you being a little behind in your reading."

The boy frowned. "You know, I think I'm tired after all. Actually, I think I'm too tired to know how tired I am."

Jon chuckled. "I thought that might be the case."

By the time they'd reached their street, the excitement of Robyn's visit had truly left behind an exhausted kid. Much staggered on his feet, and Jon picked him up and carried him the last few steps to their door.

Jon froze as he turned the knob, sensing a presence among the bookshelves. But before he could call out or wonder how he could fight off an intruder while carrying Much, a petite form stepped out from between the shelves, her features underlit by the lamp in her hand.

"You should know better than to sneak up on people, Tuck," Jon scolded the young woman without bite.

Her grin looked otherworldly as her grey eyes flickered in the flame-light. "Sorry. I was restless," she murmured.

Jon crossed the room and tucked Much into his cot, smiling as the boy took long, sleepy blinks. When he returned to Tuck, she lifted up a book she'd found, tilting her head in a question. He nodded, telling her it was fine for her to borrow it and motioned for her to follow him outside.

"I was surprised to find you gone," Tuck said once he'd closed the door behind them. "I would've thought you'd have settled in for the night."

Jon looked down at the small nineteen-year-old. Her waist-length, black hair was loose, falling in ringlets over the hood and shoulders of her dark cloak. He thought she always looked like the subject of a pre-Raphaelite painting; she didn't much care for modern fashion. But it was her cloak that told him what she'd been up to.

"You were out walking again. What's going on?" he asked.

She shrugged. "I'm not sure. I've been sort of edgy since the full moon. But I thought a good book might help me sleep."

He dipped his head once in acknowledgement. "Where are your hounds?"

"They're around somewhere. Probably out hunting for something to eat. So...where were you? It's unusual for Much not to go to bed on time."

Jon was silent for a while, thinking about what had happened with Robyn and how he should relate it. Tuck waited patiently for him to collect his thoughts.

"Do you remember when you said someone would be coming to Sherwood?"

She nodded slowly. "Yeah, the knight of wands."

"How did your reading go again?"

Tuck squinted up at the cloudy night sky, thinking. "I don't remember the exact cards, but the knight of wands will be coming to Sherwood. He will come on the cusp of great turmoil and lead us through."

"What about the part of how he will come?"

"Oh, yeah. He will stand and fight a battle, despite knowing he will lose."

Jon rubbed his jaw in thought. "I think the knight of wands came to Sherwood tonight."

"What? How do you know?"

"She was just like you said she would be. Bold, charismatic, and she jumped right in without thinking."

"She?"

"Yeah, she. Her name is Robyn."

Tuck's brow scrunched in deep thought. "She fought you?"

"Yeah."

"How big was she? How skilled? I mean, was there any chance she would win?"

He pursed his lips. "Obviously she was smaller than me. She's a couple inches taller than you but not as slender as you. She was fairly skilled. It's clear she's had training of some kind. But my guess is it wasn't with the staff." He nodded. "She fought well considering. Could she have won? Hmmm unlikely. But she was furious about something, and it made her distracted. She told me later she has the habit of letting her anger get the best of her. That reminded me of what you'd said about the knight of wands."

Tuck listened to his every word carefully, her eyes unfocused and staring into the sky as she thought hard about what he was saying.

"So...do you think Robyn could be the knight of wands?" he asked.

"Maybe. I'll have to go home and pull some cards on the matter." She shifted her weight from one foot to the other.

"Is there something else?"

She brought her curled fingers to her mouth, hugging the book she'd borrowed to her chest. Then she looked up at him, her eyes finding his unerringly in the night. "I'm worried," she admitted. "I don't think Sherwood is ready for the turmoil the knight of wands heralds. I don't even know if we have enough to make it through the winter let alone face whatever is coming."

Tuck's unease made his stomach drop, but he put that away for later. "You said the knight would lead us through though, right?"

She nodded almost imperceptibly, dropping her gaze.

"Tuck," Jon murmured, pulling her attention back to him. Then he smiled in reassurance. "I will protect you. I will protect all of Sherwood. No matter what happens. Haven't I always done?"

Tuck sighed. "You're right. You've always come through for us, Jon. You've given us all a safe place to live. A home. Thank you for reminding me not to live so much in the future and what ifs." Tuck paused. "So tell me about this Robyn. Do you trust her? Would you follow her?"

Jon thought about the fierceness in Robyn's eyes as she'd told him giving her a weapon was a mistake, the gentleness she'd shown as she'd told Much she felt safe because he was there to protect her, and the warmth that had bloomed in his chest when he saw the two of them sitting by the fire of his hearth—the warmth that still remained. "Yes," he murmured to Tuck. "Yes, I would follow her."

CHAPTER 3

*M*idshire after dark was certainly a sight to see. The residents of the coastal metropolis may be a productive lot during the daylight hours, but it was after dark that they truly lived.

Men too old, too young, too short, too tall, to serve in the war washed off the soot and sweat from a hard day's work, slicked back their hair, and put on their hats and victory suits.

Women, no longer the pre-war girls who waited for men to call, changed out of their overalls and boots and stepped into their swing dresses and heels.

The city became a cacophony of big band jazz dance halls and clubs, bars where jukeboxes were drowned out by rowdy tavern tramps, and hover trains humming over their tracks throughout the night.

A halo of golden light formed around the streetlamps as their bulbs tried to pierce the city's haze with little success.

Robyn Loxley had to walk quite a while away from Sherwood to get to a rail line that still serviced that part of town. She stood on the platform, waiting for the infrequent train as dogs howled somewhere in the distance.

The only other inhabitants of the platform were a pigeon and a seagull. She could tell some sort of drama was brewing when she spotted a cheese puff in between the two birds. The pigeon's head bobbed menacingly as it glared at its rival, and the seagull squawked like a children's play toy. She watched the two posture at each other, wondering who would be victorious. Neither of them paid any mind when the train pulled into the station. Looking back through the train window as she boarded, Robyn saw the seagull had won the prize and threw its head back, swallowing the unnaturally orange corn snack in one gulp.

Central Station was abuzz with activity when she disembarked. The turnstiles were backed up as usual, but she waited patiently as the crowd formed single-file lines to pass through. Despite the crush, Robyn managed to slip through the glass-domed atrium in less than a minute, though it took her another fifteen to clear the turnstiles to the Kapel line, the train that ran closest to her home.

The passengers gave her fleeting glances of curiosity, which she suspected had much more to do with her lack of nose and mouth covering than the unusual attire Little Jon had given her. She wondered how long it would take Winona to clean and dry her clothes. *Winona won't be pleased at having to get the stench of the canal water out,* she thought.

The Lackland mansion was not close to the train station, so Robyn had to hail a cab to get there. Of course, as a ward of the Lacklands, she had access to any of their vehicles, but she didn't mind using public transit, at least until her project was finished.

She asked the cabbie to stop just short of her destination and paid her with wet coins. The cabbie raised her eyebrows but didn't complain at the state of the currency.

Staring up at the seven-foot stone wall surrounding the property, Robyn edged toward the entrance and peeked around the corner. The house was lit up as always; the lights on either side of the smooth columns near the front door did not do the pinkish tan stone of the house justice. At the center of a round drive was a statue of Hamlet, his father's ghost standing behind him in full battle armor with one hand on the Prince of Denmark's shoulder. The light beneath the statue cast shadows that made one all too willing to believe in visitors from beyond the veil.

Dashing past the entrance, Robyn tried to make as little noise as possible as she hugged the southern wall around the mansion. She gave one quick look to both sides before climbing the black cherry tree that grew on the outside of the wall. Its long, twisted branches stretched over the stone. Sitting astride the wall, she dropped her things to the other side and walked deftly along a thick branch. Then she crouched down and hung from the wood before dropping lightly to the ground.

Robyn collected her things and skittered across the lawn to her workshed; the well-oiled door made no sound as she slipped inside. Feeling her way along the unsanded wall near the door, she flicked on the light switch. A naked bulb overhead illuminated her haven. At the center of the room, nearly complete, was her long-term project: a motorcycle she was building, she was proud to say, with her own wages. Along one side of the shed were shelves with various tools and parts, and a long workbench took up the back wall. In the back-right corner was a small sink with cold running water, a smudged mirror hanging over it.

She walked around her nearly-finished vehicle and crossed to the sink. After scrubbing her face and hands the best she could, gritting her teeth against the chill of the water, she arranged her wet clothes along the sides of the sink.

On the other wall of the shed was a small cot, not unlike the cot Much slept in at Little Jon's. She crawled in between the thick piles of blankets and closed her gritty eyelids, the exhaustion from the day finally overtaking her. Her head ached from where Little Jon had whacked her. She reached up and hissed as her fingers nudged the bump on her skull.

Robyn thought about going up to the house for some pain killers, but her limbs felt too heavy to move anymore that day. She wondered mildly if she had a concussion as she sank into sleep.

A waft of cold air on Robyn's face awoke her the next morning. She cracked her eyelids, and her bleary vision focused on her sister as she hovered over her. Marian's dark hair fell into her face, and she tucked it behind an ear.

"Hey," Robyn croaked, then cleared her throat.

Marian disappeared from view. Robyn heard the faucet in the corner turn on, and then Marian returned and handed her a cup of water.

"Where were you last night? Did you get in to see Will?" Marian asked.

Robyn sat up and drank the water she'd been offered, glad her headache wasn't as bad as it had been the night before. "No, that bastard of a warden skipped out on me."

Marian frowned at the news and her sister's language.

"But he's got another thing coming if he thinks I'm going to give up."

"I'm sure you'll figure it out," Marian encouraged. "In any case, I came to fetch you for breakfast."

"Right. How much time do I have?"

Marian took in Robyn's appearance. "I'd risk being late rather than show up filthy."

Robyn snorted. "Yeah, you're probably right."

After leaving the work-shed, Marian and Robyn crossed the expansive lawn until they reached the tall hedge. They slipped between two cypress trees and entered the gravel path of the well-maintained garden. The stones crunched beneath their shoes as they passed the greenhouse and glassed-in gazebo. Finally, they reached the pinkish sand-colored stone of the patio and entered through the large, paned doors.

Rather than following Marian to the dining room, Robyn veered toward the kitchen. Sarah was making breakfast and didn't even notice when she sneaked by to the back stairs. She hurried to the second floor and was in her room before anyone saw her.

The curtains to the balcony were drawn, so she flipped on the light switch. The white wallpaper looked cream between the printed vines in the lamplight. She crossed to her dresser and pulled out clean clothes to change into. Then she went to the bathroom, which connected her room to Marian's. After a hurried shower, she put her wet hair up in a simple twist and went downstairs.

As Robyn came down, she noticed Winona carrying a vase full of lilies. "Where did those come from, Winona?" she asked.

"They just arrived for Mrs. Lackland. I was going to deliver them to her."

"Oh, I can do that," Robyn offered. *It will be a great excuse as to why I'm late for breakfast,* she thought.

"Thank you, Robyn. I have so much to do this morning."

"I don't want to add to your list unnecessarily, but I left some dirty clothes in the work-shed if you're planning to do laundry."

"I'll be sure to fetch them when I do."

"Thanks, Winona."

"Of course."

Carrying the lilies gingerly, Robyn entered the dining room, where the Lackland family had gathered to breakfast.

"Good morning," she said cheerfully before anyone could scold her for being tardy. "Eleanor, these just arrived for you. It must be for your birthday," she told the elderly woman at the head of the table.

As usual, Eleanor was beautiful and dignified. Her long, white hair was pinned up, and her light eyes were as sharp as any woman in her prime.

"That's very kind of you, Robyn," she said. "You can put them over there on the sideboard. Does it say who they're from?"

Robyn placed the flowers where Eleanor had indicated and searched the blooms for a card. "It looks like they're from Marie," she told Eleanor, delivering the paper to her.

Eleanor placed her coffee cup in its saucer and took the card from Robyn. "Yes," she said, reading the note. "It seems another one of my daughters will be unable to make it to my birthday party. What a pity."

"That's a shame," Marian commented.

Robyn took a seat between her sister and Eleanor. The two chairs on either side of Isabella were empty as John had moved to take his brother's place at the other head of the table.

"It is unforgivable," John pronounced, "that all of my sisters and half-sisters should not be present for your seventieth birthday, Mother. Disgraceful."

"Don't make a fuss, John," Eleanor scolded. "Marie, Alix, Ellie, and Joan all have families of their own to worry about, not to mention businesses to take care of, especially now with three of them widowed and Alfonso off at war along with Dear Richard."

John frowned at his mother's mention of his elder brother. "And what of my brother's wife? Berengaria has not stepped foot in this house since they were married. She went to stay with Joan in Chicago almost immediately."

"She is distraught, my dear," Isabella defended her sister-in-law in a soothing voice. "I can't imagine how upset I would be if you had gone to war right after we were married."

John gave his wife a cold stare in response to her tenderheartedness. His nostrils flared as he took a deep breath and turned back to his mother.

"Regardless, I will ensure your momentous birthday shall be as grand as you are, Mother."

Eleanor didn't respond to her son's usual solicitations for attention but turned to Marian.

"Marian, I have invited a few old friends to the party, and I've instructed them to bring their eligible sons. You will take a look at them, won't you? I hear quite a number are very handsome, and of course they are influential as well."

Eleanor often put gentle pressure on Marian to choose a man whose family would benefit the Lacklands. Marian cast down her gaze and nodded politely. She would do what Eleanor asked as she always did.

Before she could turn her attention to the younger sister, Robyn swallowed her breakfast as fast as she could and tried to get out of there.

"Robyn," Eleanor chided lightly. "Eat slowly, or you will make yourself sick."

"Sorry, Eleanor. I'm just worried about being late for work."

"I don't know why you insist on working at the mill, Robyn. It is unbefitting," John jabbed.

"John," Eleanor admonished. "Do not discourage her. She is an intelligent, capable woman. And she can work at the mill for as long as she likes."

"Of course, Mother," John agreed, lifting his coffee cup to his lips.

All of a sudden, John spit his coffee across the table with a loud sputter, the droplets marring the white table cloth as well as Marian's and Isabella's dresses. Marian squeaked, and Isabella gasped.

Everyone turned wide eyes to John, who looked equally astonished.

Robyn realized what had happened, and mirth bubbled up inside her. She burst out laughing, the sound stark in the hush of the dining room. John squinting at Robyn, his face turning red with rage. His reaction only made her laugh harder.

"Oh my God," she said, heaving deep breaths. "I had almost forgotten. I did it weeks ago. Sarah must have finally had to replenish."

"I've had just about enough of your pranks, Robyn," John growled. "I have lost my patience. You are grown now. Hadn't you better stop this childish behavior? Isn't there something else you could be doing with your time?"

Robyn wiped the happy tears from her eyes. "Perhaps you're right, John. It did take quite a bit of time to replace all the sugar in Sarah's sack with salt. I'm sorry I ruined your coffee," Robyn said in a tone that was clear she wasn't sorry at all.

John opened his mouth to scold her again, but Eleanor cut in; her eyes sparkled though her mouth was set in a frown. "That's enough, John. She's already apologized. Isabella, go tell Sarah about the mix-up so she doesn't use the *sugar* for anything else."

John glowered but didn't say anything, and Isabella rose and left the room.

"Hadn't you better be getting to work, Robyn?" Eleanor asked mildly, though she gave Robyn a little wink before raising her black coffee to her lips.

Robyn nodded. But as she was rising to leave, John's right-hand man entered the room. Guy Gisbourne removed his hat and murmured something to John.

"All right," John answered. "Wait for me in the sitting room, and I will come momentarily."

Guy nodded and strode out.

Robyn stalled for a couple of seconds, giving Guy a chance to get where he was going.

Eleanor looked up at her, one delicate, white eyebrow raised. "Didn't you just say you were worried about being late?"

"I did, yes." Robyn smiled at the woman. "Well, I'll see you all later then. Have a good day."

Leaving the dining room, Robyn scanned the foyer for any sign of Guy. She sighed in relief when he was nowhere in sight. *Right*, she thought. *I just have to get upstairs, grab my things, and I'll be on my way. I can slip out the back if necessary.*

Creeping up to the sitting room door, Robyn only had to make it past without notice. She held her breath and rushed past the opening. She congratulated herself and moved to cross the rest of the foyer to the stairs.

"Robyn."

Her shoulders slumped, and she turned to face Guy, who stood in the doorway of the sitting room. His dark eyes smiled in that intense sort of way they always did when he looked at her.

"What is it, Guy? I'm in a hurry."

"You always seem to be on the move these days."

"Yeah, busy at the mill. Helping the war effort is a lot of work you know."

He nodded seriously. "Mrs. Lackland's birthday party is this weekend," he informed her as if she didn't know.

"Yes."

Stepping close to her, he grabbed her hand. "Would you do me the honor, Robyn?"

She gently pulled her hand from his. "I can't," she told him. "I, uh, I already have a date."

"Is that so?" he asked in a deep, serious tone.

She avoided his intense gaze. "Yes, it is."

He frowned but nodded once.

"But, uh, I have to go now. I'll see you around." Then Robyn made as quick an escape as her dignity would allow.

CHAPTER 4

Guy Gisbourne followed Robyn's retreat upstairs with his eyes. With every step she took away from him, a tension pulled at his chest, telling him to go after her. He fought the feeling, reveling in it, and stayed where she'd left him.

"She's headstrong, that one," John said, having connected Guy's gaze with Robyn's withdraw. "She always has been. If you're looking to get anywhere soon, I suggest directing your gaze to someone more...pliant."

That's one of the things I like about her, Guy thought, but he didn't say anything. Turning to John, Guy looked down at the shorter man and tilted his head, indicating he was at his disposal.

John entered the sitting room. Guy followed and closed the door behind them. Once John had settled into an armchair, he told his subordinate to begin his report with a glance.

"Collections are mostly on schedule," Guy began. "Everyone has paid on time, except for one."

John raised an eyebrow.

"A jeweler called Orwitz in Southwell has requested a month's delay. He claims the war has cut deep into his profits."

John's bland expression didn't give away his thoughts. "Give him a week."

Guy nodded his understanding. "Plans for the rally are moving forward?" he asked.

"Isabella knows what to do," John commented. "Just be there when the day comes."

Guy signaled his agreement. "The detective who gave the Accias such a hard time is still sniffing around. What would you like me to do about him?"

John quirked his mouth in thought. "Is he getting close?"

Guy shook his head. "Not really. His superiors are keeping him busy for us, and he hasn't been able to gain access to any of our businesses as of yet."

"Is he still concentrating on Lackland Steel?"

"As far as I can tell."

"Visit Captain Rorke. Express to him the importance of his continued cooperation."

Guy dipped his head.

John pointed at a nearby side table with a wooden box with a stylized "LC" burned into the lid. "The prototype is done."

Guy opened the box and found a sleek, steel gun. It had a thick barrel with a long sliding switch on one side. He knew what the gun was supposed to do, that the switch chose what kind of armor-piercing dart would be shot, that the different chemicals did everything from cause paralysis, to burning agony, to almost instant death.

"Take it with you," John said. "I want to know how it does."

Guy dipped his head but had no intention of using such a weapon.

"The Golden Arrow," John continued, lacing his fingers and resting them on his lap. "Have you found out what the problem was?"

"I found Jimmy, the runner who was working that day, hiding in some rat hole in The Doncz. After some...persuasion, he told me where we came up short."

"And?"

"It was Fallows."

John's face flushed with fury, his lips pressing into a tight line. "After all we've done for him..." he muttered. "Even making him manager wasn't enough." Glaring at Guy, John growled, "I want this ingrate dealt with...permanently."

Guy nodded, his stomach hardening at the task ahead.

"And Gisbourne?" John drew Guy's gaze back to his. "Make it slow."

CHAPTER 5

Robyn's commute to Lackland Steel was much the same as usual since the war. Workers, primarily women, flooded the sidewalks and platforms as they hurried off to their jobs. Through the train window, the sun was still rising, and it turned the bay golden through the smog. It was pleasant to see for once.

But the contentment Robyn felt was fleeting, and she eventually passed through the gates of the steel mill. She punched in without a word to anyone and made her way to the locker room.

Weaving through the lockers and benches, she passed women in various stages of undress. She tried to slip through unnoticed and managed to get her locker open and pull the fresh pair of overalls from her bag before anyone addressed her.

"Should be locked up," Mildred muttered under her breath.

Robyn ignored her, knowing the comment was aimed at her.

"How does it feel, Loxley?" she pressed.

Robyn took off her dress and reached for the overalls she'd placed on the bench. Mildred grabbed them before she could.

"I said, 'how does it feel?' How does it feel to be a traitor? Our boys are over there risking their lives, and here you are undermining the war effort on the home front." Mildred sneered, holding Robyn's overalls hostage.

"Give it a rest, Mildred," Lili snapped, snatching Robyn's clothes and handing them to her.

"Dirty Jap-lover," Mildred spat, glaring at Robyn.

Robyn took a menacing move toward her, but Lili stepped between. "She's not worth it, Robyn," she whispered.

Robyn turned her back to Mildred and stuffed her legs into her work clothes. She didn't look up as Mildred left.

"Why do you let her get to you?" Lili asked, sitting beside her friend on the bench while Robyn laced up her boots too tight with angry jerking movements.

"You should have let me deck her," Robyn muttered, her jaw tense from the effort to unclench it. "Maybe a good punch in the nose would teach her some manners."

"And who would that help?" Lili reasoned. "You only would have gotten written up by Miss Wilson, and you love this job."

"Don't try to convince me with your logic."

Lili laughed.

"I do love this job." Robyn sighed. "And I've worked hard to get it."

Lili nodded. "You have. So don't let someone like Mildred Pennyworth get under your skin."

"You're right, as usual."

"Or you could tell Mr. Gisbourne... I'm sure he would be glad to have anyone who would dare disrespect you fired," she suggested slyly.

Robyn groaned. "No way. I already have enough problems with management handling me with kid gloves as it is. If it wasn't for the war, I don't think they ever would have let me do anything more than file papers."

"Okay, then figure out another way to cope. You've been here much longer than the rest of us. And when all the men come home, and we go back to being wives and mothers and secretaries, you will still be here, working at the mill just like you want. The war will end eventually."

"But those like Mildred won't learn. They'll keep being the bullies they are."

"It's not your responsibility to change her."

"Can't I hit her just a little bit?" Robyn pleaded.

Lili turned her no-nonsense gaze on Robyn. "What do you think?"

"Will would have let me," Robyn muttered. *But Will isn't here,* she thought.

Before Lili could respond, the shift whistle pierced the thick walls of the locker room, ordering them to work.

As bad as the soot in the mill was, it was the heat that was the real trouble. The furnaces, the foundry, the whole place ran on the ability to smelt and cast steel, and that took a lot of white-hot fire. It was raw heat, like being forced to sit too close to your comfortable, winter fire for too long.

It was a dangerous job, so they all had to pay close attention. There was no time for personal feelings of animosity or deep thought; that kind of behavior could get someone killed.

The mask over Robyn's nose and mouth may have kept the dust out, but it did nothing for the smell. The sulfur scent of burning steel was something she'd never gotten used to, and if she could have taken a repair job anywhere else, she would have.

Robyn blinked her eyes against the tears that always came before her nose adjusted. Her supervisor, Philip, approached her to give her an update on how the machines were operating so far that morning.

She spent most of the day fixing a broken-down crane.

Unlike the day prior, she didn't rush out after her shift was over. She went back to the locker room with the others, washed the soot and oil off her, and changed into her day clothes. Lili and Robyn were reapplying their cosmetics in the mirror when Lili addressed her.

"You ran out so quick yesterday I didn't get a chance to talk to you. Where did you go?" she asked.

Robyn hadn't told anyone but Marian anything about her trying to get in to see Will—most had a hard enough time just knowing they were friends—so she hedged Lili's question. "Yeah, I was in a rush. Why? Did you want to talk about something?"

"Not really, I thought we could go out for a drink at The Hammer and Anvil."

Robyn hid her frown by applying lipstick. "You know I never go there."

"Right, because it's owned by the Lacklands, and the workers give you too much favor. I just thought socializing with the other girls would help you fit in better at work."

"I don't think I'll fit in any better when our fellow workers see the owner and bartender of The Hammer and Anvil bow and scrape at me. But I was planning on going to the Blue Boar Inn. Would you like to join me there?"

Lili clicked her tongue. "That place is on the other side of town," she whined.

"Exactly, and no one knows I'm a ward of the Lacklands there."

Lili looked at her watch and sighed. "I would, you know I would, but I have some things to do tonight, and I only have time for a quick one anyway."

"No problem. Next time."

The Blue Boar Inn had been a very popular pub at the turn of the century. It was the sturdy sort of tavern you'd likely find in an English village. It had a thick wooden bar, scratched and marked from decades of use; there was even a deep gouge where an overzealous prohibitionist had taken an axe to it. Tall stools surrounded the counter, and mismatched farm tables lined the walls. The rafters of the short, seven-foot ceiling were exposed but clean, without even the wispy strands of a cobweb.

The glory days of the inn may have been bygone, but it still held its own. And like every good pub, there were the same loyal customers, though it wasn't unusual to see a new face every day.

The bartender, Eadom, smiled at Robyn as she entered. "It's been a bit, Robyn. I was beginning to think you'd found a new place to grab a pint," he greeted.

Robyn returned his smile as she bent to pat Brian, the Saint Bernard, on his giant head where he slept near the door. The dog peeked through heavy lids at being pet and gave a sleepy wag of the tail before drifting off again. "Aw, come on, Eadom. You know I'd never abandon you like that. Where else can I sit on my favorite stool and have a chat with my favorite bartender?"

He leaned over the bar toward her and smirked. "Try to charm me all you like, you still got to pay."

"When have I ever stiffed you, Eadom?"

He raised an eyebrow at her.

"Other than that one time, but that was forever ago. Besides, I paid you back."

He slid over to the beer engine and pulled the handle three times, pumping dark, clear beer with a bright, fluffy head into a pint glass. Then he handed it to her over the bar.

"You're a gentleman, Eadom. Don't let anyone tell you any different."

"Yeah, yeah," he said.

Robyn drank deep; it was smooth with the slightest hint of a bite. She sighed in contentment and set her glass on the counter. "Now then," she called, clapping her hands together. "Who wants to challenge me to a round of darts?"

The other patrons avoided eye contact as she looked around the room. "Oh, come on, you cowards. No one wants to try to take on the champ?"

"Looks like they've all learned their lesson," Eadom snickered.

Just then, the front door opened and a newcomer straggled in. He wore a long, black overcoat, a charcoal fedora, and a scarf over his nose and mouth to keep the toxins at bay. Hanging up his things on a coat-rack near the door, he revealed longish, dark brown hair, tousled from his hat and curled at the tips.

"You," Robyn called to the stranger.

He looked up from eyeing Brian, his dark gaze meeting hers. Her stomach fluttered slightly. Robyn grinned at him, but he just stared blandly back.

"Want to play darts with me?"

He paused as though thinking over her offer, but his expression still gave nothing away. "All right," he agreed in a steady baritone.

She tried to hide her glee at finding a new challenger, and such a fox at that.

"Now you're in for it," Eadom chuckled. He poured the man a pint and told him it was "on the house."

"Are you kidding me, Eadom?" Robyn whined.

"Hey, I don't want to hear any of your moaning. Anyone who's willing to attempt to take you down a peg deserves a reward."

"You wound me, Eadom."

"Yeah, yeah."

"What's your name, stranger?" Robyn asked her opponent as they made their way to the dartboard, noting his ringless left hand.

"Alaric Nottingham," he answered.

"I'm Robyn." she said, grabbing the darts from the board and handed him his. He was a little over half a foot taller than her. She might have described him as tall had she not met Little Jon the night before. His suit jacket accentuated his square shoulders and narrow waist. She smiled up into his poker face. "I'll even let you go first."

"Today seems to be turning into my lucky day," he said.

"Well, don't look too much into it. Your luck is about to change," she teased.

"You think so?"

Before she could come back with a smart remark, he threw the first dart, and it landed in the triple twenty.

Robyn sized him up again, her eyes traveling from his worn-in but well-polished pre-war oxfords up his lean frame to his hidden smirk and dark eyes, which shined ever-so-slightly with mischief.

Her smile broadened. She met his gaze with a tilt of her head and a raised chin. "Where are you from, Rick?"

He paused at her shortening his name but didn't correct her. "Pittsburgh."

"Ah, that explains the accent. Why don't you let me give you a welcome gift?" Turning around, she threw her first dart, nestling it beside his in the triple twenty.

He hummed a short laugh. "Seems like this'll be the first time in a while someone will present me with a challenge."

"Game on."

Alaric Nottingham was a true contender. Robyn couldn't remember the last time she'd been so close to losing. After she'd won the first game, things got serious.

"Again," he commanded without bite. But something in his muted baritone made her want to comply.

"You mean you'd like to lose to me again? Very well, I accept," she taunted.

Robyn watched her opponent closely as they played. His lines were clean and straight, his shoulders and arms at disciplined angles. His eyes never wavered from their target. And when he wasn't staring down the dartboard, she felt his singular gaze on her, not that it affected her ability to win.

As they moved on to play best of five, Rick rewarded her wins with another round of drinks. It was still her throw when he brought her bounty back to the table nearest the dartboard. The horns of Glenn Miller blared from the jukebox, and she swayed to the music as "Vagabond Dreams" filled the small pub.

"You like music?" Rick asked as she made another shot.

"Love it. You?"

He nodded, stepping up to take his turn. "Who's your favorite?" he asked.

"Bing Crosby. His voice...it fills me with warmth."

"He's talented. I especially like his jazz songs."

"Do you play any instruments?" she asked

He shook his head. "No, but I sing a little."

"Do you?" she said. *I'd like to hear that,* she thought

"How about you? Are you musical?"

"Absolutely not." Robyn laughed. "I couldn't carry a tune if you put it in a basket. I'll leave that to the professionals, but I like to dance. Do you? Like to dance, that is."

He nodded. "It's nice if you have the right partner."

His gaze held hers for a moment longer than necessary, and her heart thumped. *Was that an innuendo?* she wondered. He looked away before she could figure it out.

"Here's something jazzy for you," she said as The Andrews Sisters' "Boogie Woogie Bugle Boy" came on.

"Yeah, that's what I like."

If she hadn't been watching him so carefully, she wouldn't have seen the slight smile in one corner of his mouth. But when the meaning of the wartime lyrics started to sink in, the little dimple turned down into a frown.

He looked into his warm beer, running his thumb down the side of the glass.

"You have friends over there?" she asked, trying to guess the reason for his mood change.

He nodded, then clenched his hands into quivering fists.

Did he lose someone already? Was he not fit for duty? Is that why he isn't there too? She kept her questions to herself. "If I win this round, will you sing for me?" she asked by way of distraction. "I'm interested to see just how good you are. I mean, you can't be any worse at singing than you are at darts," she teased.

"You're confident," he responded in a humoring tone that said he sort of liked it.

She shrugged. "I've earned it."

His eyes smiled. "All right."

Robyn won only marginally in their best of five. She laughed in triumph, beaming up at him.

He sighed, a long, low sigh of defeat. "All right, all right. What would you like to hear?"

"Surprise me," she told him, not able to contain her grin.

He looked around the bar at Eadom and the few other patrons; no one was paying them much mind. But he pursed his lips, clearly embarrassed at the thought of suddenly bursting into song in a public place. He held his hand out to her.

The feel of her fingertips on his sent a jolt of electricity through her, and she held her breath.

Her skin flushed as he pulled her in close to him, into a dancing position. Leaning in, he touched his cheek to hers. The scent of him hit her, and she resisted the urge to breathe deep. Sandalwood with the hint of orange. *His aftershave?* she wondered.

And then he started to sing, only loud enough for her to hear over the jukebox music. She supposed it appeared to others that they were dancing to whatever was playing, but she didn't hear anything but his low, smooth voice singing "Blue Orchids" in her ear.

Her face grew hot, and she didn't know if he noticed that she quivered in his arms. The pub, the patrons, Eadom, Brian, everything fell away as her senses were filled with Alaric Nottingham. His voice, his scent, the solid heat of him so close to her, her mind swirled in this shadowy stranger.

As he let the last note whisper from his lips, she pulled back slowly. His dark eyes held her in their thrall; she couldn't have looked away if she'd wanted to.

Robyn licked her parted lips and swallowed with difficulty. And as he trailed his thumb along her jawline, her eyelids fluttered. Her pulse pounded in her ears, and she couldn't steady her breath.

His lips were soft and supple as he leaned down to hers. It was a slow, tender kiss, one that made promises. And it was over far too quickly.

Pulling back suddenly, Rick seemed to realize he'd just kissed a near complete stranger.

Robyn's body felt cold, and she shivered at the chill his heat had left behind.

"I'm sorry I—"

"Don't be," she cut him off.

He met her eyes fleetingly, replacing his poker face.

He turned his attention to the dartboard, and she saw Eadom watching them from the corner of his eye.

Rick cleared his throat and suggested they play best of seven.

She looked over at the clock. "It's getting rather late, but I'll tell you what: one more game. If you win, you can take the Blue Boar Inn darts title. If I win, you'll fulfill my request, no matter what."

He paused only for a moment before declaring it a deal.

The final round was fierce, and he was winning. With one dart left, he was only three points from victory. As he lined up his shot, she moved closer to him.

"I think you may want to aim a little more to the left," she encouraged in a low whisper.

He faltered and his dart hit nineteen. He squinted his irritation and turned toward her, then froze when he saw how close she was.

"Bust," she murmured with a smirk.

"I didn't expect you to play dirty," he mumbled.

"Only when it's a means to an end."

"You want to win that badly?"

"I want you to grant my request that much," she corrected.

Robyn finished the game, winning with ease. He downed the rest of his beer and leaned his elbows on the table.

"All right, then. What is it you want so desperately?"

She smiled. "Take me on a date tomorrow."

He crinkled his eyebrows. "Pardon me?"

Robyn knew he'd heard her, so she just gave him her best cheeky grin.

He leveled his gaze at her, and she wondered what emotion was behind that steady stare. After a tense moment, he said, "You could have just asked."

"Where's the fun in that?" She laughed. "So where are we going?"

He tilted his head back a little in thought, then looked at her out of the corner of his eye. "Do you like levy?"

Her grin widened. "Love it."

CHAPTER 6

Robyn agreed to meet Rick the following evening at Legumighty Stadium. It turned out he had tickets for the levy game between the Pittsburgh Bowmen and the Midshire Mongoose.

Nothing could spoil her mood at the thought of seeing him again. She would have even been able to ignore Mildred's sneering comments had she not been scheduled for an earlier shift. Her mind was full of Alaric Nottingham as she changed into her overalls and prepared for work.

She found his surreptitious amusement intriguing, that shadow of what may have been a smile. His dark gaze was steady in a keen sort of way, and she got the idea it reflected his personality: steadfast and sombre, but not so much as to lack a sense of humor. And the kiss... Well, there was no getting it out of her head.

After work, Robyn still had too many hours to kill before she was to meet her alluring stranger. Sure, she could go home and get ready, but then she'd just be drifting around the house until it was time to leave. And that would only invite questions from Marian and the Lacklands.

Sitting on the bench in the locker room, Robyn glanced at the brown bag in her locker. It had what was left of the lunch Sarah had packed her: a few chocolate chip cookies wrapped in a napkin. The thought of a bright-eyed boy filtered to the surface of her mind. Snatching the bag, she decided to visit her new friends in Sherwood.

It didn't take her nearly as long to reach the bridge over the canal as the first time, but then she'd taken a meandering path before. As she stepped onto the bridge, a voice she did not recognize called out, "who goes there?"

"Robyn. I came to see Jon and Much," she told the voice.

At her explanation, a young man—a youth perhaps too young to yet be called a man at all—with a head of unkempt blond hair stepped from behind the wall where Little Jon had been a few days before. His bright eyes smiled as he said, "Looks like she was right again. Follow me. I'll take you to them."

She crossed the bridge to catch up to her guide.

"I'm David Doncaster," he told her as he began to lead the way. "I've heard a lot about you."

"From Jon and Much?"

David chuckled. "Yeah, well Much has talked of little else since. He was very excited when Tuck said you'd be coming back today."

How would anyone know I was coming today? I didn't even know until a little while ago, Robyn thought. "Tuck?" she asked.

David nodded. "Tuck is...sort of hard to explain, but don't worry. Jon and Much are with her now. She's anxious to meet you, too."

Robyn's skin prickled in anticipation of the unknown, and she felt the hum of excitement that comes from doing something potentially reckless. As she followed David, she looked around Sherwood again. It was more depressing in full daylight. The dereliction was so blatant, the type of squalor that was hard to look at. The shadows of dusk had left a lot to the imagination.

David led her to a Gothic-style abbey with a conspicuous lack of crosses and crucifixes. The stained-glass windows were long shattered, and the wind whistled through their empty frames. They climbed the crumbling stone steps, and David pulled the thick, wooden door open by its huge, iron knocker.

Robyn gasped as they entered. She'd never seen so much green. The columns barely holding up the roof were covered in moss and ivy. Tall grass sprung up through cracks in the floor. Somehow, the sunlight filtering through the once-glass windows looked golden as if no smog dampened its rays.

"Wow," she whispered, frozen in place.

"I know," David agreed. "It's still hard for me to believe a place like this exists in the world. But Tuck has a way of making things grow."

Robyn followed David through the nave to a side doorway with no door. Their footsteps echoed off the stone walls of the cloister. The arched windows opened toward a courtyard where a large greenhouse stood. She could see thick streaks of green through the glass.

"What...?" she turned to David, letting her question trail off.

"Our crops," he answered, following her gaze.

"Your what?" She couldn't keep the incredulous squeak from her voice.

"Tuck will explain everything."

They walked around the cloister and climbed a flight of sturdy stone stairs. Along another hallway, opened on one side with a set of arched window frames, was a series of doors. David stopped at the farthest door from the stairs and knocked loudly. A cacophony of barks answered the sound. After a moment, the door creaked open and a pack of mutts ran out, wagging and sniffing Robyn with interest. Much grinned up from the doorway.

"Señorita Robyn!" he cheered. "Tuck said you'd come today."

Robyn smiled at the boy, letting the dogs smell her while keeping the bag of cookies from their reach. "Hola, Much. I hear you've been waiting for me. I brought something for you." She handed him the paper bag with the cookies in it.

He unwrapped them with relish, his face unable to contain his joy. "Cookies," he gasped. "Gracias, señorita."

Robyn pet the boy's hair. "You are very welcome."

As Much began devouring his treat, Robyn glanced around the room. The north wall was covered in greenery, moss and ivy barely leaving the grey stone visible. A small fountain tinkled cheerfully on the west side, and the wind howled in the windowless frame to the east. To the south, a roaring fire crackled in a huge, stone hearth, beside which sat Little Jon and a young woman with black hair. She appeared to be in her late teens, her curly hair was a bit wild, though not so much that it looked uncared for. But her grey eyes told another story. She had seen a lot in her short life. She knew things others did not. Even so, her eyes were not haunted. They still held the optimism of youth.

She smiled a warm, welcoming grin, dimples blooming in her cheeks. "Hello, Robyn. We've been expecting you. I'm Tucker, but you can call me Tuck. You know Jon and Much, and you've rather unceremoniously met my hounds."

She pointed to a fluffy dog with mismatched ears, one floppy and one that stood up. "That's Kisses." The dog turned toward Tuck when it heard its name, but it quickly returned its attention to Much and his cookies.

"That's Bell," Tuck continued, indicating a slim hound with floppy ears and a short, copper coat.

"That little one is Beauty."

Robyn glanced at the squat, long mutt with golden fur and ears so long she no doubt tripped over them.

"And finally, that giant is Fangs." The monster Tuck referred to had a head that came up to Robyn's chest. He had salt and pepper fur and a tail that whistled like a whip as he wagged.

Much was having a hard time keeping the cookies away from Fangs. But when he demanded the dogs sit, they obeyed without incident.

Robyn turned back to the younger woman. "Everyone keeps telling me you expected me today. How did you know I was coming?"

Tuck gave her a cheeky smile and leaned back in her chair as if to say, "I'll never tell."

"Tuck is a witch," Much informed around a mouthful of cookies.

Robyn raised her eyebrows at him, her mind swirling with memories of priestly sermons from her youth. "You're teasing me, Much. There's no such thing as witches."

"Are you so certain?" Tuck challenged, one eyebrow quirked.

Robyn stilled at her question. It had certainly been a while since she'd attended mass, not that Eleanor still didn't pressure her to do so. But witches? She couldn't believe such bogeymen existed, or any such supernatural or divine beings for that matter. Or at least...she'd never seen any proof. "You're having me on. What's really going on? Jon, did you send someone to follow me, or what?"

She looked over at Little Jon who shook his head.

"Come on, magic isn't real. I mean, you aren't really telling me you made a pact with the devil to get magic powers like those religious fanatics say, are you?"

Tuck giggled. "Of course not! The devil isn't even real. He's just a character people use to explain the bad in the world and avoid responsibility for the sins they've committed. Magick is...it just is."

Robyn raised an eyebrow. "You're serious?"

"Absolutely."

"All right, prove it. Levitate something or throw a fireball."

Tuck laughed uproariously, a cheerful sound, nothing like the cackle one would expect a witch to have. "That's not what *real* magick is like. But wouldn't it be nice if it was?"

Robyn raised an eyebrow. "Okay then, what is *real* magick like?"

Tuck's eyes sparkled with the remnants of her laughter. "I'll show you if you're really interested."

Robyn shrugged. "I'm open-minded."

Tuck quirked one corner of her mouth and waved her hand, motioning Robyn to sit at the small table near the fire. Little Jon rose to give her his seat.

As Tuck and Robyn sat across from each other, Tuck pulled a deck of cards from a drawstring bag. Holding the deck between her hands, she closed her eyes and smoothed her features. Robyn frowned when nothing happened, thinking there would be a glow or sparkling light.

Opening her eyes, Tuck handed the deck to Robyn. "Shuffle the cards as much as you like," she instructed.

It was a little awkward at first, the cards being much larger than a standard playing card deck, but Robyn got the hang of it. After shuffling three times, she placed the deck on the table between them. Tuck took them up and overturned the first six at the top of the deck.

Gazing seriously at the cards, she silently evaluated them. Finally, Tuck picked up one of the laid-out cards and showed it to Robyn. "This is you," she said.

Robyn stared at the armored knight on a horse, staff in hand. "The knight of wands?" she asked, reading the label.

Tuck nodded. "You're bold, courageous, not afraid to go where others won't in pursuit of your goals and adventures, but you don't always think things through before you act. Still, you're charismatic, and others will-ingly follow you."

"So are a lot of people," Robyn commented, unconvinced.

Tuck pursed her lips slightly, barely suppressing her smirk, as her grey eyes danced. Dropping her gaze back to the table, she leaned forward and showed Robyn a card with a tower burning in a violent thunderstorm. "A major change is coming to your life." Then she held up a card with a single sword stuck in a stone, a crown on its hilt. "The ace of swords was reversed. This major change is likely to be brought on by a painful truth."

"How am I supposed to know if any of this is true until after it happens?"

Tuck shrugged. "That, unfortunately, is how it usually works." She looked back down at the cards and then held up a card where a man and a woman faced one another, each holding a cup. "There is a man," she declared.

Robyn's face flushed as Rick's dark eyes rose to the surface of her mind. "What does it say about him?" Robyn asked, unable to help herself.

Tuck tilted her head ever so slightly as if pricking her ear to a sound no one else could hear. "The two of cups can represent a passionate romantic relationship."

"What else?"

She held up a card of a man carrying a bindle over his shoulder, his dog by his side, as they walked dangerously close to a cliff's edge. "The fool," Tuck declared.

"Does that mean this man will make a fool of me?"

Tuck shook her head. "No, the fool is about being at a crossroads. It likely means that this big change in your life will come with a variety of choices."

"And the last one?" Robyn pointed at the card Tuck had yet to show her, where a blindfolded woman on a throne held a scale in one hand and a sword in the other.

"Justice. The decisions you make at this crossroads will have major impacts on the future."

Robyn frowned as Tuck's words left her uneasy. *But this doesn't prove anything,* Robyn thought. "So if you don't get this ability from Satan, where does it come from?" she asked the younger woman.

Tuck's eyes again reflecting wisdom well beyond her years. "I'm not special. Anyone can do it with patience, practice, and an openness to the energy around them. Sure, some people are born with innate abilities, but more often, it's how we were raised, whether our natural perception was encouraged or squashed by those around us."

Robyn didn't respond.

"You're still unconvinced," Tuck said, smoothly leaning back while lacing her fingers together. "That's all right. You don't have to believe for me to know magick is real. Besides, it's like you said, you won't know I'm telling the truth until you can prove what I've said will happen has happened."

"I guess I'll suspend my belief or disbelief for the time being."

Tuck's dimples reappeared.

"Is this how you knew I was coming then? The cards told you?"

Tuck nodded. "The tarot has shown me a lot about you lately. And when Jon told me about your visit the other day, I knew you'd finally come."

"Finally? What does that mean? There isn't a prophecy about me or anything is there?"

Tuck burst into laughter, the sound echoing pleasantly off the stone walls. "No, nothing like that. But the cards did say a time of turmoil is coming to Sherwood. And I believe it is you, Robyn, who will foreshadow this challenge."

Robyn frowned. "I don't want to bring you all trouble."

Tuck gazed steadily at Robyn. "Whether the challenge presented will be caused by you or not is uncertain and immaterial. What is important is that you are here to meet it, Robyn. The knight of wands will bring Sherwood through the turmoil ahead."

The atmosphere grew heavy, the air thick with the gravity of Tuck's pronouncement.

The weight of Tuck's expectation settled on Robyn's shoulders. "Well, I uh... I can't stay for long. I only stopped to visit with Much and Jon." Robyn looked down at her watch. "In fact, I better get going. I have plans tonight."

Tuck smiled, and the heavy atmosphere dissipated.

"Next time," Tuck said. "We have a lot to talk about, but we should do it when you have more time."

"Okay," Robyn agreed, shoving down her curiosity. "I'll come back again soon."

"How about we walk you out?" Little Jon offered, placing a large hand on Much's head.

Robyn smiled at the pair. "That would be great. Thank you."

CHAPTER 7

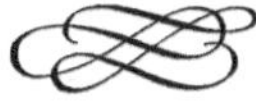

Robyn had no trouble finding Rick once it was time to meet him at Legumighty Stadium. In a sea of black and silver, the team colors of the Midshire Mongoose, he alone wore the green and brown of the Pittsburgh Bowmen. He stood near the entrance as he'd promised.

"You're brave," Robyn said as she sneaked up beside him.

The only indication she'd surprised him was the slight wideness in his eyes. "Why is that?" he asked.

She waved the end of his brown and green striped scarf. "You must be to wear this at a home game."

His eyes smiled, though she couldn't see his mouth behind his scarf. "I may not make it out alive if Pittsburgh wins."

"Well, I wouldn't worry about *that*," she teased.

Robyn thought she could hear him chuckle under his breath, but she might have imagined it; it was hard to say over the noise of the crowd.

"Shall we?" he asked, holding his arm out to her.

She slipped her arm in his, and her heart bounced at the contact, even between the layers of his clothes. She warmed at the thought of his breath on her face and how his arms had felt around her.

After the ticket taker had handed him back their tickets, she asked him if he'd ever been to Legumighty Stadium before.

"No, this is my first time."

"Should I lead the way then?" she asked. "I've been coming here since I was a kid."

He handed her the tickets, and she looked at their seat sections. Grabbing his hand, she led him to the upper balcony. His hand was warm around hers. He had long fingers, not too rough to the touch. Their seats were close enough to see what was going on, but not as close as she was used to sitting.

As they waited for the game to start, Rick offered to get some popcorn, and Robyn held their seats when he went. They didn't have any time to talk when he got back because the crowd cheered as the players skated onto the court to warm up. They practiced maneuvers on their hover skates and took discus shots at their respective goalies.

Robyn clapped along with the crowd, cheering for the boys in the black and silver sweaters. The home team smiled and waved at the fans.

Rick's cheers of "go Bowmen!" were drowned out by the cries of the mongoose fans, but Robyn smiled over at him.

"Thank you for bringing me. It's been a while since I've seen a game," she yelled to him.

"What?" he asked, bending close to her so he could hear her over the roar of the crowd.

"Thank you!" she called into his ear.

He nodded with a slight smile, showing her he'd heard.

As the referee approached middle court with the discus, the crowd quieted for the face-off. The centres for each team met in the middle, shook hands, then crouched in a ready position.

When the referee threw the discus into the air, the centres shoved each other to be the one to catch it when it came down. Unfortunately, Leo Pozmowski, the centre for Pittsburgh, caught the discus and tossed it back to his left wing, and thus the first half began.

Pittsburgh's left wing didn't hold onto the discus for long; Midshire's centre, Frank Paulson, checked him into the boards. The crowd erupted, and Richie Otterson, Midshire's right wing, took possession of the discus.

The game went on like this, the teams trading possession and attempting to throw the discus into the other team's goal net. Even though Pittsburgh was higher in the season's ranking, Midshire was keeping up.

The fight was fierce, the crowd was lively, and Robyn cheered as if her voice was the fuel keeping the home team energized. As a result, she was already hoarse by halftime. Still, she smiled over at Rick, her face hot from yelling.

"I'm impressed," Rick told her while they waited for the second half to start. "Midshire is so low in the rankings this year. And with them having traded Alderby last year, I didn't think they'd stand a chance."

"Never underestimate the home court advantage," she croaked.

He raised his eyebrows at the sound. "You want to get some water?"

Robyn nodded, and they rose to go to concessions. The lines were long, but they waited patiently.

"How long have you been a levy fan?" Robyn asked Rick.

"Since I was little. My dad used to bring me to games sometimes, and later I would listen on the radio."

"Were you listening when Pittsburgh won the cup a few years back?"

"Of course!" he said animatedly. "You couldn't go into a pub without hearing the game. And when Townsend made that final goal with seconds to spare? My heart stopped. The whole city took to the streets after that win, like a parade at midnight."

Robyn grinned at his enthusiasm, glad he was showing her something more than that steady stare, not that she didn't like that too. "Yeah, I saw pictures in the paper."

The second half had already started by the time they returned to their seats. They had even missed a goal by Midshire, tying the score.

The rest of the game was an intense blur. Back and forth, the teams were neck in neck. And they watched with rapt enthusiasm. They shouted, they cheered, they felt the frustration of near misses. Rick and Robyn even taunted each other as the game wore on, each trading comments and gestures as the teams traded places in the lead.

But with the score tied and thirty seconds to go, Midshire took possession. Otterson zoomed down the court, discus in hand. The crowd held its breath as he approached Pittsburgh's defense. But in a move that would go down in levy history, he picked up speed and skated sideways along the boards, effectively avoiding the defensemen. Paulson checked Pozmowski as he approached Otterson, and Otterson let loose a beautiful throw that sailed right past Pittsburgh's goalie.

Any trace of voice Robyn had was gone in that last roar of victory. Jumping up and down, she hugged Rick around the neck. And as she grinned up at him, he smiled back, seemingly unaffected by his team's loss.

After the game was over, Rick and Robyn were in no rush to leave with the crowd. Holding hands, they let the rest of the spectators hurry around them to wherever they were going. But when they reached the entrance to the stadium, they had to face a decision.

He gave her a hesitant smile. "Listen, I feel bad I couldn't take you to dinner because I had to work before the game. My apartment isn't far from here…"

Robyn stared up at him, trying to encourage the rest of his invitation with her eyes.

"I have some potato soup my landlady made, and I'm sure a warm cup of tea would feel good on your throat." He didn't meet her gaze, perhaps nervous she would refuse or not wanting to pressure her to accept.

She took his hand again, and when he looked at her, she smiled and nodded.

Legumighty Stadium was in Stockport, the historic district of Midshire. There wasn't much of a commercial area around the stadium, even crossing the street brought them into a neighborhood of Victorian houses and townhomes.

With every step, her hand felt warmer in his. She looked up at Rick from the corner of her eye as they walked. She couldn't see much of his face between his hat and scarf, but she took in his tall, sturdy form as best she could. It had been a while, too long, since she'd welcomed a man's touch, too caught up in everything going on in the world. But remembering the solidity of his embrace as he danced with her at the Blue Boar, remembering the tenderness of his kiss, she hoped this invitation to his apartment was what she thought it was.

In the middle of a row of houses on an unassuming street, they stopped on the bricked sidewalk before a short, iron gate.

"This is it," he told her, nodding to the yellow Victorian with white trim.

"This is yours?" she asked, unable to manage more than a whisper.

"Well, I rent an upper room from Mrs. Stanley. I was lucky to find such a nice landlady when I came to town. She even cooks and cleans."

That does sound nice, Robyn thought.

He unhitched the gate and ushered her in with a gentle hand on her back. On the porch, he held a finger to his lips. "Mrs. Stanley is probably asleep. Let's try not to wake her."

Robyn nodded and followed him in. The entryway and the house beyond were dark, indicating he'd been right about his landlady's hours. He flicked on the overhead light, revealing a small reception area with a table and a coat rack. They removed their coats and scarves and hung them on the rack. Then he motioned for her to follow him upstairs.

There was no silencing the creaks of the stairs as they ascended to the second floor. Robyn cringed, hoping Mrs. Stanley was a deep sleeper. Once on the landing, she followed Rick down the small hall and through the door at the end. The light showed what one would expect a newly-arrived bachelor's room to look like.

There was a bed with a nightstand, a round table with two chairs, and an armoire. There must have been a bathroom somewhere else because there wasn't even a mirror or wash basin. The room was tidy and the bed made. *Either Rick is quite clean, or Mrs. Stanley runs a tight ship,* Robyn thought.

As she took in the room, Rick stood in the doorway. "Make yourself at home," he said. "I'll go to the kitchen and heat up that soup."

She nodded her acknowledgment before he shut the door to go downstairs. The sparsity of decoration confirmed her initial impression of Rick: steadfast and sombre. He had nothing useless or frivolous in his personal space. She stopped at a picture frame on the bedside table. The simple pine frame was light as she picked it up.

In the old photograph, a woman with flapper short hair smiled, and her dark eyes laughed as she pressed her cheek to that of a boy of six or seven. The boy's face had that childish chubbiness that didn't quite hide the features of what would one day be Alaric Nottingham. He grinned at the camera, a gap where one of his front baby teeth had been. The pure joy in his expression made Robyn smile.

Hearing the stairs creak, she replaced the frame on the bedside table and went to open the door for Rick.

He carried a tray with two bowls of soup and two mugs of what smelled like peppermint tea. He placed the tray on the table, and they each took a seat.

"I'm sorry we're eating so late, but Mrs. Stanley is an excellent cook, so I think it'll be worth it," he said.

Robyn waved her hand to tell him it was not a problem. After tasting the soup, she smiled and nodded. He'd been right to praise Mrs. Stanley. And the warm tea was soothing on her throat, just as he'd said it would be.

"Thank you," she whispered.

"You're welcome."

There was a thick silence as they stared at their empty dishes.

"I'm not really the talkative type," he murmured like an apology. "And your throat must still be sore. Would you like me to make you more tea? Or do you want me to walk you to the station?"

He stood and reached for her mug, and she stilled his hand with hers. The question in his dark eyes as he met her gaze must have been answered because he leaned down and kissed her, his lips firm with urgency. Need slammed into her, her body flushing with heat.

She breathed in deep through her nose, rising to meet his desire on equal footing, and pulled him closer, his body hard and unyielding against her. She shivered as his tongue slipped into her mouth and licked hers.

Desire. Passion. Raw lust. All shone in his eyes as he looked at her, and she never wanted to see that reserved stoicism again. He reached for her with a hunger she knew she could satisfy, and she wanted nothing more than to do so.

Alaric Nottingham didn't need words to know what she wanted. He seemed completely tuned into what her body was saying as he caressed and stroked. So when he reached for the condoms in the drawer of his nightstand, she was already raving for him.

Pulling back only slightly, Rick stared deep into Robyn's eyes. His dark gaze focused on her as if nothing else in the world existed. And that's when she learned that words were overrated with Alaric Nottingham. With every steady thrust, his eyes never left hers. And though clouded with lust, they were still solicitous, gauging her comfort, her pleasure, her needs and desires.

In that time, the world fell away. She wasn't worried about Will or the people in Sherwood. It didn't matter that she'd only met Rick the day before. The feel of him as he filled her, his ragged breath on her face, the sound of his voice as he whispered her name, and the look in his eyes—tender yet steady—as he drove them to their mutual satisfaction, it was as if he was giving her something she hadn't known she needed.

There was something about Alaric Nottingham; he wasn't someone she'd easily forget.

CHAPTER 8

As the grey morning light lit the yellow curtains of Rick's room, Robyn could almost believe the sun was shining outside. She lay in the wrinkled sheets of his single bed, wrapped warmly in his embrace. She could feel his slow, steady breath on her neck, and she feared moving might wake him.

After a long moment, he tightened his grip on her, pressing her still naked back to his chest. He didn't speak, but she knew he was awake as he nuzzled her behind the ear, burying his face in her hair. She indulged the feeling of closeness.

"It seems we are going about this all backwards," he murmured into her hair, his voice barely piercing the silence of the still room.

"Does it matter, the order?" she asked

"Not to me."

Her heart warmed.

"But...this can't be right. We barely know each other," he said huskily.

"So we get to know each other. Who's to say what is right or wrong? You want me. I want you. We aren't hurting anyone. If it ends up not working out, then it doesn't. But why would we fight this attraction?"

The logic went against everything they'd ever been taught. Everything safe and proper and smart, and she didn't care. She wasn't ashamed.

Nothing would make her ashamed of what she felt for him. It was natural. It was mutual. It couldn't be wrong.

"I won't force you, Rick. I just want you to know where I stand. There's no need to fight it for my sake."

There was another long silence. "Then can..." he hesitated. "Can I see you again?"

Robyn smiled to herself. "What are you doing later?" she asked.

"Nothing important."

"My guardian is turning seventy today, and there's going to be a party. Would you like to be my date?"

It took him a moment to respond. "Yes."

The creaking of the stairs announced someone's approach. The pair froze, holding their breaths. Then a knock sounded on Rick's door.

"Breakfast is ready, Mr. Nottingham, and I've made enough for your lady friend as well when you're ready to come down," a woman announced from the other side of the door.

Robyn gritted her teeth.

"Thank you, Mrs. Stanley," Rick called to his landlady.

When her footsteps had retreated downstairs, Robyn whispered, "do you think she heard us last night?"

"Maybe," he said. "But it's more likely she saw your coat on the rack."

Oh, right, Robyn thought. "Well, what should we do?" she asked.

"You don't have to stay, of course, but you're more than welcome."

Her stomach grumbled its answer, and Rick let out a low chuckle that vibrated her back.

They redressed, and Robyn went to the bathroom down the hall, where she quickly made herself presentable.

When they entered the kitchen downstairs, Mrs. Stanley was placing two plates with biscuits and gravy on a long kitchen table. She was a much older woman, likely in her sixties, with dark grey hair pinned in a wispy bun. She looked up when they entered.

"Good morning, Mrs. Stanley," Rick greeted.

"Good morning, Mr. Nottingham and...?" She tilted her head at the younger woman.

"Robyn," she answered.

Mrs. Stanley smiled. "What a beautiful name. Robins were my late husband's favorite bird, you know."

"Thank you."

Robyn didn't know what she'd expected from Mrs. Stanley, but it certainly wasn't the warm, cheery woman she found.

"I'm so pleased Mr. Nottingham has finally made a friend here in Midshire. I was quite worried about him. Young, good looking fella like that ought to have tons of women after him. But, you know, you're the first person he's brought home."

Robyn glanced at Rick who stared seriously at his breakfast.

"You don't mind me saying that, do you, Mr. Nottingham?" She didn't wait for his answer but continued chattering. "I never had any children, you see. And after Martin passed, I didn't have anyone to look after. But my friend Sheryl suggested I take in boarders. 'You have that big house all to yourself,' she said. I was quite nervous at first, I tell you. But I've been so blessed with the boarders I've had so far. I can't imagine not having someone to look after. But I suppose that's what women are like. Wouldn't you say, Robyn?"

Robyn was glad she didn't really want an answer to that question. But as the older woman kept going, Robyn thought that Rick and Mrs. Stanley were a good match for housemates. He'd said he wasn't talkative, and Mrs. Stanley never seemed to be short of something to say.

Mrs. Stanley was also very solicitous that they'd gotten enough to eat. By the time she was through with Robyn, her head was spinning with stories, and her stomach was stuffed with an excellent breakfast.

As Mrs. Stanley cleaned up the dishes, Rick and Robyn thanked her for the meal and made their escape. Reluctant as Robyn was to leave Rick, she knew she had to get home before Marian sent out a search party.

"Well, I better get going," she told him.

"I'll walk you to the station," he said, offering her coat and scarf.

Their stroll was short, but his hand was warm and reassuring in hers. When they'd reached the train station, he stopped outside the entrance and faced her.

"I guess...I'll see you later then," he said.

Robyn nodded and smiled. "Thank you for a wonderful evening, Rick."

His eyes smiled, and he leaned down, lowering his scarf. She saw a slight dimple in the corner of his mouth before he placed a soft kiss on her cheek. "See you later," he promised.

"I look forward to it. Oh, and here's the address." She handed him a slip of paper she'd borrowed from Mrs. Stanley.

As she walked into the train station, she looked back and gave him a small wave.

When Robyn arrived at home, the place was a flurry, everyone getting ready for Eleanor's party that night. Amidst all the activity, it wasn't difficult to slip upstairs and into her room to change.

By the time Marian found her she was helping Winona with the decorations and trying to stay out of the kitchen and Sarah's way.

"Where have you been?" her elder sister demanded, pulling Robyn aside so Winona didn't hear her scolding.

"What do you mean? I told you I was going to the levy game last night. Did you expect to see me?"

"Okay, but what about this morning?"

"I met a friend for breakfast."

"Who? Lili?"

"I'm sorry I worried you. But as you can see, I'm fine."

Marian conceded with a frown, and they returned to work.

John wanted everything to be perfect for his mother's celebration, but he wasn't helping anyone get things done faster by shouting. Eventually, Isabella stepped in, giving them all a bit of room to complete their tasks.

When it finally looked like Winona could finish the rest on her own, Robyn went upstairs to start getting ready. Marian had already bathed, so Robyn was free to clean herself up.

Sitting down at her vanity, she looked at her reflection in the mirror. Then she looked at a photograph of Marian and her stuck in the mirror frame. Marian was a black-haired beauty with bright, green eyes, full lips, and a straight nose. If it wasn't for the shape of their faces and the similarities when they smiled, Robyn would never have thought they were related.

The picture was taken at Robyn's high school graduation. Marian and Robyn hugged each other, their smiling cheeks pressed together, Robyn's cap tipped to one side. Marian had been so proud that day. For a long while, she had worried her sister would never graduate. Though Robyn was intelligent enough, she didn't have much patience for book learning. She always preferred a more hands-on approach. But after all those sleepless nights of studying, she had made it. Her smile seemed to say, "I told you I could do it." And Marian's said, "I'd never a doubt."

Below that photograph was another: a man, a woman, and two little girls. Their parents stood, grinning on the stoop of a short house, holding the girls in their arms. You could just see the edge of a porch swing in the background. Marian had told Robyn once that this was the day their parents had purchased their first house. Robyn had been far too young to remember the occasion, and they hadn't lived there for long before the orphans had moved in with the Lacklands.

One other picture clung to the mirror. It was of a teenager drawing the tsuru on his yumi bow in his kyudo gi, obi, and hakama. That day, Will and Robyn had been the only occupants of the archery dojo. He smiled out at her from the photograph, not at all angry that she'd interrupted his concentration to take his likeness.

Robyn paused in her party preparations and reached into the drawer of her vanity. From under a canister of cold cream, beside a pair of twin daggers, she pulled out a folded letter. The paper was delicate from being overly handled, and it was ripped a little at the edges of the well-worn creases. She had no trouble recognizing Will's calligraphic script.

August 12, 1942
Robyn,

> *The time has finally come. The evacuation order was posted, and we have only a few days to report to Midshire War Relocation Center. They told us we could bring one suitcase each, but after the temple and dojo were burned, we scarcely have that.*

> *I'm sure I will already be there by the time you receive this letter. I would have called, but they are listening on the phone lines, and I don't want to bring you into this.*

> *I can picture your scowl at reading that last sentence, but let me protect you just this once.*

I don't know when I will be able to write to you again, so try not to fret if you don't hear from me.

I know we will see each other again. Be patient, and try to stay out of trouble until then.

Your most loyal friend,
Will Sukaretto

The words of Will's letter blurred, Robyn's tears making the black strokes swim. She tilted her head back and fanned her eyes with her hand, glad she hadn't put on eye makeup yet but not wanting to make her face unnecessarily puffy.

"You know patience is not something I'm good at," she told Will's photograph. "And we *will* see each other again, much sooner than you think." She folded the letter carefully and put it back in her drawer. *As soon as I can figure out how,* she thought.

Sighing, Robyn stared back at her reflection. *I don't much feel like going to a party anymore,* she thought. *But Eleanor will be disappointed if I don't come, and I do want to see Rick.*

Sniffing hard, she grabbed a tissue and dabbed her eyes before reaching for her foundation.

An hour and a half later, Robyn had her cosmetics applied and her hair done. Lifting the front of her long, black dress, her heels clacked on the marble stairs as she descended to the first floor. By design, she was still a little early. She went outside and waited by the front gate for her date.

Robyn was grateful for having grabbed her coat on the way out as she stood at the entrance to the round drive waiting for Rick. Still, she shivered as the October wind chilled her legs through the thin silk and lace of her dress. As each taxi pulled up to the curb, she squinted at the passengers to see who was arriving. Men in black-tie tuxedos escorted formally dressed women in pearls and furs. Robyn smiled politely and nodded to each of them as they greeted her. She knew their faces rather than their names, but they certainly knew her.

After a quarter of an hour, Robyn sighed heavily, puffing her cheeks and puckering her lips. She was just considering waiting in the front hall when another cab pulled up.

Her heart skipped a beat when Alaric Nottingham climbed out in a dark blue victory suit with a blue striped tie. He met her eyes under his fedora, and a slow smile graced his face.

"I seem to be under-dressed," he commented as his gaze traveled down her body. "I thought you said this was a birthday party."

"It is. The Lacklands never do anything halfway," she explained. "But don't worry about it. You look great. Besides, you're my escort, so no one will say anything to you."

He peered around her at the house over her shoulder, and his face stiffened with a frown. "I don't recall you mentioning your last name. So you're a Lackland?"

Robyn couldn't discern his tone, but she decided it was rather unpleasant. "Loxley," she told him.

"Say again?"

"Robyn Loxley," she repeated, holding her hand out to him as if they were meeting for the first time. "I'm not a Lackland. I'm a Loxley."

As he met her gaze silently, she could feel him examining her and her motives for not disclosing her full name earlier.

"Are you backing out now that you know who I am?" she asked.

"Of course not," he responded.

Rather than shaking her outstretched right hand, he took it in his and tucked it into the crook of his left arm.

Robyn hid her smirk by lowering her face as he led her toward the house.

They were met at the door by Winona, who took Robyn's coat and Rick's hat and scarf.

"This should be practically painless," Robyn assured him. "We don't have to mingle for long if you don't want to. We only have to wish Eleanor a happy birthday. But you're going to want to try Sarah's food. She's an incredible cook. I'd even say she's better than Mrs. Stanley."

Rick listened as his eyes took in the room, seeming to see everything in a practiced sweep. He looked at Robyn when she'd stopped talking. "Who are you trying to excuse from this party? Me or you?"

She chuckled nervously. "I guess you're more perceptive than I thought."

He tilted his head to the side as he stared at her.

"Let's get this over with, shall we?" she said.

Robyn steered Rick to where Eleanor, John, and Isabella were receiving guests. They stood in line as those ahead of them said their congratulations and wished the matriarch well.

"If you don't mind me asking," Rick started, hushed, "if you're not related, why do you live with the Lacklands?"

Robyn smiled sadly but responded. She barely remembered her parents or her life before, so her recounting didn't hold much sting at their loss. "My parents died in an accident when I was quite young, just four years old. Henry Lackland was my father's friend from the war. He even gave my father a job when they returned. I've been told my father saved Henry's life when they were under fire. As for the accident, I don't know a lot. I only know my parents were going out for their anniversary. Henry had let them borrow his new car to celebrate." She shrugged. "And they had an accident. After that, Henry and Eleanor took my sister, Marian, and I in and raised us. They've been very kind. They even put Marian through college and got me an apprenticeship in the Mechanics' Guild."

Rick nodded thoughtfully. "You must be grateful to them."

"I am. They've done a lot for me and my sister." She indicated toward where Marian stood, tall and elegant, entertaining a few of the men Eleanor had invited on her behalf.

He paused for a long while, then asked, "Are you involved with their businesses at all? I haven't been in Midshire for long, but it's my understanding the Lacklands own a lot of them."

"Not really. I mean, I work for Lackland Steel as a master mechanic, but I wasn't even able to use my skills until the war broke out. I think I was only hired at all because Eleanor had insisted. As for their other endeavors, I don't really know a lot about them, and I don't really care to know. I don't even go to The Hammer and Anvil, the bar where the steel workers frequent, because the proprietors know I'm the Lacklands' ward. I don't like to be treated differently from everyone else. That's why I go all the way to the Blue Boar Inn."

"Is that why you didn't tell me your last name when we met?"

She nodded. "Even Loxley is too noticeable to those who are informed. I like being just Robyn."

Rick gave her a short nod and stroked her hand on his arm. The gesture seemed to say, "I think I understand you," but the gentle touch made her shiver pleasantly.

What is that sad gleam in his eyes? Sympathy? Pity? she wondered at the look. But before she could ask, it was their turn to move forward.

Eleanor was a white-haired vision in light blue. Robyn kissed her gently on the cheek as Eleanor reached out to embrace her.

"Happy birthday, Eleanor," she told her.

"Thank you, ma chère," Eleanor answered, then turned her attention to Rick. "And who is this handsome fellow?"

"This is my escort, Alaric Nottingham."

Rick bowed his head and took Eleanor's outstretched hand gently in his. "Ma'am, congratulations, and thank you for having me in your lovely home."

"Of course, thank you for taking care of our Robyn. Enjoy the party."

Robyn smiled at her kindness. They turned to John and Isabella to thank them for putting on the celebration. John's lips were curled back in disgust at Rick's attire, but Isabella tried to make up with her graciousness.

"John, Isabella, this is Alaric Nottingham."

John's eyes widened, but he greeted Robyn's guest stiffly.

Robyn didn't think much about John's reaction as he was always uppity about something or other. But John signaled to Guy as they turned away, and Guy swooped down on them when they entered the next room.

"What are *you* doing here, Nottingham?"

Robyn had never seen so much fury in Guy's glare. "Is that how you speak to my escort, Guy?" she demanded.

Guy's brow puckered in confusion as he looked between Rick and Robyn. He narrowed his eyes at her hand in his arm. "How do you two know each other?" Guy asked suspiciously.

"I could ask you the same," Robyn shot back.

He turned back to Rick. "Couldn't get what you wanted the right way, so you try to weasel your way in. Is that it?"

Rick lifted his lips in a sneer, and the bite in his voice sent a shiver through Robyn. "Watch your tone, Gisbourne." They glared at each other in testosterone-filled silence for a moment before Rick added lightly, "This is a party after all."

"Don't think you'll get away with this, *Detective*. I've got your number."

Guy met Robyn's gaze with his usual intensity. She stiffened.

"I trust you're a victim in all this, Robyn. I know you're too soft-hearted to see the ill in people. Did he force you to invite him? Do you want me to throw him out?"

She sighed in exasperation. "He didn't force me, Guy. And I am not as innocent as you think. *I* invited *him* to the party."

Guy frowned, searching her eyes for answers. "Why, Robyn? Don't you know how much trouble he has caused the family?"

What is he talking about? she wondered. She looked over at Rick, whose gaze was passive and unreadable. "I don't know what you mean, Guy. We met at a bar. He's fun and attractive. Why wouldn't I want to spend time with someone like that?" She left out the part where she'd also invited Rick to try to put Guy off her scent.

"I knew it," Guy muttered with a sigh of relief. "You listen here, Nottingham. You may have her fooled, but I'm not buying it. Be respectful and show her a good time, and then leave. You aren't welcome here after tonight."

CHAPTER 9

$\mathcal{A}$laric Nottingham couldn't deny the twinge of satisfaction he felt as Gisbourne stormed from the room, but he kept his expression smooth when Robyn turned her attention back to him and raised her eyebrows.

"You have questions," he stated softly, his gut hardening.

"Uh huh."

"Is there someplace we can talk?"

She nodded once and took his hand. He clung to the small comfort, certain it would be the last time she touched him. She led him through the crowd to the back doors and outside. Guests were enjoying the cool night air on the patio and on the graveled garden paths.

"Follow me," she told him, releasing her grip as she no longer needed to pull him through a thick crowd.

Past a gazebo and greenhouse—which were also occupied by guests—they squeezed through some hedges and crossed a lawn. He didn't ask where they were going, and she didn't tell him. Finally, they arrived at a shed. She slid the door open and slipped inside. After closing the door behind him, Robyn turned on a light.

"No one will bother us in here. This is my space," she said as he looked around.

His attention went immediately to the motorcycle. "Yours?" he asked, not knowing much about such things, though still impressed.

She beamed with pride. "Built it myself. I would have liked to make a hoverbike. But until they install magnets in the roads, that's not really an option. They've done it in Detroit." She shrugged. "I guess, Midshire isn't ready for that yet."

He admired it, appreciating the sleek lines, but mostly steeling himself for what would come next. When he'd finished, he turned to her, ready for her questions.

"So you're a detective," she said rather than asked.

He nodded once, silently snipping the tentative threads of his attachment.

"And you know Guy because...? He said you were making trouble for the family. Are you investigating the Lacklands or something?"

He clenched his teeth, not liking the sound of Gisbourne's name on her lips. *Does she really not know about the Lacklands' criminal enterprises?* he wondered. He stared at her, studying her eyes, the eyes he'd gazed so deeply into the night before. They were the same June sky blue found in Renaissance paintings, the costly color of crushed lapis lazuli. *No, I don't think she does. She was far too open when I asked her earlier. Still, she's too close. It isn't ethical.*

"Not officially," he answered finally, thinking it was all right to tell her that much.

Robyn bit her lip, hesitating, then asked, "We met by chance. Didn't we? I mean..." She let the rest of the accusation drop.

His chest ached a little, picturing her heated grin as she'd challenged him to darts, saddened that his ignorance had landed them in this situation. "We did," he assured her.

She sighed in relief.

There was a thick silence as he tried to seal away the memories of her cheeky smirk, of her laughter, of the feel of her beneath him, still too recent to be forgotten.

"I really don't know anything," she said.

"I believe you," he answered softly. But he still didn't uncoil, willing more distance between them.

This is the end, he thought. *It has to be. It must be over before it truly begins.*

But one point still gnawed at him. There was something he had to know before he left.

"Gisbourne..." He hesitated a moment. "He seems...protective of you. Were you two ever...?" His stomach curdled as he waited for her reply.

She met his gaze steadily. "Never."

Warmth spread to his loins as her eyes clung to him. He smashed his desire down.

Robyn tilted her head. "So...we can be...friends then, can't we?" She slowly closed the distance between them, and he stifled a quiver of urge.

"I mean...you believe I don't know anything, and you're only sort of investigating the Lacklands..."

He froze when she reached his personal space, knowing he didn't have the will to move away. He stared down at her, his expression tense. "I'm not sure that's..." he murmured.

"What if I promise to stay out of it?" she suggested. "I'm not involved with any of their stuff right now, other than my job at the steel mill. We could just...not talk about it. It doesn't have to affect us, does it?"

Don't give me an out, he thought. *Don't give me a reason for you to be in my life, in my reach, when I can't have you.*

His heart pounded, and he held his breath as she reached up to him slowly, her fingertips hovering above his cheek.

His lips parted, and he let out a shaky breath. He couldn't hide his desire this time as he fought for control, barely managing to remain still as she encouraged him to touch her.

"You're worried about a conflict of interest?" She paused, lowering her hand but stepping closer, only an inch separating their bodies. Her blue gaze was trained on him, solicitous and beckoning. "I won't tell if you don't."

"I'm going to Hell," he whispered, then crushed her to him, her soft body yielding to his as he pressed his lips to hers. He'd been restraining himself since he'd awoken with her in his arms that morning.

A satisfying gasp escaped her at his insistence, and he could feel her smile against his lips. It took her a moment to catch up, but she did so with enthusiasm. She pushed back, her forcefulness a promise that she would match whatever he gave. As his arms held her against him, she pulled him closer still, one hand in his hair and the other stroking roughly against the stubble of his jaw.

"You're beautiful," he told her, his voice rough and low. He pressed kisses down the soft, tender skin of her throat and hoped she believed him.

His cock throbbed at the sound of her ragged breath, at the glazed look in her eyes.

He broke their kiss—forcing himself to pull away—and stared down at her, needing to be certain before he truly let go. "Are you sure?" he asked, his voice still graveled.

"Positive," she answered, her eyes clear and resolute.

He kissed her again, slower, deeper, less insistent, letting the heat build between them; he wanted to make this encounter last. And she seemed content to let him pick the pace, though she squirmed, grinding against him, sending jolts of desire through him.

Any other coherent thoughts were drowned in the hot breath of her kisses. Her feverish gaze watched as he removed his tie and unbuttoned his shirt, and he wished she'd never look away. He wanted her to be his, he wanted her to ache for his touch, he wanted her to mark him with her sweet scent.

They barely knew each other. But in that feverish gaze as their hungry flesh became one again, he knew they certainly would.

CHAPTER 10

*E*leanor nodded pleasantly at Mayor Ferrars while not hearing a word he was saying. She watched from across the room as John finally headed toward Guy Gisbourne, who had been waiting patiently for quite some time.

She excused herself from the mayor and followed after her youngest son, his dark red hair easy to track through the crowd despite his diminutive height. She slipped into the library right after a few men left, no doubt asked to leave for a private discussion.

"Mother," John said, noting her arrival. "Is there something I can do for you?"

Eleanor gazed at her son, his eyes always eager to please her. It's not as if she didn't love him. Of course she did. It was more that she saw him for who he truly was: cruel, cowardly, and lecherous. He had not the chivalry of Dear Richard. And further, he was not nearly as prepared to lead the family as he thought he was. She had always hoped being strict with John would help him see the error of his ways, make him a better leader. But she feared her approach may have only worsened the situation.

"I want to hear what Mr. Gisbourne has been trying to tell you for the last few hours," she said.

"Oh, it is nothing of import," he answered dismissively. "Please, go back and enjoy your party."

Eleanor leveled a stare at him. "Do not dismiss me, John." She put a hard edge on her tone, and she could see its effect in his eyes. "I am not simply an old widow, too aged and senile to be taken lightly. Do not forget who I am."

John dipped his head. "Of course not, Mother. I did not mean to suggest such. I simply didn't want to worry you on your momentous day."

Eleanor relented with a nod. "Very well. Mr. Gisbourne, continue," she ordered, taking a seat on a cushioned, straight-backed chair.

Gisbourne continued where he had left off. "She seemed genuinely surprised at finding out he's a detective. I don't think she knew before I addressed him as such. She insisted she invited him of her own free will, but it seems too much a coincidence to me."

Easily picking up the thread of the conversation, Eleanor addressed Gisbourne just as John opened his mouth to respond. "Are you suggesting Detective Nottingham duped our Robyn into bringing him here to spy on us?"

"That is my theory," Gisbourne said with a nod.

She turned to her son. "I have allowed you to handle this matter thus far. How much of a threat is he to us?"

"According to our information, he hasn't gotten close to finding out anything. He only has suspicions," John answered.

"Well, obviously he has other channels of getting close to us," Eleanor said. "Is Robyn in danger, do you think?" she asked Gisbourne.

Gisbourne frowned. "I don't know. From what I can gather about him, he seems a straight arrow. I don't think he would hurt her overtly."

Eleanor nodded absently as she pursed her lips in thought.

"If I may, Mrs. Lackland," Gisbourne added. "I think it would be much better to tell the Loxleys outright what is going on."

"Not yet," Eleanor said reflexively.

"You are already attempting to entangle Marian through marriage. She will have to know. And Robyn is an intelligent woman. She will figure it out eventually. I think they would both take more kindly to hearing it from you than someone else," he pushed gently.

"Not yet," she said again, her tone having much less conviction.

Gisbourne dipped his head.

"Would you like me to warn him away from Robyn?" John asked.

Eleanor looked at Gisbourne, analyzing his expression. "You say Robyn seemed surprised to find out he is a detective? Did she appear angry at all to you?"

"She seemed taken aback for sure. I can't imagine she will be pleased about him keeping something that important from her," he answered.

Eleanor nodded in agreement. "There is no need to take rash actions," she said, addressing John's question. "For now, we will watch what develops between Detective Nottingham and Robyn. But I do think some signal of displeasure should be sent his way as far as investigating the family. Perhaps being buried in cold cases will discourage our new friend."

"I will take care of it, Mother."

Eleanor dipped her head at her son's words. "Now, let us get back. I won't have it be said we neglect our guests."

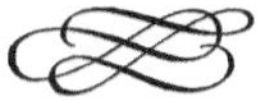

Heaving deep breaths, Robyn and Rick fell back on either side of the cot. Robyn's legs twitched with aftershocks, and it took a while before she felt capable of moving again. But when the sweat of passion had started to make her shiver in the chill of her work-shed, she forced herself to sit up.

Rick shifted his weight, seeing her purpose, as she rose and hobbled stiffly to the small sink in the corner. The cold water numbed her fingers, but she ignored it, lifting her skirt and trying as best she could to clean herself up.

A quick glance in the mirror revealed her good Detective Nottingham was watching her, his head resting on his arm. His dark eyes reflected the light of the naked bulb overhead, and his hair was tousled from their vigorous romp.

"Do you regret it?" she murmured.

He sat passive for a while, meeting her eyes in the mirror. "I don't."

She gave them both a small smile. "Good."

After she'd washed, she redressed. She tried to fix her hair and makeup, but there was only so much she could do.

When she'd finished, she knelt on the ground beside where Rick still lay shirtless on the cot. His dark eyes still watched her; she wanted to know what he was thinking.

"What do you say we get out of here?" she suggested. "We wished Eleanor a happy birthday and thanked our hosts. I know a place we can relax and talk. I could slip into the kitchen, pack some food, and we could be on our way."

He reached up and brushed a stray lock from her face, then smiled with his eyes. His gaze was almost physical. It clung to her every move, caressed her face and hair. Her heart jumped at the thrill his attention sent through her. She leaned in and pressed a long, ardent kiss to his lips. She couldn't help herself; he called to her somehow.

"You are beautiful," he whispered when she'd eventually pulled back.

And she still believed him.

After he'd redressed, she told him to go through the house to get his hat and scarf, and she would meet him on the other side.

With it being so late, there were only a handful of guests left, and none of the stragglers were in the garden. She slipped into the kitchen with ease. Unfortunately, Sarah looked over at someone entering the back door to her kitchen.

"Robyn, what in the world...?" Her light eyes bulged in her wide face to see Robyn with her hair and makeup mussed.

"No time to explain, Sarah." Robyn waved her hands at the cook's yet unexpressed questions. "Where is the basket Marian and I took that time we went for a picnic at the art gallery? Do you still have it?"

"Of course I do, but what do you need it for?" She squinted at Robyn's inquiry.

"I've been so busy tonight that I haven't had a chance to eat a bite. Do you think you could wrap up some of the leftover food and put it in the basket for me?"

She opened her mouth to ask something else, but Robyn cut her off. "I've already fulfilled my obligations for the party, and I have to go meet a friend. Would you mind putting in enough for two?"

Sarah frowned but nodded.

"Great. Thank you. I'll be back down in a minute."

Robyn quickly went up the back stairs and changed into more casual clothes, fixing her hair and makeup properly. By the time she'd gotten back downstairs, Sarah had the basket ready. Robyn thanked her and went out the servants' entrance, following the little walkway along the side of the house.

Rick waited for her where she'd met him earlier that evening. He insisted on carrying the basket, and she slipped her arm through his.

The walk to their destination wasn't too far, but the neighborhood had decidedly changed. The mansions and lawns had given way to dreary apartment buildings with cracked sidewalks and damp side-alleys with iron fire-escapes rusted to the sides of the buildings like crusty, red sores.

Robyn led Rick into an apartment building such as this. The stone, front stoop was bowed in the middle from years of feet wearing it down. In the small, deserted lobby, with only a set of mailboxes to declare its purpose, they entered the elevator. Robyn pulled the grated door closed, its clanging painfully filling the cramped space.

On the top floor, they got off in the grimy, grey hallway and stopped before the last door on the right. It had once been labeled "910," but the one had fallen off, and there was only a darkened space where it had once been, the sun having faded everything but what was underneath. Robyn approached the nearby window and felt under the little sill. She didn't have trouble finding the key Marian kept there.

"My sister is forever misplacing things, so she always hides a spare," she explained, though he hadn't asked.

They entered the little apartment. Marian had done the best she could with the place. The walls were painted white and were lined with shelves of photography equipment and drawers filled with negatives.

"This is my sister's studio. She even turned the bedroom into a darkroom," Robyn told Rick as she made her way to the small kitchen. "Why don't you unpack the basket onto the table while I make some coffee?"

He complied, and she went about her task.

He frowned as she set two steaming cups of coffee on the table and sat across from him.

"Seeing this spread, you'd never know there was a war on," he commented.

She couldn't disagree. She remembered the look he'd worn at the Blue Boar when the subject of the war came up. Now, she understood why a fit young man such as himself wasn't over there with his friends. He was in a necessary career field. Detectives needed to stay behind to protect the population at home.

"I guess the Lacklands have no problem getting around the ration board," he added softly, but there was no mistaking the underlying tone of bitterness.

Of course Robyn knew of the rations and the government's push toward lab-created foods. In fact, Legumighty was the one food they actively encouraged the population to eat. What with the war and pollution making natural foods harder to grow and raise, it was no wonder they pushed for all-in-one, nutrient-dense staples. It had everything a person needed. Too bad it tasted like petrified beans covered in congealed sawdust gravy.

His comment reminded her of the privilege she enjoyed on a daily basis. The privilege that, while she tried to avoid taking advantage of it as much as possible, still benefited her. She stared down into her warm, rich coffee and thought of all the people who were likely more deserving than she. Her empty stomach gurgled, acid churning with the upsetting notion.

Rick covered her hand with his, and she glanced up at him. His expression was serious, but his eyes were a bit soft. "When was the last time you ate? This morning?" he asked. "Let's not let it go to waste, all right?"

She nodded but only nibbled at the large portions Sarah had packed for her.

"You wanted to talk?" he asked, breaking her silence.

"Yeah, I suppose I just wanted to get to know each other a bit more."

He bobbed his head. "What would you like to know?"

"You mentioned the other day that you're from Pittsburgh. Do you still have family there? Why did you transfer to Midshire?"

He didn't respond, and she smirked.

"You don't like talking about yourself," she observed.

"Not really, but that doesn't mean I won't. After all, we... I'd like for us to get to know each other, too. Yes, I'm from Pittsburgh, and yes, I have family there. My grandfather still lives there. Like you, I lost my parents at a young age, though I was eight when my mother died and twelve when my father died."

"So you were raised by your grandfather?"

He nodded. "My parents... They didn't die in an accident," he murmured. "My mother was murdered by her employer. She was a housekeeper and heard something she wasn't meant to. Her boss...had her silenced."

Robyn brought her fingertips to her lips. "Oh my God, I'm sorry. How awful."

"My father couldn't handle her loss and found solace in the bottle. I moved in with my grandfather shortly after my mother died. And four years later, my father succumbed to the drink."

Silence reigned as Robyn struggled to find the appropriate words. Realizing there wasn't anything helpful she could say, she moved the conversation along. "Is that why you became a cop? Because of what happened to your mother?"

He tilted his head in thought. "In a way. I've never been able to stomach injustice. But, yes, I was pleased to be the one to finally serve justice to my mother's killers."

Robyn nodded in complete agreement. "I'm also someone who can't stomach injustice."

As they gazed at each other across the small table in Marian's studio, Robyn felt they understood each other. They were equals. The same. Two flames of virtue flickering dimly in a galewind of human depravity. At least that's what she thought.

After discussing such serious matters, everything else seemed to lack gravity.

Robyn's detective was surprised to discover she enjoyed monster movies, and they had a long discussion about the differences between the books and the films. He was a great reader and had read many of the classics. She enjoyed listening to him tell her what happened in the books far more than she would have enjoyed actually reading them.

She didn't care that they spoke of mundane things. She didn't care what he talked about really. She just wanted to hear his voice. Every word burned into her mind.

As the eastern horizon began to go from black to dark grey, their conversation slowed and the atmosphere grew tense. With her hands wrapped around her cooled mug of coffee, she stared out the window at the misty morning.

She didn't want to leave, fearing their separation would somehow break the spell that bound them together. She worried the light of day would illuminate their differences. Maybe he would think better of his decisions of the previous two nights. Maybe his sense of duty and honor would remind him that getting involved with the ward of a family he was sort of investigating wasn't such a good idea after all. Perhaps their passion was only meant for the black shadows of night.

"Robyn..." he started, the hesitation apparent in his voice.

She stood and turned her back to him, waiting for the words she feared would come and ruin what could have been. She didn't look his way but stared resolutely out the window with the chipped frame.

"Can I still see you again?"

Her heart swelled, and it was a moment before she felt she could control her voice enough to respond. "I would like nothing more," she whispered, turning and meeting his eyes. "Though I suppose with everything, we should probably keep our involvement to ourselves, shouldn't we?"

He frowned but nodded. "That is likely for the best."

"That's all right," she reassured them both. "That just means I won't have to share your attention."

Closing the distance between them, he crushed her to him. Slipping his fingers into her hair, he brought his lips to her ear. "Do you not see how you affect me? This feeling... I've known you for what? A few days? Why? Why do you have such an effect? What is this feeling? It can't be love. I don't know you enough for it to be love. It's a fixation. An obsession. Share my attention? As if I could think of anything else while you stand before me."

His words tumbled out of him as if his dam of self-control had broken. His stoic mask was long gone and a frenzied, frightened light shone in his dark eyes. From anyone else, it might have scared her. But with every syllable reflecting her own feelings, she was just filled with warmth, security, and passion.

His true thoughts and feelings exposed, he clamped his mouth shut. He recoiled from her as though she'd burned him. She could tell he was ready to leave. He'd said too much too soon. He looked down at his hands as if he'd cut them off for their betrayal.

Before he could turn to go, she grabbed his tie and pulled him down into a fervent kiss. She let her lips tell him everything she wanted to say.

When she took a breath, she reminded him, "You said the order didn't matter."

"I did," he agreed huskily.

He crinkled his eyebrows and bit his lip. But when he met her eyes in the grey morning light trickling through the dirty windows, his features smoothed, and he reached for her again.

They shared their passion freely. And as they conversed in grunts and moans, she finally understood why it was called making love.

CHAPTER 12

It was late morning as Robyn and Rick lay on the floor, their clothes like a makeshift, patchwork blanket beneath them. Robyn's head rested on Rick's chest as he trailed his fingertips up and down her back. Staring at the two abandoned cups of cold coffee on the table at the other side of the room, she couldn't help but think of Tuck's tarot reading.

"Do you believe in magick?" she asked him.

"What? Like levitation and fireballs?"

Robyn giggled at his response, realizing how silly it must have sounded to Tuck. "*Real* magick."

He was silent for a moment. "I don't know what would qualify as real magic, but this... What has happened to us... It has opened my mind to more possibilities."

Robyn snuggled closer to him. *But if Tuck's cards were right about Rick and me, what else were they right about?* she wondered. *She said a painful truth would lead me to a crossroads and major changes. Or perhaps I'm already at the crossroads. What choices will I have to make that will have significant impacts on the future? Have I already made them? Was being with Rick one of them?*

"What are you thinking?" Rick asked, distracting her before she could become too introspective.

"Nothing."

"I don't buy that. You've got a thinking line between your eyebrows."

"I was just thinking about this woman I met yesterday. She said she was a witch, but I'm not sure whether to believe her or not."

"Hence the question about magic."

Robyn nodded, her cheek rubbing against his bare skin as she did so.

He was quiet again for a while, then let out a long sigh. "I wish I could stay here with you all day, but I told Mrs. Stanley I'd help her. I need to pick up coal for the furnace today; she can't move it on her own."

Robyn propped herself up with her elbow. "She still has a coal furnace? Why didn't she update to diesel? It's way more efficient, and the fuel is delivered to your house."

"Apparently, Mr. Stanley was vehement about not changing things unless they are broken."

"Ah. Well, I understand if you're busy. When can I see you again?"

He brushed a loose lock from her face and gave her a small smile. "Hard to say. It depends on my caseload. But as long as nothing too serious comes up, I should be able to meet this weekend. Should I call you?"

Robyn frowned. "No, you never know who will answer the phone. It could be John or even Guy. I'll call you on Friday evening to see what your schedule is like. Mrs. Stanley shouldn't be too surprised if I call."

He nodded. "The number at the house is HIckory-5208."

"Got it."

Rick brushed a finger over Robyn's cheek. Then he leaned over and kissed her sweetly. It was soft and lingering. "I'll see you later then," he promised.

She nodded.

After Rick had left, Robyn cleaned up Marian's little kitchen before going home.

She'd thought she was free and clear when she made it into her bedroom without anyone noticing her. But when she silently shut the door, she turned around and found Marian on her bed.

"Where were you?" Marian asked quietly.

"I was..."

"Out with a friend," they said at the same time.

"Come on, Robyn." Marian closed the distance between them and took Robyn's hands in hers. "You don't have to lie to me. We're sisters. You used to tell me everything. After all, we are all we have. It's just you and me—"

"Against the world," they finished together.

Robyn hesitated.

"Please, sis, talk to me," Marian pleaded, her green eyes pouting.

Robyn pursed her lips. Marian knew Robyn could never say no to that look. "Fine," Robyn sighed. "Let me clean up first."

Marian's eyes brightened as she smiled and nodded.

When Robyn was ready, they went out to the greenhouse. The humidity took a moment to get used to compared to the crisp autumn air outside. Unlike Tuck's greenhouse, the Lacklands didn't have anything useful like crops. Exotic plants that had once grown in the jungles of Africa, Asia, and South America sat alongside each other in terracotta pots. Leaning down to smell the bloom of a white orchid, Robyn wondered how much rainforest was even left in the world.

"So what has been going on, little sister?" Marian urged. "I haven't pushed you to talk too much lately because I know you've been worried about Will, but now you aren't even coming home at night? I'm concerned."

"I'm sorry I worried you," Robyn murmured. "But everything is fine. I mean, other than Will, obviously."

When Marian saw Robyn wasn't going to elaborate, she pushed harder. "That's not good enough, Robyn."

Robyn sighed. "Yeah, I've been crazy about getting in to see Will. I thought I'd finally meet with the warden the other day, and I told you he blew me off. And just...a lot has happened since then."

"So you aren't going to try to see Will anymore?"

"Oh no, I still am. I just need to think of how."

"So what happened?"

"First, I wandered into Sherwood."

"You went to Sherwood! Oh my... Are you okay?"

Robyn waved her hand at her elder sister. "I've been there twice now, and I met some really nice people. But I can't figure out what's really going on. I didn't think anyone lived there, but I get the feeling there are quite a few people actually. I haven't seen them. I guess there's just an air about the place."

"But all of the other shanty towns have been torn down. It's wartime. There are plenty of jobs to go around. How many people could be living there?"

Robyn wrinkled her brow. "I'm not sure, but something feels weird. I'll be going back soon. I'm supposed to meet with them again."

Marian bit her lip. "I don't know, Robyn..."

"It's fine. They're fine. And something else..." Robyn trailed off, trying to intrigue Marian enough to distract her from her thoughts of Sherwood.

"What?" she asked eagerly, catching Robyn's tone.

"I...met a man."

"What? When? Oh my goodness! Is it the man you brought to the party last night? You hadn't mentioned anyone, so I just thought it was someone you'd convinced to come to put off Guy."

"His name is Alaric Nottingham."

Robyn glanced at her sister's reaction, and Marian's eyes begged for more details. Satisfied Marian didn't know the name, Robyn continued. "He's a detective. I met him at the Blue Boar Inn."

"And?"

Robyn turned to her sister, unable to hold back anymore. "Oh Marian, I don't even know what to say. He...he just...sets me on fire. It's like I can hardly think of anything else when he's around."

Marian grinned, sharing Robyn's joy. "So...how was he?"

"Earth shattering."

"He must be something if you even brought him home."

Robyn gazed at her reflection in the fogged glass window of the greenhouse, her eyes losing focus. "He is...something. More than just a few nights' pleasure...I hope. I don't know how to put it... It's like we recognized something in each other, something that defies words or rules. We just saw it and were drawn together. And all those other things were just frosting, sweet but unnecessary."

Marian was silent for a moment, her gaze drifting around the greenhouse in thought. "Does he have a friend?"

Robyn laughed. "None of those fellas Eleanor invited were your type?"

Even scowling, Marian's features were beautiful. Then she sighed.

"You don't have to marry who they want you to, you know."

"They've just done so much for us. I want to help however I can," Marian pronounced, repeating her mantra of the last eighteen years.

"Marian—"

"Oh, don't worry about me, little sister," she cut Robyn off with a smile. "That's my job. As such, I have to ask: you're being safe with this Alaric Nottingham?"

"Really?" Robyn said flatly.

"Humor me."

"Yes, yes, we're being safe."

"Good."

"But...you can't tell anyone we're seeing each other."

"Why not? I would've thought you'd want everyone to know, especially Guy."

"Well..." Robyn explained the situation to Marian about Rick's unofficial investigation, and Marian promised to keep everything Robyn told her to herself.

Robyn was relieved to tell Marian everything that was going on. She didn't like to keep secrets from her. Like she'd said, they'd been through so much together in their lives. And Robyn knew she could face anything as long as she had Marian.

After spending the morning catching up with her sister and having lunch with Eleanor and Isabella, Robyn decided to return to Sherwood. With work during the week and Rick on the weekend, she didn't know when her next chance would be.

Little Jon was the sentry at the bridge, and he smiled as she crossed it.

"Let me guess, Tuck told you I was coming?"

"Well, you said you'd come back soon anyway."

They made their way to Tuck's abbey, Robyn's curiosity quickening her pace. They found Tuck amongst the rows of crops in the greenhouse. She was past the tufted tops of the carrots, picking the last fat tomatoes from their vines and placing them in a basket on her hip. In the corner, an apple tree was heavy with fruit, its sweet aroma filling the glassed-in space.

"You're back," Tuck greeted with a smile.

"Do you need any help?" Robyn asked.

"I'm just finishing. Actually, your timing is perfect. I was about to deliver these." She bobbed her hip and the basket of tomatoes. "Come with me."

Little Jon offered to carry the basket, and Tuck thanked him and handed it over.

They left the cloister and entered a back hallway, Tuck's hounds following after like a motley parade. Then they took a flight of stone stairs leading down. They passed cellars with their shelves of jarred foods and entered a large kitchen. Bustling around a huge table in the middle of the room was an assortment of women and older children; a few more crowded a stove with their backs to the entrance. Some of them were washing tomatoes, others were peeling, and still more were pouring cooked tomatoes into Mason jars. There had to be nearly twenty people in the kitchen canning the fruits of their labor.

A few women looked up when they entered but most continued with their work, punctuated by the occasional popping of a lid as jars sealed. Robyn spotted Much standing on a stool at the stove stirring a large pot, his brow crinkled in concentration.

Little Jon placed the basket of tomatoes on the table near a teenage girl who was washing them.

"All these people..." Robyn wondered at how many Sherwood housed.

"This isn't everyone," Tuck told her. "We have plenty more scavenging Sherwood and others renovating to prepare for winter."

"But why? Why are you all here? There has to be other places to stay."

Tuck smiled sadly and shook her head. "Come with me."

Robyn and Little Jon followed Tuck from the kitchen, up the stairs, and out an ill-fitting, wooden slat door. They entered what was likely once a lush lawn, but all that was left was grey dirt with a few tufts of brown crabgrass. They climbed the hill to an old, crumbling well and looked out at the derelict borough that was Sherwood.

"What do you see when you look at Sherwood?" Tuck asked, her light voice deeper with a sort of timelessness. "An abandoned neighborhood? A shantytown? A scar on the face of Midshire? A collection of broken-down buildings and long forgotten dreams?"

She paused, and Robyn waited for her to continue.

"That's probably what anyone with a warm bed and a steady income would see. But to us? It's a haven. Sherwood saved us when we had no place to go. We created a community where all are welcome. And though we are poor, and though we struggle to meet our basic needs, we are happy. We aren't alone."

The warmth of her conviction touched Robyn's heart, and Robyn began to see potential as she stared out at Sherwood. Though she still saw the ruins of the past, her perception shifted to also see what could be of this wall or that ironwork, the potential Sherwood held.

"I think I understand," she told Tuck. "But what happened to you all? What brought you to Sherwood?"

"War," Tuck said simply.

"War and the Lacklands," Little Jon added.

Robyn crinkled her brow and tried to hear over the wind and the sudden thumping of her heart. "What was that?"

Tuck sighed, patting Fangs on the head as he leaned against her. "As war does, many of the men left home, leaving their wives and children to fend for themselves. Sure, many women have found work to support themselves and their children while their husbands kill in the name of patriotism and freedom. But...*these* women, *these* children were unfortunate because they lived in an apartment building owned by the Lacklands."

Robyn held her breath, trying to make sense of Tuck's words. *The Lacklands? Robyn wondered. The Lacklands I live with? Eleanor and John and Isabella?*

"You know of the Midshire concentration camp?" Tuck asked.

Robyn eyes bulged, but she nodded.

"It used to be an apartment building. It's where most of these women and children lived. Actually, it was company housing. The families who lived there worked for Lackland Chemical. But when Roosevelt signed Executive Order 9066, and the Lacklands won the bid to house the incarcerated Japanese Americans, the residents were evicted. On top of all that, most of the women who had taken over their husbands' jobs at Lackland Chemical were fired."

Robyn's head spun with the information Tuck presented in a sad, steady voice.

"Not everyone in Sherwood is here because of that but most are." Tuck glanced at Little Jon. "Others were considered unfit to serve, and then there are those who don't agree with killing under any circumstances."

But this doesn't make sense, Robyn thought. I mean, I know John can sometimes be callous, but would he really fire all those women and turn them out of their homes? Does Eleanor know about this?

"When did all this start?" Robyn asked.

"Shortly after Richard Lackland enlisted," Little Jon said. "Richard Lackland may be a gangster with a penchant for spilling the blood of those he thinks deserve it, but he never took it out on the innocent, or at least who he thought was innocent."

Tuck nodded.

Richard? Richard Lackland? Robyn thought. A gangster? The boy who used to read for hours and sing me songs he wrote? I mean, sure Richard has a temper, but a "penchant for spilling blood"?

Tuck seemed to pick up on Robyn's disbelief. "It's difficult to swallow, I know. To think there are people in the world who live this way, who profit off the suffering of others. It's hard to face."

Robyn nodded. "I need some time to think."

"We understand. Come back when you're ready."

CHAPTER 13

Robyn's mind was so full of what Tuck and Little Jon had told her that she mechanically made her way home. The train, the taxi, it all blurred by as she tried to reconcile what they'd said with what she knew of the Lacklands.

Could the Lacklands be gangsters? she wondered. *Are they in the mob? Are they the mob? Could they be a crime family? They do have a lot of money. But that doesn't make them gangsters. Are they doing anything illegal?*

Robyn searched her mind for anything she'd seen or overheard through her many years with them.

What sort of gangsters could they be? she thought. *Loan sharks? Illegal gambling? Drugs? Is Rick investigating the Lacklands because they're involved in serious crimes? But if that were the case, it wouldn't just be sort of an investigation, right? It would be an active investigation.*

She thought about what she knew of the Lacklands' history. She knew Fulk the ill-tempered, as the family called him, had made a fortune investing in the railroad. And she knew the family's money and influence had only expanded from there until they pretty much owned Midshire. There was no doubt they had influence.

But I've always been told their fortune came from legitimate business, she thought. *I mean, I'd heard jokes about Henry bootlegging during Prohibition, and I do recall big parties at the house when I was younger, where there never seemed to be a shortage of alcohol. But Prohibition seems so silly now, and I haven't met many people who actually followed it.*

Most of what Robyn remembered from her early years with the Lacklands was that the house was always full of activity. What with Harry, Matilda, Richard, Geoffrey, Ellie, Joan, and John, plus Marian and Robyn, there was always a commotion. Especially amongst the boys, who were constantly fighting about something.

While the Lacklands had made Marian and Robyn feel welcome, Robyn's greatest comfort had always been Marian, and Robyn Marian's.

Though Joan had been the closest girl to their age, Marian and Robyn had been particularly fond of Matilda. But then Matilda, like the other daughters, married and moved out of the house. Still, she'd made sure to stay in touch with the girls, making them feel quite loved until she'd passed.

Matilda had been the fourth child of Eleanor and Henry who died too soon, after William, Harry, and Geoffrey. Rather than bringing the surviving family closer together, it seemed every death pushed them a little more apart.

In any case, they were talking about Richard and John specifically, Robyn thought. She squinted, trying to remember when Richard had taken over the family businesses. It had been at the tail end of The Great Depression, the same year Germany and the Soviet Union had attacked Poland. *I remember Richard pouring over newspapers,* she recalled. *He wanted so badly to join the fight. He always had a fascination with the "glory of war," always reading histories of battles, always going north to hunt. "Practice" he'd called it. Maybe a "penchant for spilling blood" wasn't too far off actually.*

As she walked up the round drive of the Lacklands' mansion, she sighed. *I didn't pay enough attention back then to tell whether what Tuck said is right,* she thought. *But there may be another way.*

Robyn determined to go to the Office of Public Records after work the following day. It took all her will power to concentrate at work, her thoughts constantly drifting to her plans for after.

The Office of Public Records wasn't imposing like other government buildings. There were no great columns or long flights of granite stairs. It was a simple, square number made of brick and had tiny windows. If there hadn't been a black and white sign declaring its purpose on the side, Robyn might have thought it was a warehouse.

Just inside the front door was a small lobby where a young woman greeted her with a smile and asked her why she was there.

"I'm just here to look up a deed."

"Do you need copies?"

"No."

"All right, the registrar of deeds' office is on the third floor." She pointed her through a set of double doors.

Robyn passed by the offices that handled birth certificates, death certificates, marriage certificates and the like, making her way to a set of metal stairs at the other end of the first floor. She glanced fleetingly at the second floor, where they kept copies of old newspapers in large bound volumes, as she continued her climb.

The secretary at the registrar of deeds' office was not at her desk. Peeking around a door, Robyn saw her taking notes for the registrar. Rather than disturb them, Robyn went right to the large map of Wellington County on the wall. A grid was laid over the map, sectioning it into plots with numbers along the X axis and letters along the Y. She located the area where the Midshire concentration camp was on the map; it was located in G-52.

Beside the map was a shelf of volumes, each labeled with a number-letter combination. After pulling down G-52, Robyn placed it on a nearby bookstand and began flipping through the book of maps. It didn't take too long to locate the parcel map for where the camp was located. Repeating the book, page, and parcel number to herself, she replaced the volume and wandered deeper into the collection of shelves.

The correct book was on the very top shelf, and she had to drag a step stool over to reach it. She placed the volume on the stool and knelt beside it, then flipped to the right page.

And there it was in black and cream: 1465 Waukilby Avenue, deed holder: John Lackland.

Her heart sank, losing the hope she'd been holding onto. *John is imprisoning Will,* she thought. Her mind couldn't go much further than that point. She didn't ask whether he'd turned the women and children of Sherwood from their homes. She didn't even ask why he would want to turn an apartment building into a prison. She just sat still and let the grief wash over her.

But her woe soon turned to rage. She snapped the book shut and shoved it sideways onto the shelf, not bothering to put it back where it belonged. Her mind began to whirl, and she strode from the office, ignoring the receptionist's wide-eyed surprise as she exited the stacks.

Has John been keeping me from Will? she wondered. *Did the warden refuse me admittance because John told him to?*

Her steps thumped loudly on the grated stairs, and she didn't attempt to quiet them, the echoing clangs cathartic somehow. But as she reached the second floor, she halted when a familiar voice called out her name.

Robyn gritted her teeth and tried to swallow her fury as Rick approached her.

"What are you doing here?" he asked.

"Just a bit of research," she answered, her voice not achieving the lightness she'd attempted. "How about you?"

His eyes shifted to an opened volume of old newspapers on the table some twenty feet away. Robyn couldn't see what they said because of the angle. "Same," he said.

"Well, I'll leave you to it then. I don't want to interrupt you."

He took her hand as she turned to leave. "Is anything wrong?"

His touch seemed to push her fury back a little, calming her down enough for her mind to start working. She stifled a sigh but squeezed his hand. "No, I'm fine." She plastered a smile on her face. "I'll call you Friday, okay?"

He nodded and let her go.

Her head was too full to feel bad for brushing Rick off. *I need to think,* she reasoned. So she did what she always did when she had a problem that required thought, she locked herself in her shed and worked on her motorcycle. Working with her hands quieted her mind and let her thoughts flow at an easy, manageable pace, and it kept her from using her hands for more violent activities.

After a few hours of thinking, Robyn decided she needed more information. She sat quietly at the breakfast table with the family the following day, waiting for her opportunity.

Isabella was asking Marian's help with a rally the Daughters of Midshire were putting on to sell war bonds. Their voices barely filtered through as Robyn watched John from the corner of her eye.

"How are your eggs, Mother?" he asked Eleanor.

"Don't fuss, John. Sarah knows how I like them," she scolded.

Robyn smiled into her milk as her mark walked into the dining room in the form of Guy Gisbourne. He made John aware of his presence and left to await him in the sitting room.

Robyn bid everyone a good day and went after him. He was just settling into a wing-backed chair as she entered. He stood when he saw her.

"Good morning, Robyn," he greeted with that deep, intense voice of his.

Robyn steeled herself, fighting the urge to back out of the room, and forced a smile. "Good morning, Guy."

His eyebrows rose a little at her reception, but he didn't seem unpleased. "What can I do for you?"

"I haven't seen you since the party, and I have questions about some of the things you said to Detective Nottingham. Like I told you then, he didn't force me to invite him, but...perhaps I was being a bit naive. I was hoping...we could talk later?" Robyn looked up at him through her eyelashes.

His mouth crooked ever so slightly in as big a smile as she'd ever seen from him. "Of course, whenever you wish."

"Great," she said with a little sigh. "Tonight? We could...you know, get dinner..."

He gave her a short nod. "I'll come for you around seven then."

"Okay, see you then," she confirmed.

When her back was turned to him, her false smile fell, and she gritted her teeth. *Guy is the easiest way to get the information I want,* she told herself. She went to her room to gather her things for work, grateful the distance she usually put between herself and Guy was still polite, thinking he likely wouldn't have bought her faux interest otherwise.

Not wanting to raise eyebrows, she was waiting outside for Guy when he came to collect her that evening. He pulled up in his 1942 Packard Clipper. As much wariness as she had for the man, he certainly had an excellent eye for cars. She couldn't help but appreciate the lines of the latest model before Packard stopped production in favor of machines of war.

Guy got out and came around to open the passenger door for her. Her eyes traveled over the quality wool broadcloths and the walnut grained instrument panel. Guy glanced at her when he slid into the driver's seat. As he turned the key, her heart leapt at the roar of the diesel engine, and she couldn't help but smile. Guy's eyes lit up at her reaction. His expression as he looked at her seemed to say, "I knew you would like it."

Robyn didn't know where he was taking her to dinner, but she knew it would be someplace exclusive. And as he pulled up to the valet station at Iversen Tower, her suspicions were confirmed. Kokkenet was the premiere restaurant in Midshire. It was on the top floor of Iversen Tower, above the smog of the city. Rainbows of sparkling light from the teardrop crystals of the chandelier danced on the gold-accented, cream pillars and shined on the windows that made up the walls.

Robyn was glad she'd dressed formally as Guy took her coat and handed it to the coat-check girl.

Abe, the host, looked up from his reservation book and smiled. "Mr. Gisbourne, Miss Loxley, thank you for coming to Kokkenet," he gushed with a deep bow. "Miss Loxley, you are even more beautiful than the last time you were here."

Robyn dipped her head at him, remembering why she hadn't been to Kokkenet in a few years.

"Mr. Gisbourne, I have saved the best seat in the house for you, as requested. Please, follow me."

"Thank you, Abe," Guy said graciously.

The pair followed the fair-haired host through the round tables covered with pristine white tablecloths to the most private of tables. Guy pulled Robyn's chair out for her, and she sat as he pushed it in. She took in the table settings; flawless white china with gilded rims sat between well-polished silver. The clearest crystal wine and water glasses sparkled in the candlelight from the rose-shaped candles floating in a bowl of pink-dyed water at the center of the table. *Still as impeccable as ever,* Robyn thought.

Abe gently laid a napkin on her lap and handed Guy a thick, black leather folio menu. Guy glanced over the folder at her, and she tried to smooth her features into contentment. She knew Kokkenet had seasonal menus, so Abe was only sharing the courses of the meal with Guy beforehand. Guy nodded and handed the menu back. Then Abe bowed and retreated to his post.

As they awaited the hors d'oeuvres and their first wine, Robyn started her interrogation, lacing her fingers and leaning toward her mark. "Thank you for setting me straight at the party. I invited Nottingham, but he never told me he was a detective."

Guy nodded once. "I thought as much."

They thanked their waiter as he placed the hors d'oeuvres before them.

Robyn tilted her head. "You said he's been causing trouble for the family? What has he been doing? Is he investigating us or something?"

Guy stared at her, tilting his head ever so slightly as if trying to decide whether to let her in on the scheme.

"Come on, I'm part of the family, aren't I? You can talk to me about what's going on."

His expression didn't budge, but his eyes analyzed her.

Robyn dropped her voice and bluffed. "Look, I know I'm not... involved...with the family business, but surely you don't think I'm so stupid as to have not seen what's been going on? I mean, I've lived with the Lacklands most of my life. Do you really think I don't know about their more...risky endeavors?" She raised an eyebrow at him.

His eyes shifted to the side, and he sighed through his nose. "Mrs. Lackland didn't want you or Marian involved yet... But I knew she wouldn't be able to keep you two in the dark for long."

Robyn's pulse hammered, but she schooled her expression. "So... what's the story with Nottingham?"

Guy was silent for a moment longer, but then he began to talk as if she knew everything about the Lacklands already. "Nottingham made a name for himself in Pittsburgh, busted the Accia family. He completely destroyed their network."

Robyn had heard Eleanor speak of Lorenzo Accia. She nodded as if she knew exactly what he was referring to.

"Taking down the Accias has completely changed the game for Pittsburgh steel. We think Nottingham must have come across some of the Accias dealings with the Lacklands while he was making a case against them."

"So you think he moved here to try to follow that lead?"

Guy shrugged. "It makes sense. He makes a name for himself busting a mafia family, gets a taste for it, follows a lead to try to do it again."

Robyn's mind spun with too many thoughts.

"But he's mistaken if he thinks it's going to be that easy in Midshire. Pittsburgh has always been a shared city, shared among five families. But Midshire? The Lacklands own this town. There hasn't been a territory dispute here for fifteen years. Nottingham can try all he wants, but we have the police covered. He'll be let loose if he becomes too persistent... one way or the other." Guy smirked.

Robyn's blood ran cold at the implication. She shifted her gaze out the window, looking past their reflections on the glass to the night sky swimming with stars. The distant twinkling calmed her enough to swallow Guy's threat to Rick. "One thing," she said, turning back to Guy. "I've never been able to figure out: what do you do for the Lacklands exactly? I mean, obviously you're John's right hand man, and you check in on a lot of Lackland businesses but...?"

He leaned back in his chair, frowning as if unsure he wanted to tell her. Finally, he leaned closer, his eyes clouded with an emotion Robyn couldn't place, and whispered, "I'm the Lacklands' enforcer."

CHAPTER 14

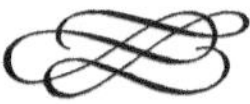

Guy couldn't see Robyn's reaction to his confession as the waiter arrived with their soup. When the waiter had left, he watched her anxiously. *How different will she see me now?* he wondered.

Robyn's eyes flicked toward Guy. "That must be a dangerous job..." she murmured.

Guy's heart leapt before he could squash the hope that her comment meant she was somehow worried for him. "I can handle it," he assured.

Robyn's puckered gaze skittered around before it landed on the flames of the floating candles. She didn't speak, and he desperately wanted to know what she was thinking. On the other hand, he didn't want to see the fear, disgust...rejection in her eyes. That same look he'd seen so often, the look that would only bother him coming from her.

But when her clear eyes met his, he smoothed his expression so as not to give away how much her sincerity had wounded him.

"Tell me," she whispered, leaning forward. "Who was the last person you had to...get rough with?"

He frowned, his face heating with a shame he wasn't used to. *Why would she want to know that?* he wondered. But her blue eyes pressed him, demanding he answer for his deeds. *She won't forgive me for this,* he thought. But he never wanted to lie to Robyn, not to her.

He leaned toward her, their faces not a foot apart. "If you tell me something first," he murmured.

She nodded. "Ask me."

"What happened in the last few days that your attitude toward me has changed?" Guy wanted to believe Robyn's interest in him was real, but he wasn't a fool. He knew she'd never shown such interest before.

She blinked in wide-eyed surprise, then shrugged. "I don't know. I guess seeing you square off with Nottingham sort of showed me what kind of man you are. You weren't afraid to stand up to him when you thought I was in trouble."

Warmth spread in his chest. He'd particularly liked how she'd referred to that pain-in-the-ass detective. Nottingham, not Alaric, not Rick, but Nottingham. Distant. Detached. "Your response didn't seem so positive at the time," he pointed out.

Robyn nodded in agreement. "Well, I was surprised. I didn't even know he was a cop. And it was Eleanor's birthday party. I didn't want to make a scene in front of all those important people."

He stared steadily at her. *Her explanation seems reasonable,* he thought. *Besides, would Robyn lie? She's so honest even in her anger—especially in her anger—so hard-working, so empathetic... She's so far out of my reach.* Even thinking that, Guy knew he'd never stop trying to get her to look at him, to get her to choose him, because what he really wanted was for her light to shine on him, for her righteous eyes to accept him, even if his deeds were far beyond forgiveness. *Do you really want to know what kind of man I am?* he wondered to himself.

"The last was a jeweler called Orwitz. He didn't pay his protection fee," Guy admitted, knowing this very well could be the last time Robyn ever spoke to him.

She clasped her hands together, unable to hide her trembling from Guy's keen eyes, the eyes that were so used to watching her.

"But I thought you said we haven't had rivals in Midshire for fifteen years? Who are they paying for protection from?" she murmured.

"Us."

"Oh." She nodded, her brow crinkled.

"And before that," he continued, not knowing why he wanted to show her the extent of his depravity. "I had to make an example of one of our managers."

Robyn stilled, clearly understanding what he meant by "make an example." "Why?" she asked breathlessly, demanding an explanation for why this man wouldn't be going home to his family.

He stopped, leaning back so the waiter could place their appetizers on the table. When the waiter retreated, Guy continued. "We found out he was taking more than his share at our casino."

That's right, Guy thought as he saw Robyn putting the pieces together in her mind. *For money. You see now. This is the kind of man I am.*

But as always, Robyn never ceased to surprise him.

"I've never been to the casino. Like you said, Eleanor didn't want us involved. And you can't exactly go to an illegal gambling house without the proprietors knowing."

Guy pounced on this new bit of information about her. "Are you fond of games of chance?"

She smiled, and his chest warmed at the expression. "I suppose I am," she said.

After the appetizers and the salad, the main course was slow roasted venison with root vegetables; it was perfectly tender and well-spiced. Guy analyzed Robyn's satisfaction with the meal, and he believed she was genuinely pleased. He nodded with approval.

As they waited for dessert, Robyn hesitated. Finally, she spoke, "I understand John turned Lackland Chemical company housing into a concentration camp."

Guy listened intently.

"Did you know I went there trying to get in to see my old school friend, Will?"

He frowned. "Yes, the warden was worried about whether to allow you in or not. As you no doubt know, you and your sister have long been under Lackland protection. And everyone aware of that is under strict orders to treat you with the utmost respect. So the warden was apprehensive as to what to do when you requested a visitation."

"So John told him not to let me in?"

Guy nodded. "He didn't want you involved in that sordid business, per Mrs. Lackland's wishes."

"I understand," Robyn murmured.

"But I assure you, they are being well taken care of. We've given them jobs at Lackland Chemical so they can earn some money. They even have radios in their living quarters," he added, wanting to relieve the apprehension on her face.

"Have you been inside then?"

"No, but I've given orders and heard reports."

"Is it..." she hesitated again. "Now that you know I've long been aware of what was going on with the family, do you think it's possible for me to see Will?"

Guy frowned as a knot of jealousy hardened his stomach. *Why does she care so much for this Will?* he wondered.

Robyn reached across the table and put her hand on his, and a flash of heat coursed through his body to his loins.

"Please," she pleaded, her eyes lost and begging for his help. "We've been friends since we were children. It couldn't do any harm for me to see him, right?"

His body flushed at her begging, his mind picturing that look in an entirely different situation, as his manhood stiffened.

He wanted nothing more than to give her everything in his power. "I think I can get you in," he murmured.

A rewarding smile lit up her face, and he sucked in a steadying breath. "Thank you," she said.

After a moment, she moved to pull her hand away, but he snatched it in his, desperately wanting her to stay with him, to keep touching him with her warmth. "Robyn, I—"

She stopped him with a warning smile. "Thank you for taking me out tonight, Guy. You've really helped me fill in a lot of blanks. I know you've been interested in me for a while, but you should know I move slow when it comes to these things. I hope that doesn't bother you...?"

Right, Guy thought. *Slow down, she's only just truly looked at you for the first time. Best to respect her pace.*

He released her hand. "Of course not, Robyn. We have plenty of time. And about the concentration camp, I should be able to work something out by this weekend. Are you free Saturday?"

"I am. Let me know the particulars when you can."

They didn't speak much during the ride back to the Lacklands'. Guy was content just to be in her presence. Robyn's eyes watched out the window at the blurring lights of Midshire.

Guy opened the door for her when they arrived and helped her out of the car. He didn't release her hand but pressed a gentle kiss to her fingers, reveling in the sensation of the sensitive skin of his lips on the heat of her flesh.

As he watched her head inside, the warmth her presence had caused in his chest went with her. She closed the door behind her, and the familiar, cold hollowness slid back into place. He told himself he would see her again, feel her warm light again. But, as always, next time felt far off. Each time, it became more difficult to let go and allow the cold to take over. Then again, he wasn't sure he could do his job without it. *This is the kind of man you are,* he told himself. *And don't forget it.*

CHAPTER 15

Robyn sighed heavily as she shut the front door, leaning her back against the wood. She had never been very good at hiding her emotions, and controlling her reactions around Guy had worn her thin.

She could still feel the ghost of his tender kiss on her fingers. She supposed she should have been surprised by how gently he always treated her, knowing his hands had bloodied so many. But the juxtaposition didn't seem like a contradiction in Guy. And for the first time, she wondered what he really felt in his heart.

As soon as she got upstairs, she went straight to Marian's bedroom instead of her own. Her sister was brushing her dark hair with a boar bristle brush and turned to her as she shut the door behind her.

"Don't you look nice. Did you have a date with your detective?" Marian asked, but her smile fell when she noticed Robyn's expression.

"No, not with Rick. Guy."

"What? But I thought you didn't like him?"

Robyn waved her hand at the comment. "I don't. But it was the only way I could get the information I needed."

"What's going on, Robyn?" she whispered, rising slowly to her feet.

"You're going to want to stay seated for this," Robyn cautioned as she started pacing the room. Robyn related what Little Jon and Tuck had told her during her last visit, what she'd found at Public Records, and what Guy had filled in at dinner.

As she recited her tale, Marian grew more and more pallid. By the end, her fingers were trembling as they covered her lips. "I don't...I don't understand," she whispered, shaking her head.

"I know. How could we have missed it?"

"John, Richard...Eleanor?"

"They're criminals. They have underground casinos. They intimidate people into paying them 'protection money.' They've even had people killed, and...and who knows what else."

"And the police...?"

Robyn shook her head. "In their pockets. We have no one to turn to."

"But Detective Nottingham doesn't seem to be corrupt."

Robyn bit the nail of her thumb. "He's in more danger than he knows."

"Do you think you can convince him to leave it alone? To protect him?"

Robyn sighed. "Probably not. I'm just going to have to trust that he knows what he's doing."

"And what about Will? And Micki, Oba-san, and Oji-san? What about all of the other people imprisoned at the concentration camp?"

Robyn clenched her teeth in frustration. "I don't know! But I can't just leave them there. Guy is taking me there Saturday. He says they're being taken care of, but there's no way Will is happy being locked up. I'll ask him what's going on when I see him, but I think we need to come up with a plan to get him out. Maybe Jon and Tuck will have an idea. Some of the people in Sherwood used to live there, right?"

Marian nodded. "I'll help too."

Robyn winced, turning to her sister.

"No, absolutely not," Marian protested, knowing by Robyn's expression what she was going to say. "You're not benching me. I know Will is your friend, but I care about him and his family, too. I'm going to help."

"Marian, I don't want you to get mixed up in all this."

"It's too late to worry about that," she said sternly.

Robyn stared at her, and Marian squinted back. *There's no point arguing when she gets like this,* Robyn thought. "Fine," she said.

Marian grinned in triumph. "So what do we do first?"

Robyn sighed. "Tomorrow we go to Sherwood."

When Robyn left work the following day, Marian was waiting for her at the gate of Lackland Steel. She wore wide-legged trousers and practical shoes, as instructed. During their commute to Sherwood, Robyn watched her sister try to stifle her agitation at the change in neighborhood as the city outside the train became more and more run-down. Marian managed to keep her expression blank, but she kept curling a lock of her black hair around her fingers. Robyn took her sister's hand and squeezed it, smiling as Marian looked over at her.

The seagull that owned the platform nearest Sherwood eyed them as they exited the train. Robyn gave Asiago, as she'd dubbed the bird after the pigeon incident, a little bow of greeting.

Marian looked between her sister and the bird, one eyebrow quirked. "Do you uh...know each other?" she asked.

Robyn chuckled but didn't respond.

After they'd climbed up and over the industrial pipe that still drained sludge into the bay, Marian frowned severely as she took in Sherwood's skyline. Robyn wondered if that was the expression she'd had before Tuck had talked to her about Sherwood's potential.

When the sentry called out for them to state their purpose, Robyn recognized his voice immediately.

"Is that any way to talk to a friend, Jon Little?" she called back.

Little Jon was grinning as he stepped out from behind the crumbling wall. "I knew you couldn't stay away." While the sisters crossed the bridge, he met Robyn's eyes with a question, then flicked his gaze between them.

When they were safely on the other side, Robyn introduced them. "We have a lot to discuss. This is my sister, Marian. Marian, this is my friend, Jon."

They nodded at each other.

"Where's Tuck?" Robyn asked.

"Training at the salle."

Robyn tilted her head, unfamiliar with the word.

Little Jon chuckled. "I'll show you the way."

Once again, Little Jon led the visitors through the streets of Sherwood. Marian looked around solemnly, jumping at every sound. But Robyn found herself cheered by the unmistakable signs of life: the smoke from a distant hearth, the reverberation of someone at work.

As they approached a square, white building with arched windows, they heard the rhythmic clanging of metal on metal. The spiked, iron fence surrounding the building was rusted into place, and the gate hung crooked and open on its hinges. They followed the uneven, bricked path up to the missing front door under the portico. The large hall they entered was well lit by virtue of missing half its ceiling. The bust of a wolf's head gazed down from the far wall at the Order of Sirius lodge turned fencing arena.

"Halt," Tuck said upon seeing them enter the room. She and Much then saluted each other with their rapiers, ending their bout. Her hounds watched attentively to one side, breaking ranks only after their salutes were over. Then they rushed over and sniffed Tuck and Much to make sure no one was injured.

"Tell me the truth," Robyn said to Tuck when they'd turned their attention to the newcomers. "Did you know I was coming?"

She pursed her lips, her grey eyes sparkling, and shrugged. "I had a feeling."

Robyn introduced Marian to Tuck and Much.

"I'm impressed," Marian praised Tuck. "Robyn told me a lot of what you've done for the people of Sherwood, and you're so young."

Tuck smiled at the compliment. "Well, I can't take all the credit. Jon is the true head of Sherwood. He's the one that finds housing for everyone and protects us from the outside. I just lend some of my knowledge."

Little Jon's cheeks flushed as they all turned to him. "Don't sell your-self short, Tuck. We would be facing a hard winter if you hadn't helped with the crops, and that sword of yours is awfully sharp."

"Maybe," Tuck said. "But I'm still worried we won't have enough to last the winter."

"We'll manage," Little Jon reassured.

As the adults talked, Much had crept to Marian's side. He tugged at her sleeve to get her attention. She bent down to meet the boy on his level.

"I help, too," he told Marian. "I'm learning to fight to protect everyone, and I helped can the tomatoes we harvested."

Marian smiled at the boy, that glorious smile Robyn had seen stupefy grown men. "I'm certain you are the most valuable resident of Sherwood. I bet everyone here feels a lot safer with you around."

Much puffed out his chest with pride.

And that was all that was needed for Marian and Much to be completely taken with each other. Marian had always wanted children, and she had such a way with them.

"You said you had something you wanted to discuss?" Little Jon asked.

Robyn nodded. "Yes, I need your help."

Tuck motioned everyone toward the side of the hall that still had a ceiling, where a long table had been pushed up against the wall. Everyone but Robyn took a chair from around the table. Robyn stood, too wound up to sit.

"I haven't been quite honest with you all, though I didn't really hide it on purpose. The truth is: my sister and I are Robyn and Marian Loxley. Our father was friends with Henry Lackland. And when our parents died, the Lacklands took us in and raised us."

She paused and looked at Tuck and Little Jon. Their eyes were wide with astonishment, but they didn't appear as though they were angry.

"So when you told me about what the Lacklands had done, I was really shocked. Marian and I had no idea they're in the business of crime." Robyn shook her head. "To be honest, I feel foolish about the whole thing. I don't know how we didn't know, even if Eleanor told the family to keep us out of it. But after I saw you last, I started to look into it."

Robyn related what she'd found at Public Records and what Guy had told her. "Everything is as you said it was. I'm sickened by what I discovered, and I want to do something about it."

"What?" Little Jon asked. "What do you need our help with?"

Robyn took a deep breath. "My friend, Will, and his family are in that concentration camp. Guy said he can get me in to visit Will, but I really want to bust him—and as many prisoners as I can—out of there."

The silence from her listeners grew thick and uncomfortable, but Robyn waited for one of them to break it.

Finally, Tuck spoke. "You're talking about breaking into a federally-mandated concentration camp to break out the Japanese people interred there? This isn't just about the Lacklands. If we're caught, we will be tried for treason. You're asking us to risk our lives and the lives of the people here."

"I know it's a huge risk. But these are American citizens we're talking about. They're being held against their will without trial. We may be at war with Japan, but that doesn't mean we should imprison Americans just because they are of Japanese descent. You can't believe that's right."

"I don't think it's right," she countered. "But why should we get involved?"

Robyn stared right into Tuck's serious eyes. "You said Sherwood was a place where everyone was welcome. Are these people not welcome? What is the law? A set of rules written by men. The law should reflect what is moral and ethical. And when it doesn't, then the law need not be followed. In fact, it is our duty to disobey a law that is so unjust. These people were taken from their homes and forced into a concentration camp, forced to abandon the lives they'd worked so hard for. As a result, the people of Sherwood were forced from their homes and fired from their jobs. For what? So the Lacklands could make more money? Money from the government contract to house the prisoners? You can bet they aren't paying them a decent wage, so they're pocketing more of the profit from Lackland Chemical as well. You want to hurt the Lacklands? You want justice for the people of Sherwood? This is one way to get it."

After another thick silence, Little Jon said, "I agree with Robyn. We need to help those people."

Tuck nodded slowly. "Whatever may come from this, it will not be said that Tucker Fry didn't help those in need despite the consequences. I'm in too."

"And me, too," Much chimed.

"You know I'll always be where you need me," Marian said lastly.

Robyn smiled, her heart swelling. "We don't have enough time to form an escape plan before Saturday. But does anyone know of a way we can talk to Will from the outside so we can plan after I see him?"

Tuck and Little Jon looked at each other and nodded. "Gylberte," they said together.

When Robyn walked into Gylberte Whitehand's workshop, she thought she'd died and gone to heaven. She practically vibrated with giddy excitement. Her gaze whirled around the room, trying to take in all the gears, tubes, knobs, and buttons. It was a machinist's fairyland.

"Gyl?" Tuck called out when the engineer didn't appear to be in.

"Here!" the group heard from somewhere unknown. Then a begoggled redhead in dark green overalls popped out from behind an odd-looking piston engine. Behind him was a huge chalkboard with equations and roughly drawn schematics of what appeared to Robyn to be a helicopter in a backpack.

"Who have we got here?" Gyl grinned, pushing up his goggles and revealing just how much grease had covered the freckles of his face. His blue eyes smiled at them.

"This is Robyn and her sister Marian. They need some tech help."

"You've come to the right place," Gyl boasted.

"Your workshop is incredible," Robyn gushed. "Is that what I think it is?" she asked, pointing at the chalkboard. "Does it work? How high can it go? How do you account for drag? How do you overcome the torque effects?"

Gyl met Robyn's eyes with a smile. "Robyn, was it? Nice to meet ya." He pulled off his glove and offered his hand, which Robyn shook heartily.

"So what can I do for you?" he asked.

"I need a way of secretly communicating with someone from a distance," Robyn told him.

"Have you heard of a telephone?"

She snorted. "They don't have access to one."

"Hmm. How about a two-way radio?"

Robyn shook her head. "Too big. I need something I can sneak into a secure location, something more inconspicuous."

Gyl rubbed his chin in thought. "No telephone... How about a radio?"

Robyn thought about it. "Yes! They do have access to a radio."

"I've got just the thing." Gyl went to a set of shelves with various bits of mechanical devices. After pulling a heavy latched box down from the shelf, he rummaged through it. "Ah, here it is."

Gyl handed Robyn a small device, which sort of looked like a vacuum tube.

"Unfortunately, it's only one way. Tell them to attach it to the radio's antenna. It's a radio frequency converter. It will allow them to pick up frequencies normal radios can't. So then all you have to do is tell them the frequency and use a transmitter to broadcast on that frequency. Should afford you some level of privacy."

"Brilliant," Robyn praised, closing her hand around the device. "Do you have a transmitter too?"

Gyl tilted his head. "No, but I can make one."

"Really? Nifty. Thank you," she murmured.

Gyl grinned. "I should have it ready by next week."

"Thanks, Gyl," Tuck said.

"Is there anything else?" he asked.

"How are the repairs coming on the border deterrent?" Tuck inquired.

Gyl sighed. "I still need to get my hands on some parts. I'll let you know when it's fixed."

"What's 'the border deterrent'?" Robyn asked.

"The border deterrent is a device Gyl created to discourage visitors," Little Jon answered. "It's broken at the moment, which is why we have guards at the entrances."

"How does it work?"

"Essentially, it's a series of speakers that send a low frequency sound-wave out from the borders of Sherwood," Gyl said. "The frequency is just right to make visitors feel uncomfortable, even a little sick. Just enough that people don't want to poke around."

Robyn pursed her lips in thought. "That's incredible. But, hey, it's a good thing it was broken, right? Otherwise we might never have met."

Little Jon nodded with a smile.

"I hope you won't mind me coming back to talk shop with you sometime," Robyn said to Gyl.

"Absolutely," he nodded. "And I can always use an extra pair of knowledgeable hands, if you can swing it."

"Believe it," Robyn told him.

Gyl replaced his goggles with a grin, then gave Robyn a two fingered salute. "Then I'll be seeing ya."

They bid Gyl adieu and left him to his work.

It was rather late when they exited the workshop. Looking up at the sky, never truly dark as the city light reflected off the low-hanging smog, Robyn and Marian knew it was time to go.

"I guess it's time," Robyn said.

"Do you have to go, Señorita Robyn?" Much asked, pouting.

Robyn hesitated, not knowing quite how to respond.

"The boy is right, you know," Little Jon agreed, meeting Robyn's eyes warmly. "You're more than welcome to stay. You don't have to rely on the Lacklands anymore. You have us now."

Robyn bit her lip as a lump rose in her throat, and she sniffed hard, keeping the unexpected tears down. "I'm grateful. I truly am. And maybe soon I'll join you all here in Sherwood. But right now, if Marian and I don't get back, the Lacklands will be scouring Midshire for us. And that won't be good for anyone."

They nodded their understanding and offered to walk the sisters out. The Loxleys agreed, and Much didn't let Marian's hand go until they'd reached the bridge.

"Are you really going to move to Sherwood?" Marian asked, as the two waited on the platform, Asiago sleeping in his nest atop the station's street lamp.

Robyn was quiet for a while, thinking carefully about her answer. "I think I will," she admitted. "With Will and the others moving there, they're going to need a lot more help."

Her sister's answering silence told Robyn she was contemplating her own decision on the topic.

Robyn cut in before she could speak. "But I think you should stay. If we're going to undermine the Lacklands, we're going to need someone there. And they'll be much more surprised by you leaving than me."

"But...but then we won't be together," she murmured.

Robyn took her sister's hand. "Even apart we're still Marian and Robyn. We each have to play our parts if this is going to work."

"You sound like you have a plan."

"I'm beginning to. And you're a much better actress than me. I'm going to need you in that house."

Marian squeezed Robyn's hand. "Whatever you need, little sister."

Robyn knew she would have to talk to Eleanor soon about moving out of the Lackland house, and the sooner she did it the easier it would be. All the next day, she thought about how she was going to broach the subject, and that evening she took the plunge.

Well after supper when Robyn knew the rest of the house had retired to their respective rooms, she knocked softly at Eleanor's door.

"Entrez," Eleanor called in French.

Robyn opened the door and slipped in. Eleanor was sitting up in bed, reading glasses perched on her nose, the soft glow from the lamp at the bedside table giving her a particularly gentle appearance. She closed her book and removed her glasses. "Robyn, what brings you here so late?"

Robyn hesitated, her mind not able to reconcile this woman, who had always been so kind to her and her sister, with the crimes she knew Eleanor and her family committed. *How much was Eleanor involved?* Robyn wondered. *Is she an unwilling participant? Did she know about what the Lacklands were into before she married Henry? One thing is for certain, she hasn't stopped it.*

"Come in, mon enfant," Eleanor beckoned, patting the bed beside her.

Robyn did as she was bid and sat down next to her surrogate mother.

"You seem uneasy, Robyn. What is it?"

"Eleanor, I don't know how to go about this," she started her speech. "You've always encouraged me to be an independent woman, to use my wits, to follow my dreams."

Eleanor smiled and nodded, patting Robyn's hand. "And you've done marvelously, ma chère."

"In light of all that, I think it's time for me to stand on my own two feet. I appreciate everything you and Henry have done for Marian and me; I truly do. But I think I need to move out."

Eleanor's aged brow creased in concern. "Are we not giving you enough freedom here? Are you unhappy?"

"Oh, it's not that. You've given me everything I've ever wanted. But I want to know what it's like to support myself. You understand, don't you?"

Eleanor nodded solemnly. "Yes, I do understand. I, who have been twice married, but yet have managed to maintain the independence of my family's fortune. It is only that I am sad to see you go. Do you need any help finding a place?"

"No, but thank you. I already have a place in mind."

She gave Robyn a sad smile. "At times like this, I think I trained you too well. You will tell me if there is anything you need? Anything I can do?"

"I will."

"When do you plan on leaving?"

"Very soon I think."

"Well, you just let me know. I will have Sarah cook up something special to give you a proper sendoff."

"Thank you, Eleanor." Robyn rose to leave.

"Robyn?"

"Yes?" Robyn turned back to the woman who had raised her.

"You will still visit, won't you?"

"Of course, and don't worry. I won't be far."

She smiled, her face smoothing out in relief, reminding Robyn of just how many of her children had left her in one way or another.

"But will you do me one favor while I'm gone?"

"Anything, ma chère."

"Please take care of Marian. She won't handle me leaving well."

Eleanor nodded. "You have my word."

"Thanks."

Leaving Eleanor to her reading, Robyn couldn't ignore the ache in her chest. No matter what this woman and her kin had done, they had been her family. And though she was prepared to go against them for what was right, it didn't stop her sorrow.

Detective Nottingham hesitated at the frosted glass door of his precinct's files room. Taking a deep breath, he squared his shoulders and turned the knob.

Miss Brimley looked up as he entered, her lips curling in a sultry smile when she saw who it was. "Alaric," she simpered. "You've come to see me."

Alaric kept his expression cool and professional. "Detective Nottingham," he corrected for the 167th time since they'd met. "And not exactly, Miss Brimley. I'm here for an old case file."

The forced distance in his tone seemed to have no effect on the woman as she slowly got up from her desk, moving as if she were an exotic dancer, her hooded eyes trained on him. "Still as unyielding as ever, I see," she cooed, undeterred.

"Miss Brimley, please. The case file."

"Which one are you looking for?" she asked with a tilt of her head.

"1924, Loxley."

Miss Brimley slunk to the file cabinet. Her long, red nails flicked the file papers as she searched. Then she pulled out a cream folder and held it up. "Here it is." She smirked. "What will you give me for it?"

Alaric sighed in exasperation. "Miss Brimley, this is highly unprofessional. You are the files clerk. I have requested a file. What right do you have to keep it from me?"

Alaric could tell by her satisfied expression that he'd made a mistake. His outburst had only encouraged her.

"Are you going to Sergeant Treadle's party next week?" she asked.

It took effort to untighten his jaw enough to answer. "I hadn't planned on it."

"You see? That's your problem, Alaric. You need to loosen up and have a bit of fun. If you promise to come to the party, I'll let you have this file."

Alaric stared at the file, the file that likely had all the answers he needed. Then he thought about Robyn and that sad smile of hers as she'd related her parents' deaths. "Fine," he agreed.

Miss Brimley held out the file to him, her hand close to her body so he had to reach in to take it. "I'm glad you're coming around, Alaric," she murmured.

He didn't thank her but took the folder and left the files room at a quick and steady pace.

Taking police files out of the precinct was against protocol. And though Detective Nottingham was usually quite strict about such things, he ignored his own twinge of guilt as he left, telling the desk sergeant he was going to lunch.

Settling into a corner booth at a nearby diner, Alaric reassured himself. *Needs must, Nottingham. You know half of the station is on the take. It's likely some of them are even working for the Lacklands directly. You can't risk getting caught by the wrong person with this file, and you don't want them asking questions about why you're looking into this.*

After ordering his lunch, Alaric opened the folder. Photographs of the twisted, charred frame of a Model T hardened his stomach. The brutality of crime scenes and the way they exposed the darkness of the human soul was something Alaric had never gotten used to. He turned over the photographs to see the investigation report.

Alaric's heart sank at what he read. He'd hoped his hunch had been wrong, that Robyn's parents had died in a car accident, just as she thought. But after reading about the gang war in the old newspapers, he knew it had been too coincidental.

He leaned his forehead on his hand, leaving the meal the waitress had set on the table untouched. *What am I going to tell Robyn?* he thought. *She deserves to know the truth. But we said we wouldn't discuss the Lacklands. She's going to be crushed. Will she even believe me?*

Anxiety churned in Alaric's stomach. He couldn't bear the thought of hurting Robyn. She'd had such a hard life already. But still, he knew they were too good to be true. He knew it had to end eventually. *How could it not?* he thought miserably. *We are on opposite sides. And she is bound to realize that sooner or later... I just didn't think it would be so soon.* His chest tightened, and his body chilled. *Why couldn't I have more time with her?*

But no matter how much the thought of losing Robyn tormented him, he knew he would eventually tell her the truth because she had the right to know.

CHAPTER 18

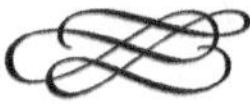

The following day, Robyn wanted nothing more than to spend the evening with Rick. Her nerves felt stretched to the breaking point. She couldn't think about anything other than her impending visit to the concentration camp and Will's subsequent jailbreak. But her good Detective Nottingham was the one thing she felt she could lose herself in. And even if she couldn't, drowning her anxiety with his touch was certainly an experiment worth undertaking.

As soon as she was out of work, she hightailed to the nearest pay phone and dialed the number Rick had given her.

He answered, his voice deep and slightly breathless. "Hello?"

"Rick? It's Robyn... You told me to call you tonight."

"Robyn, it's good to hear from you." His joyful words didn't match his sombre tone.

"Are you all right? You sound sort of down."

"I'm fine. I'm just...working through something."

"Is it anything I can help with?"

"It's just something I need to think about."

"Oh, okay. Well, when are you free?" she asked, her chest tight in anticipation of his answer.

"Hmm tomorrow?"

Robyn's heart sank. "I...I can't tomorrow. I'm going to visit a friend."

"All right."

There was silence on both ends of the line.

"I, uh..." Robyn started self-consciously. "I was really hoping to meet up tonight...if you could."

She could hear the hesitation in his answering pause. "Yeah, all right. Do you want to see a movie or something?"

"I'd...I'd rather stay in..."

When he spoke again, his voice was low and thick. "Mrs. Stanley leaves for her bridge game in fifteen minutes."

"I'll be there in twenty," she promised, then rang off.

When Robyn knocked on Rick's door, he answered as though he'd been waiting on the other side. He stood in the doorway, his tie loosened and the cuffs and top button of his shirt undone. She slipped in and shut the door behind her.

"We alone?" she whispered.

He nodded, his intense gaze trained on her like a predator ready to pounce.

"Good."

She was gratified to know she'd been right about spending the evening with Rick. Her mind dizzy with pleasure spun out thoughts of anxiety like drops of dew from a gyrating rotor. Rick didn't seem inclined toward conversation either, both of them satisfied with communicating through caresses and cries of elation.

Robyn lay silently wrapped in Rick's arms, the afterglow of love-making wearing off. And as her mind came to the surface, so did her anxious thoughts of what the following day would bring.

Rick didn't seem to notice her preoccupation as his dark eyes stared unfixed at the ceiling of his bedroom.

Maybe I should tell him what we're planning for Will and the others, Robyn thought. *He said he couldn't stomach injustice. He might be able to help, what with him being a detective and all.* She glanced up at him and the thought-line between his eyebrows. *What's he thinking so hard about?* she wondered. *He did say he was working through something... Maybe it's not such a good idea to get him involved. He may be able to help, but I'd hate to put him in a difficult position at work. The Lacklands are already watching him, fully aware he may be a problem to their enterprises. And then there was Guy's threat... No, I should keep him out of this whole thing.*

"Robyn," he murmured gruffly, then cleared his throat.

"Hmm?" She met his eyes.

"I...I found something I think you should know about."

Robyn didn't respond, waiting for him to order his words.

"When you told me about your parents, I got curious. I did a little digging, that was why I was at Public Records the other day, and discovered something...unsettling."

He paused again, glancing away. Robyn reached up and gently guided his gaze back to hers.

"What is it? You can tell me."

"The car accident that killed your parents. It was a car bomb. The Lacklands are an organized crime family, and they effectively own Midshire. But at the time, there was a turf war between the Lacklands and the Laurents. It was the Laurents who put the bomb in Henry Lackland's car, likely not knowing he would let your parents borrow it for a night out."

Robyn hadn't realized she was trembling until Rick covered her chilled hand with his.

"I'm sorry. I know we agreed not to talk about the Lacklands, but it felt too important not to say anything. I'm sure it's too much all at once," he whispered.

Her voice shook when she asked, "Are you saying my parents would still be alive if it wasn't for the Lacklands?"

He took a moment to respond. "It's possible."

"Were they...involved with the Lacklands' criminal activities?"

"Not that I can see."

Betrayal left a bitter taste in Robyn's mouth. Every trace of guilt she'd had for planning to go against them was gone. *They only took us in because it was their fault our parents are dead,* she thought. *They didn't care about us.* Fury stoked a fire in her gut, and she resolved to do everything she could to undermine their power.

The longer she remained silent the more anxious Rick looked, his eyes searching her wrathful face. He released her hand, giving her space. His sudden distance was like the cold water of Sherwood Canal.

Robyn breathed deep to steel her nerves and push back her rage.

"Thank you for telling me," she murmured, stroking his chest. "I just... can't believe I didn't know for so long." She played up her ignorance, knowing Rick still believed she knew nothing of the Lacklands' shady endeavors.

The tension in his face relaxed at her reassuring gesture. "Don't be too hard on yourself. Hiding the truth is what they're good at. If not, they never would've gotten this far."

"I guess..."

He pulled her closer in his embrace, and she didn't resist.

"What are you going to do?" he asked, rightfully assuming this revelation would have a major impact on her life.

Robyn sighed. "I'm moving out. I can't stay there anymore. I can't take money from them, live with them."

"But where will you go?" He hesitated. "If you need a place to stay..."

"Don't worry," she assured him. "I have a friend I can stay with."

He nodded faintly.

Robyn was silent for a while, thinking about how this new information affected her plans. "The more difficult part is going to be leaving my job. I don't want to raise suspicion that I know about them. Moving out won't be hard, but quitting my job at the mill? I need a good cover story to get out of that without alarming them."

"I see what you mean. Perhaps another job somewhere else will open up?"

"Another job at a place in Midshire not owned by them?" she asked sarcastically. *And not extorted by them?* she asked internally.

"Hmm. You could tell them you're moving farther away."

"But I still need to see my sister. And who knows how many people could offhandedly mention they saw me around?"

"Are you going to tell your sister what I told you? Will she also want to leave?"

"No, it would hurt her too much. She's a lot more sensitive than I," Robyn lied. *Of course, I'm going to tell Marian,* she thought. *But he doesn't know why I need her to stay with the Lacklands.*

"I see... Or...or you could tell them you're getting married. That's a common reason for women to leave their jobs."

Her heart thumped in her chest. *Surely...he's not...?* she wondered. She rose from where she lay on his chest to look more directly into his eyes. "That's not a proposal, is it Detective Nottingham?"

His face flushed, and she couldn't help but admire this new expression; she wasn't likely to see it often. "N-no, that's not..."

Robyn giggled, poking him in the ribs. "I know, but you should be more careful with your words, Detective. A girl might get the wrong idea."

He nodded silently. "But you could lie and say you're getting married."

Robyn pursed her lips. "I could, but I don't know how that would go over. They'd surely want to meet him," she glanced sideways at him, "and as you aren't volunteering..." *And who knows how Guy would respond?* she thought. *Besides, I might need to pump him for information again, and I certainly can't be as effective if I'm "getting married."* "I'll think of something," she assured him.

Rick trailed his thumb along her cheek. "You're all right, aren't you, Robyn?" he murmured anxiously.

Smiling slightly, she met his eyes. "I am. It's hard to hear. It's like everything I've known my entire life is wrong, but I'm resilient. I'm not so easily broken, Detective."

"I see that," he complimented.

"I'll be fine," she promised. "There's no need to worry."

"I like worrying about you," he whispered.

Heat gathered in Robyn's core. But as he kissed her, a kiss that started sweet but built in urgency, a clock chimed downstairs.

She pulled away slowly. "I've got to go. It's getting late."

"You could stay..."

She averted her gaze from his, not sure she'd have the ability to leave if she kept looking into those intense, dark eyes. "I can't. I'm meeting a friend tomorrow, one I haven't seen in too long. I can't be late."

"I understand," he said, his disappointment not quite stifled in his tone. "When can I see you again?"

"Hmm, I'm not sure. I think I'm going to be busy, what with moving and everything." *Not to mention committing treason,* she added in her mind.

"Well... Halloween is next week... And it seems my sergeant and his wife always put on a party. Do you think you'd like to go with me?"

Robyn's chest warmed. "I thought we were going to keep quiet about us?"

He shrugged. "Well, it's a costume party after all, and you said you like just being Robyn."

With everything going on right now, I really don't think I should, she thought. But as Rick gazed at her with that expression of boyish hope, she couldn't refuse him. "I'd love to," she answered.

His smile was small but telling.

"I'll call you for the details?"

He agreed.

CHAPTER 19

This time when Guy came to the house to meet Robyn, she wasn't concerned about waiting outside. Marian already knew he was taking her to see Will, and the Lacklands would likely be pleased if they thought they were going on a date. She'd convinced Guy not to tell John or Eleanor she knew about the family business, unless they asked directly, as it would only upset them. So they didn't correct John when he told them to have a good time, smiling on as Guy helped Robyn into her coat.

"Thank you so much for this," Robyn said from the passenger side of his Clipper as they drove to the concentration camp. "I can't tell you what it means to me."

He glanced over at her. "You can always come to me, Robyn. Whatever you need. I hope you know that."

Robyn nodded. The more she was around Guy in a one-on-one situation, the more she began to wonder about him. *What happened to him in his life that he ended up here?* she asked herself. *Is he an inherently violent person who is capable of a gentleness he only shows me? Or is he a gentle person, hardened by circumstance and forged into a killer?*

"We have known each other for a while," she stated in a conversational tone.

"Nearly a year."

"Where were you before you started working for John?"

He frowned at the turn the conversation was taking. "I've been a lot of places."

"Have you always done the same type of work?" she pushed.

He shrugged. "It's what I'm good at."

His tone suggested he wasn't going to elaborate. Robyn tried again. "Are you from Midshire originally?"

"No, Charleston."

"South Carolina?"

"Oregon."

"Oh, I've never heard of it. Is it nice?"

"It's a few miles west of Coos Bay. It's just an insignificant fishing village."

Robyn couldn't quite tell if his tone was sad or bitter, but his knuckles were white on the steering wheel.

"So were you glad to move to Midshire then?"

She nearly flinched when his intense gaze met hers.

"It has its perks."

Her face flushed, suddenly embarrassed by his attention. "I-I've never been anywhere else," she murmured, looking away.

Silence settled in for the rest of the drive. Robyn was no closer to understanding Guy Gisbourne than she had been in all the months before.

He confused her. *Should I trust the instinct that has told me to stay away from him since the moment we met?* she wondered. Every time he met her eyes, she got a shot of adrenaline, telling her that this man was dangerous. And certainly he was, which was only confirmed when she'd found out what his real job was.

I know he's kind to me because he wants me, she thought. *I'm not an idiot.* But Guy wasn't the first dangerous man she'd met in her life. And the others, while polite, no doubt because of her affiliation with the Lacklands, were never so gentle. She'd seen the way dangerous men treated the women they desired. They were intense all right, just like Guy, and they may be generous with their money and their regard, but she never would have called them gentle.

Still, this tenderness didn't draw her in so much as intrigue and disorient her. It was the feeling of wondering how far you could lean over a ledge without falling, the feeling of how close you could get to a flame without being burned.

It was nothing like the thrill Rick gave her. Rick was the thrill of discovery, adventure, that feeling that pulls you along the unknown path, ever seeking to mount the next hill, to turn the next bend. But not danger. Guy seemed to come with the promise of inevitable destruction.

I suppose some women are into that, trying to tame what's wild, trying to redeem what's corrupt, she thought. She glanced sideways at Guy, his gaze fixed on the road. *Guy Gisbourne hurts people for money, kills people for money,* she reminded herself. *Is he redeemable? Does he even have a sense of moral justice?*

As he pulled up to the apartment building turned concentration camp, Robyn stared at the stories upon stories of barred windows. She wondered what it had looked like before. *Had the women and children of Sherwood seen its gate and small courtyard as welcoming?*

Charles still stood near the door, weapon in hand, his eyes suspiciously glaring at Guy's car.

Guy slid out from the driver's seat and came around the car to open Robyn's door. And as he held out his hand to her, his eyes solicitously watching her footing, she couldn't believe he didn't have some code of ethics dictating his behavior. *What exactly happened to you, Guy Gisbourne?* she wondered.

But Robyn had no more time to ponder her escort's philosophical leanings as a short man with a red, pinched face exited the front door. He was accompanied by the fellow who had given her the warden's letter.

"Warden James Weldon," the squat man introduced himself to Robyn with a deep bow and a welcoming smile.

Gone were the snotty words of the warden's letter as if they'd never existed. Robyn might have thought he didn't know she was the same person had it not been for his companion in the tailored suit, whose dry gaze held the undeniable hint of recognition.

She frowned at the pair, refusing to meet the warden's change in attitude with any sort of pleasantness on her part. Guy smirked, obviously finding her reaction amusing.

"Is everything arranged?" Guy asked the warden.

"Oh yes, absolutely, Mr. Gisbourne. Everything is as you requested."

"Good."

Warden Weldon released a little sigh of relief at Guy's threatening word of approval.

"Well?" Guy demanded, raising an eyebrow when the warden hadn't moved.

Weldon flinched and scurried as fast as his short legs would take him, nearly tripping on the front stairs. "This way, Mr. Gisbourne, Miss Loxley."

Robyn raised her chin and didn't even glance at Charles as they passed him, entering Midshire War Relocation Center.

The first thing that struck Robyn as they passed the wall of unused mailboxes in the lobby was how very clean the place was. She'd expected the prison to be filthy, dark, and dingy, but it was reminiscent of those radio advertisements for cleaning products: *Make your home a more pleasant, more inviting place to be with Chem-Lax! No hard rubbing! No rinsing! Only Chem-Lax cleans wood, walls, tile, and linoleum! Ask your nearest hardware, paint, or department store about Chem-Lax today!*

But when they got off the elevator on the second floor, she saw exactly why it was so spotless. A group of inmates, elderly and children, were working hard to clean and polish the floors and fixtures of their prison.

As Robyn passed one stooped, elderly woman on her hands and knees, the prisoner looked up at her. Her dark eyes, clouded with cataracts, had no trouble finding Robyn's. Her face spoke of a lifetime of struggle, of smiles and tears, of countless hours working for her family. And though her eyes haunted Robyn, she did not look beaten. She did not look defiant either, just resigned.

"We try to build a community here," Weldon said, gesturing to the people cleaning with an expression of high-chinned pride. "All must pull their weight and do their part. These elderly and children are unfit to help at the lab, so they work at home, providing a clean and welcoming space for their fellow countrymen."

Robyn tasted the metallic bitterness of blood as she bit down hard on her tongue. Her indignation must have shown clearly on her face because Guy cut the warden off.

"We don't need commentary. Just lead the way."

"O-of course, Mr. Gisbourne. This way, Mr. Gisbourne."

Weldon led them into an apartment labeled with his name and position, which had been turned into an office.

"Please, make yourselves comfortable," he said, gesturing to a pair of armchairs before wringing his hands compulsively. "Can I get you anything to drink?"

Robyn was in no mood to deal with pleasantries, and Guy seemed to pick up on that.

"I'm losing patience, Mr. Weldon. The internee. Where is he?" Guy demanded.

The warden's red face paled. "The guard is waiting for my signal, Mr. Gisbourne."

"Then give it."

Weldon's head wobbled on his shoulders as he nodded. "Right away, sir." Then he gestured to his assistant in the tailored suit, who turned on his heel and left the room.

Robyn stepped close to Guy, lifting her face. Seeing her purpose, he leaned down closer to her.

"Guy, I don't care for this man, and I'm afraid Will won't talk to me if he's here. Could you get him to leave?" she pleaded.

Guy's gaze lingered on her face, close to his as she whispered to him. His eyes were so dark, she could never tell if they were brown or black. Her head spun, and she felt like she would fall into them like Alice down the rabbit hole.

"Warden?" he called, not taking his eyes off her.

"Yes, Mr. Gisbourne?"

"Wait in the hall. You can send him in when he arrives."

"But—"

Guy's gaze flicked to glare at the man.

"O-of course, sir." Then he skittered out the room.

"Thank you," Robyn said sincerely, giving Guy a tentative smile.

Guy's features smoothed out into an expression of momentary contentment as he met her eyes. The look produced a glimmer of warmth within Robyn that she'd never experienced in Guy's presence. And though it was just a glint, it seemed comfortable compared to the cold wariness she usually felt around him.

She wasn't so ungenerous that she couldn't acknowledge the things he'd done for her. For one thing, he had always been, and continued to be, completely honest with her. And he had gone against John and Eleanor's wishes, despite the real possibility of incurring their wraths, just to ease her mind.

For the first time, Robyn thought that perhaps she had misjudged Guy, perhaps they could be friends. Maybe he could be redeemed after all.

A knock sounded on the door, halting her train of thought.

"Enter," Guy ordered.

The door opened, and a hulking man led Will in. "14598C, as requested," the guard announced.

Robyn held her breath as her heart pounded painfully at the sight of her best friend. He was thinner than she remembered, not sickly, but most definitely thinner. His hair had grown some two inches, and his face had lost that warm glow it had always had.

"Robyn..." Will whispered, his almond eyes wide.

Guy placed a hand on Robyn's shoulder. "We'll give you a minute," he murmured before gesturing for the guard to leave Robyn and Will alone.

By the time the door clicked and locked, Robyn already had her arms wrapped around Will, her face buried in his neck. She inhaled deeply his familiar scent, and her exhale came out as a sob. Her nose and throat burned with the hot tears she couldn't hold back.

She hadn't planned on wasting their time with tears, but then again, she never planned on crying. His warmth just brought it out of her.

She didn't get a hold of herself until she felt his silent trembling against her. She pulled back and looked into his dark eyes, smiling through her tears. His answering smile was just as watery.

"I've been so worried," she whispered.

"Didn't you get my letter? I told you I didn't want to bring you into this. What are you doing here?" he scolded her without ire.

"Did you really think I could stay away?"

"I should've known you wouldn't leave it alone. The United States government is no match for you."

Robyn grinned, but he squinted slightly at her.

"Still, I didn't think you'd get Guy Gisbourne involved. I thought you didn't like him."

Robyn waved her hand at the comment. "Listen," she whispered low. "I'm sure we don't have a lot of time. Some friends and I are going to get you out of here. You, Micki, and as many people as we can."

Will froze. "What are you saying, Robyn? This is a prison. There are armed guards. We're here by executive order."

"Are you saying you don't want to leave?"

He frowned. "I didn't say that, but some of the others won't. We'd have to go into hiding, change our names, pass ourselves off as Chinese at best. And that's only *if* we get out alive. Sure, none of us *want* to be here, but that isn't the same as escaping."

Robyn bit her lip. "But what about you? Will you come with us?"

Will scowled at her. "Of course I will. What, do you think I want to stay in this place?"

"Will you try to convince the others?"

"I'll see what I can do. What's your plan?"

"I don't have one yet."

Will stared at her. "Are you serious?"

"Shut up, I'm working on it. You know I'm not a planner. Here." Robyn pulled the device Gyl had given her from her pocket and handed it to Will. "Guy told me you have a radio?"

He nodded. "We share it with the other two families in our apartment though."

Robyn clicked her tongue. "It's the best we could do." Then she told him to attach it to his radio's antenna, what frequency she'd be broadcasting from, and what time to tune in every night.

He listened carefully, his expression tense, as she relayed all the details.

"Don't worry. We're going to get you out of here," Robyn promised.

Just as she squeezed his hand in reassurance, the door opened, and Guy entered. Then the guard's head appeared over his shoulder in the doorway. Will patted Robyn on the arm silently before turning to his prison-keeper. But as Guy stepped aside for him to pass, Will stopped in front of him.

"Thank you. I'm sure you know how she likes to worry."

Guy nodded his acknowledgment, and the guard reached out and grabbed Will by the shoulder, pulling him forward. Robyn advanced, ready to protest, but Will looked back at her and shook his head. "I'm sure our boys will win the war soon. I'll see you then."

"Don't you doubt it, nip," the guard muttered as he pushed Will out of the room.

Robyn ground her teeth, her eyes glaring at the guard's retreating back, too irate to notice the warden and his assistant had returned as well. A soft touch on her shoulder made her flinch.

"Let's go," Guy murmured, leading her with a gentle hand on her lower back.

CHAPTER 20

ill Sukaretto clenched his jaw as Clauson pushed him from the room. His indignation reappeared with Robyn out of sight, knowing he had to be cool in her presence if he wanted her to keep her explosive temper under control. After over fifteen years of friendship, he was used to having the cooler of their two heads.

As the doors of the elevator shut on Will and Clauson, the guard hit the button for the basement.

"I thought I was going back upstairs," Will commented, the radio frequency converter burning a hole in his pocket.

"Warden says you're to work this afternoon. You'll be transported with the rations," Clauson snapped.

Will's heart thumped as he thought of the pat-down all prisoners had to endure when leaving the factory.

The temperature dropped at least ten degrees when the elevator doors opened. It was chilly on the upper floors, especially as winter approached, but the basement was downright frigid. Will thought wistfully of the two thin Army blankets on his cot upstairs as he blew frosted breath onto his cold fingers.

Clauson delivered Will to the kitchens, where old women and young teens were counting out Legumighty for the lab workers. Clauson left with only a nod to his colleague, the guard who would be transporting the food.

Micki looked up from the counter where she was packing Legumighty into boxes. Her young brow smoothed when her brother came to stand beside her.

"So? What was that about?" Micki asked in Japanese. "Why did the warden want to see you?"

"You won't believe it," he answered in the same language. "Robyn found a way in to see me."

"What? Robyn-chan was here? How?"

Will shrugged. "You know Robyn. Looking back, it was foolish to think she wouldn't find some way in."

Micki giggled her agreement.

Will glanced at the guard across the room, who was eyeing them suspiciously, as they always did when the inmates spoke the language of their forefathers. "And she gave me something while she was here," he said, dropping his voice low. "Do you think you can put it upstairs for me? Without anyone seeing...?"

His sister smirked. "Are you doubting me, Onii-san?"

Will had never been so grateful for Micki's light fingers. In fact, he used to find it quite annoying, especially when she'd steal his sweets.

"It's in my right pocket," he told her, knowing she'd find a way to purloin it without him noticing, let alone the guard.

When Micki and the rest of the kitchen crew had finished counting and filling the boxes, Will and a few of the boys hauled the boxes into a cargo van.

As the rest of the kitchen crew prepared the rations for those left at the camp, Will settled in among the boxes of Legumighty to be transported to Lackland Chemical, satisfied to find his pockets empty.

On the short ride to the lab, Will bemoaned the van's lack of windows. His ride to and from the lab every day was the one thing he looked forward to. Looking out the windows of the bus made him almost feel a part of Midshire again. He could almost fool himself into believing he was on his way home to the dojo as he watched the streets, filled with familiar haunts, pass by. The five and dime where Robyn and he used to get candy after school, the corner market where he would carry his mother's shopping basket, the vacant lot where he and the neighborhood kids used to play street levy, Midshire hadn't changed at all, and yet, there seemed no place for him there anymore.

No, he thought. *I can't think like that. A country is made up of people. There may be those who don't want me here, but there are also those, like Robyn, who will fight for me to stay.*

Warmth spread to Will's limbs as he thought of his long-time friend. Their adventures, their memories at the dojo, the pranks they used to play on each other, it was the thought that Robyn, at least, was still out there, living free and seeing the clouded sky that made Will capable of enduring it all. If he died today, someone out there would mourn him, someone out there had loved him.

When the van arrived at the lab, Will was unloaded with the boxes meant for the workers' lunch. He was given one packet of Legumighty as he was directed through the unused kitchen to the cafeteria. He took a seat and watched as workers lined up for their rations. He made eye contact with his parents, who sighed in relief at seeing their son safe after his visit with the warden.

As Will choked down his lunch, Yuki, Alice, and Ritsu sat down at Will's table.

"Look at that, he's alive," Ritsu said to the women. "I told you he'd be fine."

"Well, we didn't know what was going on, did we?" Alice snapped.

"Are you all right?" Yuki asked, her big, brown eyes analyzing Will solicitously.

"I'm fine," Will assured her. "I'm better than fine actually."

"Oh?" Alice tilted her head.

Will nodded. "I got a visit from Robyn."

"The illustrious Robyn we've heard so much about." Ritsu smirked. "And did you get a kiss from your lady love?"

Will frowned. "I've told you it's not like that," he said.

"And I've told you I don't buy it," Ritsu answered in the same tone.

"But how did she manage to get in?" Yuki asked, ignoring Ritsu.

"I'm not sure exactly, but...she'll be back," Will whispered significantly.

"Are you saying what I think you're saying?" Alice asked.

Will nodded, meeting each of their gazes in turn. "So...are you in?"

"Are you kidding?" Ritsu laughed.

"Obviously," Alice agreed.

They all looked at Yuki, who hesitated. "Wouldn't it be better if we just waited for the war to be over? They'll let us out eventually," she murmured.

"I'm not going to lie to you, Yuki," Will said. "It's going to be dangerous. You don't have to if you don't want to."

Yuki looked down at her hands, then nodded. "No, you're right," she answered, her voice trembling ever so slightly. "Freedom... It's why our parents came all the way here, why they worked so hard, right?"

The others nodded in agreement.

A bell echoed off the bare walls of the cafeteria, and everyone rose to return to work.

As they passed through the scrub area, a long room with hooks along the walls and sinks in the center, those who had spent their meager wages on protective masks and overalls put their gear back on to return to the lab.

"Hey," Will muttered, putting his hand on Yuki's shoulder. "You can keep using my mask for the rest of the day," he told her.

"But...you need it," she protested weakly.

Will smiled. "I'll be okay for one day. Besides, you have asthma, and you're close to saving up enough for a mask, aren't you?"

She nodded slightly. "Thank you."

"What are friends for?"

CHAPTER 21

Guy Gisbourne escorted Robyn through the concentration camp and out the front lobby. Keyed in to her trembling back beneath his hand, he ignored whatever Weldon was chattering about.

When Guy opened the car door for her, Robyn didn't get in. Instead, she stomped through the courtyard and out the gate.

Guy didn't glance back at the warden, his assistant, or the guard to see their reactions but followed after her.

It wasn't difficult for him to catch up with Robyn's shorter stride, but he approached cautiously, seeing the tension in her rigid gait.

"Robyn, let me take you home."

Robyn halted, and he thought she would turn and head back to the car. But she whirled around, her ferocity glaring up at him. "You lied to me, Guy Gisbourne," she growled.

A thrill raised the hair on his arms.

"You said they were being taken care of."

He opened his mouth to speak, but she cut him off.

"Is that what you call being taken care of?" she demanded, her voice raising in pitch and volume. "Did you see Will? Did you? Did he look well to you? And those elderly and children, forced to clean their own prison!

Are they being fed properly? And what about the temperature? It was freezing in there!"

Guy felt the full force of Robyn's fierce empathy. He had been judged and found wanting. His chest ached at the verdict in her eyes.

"I knew I'd been right about you," she spat, each word slicing into his heart.

She turned on her heel, and he was certain she would never look at him again.

"Robyn, wait." He grabbed her wrist to stop her from leaving.

She snatched her hand away. "Leave me alone, Guy. This was your responsibility. You oversee all Lackland enterprises, don't you? You allowed this to happen, and I blame you personally. I never want to see you again."

When she stormed away, Guy didn't attempt to stop her.

"I will fix this," he called after her, but she gave no indication she'd heard him.

Clenching his fists, Guy channeled his sorrow into rage. Not at Robyn, never at Robyn, but at the root of the problem.

When he'd returned to the courtyard, the warden and his assistant were still waiting by his car to see him off. He marched up to them and stepped right into the warden's personal space.

The warden flinched and cowered at the glare Guy directed at him.

"The state of this camp is completely unacceptable. You have been falsely reporting the conditions here, Weldon. As such, you are dismissed. Leave the premises immediately." Guy turned to the assistant in the tailored suit. "What's your name?"

"Karl Wisely," the assistant answered.

"Well, Warden Wisely, I expect better from you than your predecessor."

"Certainly, Mr. Gisbourne."

Guy turned to leave, but the new warden wasn't finished.

"However, I would be remiss in my duty if I did not inform you that we are low on supplies, should you wish conditions to improve, that is."

Guy's glare flicked to Wisely, who met his gaze passively. "Such as?" Guy ground out.

"Fuel, for one. Not to mention food and medicine."

"Are you not issued funds for these things?"

Wisely nodded. "We have nearly three thousand internees at this camp. This is a repurposed building. It was not built to house internees, and it certainly wasn't built for this many people. And with the conditions as they are at the chemical lab, we have quite a few sick. Masks and overalls are expensive, and many of the internees use their wages on necessities like soap and toothbrushes. If you want these people healthier, you need safety equipment for everyone at the lab, better food, more medicine, and more diesel for heat at the very least."

Guy frowned, wondering if John knew about this or if Weldon had left that out of his reports to him as well. "I will see what I can do. Do the best you can with what you have for now," Guy instructed Wisely.

Guy couldn't get the look in Robyn's eyes out of his head as he drove to the Lacklands'. The outrage, the pain... *I will* make this right, he swore to himself.

John Lackland was in his bedroom preparing for a night out when Guy arrived, but he called for Guy to enter. John met Guy's gaze in the mirror as he tied his tie.

"Back already?" he asked Guy.

Guy recalled that John had assumed Robyn and he were on a date. "Yes," he answered. "Some urgent business."

John's reflection raised his eyebrows. "Oh?"

"Sir, have you been to the concentration camp?" Guy asked.

"No, why would I?"

"It has come to my attention that the internees are not being well cared for. The money provided isn't enough to give them healthy and humane conditions."

"How so?" John asked unconcerned.

"Well, Wisely told me they are overcrowded. That due partly to the conditions at the lab, they are sick. They don't have enough money for proper food, medicine, or even fuel."

"And? The government doesn't exactly give us enough to house the wretches. If we didn't have them work at Lackland Chemical, we'd barely be making a profit. We have to garnish their wages just to feed them Legumighty. Can you imagine what it would cost for *real* food?"

"But surely there is enough to spare for diesel? Winter is coming after all."

"So you'd have our servicemen go without fuel and medicine and decent food so a few thousand spies can live comfortably on the government's dime? There's a war on, you know. Or haven't you heard?" John said mildly.

Guy knew John didn't care about the war. He only saw how he could profit off it. In fact, he'd once told Guy he hoped it would never end, then perhaps Richard wouldn't come home.

"Then what about Lackland Chemical?" Guy grasped at straws. "Wisely said they don't have enough safety equipment for everyone."

"I'd imagine so," John stated. "We give them wages. If they choose to spend that money on something other than masks and overalls, well, there isn't much we can do about that. Is there?"

"We could give them the safety equipment."

At this, John turned around, his eyes cold. "The previous workers had to purchase their own equipment. Why would we treat these traitors any better?"

But if you're garnishing their wages for food, then it would take them longer to afford safety gear, Guy thought. "There must be something we can do, sir," Guy offered.

"Tell me, Gisbourne," John said condescendingly. "Have you seen the other camps?"

"No," Guy answered.

"I have. And I tell you they are far worse than ours. Thin-walled Army barracks, more than twice as many internees. At least our internees have decent walls."

Guy didn't respond.

"I'll tell you what, Gisbourne. You want conditions to be better for them at the lab and at the camp? Then you pay for it. Sure, pay for it out of your own money. But you wouldn't like that, now would you? You want it to come out of my pocket but not yours," John sneered. "I don't want to hear about this again," he added with finality.

Guy left John's room. *"I never want to see you again."* Robyn's pronouncement rang in Guy's ears. *I have to do something,* Guy thought.

CHAPTER 22

"*I* will fix this!" Guy called, but Robyn didn't look back as she strode down the street.

Her heart pounded in her chest, pumping rage in her veins. Her fingers ached from squeezing her fists too tight. She'd known going to the camp wouldn't be pleasant. But now that she'd seen it with her own eyes, she couldn't get Will's sad smile out of her mind. She clenched her eyes shut and shook her head, sighing.

Maybe I should tell Rick about this. It can't be legal to detain people like that. They didn't even have a trial, she thought.

Then her arms hung at her sides, deflated with hopelessness. *No, what can he do about it? Legal or not, they're detained by executive order,* she thought. *Rick can't do anything about that. He could potentially look into the conditions, but there's no way the Lacklands would let him get anywhere near with the target on his back.*

Biting her lip, she crinkled her brow. *I shouldn't have said that to Guy,* she thought. *I let my anger get the best of me again. I can blame him all I want, but I just burned the best bridge I had into the Lacklands' organization.*

Robyn sighed again. *Oh, well,* she thought. *Not much I can do about it now, and I've got too much to do to worry about it. Will is relying on me.*

When Robyn arrived back at the Lacklands', she was glad to see Guy's car was not in the round drive. She walked around the house to her work-shed, needing the quiet mind that came from working on her motorcycle. But as she stared at her project, she frowned. As soon as she put the chains on, her bike would be complete.

I guess there really isn't anything left to do here, she thought hollowly.

An hour later, Robyn wiped her greasy hands on a rag and reached for the handlebars. She wheeled her creation out of the shed onto the lawn. Then she sat astride, the weight of her bike solid and heavy between her thighs. Reaching down, she opened the decompression lever, then kicked the kicker with her right foot. She kicked hard a second time but nothing happened.

She cursed under her breath, trying to figure out where she could have gone wrong, but tried again. On the fourth kick, the diesel engine rumbling to life, accentuated by loud knocks.

Warmth spread through Robyn's chest, and a slow, satisfied smile slid onto her face.

Kicking up the stand, she squeezed the clutch and flipped the gear lever with her foot. Slowly releasing the clutch, the motorcycle eased forward. As she pulled the throttle and the bike sped up, she let loose a whoop of satisfaction. She sailed across the lawn and tested the brakes not a foot from the hedge.

Robyn glowed with satisfaction at a job well done. Squeezing her new ride along the side of the house, she parked it in the round drive, promising herself a more stimulating and thorough ride after she had packed.

When Robyn strode down the hallway toward her room, she skidded to a halt as she passed Marian's door. Taking a deep breath, she knocked. A call from inside bid her come in.

Marian was standing on her bed, staring down at photographs scattered on her bedroom floor. She looked up when Robyn opened the door.

"What do you think?" Marian asked, motioning for Robyn to climb onto the bed beside her.

Robyn slipped off her shoes and carefully crossed the room, trying not to step on the matte prints. When Robyn reached the bed, Marian stretched and pulled Robyn up by the hand.

Standing beside her sister, Robyn looked down at the assembled photos. Each photo didn't mean much individually, a bit of sky here, the corner of a building there. But when the photographs were placed together, they formed a sort of mosaic of an elderly woman's face. Her face was weathered and spotted, deep wrinkles lined her brow and beneath her eyes. Her mouth was quirked in an amused smile, and her dark eyes glinted as if she was humoring the young photographer. She wore a scarf tied under her chin, wispy grey hair peeking out above her forehead.

"Who is she?" Robyn asked, unable to look away from the woman's sprightly gaze.

"I found her down at the docks. She's the mother of a fishmonger. Her late husband owned a fishing boat, and now her son runs it. She helps her daughter-in-law sell fish at the market."

"She looks like she's seen a lot in her life," Robyn mused.

Marian nodded.

"How do you think she's managed to still look so good-humored about it all?"

"Perhaps when you've seen so much, you can find joy in every situation."

"It's probably more her disposition," Robyn countered.

Marian shrugged. "Maybe. In any case, I wanted to portray the many experiences that make up a person. If you look at just her brow, for instance, you would think this woman is troubled, worried, she has problems. But when you see the whole picture, you understand that those are problems of the past, long days and nights furrowing her brow in concern."

Robyn patted her sister on the shoulder. "You're really getting good at this whole photography as art thing, aren't you?"

Marian smirked. "What are you saying? I wasn't good before?"

Robyn raised her hands with a grin. "I didn't say that."

They both chuckled.

"Anyway, how did your visit with Will go?"

Robyn related what had happened at the concentration camp and after.

Marian's troubled expression turned soothing. "I know you're worried. I am too. But let's focus on helping them rather than getting distracted by the anger we feel at the injustice of it all."

"You're right," Robyn sighed.

"Aren't I always?" Marian teased.

"But Guy..."

Marian wrapped her arm around Robyn's shoulders and squeezed. "Let's not worry about that now. For all you know, we won't need anything else from Guy. And you didn't want him to get attached, did you? I mean, I know he isn't exactly a *good* person, but that doesn't make playing with his emotions okay, right?"

Robyn pursed her lips. She didn't know how to tell her sister she'd actually started to like Guy, didn't want to acknowledge it in her mind let alone say the words aloud.

"Besides," Marian continued. "You already have a super-secret spy." She lifted her chin and turned her head to the side in a dignified expression.

"All right. I'll leave it in your hands then."

"Good."

Robyn sighed. "I think it's time," she pronounced. Meeting her sister's eyes, she asked, "Would you help me pack?"

Robyn knew she couldn't take much with her to Sherwood, just whatever she could carry on her motorcycle. She brought her overalls, her boots, the outfit Little Jon had given her, a few every day clothes, and a single pair of heels.

She frowned at the extensive collection of clothes and cosmetics she was leaving behind.

"Don't worry," Marian assured. "If you need anything else later on, I can bring it to you."

From her vanity, Robyn grabbed her photographs, the letter Will had written her, and the pair of double daggers from the drawer. She tucked them into the lone rucksack on her bed.

As she turned around, scanning the room to see if she'd left anything behind, Marian held out her bow and a quiver of grey goose feather arrows, which Robyn kept in her closet. "You might need them," she said, handing the weapons to Robyn.

The familiarity of the bow's leather grip soothed Robyn's humming anxiety. She trailed her finger along the polished wood of the upper limb.

The bow was truly a work of art. Robyn and Will had painstakingly carved it out of yew together. It was one of a kind. She hadn't pulled the bowstring since Will was taken away. But in that moment, she vowed to use it to save him.

Robyn grabbed the lot and started across the room. On the threshold, her hand on the light switch, Robyn looked over her shoulder at the room she'd slept in most of her life. Taking a deep breath, she turned out the light and shut the door behind her.

With it being a Saturday night, the Lacklands were out at the theatre. *La Traviata* was playing, so there was no one but her sister to see her go. After Marian had helped Robyn mount her few belongings to the back of her motorcycle, she rested her hands on her little sister's shoulders.

"You call me," she ordered. "I'll meet you anytime, day or night."

Robyn nodded, swallowing the lump in her throat, the moment of separation finally real.

"I know you'll do great. You're the strongest, most capable woman I know," Marian told her.

Tears stung Robyn's nose as Marian's voice thickened. Sniffing hard, Robyn embraced her sister, squeezing her eyes shut to stop the tears from falling.

"You know where I'll be," Robyn reassured. "You're more than welcome in Sherwood."

Robyn felt Marian nod.

"And Marian," Robyn added seriously, pulling back and staring into her sister's eyes. "I want you to be careful, all right? What I'm asking you to do could be really dangerous. Do what you can, but don't take unnecessary risks, okay?"

Marian frowned at Robyn's hypocrisy but didn't protest. Robyn squinted at her sister, noticing she hadn't agreed.

"You better get going before they come home," Marian murmured. "Give Much a hug for me, will you?"

Robyn nodded, squeezing her sister's hand, then got on her bike. She didn't feel the same thrill she had only hours before at the sound of the engine she'd built, somewhat dampened by the sorrow of parting. She put on her cap and wiped her misty eyes so her goggles wouldn't fog.

Marian raised a hand in farewell as Robyn kicked up the stand. Robyn nodded once before chugging out of the round drive and onto the road.

Once she was on the street, Robyn took stock of how her machine was running, and a level of satisfaction hummed around the ache in her chest as she rumbled along efficiently.

She was grateful for her cap, goggles, and scarf as the cool October wind whipped her face. Sure, she wanted to feel the wind blowing the hair from her face, taking her breath away as it flowed into her lungs; it would have been thrilling. But she wasn't keen on her face getting wind burn or a lungful of exhaust from the car ahead of her.

Still, she couldn't argue that the bike had given her a level of freedom she hadn't had before. No longer did she have to switch from cab to train to train to train to get where she was going.

Following the grid-like pattern of the city's streets, it didn't take her long to get to The Doncz, the borough between Sherwood and the rest of Midshire. As she made her way to the bayfront, she located the industrial pipe that eventually acted as a barrier to Sherwood, raised on iron stilts in that part of the city. She rode under it, and drove between the pipe and the canal the rest of the way, the knocking of her motorcycle echoing off the cement walls of the canal on one side and the metal pipe on the other. Still, she barely heard it over the rest of the sounds of the city.

As she approached the bridge, she saw Little Jon already waiting for her.

When she'd parked and turned off her motorcycle, she lifted her goggles onto her cap.

"Let me guess, Tuck told you I was coming?" she asked him.

He shook his head. "No, I heard your bike and saw it was you." He gazed at the motorcycle in admiration. "Is it new?"

Robyn nodded. "Finished it today," she answered with pride.

"You built it yourself?" He gave a low whistle. "You sure are something, Robyn Loxley."

She grinned. "Thanks."

After she had grabbed her things and covered her motorcycle with a tarp, she turned to Little Jon expectantly. "I hope you have a place for me to stay after that heartfelt invitation."

He smiled. "Yeah, most of the women stay up in the abbey's dormitory.

There's room for you there for as long as you want, or until you find some-place else in Sherwood you like."

Robyn's heart warmed at Little Jon's open expression. She looked up at him and smiled. "Walk me home?"

He nodded. "Of course."

CHAPTER 23

As Robyn and Little Jon strolled through Sherwood, she felt none of the apprehension she'd experienced on her first visit. The soft crunch of pavement beneath their boots seemed loud in the shadowed night.

"Do you really think I'm this knight of wands Tuck talked about?" Robyn murmured to Little Jon as they walked.

He looked over at her, his expression soft and open. "I do," he said.

"Why?"

He stopped and turned to her, and she followed suit, tilting her head back to meet his eyes. "Because I believe in you, Robyn," he said simply.

She frowned. "I appreciate that. I do. But, let's be honest, you haven't known me very long. Why would you follow me? Commit treason with me?"

He tilted his head. "It's the right thing to do. When you know something is right, you should choose that path. That path has never been the easy choice. And I may not have known you very long, but it has been long enough for me to see what kind of woman you are."

"And what kind of woman is that?"

He smiled softly. "You're like...a grizzly bear."

Robyn squinted. "Excuse me?" she asked flatly.

Little Jon chuckled. "See? Grizzlies have a bad reputation, but they're charming when you pay attention. They're shy but curious. They're playful. And they only attack when they're surprised or afraid or when they're protecting their cubs. It's not that they like confrontation; they would much rather avoid it. It's that they feel there's no other choice. So they make themselves big, growl loudly, bite, and swipe with their huge claws. But really, they'd rather forage and play and explore and sleep."

Robyn stared at Little Jon, wondering how he'd seen through her in such a short time. The hulking man looked as though he could take on a grizzly bear and win. *And I suppose he did,* Robyn thought, laughing to herself. "I always thought of myself as more of an otter: sleek, clever, and adorable," Robyn countered.

Little Jon smirked. "You're not so stealthy as an otter," he teased.

"Well, given your first impression of me, I can't argue with that. But I can be stealthy."

He raised an eyebrow. "Mmhmm," he hummed, unconvinced.

Robyn grinned. "Challenge accepted, Jon Little. Challenge accepted."

He laughed that deep-chested rumble, which made her smile, and they began walking again.

"In any case, I'm starting to question your decision-making skills following someone like me. Even Tuck's cards said I don't think things through."

Little Jon shrugged. "How long have you been wanting to get your friend out of the camp? You didn't just rush the gates, did you? You're trying to plan a way to get him out safely, right?"

"Hmm. That's true..."

When Robyn and Little Jon arrived at the abbey and opened the heavy front door, they found Tuck in the nave. She stood, her arms spread wide and her eyes closed, barefoot in the middle of the mossy floor. The candlelight flickering at her feet barely reached her face, but they could see her mouth open, a gossamer melody flowing from her lips. Her hounds sat in a rough circle around her.

They crept forward, unable to hear her words until they were nearly upon her. "Until we meet again," she finished, opening her glassy eyes.

It took Tuck a moment to focus on them. She blinked, her eyebrows pulled together, a few times before recognition cleared her expression.

"I hope we aren't interrupting..." Robyn murmured.

Tuck smiled and waved her hand. "Not at all. I was just finishing." She took in Robyn and the belongings she carried. "So you're here to stay then?"

Robyn nodded. "Jon said you have a room for me?"

"Of course, I have a few, in fact. Would you like to be in the dormitory with everyone else or upstairs with me? You saw my room before. There's another in that same hallway. Those rooms are bigger, but the dormitory tends to be warmer. Also, it's closer to the kitchen."

Robyn thought about the wind whipping through the open windows of Tuck's room. "I think I'd prefer the warmth what with winter coming and everything," she said.

Tuck nodded. "All right. Follow me." Tuck picked up one of the candles from the floor and smothered the rest before leaving the nave, her hounds ever at her heels.

Robyn and Little Jon trailed Tuck through the cloister to the door they'd taken to the kitchens. Instead of going down, they took the set of stairs up. The flight led to a long hall, much longer than the hall Tuck's room was in. Robyn marveled at the Romanesque, pointed-arch, vaulted ceiling, barely illuminated by the lanterns hung outside each door.

"Most everyone should be asleep by now," Tuck informed in a hushed voice. "Do you mind being near the stairs?" she asked, pointing to the first door on the left.

"Not at all," Robyn answered.

Tuck nodded and reached for the lantern hanging outside the door, grabbing it by the hanging ring. After Little Jon had opened the door, Tuck went in first, holding the lantern high so they could see the room. Her hounds sniffed every inch with determined curiosity.

The space was simple and small with rough, stone walls. The bed was a rectangular frame with strips of leather weaved in a square pattern and nailed into the frame to create a sort of net. There was also a small writing table and a little square stool, a blanket folded neatly on the seat. Closed shutters rattled in the hole that was the window.

Turning around in the small space, Robyn saw Little Jon had chosen to stay in the hall, only bending down to stick his head in. She stifled a laugh at the thought of the giant man in the tiny space.

"I know it's not much," Tuck said, "but it's better than nothing."

Robyn nodded, not upset by the humble room. "It's fine," she answered honestly. *It may not be my huge, comfortable room in the Lacklands' mansion,* she thought. *But considering where they got the money to afford that place, I'll take this simple living space any day.* "Thank you," she added.

Tuck placed the lantern on the table. "Do you want me to come get you for breakfast tomorrow morning?"

"Please."

"All right. And you best be off, Jon. Much will be worried," Tuck said, turning to leave.

"I'll see you tomorrow then," Jon told them.

"Thanks again," Robyn said with a smile.

Tuck and Little Jon returned her warm expression and left her to rest.

Her friends gone, Robyn settled into her new space. She placed her things at the foot of her bed, wrapped herself in the blanket, and lay on the cot, using her scarf as a pillow. The netting yielded to her weight, forming around her. *It's more comfortable than it looks,* she thought, watching the lantern light flicker off the rough-hewn walls.

Robyn sighed, trying to release the anxiety tightening her chest. "Every day is a new adventure," she murmured.

CHAPTER 24

The next morning, Robyn awoke to the shuffling of feet and the opening and closing of dormitory doors. She blinked rapidly, trying to clear her sleep-addled mind. When she realized where she was, she sat up in her monk's cot. Her stiff back ached from sleeping so hard, so she rose and stretched her arms above her head, her vertebrae cracking with relief.

She went to the window and opened the shutters, the chilled autumn air filtered in with the morning light. Looking back into the illuminated room, Robyn noticed there was no mirror by which she could get ready. *It's fine*, she thought, realigning her expectations to her new environment.

Robyn changed into her work overalls and finger-combed her hair. On the way out of her room, she hung her dead lantern on the hook outside the door.

The dormitory hall was quiet, no hint of the earlier activity. Robyn crept downstairs to see where everyone had gone. The moment she reached the ground level, she was amidst a flurry of activity.

Women and children walked purposefully up and down the stairs to the kitchen and cellars, carrying food past her down the hall. Robyn followed the trail through the cloisters to the door of the refectory. Two long tables with small, square stools ran the length of the room.

"Excuse me," a teenage girl said, trying to pass through the door Robyn blocked.

"Oh, sorry," Robyn apologized, stepping out of the way.

The girl carried a plate of biscuits across the room and placed it on the head table, where all the food was being assembled. When she'd made her delivery, she came back toward Robyn.

"Could you tell me where the toilet is?" Robyn asked her as she passed by again.

"Just down there," the girl pointed farther down the cloister toward the path to Tuck's room.

Robyn nodded and thanked her.

Following the girl's directions, Robyn traveled down the hall. At the far end, she heard the sounds of water and chatter and pursued the noise. Upon opening a warped wooden door, Robyn froze, her mouth hanging open. The room was thick with steam emanating from a long, clear pool spanning the length. Naked women and young children soaked in the Roman-style bath, chattering and giggling as if they had no troubles. Others sat on stools over drains and scrubbed themselves with soap before pouring buckets of water over their bodies to rinse.

"Shut the door, will ya?" a woman nearby called as she dried herself with a towel.

Robyn stepped into the bathroom with a nod of apology. "The toilet?" she asked the woman, who pointed at another door at the far end of the room.

The humidity seeped into Robyn's clothes, making them feel slightly damp as she made her way around the bath. Her bones and muscles ached as if begging for a long soak.

When she opened the far door to use the toilet, she tilted her head and scrunched her brow. "What the...?" she trailed off, mumbling to herself. She'd expected a pit in the ground with a holed board to sit on, but someone had redesigned the room to have flushing toilets.

"Gylberte's amazing," a short, middle-aged woman with dark hair and an olive complexion said at Robyn's side.

Robyn turned to her. "Gyl did all this?"

The woman nodded with a smile. "You're new here, right? I'm Giulia. Welcome to Sherwood."

"Thank you," she answered, shaking the woman's outstretched hand. "I'm Robyn."

"Well, you better get going, Robyn. They'll start serving breakfast soon," Giulia urged.

"Right." When Robyn had finished, most of the women in the bath were drying off and getting dressed.

Robyn walked around the pool and left. When she entered the refectory again, she joined the line that had formed along one wall. It traveled up to the head table, where people filled their plates. Others sat, already eating, at the long tables.

Once she had her food—vegetable soup and a biscuit—she looked around for Tuck or Little Jon, or anyone else she knew. Giulia waved at Robyn, an empty seat beside her, and Robyn made her way toward the woman.

"Sit with us, Robyn," Giulia urged with a smile.

Robyn thanked her again, taking the empty stool.

Two ladies on the other side of Giulia watched Robyn, curiosity sparkling in their eyes.

"These are my friends: Ilse Fischer," she introduced the lean, woman with grey-streaked, brown hair and big brown eyes who sat beside her.

Robyn nodded to the woman, who smiled back at her.

"And Nan Kirklees," Giulia finished, indicating a reddish blonde with blue eyes around the same age as Robyn.

Nan tilted her head, her brow crinkled in thought as she stared at Robyn.

"Have we met before? Robyn was it?"

Robyn looked more closely at the woman. "I don't think so," she answered.

Nan frowned. "What's your surname?"

Robyn hesitated. *I suppose it's better to be honest. They're all likely to find out eventually,* she thought. "Loxley," she said.

"Loxley... As in William Loxley?"

"My father's name was William, yes."

"And your mother?"

"Joan Ellis."

"Really? My mother was Beatrice Ellis!" Nan pronounced. "She often spoke of her younger sister and showed me pictures... She was so sad when she died."

Robyn had heard Marian speak of an aunt who was their only surviving relative. She'd asked Marian once why they didn't live with their aunt and had been told she couldn't have afforded to support them.

"Welcome to Sherwood, cousin!" Nan said with a happy grin.

An unexpected warmth spread in Robyn's chest. "Thank you. Marian will be so surprised when I tell her you're here. We didn't even know we had a cousin. How is your mother? Aunt Beatrice? I don't really remember her."

Nan's smile slid from her face. "She died when I was ten... Polio."

"Oh, I'm sorry," Robyn murmured. "And your father?"

Nan shook her head. "The Great War."

Robyn's stomach sank, reminded of how much she'd benefited from the Lacklands. *Did Nan live on the streets? How did she end up in Sherwood?* Robyn wondered.

"I grew up in The Cottage," Nan answered Robyn's unspoken question.

Robyn shuddered at the colloquial name for the orphanage formally known as Saint Benedict's Asylum for Abandoned Children. It didn't have a pleasant reputation and was known for many of its charges pronounced dead or missing. Of course, it's likely most had run away, far happier fending for themselves than living under the watchful eyes of the nuns at The Cottage.

Robyn smiled weakly. "Well, I'm glad you're here," she said to her cousin.

"And I you," Nan responded.

Robyn wanted to stay and get to know her cousin better as well as Giulia and Ilse, but she had to be at work. She ate quickly, which she felt was a disservice to the food as it truly was delicious even in its simplicity. Then she bid them farewell, promising to spend more time with them later.

Just as she was exiting, Tuck entered, scanning the room with her eyes.

"Robyn, I was wondering where you were. I came to wake you for breakfast, but you weren't there," Tuck said.

"Yeah, sorry. I should've found you and told you I was awake."

Tuck took in her attire. "Off to work?" she asked.

"Off to quit my job at Lackland Steel to be precise," Robyn corrected.

Tuck nodded with satisfaction, and Bell gave Robyn's hand a kiss of encouragement.

"I'll be back in a bit," Robyn said, patting the dog in thanks. "After all, we've got a lot to do before the refugees get here."

"Right. See you later."

As Robyn left the abbey, she found Little Jon and Much walking around the side out of the gathered fog, a basket in Little Jon's hand.

"Good morning, you two," she called to them. "What brings you here so early?

"Breakfast," Little Jon answered, holding up the basket. "The abbey cooks for all of Sherwood, but they don't have room for everyone to eat here, especially not the likes of me."

Robyn smiled at the thought of Little Jon trying to sit on one of those tiny square stools. "You on guard duty today? Want to walk me out?"

"I'd like to, but I'm helping salvage today. David is watching the bridge."

"I can walk you to the bridge," Much piped in, after swallowing a big bite of biscuit, the evidence still in the corner of his mouth.

"Why do I get the feeling you're trying to avoid eating your soup," Little Jon teased.

"I'm not!" Much protested.

"So you will eat all of the vegetables when you get back?"

Much pursed his lips.

"You want to be big and strong like Jon one day, don't you?" Robyn asked the boy.

"I will be. I'm growing every day," he asserted.

"Jon, how did you get so big and strong?" Robyn asked.

"Vegetables," Little Jon answered seriously. "And milk."

Much frowned, doubt clouding his expression at their assurances. "Even green beans?"

Little Jon nodded. "Especially green beans."

Much sighed. "Fine. I'll eat all the soup. But can I walk Robyn to the bridge?"

"Sí," Little Jon approved. "But no detours," he called after the boy as Much led Robyn down the path.

Robyn couldn't help but smile at the warmth she felt as she watched them interact.

Once they were alone, Much launched into an inquiry. "When are we going to break your friend out?"

Robyn answered as best she could. "I hope soon, but we have to be careful and make a plan first."

"Why is he in prison anyway? Did he hurt someone?"

"No, he didn't. You heard about the attack on Pearl Harbor, didn't you?"

He nodded. "Jon read about it in the paper."

"Well, when Japan attacked Pearl Harbor, some people started to worry about Americans who came from Japan or whose families came from Japan."

"¿Por qué?"

Robyn sighed, not quite understanding the answer herself. Such a simple question didn't have an equally simple explanation.

"They're afraid," she said, thinking that summed it up pretty well.

"What are they afraid of? Should we be afraid? Jon doesn't seem afraid."

Robyn thought for a moment. "Fear is a feeling that makes people do a lot of irrational things. Sometimes, it tells you when you need to be cautious and careful. It's really important when you're in danger. But other times, it needs to be faced. I think, when it comes to people, it's always better to give them a chance before you assume and act on fear. No, you don't need to be afraid of the people coming to stay with us. In fact, they're likely more afraid than we are, given what's happened to them."

"I was afraid when I lost my parents," Much said. "And I was afraid of Jon when we first met. But I'm not anymore. I'll help make them less afraid."

Robyn stroked the boy's hair. "That's very kind of you, Much."

They found David sitting on the ground, his back to the wall, reading a book when they reached the bridge.

"Hello, Robyn," he greeted. "So you're here to stay? Glad to hear it. Tuck and Jon seemed happy. And what are you doing here, Muchisimo?"

David asked Much. "Have you come to challenge me to another round?" Then he crouched down, shifting his weight from side to side.

Much grinned and launched himself at David, who began playfully wrestling with the boy.

Robyn chuckled under her breath, having clearly been forgotten. "Well, I'll see you fellas later then."

"Adiós," they called to her as they wrestled.

Then Robyn crossed the bridge and uncovered her motorcycle. It took a few minutes before the engine would start in the chilled, foggy morning by the bay. But it soon rumbled to life, and she was on her way.

It wasn't long before she parked her bike around the block from Lackland Steel. She didn't bother to punch in but went straight into the mill to find Philip. As the shift hadn't started yet, he wasn't on the mill floor. She went down the administration hallway and knocked on his office door. There was no answer.

Robyn sighed with a frown.

Miss Wilson giggled from her office next door. *Well, she is in charge of female employees,* Robyn thought. *I could just tell her and have her pass on the message.*

Robyn knocked on Miss Wilson's door as she opened it. Miss Wilson smoothed out her skirt as Philip jumped away guiltily.

"Good morning, Miss Wilson, Philip. I'm glad you're together," Robyn started, ignoring the compromising position. "I'm here to tender my resignation."

Their eyes widened in shock.

"You're resigning?" Miss Wilson asked. "Does Mr. Gisbourne know about this? Mr. Lackland?"

Robyn frowned. "I thought it more professional to tell my supervisor and you first, Miss Wilson."

"Right. Of course," she responded, correcting herself.

"But will you be all right, Robyn? You aren't...in any trouble, are you?" she asked, delicately insinuating. "I know how much you love this job," she added.

"No, I'm fine," Robyn assured, scrambling for a reason. "I..." Gyl's chalkboard surfaced in her mind. "I got an offer to work with an inventor, a scientist. He's researching some amazing new inventions and needs an extra pair of hands."

"We'll be sad to lose you," Philip said half-heartedly.

"Yes, I'm sorry about the short notice, but he really does need me right away. You understand." Robyn gave lip-service to the usual excuses, knowing full well they wouldn't dare say anything against her.

"Of course," Miss Wilson said.

"Well, I'll clean out my locker and be on my way then..." Robyn trailed off, inching toward the door.

"Good luck to you," Miss Wilson added.

CHAPTER 25

Robyn was cleaning out her locker when Lili shuffled up beside her. Robyn stuffed the hairbrush and cosmetics she kept at the mill into a bag.

"What's going on?" her friend asked with a furrowed brow.

Robyn steeled her resolve and forced an excited smile. "I just got a great opportunity."

"You're leaving the mill?"

Robyn nodded quickly. "I'm going to work with an inventor. Isn't that great?"

Lili eyed Robyn as if trying to determine her sincerity, but Robyn's smile didn't slip.

Lili smiled in return. "That *is* great. I'm happy for you, but I sure am going to miss you."

Robyn wrapped her arms around Lili's shoulders. "Thanks, Lili," she murmured. "I'm going to miss you, too."

"Well, you know where I'll be. We can have lunch or go get a drink anytime you want."

"Absolutely," Robyn said, knowing she wasn't likely to take that offer. *Lili doesn't need to get involved in any of this,* she thought. "Well..." Robyn continued, throwing her bag over her shoulder. "I'll be seeing you then."

"Good luck," Lili said with a sad smile.

"You too."

Robyn didn't bother to acknowledge Mildred or the rest of the women gathering in the locker room to start their work day. They were no longer her concern. They were part of her old life, the life where she was naive and undisciplined. She couldn't afford to be either anymore.

When Robyn stepped through the gate of Lackland Steel, she sighed in relief. *Now, the real work can begin,* she thought, looking up into the dark grey sky.

"Hello, Robyn," a deep voice greeted.

"What do you want, Guy?" she asked, recognizing his voice without turning toward him.

He didn't answer, so she glanced over at him. His expression lacked that assured intensity it usually had. His face was straight and serious with a trace of sadness around the eyes.

Robyn's heart twinged, knowing it was her words that had put that sadness there. But she refused to allow her sympathy to show, keeping her expression rigid while waiting for his response.

"How are you?" he asked.

"Wonderful," she spat.

He hesitated.

"Look, I've got places to be." She turned to walk away.

"Wait," he called.

She stopped but didn't turn back.

"...Aren't you going into the mill?"

"No, I've taken another position somewhere else."

"What? You're leaving the mill? But...but... It isn't because of me, is it?"

Robyn stifled a sigh and faced Guy. "No, I have my own reasons." She wanted to tell him that he should give up, that he'd never have a chance, never had one to begin with. Had she not only reached out to him to get information? She wanted to rail at him and tell him they were too different. She stood up against injustice while he propagated it. But as he met her glare with that open expression of vulnerability, she couldn't say any of that.

Her eyes softened, and she met his gaze steadily. "I hope you find peace one day, Guy. I hope you can live without spreading fear and violence. Because even if you feel no guilt, even if you don't know it, those transgressions are eating you alive. And every time you hurt someone, you become a little less human."

She turned to leave again. But before she could take a step, Guy embraced her from behind, burying his face in her hair. A thrill shot through her, and she froze.

"I do know it," he whispered, his humid breath tickling her ear. "I didn't think I had any humanity left...until I met you. You make me want to be a better man."

After the initial shock had passed, Robyn squirmed against him, and he released her.

She whirled around. His expression was once again intense and unapologetic, her sympathy seemingly emboldening him. *If my words really have an impact, perhaps I can save his next victim,* she thought. Her recent discussion with Much rose to the surface of her mind, and she wondered if she hadn't let fear control her actions toward Guy. Had she not told the boy that when it comes to people, it's always better to give them a chance?

Robyn sighed. "Look, if you really want to be a better man, then you have to stop hurting people."

"But that's...my job..."

"Is it? You oversee all Lackland businesses, and you're telling me your job is only to hurt people? You're in a position of power. You don't have to use that power to hurt others. You could use it to help."

Guy's mouth quirked in thought. "And if I do that, you will see me again?"

Robyn's heart thumped. "We'll see."

His eyes lit up. "I will find a way to make this work, Robyn. You mark my words."

"I hope you do," she responded. "But now, I really have to go."

"I'll see you at the Lacklands' then?"

"No, I moved out. I'm trying to be an adult and make it on my own."

Guy nodded, then dug into his jacket pocket. "Here's my address and telephone number should you need me."

Robyn took the calling card he offered and put it in her pocket. "Well, goodbye then."

"See you later," he promised.

Robyn didn't respond but turned and walked away. Rounding the corner, she stopped and leaned her back against the wall with a heavy sigh. She squeezed her eyes shut and shook the swirling thoughts from her head. *I can't worry about this now.* Straightening her posture, she walked the rest of the way to her motorcycle.

As Robyn drove back to Sherwood, a sense of freedom permeated her. It was as if the wind blew away her previous life. By the time she crossed the bridge, her desire for justice soothed any anxiety she might have felt at abandoning everything she'd ever wanted and known.

But while she was willing to give up her previous ambitions, she wouldn't part with the people she cared about most. She would never abandon her sister, and she would absolutely save Will. And as she made her way through the streets of Sherwood and heard the distant clangs and shuffles of people doing their best to support each other and survive, she smiled to herself.

The crumbling buildings and desecrated paths were familiar, and the inhabitants were hers to protect. Tuck and Little Jon had told her she would lead them and so she would. She would save Will and the other prisoners, and she would provide for the people of Sherwood. No one would go hungry this winter on her watch because she had a plan.

CHAPTER 26

Guy watched Robyn until she'd turned the corner down the block, his heart still pounding as her warmth in his arms faded. He smiled to himself. *I still have a chance,* he thought. *She's so kind and forgiving.* Her good-heartedness made him only want her more.

With a revitalized determination to get to work, Guy turned back toward the gate of Lackland Steel, glancing sideways as something caught his attention. Half a block down, rooted to the pavement, stood Detective Alaric Nottingham. His frame was taut and his hands clenched into fists, but it was his eyes that effectively communicated his barely-contained rage.

Guy squinted at the cop and swaggered toward him. "What's this, Nottingham? Resorted to stalking now?" Guy prodded when he'd reached the detective. "That's a crime, you know. Is this what our tax dollars are paying for? Maybe I should call your superiors."

"Maybe you should also tell them about how you just harassed an employee. It would save me time in filling out a report myself," Nottingham growled.

Guy glared at the accusation. "If Robyn doesn't like when I touch her, she'll let me know herself."

Nottingham's jaw tensed as he clenched it. "That's Miss Loxley to you," he hissed through his teeth.

Guy raised his eyebrows. "Is it? I've known her for much longer than you have, and I have more of a right to call her Robyn than you do."

"You think so?" Nottingham challenged.

Guy stepped closer to the detective, their chests nearly touching. "I do. And what do you have to say about it?"

Nottingham didn't back down. "I say, watch yourself, Gisbourne. She's not yours to claim."

"And she's yours?"

"More than yours."

Guy barked out a harsh laugh. "You get attached too easily, Detective. You have a few drinks, a few dances at a party, and you think that means something?"

Nottingham exhaled sharply through his nose in an incredulous laugh, shaking his head slightly. "You think that's all there is? You're more of a fool than I'd expected, Gisbourne."

Guy's face flushed with fury, and he grabbed Nottingham by the coat lapels. "Listen to me, you—"

"No, you listen, Gisbourne," Nottingham said, cutting Guy off and extricating himself from Guy's grasp. "You keep your hands to yourself, hear me? You don't touch me, and you don't touch Robyn. You got that? Or you'll be explaining to your pocket police officers why I brought you in for assault."

Guy frowned. *That would be inconvenient*, he thought. "I don't want to see you hanging around here again, Nottingham. What's your excuse anyway? You have no business here."

Nottingham smirked. "What do you mean? Can't a fella get breakfast from his favorite diner on the way to work? We still live in a free country, don't we?"

"Well then, hadn't you better be on your way? Wouldn't want to be late."

Nottingham's stony expression returned. "That's right. Go about your day, citizen... And remember what I said."

Guy's lip curled as Nottingham turned his back to him and walked in the opposite direction from Robyn. Guy faced the entrance to Lackland

Steel, his chest tight and his mind whirling with Nottingham's implications, but went back to his car.

"It can't be true," he murmured to himself, heading toward the bay, gripping the steering wheel so hard his fingers ached.

He could still picture the blood draining from her face when he'd insinuated Nottingham would be taken care of if he got out of line. *But that's because she's so tender-hearted. She can't handle the thought of anyone being hurt.*

Nottingham's taunting laugh echoed in Guy's ears. He clenched his jaw. *No, she said she takes it slow, and she hasn't known him that long. No, she wouldn't lie.* His words didn't even convince himself.

As Guy parked near the pier in Stockport, the knot in his stomach eased a bit at the sight of the grey waves of the bay. He got out of his car and walked out onto the pier. At the very end, he breathed deep the sea air. Closing his eyes, he let the wind caress his cheeks and the waves crash in his ears.

Seagulls called each other overhead as the tension drained out of Guy, as it always did when he was near the ocean. Staring out into the wide expanse of water, he sighed. "Hello, Dad, Mom."

His heartbeat slowed, and his breathing evened out as the years slipped away. His short time at the orphanage, his years on the streets, even the horrible few he was inside, the sound of the waves washed them away. He didn't have to fight here, didn't have to protect himself, didn't have to use the deadly skills he'd honed over most of his life, the skills people like John Lackland found so valuable. Here, by the water, the seabirds chattering and the salty air in his lungs, he was just Guy.

He had long come to terms with what the ocean had taken from him, his father, who had never come home from that fishing expedition and his mother, who couldn't bear to be apart from her husband. When he was young, it had been hard to understand why his loving mother had thrown herself into the sea. But now? He understood too well what he'd be willing to do for the one he cared for most.

"Robyn says I should use my position to help people," he told his parents. "And I'm sure she's right. She's so honorable and true. If she would just... I know if I can get her to accept me, then I could be as good a man as you wanted me to be..."

Guy shook his head against the image of Robyn and Nottingham holding hands at Mrs. Lackland's birthday party. *No, I should trust her. Every strong relationship is built on trust,* he thought. "I hope I can bring her here to meet you one day." His voice was hardly audible above the sound of the waves.

CHAPTER 27

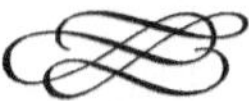

*A*laric Nottingham unclenched his jaw and sighed, slumping into the driver's seat of his car. *I shouldn't have done that,* he thought. *We agreed to keep our relationship hidden.*

Though he regretted his mouth getting the better of him, he knew he would've stepped in had Robyn not wiggled out of Gisbourne's grasp. Alaric clicked his tongue as the image of Gisbourne wrapping himself around Robyn resurfaced in his mind.

He could tell by her initial rigidity and swift release that Robyn had not appreciated the contact, but he couldn't ignore the niggling anxiety he felt at watching them converse so familiarly. He repeated to himself that Robyn had told him she and Guy had nothing between them. He trusted her. And besides, as much as he postured at Gisbourne, she really wasn't Alaric's either.

"That's right, Alaric," he muttered to himself. "No matter how you feel about her, no matter how many times she shares herself with you, that doesn't make her yours."

His chest tightened at the thought that his deeper feelings could very well be unrequited. He'd made the mistake of letting some of those feelings slip too soon. And though Robyn hadn't rejected them, she hadn't echoed them either.

Attraction she'd said, he thought. *Attraction doesn't cover it, at least not for me.*

He closed his eyes and took a deep breath, then let it out in another sigh. "Don't push it. Take it slow. Be still and constant. Let her come to you. You don't want to scare her," he murmured.

He scowled at himself, the inevitability of the situation too much to bear. "Don't want to scare her? Yeah, right." The truth was he'd been terrified from the moment Robyn had leveled her steady, blue gaze on him, terrified by how she made him feel, panicked and thrilled by the power she didn't know she had over him, worried about what would be left of him if she ever directed her eyes elsewhere. Engaging her had been the most reckless and unhealthy thing he'd ever done, and he would do it a thousand times over given the chance.

He glanced over at the paper bag in his passenger seat, holding the cape and mask he'd gotten for the Halloween party later that week. A warmth spread through his chest and eased his anxiety as he thought about their upcoming date.

He hadn't expected to see her that morning. After all, it had been his routine to monitor Gisbourne's comings and goings when he had a free moment, and he'd never seen Robyn at Lackland Steel before. He would've remembered that.

She was leaving, he thought. *Today must have been when she decided to quit. I hope it went okay.*

A car horn blared from farther down the block, reminding him that commuter traffic was in full swing. A quick glance at his wrist told him he was already late for work. He started his engine and pulled out into the fray.

Alaric hadn't even gotten the chance to sit down before Preston, the detective Alaric was sometimes partnered with on cases, began to razz him.

"You know, just because you've been assigned to cold cases doesn't mean you get to come in when it pleases you."

"Yeah, yeah," Alaric responded, not in the mood to joke as he sat at his desk piled with file folders so high he couldn't see the hinged picture frame with photos of his grandfather and parents.

"Seriously though." Preston dropped his voice so only Alaric could hear. "They're looking for any reason to get rid of you what with you pursuing the Lacklands at every turn. Don't give them any more ammunition."

Alaric met Preston's concerned gaze. "Thanks for the advice." *My only mistake was not covering my investigations more carefully,* Alaric thought.

Preston slapped him on the shoulder. "You've got a visitor by the way. They might not have noticed your late arrival if not for that."

Alaric stood, and Preston waved his thumb in the general direction of Lieutenant McMurphey's office. Alaric nodded his thanks.

Lieutenant McMurphey was a surly man with bags under his eyes and a lip that was more frequently curled in distaste than not, especially when his gaze was directed at Alaric Nottingham.

But this time when Alaric knocked at McMurphey's office, his face wore an unnatural smile. "Come in, come in, Nottingham," he called amicably.

Alaric entered the small cube of a room and noted the two visitors: a slight elderly woman, bent and delicate, and a teenage girl, her dark hair cut short and the brim of her paperboy's hat doing little to hide her battered and bruised face.

"Mireilla," Alaric said, greeting the girl, whose blue eyes appeared even more brilliant surrounded by the purple of her shiner.

The girl's split lips smiled ever so slightly.

"C'est lui?" the woman asked the girl, looking between Alaric and Mireilla.

"Oui, Mémé," Mireilla answered.

Then the woman turned her steady, wrinkled gaze on Alaric. "Monsieur," she addressed him, her serious tone strong in her deceptively weak body. "You have saved my granddaughter," she declared in a thick accent.

"I have done nothing short of my duty, Ma'am."

Her face lit in a smile of approval. "I cannot thank you enough. My Mireilla is the only one I have left. I wanted to see the face of her savior."

"I'm only sorry I didn't catch those who did this to her."

"Do not worry about that, Ma'am," McMurphey interjected. "We have our very best on the case."

The grandmother turned her steely gaze on McMurphey, her eyes keen with the knowledge of how Midshire really worked.

Everyone in the room knew the perpetrators wouldn't be caught. And as much as it irked Alaric, he was glad he'd found Mireilla in time to save her. Had he not been spending his free time trying to find the Lacklands' underground casino, she wouldn't have been as lucky as she was.

The grandmother reached out her hand to Alaric, and he took her yielding, delicate fingers in his. With a gentle squeeze, she said everything she needed to.

"Allons-y, Mireilla," the woman ordered, waving her hand at her granddaughter.

"Oui, Mémé," Mireilla answered, ducking her head obediently.

As the girl passed, she met Alaric's gaze. "Listen to your grandmother, and try to stay out of trouble," Alaric murmured to the girl. By which he meant, don't gamble and steer clear of bookies, especially those of the Lackland variety.

Mireilla nodded. "Don't worry, Detective. I've learned my lesson."

I hope so, Alaric thought, but he wasn't entirely convinced by her declaration.

Once the pair had left McMurphey's office, Alaric turned back to his superior.

"Well?" McMurphey demanded, his familiar scowl back in place. "Don't you have some cold cases to solve?"

"Yes, sir," Alaric answered, resisting the urge to grind his teeth.

CHAPTER 28

Robyn heard the loud boom even from outside Gyl's laboratory. She rushed inside, squinting her eyes against the smoke-cloud billowing from every broken window.

"Gyl?" she called as loud as she could through the fabric of her scarf, which she pressed to her nose and mouth.

She received no answer.

"Gyl!" she shouted.

But still he didn't respond.

Finally, the smoke began to clear. Gyl sat on the floor, stupefied and blinking, with a wrench in his hand. The remnants of whatever he'd been working on was black with soot before him, the metal twisted outward.

Robyn reached the scientist and crouched down beside him. "Gyl, are you all right?"

He tilted his head. "That wasn't supposed to happen."

"Are you hurt?" Robyn demanded, focusing the man's attention.

He looked over at her. "Hurt? No. But damn it all if I don't have to start over."

Robyn rocked back with an incredulous laugh. She plopped down beside him, the ridiculousness of the scene too cartoonish to take now that she knew he was safe. Her laughter became heartier as she indulged it.

Gyl pouted beside her. "Are you laughing at me, Robyn?"

Robyn turned to him, his red hair a ruddy brown from soot and his goggles smudged from dirty fingers trying to wipe them clear. She burst out in another fit of laughter. "If you could only see your face," she managed between giggles.

Gyl grinned an indulgent smile, unable to be upset in the face of her mirth. "Well, every setback is a learning experience in science anyway as the good Gaffer Swanthold always said."

"Gaffer Swanthold? Who is he?" Robyn asked.

"My mentor at MIT."

"MIT? Wow, you graduated from MIT?"

Gyl smirked. "Well...I didn't graduate exactly."

Robyn raised an eyebrow at him, waiting for him to continue.

"Let's just say they didn't appreciate the aesthetic effects an experiment gone awry could have on a physics lab."

Robyn chuckled. Seeing the effect of his latest experiment gone awry, she could only imagine what he'd done to the campus.

He got to his feet, not even bothering to dust off his overalls. Then he held out his hand to help Robyn up as well. She took his offer with a thank you.

"If you've come for your transmitter, I'm afraid it will be a few more days," he told her, looking around at the damage his setback had caused.

"Actually, I'm here to see if you have a telephone."

Gyl lifted his goggles onto his head and met her eyes seriously. "Are you saying that out of all Sherwood, you think I would be the one to repair the telephone lines and *steal* service from Midshire?"

"Aren't you?"

He grinned. "Of course, I was just making sure my reputation was still intact."

Robyn chuckled. "Well...can I use it?"

He nodded. "It's in the study," he said, pointing to a set of metal stairs, which led to a catwalk-type second floor.

"Thanks." When Robyn had reached the upper floor, she stopped at a door she would have expected to be on a submarine. It was heavy and metal and had an airlock handle in the center. She grabbed either side of the wheel and turned it hard. With a clang, the door unlocked, and she yanked to open it.

The study looked more like a bunker to Robyn. There were no windows and only one door; it seemed rather like a metal box. There must have been a vent somewhere because the air wasn't stuffy or stale. There was also a desk and plenty of books. It was clear Gyl really did use it as a study at least. He even had an overstuffed couch, and the lamps gave off a soft, yellow glow.

Robyn spotted the telephone on the desk and sat in the simple, wooden chair by it.

She pulled the telephone book beside it toward her and looked up the number she wanted. But as she lifted the receiver and heard the dial tone, she bit her lip, suddenly uncertain of her decision. With a deep breath, she dialed the number.

"MPD Central, is this an emergency?" a terse female voice answered.

"No, I'd like to speak to Detective Alaric Nottingham, please."

"Please hold while I transfer the call."

"Thank you."

A few moments later, a smooth, serious baritone picked up the line; Robyn would recognize that voice anywhere. "Detective Nottingham."

Even through the telephone, on the other side of the city, Rick's timbre moved her. She smiled into the mouthpiece.

"Has anyone ever told you how sexy your voice is, Detective?" Robyn asked.

Rick made a choking sound, then coughed to cover it up. "It's not nice to do that to a fella when he's at work, Miss," he answered low.

Robyn chuckled. "Well, I just couldn't help it. Try harder not to sound so enticing."

"Now, how am I supposed to do that when I'm on the phone with you?"

Robyn flushed and shivered. "Don't tempt me, Rick. You don't want me to come down there... I don't know what I'll do... And we wanted to keep our relationship secret."

Rick paused. "Speaking of which, do you need something? I'm surprised you called me at work."

"I just wanted to let you know I quit my job at Lackland Steel this morning."

Another pause. "How did it go?"

"Not too bad. They were shocked, but they bought my excuse. I..." Robyn stopped short of telling Rick about her encounter with Guy. "I also wanted to ask about the Halloween party this weekend. When should we meet?"

"Right. I'm glad you called about that actually. I got your disguise prepared. It will go perfect with that dress you wore before. The one from the party. If you give me your new address, I can pick you up...around seven?"

"No...it's fine. I can meet you at your place. I have stuff to do on that end of town anyway," Robyn lied.

"Okay."

"Seven, you said?"

"Yes."

"All right, I'll be there at seven."

"Great."

Robyn hesitated, reluctant to say goodbye.

"Is there anything else?" Rick asked.

"No, everything is fine. I'll see you Saturday."

"Okay, see you then."

Robyn hung up the receiver, then picked it back up to make another call.

"Lackland residence," Winona answered the phone.

"Hey, Winona. It's Robyn. Is Marian there?"

"Oh, Robyn! We were all so sad to hear you had gone. Is everything all right?"

"Everything is fine, Winona. Could I talk to my sister please?"

"Yes, I'll get her."

After a few minutes of waiting, Marian picked up the line. "Miss me already?"

"You know I do, but that's not why I called."

"What do you need?" Marian asked low.

"You know that dress I wore to Eleanor's party? The black one with the silk and lace?"

"Yeah."

"Could you bring it to your studio sometime this week?"

"Um...sure. But what do you need it for? Your...new place doesn't seem like the gala type."

"I'm going to a Halloween party with Rick this weekend, and that's what he told me to wear."

"Oooo," Marian teased. "So you have a date with Mister—"

"Don't say his name," Robyn cut her sister off quickly. "You don't know who might be listening in that house."

"Oh," Marian whispered. "Sorry."

"It's fine. Just be careful. Will ya?"

"I will. I promise."

Robyn sighed, trying to relieve the sudden anxiety tightening her chest.

"Do you need any help getting ready? Or do you just want me to leave it for you?" Marian asked.

Robyn didn't need any help, but she did want to see her sister. "I'd love some help. Thanks. Saturday?"

"Okay. Come around lunchtime. I'll bring food."

"Great. See you then."

"Okay. Love you. Bye."

"Love you, too. Bye."

CHAPTER 29

Tuck picked up the card at the center of the spread and gazed steadily at it, letting her mind drift away. The queen of wands sat on her golden throne, a crown of sunflowers atop her fiery hair and a gleaming scepter in her hand.

So soon? Tuck wondered. *Though big life changes do have major impacts,* she reasoned.

She gathered the rest of the spread and reshuffled the deck, asking what was in store on her own path. Placing the top three cards on the table before her, she overturned the wheel of fortune, the ace of cups, and the king of cups.

She stared down at the result of the path she was currently on, trying to determine the meaning.

Tuck sighed. It seemed no matter how hard she tried, she could never separate herself enough to read her own cards, too willing to believe the best and brush off the worst. While she had no problem picking up and examining the threads of someone else's current fate, she couldn't see her own clearly.

She could still hear Sophie advising her to let go. "Don't try so hard," she would say.

Tuck frowned at the thought of her mentor and wondered how she and the rest of the grove were now, the men and women she'd known her entire life. Most of them had left Midshire, driven out by the Lacklands at the Church's behest, including Tuck's own mother.

So righteous, those Lacklands, professed Catholics who didn't seem to have any problem committing sins. And the Church didn't seem to mind either, so long as the family kept coming to mass and giving generously to the coffers.

How much would I have learned by now had they not disbanded the grove? Tuck wondered. *Would I have been an ovate by now?* She scowled down at the cards, snatching them up and putting them back in the deck. "Yeah, right," she muttered. She knew her frustration was the impatience of youth. It was unlikely at her age she would be advanced enough to be an ovate. But with the grove scattered to the winds, she wasn't likely to ever get there now.

A knock sounded on her door just as she was placing her deck of cards into their bag. Her hounds vocalized their warnings that someone was there as if she couldn't hear the knock herself.

"Come in," Tuck called over their barks and howls.

Robyn entered, her cheeks rosy and her eyes bright. She bent down to greet the dogs and received many licks and wags.

"It went well then?" Tuck asked.

Robyn nodded, and Tuck could feel the waves of joyous freedom rolling off her friend.

"I've got an idea of how to go about helping the prisoners. You said a lot of the people in Sherwood used to live there?"

Tuck nodded. "When it was an apartment building, yes."

"I'd like to get everyone in Sherwood together and ask for help. With them having lived there, someone has to know the best way to get them out."

Perhaps the queen wasn't so far off after all, Tuck thought. "I agree. I'll call a meeting tonight after men's bath hours."

"And when is that?"

"Six to nine," Tuck answered.

"Sounds good. In the meantime, I think I'm going to take a look around Sherwood. I haven't really explored, and I want to see if there are any suitable places to house the prisoners when they get here."

"That's a good idea. Would you like some company?"

"Sure," Robyn said, smiling.

After Tuck had put on her jacket and cowl hood, they made their way from the abbey. The hounds ran on ahead, looking back every so often to make sure they were still following.

"How many prisoners do you think will come to Sherwood?" Tuck asked as the pair walked through the streets.

Robyn frowned. "Will said he would try to get as many as he could, but he wasn't convinced very many would want to come, want to risk escaping."

"If tons of prisoners go missing all at once, don't you think the government will notice and come looking for them?"

"Knowing John Lackland, he'll want to keep the fact that he lost his charges from the government. But should a lot of them decide to come, we can always move them to safer ground. Canada maybe?"

"That's a long way. We'd have to get them through Oregon and Washington first. Let's hope you're right about how John will react."

"I am. He hates showing weakness, and he avoids taking blame at all costs."

Tuck nodded. "Do you know how many people are in the camp?"

"Well, the apartment building looks about ten stories. There were probably thirty apartments on each floor if the one I saw is any indication. And Will said he shares an apartment with two other families. I know he has a family of four. So rough estimate? Thirty-six hundred?"

Tuck winced. "That's a lot of people. We only have just over a hundred in all of Sherwood."

Robyn nodded. "We need a better estimate. For now, do you know of any place in Sherwood that could house a lot of people at once?"

Tuck thought for a moment, tilting her head. "Follow me," she said.

She led Robyn about a half a mile north. The state of the surrounding buildings deteriorated worse and worse as they went. Finally, all that lay before them were giant piles of rock and brick, wood and dust.

At the very edge, on the line between ruins and complete desolation, there was a wooden guard tower, not unlike the ranger stations one used to find in the forests before they were the subject of fairy tales alone. It looked out of place, like a skyscraper in a sea storm.

"Jon and some of the others built this a while back when they thought we might need to keep watch on the northern border," Tuck informed, taking the first of the stairs to the top. "But with Sherwood being the north-most borough of Midshire, they ended up not really needing it. Still, I like to come here sometimes to think."

At the top, Tuck and Robyn went into the single room. It was bare except for a small table, a chair, and a cot in the corner. Tugging a rope hanging from the ceiling, Tuck pulled down a trapdoor, which folded out into a ladder. Robyn followed her up the ladder and onto the top platform of the tower.

The hounds howled their displeasure at being left behind, but a sharp word from Tuck quieted them.

At that height, they could see over the massive piles of rubble, see just how far the destruction extended.

"Did you ever hear about what happened to Sherwood Forest?" Tuck asked. She pointed past the once-lively city to the burnt earth beyond, charred sticks that were once lush, green trees still stood, ghosts with a tale to tell.

Robyn looked out at the desecration. "No, I've...never been this far north.

Tuck nodded. "It happened before either of us were even born. But my mom and the rest of my...family told me about it."

Tuck stared out at the corpses, never given the chance to live again. With so much pollution, with not enough sunshine or clean water, she wondered if even weeds could grow in those conditions. Her chest ached at the sight.

"During the Great War, the Lacklands controlled this part of the city; they were still fighting the other families for control of Midshire at the time. It was lucrative for them, what with the canal built to connect the river to the bay. They had a munitions factory up here, right where the forest connected to the river. But as often happens in unsafe conditions, the factory went up in a massive explosion. My mom said the fire burned for days. It took the forest and most of Sherwood with it. The survivors left after that, letting the rest of Sherwood fall into ruin. Some people returned during the depression, having no place else to go. But most left when war broke out again. And now... Well, I already told you how many of us ended up here."

Robyn's eyes were soft and sad as she listened to the story. "They have to be stopped, Tuck," she murmured. "For too long they have had control of Midshire. They have it in their heads that they are entitled to the place and the people like some sort of divine rule. No, I won't let them do this anymore. I will end this."

Tuck gazed over at her friend, who still looked out at the horizon. "I know you will," Tuck answered.

CHAPTER 30

$\mathcal{A}$top the guard tower, Robyn took in all of Sherwood. "Is there a hotel or apartment building where they can stay?" she asked Tuck, scanning the remaining buildings for signs of housing.

Tuck shook her head. "Most of that was on the north side. Even the old hospital was up here. Why do you think most of us live in an abbey? Jon lives in a bookshop, you know."

Robyn nodded. "That makes sense."

"Oh!" Tuck exclaimed, squinting toward the bay. "That might work."

"Where?"

"There," she pointed. "The old shipyard. There are plenty of old ships there. They took all the seaworthy ones to the newer yard in Stockport. But we don't need them to be able to float to live on them, right? There are a couple propped up, you know? In warehouses."

"And they're big?"

"Oh yeah, really big. With cabins and galleys and everything."

"Sounds perfect."

"Well, it is sort of out of the way though."

"It's not like they have to stay there if they don't want to. They can go wherever there's room. I just want to make sure we have someplace safe for them for certain."

Tuck nodded her agreement.

"So you'll gather everyone in Sherwood tonight?" Robyn asked.

"Yes, I'll send word for them all to come to the abbey."

Robyn nodded her approval.

At nine that evening the inhabitants of Sherwood gathered in the abbey's nave. There were no longer pews, so they crowded in and stood in loose groups. Robyn, Tuck, and Little Jon stood on the raised platform that used to be the altar.

The people of Sherwood murmured to each other with furrowed expressions, wondering why they had been gathered.

"All right, everyone," Tuck said from beside Robyn, but no one seemed to notice her call for attention.

Tuck looked up at Little Jon, who then slammed his quarterstaff against the stone floor with a few loud thumps. "'Ey, up here!" he shouted.

The din silenced.

"All right, everyone," Tuck said again. "I know we don't normally introduce new inhabitants, but I'd like you all to meet Robyn. She's the one I told you about. The one we've been waiting for."

"Oh, give it a rest, ya loony bat," someone from the crowd shouted.

Tuck frowned. "I'm well aware that not everyone subscribes to my insights, and that's fine. But please listen to what Robyn has to say."

"Yeah, shut it, Scott," a woman called to the heckler. "Everyone knows you're all talk. Don't believe in Tuck? Doesn't seem to stop you from visiting her every time you've got a bellyache."

"Yeah, if Jon and Tuck vouch for her, then that's all I need to know," someone else agreed.

The rest of the crowd murmured approval.

Robyn stepped forward toward the assemblage. "I'm Robyn Loxley," she declared. "And I don't know that I believe in some great destiny Tuck has ascribed to me, but I will tell you this: I want to help you, the people of Sherwood. It's my understanding we are facing a harsh winter. I have a plan on how to get more food, more blankets, more fuel, whatever we need to survive. But before that," Robyn paused.

She gazed out at the crowd, making eye contact with as many individuals as she could. Roughly one hundred people, mostly women and children, looked back at her, waiting with hopeful eyes for her to continue.

"But first, I need your help. I know many of you used to live in Lackland Chemical company housing, the apartment building that was turned into a concentration camp. Any information you have on the building, its layout and structure, would be very much appreciated. You see, as unjust as the Lacklands have been to you, firing you from your jobs, evicting you from your homes, even worse has been done to the people who are there now. They were taken from their homes. They were coerced into selling or abandoning their properties and businesses, many of which have been ransacked and vandalized. They were forcibly relocated to overpopulated camps and compelled to work at the chemical plant. And, trust me, I've seen the camp. Old women and children clean while the more abled are at the plant. And I can tell you, they aren't being fed properly. Being in the situation you're currently in, I'm certain you can empathize with their plight."

A few of the faces nodded, pity softening their expressions.

"But the Japanese attacked us. If it wasn't for them, the men wouldn't have been sent to war. They'd be home with us. And the Lacklands wouldn't have evicted anyone," Nan shouted back in a dissenting voice.

Robyn stared at her cousin. "You're right, cousin. The Japanese government did attack us. And maybe America wouldn't have gone to war had that not happened. Then again, maybe we would have. But I'll tell you one thing. These people our government has imprisoned? They are Americans. They have come here as immigrants, or their parents or grandparents came here as immigrants. Why is that? The same reason all of our ancestors did. To find a better life. These people have embraced what it means to be American. Did they not fight for America in the Great War?"

"And what of it? Things change. How do we know they aren't enemy spies?" Nan spewed the usual rhetoric.

"How do we know anyone's not?" Robyn countered. "Our family is British, right, Nan? What if America was at war with Britain? Would it be all right for them to round up anyone of British descent?"

"Britain is our ally," Nan answered simply.

"At the moment, yes. But they weren't always. Okay, what about Germans and Italians? We're at war with Germany and Italy too, aren't we? Some Germans and Italians are being detained and imprisoned as well. What about your friends, Nan? What about Ilse and Giulia? Would you not defend them should the government decide they're a threat?"

"But they aren't a threat. They've lived here for years, well before the war," Nan argued.

"Exactly, and so have those imprisoned at the Lackland camp. Most of them have lived here their entire lives, Nan. Most of them were born here. Don't you see how dangerous it is for the government to dehumanize groups of people? But look, I'm not here to be a dictator. Yes, I want to help them. I want to bring them to Sherwood, a place where everyone is welcome. And I want to stick it to the Lacklands. I want to take away their source of cheap labor. I want to punish them for what they did to all of us. I want to show them they can't treat people this way, show them we have rights. But I'm not going to force them on you. How about a vote?"

The crowd murmured.

"All in favor of helping the prisoners and bringing the Lacklands to their knees?" Robyn called.

A vast majority of the crowd raised their hands, at least ninety-five percent. Nan was not among them.

Robyn glowed at the group. "You are true defenders of freedom. You exemplify everything that is good about America, everything our forefathers fought to preserve. And now? It's our turn."

Cheers echoed off the green-covered stones as the people of Sherwood cried out in approval.

Robyn was positively bombarded when the meeting came to a close. People swarmed her, wanting to shake her hand or embrace her. Some offered to tell her what they knew about the camp building. And just as she was realizing she would need to make a schedule to give each person the proper amount of attention, Little Jon called to her, waving his great hand to beckon her to him.

She turned back to the swarm with a smile. "Thank you so much, everyone. I really appreciate your help. Would you mind leaving your name with Tuck, and I'll come see each one of you," she said.

Tuck's eyes widened as the hoard turned their attention to her. She cleared her throat. "Right. How about you gather in the refectory while I grab a pencil and paper?"

As the crowd cleared, Robyn made her way to Little Jon and the woman beside him. She was plump and pretty with the same shade of hair as Little Jon, though hers fell in ringlets about her face and neck.

"Robyn, I'd like you to meet Artheia Bland, my cousin," Little Jon introduced, beaming with pride.

Robyn shook Artheia's sturdy hand. "Nice to meet you, Artheia. What can I do for you?"

"Artheia was the cleaning lady for Lackland Chemical employee housing," Little Jon explained.

"Ask me anything," Artheia said with a cheery smile. "I know that building with my eyes closed."

"Wonderful!" Robyn exclaimed. "Tell me everything."

Robyn, Little Jon, and Artheia talked long into the night. They were later joined by Tuck. Eventually, with bleary eyes and heavy heads, they had to adjourn but promised to meet again the following day.

After the satisfied sleep that comes only from exhaustion, Robyn awoke and went downstairs for a bath and breakfast. As she scanned the refectory for a seat, she met her cousin's gaze.

Nan pursed her lips, then rose from her seat, taking her breakfast with her as she left the room.

Robyn's stomach sank.

"Don't mind her," Giulia murmured to Robyn as she watched her cousin retreat. "She'll come around. She's just angry. You understand. She thinks if the Japanese hadn't attacked Pearl Harbor, then America wouldn't have joined the war. And if we hadn't joined the war, Roger wouldn't have gone away."

"Roger?" Robyn asked.

Giulia nodded. "Her sweetheart. She sort of sees him as her savior. He was there for her when she needed someone most."

"So why do you think she'll come around then? If she's that angry."

Giulia smiled gently, but her eyes were sad. "It's what I have to believe. She has a good heart, so full of love. If she can love him so fiercely, it is my hope she can extend that love to others."

"I hope you're right," Robyn said.

Later that morning, Robyn met Artheia and Tuck at Little Jon's bookshop home to discuss potential plans in more detail.

"So you're saying our best bet is to get them out from the roof?" Robyn asked Artheia, as they leaned over a drawing Artheia had made of the building and surrounding area.

Artheia nodded. "If the fire escapes have been taken down as you said and the bottom floors are guarded, the best way to sneak them out is on the roof. If you didn't care whether you alerted the guards or whether you hurt anyone, then going out the back door would be best. But to do it in stealth without harm? I say the roof."

Robyn paused, recalibrating her earlier plans. "Okay," she murmured.

"We're really going to have to know how many are coming if we plan on getting them off the roof," Tuck pointed out.

Robyn nodded.

"You say the neighboring building is fairly close?" Robyn asked Artheia, pointing at the drawing before them.

Artheia nodded. "Yes, it's not close enough to jump across, and it's a few stories shorter than the camp, but it's close enough to see in each other's windows."

Robyn stared off into space, considering next steps. "I may have an idea, but Tuck's right. We need to know how many are coming."

"What's the plan?" Little Jon asked.

"First, we have to get the transmitter from Gyl," Robyn said. "Then we go to the building next door. Artheia, would you mind coming on this scouting mission with us?"

"I'm not very skilled with anything other than a broom and a rag, but if I can be of assistance..."

"I recall you besting me once in our youth with that broom," Little Jon countered with a chuckle.

Artheia raised her chin in defiance. "You shouldn't have stolen my pie. You knew apple was my favorite, and I was saving that piece for later!"

"How many pies have I given you since then?" Little Jon argued.

"No amount of penance pies will make up for the disappointment I felt that day." Artheia glared at her cousin, who winced as if her retribution could still be felt all these years later.

Robyn laughed at their exchange. "Anyone who can make Jon cower in that manner can be on my scouting team any day."

Artheia gave them a small smile, her cheeks pink with embarrassment.

"All right then," Tuck said. "We just have to wait for Gyl to finish the transmitter."

Everyone else nodded in agreement.

It was another two days before Gyl had the radio transmitter ready. In that time, Robyn visited all the people who Tuck had written down; most of them corroborated what she'd learned from Artheia. Then she got the message that the transmitter was finished.

Robyn stared at the buttons, knobs, and switches, then looked up at the inventor.

"Hadn't you better go with us?" she asked, her tone urging him to agree.

"You want me to leave the laboratory?" He raised his eyebrows above his goggles.

"Well, we could definitely use your keen mind while scouting how to get possibly thousands of people off a roof."

"Yet another problem that needs a scientific solution?"

"Could be."

Gyl grinned, rubbing his hands together eagerly. "When do we leave?"

CHAPTER 31

Robyn and her band decided their scouting mission would head out Sunday evening when most people would be home preparing for Monday's work. So when the grey sky lightened on All Hallows' Eve, she was free to let the excitement of seeing Rick take hold. In fact, her anticipation for that evening was the only thing keeping her mind off what would come the following day.

As promised, she met Marian at her studio around lunchtime. Robyn found the door unlocked.

"Hello?" Robyn called as she entered the space, smirking as she thought about the last time she'd been there.

Her sister poked her head out of the kitchen. "Robyn, you made it." She grinned and crossed the room to embrace Robyn tightly.

"Did you miss me?" Robyn asked, echoing Marian's question from earlier in the week.

"I knew I would, but I didn't know how much." Marian held Robyn at arm's length, inspecting her. "You seem to be doing well," she said with approval.

"I am. And you?" Robyn noted the puffiness under her sister's eyes, the circles expertly covered with cosmetics. "Are you not sleeping well?"

Marian gave her a reassuring smile. "I'm fine. I've been helping

Isabella with the bond rally. And trying to listen at keyholes without getting caught is hard work, you know."

Robyn's brow furrowed. "But you're being careful?"

Marian waved her hand dismissively. "Yes, yes, I'm perfectly fine. But you know, I think something is going on between John and Guy."

"What do you mean?"

Marian quirked her mouth. "I don't quite know as of yet. But it seems like they're much more strained in how they speak to one another, though maybe it's just Guy. He seems...less forthcoming? I don't know. As if he only answers direct questions, and he does so in as few words as possible. His visits seem shorter, too. I really had to scurry to make sure they didn't catch me the other day."

Robyn crinkled her eyebrows. "And John?" she asked.

"He doesn't really seem to notice, or maybe he doesn't care. Just gives his orders like he's the king of Midshire."

"Anything I should know about?"

Marian shook her head. "Things seem to be running smoothly for them at the moment. John keeps asking after a new manager at their casino, how he's doing and the like."

Robyn nodded.

"Oh, Guy did mention some potential trouble with a girl and some bookies. Apparently, there was a detective who interceded. But John didn't seem worried when he told Guy to remind his superiors where their loyalties ought to lie."

Robyn hummed in thought.

"Anyway, enough of that. You're going to a party tonight, right? Did Rick tell you what you would be dressed as?"

"No, he just told me to wear the dress I wore for Eleanor's birthday."

"Okay, well, let's dress you up nicely, and you can adjust when you find out."

Robyn and Marian had lunch and then spent the next few hours doing Robyn's hair and cosmetics. They talked about what they'd been doing since they saw each other last. A week was a long time for two sisters who'd never been apart.

Marian was shocked to hear their cousin was in Sherwood. She wanted to meet her as soon as possible. But when Robyn told her how angry Nan was, she agreed to wait for a more opportune time. Marian was also excited to invite Robyn to her upcoming photography exhibition. Robyn congratulated her sister and promised to be there.

Robyn was ready well before seven. She might have just stayed and chatted with her sister, but Marian said she'd promised to be home soon. So Robyn decided to head over to Rick's early. After all, if he wasn't in, she could always visit with Mrs. Stanley.

It was a little sad to see the lack of Halloween enthusiasm of past years. There were no parades—not if the city council had anything to say about it—and hardly any trick-or-treaters—not many treats to give them anyway what with the sugar shortage. It was less than a year since America had joined the war, and Robyn was already dispirited by the effects. *Such a small thing to have to give up, Halloween,* she thought. *But so telling.* Still, many people were having private parties to keep their spirits up, so it wasn't as if there were no autumn celebrations.

Rick's polite expression warmed into a smile when he answered the door and recognized his date. Robyn shivered at the look in his eyes.

"You're early," he murmured, pleased by the surprise.

"I am."

"Come in." He opened the door wide for her.

"Mrs. Stanley?" she asked him softly.

"In the kitchen."

His eyes flicked to the stairs in a question, and Robyn nodded before heading up to his room.

Upon entering his bedroom, Robyn immediately noticed the white tie attire he had draped over a chair. On the other was a black cape, and on the table was a black satin and lace masquerade-type eye mask.

She picked up the mask and held it to her face. "Is this for me?" she asked, turning back to Rick.

He nodded.

"What am I supposed to be?"

"Well, I knew you liked monster movies, so I thought it would be fun if I went as Dracula. You could be Lucy or Mina."

"I'm the helpless victim?"

"Well, in the book there are three female vampires who live at Castle

Dracula as well, not to mention Lucy becomes a vampire. So you could also be one of them."

Robyn smiled. "Do you think I could pull off one of these female vampires?"

Rick stepped close to her, and she tilted back her face to look up at him. "Jonathan Harker has some very impure thoughts about them. He fantasizes about them kissing him. But his desire for them is nothing compared to what I feel for you," he murmured.

By the time Rick was finished fully expressing his desire, the work Robyn and Marian had done earlier that afternoon was all but erased. Though considering what she now knew about her costume, Robyn would have had to undo most of it anyway. And even if she didn't, the elation she'd felt while she was tangled in him was well worth the cosmetic reapplication.

As Rick dressed in his Dracula dress suit and cape, Robyn fully loosened her hair, which tumbled to her shoulders. Then she applied some deep red lipstick and skipped the rouge. With a little assistance from Mrs. Stanley's kitchen supply, she even made a trail of blood out of the corner of her mouth with a mixture of lipstick and liquid dish detergent. After putting on the eye-mask Rick had given her, she analyzed her own reflection. She smiled a wicked grin, confident John Lackland himself wouldn't even recognize her.

"How do I look?" Rick asked.

Robyn turned around to see him. He was crisp and clean like one would imagine a Romanian nobleman to be, his hair slicked back with pomade. "You look like a sinister Fred Astaire," she answered with a grin.

"Oh, you're a saucy one," Rick razzed.

"You like that, do you?"

"I like everything about you," he murmured sweetly.

"Now, don't you start that. Unless, you don't want to go to the party after all?" Robyn raised an eyebrow at him.

Rick sighed. "I really should, though to be honest I'd rather stay in with you. But Preston is always telling me to get more involved with the fellas at the station. He seems to think it'll help me fit in."

Robyn pounced on this little bit of information he'd let slip about himself. "Do you not fit in?"

Rick shrugged. "Well, I'm the new guy, right?"

Robyn knew it had to be more than that. *And you're incorruptible*, she thought. *From what Guy said, your fellow officers are less than savory. But you won't tell me that. Are you still trying to keep me out of the whole Lackland mess? If only you knew just how deep I was in already.*

"I will be on my best behavior then," Robyn promised. "If I can charm them the right way, perhaps they'll be more accepting of you."

"Well...don't charm them too much."

Robyn laughed at his apprehension. "Nothing to worry about, Detective. There's only one copper whose attention I want to keep."

Rick stared at her, his expression soft and open as if he'd been waiting for any breadcrumb of favor she'd throw his way.

It wasn't that Robyn disliked the light of admiration shining in his eyes, it was more that she was confused by his reaction. She tilted her head slightly. *Why should such an offhand comment trigger that sort of response?* she wondered. *Have I been unclear in my affections?* Robyn slipped her hand into his, lacing their fingers together with a smile. "Shall we go?"

CHAPTER 32

$\mathcal{A}$laric could tell by Sergeant Treadle's expression as he opened the door that his superior hadn't thought he would show.

"Nottingham?" Treadle stumbled for only a second. "You made it. Welcome."

"Thank you, sir," Alaric stated, already slipping into the reserved demeanor he wore in public. He could feel Robyn's gaze on him as she took in his tone.

Alaric ushered Robyn in before him with a hand on her lower back. They handed their coats and scarves to Treadle, then turned toward the gathering.

Alaric recognized men from his precinct; most were from his unit. They were gathered in small groups, drinks in hand, talking and laughing. Their costumes ranged from scarecrow to Frankenstein's monster to knight in cardboard armor. They hadn't been there a minute before a woman in a short red dress, barbed tail, and devil horns noticed his arrival.

"Alaric," she called, handing Paynton her drink and sauntering over.

Alaric stiffened at hearing her voice and cringed as she came toward him. Her eyes flicked to Robyn only momentarily. When she reached him, she stepped in close, running her fingertips along his chest. "I knew you'd keep your promise. You're a man of your word after all."

"Miss Brimley, how many times have I asked you to address me as Detective Nottingham?" he asked, stepping out of her reach and moving closer to Robyn.

Miss Brimley smiled in that undeterred way she had. "Oh, Alaric, you're such a kidder."

Alaric frowned.

"Rick?" Robyn said sweetly in a tone he'd never heard when he wasn't making love to her. "Won't you introduce us?"

Alaric risked a glance at her. She smiled up at him, her expression smooth and unruffled. "Of course. Robyn, this is Miss Brimley. She works in the files room at the station."

Robyn dipped her head at the woman, who squinted ever so slightly back.

"It's nice to meet you, Miss Brimley. I'm glad to hear my Rick works with such friendly colleagues."

"Oh, yes," Miss Brimley agreed. "We are great friends. He visits me quite frequently in the files room. But I'm surprised. He's never mentioned you."

"I'd imagine not," Robyn answered without hesitation. "He's such a professional. He would never mix business and pleasure. Well, as I said, it was nice to meet you, Miss Brimley. Rick, could we get something to drink? I'm parched."

Alaric nodded and led the way after Robyn slipped her arm in his. As soon as they walked away, Alaric looked sideways at Robyn. "Robyn, I assure you, there's—"

"I know," she cut him off. Then she smiled softly, her eyes sending a message of reassurance. "You don't have to tell me. I've met enough women like her to know who she is. You probably brought me as a way of putting her off too, right? Besides, I can tell the difference in how you look at me as opposed to her."

Alaric's heart swelled. *What have I done in my life to deserve this woman?* he thought, gazing down at her.

She smiled wider and stood on her toes, kissing him lightly on the mouth.

Before he could say anything, Preston wrapped his arm around Alaric's shoulders. "See? I told you you should get out more. Here not five minutes and already captured this lady's heart."

"Whoa!" Robyn exclaimed. "Where did you get that?" She indicated the Midshire Mongoose sweater Preston wore as his costume.

Preston grinned. "My nephew plays for the Mongoose. He gave it to me for Christmas last year."

"That's incredible! Who is he?"

"Richie Otterson."

"Richie Otterson! We saw him make the winning throw against Pittsburgh."

Preston nodded. "Boy, was I sorry I missed that game. But seeing as how Alaric took you, I don't feel so bad. I'm glad you enjoyed it."

"Are you kidding? We had a great time. Didn't we, Rick?"

"Yes, we did," Alaric answered with a smile.

"Oh, you're saying that even though Pittsburgh lost?" Preston marveled. "This girl must be quite something if you can have fun despite your team losing."

She is, Alaric thought. "Robyn, this is Eugene Preston. We are often partnered on cases together."

"It's nice to meet you, Eugene," Robyn said, holding out her hand to shake his.

"Enough with that Eugene stuff," Preston groaned, taking her hand. "Just call me Preston."

Robyn chuckled. "All right, Preston."

Alaric and Robyn spent most of the night talking with Preston. More accurately, Robyn and Preston spent most of the night teasing Alaric. But he didn't mind. He was happy to see Robyn enjoying herself, to see her laughing and joking, to see her lighthearted. It reminded him of the first night they'd met at the Blue Boar Inn. And with everything that had come to light since then, he was relieved to see she was still Robyn, despite it all.

It was a good night, one that promised many more to come. And Alaric was high on the knowledge that Robyn did, in fact, care for him. His honesty had paid off, and she'd said she wanted only his attention. No one else's. She even warned Miss Brimley away, effectively claiming Alaric for herself. For the first time in a long time, Alaric Nottingham felt content, at ease, happy.

"Did you have a good time?" Alaric asked Robyn as they got out of his car at his flat.

"I did. It was fun. Thank you for inviting me."

"Anytime. But you know..." he paused as they stood on the sidewalk, "it doesn't have to be over. You could stay."

She smiled sadly. "I wish I could. But I have something important to do tomorrow, and I need to rest."

He nodded sadly. "I understand."

Bending down, he kissed her goodnight. It started sweet and gentle. But as it went on, she deepened it, pressing her lips harder to his and pulling him closer. Alaric's blood heated. He knew allowing it to continue would only make it harder when she left, but he didn't care. He wanted every moment.

When she broke their kiss, her heavy breathing caressed his face. "Okay," she murmured. "Okay, but I have to leave early."

CHAPTER 33

obyn awoke early the next morning, warmly wrapped in Rick's arms. She was glad she'd decided to stay. She knew if she'd gone back to Sherwood, she only would have been anxious about the mission. And being with Rick always had a way of taking her mind off things. Unfortunately, she had no time to spare. She had to prepare for that evening.

As gently and silently as she could, Robyn extricated herself from Rick's bed and dressed. But as she stopped to gaze at him one last time, she couldn't bring herself to leave without saying goodbye. Locating a pencil and paper, she wrote him a little note.

> Rick,
> I didn't want to wake you, but I had to get going.
> I'll call you soon. Thanks again for last night.
> Robyn

She placed it on the pillow and left. She was relieved when she got out before Mrs. Stanley was up and about.

Robyn and her band spent the rest of the morning and afternoon preparing for the mission, gathering supplies and going over the plan a few more times.

As dusk darkened the grey sky, they gathered near the bridge of Sherwood Canal.

"Here," Tuck said as she passed fabric to Robyn, Gyl, Little Jon, and Artheia.

"What's this?" Robyn asked, holding up the cloth she'd been handed.

"It's a hood," Tuck said. "They know your face around that area, right? And it's best if they don't know ours. I made them from bits of cloth I found."

Robyn smiled at the young woman. "Great idea, Tuck. Thank you."

Tuck nodded.

"What about mine?" Much asked.

Tuck glanced at Little Jon.

"This time, you're going to stay with David and watch the gate," Little Jon told the boy.

"But I want to go, too!" Much protested.

"We're going to need your help next time," Little Jon promised.

"We don't know what's going to happen while they're gone, Muchisimo," David added, patting Much on the shoulder. "With all of our strongest people gone from Sherwood, we need to stay and protect those left behind. Don't you think?"

Much frowned. "Well, I wouldn't want to leave them unprotected."

"Exactamente," David agreed.

Robyn pulled on her new hood over the poncho Little Jon had given her and readjusted her quiver across her back. The hood's cowl made her scarf unnecessary, so she took it off.

"Would you mind looking after this for me until I get back, Much? This is my favorite scarf, and I don't want anything to happen to it." she asked the boy.

Robyn wrapped the scarf snuggly around Much's neck, his dark eyes shining as though he'd been given a sacred duty. He nodded, and she ruffled his hair.

Everyone else put on their cowl hoods and armed themselves for a potential fight, Tuck with her sword, Little Jon with his quarterstaff, Gyl with a strange looking gun that only he knew what it did, and

Artheia with what looked suspiciously like a mop handle with the mop removed.

Then they bid Much and David farewell, promising to return before dawn. Tuck had to tell her hounds to stay more than once before they complied, though they whined in protest.

The building closest to Midshire War Relocation Center was a small theater and institute for the arts. The ground floor held the theatre, and the upper floors were used for teaching and practicing dance, singing, painting, and the like. None of them had ever been inside, but Artheia knew there were fire escapes on either side of the building.

The band scurried up the fire escape on the far side of the theatre, carefully trying to keep their ascension quiet. On the roof, they crouched down and made their way toward the ledge on the other side, moving from shadow to shadow.

Reaching the ledge, they knelt and peered over the side and into the concentration camp windows.

Artheia had been right, Robyn could see into each of the barred windows facing her, like looking into so many television sets. Men, women, and children went about their lives cleaning, playing cards, and sitting around the radio. Robyn scanned the windows but didn't see anyone she recognized.

She analyzed what she could see of the roof a few stories above them, then turned to Gyl, who was doing the same.

"Okay," Robyn murmured. "Everyone, look around for anything that might be important later." She looked at her watch. "It's time. Gyl, let's fire this thing up."

Gyl pulled the radio transmitter from his back and placed it between them. He switched it on and turned some knobs before handing Robyn a telephone handset.

"You won't be able to hear them, of course. But as long as they added the converter to their antenna and the radio is on and tuned correctly, they'll be able to hear you."

"But no one else listening to the radio will be able to, right?" Robyn asked.

Gyl nodded. "Right. When you're ready."

Robyn indicated her readiness, and Gyl toggled a switch.

"Go ahead," he murmured.

Robyn began talking into the telephone. "Will? I hope you can hear me. The time is drawing near. We need to know how many people will be coming. I'm sure it'll take a bit for you to figure that out, but listen. Just so we know this transmission is getting through, I want you to hang three socks in your window tomorrow. And when you know how many are coming, figure out some way of communicating that. We'll check the window every day until we get the answer. It won't be long now. Stay safe."

Robyn handed the handset back to Gyl, who toggled the switch off. Then she motioned for everyone to regroup. "Did you get a good look around?" she asked them.

They nodded.

"Good. Let's head back to Sherwood and go over what we learned. Tomorrow, Tuck and Much can come back and locate the window we need to be watching." Robyn explained, thinking the pair would be the most inconspicuous during daytime hours.

Then Robyn and her band left as swiftly and as quietly as they'd come, retreating back to the safety of Sherwood.

CHAPTER 34

"Stay safe," the radio said, and then there was silence punctuated by the occasional crackle of static. Will reached out and turned the radio off before facing his family and the others who lived in the apartment.

As expected, his mother's brow was knit with worry, and she glanced anxiously at her husband. Will's father didn't notice. His eyes were fixed on the floor as he squinted in deep thought at Robyn's words. Micki practically vibrated with excitement. Will could feel his little sister's gaze on him like an incessant poking. He ignored it and took in everyone else's reaction.

Mr. and Mrs. Fujino exchanged glances before turning their expectant eyes on Will. Yuki sat on the floor beside them, her head bowed. She hadn't moved since the transmission had started.

The widowed Mrs. Ichikawa spoke first, her infant daughter cradled in her arms and her twin boys each clutching a side of her skirt. "What does this mean, Will?" she asked softly.

Will stood and addressed the group. "My childhood friend wants to help us escape. We know it'll be dangerous." Will shook his head. "I don't have to tell you that what's happened to us is wrong. You all know it.

We've all suffered. I'd rather take my chances out there than wait around for them to decide what else they want from us."

Will analyzed their expressions, but the only thing he could gather was their anxiety.

There was a tense silence before his father nodded. "Take Micki and go, Will. Robyn will look after you. I don't want you to live like this. Your mother and I will stay. We will only slow you down. And if too many people go, you'll be less likely to get away."

Will looked at his mother, who gave him a tearful nod. "Take care of your sister," she said.

Yuki took a deep breath and stood. She moved to Will's side and faced her parents, head still bowed. "Otousan, Okaasan, I'm going with Will," she told them.

"Yuki-chan, you are not well," Mrs. Fujino urged. "How will you keep up with your asthma?"

Yuki straightened her spine. "Okaasan, I know you're worried because you love me. But you and Otousan went through so much for the promise of freedom. I want to make you proud."

Mrs. Fujino opened her mouth to protest, but Mr. Fujino cut her off with a raised hand. He stared hard at his daughter. And though Will could see Yuki's hands shaking, she didn't look away from her father's gaze. With a silent nod, Mr. Fujino pronounced his judgment, and the matter was settled for the family.

All the while, Mrs. Ichikawa gnawed her lower lip. "I don't want my children to grow up in here," she said, tears spilling down her gaunt face. "But we will only slow you down. We would endanger everyone else if we came with you."

Will approached Mrs. Ichikawa and spoke to her with confidence. "I don't want Hibiki and Naoki or little Kiku to remember this place. Come with us, Ichikawa-san. We will keep you and your children safe."

"I'll help," Micki added.

Yuki nodded. "Me too."

Mrs. Ichikawa smiled tearfully, thanking them with repeated bows. And as Will's mother comforted Mrs. Ichikawa, Will, Micki, and Yuki each removed a sock and hung it in the window.

The following day, Will went to work at Lackland Chemical. The nature of making chemical grenades hadn't become any safer, but the safety equipment had improved as of late. A few days after Robyn had come to visit, Guy Gisbourne had delivered boxes of protective masks and overalls without a word. Will likely wouldn't have noticed him had he not recognized his intense glower.

He'd also heard from the infirmary that the medicines had been mysteriously restocked as well, and internees were being treated without having to pay for the pleasure.

Personally, Will had always disliked Guy. He found him unsettling, and it was downright creepy the way he looked at Robyn. But he would give credit where it was due. And for whatever reason, Guy seemed to suddenly have taken interest in their welfare. Of course, he couldn't do much about the overcrowding or the shortage of diesel to heat the building what with the rations, but Will recognized and appreciated his efforts.

That evening, as Will was trying to figure out how to discretely ask people about escaping without alerting those who would snitch, the "mayor" called a meeting.

As usual, everyone headed up the stairs to the top floor in a great stream of bodies. All the inner walls of the top floor had been knocked down, creating a huge open space for gatherings such as this. Sometimes dances were held, but mostly it was used as a space for simple exercise.

After everyone had gathered, the mayor—the prisoner who the other inmates had appointed to speak for them—stood on a chair to address the crowd.

"Good evening," he greeted with a bow. "I called you here because I've heard some grumblings I'd like to address. I know many of you had hoped that after our victory at Midway, it wouldn't be long before we were released."

The mayor paused as a murmur ran through the crowd. "I'd like to remind everyone to please be patient," he continued. "It is for our own safety and the safety of our fellow Americans that we are here. Our fellow Americans are justifiably upset at the attack on our country, as are we all. And those who look like us have been harmed in the wake of this great fear and grief. Remember, our president has relocated us here to protect us from those who might harm us. And I believe we are all agreed in the fact that precious resources should not be wasted on ferreting out any Japanese spies—and we all know they exist—who might harm this great nation of freedom and opportunity. If my being here for the remainder of the war can help the cause, then I say, 'anything I can do to help my nation!' And let us not forget that we are being taken care of. We have beds to sleep in, food in our bellies, and work that helps our boys on the front."

Will's stomach curdled at the propaganda spewing from the mayor's lips. *Does he really believe this?* he wondered. He scanned the room to look at the response of those around him, his eyebrows raising with every passing moment. The majority of the crowd listened intently to the mayor's words and nodded seriously. Only a few by comparison frowned. Will made note of every person who wore expressions of anger, resentment, or disgust. *These are the people who will want to escape with us,* he thought.

CHAPTER 35

Over the week that followed, Robyn, Little Jon, Tuck, and Much took turns checking Will's window in the evening. During the day, Robyn helped Gyl collect and prepare the equipment they needed for the rescue.

It was Robyn's turn to take a walk on the street that ran along the backside of the camp. She wore the hood Tuck had made her—it being quite effective against the November wind—but she carried a grocery basket on her arm in case someone grew suspicious. She strolled along the opposite side of the street showing no inclination to rush.

Glancing up at the fourth story window second from the left, Robyn slowed her pace and squinted. In the bottom right corner of the window, white spots of soap dotted the glass in an odd pattern. Four open circles had been drawn in a row above a line with two dots on either side. Below the left dot, a column of four open circles had been drawn. Under the line were eight circles drawn in two columns of four; the left column's circles were open while the right's were solid. Finally, the fourth column, below the right dot, had two solid circles above two open circles.

Robyn smiled to herself, remembering one winter afternoon when Oji had been teaching Micki how to count on the soroban. At Robyn's display of curiosity at the wooden beads, he happily showed her as well. *Forty-two,* Robyn thought. *We can work with that.*

On the following Sunday, when the stage crew and actors of the theatre had long returned to their homes, Robyn, Gyl, Little Jon, and Tuck returned to the roof to transmit their plans to Will.

Three days later, as Robyn and her band clambered up the theatre fire escape, ready to commit their act of treason, Robyn recalled the president's words she'd heard over the radio earlier that day as he delivered his Armistice Day address to the nation from Arlington National Cemetery.

"We stand in the presence of the honored dead," he'd said. "We stand accountable to them, and to the generations yet unborn for whom they gave their lives."

Robyn's heart had swelled at those words. *We are accountable to the honored dead,* she thought. *It's our responsibility to uphold and improve the morals and values of those great men and women who came before us, who died for freedom from tyranny. And we do owe the future generations an America that strives to make itself better than it has ever been. They may call it treason in this moment, but later, perhaps much later, they will see that what we do today is in the spirit of liberty and equality. Today, we act in accordance with those high ideals, no matter the cost, as those before us have done.*

Standing sure-footed on the ledge of the theatre roof, her hood shadowing her face, Robyn pulled back her bowstring and shot a modified arrow; the attached ropes wiggled like tadpole tails as it soared through the air. Its hooks securely found purchase in a chimney atop the concentration camp.

Gyl quickly secured the other end and attached a bag to the pulley rope. Then he pulled the rope until the bag was transported to the other end.

And there it hung. Robyn strained her eyes against the darkness of midnight, holding her breath so she might hear even the slightest sound.

"Do you think—" Little Jon whispered.

Tuck shushed him before he could finish.

Then, slowly, the shadows on the other rooftop began to shift and flow, a smiling face under a mess of dark hair appeared, flanked by a group of anxious strangers. Will raised his hand and waved. Robyn mimicked the gesture, though releasing her breath didn't ease the tightness in her chest.

Getting to work, Will quickly took down the bag Gyl had sent over and began fitting Micki with the first harness. A minute later, Micki stood on the ledge, staring down at the alley between the buildings.

Will grabbed her hand, and she looked back at him. He said something with a nod. Then Micki turned her gaze toward Robyn. Robyn smiled and motioned the girl toward her. Micki nodded rapidly, then jumped from the building.

Micki whizzed down the rope, her face red as she held in her screams. Robyn caught her on the other side.

"You made it," Robyn soothed, stroking the girl's hair.

"Onee-chan," Micki murmured with relief, embracing Robyn.

"I know, Micki-chan" Robyn hushed. "But listen, we're going to need your help here, okay?"

Micki nodded, and Robyn removed her harness.

As Robyn sent back the harness, Will had already fixed another to a young woman and was in the process of helping someone else with the third.

The more people who came over, the faster Will and Robyn got at harnessing and unharnessing them. When ten people had made it across, Robyn looked at Tuck and nodded.

"All right," Tuck whispered to the lot. "We're going to guide you in groups so as not to draw too much attention. I'll lead the first. Follow me."

Micki hesitated, looking back across the divide, her brow crinkled with worry. "But my brother," she protested.

"Micki-chan, Will sent you over first because he wants you out of here as soon as possible. Don't worry. We'll meet up with you later. Trust me," Robyn assured. "Good luck," Robyn said to Tuck, her voice sounding much more confident than she felt.

And they disappeared down the fire escape on the far side.

Another ten and Little Jon's group was ready. He hesitated to leave.

"What if you run into trouble?" he asked Robyn anxiously.

"Then I've got a quiver of arrows ready to loose, haven't I?" Robyn reassured.

Little Jon nodded. "See you back in Sherwood."

"You bet."

Another ten and it was Gyl's turn. "Do you remember what I said?" Gyl asked Robyn.

"No problem," Robyn answered.

Gyl nodded and led his group away.

Will came over last, carrying the bag. As he landed, Robyn embraced him. The tightness in her chest finally loosened as he stroked her hair.

"I told you," a man from Robyn's group whispered to two women beside him.

Pulling back from their embrace, Robyn straightened her spine. She took the controller Gyl had given her from her pocket and pressed the button. The hooks holding her arrow to the camp chimney disengaged, and she pulled it back across the gap before stuffing the lot into the bag.

"All right," she said. "No time to lose."

Having sent most of the vulnerable ahead first, Robyn was left with a group of twelve fit, young people. It didn't take them long to descend the fire escape on the far side.

Safely on the ground, just before the mouth of the alley, Robyn turned to the group.

"The hard part is done," she encouraged. "But we aren't home free yet. Stay close, and be as quiet as you can. We'll be taking back ways to avoid being seen. But by morning, you all will be safe in Sherwood. Let's go."

CHAPTER 36

The air of Sherwood was undoubtedly dirtier than the processed air of the concentration camp. But as Will stepped onto the solid ground on the other side of the canal, he thought it had to be the sweetest, freshest air he'd ever breathed in his life.

Robyn was approached by a teenager with messy blond hair and a small, dark boy, whose grin couldn't have been any wider.

"Everyone get here okay?" she asked the youth.

He nodded. "You're the last."

She sighed, then laughed in that relieved sort of way she'd always done when they'd escaped some adventure unscathed as children. "We did it," she said, turning her sparkling eyes to Will.

Her joy traveled through the last group of freed prisoners, and they gave a collective sigh of relief, their anxious faces smoothing into smiles.

"You were right," Ritsu told Will, throwing his arm around his shoulder. "Your Robyn certainly is something else."

"She's not mine," Will corrected again. He'd lost track of how many times he'd done so.

"So you say," Ritsu snickered.

"As much as it pains me, Will. I'm going to have to agree with Ritsu on this one," Alice added. "We all saw that heart-felt embrace."

Will sighed, defeated. He'd never been able to explain his relationship with Robyn properly to others. Not lovers. But more than friends. Too charged for siblings. *I barely understand it myself,* he thought. *How could I possibly explain it to someone else?* And he had tried to understand it, of course he had. But no label ever seemed to fit quite right.

"I believe you," Yuki murmured.

"Thanks, Yuki."

"I'm sure you're all tired," Robyn said to the group. "Sherwood has a sort of open living arrangement. Feel free to stay wherever you like that isn't already occupied. We've found a place for you all to stay for now, until you get settled where you want. I'll take you there."

Will easily fell into step with Robyn as she led the way, the familiarity a comfort in this new and uncertain situation. She looked over at him, her smile gentle and her eyes soft with affection.

"I'm so glad you're here, Will." She'd always been good at saying exactly what she felt.

"Thanks for coming for me," he murmured.

Her smile widened. "Was there ever a doubt?"

"Well...I had hoped you'd listen to me for once..."

She pursed her lips.

"But I'm glad you didn't."

"And the adventure isn't over yet. We've got over a hundred people here in Sherwood we have to get ready for winter. And I want to help those left in the concentration camp. If Lackland Chemical is anything like the steel mill, I'm sure you don't have enough safety equipment. I mean, they made us pay for ours. And look at you, how much weight have you lost? They weren't feeding you well, were they?"

"You're right, but things have gotten somewhat better as of late thanks to your friend."

She tilted her head at him.

"Guy Gisbourne. He brought masks and overalls to the plant for the workers. He even brought medicine to the camp. I know I've never had anything good to say about him, but I'm not spiteful. He's helped us, and I give him credit for that."

Robyn's eyes softened though her brow was still crinkled in thought.

"But I still don't like him," Will added.

Robyn laughed, and Will's heart warmed at the sound.

It wasn't a short walk from the bridge, and everyone was tired. They hadn't slept since the night before, and they'd spent the whole day working before they'd tramped across Midshire.

"I know," Robyn apologized. "It's a ways, but it's all we could think of to house everyone at once. Don't worry. We're almost there."

"There" turned out to be an abandoned shipyard. Beside a hulking man, who looked as though he could crush Will's head between his bare hands, Micki waited outside a warehouse. Spotting their approach, she ran to Will and hugged him. Will stroked his sister's hair, taking comfort in her rare display of affection.

They continued to follow Robyn toward the giant.

"Will, I'd like you to meet Little Jon." Robyn's face reddened the moment she'd said his name. "I mean, Jon Little," she corrected, embarrassed.

Will took in the seven-foot man and his bemused expression and burst out laughing. "No, no, I think you got it right the first time," he chuckled. "Little Jon is so perfect. I don't think I can ever call him anything else."

Robyn's blush deepened. "I'm sorry, Jon. It slipped out. It's just so ironic and—"

Little Jon held up a massive hand, silencing her apologies. "'Salright," he said graciously. "I don't mind. You aren't the first, but at least I know you say it with affection."

"I do," Robyn promised.

"Then you call me whatever you like, Robyn."

Will looked between them and smiled, recognizing that fierce loyalty Robyn evoked in people all too well. "Sorry if there was any misunderstanding, big fella. I'm Will. Any friend of Robyn's is a friend of mine." Will held out his hand to Little Jon, putting a lot of trust in the man who could easily crush his hand beyond use.

"I hear you've known each other a long time," Little Jon said, taking Will's hand.

"We've been friends most our lives," Will agreed.

Little Jon smiled congenially. He released Will's hand, then he gestured to the warehouse behind him. "Tuck's in there, making sure everyone is getting settled."

"Thanks, Little Jon," Robyn said with a grin. Then she motioned for the group to follow her.

Will and the others entered the building to find it housed a massive ship, long put up on stilts to be repaired. It was rusted and dirty and beautiful. It was freedom and safety and community.

"I've gotten everyone else settled aboard. There are individual cabins for everyone. And I already showed them the galley where we put the food for tomorrow."

Will turned to look at the woman who'd spoken. His heart pounded loud in his ears, and his mouth hung open like a suffocating fish. She was petite, someone you could pick up and carry around like a child does a doll. Her perfect curls glistened down her back, and her eyes were shiny and captivating like a distant, swirling galaxy through a telescope.

He was aware that Robyn was speaking, though he could not internalize what she'd said. Then the woman met his gaze, and an attractive flush dusted her cheeks. His mouth dried.

"It's nice to meet you, Will," she murmured, her blush deepening the longer they held eye contact.

His name sounded so glorious on her tongue. He wanted her to say it again.

"Oof," he groaned as Robyn elbowed him in the side, reminding him to speak.

"The pleasure is mine…?" He hadn't been listening when Robyn had said her name.

"Tuck," the woman provided.

He felt an idiotic smile spread across his face. "Tuck," he whispered.

Her eyes sparkled, and he was only vaguely aware that Ritsu, Alice, and Yuki gossiped behind him.

CHAPTER 37

Marian Loxley blinked drowsily in the darkness of her bedroom as a telephone pierced the sleepy silence of the Lacklands' mansion. When the ringing was abruptly stopped, she closed her eyes and turned over.

"What?" John Lackland screamed.

Marian shot out of bed. A call just before dawn and John sounding that angry? She knew she had to hear this conversation. Any sneaking was swiftly foiled as Eleanor and Isabella joined her in the hallway. Eleanor's deep frown no doubt expressed only a fraction of her displeasure. Isabella's brow was puckered with worry. The trio made their way to the top of the stairs and looked down at John as he listened to the caller.

"No," he commanded. "Don't send out a search party. I will send Gisbourne to you to check things out."

He paused as the caller responded, then he hung up with not so much as a goodbye.

"What's happening, love?" Isabella asked her husband, who glared up at her.

He didn't respond but picked up the phone and dialed.

It was a few moments before someone answered.

"Gisbourne, there's a problem at the camp. Get down there right away and see what's happening."

He was quiet as Guy spoke.

"It seems some of the prisoners have escaped. I want to know how many and how it happened. And Gisbourne, I don't need to emphasize that this information is not to get out. Do I?"

Another pause.

"I expect to see you later this morning, and you better have answers for me."

John slammed down the telephone and strode from the room. "Sarah!" he screamed to the cook, who may or may not have been sleeping. "Breakfast, now!"

Marian glanced over at Isabella and Eleanor. Isabella lifted her nightgown and scurried down the stairs to comfort her husband—or more likely, to be the target of his ire. Eleanor gazed back at Marian, her light eyes soft with sadness.

"I guess it's time," the woman murmured. "Marian, follow me to the sitting room. We have some things to discuss."

Twenty minutes later, Marian and Eleanor sat across a short table from one another, coffee, toast, and tinned mackerel between them. Marian waited for the older woman to speak, allowing the coffee cup to warm her chilled fingers.

"I'd hoped I could keep you girls out of this for a while longer. I wanted to make sure you were ready." She brought her hand feebly to her eyes, and it was the first time Marian had ever thought she looked old.

Eleanor shook her head. "But it was only a matter of time."

Marian didn't respond but waited for Eleanor to continue. Eleanor sighed, then met Marian's eyes with a resigned look.

"Sometimes, in order to protect your interests—your family—you have to do things you wouldn't normally do. And the more wealth, the more power, you accumulate, the more precarious and vulnerable you become. You become a target. And so you try even harder to protect what is precious to you. The Lacklands, my family—the Aquitaines—even those of my first husband, Louis, we are all such families."

Marian didn't dare speak, too afraid of giving anything away.

"It requires a great deal of strength to be part of such a family,"

Eleanor stated. "You have to be able to do whatever it takes. *Nothing* is too far when protecting your family."

Eleanor held Marian's gaze steadily, pressing her fierce loyalty on her, her familial expectations.

Finally, Marian had formulated her response, one that reflected how Eleanor would expect her to react. She placed her coffee carefully on the table between them. "Eleanor, you have always been so kind to my sister and me. You took us in when we had nowhere to go. You loved us, fed us, clothed us, educated us. I can never accurately express my gratitude. But as always, I will dutifully help you in any way I can. Whatever you need, you just say the word."

Everything inside Marian screamed in protest. *You're the reason my parents are dead,* she thought. *You may have taken care of us, but how many others have suffered because of you and people like you?* But she kept her voice steady and her expression neutral, her entire life a practice for this moment, because Robyn needed her on the inside. They could much more effectively take down the Lacklands if she played the dutiful ward.

Eleanor smiled, her eyes soft. "As expected, Marian. You are as loyal and devoted as ever."

Marian dipped her head. "How can I help?"

"Well," Eleanor started, "now that you mention it. We have a number of important people coming to Midshire, key members of some of the families we are trying to foster alliances with. Most are men Dear Richard has previously established relationships with. But what with the war and all this uncertainty, John decided renewing our shared interests was a good idea." Eleanor frowned. "I don't have complete faith that John is up to this task. Your help would go a long way to putting me at ease."

"What do you want me to do?"

"John has a series of events and gatherings planned to entertain our guests, one of which was your photography exhibition. If you could show these people special consideration, that would be a great help."

Bile rose in Marian's throat, but she swallowed it with a smile. "Of course."

"I hear, he even has a great banquet planned for before the event. He's shipping in delicacies not easily acquired at the moment. This may well boost your ambitions as well."

"Oh? Is there anything I can do to help with the banquet?"

Eleanor shook her head, waving a hand at her offer. "It's all taken care of. Guy Gisbourne is overlooking the arrangements. Everything should be in place by the beginning of next week. No need to worry."

Marian nodded as if satisfied by this news.

Eleanor met her gaze with a sidelong glance. "Some of these men are very eligible bachelors. Perhaps giving them some serious consideration wouldn't be uncalled for."

"I will pay close attention," Marian assured her.

The older woman sighed in contentment. "I must say, I'm rather relieved having told all. Do you think Robyn would react similarly?"

Marian took a sip of her now-cold coffee. "What with Robyn having just moved out and started a new job, I think it would be best to keep her happily ignorant of these matters."

Eleanor nodded. "Of course. Though I do love our Robyn's fiery nature, she is not near as sensible and level-headed as you are, ma chère. I agree with you. Let us continue to keep her out of this for now."

CHAPTER 38

*E*arly the next morning, before breakfast, Robyn left Sherwood in search of the nearest newspaper stand. She passed the girl at the stall three cents and took a copy of *The Midshire Sentinel* from the top of the stack, folding it carefully under her arm. As fast as she could without breaking into a run, Robyn returned to the privacy of her cell in Sherwood's abbey.

She lit her lamp, striking a match as weak morning light struggled through the thick clouds. Finally, having held herself back until this point, she scoured her acquisition.

"Allied troops in Tunisia...French fleet...Nazis struggling with Russia's winter..." she muttered to herself as her gaze skipped over the page. "Surely, it would be on the front page if it was in here. They'd know they had escaped by now. Will said they were checked at dawn."

She read every headline, scanning every inch of the morning edition. When she reached the last advertisement on the last page, she sighed out the last of her anxiety. "We did it." Her voice sounded surprised even to her own ears.

Triumph, pride, and giddy success warmed Robyn's chest. It welled up her throat and burst forth in a loud guffaw. And she felt strong. She felt fierce. She knew she could do anything. Snatching up the proof of their victory, Robyn ran from the room, whooping and shouting and waking all of Sherwood.

"We did it!" she cried, bursting into Tuck's room, the closest of her co-conspirators.

Tuck shot out of bed as if her blanket was aflame, her wide eyes shifting wildly to discern the danger. If anyone had still been awake in all of Sherwood, the hounds' barks and howls of protest certainly would have been enough to remedy that.

"We did it," Robyn repeated, grinning and waving the paper at her. "I was right about John Lackland. He'd never want to let anyone know, coward that he is."

Tuck sighed, her hand on her chest. "You scared me to death, Robyn," she complained.

"Sorry," Robyn apologized in a tone that said she didn't really regret her actions. "But look! Look at this!"

Tuck sat back on her bed and took the newspaper from Robyn, staring seriously at the front page. "And there's nothing in here about the escape at all?"

Robyn shook her head. "They don't even mention the camp."

Tuck smiled. "That's great. Of course, that doesn't mean there won't be something in a later edition. He's not safe yet."

Robyn smirked, knowing exactly who her friend was referring to; she'd have to be a complete idiot to not have seen the exchange between them the night before. "You're right," she said. "Perhaps you should go check on *him*."

"Them," Tuck corrected. "I agree. We should go check on *them* after breakfast."

"Of course," Robyn agreed sweetly.

Tuck went to a chest at the foot of her bed and began digging through her clothes. "We should bring them some extra clothing from storage as well," she told Robyn.

"He's free, you know," Robyn offered.

Tuck froze. "Who is?" she asked, digging more slowly.

"Will."

Tuck bit her lower lip at the mention of his name, and Robyn couldn't stifle a smile.

"Oh... Is he...? How do you know?"

"Come on, Tuck. I've known him most my life. You think I can't tell? He likes you."

"D-does he?"

Robyn nodded. "Definitely."

"But...when you talked about him all this time, I thought... I guess I assumed...you two were...?"

Robyn shook her head and waved her hand dismissively. "Not at all. We... Well, it's hard to describe. But no, we aren't like that."

"Really?" Tuck hesitated.

Robyn took her friend's shoulders and faced her. "Honest. He's wonderful and amazing and kind and generous, but there's nothing like that between us. And I'm telling you, I have never in my life seen him look at anyone the way he looked at you last night."

Tuck blushed, and she brought her hands to her cheeks self-consciously. "I've never felt this way before," she admitted, her voice a little shaky with nerves.

Robyn nodded seriously. "I understand. Just be honest. He's the gentle sort. He appreciates honesty, especially when it comes to feelings."

"But...what if he ends up rejecting me?"

"Well, I don't believe that will happen for a second. But if it does, you'll know that you did all you could. Better live big and fail than never take a risk and wonder 'what if' for the rest of your life."

Tuck took a deep breath. "You're right. I'm being silly. I've never been scared of anything in my life. I can handle this."

"That's right." Robyn agreed with a nod of approval. "Now, get dressed so we can eat breakfast and you can go win his heart."

After breakfast, just as Robyn was loading Little Jon's arms with bags of clothing for their new residents, David appeared with a surprise visitor.

"Señorita Marian!" Much called, rushing to the woman as she knelt down to embrace him.

"Much, it's wonderful to see you," Marian said, squeezing the boy tightly. "Have you been good since the last time I saw you? Have you been minding Jon? Eating your vegetables? Doing your schoolwork?"

"Sí, I've been very good."

"Except for green beans," Little Jon added, not letting the boy get away with his small lie.

Much flashed his guardian a glare as if he had committed the grossest betrayal in the history of betrayals.

"You haven't been eating your green beans?" Marian asked the boy.

Much lowered his gaze. "I don't like how they squeak my teeth," he complained.

"You don't like when they squeak?" she asked.

Much shook his head.

"Well, if it's the squeaking you don't like, then you only have to cook them a little bit longer. The squeak goes away."

"It does?"

She nodded.

"Okay. Well, I guess I can eat them if they don't squeak."

"Bueno." Marian smiled and stroked the boy's hair.

"We're going to take these clothes to Will and the others," Robyn told her sister. "Are they talking about the break out on your end? Is that why you're here?"

Marian nodded and took a basket of clothing. "Yes, among other things."

Robyn could tell by her sister's tone she had something important to discuss. "All right. Follow us. You can tell us on the way."

As Robyn, Marian, Much, Little Jon, and Tuck carried clothing toward the shipyard, her sister told Robyn about what had been happening at the Lacklands'.

"You said they've been talking about the camp?" Robyn asked.

"Yeah, all was in an uproar this morning. John got a call from the camp. He was so furious that he didn't even attempt to keep his feelings quiet. I heard everything. He called Guy and ordered him to find out what happened. Later, Guy made his report. They have no idea how they escaped. John told Guy to make discreet inquiries and to tighten security for the inmates remaining. And Guy is going to interrogate them to see if anyone left behind knows anything."

Robyn nodded, internalizing everything her sister said.

"But there's more," Marian added. Then she proceeded to tell Robyn about Eleanor coming clean, the visiting mafiosi, and the plan for her photography exhibition.

"They're having food shipped in?" Robyn asked.

Marian nodded.

Robyn grinned. "I think we should redistribute those nibbles to people who could really use them. Wouldn't you agree?"

Marian smiled. "I would in fact. Eleanor said they should arrive before the beginning of next week. Would you like me to find out when?"

"Guy is overlooking the operation?"

Marian agreed.

"Then, no. I'll figure it out. You continue to look innocent and listen in."

"I can do that."

When they arrived at the shipyard, the freed prisoners were already up and about. Will and a small group of young people were coming toward the door as Robyn and the others entered.

"Hey there." Robyn smiled to the lot. "We've brought you some extra clothes we had in storage."

"Thanks," Will said. "We were just leaving to take a look around Sherwood."

"That's a great idea. Tuck, you know Sherwood better than anyone. Why don't you show Will and the others around?" Robyn and Will turned to Tuck.

Tuck cleared her throat. "No problem," she managed. "Let me check on the kitchen provisions before we go."

Robyn handed off the clothing she carried to one of Will's companions and motioned Will aside as the others headed toward the ship to make the delivery.

"I have something for you," Robyn told her friend, digging into her bag.

She pulled out the twin daggers she'd brought from the Lacklands'.

Will's eyes lit up. "My daggers," he gasped. "I hid them when they took us to the camp. How did you know?"

Robyn raised an eyebrow at him. "Did you really think it would be so easy to hide something from me?"

Will grinned and took the weapons, caressing them as though they were priceless treasures.

"Speaking of which," Robyn started.

"Of what?" Will said, not looking up.

"Of not being able to hide things from me. Tuck...?"

Will's gaze shifted to Robyn's, but he didn't speak.

"Don't think I missed that exchange last night. Even your friends noticed. I heard them. You like her."

Will pursed his lips. "Like her? Come on, we just met," he argued unconvincingly.

Robyn's light tone grew serious. "A moment is all it takes, Will."

Her friend tilted his head, squinting. "Have you...? You have! You met someone while I was gone. Didn't you? Don't lie. I can always tell when you're lying. Who? Ugh, it's not Guy. Is it?"

Robyn's heart jumped. "No, it's not Guy. But we aren't talking about me."

"Now we are. Who? Do I know him? You didn't get back with Chadwick. Did you?"

"Stop trying to guess. He's no one you know. We met at the Blue Boar. He's new to Midshire, a detective, from Pittsburgh."

Will frowned, his expression clouded with deep worry. "A detective? Robyn...you committed treason...and I assume he can't ever know that."

Robyn sighed. "No—I don't know. It's...complicated. He's very straitlaced, but I think he would understand. The police in Midshire all answer to the Lacklands—that's a whole different story I have to catch you up on—but Rick... He...really believes in justice, you know?"

"To the point of breaking the law?" Will asked.

"I don't know... I think so... I mean, justice and the law aren't necessarily the same."

"So you'll tell him then?"

Robyn bit her lip, thoughts and possibilities whirling in her head. "Probably, when the time is right, when it is more dangerous for him to be in the dark."

"That's a thin line you're walking, Robyn," Will pointed out softly. "A lot could go wrong. I hope you know what you're doing."

Me too, Robyn thought. "Now that you've quite thoroughly changed the subject, I just have one thing to say to you," Robyn told her life-long friend.

"And that is?"

She nodded toward the ship, where Tuck was descending down the ladder to the warehouse floor. "That girl likes you. I believe the words she used this morning were: 'I've never felt this way before.' And as your friend I'll tell you I've never seen you look at someone the way you look at her. So let's not play games and deny your attraction to each other."

Will nodded, his gaze clinging to Tuck as she crossed the expanse of warehouse floor.

"And Will?" Robyn demanded his full attention.

He looked back to his friend.

"She's young and most definitely inexperienced. Be gentle with her."

Will didn't respond as Tuck was now in earshot, but Robyn could see he had taken her words to heart. His uncertainty, his dumbstruck awe had settled. He knew Tuck was receptive to him, which gave him confidence.

Will smiled gently at the girl as though she were precious and break-able and he looked forward to discovering her little by little.

Tuck, who smiled so wide that it must have been painful, addressed those who would be joining her. "Welcome to Sherwood," she said. "Would you like to see your new home?"

CHAPTER 39

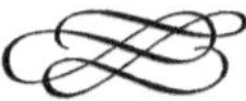

As Tuck took Will and his friends on a tour of Sherwood, Little Jon stayed behind to help with any necessary repairs to the ship. Marian had to return before she was missed, so Robyn walked her sister to the bridge, then headed to Gyl's to use his telephone.

Gyl was tinkering with his first helipack prototype, muttering to himself as he went.

"I'm here to use your telephone," Robyn said.

She didn't receive an answer or any kind of acknowledgment whatsoever, but then again, she hadn't expected to with Gyl in that state.

In Gyl's submarine of a study, Robyn dug into her bag for the calling card Guy had given her. She dialed his number. After eight rings with no answer, Robyn shook her head at herself. *What did you expect?* she thought. *He's not going to be home right now. He's probably running around trying to figure out what happened last night.*

Just as she took the receiver from her ear to hang it up, she heard a breathless voice call out from the earpiece.

"Hello?" Guy shouted. "Hello? Are you there?"

"I'm here," Robyn assured.

"Robyn? Is that you?"

Robyn nodded. "Yes, it's me."

Guy's tone was colored in relief. "I'm sorry I almost missed your call. I've been out since early this morning. Just came back for a quick shower and a change of clothes."

"Is this a bad time?"

"No, no. It's never a bad time for you, Robyn," Guy said honestly.

Robyn's heart twinged a little at the sincerity in his voice. *I'm a terrible person,* she thought. *He really cares about me. And from what Will said, he's trying to help people. To change. I don't know if I can do this after all. But the people of Sherwood... It's not really him I'm trying to hurt. It's the Lacklands.*

"Robyn? Are you still there?" Guy called anxiously.

"Yeah," Robyn murmured.

"What can I do for you? Do you need something? Are you all right?"

Robyn stifled a sigh and clenched her eyes shut as if that would make her feel better. "I'm fine. I just... I was wondering if you were busy this weekend."

Guy didn't speak for a good five heartbeats. "I sort of have my hands full at the moment... But I can move things around if you want to see me. Except for Saturday evening, I have something to do that night. But otherwise, I'm yours."

Robyn swallowed the lump that rose in her throat. "Tomorrow then?" she croaked. "Tomorrow morning or afternoon?"

"Tomorrow morning is perfect. Do you want to meet for breakfast? I could pack a picnic. Perhaps we could go to the beach afterward?"

"Breakfast sounds good, but the beach is a little too far from where I am now. Should we just meet at a diner?"

"All right," Guy agreed, his disappointment barely noticeable. "Pippa's? In The Doncz?"

"Great. Pippa's makes the best omelets."

"About nine?"

"That's fine. See you then." As Robyn started to take the handset away from her ear to hang up, Guy spoke again.

"And Robyn?"

Robyn hummed into the phone to tell him she was still there.

"I'm glad you called."

"See you tomorrow morning, Guy." Robyn hung up the telephone and buried her face in her hands, rubbing her clenched eyes. "Why is this so hard?" she asked herself. "He's hurt people. Killed people. *Killed people,*" she emphasized just to make sure she understood. "He's a thug, Robyn. A gangster," she said.

But people can change...can't they? she wondered, not daring to say that bit aloud. *He helped the prisoners, gave them medicine and protective masks. Maybe... Nothing is ever going to erase the bad he's done. But without the possibility of redemption, are we all just walking amalgamations of our past slights and sins? I've lived with the Lacklands most of my life, benefiting from their crimes and cruelties. I've ignored, willfully or otherwise, their activities. I was a bystander, and therefore an accessory, to what they've done. And when I realized the wrongs I'd been party to, did I not rebel in search of redemption?*

Robyn shook her head, pushing her thoughts away. "I may not be on the level when reaching out to him. I never would have given him a chance had it not been for the information he has. But that doesn't mean I can't be friends with him. Yeah, friends. His efforts at changing have earned him a tentative friendship I would say."

Though a nagging in the back of her mind told her that if she wanted to be Guy's friend, she should be more honest with him. She determinedly ignored the thought, refusing to acknowledge it altogether. Then she picked up the telephone and waited for her lover to answer the line.

"Detective Nottingham," his stalwart baritone stated as if assuring the caller that he was there to protect and serve.

"I'm sorry I had to leave you the way I did, Detective," Robyn apologized, her voice husky with the memory of his naked form sprawled on his bed. "I'd like to make it up to you, if you'll let me."

Robyn smiled as Rick released a steadying breath into the telephone.

"How about I come over tomorrow? What do you say?"

"Yes," he murmured softly, holding onto the S ever so slightly.

She could practically feel his breath in her ear and was gratified that his voice drowned out her earlier contemplations quite completely. The tightness in her chest eased, and her breathing became loose and free. Nothing could compare to this feeling, this filled up feeling that was like pleasantly drowning. And as she thought of him, clear-gazed and broad-shouldered, his moral compass never failing to find true north, she knew she could indulge in any feelings she had toward him without guilt.

"See you tomorrow," she promised.

Pippa's was an old steam train car turned diner. It was long and rectangular and only barely wide enough for customers to walk alongside the leather stools, which sat close to the counter. The grimy train windows all down the sides didn't allow much outside light in, but the inside glowed a warm yellow as the overhead incandescent bulbs reflected off the honey-colored walnut counter, which practically spanned the length of the diner.

Robyn arrived early and took the stool at the very far end of the counter adjacent to the emergency exit that once connected one railcar to another.

"Good morning," the woman called to Robyn over her shoulder as she stood over a griddle frying bacon and eggs.

Robyn inhaled the scent appreciatively, wondering when the government would decide to ration bacon as well. She greeted the proprietor with a smile and a nod.

"Go on," the woman at the griddle said to a teenage girl, who leaned on the counter behind her.

The girl pouted, slumping her shoulders. "Do I have to, Auntie?" she whined.

The aunt's eyes softened with sympathy. "Go on, love. Your mum would be so glad to know we're taking care of her place once she'd gone. And your grandmother wasn't too pleased with that last spot of trouble you got yourself into, was she? Give it a try. It isn't so bad. You might even like it." She smiled encouragingly to punctuate her pep talk.

The girl nodded and headed toward Robyn, walking rather awkwardly as if she wasn't quite used to wearing a dress and apron. "What can I get for you?" she asked Robyn, her little pad and pencil ready.

Robyn looked up from the menu and met the girl's cautious blue eyes, one of which was surrounded by the hint of a fading bruise. The pin to keep her short, dark hair from her face wasn't doing its job, and her little cap was crooked. Her name tag identified her as Mireilla.

"No coffee?" Robyn asked the girl on the off chance she'd be lucky.

"I'm afraid not," she answered. "But we have Postum and chicory," she offered

"Chicory," Robyn answered.

"Anything else?"

"I'm waiting for someone. I'll order when he gets here."

Mireilla nodded and went to fetch Robyn's coffee substitute. Moments later, the waitress placed a cup full of warm not-coffee-but-looks-like-coffee before her, looking quite proud that she'd made it ten steps without spilling or breaking anything.

Robyn smiled, remembering all too well how awkward she had been when she was still getting used to her developing body. "You worked here long?" she asked the girl.

Mireilla shook her head. "No, but I used to come here all the time. My mother was Pippa." Her blue eyes saddened. "But now that she's gone, Auntie Eva runs the place."

"So you're just helping your aunt then?"

Mireilla shrugged. "Your fella isn't late, is he? Think he'll show?"

Robyn nodded. "He'll be here."

"You're so sure? Must be someone special to have you so confident in him. You must like him a lot."

"We're just...friends." She tasted the word on her tongue, still not quite sure it was the right word.

"If you like someone, you should tell him," Mireilla said sagely. "You never know if it'll be too late when you get around to it, especially with the war on."

Robyn tilted her head at the girl. "That's very true," she agreed.

"I liked a boy once..." she murmured. "And I was too scared to tell him. But when he up and joined the Navy, it was too late. Now I don't know if I'll ever get the chance."

Robyn looked at the girl more closely, wondering what sort of living she had done so far.

"In any case, he probably won't even be the boy I liked when he comes back...if he comes back."

So much loss for someone so young, Robyn thought. *Though I suppose it was the same for me and many others. She can't be that much younger than me either. Five years? Six?*

Just as Robyn was about to ask how old Mireilla was, Guy came in through the far door.

As he pulled down his scarf to reveal his face, Mireilla blew out sharply in appreciation. "Is that him?" she whispered.

Robyn nodded.

"I can see why you like him," she murmured. "Good luck."

Robyn didn't respond. Objectively speaking, the girl wasn't wrong. Guy was an attractive man, tall, smooth yet rugged, with a gaze that made you believe you were the only woman in the world. Too bad that singular attention promised trouble, danger. Robyn met Guy's piercing stare, and a shiver ran through her. She'd be lying if she said it was unpleasant. *Guy is untamed,* she thought. *Any woman who chooses him is certainly in for the thrill of her life, like climbing into the cage of a starving circus tiger.*

"Robyn," Guy purred, completely ignoring Mireilla's presence.

As he took the stool beside Robyn, she immediately regretted her decision to come to Pippa's. Sure, she wasn't alone with him, but he was dangerously close with his arm brushing hers. And she was all too aware of the contact.

"No coffee?" Guy guessed, looking down into Robyn's forgotten cup.

"Chicory," Robyn answered.

Guy frowned but consented to the roasted root tea.

After Mireilla had delivered the brew, she took their breakfast orders and scurried off to the far end of the counter, winking her encouragement at Robyn.

"I can't tell you how happy it made me that you called," Guy said, turning toward Robyn as much as the counter would allow.

And while Robyn could repeat 'friends' to herself as many times as she liked, she wasn't convincing anyone, certainly not Guy. *In for a penny,* she thought. "You said on the phone that you have your hands full. Is everything all right?" she asked.

Guy frowned. "I'm handling it," he assured her with a confidence that almost made her fear for her new friends in Sherwood.

"That's good," she murmured into her chicory. After taking a sip, her lips curled as she shook her head at the taste.

"It's not the same, is it?" Guy said, nodding to the cup.

"Not at all," she agreed.

"Why don't you ask the Lacklands for some coffee? I'm sure they wouldn't mind giving you some for your new place."

"It's fine. I'll make do. Everyone else is, right?"

Mireilla delivered their breakfasts and was gone in a heartbeat.

Guy smiled warmly, an expression that made Robyn look twice.

"That's one of the things I admire about you, Robyn," he murmured, his tone deceptively benign. "You're always thinking of others."

Robyn hung her head. "Thank you," she said miserably as guilt curdled her stomach.

"Are you going to Marian's photography exhibition?" he asked.

"Of course."

"Mr. Lackland is planning a special menu for the event. I'm going to pick up the food tomorrow night. I'm sure you'll enjoy it."

"Tomorrow night?" Robyn wondered. "Where would you be picking up food in the middle of the night?"

"Well...some of the food is...not easily gotten hold of at the moment, so he had it shipped in."

"Oh, obviously... I imagine the night watchman at the Stockport docks is...?"

"Going to be well paid to take a break." Guy assured her no harm would come to the man, whoever he may be.

Robyn bit her lip. "I hope you aren't doing anything dangerous," she said.

Guy covered her hand with his, and Robyn's pulse sped up. "Don't worry. This sort of thing is easy. Everything will be fine."

CHAPTER 40

Robyn arrived at Rick's with a sore heart and a guilty conscience. When he opened the door for her, she didn't bother to ask whether Mrs. Stanley was in. She just pulled him down for a kiss right there on the threshold, in full view of any neighbor or passerby who may be watching.

He didn't resist, didn't protest, just gave her what she needed as he always did. And though he was as generous with his attentions as he had been before, this time was different somehow. Robyn's heart seemed heavy in her chest. But as ever before, Rick's touch drowned out all thoughts and worries.

She was not disappointed. Oh no, she could never be disappointed in Alaric Nottingham. She was content for the moment to share this sensation with him. She was content to be surrounded by him, filled up by him, to be shattered by the vigor of his passion and pieced back together so tenderly with his gentle caresses.

As he collapsed on her chest, spent with exhaustion from the most wanton and boundless sex she'd ever had, she softly kissed his cheeks, his nose, his eyelids.

Robyn smiled as Rick slid his arms under her to clutch her to him, his head resting heavily on her breast. She stroked his mussed hair, her own eyes growing heavy with satisfaction and fatigue. In that moment, as she drifted off to sleep, she couldn't think of anything else she wanted in all the world.

Robyn awoke before Rick, but that was all right with her. She gazed down at him for a while, reveling in the present moment. Then her eyes began to wander his bedroom. Glancing at the nightstand, she saw his detective's shield, a long-barreled Colt revolver beside it. Robyn frowned. *Is it time to tell him what I've done? What I'm going to do?* she wondered, more uncomfortable with the thought of keeping it from him after her talk with Will.

I said I'd tell him when it's more dangerous for him not to know. But John won't tell anyone about the internees, and I have to think about the safety of Will and the people of Sherwood. So far, the Lacklands have no idea I'm connected to any crime against them. And I think I've convinced Guy I'm not involved with Rick anymore, which should afford him some safety if the Lacklands discover what I've done to them.

On the other hand, Rick isn't likely to stop investigating them, and he's up against a lot of opposition in that regard. Perhaps telling him would get him to ease up, therefore putting him in less danger.

But it's a gamble. If he doesn't react the way I think he will, I would've just made things a whole lot worse. I'll have made things even worse for him and put Sherwood in more danger. I need to be absolutely sure of how he'll react before I tell him.

Rick stirred from his sleep, and Robyn smiled as he looked up at her.

"That, uh, sure was something," Robyn said, clearing her throat.

Rick gave her a tired smile. "I still have a few tricks up my sleeve."

"Oh?"

Rick's face straightened. "Now, don't give me that look."

"What look?" Robyn asked innocently.

"*That* look. I can't think right when you give me that look."

Robyn chuckled. "I didn't know I had such influence."

Rick eyed her, unconvinced. "Well...you do. And I'm not prepared. I'm still recovering."

Robyn pouted. "Well, you shouldn't have dangled the carrot if you weren't prepared for me to chase it."

"You're right. I'm sorry," he said, crawling up her body and kissing the side of her head before collapsing again beside her. "Just give me a moment," he murmured. "Let's talk about something else. How are you liking your new job?"

"I like it," she said. "And my new place is good, too. There's a real community there. You know?"

"That's good. Where abouts is it?"

"Oh, it's on the north side," Robyn hedged. "How about you? Are you fitting in better at work?"

Rick frowned. "Not exactly. But that's to be expected when I keep poking my nose in Lackland affairs. I've been relegated to cold cases for the foreseeable future."

"So you aren't actively investigating them then?" Robyn hoped.

"No, I still am. I just have to be even more careful than I was before and do it mostly in my free time."

"Oh."

Robyn could feel Rick's keen gaze on her expression. "I've mostly been following Guy Gisbourne. I have a hunch he's the easiest to get at. John Lackland stays pretty shut up, and Gisbourne does a lot of the running around."

He isn't wrong, Robyn thought.

"He still giving you a hard time?" Rick asked.

Robyn tilted her head at the question.

"At the party," Rick clarified. "You seemed to be at odds."

"Right." Robyn nodded slightly. "Guy is..." She sighed. "I don't quite know what Guy is. He's..." She struggled with the words. "Lost? Not exactly lost, but I have no better word for it. Guy isn't what I expected him to be." She finished helplessly.

Rick paused, his eyes never leaving her face. "So...you're...still in contact with them all then?"

Robyn wrinkled her nose. "Not really. I mean, I try to see Marian as much as I can. I haven't talked with the Lacklands at all since I left. But I have met Guy once or twice."

Rick was silent for a long time. "You can tell me if you two are friends, you know," he murmured finally.

Robyn didn't meet his gaze, guilt burbling in her stomach. "Friends...? I don't know about that," she said vaguely. "But enough about Guy."

Robyn waved her hand as if to dispel the thought of him. "I want to hear more about those tricks up your sleeve." Then she gave him the look he'd warned her about.

The cold detective's glint in Rick's eyes melted away as heat replaced it.

Robyn smiled at the change. "It seems the carrot is ready to be chased again," she simpered, trailing her fingertips down his naked torso.

CHAPTER 41

The next morning, Robyn called her most trusted together at Gyl's workshop to hatch a plan for that evening's heist.

"Tonight, at Stockport docks, a shipment of high-quality food bound for the Lacklands' table will arrive," Robyn explained. "I think we should commandeer it for the people of Sherwood."

Everyone gathered was in favor of Robyn's proposition.

"Do you have a plan?" Will asked.

Robyn smiled. "I do, but I'm going to need all of your help."

"You can always count on me, Robyn," Little Jon assured. The rest echoed Little Jon's sentiment.

"Here is what I'm thinking: the food will be loaded onto a truck or into a van. After it's loaded but before it drives away, I'll create a distraction. When I say distraction, I refer to one that cannot be ignored."

Robyn looked significantly at Gyl.

"How about of the explosive variety?" Gyl asked.

Robyn nodded. "That works. So I'll draw everyone's attention farther from the truck. It's likely Guy will order the truck to go so as not to jeopardize his mission. While everyone is distracted, I want Will to incapacitate the driver while Tuck gets behind the wheel and drives the goods south, away from Sherwood."

"Incapacitate?" Will asked for clarification.

"Nothing too bad. Chloroform or the like," Robyn answered.

Will nodded.

"Tuck will drive the truck south to a meeting point where Little Jon and Gyl will be waiting. They will transfer the bounty to a nondescript vehicle and drive the lot back to Sherwood."

"Sounds simple enough," Little Jon said.

"Right. I have it on good authority that the night watchman will be otherwise occupied. So the only people at the docks will be those working for the Lacklands. The downside is that I don't know the exact time of the exchange. I only know it's sometime tonight."

"So we'll have to keep watch," Gyl mumbled in his thinking voice.

"Exactly," Robyn agreed. "But I'll recognize Guy's car, and it'll take them a bit to unload the shipment. We should have enough time to get into position on our end."

"Tuck, I think I can rig something small up that will give us warning of when you're almost to us so we can be ready," Gyl said, eyes staring off into the distance as he thought about the problem at hand.

"And the explosion?" Robyn reminded.

Gyl waved his hand at her as he turned his back, already getting to work. "Easy. I'll tip some arrowheads for you."

"All right then," Robyn announced cheerfully. "Let's get more specific."

For the next few hours, Robyn and her band went about choosing the best place to switch vehicles, where they should keep watch at the docks, and what to do in case things should go pear-shaped.

Around lunchtime, they went their separate ways to rest and gather the things they'd need for that evening. They all met back at Gyl's at dusk.

Gyl carefully handed Robyn an ammo belt with three small pouches, each holding an explosive arrowhead. "It'll be heavier than a normal arrowhead, so you'll have to adjust for that when you fire. But I've made them so that they should slip right over your normal arrowheads."

Robyn nodded her understanding.

Next, Gyl turned to Will and handed him a simple facemask, which covered the nose and mouth, and a spray can. "Chloroform is good, but this is better," Gyl said. "It's fast acting, and doesn't have as many side effects. It also doesn't knock someone out for as long. But you don't have to be as close, meaning you don't have to physically hold a cloth over the driver's face. Still, wear this, or you'll be fast asleep alongside him." He also handed a mask to Tuck just in case.

Then Gyl handed Tuck a small remote, which fit neatly in her hand. "When you're behind the wheel, press this button. It will send a signal to our end telling us to be ready," Gyl instructed.

As Gyl went to gather his own supplies, Tuck shuffled up to Will. "Um, Will?" she murmured.

He turned to her.

"I made these for everyone else, and I thought you should have one, too" she explained, holding out a cowl hood to him.

While Tuck had done an excellent job on everyone else's hood, it was plain to see she had taken extra care with Will's. The hems were straighter and the stitches even. His hood also had a dark red trim along the edges.

"You made this?" Will asked her.

Tuck nodded.

He smiled down at her, that soft, charming smile that was open and honest and needed no words as accompaniment. Still, he whispered his thanks in a low, intimate voice.

Robyn smiled at the pair, glancing away to give their moment privacy.

By nine o'clock, Robyn, Tuck, and Will watched the road to the docks from behind a stack of crates. They'd seen Gyl and Little Jon to their post, and now they waited, hoods up, ears pricked, and weapons at the ready.

It was another two hours before anything of interest happened. The night watchman, who had been meandering about the docks without paying much attention to anything, looked at his watch and left his post entirely. From the looks of it, he was heading straight for Saxony Avenue, where a pub with particularly good pickles served its patrons late.

A quarter of an hour later, Robyn nudged her companions. "That's it," she hissed.

"You're sure?" Will whispered back.

"Oh, I'd recognize that Clipper anywhere," Robyn answered.

They watched the headlights disappear. As the women stood to get into their respective positions, Will snatched each of their hands and dragged them back down.

"Wait," he urged.

"Oh no," Robyn groaned, squinting at the driver of another car as he coasted by without his lights on.

"What?" Will asked.

"That's Rick."

"Rick? Who's Rick?" Tuck whispered.

"Don't tell me that's the detective you were talking about," Will said.

Robyn nodded.

Her friends cursed under their breaths.

"What do you want to do?" Will asked. "Should we call it off and go back to Little Jon and Gyl?"

Robyn's head spun. "No," she whispered finally. "No, Sherwood needs that food. This changes nothing."

The pair stared at her, unsure of her resolve.

"Find the truck and get into position. It won't take them that long to unload," Robyn ordered.

CHAPTER 42

This is it, Alaric thought as he stood on a pier, peeking around the bow of the ship that separated him from Gisbourne and the men who were unloading cargo onto a truck. *No night watchman, past eleven at night, no legitimate business happens at the docks this way.*

Just as Alaric was deciding to follow the truck rather than Gisbourne, the men finished packing the load and shut the door. The captain of the vessel that had brought the goods turned to Gisbourne, who took an envelope from his jacket pocket and handed it to him. The captain nodded his thanks.

Alaric took a step to creep back to his car unnoticed when a loud boom came from behind him. The aftershock of the explosion shook the wooden planks of the pier on which he stood. He turned around to see a pillar of fire and smoke farther down.

Heavy feet thumping on wood announced Gisbourne and his men before Alaric saw them.

So much for stealth, Alaric thought as they charged right by him toward the smoke and fire.

Gisbourne's gaze met Alaric's as he passed, his squint promising retribution.

Alaric cursed under his breath and jogged to where Gisbourne was. He grabbed the man by his elbow. "What's going on?" Alaric demanded.

"If I find out this is your doing, Nottingham, I won't bother to go through your superiors to deal with you."

"As much as I'd like to take credit for disrupting your, no doubt, illegal activities, this wasn't me."

"Do something useful, *Detective*. Go to the watchman's office and call the fire department."

Alaric let go of his mark, and Gisbourne raced back toward the truck, letting his men address the fire.

He ran to the watchman's office, alongside the road to the docks, to call the fire department and the police.

Just as he reached the door, he heard pounding footsteps heading away from the docks. Following the sound, he saw a hooded form run around the back side of the office. He drew his weapon. "Stop right there," he ordered. "Don't move. I have my weapon drawn."

The figure halted as directed.

"Put your hands in the air," Alaric said, slowly moving toward the suspect.

The man had a quiver of arrows across his back and a bow in his hand.

"Drop your weapon and turn around. Slowly."

"I'm really sorry about this, Detective," a man said from behind him.

Alaric spun around and was sprayed in the face with a foul-smelling liquid. All he managed to see before he lost consciousness was a man whose eyes were shadowed by a hood and whose mouth and nose were covered by a mask.

Ten minutes later, with a pounding headache and a bitter taste in his mouth, Alaric awoke on the ground behind the watchman's office. He only vaguely recognized that he hadn't fallen in some awkward position. He was lying quite comfortably on his back with his scarf tucked carefully under his head.

After staggering to the office, he made the calls. Then he returned to the dock to see what had happened while he was out.

Gisbourne lay sprawled out on his stomach; the driver of the truck, similarly arranged, wasn't far away.

Alaric ran to Gisbourne and bent over him to see if he was breathing. He was. He shook him to no avail. The man was out cold.

Once the fire truck had arrived, it didn't take the firemen long to put out the flames.

And by the time the police showed up, Rick had mostly recovered from his assault by spray can. Gisbourne and the driver had come around but were still a little dazed. Gisbourne frowned severely as the officers secured the scene.

"I can handle it from here," Alaric told Gisbourne, holding up his hand to stop the man's protest. "In case you hadn't noticed, Gisbourne, there's smoke still coming off those crates over there, where a fire was so recently raging. You think explosions like that just *happen*? I might also point out that you are a civilian, and I am the authority here."

Gisbourne's lips curled, and Alaric thought there was a real possibility he would spit at him.

"I'm going to investigate this explosion, helped by the officers I've called from my precinct. I'm also going to investigate the theft that just occurred. You were here to pick up a delivery. Were you not? It must've been urgent for you to come all the way down here so late at night. I would've thought your employer would want the criminals who stole it apprehended. Not to mention those bandits assaulted me. That makes this awfully personal."

Gisbourne squinted at Alaric's words, licking his teeth as though tasting the flavor of what he was about to say. "I trust you'll catch these villains then?" he asked uncertainly.

Alaric frowned, having realized that staying on the case would mean he would effectively be working for the Lacklands. "I'll uphold my duty as a sworn keeper of the peace."

Gisbourne eyed him in silence for a moment. "Let me take this opportunity to remind you to stay within the confines of this investigation, Detective."

Alaric heard the "or else" without Gisbourne having to speak it aloud.

"What's the story here?" Preston asked, standing beside Alaric as he stared down at the aftermath of the explosion and fire.

Alaric frowned. "I'm not quite sure yet," he admitted.

"Any suspects?"

Alaric nodded. "Two for certain, likely three," he murmured, thinking someone must have driven the truck away. "They wore hoods, so I couldn't see their faces. One had a bow and a quiver of arrows. The other, definitely a male, had a spray can."

"A spray can?" Preston asked flatly. "And...a bow and arrows... Doesn't sound too threatening in the age of missiles and machine guns, does it?"

Alaric ignored his sometimes partner. *What exactly was on that truck that they wanted so badly?* he wondered.

CHAPTER 43

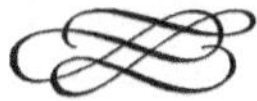

THE MIDSHIRE SENTINEL
November 15, 1942

Explosion in Stockport Covers up Theft
By Alan A. Dale

An explosion, which shook Stockport docks late last night, appears to have been a diversion to distract from another crime, the theft of luxury food items. The food, which was set to be served at a photography exhibition by local artist Marian Loxley, ward of the Midshire Lacklands, later this week is suspected to have been snatched by two, possibly three, hooded brigands. Why this particular shipment of goods was targeted and why the perpetrators went to such lengths is still unknown.

A detective, who was on scene when the crime was committed, the driver of the delivery truck, and one unidentified citizen were attacked while trying to thwart the suspects. They sustained no injuries.

When asked if Marian Loxley or the Lacklands were the targets of this heist or if it was merely a coincidence, the detective in charge of the investigation gave no comment. His response was similar when asked for clarification as to what exactly was meant by luxury food items and if these items are currently restricted or rationed.

*R*obyn read the morning edition in the abbey's kitchen over a cup of glorious coffee as Tuck and the kitchen ladies took stock of their evening's bounty.

"Well," Tuck sighed finally, sinking onto the stool beside Robyn. "We may not have as much as I'd like, but I think we'll have enough between what we grew ourselves and what we obtained last night."

"Until spring?"

Tuck frowned. "Maybe. It would be easier if we had money to use our ration books. But I think we can stretch it if need be. Cabbage soup can go a long way."

Robyn smiled at her friend and patted her shoulder. "Don't worry, Tuck. The Lacklands have more than enough to spare. Speaking of which, have you seen this article?" she asked, showing Tuck the paper. "I think we should reach out to this Alan A. Dale."

"Really? Why is that?"

"I get the feeling he has a lot more to say about the Lacklands that he's holding back. A friend in the press could go a long way to turning the public against them. He may even know more than what his editor is allowing him to print."

"Maybe, but I bet your detective knows even more than he's telling the reporters."

Robyn's chest tightened at the mention of Rick. She hadn't wanted him involved. If she was lucky, Guy would use his influence to shut Rick out of the case. She could still picture him there on the ground, his jaw slack and his eyes rolled back. She knew Will was trying to protect her.

Rick could have shot her if he hadn't acted, but that didn't ease her regret. After spraying Guy and the driver, they were fortunate there had been enough left for Rick at all. She hadn't seen the result of Will's spraying of Guy, but she trusted that it had been necessary as well.

Though the paper had claimed they hadn't sustained any injuries, she would continue to worry until she saw them for herself. Robyn went to Rick's as soon as she could get away from Sherwood.

Mrs. Stanley answered her knock at the door. "Oh, hello, Robyn," she said with a smile.

"Is Rick in?" Robyn asked.

"Yes, he's upstairs. Would you like me to call him down?"

"No, it's fine. I'll go up."

Mrs. Stanley smiled and nodded, her wrinkled cheeks pink with thoughts of what two young people might do while they were alone together.

Robyn knocked gently on Rick's bedroom door. When there was no answer, she opened it slowly. Rick lay, still mostly clothed, atop his covers. He'd managed to take off his jacket and unbutton most of his shirt, but he still had one shoe on.

Robyn gazed down at him, analyzing every line of his face. *He seems all right*, she thought. She carefully removed his other shoe and unbuttoned his shirt the rest of the way. Then she picked up his discarded jacket from the floor, and hung it on the back of one of his chairs.

"This is a pleasant surprise," Rick croaked, peeking at her from under his heavy eyelids.

He reached out to her, and she sat beside him on the bed.

"I know we didn't have plans today, but I felt like I had to see you," Robyn said. "What's wrong? Aren't you feeling well? You're still sleeping even though it's so late."

Rick seemed too tired to notice the lack of sleep on Robyn's face. "No, I'm fine. I was just working late," he yawned.

"Oh? I didn't think cold cases were so demanding. Or were you…investigating on your own time again?"

He nodded. "Yeah, and I even managed to catch a fresh case thanks to your friend."

"My friend?"

"Gisbourne," he clarified.

"Did you? Is he redirecting your efforts away from anything Lackland related?"

"No, it seems the Lacklands were robbed last night. It should have been in the papers by now."

"I didn't see that," Robyn lied. "I would've thought Guy would warn you off investigating anything that had to do with them."

Rick shrugged. "I guess he recognized that I do my job even for people I don't like."

Robyn's stomach bottomed out. "So what was stolen?" she asked.

"A truckload of food for your sister's exhibition."

"Oh, no. Marian will be disappointed. I'll have to call her and see if the event is still happening."

"It is, and I'll be there, on duty of course. It may be that these thieves are targeting the Lacklands or your sister in particular."

Robyn didn't attempt to hide her frown. "But if they just stole food, perhaps it isn't really related to Marian at all. Maybe it's a coincidence. Maybe they need it to feed their families."

Rick's eyes turned chilled again with his keen detective's stare. "It doesn't matter what they stole or why they stole it. It doesn't even matter who they stole it from. The laws were created as rules for how people live together in society. They were created by the people through their elected officials. So whether someone agrees with it or not, those rules are for the benefit of all citizens. And we have official ways of changing laws that don't work or need to be changed. I believe in the system. It's through the system that my mother got justice, through proper investigation and execution of the law."

Robyn's heartbeat pounded in her ears, and her chest ached as though she were underwater and had exhaled the last of her breath. *Is this what he meant when he'd said he couldn't abide by injustice?* she wondered. He'd made his declaration with such force and precision that it was clear to Robyn he'd thought about this thoroughly, that there was no convincing him of any other perspective. Her mouth dried as she tried to swallow.

Rick reached up and stroked her cheek with the back of his fingers, his eyes soft and warm again. "I know you're scared for your sister, that you want to believe any reason why this may not have anything to do with her." He pulled her into an embrace, and she rigidly complied. "But don't worry," he murmured in a soothing tone. "I will find out who is behind this and bring them to justice. I won't let anything happen to you or Marian."

Robyn pulled gently away from Rick's embrace, not feeling the intended comfort.

"Well," she murmured. "I better get going."

His eyebrows crinkled. "Already?"

"Yeah," she said, standing. "I mean, I'd stay. But based off what you just told me, I should probably go see how Marian is doing."

He nodded slowly, her lie easily convincing him. "I guess I'll see you this weekend at Marian's event then."

"Right. See you then."

He snatched her hand as she turned away and pressed a kiss to it. Her chest throbbed as he met her eyes so tenderly. And then she left.

CHAPTER 44

Robyn hadn't known where her next destination was located, so she hailed a cab near Legumighty Stadium. But when the cabbie dropped her off in front of an old warehouse on the waterfront, Robyn wondered if there had been some mistake.

She dug into her pocket and pulled out the calling card, double checking to make sure the addresses matched.

Tilting her head, Robyn entered the front door and took a set of concrete stairs to the fourth floor. The hallway she walked down was narrow and dimly lit, but she found apartment 404 with ease.

Taking a deep breath through her nose, Robyn lifted her hand and knocked firmly on the door as she exhaled.

A few moments later, Guy opened the door with a jerk, his black eyes glaring out at whoever dared disturb him.

He hadn't opened the door all the way, but he'd opened it enough for Robyn to see that he wasn't presentable. He wore striped pajama pants with no shirt or shoes to speak of. His hair was disheveled as if he'd gotten into a fight with a pillow and suffered an embarrassing defeat.

Robyn froze at the sight of his bare chest, toned and lean. Her heart hammered, and she redirected her eyes to his.

"Robyn?" His voice was deep and graveled as if still half asleep, but his eyes warmed in recognition.

"May I come in?" she asked, relieved that her voice was even.

He stared for a moment longer and opened the door for her to enter. Robyn followed him farther into his apartment, taking in the space around her. After a short, narrow hallway, the apartment opened up into one large room, a small kitchen to the right, and a living room straight ahead. The couch and chairs all faced huge paned windows, which overlooked the bay. Past the kitchen was a metal spiral staircase.

"Wait here," Guy instructed.

Robyn nodded and watched as he headed for the staircase. She followed him with her eyes to the upstairs loft, easily seeing his bedroom beyond the simple metal railing.

She noted the rumpled blanket on the couch just as he returned to the living room, now wearing an undershirt that left little to the imagination.

"Would you like something to drink?" Guy asked, his gaze flicking to the pristine kitchen area.

Robyn thought it was more unused than the result of a good house-keeper. "No, thank you," she murmured.

But as he turned his dark eyes back on her, she wished she would have given him something to do with his singular attention.

"I'm sorry to show up like this," Robyn apologized, trying to remember why she was there to begin with.

But a red lump peeking out from Guy's hairline reminded her.

"I read about the food theft in the paper this morning, and I wanted to see if you were all right. It said there was an explosion and some people were attacked. Were you one of them?"

Guy smiled gently, his eyes soft as he met hers, and nodded. "Yes, I was one of the ones attacked, but I'm fine. You came all the way here to check on me?"

The large room suddenly felt very small as Guy moved closer to her.

Robyn's mouth dried up. She didn't respond, didn't even nod.

"It was sweet of you to worry for me, Robyn," he murmured, trailing his fingertips down her arm. He took her hand gently in his and brought it to his mouth, brushing his lips against her fingers.

She trembled and hoped he didn't notice. "The paper said the driver and a detective were also attacked. Do you know if they're all right?" she asked, gently pulling her hand from his.

Guy smirked at her retreat but answered her. "Yes, they're both fine. Incidentally, the detective was our old friend Nottingham. I believe he has taken it upon himself to follow me around."

Robyn frowned. "But surely caught in the act, he'll back off now."

Guy shrugged. "He's investigating the thieves...the hoods who stole the shipment."

"And you allowed him to stay on the case?" Robyn whispered, her disbelief genuine.

Guy snorted. "He certainly thinks he is, but his superiors will have a tight leash on him."

"Even so, what if he uses his limited investigation as a way to find out more about the family?"

The look in Guy's eyes made Robyn think his next words would be another threat on Rick's life.

"Don't worry," he assured her. "I'm watching him closely. If he goes too far, I'll have him taken off the case. He's only allowed this far as a way for us to keep an eye on him. And who knows? The man is dogged. Perhaps he will find these hoods after all."

Robyn blinked, a line forming between her eyebrows. *Is this Guy Gisbourne I'm talking to?* she wondered. *I had counted on him keeping Rick well away from the matter.* She couldn't reconcile his tame response with the man she'd known for the last year.

"Trust me," Guy urged.

Robyn nodded, her confusion nowhere near resolved. *Perhaps he has changed more than I supposed,* she thought. She looked over at him again. Her gaze searching his dark eyes for any indication that Guy Gisbourne was trustworthy. Not just with her; she knew he would never lie to her. But truly trustworthy, a man she could depend on.

He wasn't the same as her, not in the way she had recognized Rick. But then again, Rick hadn't been the same either, had he? She thought she had recognized a kindred spirit, but his speech that morning told her she had been very much mistaken. Had she also been mistaken about Guy? Perhaps there was more to him than she had given him credit for all this time. If she came clean with him now, would he support her? Would he be able to see past her initial motivation for reaching out to him? For using him?

Before she could truly consider that train of thought, the look in Guy's eyes changed. It had the same intensity it always had, but there was a purpose there, a plan of action. And just as he made a move toward her, just as she tensed to deal with the consequences of that look, a loud ring pierced the air.

Frowning, Guy made his way to the telephone and raised it to his ear. "Hello?" he snapped.

Robyn let out her breath, her nerves settling as she did so. She quickly realized who had called when Guy said, "yes, sir," in that confident tone.

Robyn bit her lip and nodded to herself. Catching his gaze, she jerked her thumb over her shoulder, motioning that she had to go.

He frowned and started to protest, but she smiled softly and dipped her head.

He nodded reluctantly and returned to his conversation with John.

CHAPTER 45

When Robyn arrived back in Sherwood, she didn't return to the abbey. She went straight to the guard tower and sat on the top, her feet dangling off the edge as she looked out at the desolated Sherwood Forest.

That's where Little Jon found her sometime later. He sat beside her, silently keeping her company.

Finally, she spoke, not looking at him as she did so. "Have you ever cared deeply for someone, Little Jon?" she wondered softly.

"Are you asking if I've ever been in love?" he murmured.

Robyn flinched at the word, shying away from it, but she didn't protest.

From the corner of her eye, she could see Little Jon's gaze directed toward the horizon as he answered. "I have," he said simply.

She didn't speak for a long while. "What if you knew you could love someone, you could feel you were well on your way to doing so, but circumstances got in the way?"

"Sometimes...love just isn't enough," he said sadly. "If the circumstances are such that they can't be adjusted, and if neither person is willing to cross that line that divides them, then...sometimes things just don't work out."

Robyn closed her eyes at his truths. She felt a large, warm hand stroke her hair at the back of her head.

"Still, there are many types of love that people live for, right?"

Robyn smiled up at her friend. She knew he was right, no matter how much the lost potential hurt. Had she not gotten into this entire situation because of her love for Will? Had that love for her best and truest friend not grown into her love for Sherwood and the people who live there?

"Thank you," she murmured, leaning against him, her shoulder and head resting on his arm.

"Anytime, Robyn."

They sat there a while longer, each taking comfort in the other's presence. Finally, a shout from the ground below called for their attention.

"Hey!" Tuck yelled up, her hands cupped around her mouth. Her hounds howled in imitation. "I found Alan A. Dale."

"Back to work," Robyn declared. Recharged with purpose, she pushed her heart's dilemma to one side. "How far is he?" she asked Tuck once they'd joined her on the ground.

"Not far," she assured. "Looks like the address is in The Doncz."

"Right." Robyn nodded. "Let's go."

The address Tuck had for the journalist turned out to be a flat above a bebop bar, which was ablaze that Sunday evening with the fast rhythms of a sax going full improv. Around the side of the building, in a rather dark and dirty alley, a flight of wooden stairs led to a door on the second floor.

Tuck knocked, and the door was opened only wide enough for the trio to see one dark eye looking out at them.

"Who is it?" the man said through the crack.

"It's Tuck. We talked on the telephone earlier. I'm here as promised, and I brought my two friends with me."

The door shut, then opened again with the chain removed. A tall, black man, though not as tall as Little Jon, stood in the doorway. His tie was loose at the neck, and his shirt sleeves were rolled to the elbow. He was about Robyn's age, but he wore thick, rounded glasses, which he adjusted on his nose as he looked at them.

"Come in," he invited.

They shuffled into his apartment. His living room was clean and tidy with well-used armchairs and an old radio in the corner.

Once he'd closed and locked the door behind them, he motioned them on ahead. They followed his movement down a hallway and into an office, which seemed to belong in someone else's apartment entirely. The walls and desk of the office were strewn with papers. Notes and newspaper clippings were tacked to the wall in an organization scheme that seemed to be understood by Alan A. Dale alone.

"You said on the telephone you have information about the robbery last night?" the reporter started, leaning his legs against the desk.

"First, we have some questions for you, Mr. Dale," Tuck said, turning to Robyn.

"How do you feel about the Lacklands, Mr. Dale?" Robyn asked.

The man frowned. "Just call me Alan. How do I feel about the Lacklands? What do you think?" He pointed to his wall of research behind him.

Upon closer inspection, Robyn saw there were article clippings about bodies found, shop owners beaten, unpopular policies passed, and unions disbanded.

"The Lacklands are a scourge on Midshire. I've been trying to tell the people about it since my first byline. Do you know how many times I've been fired?"

"Yet you still find jobs," Tuck pointed out.

"Well, I'm a good reporter, and I've learned to be more careful with my word choice."

Robyn smiled at the man. "How would you like our help in letting the people know what the Lacklands are really up to?"

"You got some inside information or something?" Alan asked uncertainly, having learned that if something sounded too good to be true it probably was.

"I'm Robyn Loxley," she stated. "And I robbed the Lacklands last night."

Alan stared at her silently for a moment, his expression not betraying his thoughts. Finally, he sighed. "I'm going to get fired again."

CHAPTER 46

*L*ater that week, Tuck and Will stood watch from an alley across the street from an art gallery in Thanes. Robyn glanced in their direction only for a moment before she went into the photography exhibition.

"Do you think she'll be okay?" Will whispered from under the hood Tuck had made him.

She glanced at him.

"I mean, I know she's been dealing with them most of her life, but it sort of feels like she's going into the lion's den unarmed."

Tuck thought about the cards she'd pulled earlier that day. The king of wands had smiled out at her, his crown—a beacon to all who needed a leader—and his scepter—a torch to light the unknown paths ahead. His confidence was reflective of what he was capable of, what he promised.

"She'll be fine," Tuck assured. "Besides, we're here to help should she need it."

Will nodded. "You're right. She may have a knack for getting into trouble, but she always seems to find her way out again, especially when she has friends looking out for her."

Tuck stared at Will's profile as he watched the entrance Robyn had disappeared into. "You two have always been close," she murmured.

Will smiled more to himself than to her. "Yeah," he agreed. "We were in school together. The cheeky urchin came right up to me during lunch, sat down, and stole a pickled plum from my lunchbox." Will chuckled. "You should have seen her face when she popped it into her mouth. She certainly wasn't expecting that. Served her right."

"And you've been together ever since?"

"That's about the sum of it. Robyn has always had a way of charming people, and it never took much convincing for me to join in on her adventures. We were in school together, and then we started playing outside of school. Eventually, she came to our dojo and fell in love with martial arts. After that, there really wasn't a realm of my life Robyn wasn't a part of."

Tuck smiled around the knot in her stomach. *Robyn is my friend,* she thought, admonishing herself. *And I trust her.* And it was true. She did trust Robyn. She knew if Robyn had said only friendship had ever existed between her and Will, then that was the end of the story. If Tuck only felt more confident in his estimation of her, she was sure her jealousy would melt away forever.

She silently kept watch beside him, observing as countless men and women, all in suits and gowns that looked more expensive than any bit of clothing had a right to be, entered the party.

"Is it strange for you to be out here?" Tuck asked.

"What do you mean?"

"Well, being Robyn's oldest friend, you must have accompanied her to these sorts of things in the past."

"Me?" He chuckled a warm sound that made her heart light. "Nah, she usually had a date for things like this. Never had a shortage of fellas looking to catch her eye, that Robyn. Though the silly girl didn't really notice half of them, poor guys. Speaking of which, her detective ought to be in there and Guy, too. I hope our girl manages to stay out of the thick of it."

Our. Tuck repeated the word in her mind. She liked the sound of that. It made her feel brave, and she cleared her throat. "Have you ever been 'in the thick of it'?"

Will looked at her seriously, his eyes finding hers without err. Her heart jumped. "Do you mean have I ever had two girls vying for my heart at the same time?"

Tuck nodded only slightly.

"Not in the least."

"Oh," she murmured.

Will frowned. "That's not to say I've never been involved with someone before," he admitted. "It's just never been that deep, you know?" He smiled apologetically as if he wished he could have answered differently.

Tuck nodded her understanding, looking down at the cracked pavement beneath their feet.

"And you?" Will asked hesitantly. Tuck looked up, meeting his gaze again. "Have you ever...wanted someone's heart?"

She shivered under the weight of his question, the interest in his eyes. She waited to answer, certain her voice would tremble if she spoke right away, hoping she would manage to hear her own words over the pounding of her heartbeat. Realizing she wouldn't be able to steady herself anytime soon, she whispered, "Not until recently."

Three. Four. Five heartbeats thumped in her ears as Will held her gaze in the alley.

A car pulled up to the curb near the mouth of the alley.

Will launched himself at Tuck, driving them both farther into the shadows. With her back up against the wall and Will's body close to hers, Tuck gazed up at Will. His breath was warm on her face though he was not looking at her. He stood, straight and still, blocking her from anyone who may be a little too curious.

The car door closed, and they heard the shuffle of footsteps crossing the street. Tuck peeked around her hood as a tall man with a confident gait entered the gallery.

"Guy Gisbourne," Will murmured, his eyes directed at the new arrival. Then he looked anxiously down at her. "Are you all right? I didn't make you hit your head. Did I?"

She met his eyes again, barely hearing his words over her own heartbeat. *He couldn't hear it. Could he?* she wondered. She felt light-headed, her breath shallow.

"Tuck?" Will asked, his voice more urgent when she hadn't responded.

"I'm fine," she managed, sounding a little more breathless than she would've liked. "I didn't hit my head," she assured him.

He sighed in relief, but he didn't step away. His dark eyes reflected only a soft shimmer of the dim light, his face cast in deep, angular shadows. "Me too," he murmured. "I've never wanted someone's heart either... not until recently."

Tuck's breath hitched, then she let it out in a heavy rush. She couldn't have looked away if she'd wanted to.

Will's hands, which rested protectively on the wall on either side of her, moved gently to her shoulders.

She shivered at the weight.

He paused, his gaze analyzing her expression. She didn't know what he found there, but his hands traveled down her arms to her hands, where he laced her trembling fingers with his. His long fingers warmed her chilled ones.

Her chest ached at the pounding of her heart, heaving painfully with every breath.

As he leaned toward her, his eyes watched hers, giving her every chance to turn away. Her eyelids fluttered closed. She barely heard him as he whispered her name before his lips touched hers.

CHAPTER 47

Robyn stood before the large photo mosaic of the fisherman's mother, not really seeing it. She'd already greeted Eleanor, John, and Isabella, grateful they were too busy entertaining to ask her more than how she was doing. Then she'd spent a while marking John's guests. She remembered having seen most of them at one time or another, though she couldn't recall many of their names. This time, she carefully noted them in her mind.

Of course, not everyone there was part of a powerful family. It was an art exhibition after all. There were critics and other artists carefully analyzing Marian's work, none the wiser as to the company they were keeping.

For the first time since Robyn had arrived, her sister came up to her, having managed to slip away from the sons of some of the most powerful crime families in the country.

"You really did a beautiful job, Marian," Robyn told her.

Marian smiled. "Thank you." Then she sighed, glancing around. "I certainly didn't expect my exhibition to be like this though."

"Do you regret it?"

"You know I don't. I'd do anything for my baby sister." Marian reached up and pinched Robyn's cheek playfully.

Robyn laughed.

"There's that beautiful smile. I expected to see it before now with all your recent successes."

"Yeah." Robyn's grin softened, her eyes drifting to where Detective Alaric Nottingham stood, watching the crowd.

Marian followed her gaze. "Problems?"

Robyn sighed. "You could say that. My heart feels a bit mixed up."

Marian patted her sister's shoulder sympathetically. "This is just a moment passing in time. Who knows what the future will bring?"

"Such a poet."

"What can I say? I live art."

Robyn chuckled at her sister.

"Why don't you go see if the good detective would like some refreshment? Standing there looking so stern and observant has to be thirsty work, and I have so many people to entertain already. Would you mind helping me out, sis?" Marian gave Robyn a little push before fluttering away to mingle with someone else.

Robyn wound through the crowd to the man in question, her chest tightening with every hesitant step. "Can I get you anything to drink, Detective?" Robyn asked.

He met her gaze, eyes flashing only momentarily with a look she recognized all too well. "No, thank you, Miss Loxley. I have to keep my wits about me."

She stepped closer to him so only he could hear her. "Do you really think they'll show up tonight? It's not exactly an open guest list."

"They weren't exactly invited the last time they showed up. Besides, they could already be here for all I know. They could be any one of these people." His eyes scanned the crowd suspiciously, then rested on Robyn.

She stiffened.

"You look beautiful tonight," he murmured.

"Thank you," she said softly back.

"What do you say about coming to my place after this?"

Guilt gnawed at Robyn's stomach. *He has no idea we're enemies in this,* she thought miserably. *Being with him under these circumstances feels...wrong.*

Robyn shook her head slightly. "I'm sorry," she said. "I—"

"I didn't allow your presence so you could socialize," Guy interrupted. "Don't you have some hoods to catch?"

Rick glared icy daggers at Guy, clenching his jaw.

"It's my fault, Guy," Robyn jumped in. "Marian asked me to help her hostess, and I was just asking Detective Nottingham if he'd like me to get him something to drink. He's trying so hard to keep us all safe after all. We wouldn't want to appear ungracious."

"Thoughtful as ever, Robyn," Guy praised. "But as we wouldn't want to distract the detective from his work, I suggest we leave him be. I recall you're a fan of art, Robyn. Why don't you show me around? I'd like to hear your thoughts on Marian's pieces."

Guy offered Robyn his arm. Her nod was more of a flinch than agreement. As Guy led her away, she looked back at Rick. His face was perfectly schooled, but his fists shook with barely contained rage.

As he handed her a glass of wine, Guy smiled down at her, high with victory. "You left in a rush the other day," he commented.

"Sorry about that," she said, not having an explanation to give him. Images from her visit rose to the surface of her mind and her stomach fluttered. *What would have happened if I'd stayed?* she wondered.

Her eyes drifted to Rick across the room. His presence was usually an anchor to her emotions, but her chest tightened.

"He seems comfortable with you," Guy commented, following her gaze.

"You think so?" Robyn shrugged, letting her eyes drift anywhere else.

"Have you seen him since Mrs. Lackland's birthday?"

"I've run into him a few times here and there," she said, thinking she couldn't get away with a complete lie.

"He hasn't been pestering you?"

She shook her head. "On the contrary. He has been quite hospitable." Robyn resisted the urge to squirm as Guy eyed her carefully.

"You could tell me if you two are friends, you know. As much as I hate to admit it, there is something...admirable about his stalwart nature."

Friends doesn't even come close, Robyn thought. "No," she stated with confidence. "We aren't friends."

CHAPTER 48

Marian stretched her back and limbs as she lay in bed the morning after her photography show, sighing while she stared up at the ceiling. Her exhibition had been a success by all accounts, despite John having used it to further his own standing in the criminal underworld. She frowned at the thought that some of her art would be gracing the homes of some very dangerous men and women by week's end. But how could she have refused the sales in those circumstances?

Still, everyone had behaved themselves. She might have never known who they really were had she not been informed beforehand. She may have even considered a few of them in the way Eleanor always wished she would. She found Owen MacKenzie particularly charming. Too bad he was set to become the next head of his family. She didn't want to think about the harm he'd done in his still young life. And she wanted to think about what he would do later on even less.

What would Mom and Dad think about all this? she wondered. *Dad had been the honorable sort, even put his life on the line to save a fellow soldier. And Mom had always been generous, often sharing a meal with a stranger even when they had little to spare.* She didn't think her dad would have taken a job with Henry had he known what the Lacklands were into. They definitely wouldn't have wanted their daughters raised in it. *Which I suppose could be why Eleanor tried so hard to keep us in the dark for so long,* she thought. *Should I be grateful for that?*

She was so thankful Robyn had told her everything before she entered into a marriage with a man such as this. She could too well see how she could have traveled down that path. Had she not always done what the Lacklands had asked of her before?

She sighed again. Worrying for Robyn had always been a full-time job, and she'd really been pushing Marian's limits of late. But Marian could see the changes her sister had undergone. She'd always been confident, but never in a way such as this. She'd grown into a leader, a person who looked out for the welfare of others. Marian knew their parents would be proud.

She'd be perfectly content, downright pleased even, had she not seen the pain, the conflict, in her little sister's eyes the night before when looking at Detective Nottingham. Robyn had always felt too deeply. She couldn't fool Marian by hiding her tears.

Marian sat up from her bed and went about getting dressed. No matter how much she wanted to be in Sherwood with the person she cared for most, Robyn needed her here.

As she made her way downstairs for breakfast, she passed by Isabella's room and paused, surprised to hear John's voice coming from inside. Despite the fact that they were married, Marian had never known them to spend the night together.

"Don't worry, love," Isabella soothed. "I have everything in hand."

Marian could picture John's scowl as he looked at his wife. "I'm trusting you with this, Isabella. This is a big undertaking for me. If I make this kind of money for the family, my position will be much more secure. It's possible I could keep it even should Richard return from the war."

"Everything is already set. The rally is booked, and everything is on schedule. All I have to do is hand the money off to Guy once it's collected. No problem."

John sighed. "You're right. I shouldn't worry. Even you couldn't mess this up. Gisbourne can handle the rest just fine. By next week, our account will be flush, and the patriotic people of Midshire will be none the wiser. It will be a Thanksgiving to be truly thankful for."

"Exactly," Isabella agreed. "And should I prove myself in this way... You will do as you promised?"

"We shall see," John said sternly.

Isabella snorted in a rare note of defiance. "If only you'd said the same to Adela and Clementina. Do you know how foolish I look to others? Three years of marriage and still no children whilst you clearly have no trouble helping your mistresses, women already married at that, become mothers."

Marian flinched, picturing John's face turning purple.

"A babe," Isabella added, contrite. "Is that too much to ask, husband?"

"I said we shall see." John put an end to the conversation.

Marian hurried along down the hall as swiftly and quietly as she could. *I have to go to Sherwood as soon as I can,* she thought as she sat down at the breakfast table, joined shortly after by John and Isabella. *How low can these people get?* she wondered, hiding her disgust in her coffee cup.

CHAPTER 49

Robyn laced her hands together, elbows resting on Gyl's desk. She stared at the telephone, willing herself to pick it up and dial. If this latest attack on the Lacklands was going to work, she'd need to play her part, too. She sighed and picked up the handset.

"Hello?"

"Guy? This is Robyn."

"Oh, hello, Robyn." His voice immediately warmed.

Robyn's heart jumped. "Hey, so I was wondering...are you busy this week?" she asked softly.

"Well, I'm sure you know about the rally Wednesday. I have to go to that, of course. But otherwise, there's nothing I can't move around for you."

"I thought you might be going out of town to see family. You said you were from Oregon before, right?"

"I don't have any family," he stated.

"Oh, I didn't know that. Well, I was hoping we could get together that day. I'd forgotten about the rally actually."

"I'm sorry. I really need to be there." His tone suggested he'd never been more sorry for anything in his entire life. "I assume you're going to the Lacklands' for the holiday?"

"I thought about it, but I decided not to."

"Perhaps we can meet on Thursday then. No one should be alone on Thanksgiving."

Sadness weighed on Robyn's heart. *How many holidays had Guy spent alone?* she wondered. "Yeah, okay," she accepted. "We can have that picnic you talked about before."

"Thoresby Beach? Around one? We can take a walk, then go inside for the picnic." he suggested.

"That's fine."

"Great. I'll see you then."

"Well, now that you reminded me about the rally, maybe I'll go, too. Marian is going to be there, right?"

"Yes, she's been helping Mrs. Lackland organize it."

"Right. So I might see you there."

Guy promised to keep an eye out for her before ringing off.

"Damn," Robyn muttered to herself before sighing heavily. "Well, we'll just have to adjust our plan." With a smirk, she recalled all the times her candies had mysteriously disappeared. She knew exactly who to ask for help. She stood from the desk and returned to the others.

The day before Thanksgiving, the riverfront in Thanes was packed with excited people, all crowded around the outdoor stage where performances were soon to commence. The bridge over the river was jammed with cars, heading to Midshire from Trentfield.

They hadn't managed to get any big stars to attend, but there were a number of musicians and comedy acts set to perform.

From where she stood, Robyn could see Marian and Isabella at a table where people paid for admission, under the impression their money was going to a good cause.

Robyn and her band all wore their hoods, blending quite well with everyone else's cold weather attire. Robyn, Tuck, Little Jon, and Much appeared to be four excited event-goers. Will and Gyl were stationed farther away in the getaway car.

Little Jon and Much were not far from the table, ready to play their parts at any moment. Tuck was also close by, though not with them, armed with the knowledge Micki had so recently imparted. Robyn was on the lookout for a tall man with intense, black eyes.

It didn't take her too long to find her mark, and she spent the better part of an hour keeping herself somewhere between him and the admission table, glancing every so often at Marian to see how things were progressing.

Finally, during a set change, Marian gave Robyn the signal. Isabella was sealing their ill-gotten gains into an envelope. After she'd done that, she looked around for Guy. Robyn moved into position as her band went to work.

Heading toward Guy, Robyn heard Much cry out as he bumped into Isabella and fell. Isabella and Marian rushed to his aid, hushing the child and checking for injuries.

Robyn reached Guy and tapped him on the shoulder, hoping Tuck would have no trouble switching the envelopes, and Little Jon would carry the still tearful Much away.

Guy turned around.

"I knew I'd find you eventually," Robyn said with a smile.

"Have you been looking for me for long?"

"Not very. It's a good show so far. Are you enjoying it?"

Guy nodded. "Yes, your sister and Mrs. Lackland did a good job of organizing it. I was about to go see them if you'd like to join me."

Robyn looked toward the table as Little Jon lifted Much into his arms.

Guy started to follow her gaze, but she called his attention back to her.

"I'm looking forward to our picnic tomorrow. Is there anything you'd like me to bring?" Robyn asked.

"No, don't trouble yourself. Your presence is all I could ask of you."

Robyn glanced again. There was no sign of Little Jon, Much, or Tuck. "Well, I don't want to keep you. You're working after all."

Guy tilted his head. "Don't you want to say hello to your sister and Mrs. Lackland?"

Robyn smiled. "It's fine. I saw them earlier when I got my ticket, and they're busy working too, right? I'll just see you tomorrow."

"Okay," he agreed.

Robyn slowly moved through the crowd and made her way from the riverfront. She weaved through side streets and alleys until she reached a corner soda shop. Sitting on the free stool on the other side of Little Jon, she ordered a root beer float.

"Everything all right?" she asked him, as the soda jerk went about making her order.

He smiled down at her. "Perfect."

Robyn paid the jerk his thirty-five cents and took a sip of her cold, creamy soda.

"Tuck get out okay?" she murmured.

Little Jon nodded. "Should be on her way home now."

Robyn leaned forward, looking down the counter to Much on Little Jon's other side. He clutched a spoon in his fist as he brought the last of his chocolate sundae to his already smeared mouth.

She smiled at the boy, happy to see him enjoying a childish pastime for once.

CHAPTER 50

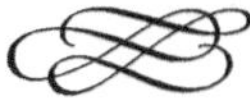

Tuck stared down at the newspapers scattered across her bed, the headlines glaring back at her in bold, all capitalized letters: "Brigands Strike Again," "Villains Steal from Soldiers," "Traitors at Home," "Bandits Help Axis," "Rally Funds Swiped." She'd already read them all, read each word as the news, with their limited knowledge of events, twisted the truth into something hideous and loathsome.

Her stomach felt heavy and hollow, and she closed her eyes as more tears trailed down her already wet and swollen face. Kisses lay half in her lap, and Beauty licked her cheek. Fangs and Bell stood on the floor, resting their heads on the bed. Their dark eyes watched her, sharing her sorrow.

When she heard a knock on her door, she didn't answer, even her hounds didn't respond. She hugged Kisses to her chest, her soft fur warm and comforting. The door opened without Tuck inviting her visitor in.

"Tuck?" Robyn called. "What's the matter? Are you all right?" Robyn climbed up beside her. The papers rustled near her feet.

"No," Tuck answered, her voice thick with her running nose. "I'm not all right."

"Is it the papers?" Robyn asked softly.

Tuck met her friend's eyes. "I don't understand. How can they get it so wrong? Day after day, the Lacklands strangle this city, hurt people, and they never say anything. But we act to stop them, and this is what we get?"

Robyn frowned, reaching out and rubbing Tuck's back. "Alan is working with Gyl to get his story printed. I brought you a copy. We're going to deliver them around the city tonight." Robyn held out the sheet of paper to her, but Tuck shook her head.

"It won't matter," she answered morosely. "It doesn't matter that what Alan wrote is the truth. People aren't going to believe our version."

"Some might," Robyn offered.

"Do you want to know what really gets me?" The tears were rising in Tuck's throat again, but she pushed through. "Good will never win. Good will never win, Robyn, because bad is willing to do things we never will. Sure, we took food and money from bad people, and we gave it to those they'd harmed. We gave it to people who needed it far more, people who may not have survived without it."

Tuck shook her head. "But it doesn't matter because they're willing to go even further. They're willing to kick families out of their homes, to extort money from those who are barely getting by, to bribe elected officials and police officers, to kill. They're willing to force my grove, my family, out of town because the church didn't want us here, because they were offered the possibility of salvation if they did so. So we stole the money that they had already stolen. We aren't willing to go to the lengths they are to get what we want. That's why we will lose, Robyn."

Robyn was silent for a while. She met Tuck's gaze seriously, and her voice was steady when she responded. "You're right, Tuck. We aren't willing to do all that. And maybe that means we will never truly overcome. Maybe the Lacklands and those like them will never be beaten in this fight. But that doesn't mean we lose. For every family we welcome into Sherwood, for each person, each child, we feed and clothe and teach, we win. Good may not win by beating bad. Good wins when good survives. Good wins anytime someone protects someone weaker than her not because it benefits her, but because it's the right thing to do. Tell me something, Tuck."

Robyn paused, making sure Tuck was ready to hear her question. "Who will speak for these people if we will not? What would have happened to the people of Sherwood had you and Little Jon not taken them in? I know you're disheartened. People are bound to misunderstand what we're doing here. But you can't stop the fight. Because if you stop, then they truly do win."

Tuck sighed out a shaky breath, the last of her tears dripping off her chin. "I wish it could be different," she murmured.

Robyn smiled softly. "I know, but that's why we're here, to *make* it different."

Tuck sniffed hard and nodded. "You're right. Some people aren't in a position where they can speak out like us. They're relying on us to stand up and fight back for them."

"That's right. Now, take a look at this letter Alan wrote." Robyn offered her the sheet of paper again, and this time, Tuck took it.

An Accurate Account of the Rally Theft
November 26, 1942

Good people of Midshire,

By now, many of you have read accounts of how the bond funds were stolen from the rally by persons unknown. The accounts portrayed thus far are false, for the funds were stolen from the citizens far before it was first reported.

In fact, the funds were never intended for the troops at all, but to line the pockets of the Midshire Lacklands.

Thus far, you have read only what they have wanted you to read, so tight is their grasp on the throat of the First Amendment in Midshire. That ends now.

The funds stolen from the original thieves will be distributed amongst the most needy and put to use in ways that will benefit all.

For now, good citizens, know that there are those out there willing to fight the tyranny that is John Lackland and his ilk.

Take heart and resist.

`The Hooded Brigands`

Tuck smiled down at the paper. "Do you think it will work? Do you think it will change anyone's mind?"

"I think most of Midshire already knows what the Lacklands have been about for a long time. And once they read this and know who we are really against, and once they hear about how we're giving donations to charities, I think it will change some minds, yeah."

"What does he mean, 'put to use in ways that will benefit all'?"

Robyn grinned. "I've got something special planned."

CHAPTER 51

Robyn left Sherwood with a spring in her step, even humming a little tune. It was Thanksgiving, and the people of Sherwood had much to be thankful for.

Thoresby Beach was in The Doncz, not very far from Sherwood, but well away from the commercial traffic of the docks in Stockport. It was one of the cleanest beaches in Midshire, which wasn't saying much. Its sand was a shiny black that might have been beautiful if it had occurred naturally. There were few seabirds on the shore, most having traveled farther into Midshire for food. Still, the wooden planks of the pier were sturdy, and the water out to sea did have a sort of blue tint to it.

Robyn arrived before Guy. She walked some twenty feet onto the pier and sat on the edge, the heels of her feet thumping against the side as she swung her legs while she waited. She faced north toward Sherwood, not able to see it through the buildings but knowing it was there.

She'd determined to have a pleasant time with Guy. Sure, he hadn't lived the most honorable life, but he was trying to change. And sure, she'd initially—and repeatedly—reached out to him to get information about the Lacklands, knowingly manipulating his feelings toward her. And certainly, her actions as the leader of The Hooded Brigands had no doubt put him in hot water at work. But should all that get in the way of a pleasant meal with a lonely friend on Thanksgiving? If it should, Robyn had pushed it out of her mind.

Upon hearing heavy footsteps on the pier, Robyn pried her eyes away from the dark ocean swells and turned toward the sound. She stood with a smile and went to meet Guy as he approached.

"Hey, where's your basket?" she asked.

Guy's eyes blazed under the brim of his hat as he reached Robyn and grabbed her by the front of her coat, lifting her slightly from her feet.

"Are you making a fool of me, Robyn?" he demanded.

Robyn's heart hammered in her chest as real fear shot through her veins. "W-what do you mean?"

"Do you think I'm simple?" he growled. "Did you honestly think I wouldn't put it together? Every time you reach out to me, the Lacklands are robbed. I take you to the camp? The prisoners escape, including your friend. I tell you about the shipment of food? It's stolen. You call the day before the rally? The funds are taken right from under my nose. Explain this to me. Now."

Robyn took a deep breath and let it out slowly. Though her heartbeat still pounded in her ears, she met Guy's eyes with a steady look of defiance. "Take your hands off me, Guy Gisbourne," she ordered.

His grip eased her more steadily on her feet, but he did not let her go. "Please, Robyn. Make me understand." His voice held the faintest hint of a plea.

"Is this how you become a better man?" she challenged. "You pursue me for almost a year and the moment I respond you turn on me with suspicion and accusations?"

The hardness in Guy's eyes faltered.

"Is this truly how you see me?" Robyn pushed.

Doubt loosened his hold on her a little more. Then he shook his head, and his grip tightened again, the hard glare returning. "No, there's too much coincidence. Too much doesn't add up. If you want me to believe you, you're going to have to prove it."

"Did I come to visit you at your apartment to steal from the Lacklands then?" she challenged. "What would I have to gain from doing that?"

His expression wavered, and she could tell she was convincing him.

And when his black eyes met hers, she saw what she had done. Pain.

Uncertainty. Vulnerability. Robyn's heart gave one hard beat. She reached out and grabbed Guy by the scarf, then pulled his lips down to hers.

He stiffened for a moment, eyes wide, then released her coat to wrap his arms around her, crushing her to him.

Robyn's chest tightened, her whole body screaming. His hard body was too hot as he enveloped her, his limbs too heavy to escape. His lips were too eager as they devoured hers. She couldn't breathe, surrounded on all sides as he claimed her so willfully.

Robyn didn't know for how long the kiss lasted. A moment? An eternity? However long it was, it was enough for a little part of herself to be lost. He'd taken it, suffocated it, smothered it to death. *No, that's not right,* she thought. She'd given it to him.

As they broke apart, Robyn heaved heavy breaths, the cold, ocean air scraping against her throat. Her insides quivered, and her entire body was flushed.

She analyzed Guy's eyes. They were soft with regret but simmering with pleasure, and she could still see a sliver of distrust there.

"This isn't how I wanted our first kiss to be," he said, his tone tinged with remorse. And it sounded sincere despite the hint of suspicion. "I'm sorry."

Robyn couldn't bring herself to speak. Her head swam with confusion, too muddled to order her thoughts, her feelings. She just nodded slightly.

Guy hesitated, turmoil warring in his expression. "I've ruined it, haven't I? The picnic."

"I understand," Robyn murmured honestly. "You were feeling taken advantage of. For that, *I* am sorry."

Guy watched her closely, then shook his head. And when he sighed, his last bit of doubt in her seemed blown away by the sea breeze. "No, Robyn. I was out of line. And I never should have laid my hands on you in anger. I don't think I'll ever forgive myself."

Robyn couldn't say much to that. He most certainly shouldn't have physically intimidated her. There was no excuse for that. But had she not done him wrong as well?

"I...I think I'm going to head home," Robyn told him.

Guy nodded. "Another time," he said, taking her hand ever so gently.

"Now that I know how you feel, I can be more patient. We have many, more pleasant, days ahead of us."

She squeezed his hand in goodbye, trying to apologize for everything she'd put him through. Then she released it and headed back up the pier.

Robyn had survived. She'd thrown suspicion elsewhere, away from herself, away from Sherwood. But as her chest ached and her stomach quivered, she wondered just how deep she was in with Guy Gisbourne. And as she glanced back at him, his black eyes still following her even at this distance, Robyn vowed to never reach out to Guy for information on the Lacklands again.

CHAPTER 52

Alaric could think of a hundred things he'd rather be doing on Thanksgiving than working, most of them involved Robyn. Unfortunately, he had no way of contacting her, and he had less seniority than the other fellas at the station. At the very least, he would have preferred to stay home and eat Mrs. Stanley's Thanksgiving dinner. But allowing his colleagues to spend time with their families would go a little way into making them like him, he hoped. Not that he wanted them to like him exactly. It was more that investigations went a lot smoother when your coworkers and subordinates didn't hate you.

He really hadn't planned on following Guy Gisbourne. But when he was heading back from lunch, he happened to see his Clipper pulling into the deserted lot near Thoresby Beach. Curiosity and old habits took over, and he parked down the block. Guy was walking at a good pace far ahead, his shoulders bunched and tense with emotion.

Alaric slipped behind a dead palm, somehow still standing in the black sand, and peeked around it toward the pier. Two figures embraced on the pier. Their faces pressed together in a passionate exchange.

"Huh, I didn't know you had a girl," Alaric murmured. He squinted through the misty haze of ocean spray, hoping the couple would turn in such a way that he could see the girl's face.

They pulled away from each other, and Alaric's world crashed all around him, sounding a lot like the waves of the Pacific, a pounding heartbeat, and a strangled groan that seemed to be coming from his own lips.

His stomach rolled as bile burned the back of his throat, but all he could do was stare, his mouth hanging open in horror.

His thoughts spun, too incoherent to comprehend.

Guy captured Robyn's hand. When she pulled away, it seemed a regretful gesture.

As Robyn left Guy alone on the pier, Alaric couldn't bring himself to follow his lover or to confront his rival. His feet were too heavy, shoes sinking slightly into the black sand. Leaning his back to the dead palm, he slid down to the ground, not even registering the filth on his clothes.

I'm a fool, he thought, his chest aching as though he was being crushed by heavy stones. *How long? How long has she been with Gisbourne? The entire time? Maybe the whole thing was a farce. Maybe he was tired of me poking my nose into Lackland business, and he sent her to distract me, to muddle my mind.*

Alaric pictured the fervent look in Robyn's eyes as she kissed him, as he caressed her, as they called out in mutual pleasure. Even now, he could feel the warmth of her body beneath his. He could smell the scent of her as he'd buried his face in her hair. Alaric leaned over and retched, his lunch marring the shiny black sand of Thoresby Beach.

He clenched his eyes shut as he fell back against the tree trunk. *Is it really true?* he wondered. *Have I really been duped so completely?*

He imagined her smile, her laugh, the words she'd whispered to him. He remembered how she'd accused him of trying to get close to her to further his investigation. *It can't be,* he told himself. *It can't have all been a ruse. It's obvious she has lied to me, that something is clearly going on between Gisbourne and her. But that doesn't mean her time with me was a lie. She's the one who suggested we not talk about the Lacklands to begin with. She even moved out of their house. But...I don't know where she moved to. What if she moved in with Gisbourne?*

Alaric shook his head at his own train of thought. *No, I've followed him too many times from his place. I would've seen her at least once if she lived there. She lied about Gisbourne, yeah. But she never said we were to be exclusive. That was my own foolish heart getting ahead of me.*

Alaric remembered Robyn's hesitation when he'd asked if she was friends with Gisbourne. He'd known something was off at the time, though he hadn't known exactly what.

But I was sure, he thought. *I was so sure we were heading somewhere.*

"Clearly, I was wrong," he muttered with a sigh. "Because if she did feel anything for me, she never would have k—" He cut himself off abruptly, not being able to stomach the sound of the word.

Closing his eyes, he listened to the ocean waves crashing on the shore. It was nothing like the quiet flowing melodies of the three rivers at home. But it was much more effective in drowning out his thoughts. He breathed deep, matching his inhales and exhales with the ebbs and flows of the breaks.

The suffocating weight on his chest eased, though it didn't go away. *I'll talk to her,* he thought. *I'll tell her honestly what I feel for her and what I want from our relationship. She wasn't forthcoming about her and Gisbourne, but that could be because she knew we were at odds and didn't want to complicate things. Based off what Gisbourne said before, it's likely he doesn't know about her relationship with me either. She never said we weren't to see other people. That's just...just what I want. I obviously can't take the thought of her being with someone else. I should tell her that.*

He stood up and looked back at the pier where his lover and rival so recently expressed their passions in full view of anyone watching. It was empty. His heart squeezed in protest. *I'll talk to her,* he thought. *Just not now.*

CHAPTER 53

Robyn adjusted her quiver and bow. She took the stack of papers Alan offered her and stuffed them into her bag. She glanced around the nave at the gathered volunteers, some thirty people all dressed with their faces shadowed by hoods, hats, or scarves. They each took their stack of papers as though they were accepting a solemn undertaking, and so they were.

"All right," Robyn called to the assemblage after they were properly equipped. "You have your assignments. Get in and out as quickly as possible. Stay with your partner, and be safe."

They murmured their acknowledgment and headed out, each destined for a different neighborhood of the four boroughs south of Sherwood.

"You ready?" Robyn asked Little Jon as he knelt down before Much.

Little Jon nodded and stood.

"How about you, Much?" Robyn looked down at the boy. "Are you ready to keep track of everyone who returns?"

Much nodded, clutching his pad and pencil with all the volunteers' names.

Robyn stroked the boy's hair. "Good." She looked up at Little Jon. "Let's go," she said.

Little Jon and Robyn were destined for Southwell, the southernmost borough of Midshire. The streets were quiet and deserted as the people of Midshire slept, exhausted from a holiday of food and family.

"I used to live here," Little Jon murmured as they walked down a street with closed shops, which would soon be bustling with holiday shoppers. "When I first moved to Midshire."

"You did? You aren't from here originally?"

Little Jon shook his head. "No, I moved here to help out my mother and siblings. Dad died in the war. Being the eldest, I helped Mom as much as I could, but ten kids are too many to support on your own. So when I was old enough, I moved to Midshire to get a job, ease her burden. I sent as much as I could spare home."

"Let me guess, you worked for the Lacklands, and they fired you."

"Not exactly. I worked for a shipping company they put out of business."

"Do you miss them? Your family?"

"Of course, but they're doing fine. And I've got Much to look after. And I have Artheia and Tuck and you..."

Robyn smiled at her friend. "You're right. You're my family too, Little Jon."

Little Jon returned her smile, and they shared a warm moment of kinship.

Then Robyn pointed to their first target, a newspaper stand. She pulled an arrow from her quiver and Alan's letter from her bag. She speared the paper, and shot the arrow into the wooden side of the stand.

They didn't speak for a while but quickly made their way through the neighborhood, posting the notice anywhere people were likely to see it: corner shops, train stations, newspaper stands. To cover more ground, they'd split up, but they were never out of each other's sight for long.

Having posted her last copy, Robyn waited for Little Jon to return from down the street. When he reached her at the mouth of a rather dark alley, they heard a crash behind him.

Robyn drew her bow, and Little Jon brandished his quarterstaff, probing the alley with their eyes, ready for whatever might emerge.

"Who goes there?" Little Jon growled.

"Don't shoot," a soft voice murmured as a thin teenage girl in slacks and a paperboy hat stepped into the light with her hands raised, a rumpled paper in her fingers.

Robyn lowered her bow, staring hard at the girl's short, dark hair and blue eyes. *I've seen her somewhere,* Robyn thought. *Where was it?* "Mireilla," Robyn said, finally recalling the awkward waitress at Pippa's.

The girl's blue eyes widened. "How do you know me?" she asked, squinting in the dark, trying to see into Robyn's hood.

"Why were you following my friend?" Robyn demanded.

"I go out the window on the fire escape sometimes when I want to be alone. I saw him," she indicated toward Little Jon, "post something on the corner, so I went down to see. Are you the hoods the paper was talking about? The ones that blew up the pier in Stockport? Did you really steal that money from the Lacklands?"

Her gaze was clear and curious.

Robyn glanced at Little Jon and then back at Mireilla. "Go home, Mireilla, before your family misses you."

Little Jon and Robyn turned to leave.

"Wait!" Mireilla called. "I can help."

They paused in their retreat. Robyn looked hard at the girl. Whatever it was, she was telling the truth.

"You're trying to steal from the Lacklands?" Mireilla asked quickly before they had a chance to go. "I've been to their casino. I know where it is and how to get the password. If you want to hit them where it hurts, that's the mother lode."

Robyn considered what she said but hesitated.

"Please," Mireilla begged. She smoothed out the paper in her hand and pointed to Alan's letter. "This is important. I want to be a part of it, and I can help."

Robyn looked again at Little Jon, who shrugged by way of opinion. Robyn nodded. "Fine. Tomorrow, come to the bridge of Sherwood Canal. When asked why you're there, tell them Robyn sent you."

Mireilla nodded seriously. "I'll be there," she said.

The following day, David escorted a nervous-looking Mireilla into Gyl's workshop.

"'Ey!" David shouted, drawing Gyl's and Robyn's attentions as they worked on fixing the border deterrent.

"I got it, Gyl," Robyn said, stepping away from the machine as Gyl returned to work. Robyn made her way toward her visitor, pulling off her goggles.

Mireilla's eyes widened in recognition. "You..." she murmured.

Robyn smiled. "Welcome to Sherwood, Mireilla."

CHAPTER 54

Guy Gisbourne was conflicted. He couldn't remember the last time he'd felt this good about himself. He strongly suspected it had never happened. But as he entered John Lackland's study and saw the paper clutched in his boss's hand, he knew he was in trouble.

"Why do you think I hired you, Gisbourne?" John asked too calmly.

Guy paused, uncertain if John really wanted him to answer. It turned out he did not.

"All over I heard tales of the ruthless Guy Gisbourne, the man who never flinched and who never failed to carry out his contract. I brought you to Midshire on a full-time basis, gave you a steady job, one that pays quite well I might add. So pray, explain to me." John crushed the paper between his hands and threw it at Guy. "Why have you done nothing about these brigand hoods?" he roared.

Guy stood still, remaining calm in the face of John's rage. He wasn't one to make excuses or grovel. "They will be caught," he stated.

John's face was red and his eyes wild as he ran his hands through his hair. "They better be, Gisbourne, or it will be your head."

Guy leveled a cool stare at John but didn't say anything. John Lackland hadn't the balls or the stomach to take on Guy. But what he did have was a network of capos and soldiers vying for his favor. Guy may be capable of taking them on one-on-one, but he'd never survive should John Lackland unleash all the powers at his disposal on Guy's tail.

"And I want you to go to The Golden Arrow. While the families were there, MacKenzie complained that the whiskey was watered down. Find out what's going on."

Guy nodded once.

John stared at him, finally curling his lip. "I don't know what's gotten into you lately, Gisbourne, but I don't like it. There's talk among some of the boys that you've gone soft. I'm told you've started negotiating now? Al said you stopped Geoff from teaching someone a lesson the other day."

Guy frowned, disgusted by the cutthroat politics of the organization. *This is why I took contracts,* he reminded himself. "Geoff didn't seem to understand that a tailor with crushed fingers isn't going to make us much money."

John frowned at the new information. "Look, you want to give to charity or donate medicine to the Japs at the concentration camps? Whatever. It's your money. But when your generosity interferes with my business, then it becomes my problem. You hear me? To everyone else, you look like you're slipping. So go to The Golden Arrow, find out who's watering the booze, and make an example of him. We have too much to lose to show weakness now."

Guy hesitated at the direct order, so in contrast was it to what Robyn had told him, who he was trying to be. He could still feel the warmth of her in his arms from the day before, the taste of her on his tongue. He brushed his twinge of unease aside. *Just this once,* he thought. *Just once shouldn't be a problem. Just enough to assure John and the boys.*

"I'll take care of it," Guy promised.

CHAPTER 55

Over the first week of December, the daytime temperatures in Midshire had dropped into the fifties, signaling that winter was truly approaching. All around the city, there were whispers of the hoods. They'd given to orphanages and hospitals; they'd given to the American Legion and other organizations that helped veterans. And the people loved them for it, though not openly for fear of Lackland retribution. Less well known, they'd dropped care packages of soap, toothbrushes, and good food on the roof of the concentration camp, telling Will's parents with the transmitter to quietly distribute them among the prisoners.

Across the street and around the corner from The Golden Arrow, Mireilla fussed over Robyn's hair, tucking the signal which would get them into the casino into her updo. Tuck, Will, and Little Jon looked on in their hoods.

"Don't worry, Robyn," Will assured. "Little Jon and Mireilla will be watching from up there." Will pointed to the roof of the building across from The Golden Arrow. "And Tuck and I will be on the other side of the building in the alley. So however you need to signal us, we'll see it."

Robyn nodded, and Mireilla clicked her tongue as her head gesture thwarted her efforts.

"There," the girl pronounced finally, stepping back to admire her work. Then she handed Robyn another paperwhite narcissus she'd fashioned from actual paper.

Robyn took the offering and approached Gyl who was dressed formally in a suit. She smiled at the inventor as she reached up to put the flower in his buttonhole.

"What do you think?" Gyl grinned. "I clean up nice, eh?"

"To tell you the truth, I think you're more dashing covered in grease and soot," Robyn said.

Gyl's grin widened.

"Okay," Mireilla coached. "When the hostess asks if you have a seating preference, you're going to show her the flowers and ask for the best seat in the house."

Robyn and Gyl nodded their understanding.

"They're going to get suspicious if you go down there and don't place any bets, so make sure to stop at a few of the tables as you look around. It's all right if you win a little, but don't try too hard because that will make them pay even more attention to you." Mireilla took them both in. "You look great," she pronounced with a smile of satisfaction.

As Robyn took Gyl's arm and strolled toward The Golden Arrow, she wasn't worried that someone would recognize her. Anyone who knew Robyn Loxley in this place would try extra hard to take care of her every desire. They entered the small restaurant with their heads held high.

The Golden Arrow was a restaurant above a casino. Though gambling was illegal in California, the Lacklands had only made a cursory effort to hide their establishment. It was enough to get in if you just knew the right person to ask.

The restaurant was dimly lit with white table cloths and candlelit centerpieces. The special that day was a marinated grilled swordfish steak. Robyn wondered if the people at the tables in the restaurant beyond knew about the casino under their feet. The hostess looked up from her book.

Robyn turned her head toward Gyl, consequently turning the paperwhite narcissus in her hair toward the woman.

"Party of two? Do you have a seat preference?" she asked, her eyes lingering on Gyl's lapel.

"The best in the house," Gyl said in a mock tone of superiority. Robyn swallowed a laugh.

"Very well, sir," the hostess said with a nod. "This way."

As they followed her, Robyn elbowed Gyl in the side. His grin and laughing eyes said her silent censure hadn't bothered him in the least.

The hostess led them through the restaurant to the kitchen's swinging door. The cooks didn't even look up as they entered, immediately turned left, and descended a flight of carpeted stairs.

"Here you are, sir," the hostess pronounced at the bottom of the stairs. "The best seat in the house."

Gyl's eyes analyzed the casino before him in the calculated gaze of someone trying to solve a problem. Robyn was glad she'd chosen him to accompany her in casing the place. It was his keen mind that set him apart from the others, not to mention Little Jon and Will were much too conspicuous to go unnoticed. Nodding at the hostess before she left, Robyn followed suit and took an initial look around.

The casino was small in comparison to what Robyn had heard of places like Reno or Vegas. Still, the joint was packed with maybe two hundred people. From Robyn's point of view, she could see three craps tables, one roulette wheel, two blackjack tables, and six round tables along the back where people were playing poker. The air was hazy with cigarette smoke, and the full bar was packed.

Near the entrance, there was a barred cashier's box. The pair stopped there first. Gyl asked for two dollars' worth of chips. More than what Robyn would have liked to spend but enough that the cashier didn't raise an eyebrow.

As they made their way through the crowd, they looked around for doors to potential exits. Gyl stopped at the roulette table, the table he had to pay the least amount of attention to.

"I'll get us some drinks," Robyn said, leaving Gyl at the table and wading toward the bar, glancing around as she went.

To one side of the bar was a door that likely led to a storage room. *It's possible there's a set of stairs in the storage room that lead outside for easy loading and unloading of booze,* Robyn thought.

When she'd managed to get the bartender's attention, she ordered a grasshopper and a vodka tonic. After she had a drink in each hand, she took the long way back to Gyl.

At the far end of the room, behind the poker tables, there was a short hallway with three doors. Robyn marked them and went to deliver Gyl's drink. He turned to her and left the roulette table as she held out the vodka tonic to him.

She slipped her arm into his, and he tilted his head toward her so she could whisper to him as they walked toward a craps table. "Did you see the hall at the far end of the room?" she asked.

He nodded slightly.

"I'm going to check it out, see if any of those doors lead to an exit. I want you to see if there's a way out in the room near the bar."

"Right," he agreed, placing himself around the craps table at just the right angle to see into the room should the door open.

Excuse at the ready, Robyn made her way to the hall. Glancing back toward the poker players, she tried the door on the left.

It was locked.

But after a few seconds, someone from inside called out. "Occupied," she moaned in a breathless voice that announced the washroom's dual occupancy.

Robyn moved to the door across the hall. She turned the knob softly, and opened the door to an empty office, no exit in sight. She shut the door and crept toward the last at the end of the hall.

Opening the final door, Robyn took in the room that was likely used for high-stake games and meetings. The round table was pushed to the side and a pair of smirking men sat near it, their chairs facing the center of the room where a bloodied man was strapped to a chair, his head hung forward in unconsciousness. A tall man with strong shoulders—his back turned to Robyn—stood over his victim, wiping blood from his knuckles with a handkerchief.

Beyond the brutality, Robyn marked a set of stairs leading up. "Oh, I'm sorry. I was just looking for the washroom," Robyn murmured as she began shutting the door.

The perpetrator turned, his cold, black eyes glaring over his shoulder at the intruder.

Robyn gasped, her heart leaping into her throat. She reflexively brought her shaking fingers to her mouth as her eyes burned with unshed tears. "Guy..." she whispered.

His unfeeling eyes widened in recognition. He grimaced, then opened his mouth to speak. "Robyn—"

She didn't stay to hear whatever it was he had to say. She dashed from the room, as fast as she could in her heels, and ran down the hall. She could hear him calling her, pursuing her as she threw herself into the crowd.

Gyl saw her coming and abandoned his place at the craps table, steadying her by the arms when she reached him.

"What is it?" he asked, raking her with his eyes to see if she was hurt.

"I need to leave," she told him shortly through heaving breaths.

She glanced behind her as they reached the bottom of the stairs. Guy stood in the middle of the room, his brows crinkled and his mouth open as though he were in pain. Robyn met his eyes, betrayal and disappointment bubbling in her gut. His black gaze seemed troubled and lost. She turned her back on him and left The Golden Arrow.

CHAPTER 56

Alaric pulled up the round drive of the Lacklands' mansion and got out of his car. Everything about this situation got under his skin. He hated that he was effectively working for the people he wanted most to take down for their crimes, but justice had to be served.

A maid answered his knock with big, expectant eyes.

"Is Miss Marian Loxley in?" Alaric asked.

The maid shook her head. "No, Marian isn't here right now. She's at her studio. Is it urgent? I could call her if you like."

"That's not necessary." He thanked her and got back in his car.

It didn't take long for Alaric to reach Marian's studio. Raising his hand to knock on Marian's door, Rick tried to push the images of Robyn and him on the studio floor from his mind.

It took Marian a while to answer. She tilted her head and wrinkled her brow upon recognizing her visitor. "Detective Nottingham?"

"Miss Loxley, do you have a moment?" he asked, taking in her rumpled appearance.

"Um, yeah, sure. Come on in." She opened the door for him. "I'm sorry about my dress. I was in the dark room. You never want to wear nice things when dealing with those chemicals."

"Don't worry about it."

"Would you like a cup of coffee?"

He nodded. "That would be welcome. Thank you."

He took a seat at the table, where he'd sat on his previous visit. His heart gave a pang as Marian moved around the kitchen, her graceful motions a reflection of her sister's. When the coffee was ready, she set a cup before him and sat opposite, where Robyn should have been.

"How can I help you, Detective?" she asked, wrapping her fingers around her own warm mug.

"Miss Loxley, how closely have you been following this hood business?"

Marian tilted her head. "Not very, but it's hard not to hear about it. I live with the Lacklands after all."

"That's precisely why I wanted to speak with you. John Lackland and his wife and mother are less than forthcoming in regards to my investigation. Have you noticed anything strange or suspicious as of late? Anyone lurking around? Things out of place?"

Marian pursed her lips and gazed out the window in thought for a while. "I'd like to help you, Detective. Robyn speaks so highly of you." she said finally.

Alaric flinched at the name.

"But I really haven't noticed much. Before, I was so busy with planning my art show and then the rally. And after those letters were posted on Thanksgiving... Well, the telephone has been ringing off the hook. The family has been very selective of who they allow to visit since then, and the people who are admitted are those we've known for a long time."

"You mentioned the rally. When I spoke to Mrs. Lackland, she said that there was a point when she may have dropped the envelope of money before giving it to Gisbourne because a child ran into her."

Marian tilted her head. "Well, I remember the child running into her, but I don't know if she dropped the envelope or not. I was much too busy attending to the boy." Marian shrugged. "If Isabella said that's what happened, then she's probably right."

"Do you think this boy and the man he was with could have been involved? Perhaps distracted you and Mrs. Lackland while a switch was made?"

Marian crinkled her eyebrows in confusion. "I can't even imagine that to be the case. The little darling was injured; I even saw he'd scraped his knee when he fell. And his father was so concerned, so gentle as he comforted him. Is that what Isabella thinks happened? That they tricked us?"

Alaric frowned. "Not that she said to me."

"I should think not. Isabella loves children, you know. She might have shed more tears at his getting hurt than the boy did himself."

Alaric lifted his coffee to his lips, wondering why he'd had a feeling that Marian might know something the others didn't.

"How do you feel about the letter the hoods posted all over the city?"

Marian's green eyes hardened like emeralds. "I don't appreciate the libel they're spreading around. The accusation that the Lacklands were going to keep the bond money for themselves is entirely false. After every-thing they've done for this city, it boils the blood to think about."

So she hasn't even told her sister what the Lacklands are really like, Alaric thought. He stifled a sigh. *That makes this whole conversation entirely useless. She wouldn't even be able to tell me about the Lacklands' potential enemies.*

"Well, if you do see something strange, you can call me at the station."

Marian gave him a short nod, her face still squinched in irritation at the audacity of the hoods.

As Alaric rose from the chair to take his leave, he thanked Marian for her hospitality and wished her a good evening.

He took his time going down the stairs. And when he'd climbed into the driver's side of his car, he leaned his forehead against his hands on the wheel without starting it. "I'm all fucked up," he told himself. "Why did I even go there? Was I hoping by some chance she'd be there? Get it together, Nottingham."

He sighed and turned his face to the window. A hooded figure entered the alley beside Marian's building and started scaling the fire escape. Alaric squinted against the relative darkness of the alley. The figure opened a window on the top floor and slipped into the apartment.

Alaric paused, staring at the still-opened window, waiting for some sound of alarm, a scream, anything. Then he got out of the car and re-entered the building.

CHAPTER 57

Robyn and Gyl left The Golden Arrow through the kitchen's back door. They exited the alley and crossed the street to where they knew Will and Tuck would be lurking.

Will took one look at Robyn's face and demanded to know what was wrong.

Robyn shook her head. "It's nothing. I was just surprised by something I saw. It shouldn't affect our plans."

Will frowned.

"Listen, you guys stay here. Finish casing the place. Watch what they do at the end of the night, how they transport the money and whatnot. I'm going to head back to Sherwood."

Tuck's eyes widened. "Are you sure you're feeling all right?"

Robyn managed a small smile. "I'm fine. I promise. Gyl and I got a lot of information from inside. Let's meet tomorrow and compare notes, see how best to proceed."

Will and Tuck reluctantly agreed. On the ride back to Sherwood, Gyl didn't pressure Robyn to talk about what she'd seen. She was grateful because she wouldn't have known what to tell him if he had.

She understood her reaction, though she didn't want to admit what it meant. She'd known what sort of man Guy Gisbourne was, but he'd been so sincere when he'd promised he would make things right, when he'd told her he wanted to be a better man, when he'd told her she made him want to be a better man. She'd found herself believing him, trusting that he would never lie to her, despite everything he'd done. She was surprised how much it hurt to see him standing over that man he'd beaten so brutally. As she confronted the sharp ache in her chest, she had to face the fact that she'd liked Guy much more than she'd thought.

Upon reaching Sherwood, Robyn returned to her monk's cell and changed her clothes. Lying on her cot, she stared at the lamplight dancing on the wall, restlessly moving her foot from side to side. Sighing, she rose from her bed and put on her hood. Then she made her way to Gyl's to use his telephone.

She hesitated for a good thirty seconds before dialing Rick's number. She wasn't going to see him, wasn't going to meet him. Because if she did, she knew she'd want the solace of his embrace, of drowning in his fervent touch. *But to just hear his voice. That should be all right. Shouldn't it?* she convinced herself.

Mrs. Stanley answered, her voice snapping at being called from bed.

"Mrs. Stanley, I'm sorry to bother you. It's Robyn. Is Rick in?"

Mrs. Stanley called Rick's name loudly, then put Robyn on hold when there was no answer. "His car isn't there, dear. He must be out."

"Oh, okay," Robyn murmured, wondering where in the world Rick could be at this hour. *Likely investigating your crimes,* she told herself.

Robyn hung up with Mrs. Stanley and dialed again, knowing it was still early for the Lacklands.

Winona answered and told Robyn Marian was at her studio.

Hanging up the receiver, Robyn suddenly wanted the unconditional love her sister's presence provided. She determined to visit Marian at her studio.

The drive on her motorcycle was brisk with late autumn chill. It refreshed Robyn, fortifying her in its simplistic sensation. By the time she'd parked around the corner from Marian's studio, Robyn was already feeling more at ease. She grinned when she reached the mouth of the alley beside Marian's building. Thinking she'd give her sister a good scare,

Robyn headed into the alley and climbed the fire escape to Marian's window. Then she slipped in.

Marian was washing a pair of coffee cups in the kitchen when she looked over and gasped. As she dropped a cup in the sink, warm, soapy water splashed up onto her face and the clothes she wore when working in her darkroom.

Robyn laughed heartily.

"Jesus Christ, Robyn! You scared me to death," Marian complained.

Robyn's grin was unapologetic.

Marian sobered, fear creeping back into her relieved eyes. "Wait, did you just climb into the window dressed like that? You weren't seen. Were you?"

Marian ran to the window and stuck her head out.

"Seen? Maybe, but I didn't see anyone."

Marian cursed.

"What?" Robyn asked.

"Detective Nottingham was just here. He came to ask me questions about if I'd noticed anything strange around the Lacklands. He just left, and now he's coming back."

Dread squeezed Robyn's heart. *I can't be here,* she thought, panicking.

"Okay, he came back into the building. Now, get out of here. Hurry," Marian urged, pushing Robyn back through the window and closing it behind her.

Robyn scrambled the rest of the way up the fire escape to the roof, her heart pounding in her ears. After running across the roof, she climbed down the fire escape on the other side and made a break for her motorcycle. The cold weather made it so she had to kick it more than a few times for it to start. Looking back as she drove away, Robyn heaved a sigh to see she wasn't being followed.

By the time Robyn crawled into her cot back in Sherwood, everyone else had already returned from the scouting mission at The Golden Arrow. And as the adrenaline from a long, eventful night drained out of her, Robyn fell into a hard sleep.

A jolt of panic awoke her late the next morning as a fist pounded on her door. She muttered under her breath about Tuck being petty for exacting payback and opened the door with a jerk.

She squinted at Gyl, his brow wrinkled as he gnawed on his lip.

"Robyn, I just got a call. I couldn't even believe it. It took me a while to figure out where the ringing sound was coming from. I've never given anyone the number. Then I remembered that you had," Gyl babbled.

Robyn shook her head with a heavy sigh. "What is it, Gyl?"

"It's your sister... She's been arrested."

CHAPTER 58

Detective Alaric Nottingham stared at Marian Loxley across the small, wooden table of the interrogation room. The dim light from the overhead bulb cast her face in long shadows. He had underestimated her. *She's calm, too calm,* he thought as he watched her sip water from the mug he'd given her.

"You're going to sit there and tell me that a hood didn't climb into your studio window?" he demanded.

Her green eyes met his, giving nothing away.

"I saw it with my own eyes. I even double checked by counting the windows."

Still, she didn't speak.

"Who is he, Miss Loxley? You obviously know him. Is he your lover? Who else would climb in through your window so late at night without you raising an alarm?"

Alaric ground his teeth together, knowing that after the phone call she'd made, he wouldn't have long before he had to let her go.

"Are you involved in all of this? Have you been feeding him information? Why are you helping him? Has he threatened you? Do you love him?"

Marian just blinked her cold, emerald eyes at him slowly, looking entirely unperturbed.

"I'm going to catch him eventually, Miss Loxley. It's only a matter of time. The question is: do you want to go down with him, or not?"

A little hint of color rose in Marian's cool cheeks as he threatened the man she was so loyal to. But just as he opened his mouth to follow that train of inquiry, the door to the room burst open.

"What's the meaning of this?" Robyn demanded, eyes blazing in a fury he'd never seen.

His heart leapt in his chest.

She turned her fiery gaze on him. "This interview is over," she declared. "Any further questions can be directed through my sister's lawyer, who you will find waiting for you outside. Marian, grab your coat. We're leaving."

Alaric made a move to protest, and Robyn stepped right up to him, her rage rolling off her in waves. "I can't believe you would do this," she spat.

Alaric stood up straight and met his lover's eyes. "I can't ignore evidence just because of how I feel for you. And all evidence points to the fact that your sister is involved with one of the hoods. I saw him climb into her window last night."

"How you *feel* for me? You wouldn't have *arrested my sister* if you *felt* anything for me. I'm sure there's a completely reasonable explanation for this. You could have just asked her! Did you even think about how this would make *me* feel?"

Alaric's face flushed, anger bubbling up inside him. "You want to talk about considering someone's feelings, Robyn?" he growled. "How do you think I felt when I saw you and Gisbourne with your tongues down each other's throats? You don't get to lecture me about feelings. I've got a job to do, and I'm going to do it."

Robyn froze like Alaric had slapped her, the color draining from her face. "That..." she mumbled, "has nothing to do with this."

"You're right," he agreed. "It doesn't. So I'd appreciate you not bringing our personal relationship into my investigation."

She stared up at him, a war of rage and sorrow in her eyes. He was sure if he'd looked in a mirror, his wouldn't be much different.

After a long moment, a haunted look of sadness won the battle in her gaze.

Before he could say anything else, she turned and ushered her sister from the room. Once they'd left, a shrewd looking lawyer entered, glasses on his nose and briefcase in his hand. After listening to his exhaustive speech, Alaric took a moment at the table, resting his forehead against his clasped hands with closed eyes.

When the other chair skidded against the floor, Alaric looked up to see Gisbourne sitting across from him.

"Did you come here to gloat?" Alaric asked. "Because I'm not in the mood. And the Lacklands' fancy lawyer already gave me an earful."

Guy Gisbourne's black eyes stared at him, analyzing him. "I don't like you," he declared without ceremony. "But as much as I don't like you, I don't like these hoods even more. What do you say to combining forces?"

Alaric looked back at Gisbourne, but his expression showed no indication of deception. "What do you have in mind?"

Gisbourne leaned forward. "You're concentrating your efforts in the wrong area with Marian Loxley. The hoods have it in for John Lackland, right? They're stealing from him specifically."

"Okay."

"So why don't we set a trap? Give them a mark they can't resist?"

"And what would that be?"

Gisbourne smiled, the kind of hot and cold smile that sent a shiver and a thrill down your spine. "The Golden Arrow."

"The restaurant?" Alaric asked. *It wasn't far from there that I found Mireilla being beaten by bookies*, he thought.

Gisbourne rolled his eyes. "How did you become a detective?" he scoffed. "The Golden Arrow has the only casino in Midshire. If the hoods want to hurt John Lackland, that's where they'll strike."

"But how will we know when? We can't have men watching it day and night. They'll just wait until we grow lax."

"So we have an event, a big party with high stakes, every chip you buy is worth double its value when you cash in, one night only."

"That certainly would bring people and money in."

"Exactly," Gisbourne agreed.

Alaric nodded. "All right. Let's try it."

CHAPTER 59

Robyn watched her sister as she took photographs of the children playing in the relative warmth of the dock warehouse. Marian hadn't fought Robyn when she'd insisted she move to Sherwood after she'd been arrested.

Even the Lacklands had thought it a good idea for Marian to move in with her sister. They hadn't for a moment believed Marian had anything to do with The Hooded Brigands, punctuated by the fact they had sent their well-paid lawyer to remind Rick who he was messing with. And even if John or Isabella had suspected, they never would have stated the notion aloud, too afraid of Eleanor's retribution.

Marian had taken a look around Sherwood and decided to stay at the docks. Over the last few weeks, the people of Sherwood had really cleaned the ship up. Had it been able to sail, it might have been a cruise ship bound for a tropical vacation.

Only around half of the freed prisoners had decided to settle there. The rest had found other accommodations around Sherwood. And after seeing the ship all shiny and polished, some of the abbey residents traded their monk cells for cabins. And some of the ship's residents had relocated to the abbey, Will for one, though Robyn had a strong suspicion as to why he'd made that decision.

Robyn smiled as her sister put down her camera and joined in on the children's games, her own inner turmoil momentarily forgotten in the echo of childish laughter.

Robyn hadn't been sleeping well the last few days. Every time she closed her eyes, she was faced with Rick's pain as he confronted her about kissing Guy. The comfort of his arms felt much too far away. She knew she'd been relying on him to help her keep balance, to help her deal with the anxiety-riddled realities of what she was doing in Sherwood. She may have no guilt toward the Lacklands, but leading the people of Sherwood, considering their safety and well-being, was a stressful job. And with Rick, she could always be just Robyn.

Yes, she'd known she'd been relying on him, but she hadn't known just how much. She wanted nothing more than to show up at his door, without a word, and express her feelings for him. The scenario played over and over in her mind as if compelling her to act it out. *Would he welcome me?* she wondered. It didn't really matter because she knew she wouldn't do it. No, it was far better for her to stay away from Alaric Nottingham because if she didn't, she might do something reckless.

And then there was Guy. She was still disappointed in Guy. And one look at his face as she'd passed him at the police station had told her he knew it, too. She still hoped that one day he would find peace, that he would use his influence to help others rather than hurt them, but now she knew that was entirely in his hands. Her influence on him did not translate to responsibility for him. If he wanted to become a better man, as he'd said, then he had to do it for him, not for her. Still, that hadn't stopped her active mind from imagining even more fantasies of what would never, could never, be.

"Robyn," Mireilla called breathlessly, entering the warehouse and making her way to where Robyn sat with Will, Tuck, Little Jon, and David.

"Mireilla, I didn't know you were visiting today. I didn't expect to see you until this weekend." Robyn commented. "How's your family?"

"They're fine," Mireilla answered. "This weekend is what I came to talk about."

Robyn frowned, tilting her head, more than a little surprised that

Mireilla of all people would be having second thoughts about robbing The Golden Arrow. "What about it?" Robyn asked.

"I've just heard that the casino is having a huge event the week after next, the twenty-second, a winter solstice party. There's going to be a massive haul. They said every chip you buy is worth twice what you paid when you cash in. I thought you ought to know. Maybe we should change our date to that night."

Robyn thought seriously about this new information.

"This is a trap if ever there was one," David pointed out.

Will nodded. "I agree. They've guessed that The Golden Arrow is our next target, or they're trying to entice us."

Robyn considered their well-laid plan. It was simple. Every night when The Golden Arrow closed—long after all the employees had left—the house's winnings were transported by three armed men from the casino. The three men got into a car, which was parked in the alley near the back door. Then they took the cash to wherever John Lackland had instructed. So when the three men left the casino, Gyl was to drop a modified gas grenade, which Will had learned how to make at Lackland Chemical, filled with the concoction they'd used at the docks. When the guards were sound asleep, Tuck would enter the alley, take the cash, and meet up with Will and Gyl in the escape car. Little Jon and Robyn were to keep watch until Will, Tuck, and Gyl were clear, then make their own ways back to Sherwood.

"That's a great idea, Mireilla," Robyn praised.

Mireilla smiled while the rest of the group hesitated.

"Are you sure about this, Robyn?" Tuck asked. "They know we're coming."

Robyn smiled with confidence. "But they don't know we know that they know. Guy and Rick were both there at the docks, and there were tons of people at the rally. We can do this. We know they'll be looking for us, so we just have to keep track of where they are."

Her friends considered her words.

"I'm with you, Robyn," Little Jon pledged.

Robyn looked to the rest, who nodded despite their unsure expressions.

"All right. Then we wait until the longest night of the year."

CHAPTER 60

$\mathcal{A}$ laric had been trying to ignore Gisbourne's look of disgust. But over the last few hours, it had only deepened. Finally, he sighed and turned to the man in his passenger seat. "What? Why is your face doing that?" he demanded.

"We should've sat in my car," Gisbourne muttered.

"Really?" Alaric said flatly. "That's what this is about?"

Gisbourne looked out the window. "My car is nicer."

"Yeah? Well, I guess that's because criminals are paid more than cops."

Gisbourne didn't reply.

"Just...pay attention. Will ya? You said the money is most vulnerable when it's moved from the casino to the car, right?"

He gave an answering nod.

Alaric stared at the car parked in the alley beside The Golden Arrow. *Any time now,* he thought. He wondered if he'd been right to insist that Gisbourne keep the same three guards as always. His reasoning was sound. If there were more men, that might alarm the hoods, make them abandon their aims for the night. But as his eyes swept the quiet street, he wasn't too sure about his decision.

"There," Gisbourne stated, nodding toward the side door in the alley across the street.

Alaric tensed as the three men exited, business as usual. Alaric's hand hovered over the handle of his car door, ready to spring into action.

As he watched, something small fell from The Golden Arrow's neighboring roof, and a thick, white mist filled the alley.

Gisbourne opened the passenger door to jump out.

"Wait," Alaric commanded, grabbing a fistful of his jacket to keep him inside. "Shut the door. If that's what I think it is, we're going to have to wait until it clears."

"But they could be getting away!"

"Do you want to be down for the count again?" Alaric snapped. "Wait," he repeated.

Gisbourne shut the door with a curse, his muscles as tense and ready to spring as Alaric's.

When the mist had cleared enough, they saw the three guards laying on the ground, no hoods in sight.

Alaric clicked his tongue, pulled his scarf from his neck, and wrapped it tightly over his nose and mouth twice. "Do your best not to breathe it in," he advised before getting out of the car.

He drew his weapon, and Gisbourne followed suit.

Alaric's gaze swept down the street and along the rooftops for any sign of movement as they made their way toward the downed men. He gritted his teeth, still not seeing the hoods.

Gisbourne cursed again, and Alaric echoed the sentiment.

When they reached the guards, Gisbourne knelt down to one of them to feel for a pulse. That's when Alaric saw him, a hooded figure who dashed across the other end of the alley.

"There!" Alaric shouted, breaking into a sprint, in full pursuit.

He could hear Gisbourne's footsteps pounding the pavement behind him. Once he'd reached the other end of the alley, Alaric spotted the hood turn a corner. He gathered speed.

His breath was hot as his scarf smothered him. He reached up and wrenched the cloth from his face, taking huge gulps of cool air. His heart pumped twice as fast as his legs as he rounded the corner.

The hood paused astride his motorcycle just as he was raising his foot to try to kickstart it again. One heartbeat later, he sprung off the motorcycle and made a run for it.

Alaric launched himself at the suspect, tackling him to the ground. In the tussle, the hood started to slip from Alaric's grasp. There was the deafening bang of a gunshot, and the hood stilled. Gisbourne lowered his weapon from the sky and trained it on the hood.

Alaric got to his feet, hauling his catch up by the arm. "It's over," he said, and the hood didn't struggle.

"Who is it?" Gisbourne asked, his weapon still aimed to kill.

"Let's find out." Alaric reached up and pulled back the hood. He froze, his mind incapable of comprehending what he saw. He didn't blink, didn't dare breathe; his heart didn't even beat.

But as he met the hood's beautiful blue eyes, the eyes he knew better than any others, the eyes that at that moment were unmistakably shadowed with guilt, the world shattered as if he'd never truly known anything in his entire life.

"W-what...?" he murmured, confusion muddling his ability to put complete phrases together.

"Let me explain," Robyn pleaded, her eyes shifting from his to Gisbourne's, then back again.

He didn't have the presence of mind to stop her from doing so.

"I never planned this," she assured. "Meeting you was as much of a chance for me as it was for you. I didn't even know about what the Lacklands were doing then. I didn't know about their criminal enterprises. I swear."

Alaric's heart grew heavy, weighed down as he began to realize the extent of her betrayal. "You..."

"No," Robyn said firmly. "No, whatever you're thinking, it isn't true."

Her eyes filled with tears. And as they spilled down her face, somewhere in his mind he recognized that this was unusual.

"Rick," she whispered.

The usual thrill he got from her calling him that, the only person who had ever called him that, twisted into something painful. His mind pushed the feeling away.

"No," she said. "Don't do that. I can tell just by looking at you that you aren't listening." Her cold fingers shook as she covered his hand, which still held her firmly by the arm. "I never meant to hurt you."

But as she said it, her eyes were locked with Gisbourne's.

Alaric sobered as his fondest hope soured into his worst nightmare. Reality crashed into him, his mind whirling with thoughts and possibilities and what he had to do.

"Robyn Loxley," he said. "You're under arrest on suspicion of robbery—"

Before he could finish his list of charges, she struggled in his grasp. The sensation was foreign and uncomfortable as he kept a firm hold on her.

"You call this justice?" she spat, her anger flaring. "You're arresting me? For what? Stealing from the biggest, most ruthless crooks in Midshire? I've helped people with the money I stole from them. People who deserved justice and who never would have gotten it."

"You aren't a cop. You aren't a judge. You don't get to dole out your own brand of vigilante vengeance," Alaric argued.

"What would you have me do, Rick? The channels you're so unwilling to step outside aren't working! You're following the law, and look at you. You're working for them just like everyone else. There's no democracy in Midshire. They decide what laws are passed or not. The only crimes prosecuted are the ones they deem offensive. I'm only trying to survive in the lawlessness they created, to help others survive. They have stolen far more than I ever could. Where's the justice? When the system is broken, following the same broken processes over and over isn't going to fix—"

"So you'd have anarchy?" he interrupted.

"No, not anarchy. Resistance. They need to know they can't act however they want. That even if the establishment won't do anything about it, the people will. Because there is a higher form of justice than what can be bought. People have the right to live freely and without fear. And when that right is threatened, they have the right to take it, to fight for it."

Alaric hesitated, her words forcing their way into the cracks of what he'd always known to be true. *How do you fix a system if all you're doing is operating within it, if the means of change are wholly ineffective?* he wondered. He met Robyn's eyes again, so certain in the face of his own uncertainty. His heart recognized her even as it seemed he was seeing her for the first time. *Robyn. This is Robyn,* his mind repeated. His hold on her loosened, and his arm dropped to his side.

Robyn didn't have to thank him, didn't have to say anything. As she looked up at him, her eyes said it all: Thank you. I'm sorry.

As she took a step, preparing to go back to wherever she'd been hiding, Gisbourne cocked his weapon with a menacing click.

Robyn turned her gaze on him.

"I ought to kill you where you stand," Gisbourne said.

She didn't speak, just met his eyes with that steady gaze she must have learned from her sister.

"You made a fool of me, used me, manipulated me," he accused.

Unlike with Rick, she didn't defend herself. "I'm sorry, Guy."

"I've killed people for less," he told her, wholly ignoring her apology.

Rick tensed, but Robyn nodded her understanding at Gisbourne.

"Why shouldn't I kill you?" he asked her, his voice soft with the slightest hint of a quiver.

"Because that isn't who you want to be," Robyn assured him.

"Don't use my own words on me," he spat. "You're not who I thought you were. I never should have trusted you."

"I'm sorry," she said again. "I'm sorry I hurt you. But I truly do want peace and happiness for you, Guy. And I believed everything you ever told me. You can be that man you want to be."

"For who? I've no one to be better for."

"For yourself."

Gisbourne's weapon trembled in his unsteady hand.

Robyn didn't flinch, just met his eyes with a calm confidence.

He lowered his weapon. "The next time we meet, you will be nothing to me," he told her. Then he turned his back on her and walked away.

Rick glanced back at her to find her gazing after Gisbourne's retreating form.

"Maybe one day, we won't be on opposite sides," she whispered.

He wasn't certain if she was referring to him or Gisbourne. "And should that day come?" he asked, unable to hide the doubt in his tone.

She gave him that same cheeky grin she'd given him when she'd challenged him to darts. "We'll have to wait and see."

EPILOGUE

Robyn sat atop the guard tower in Sherwood, the heels of her boots thumping against the roof as she dangled them off the edge. She smiled wistfully as she watched Tuck and Will, hand-in-hand, as they went around watering the newly planted saplings they'd brought down from Canada, where it turned out there were still forests. They didn't look like much now, but Robyn knew with loving care, Sherwood Forest would flourish again, much like the people of Sherwood had.

Robyn knew that the peace they all felt at that moment wasn't going to last forever. They had managed to hide in plain sight, but she didn't for a minute think they wouldn't come to Sherwood eventually, especially knowing Nan had left, having slipped out in the middle of one dark, winter night. Would Nan betray her family and reveal their location? They didn't know. But on that rare spring day, where sunlight filtered through the clouds in sparkling beams, that problem felt far away.

"You hiding up here?" Little Jon asked, poking his head up through the trap door.

"Well if I was, I wasn't doing a very good job of it," she countered.

He chuckled and climbed up to sit beside her. "Just got word that a shipment John Lackland ordered from out east is arriving in a few days," he murmured.

"Any idea what it is?"

He shook his head. "Whatever it is, it's important to him."

"Stockport docks?"

"Nope. Midshire Central."

"A train, huh?"

He nodded.

Robyn grinned. "Never robbed a train before."

Little Jon smiled back at her.

She thought for a moment. "Do you think they'll be there?" she wondered.

"I wouldn't be surprised. After all, the one will be securing his boss's property, and the other..."

Robyn finished his thought. "The other is the detective in charge of catching Robyn Hood."

AFTERWORD

Thank you for reading! I do so hope you enjoyed it. If you have a moment, I would very much appreciate a review on the store where you bought it. Tell other readers what you thought, and help them make a decision on this book.

If you'd like to stay updated on news about my books and events, you can subscribe to my newsletter on my website:

www.dlieber.com

On my site, you will also find my blog, where I post all my fun little tidbits.

Thanks again! I hope you will travel through my worlds with me again in the future.

D. Lieber

ABOUT THE AUTHOR

D. Lieber has a wanderlust that would make a butterfly envious. When she isn't planning her next physical adventure, she's recklessly jumping from one fictional world to another. Her love of reading led her to earn a Bachelor's in English from Wright State University.

Beyond her skeptic and slightly pessimistic mind, Lieber wants to believe. She has been many places—from Canada to England, France to Italy, Germany to Russia—believing that a better world comes from putting a face on "other." She is a romantic idealist at heart, always fighting to keep her feet on the ground and her head in the clouds.

Lieber lives in Wisconsin with her husband (John) and cats (Yin and Nox).

LINKS

Website: www.dlieber.com
Goodreads: www.goodreads.com/dlieberwriting
Bookbub: www.bookbub.com/profile/d-lieber

www.ingramcontent.com/pod-product-compliance
Lightning Source LLC
Chambersburg PA
CBHW021238200726

48288CB00014B/3